ABOUT TIME

THE UNAUTHORIZED GUIDE TO
DOCTOR WHO

1980–1984

SEASONS 18 TO 21

LAWRENCE MILES & TAT WOOD

Also available from Mad Norwegian Press...

Chicks Dig Time Lords: A Celebration of Doctor Who by the Women Who Love It

Running Through Corridors: Rob and Toby's Marathon Watch of Doctor Who
by Robert Shearman and Toby Hadoke (three volumes, forthcoming)

*Wanting to Believe: A Critical Guide to The X-Files, Millennium
and The Lone Gunmen* by Robert Shearman

More Digressions: A New Collection of "But I Digress" Columns
by Peter David

AHistory: An Unauthorized History of the Doctor Who Universe [Second Edition]
by Lance Parkin

AngeLINK Novel Series
by Lyda Morehouse, winner of Philip K. Dick Award, Shamus Award,
Barnes and Noble "Maiden Voyage" Award.

Resurrection Code (all-new prequel, forthcoming)

Time, Unincorporated: The Doctor Who Fanzine Archives
Volume 1: Lance Parkin
Volume 2: Writings on the Classic Series
Volume 3: Writings on the New Series (forthcoming)
Volume 4: Writings on the Doctor Who Universe (forthcoming)

The About Time Series
by Lawrence Miles and Tat Wood

About Time 1: The Unauthorized Guide to Doctor Who (Seasons 1 to 3)
About Time 2: The Unauthorized Guide to Doctor Who (Seasons 4 to 6)
About Time 3: The Unauthorized Guide to Doctor Who
(Seasons 7 to 11) [2nd Edition now available]
About Time 4: The Unauthorized Guide to Doctor Who (Seasons 12 to 17)
About Time 5: The Unauthorized Guide to Doctor Who (Seasons 18 to 21)
About Time 6: The Unauthorized Guide to Doctor Who
(Seasons 22 to 26, the TV Movie)
About Time 7 (forthcoming)

Copyright © 2004 Mad Norwegian Press (www.madnorwegian.com)

Cover art by Steve Johnson.
Jacket & interior design by Christa Dickson (www.christadickson.com)

ISBN: 0-9759446-4-9
Printed in Illinois. First Edition: December 2004. Third Printing: June 2010

table of contents

table of contents

Essays

how does this book work ?

About Time prides itself on being the most comprehensive, wide-ranging and at times almost *shockingly* detailed handbook to *Doctor Who* that you might ever conceivably need, so great pains have been taken to make sure there's a place for everything and everything's in its place. Here are the "rules"…

Every *Doctor Who* story gets its own entry, and every entry is divided up into four major sections. The first, which includes the headings **Which One is This?**, **Firsts and Lasts** and **X Things to Notice**, is designed to provide an overview of the story for newcomers to the series (and we trust there'll be more of you, after 2005) or relatively "lightweight" fans who aren't too clued-up on a particular era of the programme's history. We might like to *pretend* that all *Doctor Who* viewers know all parts of the series equally well, but there are an awful lot of people who - for example - know the '70s episodes by heart and don't have a clue about the '60s. This section also acts as an overall Spotters' Guide to the series, pointing out most of the memorable bits.

After that comes the **Continuity** section, which is where you'll find all the pedantic detail. Here there are notes on the Doctor (personality, props and cryptic mentions of his past), the supporting cast, the TARDIS and any major Time Lords who might happen to wander into the story. Following these are the **Non-Humans** and **Planet Notes** sections, which can best be described as "high geekery"… we're old enough to remember the *Doctor Who Monster Book*, but not too old to want a more grown-up version of our own, so expect full-length monster profiles. Next comes **History**, which includes all available data about the time in which the story's supposed to be set.

Of crucial importance: note that throughout the **Continuity** section, *everything* you read is "true" - i.e. based on what's said or seen on-screen - except for sentences in square brackets [like this], where we cross-reference the data to other stories and make some suggestions as to how all of this is supposed to fit together. You can trust us absolutely on the non-bracketed material, but the bracketed sentences are often just speculation.

The only exception to this rule is the **Additional Sources** heading, which features any off-screen information from novelisations, writer interviews, etc that might shed light on the way the story's supposed to work. (Another thing to notice here: anything written in single inverted commas - 'like this' - is a word-for-word quote from the script, whereas anything in double-quote marks "like this" isn't.)

The third major section is **Analysis**. It opens with **Where Does This Come From?**, and this may need explaining. For years there's been a tendency in fandom to assume that *Doctor Who* was an "escapist" series which very rarely tackled anything particularly topical, but with hindsight this is bunk. Throughout its history, the programme reflected, reacted to and sometimes openly *discussed* the trends and talking-points of the era, although it isn't always immediately obvious to the modern eye. (Everybody knows that "The Sunmakers" was supposed to be satirical, but how many people got the subtext of "Destiny of the Daleks"?). It's our job here to put each story into the context of the time in which it was made, to explain *why* the production team thought it might have been a good idea.

Up next is **Things That Don't Make Sense**, basically a run-down of the glitches and logical flaws in the story, some of them merely curious and some entirely ridiculous. Unlike a lot of TV guidebooks, here we don't dwell on minor details like shaky camera angles and actors treading on each others' cues - at least unless they're *chronically* noticeable - since these are trivial even by our standards. We're much more concerned with whacking great story loopholes or particularly grotesque breaches of the laws of physics.

Analysis ends with **Critique**; though no consensus will ever be found on *any* story, we've not only tried to provide a balanced (or at least not-too-irrational) view but also attempted to judge each story by its own standards, *not just* the standards of the post-CGI generation.

The last of the four sections is **The Facts**, which covers ordinary, straightforward details like cast lists, viewing figures and - where applicable - the episodes of the story which are currently missing from the BBC archives. We've also provided a run-down of the story's cliffhangers, since a lot of *Doctor Who* fans grew up thinking of the cliffhangers as the programme's defining points.

Additionally, as producer John Nathan-Turner's "guest star" policy will be a significant feature of the series from now on, we've added an **Oh, Isn't That..?** category to discuss the backgrounds of various actors and actresses who'll appear.

The Lore is an addendum to the Facts section, which covers the off-screen anecdotes and factettes attached to the story. The word "Lore" seems fitting, since long-term fans will already know much of this material, but it needs to be included here (a) for new initiates and (b) because this is supposed to be a one-stop guide to the history of *Doctor Who*.

A lot of "issues" relating to the series are so big that they need forums all to themselves, which is why most story entries are followed by mini-essays. Here we've tried to answer all the questions that seem to demand answers, although the logic of these essays changes from case to case. Some of them are actually trying to find *definitive* answers, unravelling what's said in the TV stories and making sense of what the programme-makers had in mind. Some have more to do with the real world than the *Doctor Who* universe, and aim to explain why certain things about the series were so important at the time. Some are purely speculative, some delve into scientific theory and some are just whims, but they're *good* whims and they all seem to have a place here. Occasionally we've included footnotes on the names and events we've cited, for those who aren't old enough or British enough to follow all the references.

We should also mention the idea of "canon" here. Anybody who knows *Doctor Who* well, who's been exposed to the TV series, the novels, the comic-strips, the audio adventures and the trading-cards you used to get with Sky Ray ice-lollies, will know that there's always been some doubt about how much of *Doctor Who* counts as "real", as if the TV stories are in some way less made-up than the books or the short stories. We'll discuss this in shattering detail later on, but for now it's enough to say that *About Time* has its own specific rules about what's canonical and what isn't. In this book, we accept everything that's shown in the TV series to be the "truth" about the *Doctor Who* universe (although obviously we have to gloss over the parts where the actors fluff their lines). Those non-TV stories which have made a serious attempt to become part of the canon, from Virgin Publishing's New Adventures to the recent audio adventures from Big Finish, aren't considered to be 100% "true" but do count as supporting evidence. Here they're treated as what historians call "secondary sources", not definitive enough to make us change our whole view of the way the *Doctor Who* universe works but helpful pointers if we're trying to solve any particularly fiddly continuity problems.

It's worth remembering that unlike (say) the stories written for the old *Dalek* annuals, the early Virgin novels were an honest attempt to carry on the *Doctor Who* tradition in the absence of the TV series, so it seems fair to use them to fill the gaps in the programme's folklore even if they're not exactly - so to speak - "fact".

You'll also notice that we've divided up this work according to "era", not according to Doctor. Since we're trying to tell the *story* of the series, both on- and off-screen, this makes sense. The actor playing the Main Man might be the only thing we care about when we're too young to know better, but anyone who's watched the episodes with hindsight will know that there's a vastly bigger stylistic leap between "The Horns of Nimon" and "The Leisure Hive" than there is between "Logopolis" and "Castrovalva". Volume IV covers the producerships of Philip Hinchcliffe and Graham Williams, two very distinct stories in themselves, and everything changes again - when Williams leaves the series, not when Tom Baker does - at the start of the 1980s.

There's a kind of logic here, just as there's a kind of logic to everything in this book. There's so much to *Doctor Who*, so much material to cover and so many ways to approach it, that there's a risk of our methods irritating our audience even if all the information's in the right places. So we need to be consistent, and we have been. As a result, we're confident that this is as solid a reference guide / critical study / monster book as you'll ever find. In the end, we hope you'll agree that the only realistic criticism is: "Haven't you told us *too* much here?"

And once we're finished, we can watch the *new* series and start the game all over again.

18.1: "The Leisure Hive"

(Serial 5N, Four Episodes, 30th August - 20th September 1980.)

Which One is This? Big baggy reptiles truss themselves up inside human-suits and try to sabotage a Theme Park in Space, while the Doctor gets his arms and legs ripped off (but not really) and then grows old. Disgracefully.

Firsts and Lasts All change. "The Leisure Hive" marks the beginning of John Nathan-Turner's producership on *Doctor Who*, and he'll become the original series' last and longest-serving producer, steering the programme - through good times and very, very bad - for the next nine years.

The difference is palpable, which is why many see the gap between Season Seventeen and Season Eighteen as one of the biggest stylistic jumps in the programme's history (the only bigger one being the leap from black-and-white to colour in 1970). Darker, flashier, less comedy-prone and more likely to use "big" made-up pseudo-scientific artefacts instead of random pieces of technobabble pulled out of the Doctor's pockets, this is the start of what might be called the "slick" era of *Doctor Who*. New script editor Christopher H. Bidmead starts to impose his divine will on the series, and former series producer Barry Letts gets a credit as executive producer, keeping an eye on the change-over.

But the first noticeable change to the series is the new title sequence, complete with re-arranged theme music, replacing the "time tunnel" with the "starfield". (This comes in the wake of the late '70s pop-SF boom, in the same way that the earlier version came in the wake of *2001*. Even the new logo, with its joined-together letters, hints at the *Star Wars* influence... although it looks more prog-rock than anything. Tellingly, the new version of the theme is supposed to be rousing and dramatic rather than strange and slippery, while Delia Derbyshire pointed out that it was closer to Ron Grainer's original composition than her 1963 rendition. It is, incidentally, in a different key.)

The sound of the incidental music changes as well, thanks to new Radiophonics Workshop tune-engineer Peter Howell, whose style is more inclined towards ethereal "boopleoopleoopleoople"

Season 18 Cast/Crew

- Tom Baker (the Doctor)
- Lalla Ward (Romana, 18.1 to 18.5)
- John Leeson (voice of K9, 18.1 to 18.5)
- Matthew Waterhouse (Adric, 18.3 to 18.7)
- Sarah Sutton (Nyssa, 18.6, 18.7)
- Janet Fielding (Tegan Jovanka, 18.7)

- John Nathan-Turner (Producer)
- Barry Letts (Executive Producer)
- Christopher H. Bidmead (Script Editor)

twinkling noises than dramatic "dann-dann-*doo*!" orchestral stabs. In fact, just about *everything* changes here except for the lead cast. Tom Baker and Lalla Ward are still in place, while K9 gets his old voice back as John Leeson returns to the programme to do the honours.

Making its last appearance here is the randomiser, the oh-so-contrived method of taking the Doctor to random destinations, which made its first appearance in "The Armageddon Factor" (16.6). New props include the re-built TARDIS exterior, and the Doctor's new coat, a sombre burgundy number that helps set the tone for the more funereal nature of some of this season's stories. For the first time, people on different planets communicate by hologram instead of using old-fashioned video-screens (21.6, "The Caves of Androzani" and 22.6, "Revelation of the Daleks" will make this a space-industry standard).

In the background are two figures who'll be around for a while. One of the zero-gravity squash players at the Leisure Hive is Graham Cole, who is to early '80s *Doctor Who* what Pat Gorman was to the '60s and '70s, the all-purpose walk-on and third-monster-from-the-left (later he'll become a familiar face in *The Bill*). And milling around as the tachyon regenerator pulls visitor Loman apart is Ling Tai, who's going to pop up a lot until 1984, at which point she'll get to present *Crackerjack*. After that she'll be officially famous enough to qualify as a "guest star" (in 26.1, "Battlefield").

Indeed, the new producer's "guest star" policy is going to be a significant feature of the series from now on...

Four Things to Notice About "The Leisure Hive"...

1. Fear. Look at this from an eight-year-old's point of view. Love it or hate it, late '70s *Doctor Who* just wasn't very scary, or certainly not deliberately. While those raised in the '60s and early '70s still speak of hiding behind the sofa as soon as the spooky opening sequence started, or being alarmed by the harsh monochrome settings and the weird background noises, by the late '70s the programme was "clever" rather than "alarming".

But episode one of "The Leisure Hive" ends with the Doctor being put into a machine that rips off his arms and legs, while the camera zooms forward and practically shoves itself down his throat as he screams. With the hindsight of adulthood, the effects are weak and episode two reveals that it was all just a big illusion anyway, but at the time this *really* freaked out the younger audience and made it clear - more clear even than the new titles or the buffed-up visuals - that something had profoundly *changed* about this universe. Suddenly it wasn't all fun and games any more. (The cliffhanger of episode two goes even further, but we'll come back to that later on...)

2. Less scary are the monsters here, but you've got to give the designers bonus points for trying. The Foamasi, chunky reptile-people with chameleon-eyes, were designed so that each costume has two layers; the outer layer is semi-transparent, supposedly giving the illusion of lizard-skin. Unfortunately, this neat touch is completely lost to the cameras under studio conditions, and the result is yet another alien entity which looks good in still photographs but resembles someone trapped inside a bean-bag when required to walk around the place. The Foamasi are particularly notorious in this respect, thanks to a rather ill-judged scene at the end of episode three in which one of the human characters turns out to be a Foamasi wearing a human-skin. Since the Foamasi are noticeably fatter than humans from every angle, this is difficult to accept.

In opposition to the Foamasi are the Argolin, a rarity in *Doctor Who*, and you could probably add "and quite right too". Most aliens in *this* series are either entirely human-shaped or played by people in all-over body costumes, and the programme has never favoured the *Star Trek* route of giving aliens funny ears or prosthetic foreheads. The Argolin are the exception, being green-tinted folk with pointy bits on the tops of their heads. It's the last time the programme will try this sort of thing

until the dark days of Season Twenty-Four (see 24.1, "Time and the Rani"), and in future the series will be much more choosy about its use of exotic make-up (see 18.2, "Meglos").

3. Things everybody knows about "The Leisure Hive", number one: it was written as a "Mafia" story, shamelessly influenced by *The Godfather* (but see **The Lore**). The plot is about an alien leisure complex that suffers an attempted "hostile takeover" from a galactic organised crime group, suggesting Las Vegas in the days of the mob, which is why "Foamasi" is - all together now - an anagram of "Mafiosa". The Argolin get an offer they can't refuse, though sadly there's no reptilian equivalent of anyone getting a horse's head in their bed. (The Myrka must be glad to hear it; see 21.1, "Warriors of the Deep".)

4. Though the stories of this era tend to feature less padding than - for instance - those of the Jon Pertwee years, "The Leisure Hive" introduces a style of *Doctor Who* that's actually slower-paced in some respects, comfortable with long, lingering atmosphere-building shots and extended sequences with no dialogue or explosions. (Just look at episode two, in which the Foamasi pursue the crooked Stimson through the half-lit Hive.) This approach becomes apparent right from the very first shot of the story, which makes us look at deckchairs for a minute and a half.

The Continuity

The Doctor Upon entering the tachyon generator on Argolis, the Doctor is aged by an estimated five-hundred years. This means that he emerges from the booth as a horribly old man, balding, white-haired and with a colossal beard. [He looks as if he's on his last legs, so assuming that there haven't been *too* many off-screen adventures for the Doctor, this seems to indicate that the natural life for a Time Lord's regeneration isn't much more than five-hundred years. The First Doctor, who didn't appear quite this ancient but who exerted himself more, died after 450-odd years. This might hint that a Time Lord's "natural" life-span is around 6,500 years, barring accidents, so all this adventuring has *really* knocked the years off the Doctor's existence. The incident with the generator also demonstrates, beyond doubt, that the Doctor *is* capable of growing facial hair even if he's never seen to shave (see 14.1, "The Masque of Mandragora', 6.5, "The Seeds of Death"). Perhaps

The John Nathan-Turner Era: What Was the Difference?

Being the Case for the Defence. For the opposing view, see **The John Nathan-Turner Era: What Went Horribly Wrong?** *under 21.7, "The Twin Dilemma".*

It was clear, from the start, that *something* had changed.

The new title sequence was a big clue, natch. By 1980, the old "time tunnel" opening to *Doctor Who* had been around for seven years, long enough that a generation had grown up taking it for granted in the same way as (say) the telephone dialling tone. For those of us who were eight or nine or ten, the new "starfield" was puzzling, but it was only the beginning. The rest of "The Leisure Hive" left us feeling… a little bewildered. Not that we'd have been able to vocalise it properly, but there were things about it that seemed new and odd and even *scary*. It looked and sounded peculiar, and even seemed to move in a peculiar way (though not so much as later stories in Season Eighteen). And since those who are eight or nine or ten don't have a tendency to look at the names on the end credits, the fact that a new producer had taken over simply wasn't an explanation. Besides, even if it had been - even if you were old enough to remember Williams taking over from Hinchcliffe, and to realise what a New Man at the Top meant - then the gap between "The Horns of Nimon" and this seemed far, far wider than the gap between "The Talons of Weng-Chiang" and "The Horror of Fang Rock".

The late John Nathan-Turner was the last producer of the original series of *Doctor Who*. He oversaw the programme for more than a third of its lifetime, and it was on his "watch" that it floundered and died. This has made him an object of unparalleled hatred in fandom, and anyone with even the slightest connection to the *Doctor Who* underworld will know of the various slaggings-off and death-threats he received in the fan-press during his reign. A fair amount of this stick was justified, as even the most generous viewer *has* to accept that the mid-to-late '80s saw a long string of ugly, misguided decisions that not only hastened the programme's demise but seriously damaged the general public's memories of what the series had been in its prime… whenever you think that was.

But here we're not talking about 1985, or 1986, or 1987. Whatever mistakes Nathan-Turner may have eventually made, the fact remains that in 1980 a great many people thought the programme was in need of a renaissance, and that the

New Man *did* provide it. As ever, fandom's view remains divided - as does the authorship of this present volume, inevitably - but at the time Season Eighteen was widely seen as both a success and a redefinition. It didn't get great ratings (often through no fault of its own, as we'll see elsewhere in this volume), yet it gained the series a new following, and came as a slap in the face to those who'd begun to assume that this was just a low-rent SF series about one actor, one metal dog and a lot of ill-fitting monster outfits.

What follows here isn't so much an apology for the early Nathan-Turner productions as it is an explanation of *why* the programme changed so much once he took over. Why do stories like "Full Circle", "Warriors' Gate" and "Logopolis" still seem so different to what had gone before? Why is there such a gulf between this and the tail-end of the Graham Williams era? The standard fan-guide answer is that Season Eighteen was "glossier", that it had "higher production values", but this is vague and only a fraction of the story.

Give more money and better effects to a Season Seventeen story, and it'd still be a Season Seventeen story. Something far more profound has changed here. What?

In context of the times, one factor needs to be mentioned before all others: the impact of cinema. It's a theme that'll haunt these volumes time and time again, but it's worth reminding ourselves that traditionally *Doctor Who* had little or nothing to do with the way things were done in the movies. In the '60s and '70s, most "big" American drama series - including that old favourite, *Star Trek* - came from a culture of cinema, attempts by American television to replicate Hollywood in the TV studio. The BBC did things differently. While the US gave us westerns, BBC drama sprang from a tradition of televised theatre, a tradition of bringing highbrow culture to the masses and occasionally hiring *playwrights* to work on the scripts.

Even the modern BBC shows signs of this heritage, which is why BBC sit-coms tend to be written by individual authors rather than "teams", and ultimately why so many series are made in little batches of six rather than big-budget blocks of twenty-two. From its first ever episode in 1963, *Doctor Who* was written and staged as if it were a televised play, albeit with its own highly advanced forms of technical trickery. Things changed a little with the shift to colour in 1970, when the ITC

continued on page 11…

it grows very slowly, though, if it takes five centuries to reach that length.] He describes himself as 1,250 in this state, meaning that his real age is still around 750 [760 is more like it].

Proving that he keeps changing his mind about things, the Doctor here says he's sick of not knowing where he's going and is happy to leave the randomiser on Argolis.

• *Inventory.* He's definitely changed his coat, and it's not one of the "spare" coats that's been seen lying around the TARDIS before now. He's got a new scarf as well, as needlessly long as the old one but a lot more low-key. He writes on the outside of the TARDIS with a chinagraph pencil, as used by real scientists on petri dishes and test-tubes. The sonic screwdriver is once again used as a cutting-tool, capable of making a hole in the back of the tachyon generator machine.

The Supporting Cast

• *Romana.* Has no problems helping the Earth scientist Hardin perfect his tachyon experiments, even though this must surely change local history. She claims that the tachyon generator would make her 650 if it surged [indicating that she's around 150... see 17.2, "City of Death"].

• *K9.* Sea-water makes his internal workings explode and causes him to shut down, but what's *really* noticeable is that he doesn't hesitate to roll into the ocean when Romana orders him to fetch a ball, even though he must know it'll damage him. He's programmed with a long list of holiday planets.

The TARDIS The Doctor over-rides the randomiser in order to get to the opening of the Brighton Pavilion, but he gets the wrong century and the wrong season. He states that this is the second time he's missed this event. [Quite possibly referring to 15.1, "Horror of Fang Rock". Also, compare this with the Doctor's TARDIS-piloting skills in 18.3, "Full Circle".] The randomiser is eventually used to make the tachyon generator on Argolis fully-functional, and the Doctor leaves it behind when he departs.

The Time Lords Gallifrey abandoned the science of tachyonics - the manipulation of faster-than-light particles - when it developed warp matrix engineering. Or so says Romana.

The Non-Humans

• *Foamasi.* As bipedal reptiles with beak-like faces and horrible-looking claws, the Foamasi are in fact quite civilised, though their natural language is a series of squeaking, chirruping noises and they can only talk to humans by using badge-like voice synthesiser devices. Even the Doctor can't understand what they're saying, and their names are unpronounceable even with the synthesizers in effect. [Is their native tongue too peculiar even for the Doctor's 'Time Lord gift' to interpret?] Though the Foamasi devastated Argolis in the nuclear war of 2250, and apparently won the conflict - see **Planet Notes** - the two sides have since made their peace, so the ambassador from the Foamasi government treats the Argolin with decorum.

On the other hand, the Foamasi of the West Lodge are gangsters, with plans to run the Argolin Leisure Hive into the ground and buy the planet cheap. To this end, two of the West Lodge's agents are walking around the Hive in human suits, good enough to fool even the Doctor. At least one of the suits is exactly modelled on a real human, the Hive's Earth agent Brock. [The human suit is portrayed as just being a false "skin", but the Foamasi within is clearly much bulkier than the human outside. It's possible that some sort of holographic or mind-bending technology is involved in the suit's construction, although the novel *Placebo Effect* claims that the Foamasi have hollow bones and flexible skeletons, allowing them to squeeze into tiny spaces.]

Officially there are no private enterprise groups among the Foamasi, as the government has owned the whole Foamasi planet since the war [so the West Lodge is a criminal business just *because* it's a business], and the West Lodge has been looking for a new base of operations ever since the government's last clampdown. For years the Foamasi government has been trying to 'force' restitution money on the Argolin, who haven't accepted this apparent apology for genocide.

Though obviously a sophisticated, space-faring species with plenty of technology at their disposal, the Foamasi don't wear clothes when they're not disguised as humans. It's said that reptiles are resistant to radiation [not in *our* world], which means the Foamasi are the only life-form in the galaxy which could live on the surface of Argolis [an exaggeration, even if this refers to *intelligent* life-forms]. The ambassador uses a grenade-like

The John Nathan-Turner Era: What Was the Difference?

...continued from page 9

action serials started to influence the Jon Pertwee run (the action serials, like most American output, being determined to ape the bangs, flashes and high-speed chases of either Hollywood or James Bond), but you can still watch any '70s episode and see traces of the old "live broadcast" system in the Doctor's endless confrontations with Shakespearian villains.

Yet by 1980, Hollywood was being overtaken by New Hollywood. Here in 2005, it's easy to forget, but in the 1970s American cinema was actually starting to look exciting. The old studio heads had proved that they knew next to nothing about the tastes of the post-'60s generation, and the new-blood directors were fighting their way to the surface of the swamp. *Doctor Who* had always, quite rightly, snubbed the crassness of populist cinema. But what happened when populist cinema unexpectedly became worth seeing? What if, like most of the decent movies made from the late '60s onwards, it started to make audiences question the rules of storytelling?

Then came the clincher. In 1977, *Star Wars* was released, and in 1978 it hit Britain like a freighter full of anti-matter. Again, those who weren't "there" at the time may have difficulty understanding what a difference this made. It changed almost everything, as far as the popular media was concerned. Not just by making vast leaps forward in special effects, editing, use of sound and the way film was paced. And not, as cynics now like to claim, by changing the way movies were marketed (it received no hype at all on its US release, and became an overwhelming success through word-of-mouth alone) or the way they were merchandised. It introduced an entirely new dynamic into film-making; a new sense of mythicism; and more importantly still, a new way of using *space*, of presenting us with nigh-tactile, multi-dimensional environments. It was by no means the first or the only film to toy with modern techniques, but it was the biggest and the brightest, and most crucially it was a fantasy.

Bear in mind, before this other worlds never really seemed fully-formed, at least not on a sensual level. A great script (let's say, by Robert Holmes) can suggest whole worlds beyond the one you see on screen, but in a theatre-based medium these implied worlds are confined to the conceptual. Above all else, *Star Wars* - like many of the New Hollywood films preceding it, and in con-

text of "The Leisure Hive", *The Godfather* obviously springs to mind - was an exercise in what we might call "total cinema".

At this level of film-making, there's no division between the story and its medium, and even the movie's sense of movement becomes part of the plot. Many grown-ups found themselves involved in ways they couldn't quite understand, while children soon realised that they had an instinctive knowledge of every facet of the mythology. Anything else was bound to look static by comparison. Though it's true that cinemas were soon full of bad space-opera trying to ape *Star Wars* and missing the point, better film-makers saw the movie and realised what they could do with the form. The most obvious example is Ridley Scott's masterpiece *Alien*, another film we'll be mentioning an awful lot in this volume, which took the *Star Wars* approach and applied it to a rather more adult set of themes.

Where, then, did this leave poor *Doctor Who*? Cinema had changed the expectations of the viewers, not because the audience now wanted more spectacle (although that's what a lot of misguided TV executives thought, at the time) but because it had shown them new ways of relating to a story. Earlier *Doctor Who* seasons tended to take the "literary" approach, and suddenly that just wasn't enough. A story like "The Pirate Planet" (16.2) might be *ingenious*, but even with an old hand like Pennant Roberts behind the camera it's not a great work of dynamic, visual art. In a world beyond Coppola and Lucas and Scott, other productions tended to use the visual nature of film as a story-engine in itself, an increasing sense that theme, narrative, movement and design were all part of a unified process. The SF-ness of a massive must-see film like *Star Wars* no doubt helped the ratings of everything vaguely SF-ish on television, *Doctor Who* included, but after a while TV's lack of scope began to become obvious.

Through a combination of accident and design, *Doctor Who* responded to this big artistic shift in the only way it could. Film-makers had got to grips with "total cinema", so now the series began to venture into the realm of "total television". 1980 was the year that saw the programme take its greatest single step away from televised theatre, not precisely because it was trying to copy the movies (the series wisely stayed away from space-battles in the *Buck Rogers* mould) but because it

continued on page 13...

weapon which, when thrown at his two prisoners, binds them up in a web of filaments. One of these prisoners is the Leader of All Sectors in the West Lodge [i.e. the Godfather]. The West Lodge would supposedly be finished if he were to face trial, but he's killed when the Foamasi shuttle is destroyed [but see **Things That Don't Make Sense**].

Planet Notes   The last few holiday planets mentioned on K9's seemingly-alphabetical list… Yegros Alpha, specialising in atavistic therapy on primitive asteroids; Zaakros, the galaxy's [i.e. Earth's galaxy's] largest flora collection; and Zeen 4, known for its historical re-enactments. Planets like Limnos 4 and Abydos possess non-gravity swimming pools, robot gladiatorial games and sleep-reading stations that provide accelerated learning experiences covering every subject of the technic-index, all of which are providing tough competition for Argolis in the twenty-third century [compare with 4.7, "The Macra Terror"].

• *Argolis.* In 2250, Argolis was devastated by a twenty-minute nuclear war with the Foamasi, in which 2,000 missiles turned the surface of the planet into a desolate, irradiated wasteland. Those Argolin who lived through the war were rendered sterile, and pioneered the science of tachyonics in order to try to create the next generation. They also built the Leisure Hive, a great star-shaped complex in the middle of the wasteland, which made Argolis the 'first of the leisure planets' [in this era] according to K9's files. The war was forty years ago, though the planet's surface won't be inhabitable for another three centuries.

The Argolin tried to 'clone' themselves by donating cells to the tachyon recreation generator they developed, but most of the experiments were failures and the offspring were mutants. The only surviving child - and thus the only native young person on Argolis - is the ambitious and war-like Pangol, and *he* doesn't seem entirely stable. A twenty-year moratorium was called on the experiments until Pangol, a 'thoroughly proficient' tachyon engineer, came of age.

At this point in time, the Leisure Hive is expected to face bankruptcy, but Pangol is determined to perfect the tachyon technique which will create a new army of Argolin in his image. Though Argolin are humanoid in appearance, their skins are green-tinted; they have pointed crests on the tops of their heads; and these crests are surrounded by small bead-like nodules, which drop off as the

Argolin approach death. [It doesn't really come across on-screen, but they were *supposed* to be plant-people.] The war still curses the Argolin survivors, as they have a slow, steady metabolism for most of their lives but then age to death in mere hours. Still an advanced culture despite the years of hardship, the Argolin seen here wear toga-like robes, colour-coded to suit their roles in the Hive [which appears to be the only remnant of civilisation on the entire planet]. They know of Earth history, specifically Greece and Rome. The board which runs the Hive is apparently made up of Argolin, but the *real* Brock is offered a directorship, which he turns down.

The Leisure Hive has an 'experiential grid', which offers twenty different environments to those seeking physical and intellectual 'regeneration', and all the visitors seen here appear to be human [reasonable, since this is humanity's expansionist period, and a sure sign that the planet's in our galaxy]. Part of the Hive's purpose is to promote cross-cultural understanding after the horrors of the war, and one of the environments is said to simulate a high-gravity planet with an indigenous life-form.

Among the attractions seen here is a zero-gravity squash court, but sight-seers are also given demonstrations of the tachyon recreation generator. When a subject enters the generator, a "solid" image of that subject can be manipulated on the machine's viewing-screen, something which the Argolin use as a party-trick but can tear people to pieces if it's sabotaged. Pangol's purpose for the device is to create "photocopies" of anyone who enters it, or anyone who's been programmed into the workings, although these duplicate 'solid images' are unstable and last for only a few minutes before disappearing completely [which smacks of the fake-cloning process in 15.2, "The Invisible Enemy"]. In theory, a tachyon image can never be permanent. The experiments by the Earth scientist Hardin suggest that the machine can be used to make people younger or older, though Hardin has never made this work properly before Romana gives him a hand.

The Argolin were once led by Theron, whose ambition caused the war but who seems to have united Argolis as a single state. The helmet of Theron, a suitably classical-looking relic, is a sacred symbol and a reminder of the horror of violence. Suspected criminals are required to swear their innocence before it when the chairman of

The John Nathan-Turner Era: What Was the Difference?

...continued from page 11

began to explore the possibilities of television as its own medium.

Several things allowed this to happen. The first was the attitude of John Nathan-Turner himself, and it needs to be stressed that unlike the producers before him, Nathan-Turner was a TV obsessive. Though he *did* have a handful of definite ideas about the direction the programme should take, he had no masterplan for changing the series' artistic vision, but in this atmosphere he didn't need one. Though his critics have often mocked him for being an "accountant" obsessed with number-crunching - he was, remember, the man who worked out that it was £25 cheaper to film "City of Death" in modern-day Paris than to build sets for 1920s Monte Carlo - this isn't in itself a problem, provided that the directors and script editors know what they're doing. You can say this about the man: he was good at squeezing the pound. He wanted the programme to look less scrappy, and in this he succeeded brilliantly.

It sounds like pure bean-counting, but what this effectively *means* is that the programme-makers had more scope at the very point when "more scope" was the order of the day. "Higher production values" isn't just about making things "look nice", it's about understanding how to *use* a visual form to tell a story. Both "The Sun Makers" (15.4, made in 1977) and "Full Circle" (18.3, made in 1980) feature copious "corridor" scenes, yet "The Sun Makers" reveals its meaning almost wholly through dialogue and uses corridors purely to connect scene A and scene B (with perhaps a couple of guards thrown in halfway between the two as a way of livening things up... or not), whereas "Full Circle" uses the sense of *space* within the Starliner to define the story's environment and underline what the whole thing's actually about. As we'll see when we get there. There are some stories in this period - "Warriors' Gate" (18.5) is the most obvious example - which simply wouldn't have been possible without this stretching of the visual, and which would have been unthinkable just a year earlier. Most stories from the '60s make perfect sense if you take away the pictures and listen to the soundtrack, even if you lose a lot of the thrill. Most stories from the '80s don't.

A final word on this subject. There's a school of thought which holds that film-making is all about the use of space; that when we see a fully-formed cinematic "world", we primarily become familiar

with the meaning, the history and the "rules" of that world not through dialogue or even characterisation, but through the way the director manipulates the spaces we see on the screen. In effect, the place where we feel we "are" dictates our *mental* space, so we come to understand the story as much because of its environment as because of what actually happens. One of the reasons that Orson Welles' *Citizen Kane* is considered to be such a classic is Welles' use of these environmental techniques. In a time when most movies still looked as if they were shot on stages, Welles used long tracking-shots to suggest a sense of movement through the film's "world"; overlapped conversations to make three-dimensional "soundscapes"; and, most famously, insisted on building sets that had proper ceilings. This sounds like a trivial point, but it's a massively powerful way of telling the viewer what kind of space s/he's in, not merely setting the mood but enclosing the audience inside the story. What's on the screen becomes part of a much bigger, all-enveloping structure. '70s cinema took this process to extremes, especially with the use of pseudo-documentary techniques, although by definition it's not something the viewers are consciously supposed to pick up on.

With this in mind, compare a '70s "space opera" episode of *Doctor Who* to the way Peter Grimwade directs 19.6, "Earthshock". The '70s generation, brought up in a world where culture was less linear and the media was becoming something to "navigate" rather than "read", were obviously more likely to respond to this spatial approach to TV and film production. Grimwade, whether he was conscious of it or not, might even be described as the first "modern" *Doctor Who* director in this sense. He didn't have to be a great visionary. He just had to go to the pictures. (You may also want to consider 21.1, "Warriors of the Deep", which was originally supposed to be like "Earthshock" but ended up being made by the returning '70s director who was responsible for "The Pirate Planet"... and as a result, everything looks as if it's shot on stage-sets again.)

On top of that there's the arrival of Christopher H. Bidmead as the new script editor. His approach to the series is interesting, and entirely in keeping with the mood of the times, though unlike Nathan-Turner he was a stickler for details. Key to understanding Season Eighteen, as has already

continued on page 15...

ABOUT TIME 1980-1984

the Leisure Hive [effectively the ruler of the planet] sits in session as a judge. The boardroom serves as a court. When Theron wanted to try someone, however, he used the more Medieval technique of throwing them into fire or water.

Pangol hopes to repopulate the planet with copies of himself and lead the Argolin back to war, but in the end the tachyon technology just turns him back into a baby with the same Argolin hairstyle, while his "mother" Mena becomes a much younger woman and resumes her duties as chairman. But the generator is destroyed [so the Argolin may still be doomed, though Hardin's work is so advanced that he may well be able to re-build it].

Despite its supposedly peaceful purpose, the Hive is equipped with weapons which can blast departing shuttlecraft to pieces.

History

Dating. The war of 2250 was forty years ago, so given that people tend to round up or down when they're making statements like this, it's now somewhere around 2290. The Doctor's trip to Brighton is apparently in the present day.

By the time of the Leisure Hive, humans are advanced enough to take holidays on other planets as a matter of course. Hologram-like 3D communications are possible between planets, and recordings are made on holo-crystals. People are still wearing spectacles. According to Romana, this part of the galaxy [perhaps meaning the human-occupied part] doesn't discover 'unreal transfer' - a way of manipulating solid objects - until 2386.

The Doctor and Romana believe that tachyonics was first theorised on Earth [what, before Gallifrey?], but that humans didn't do anything with it. Nonetheless, it's a human, Hardin, who's worked out how to manipulate time using tachyonics.

The Analysis

Where Does This Come From? We should start in 1978, the year that popular SF sprouted two enormous and all-devouring heads. This was the year that Douglas Adams finished the first series of *The Hitch-Hiker's Guide to the Galaxy*, which opened out the whole *language* of science fiction, as well as profoundly changing the way future generations - in Britain, at the very least - would think of

the genre. But at the time this went unnoticed by many people, because 1978 is also the year that *Star Wars* battered the country into submission.

Early '80s *Doctor Who* is, at times, rather torn between these "ideologies" (see also **The John Nathan-Turner Era: What Was the Difference?**). While he was script editor under Graham Williams, Adams had a distinctly literary approach towards the series, and a quick look at Volume IV will demonstrate the extent to which the late '70s production team was influenced by current trends in written SF. But now John Nathan-Turner's in charge, and Nathan-Turner is a man obsessed with television as a medium in itself. From this point on things are going to get a lot more *visual* around here. So naturally, this means plundering the cinemas as well as the canon of British TV.

Star Wars has been mentioned before now, and it'll be mentioned again, simply because it had such an impact on the audiences, film-makers and pop-culture-producers of the early 1980s that its influence was almost inescapable. Younger readers might not realise the full extent of this, now that we live in an age when almost every Hollywood blockbuster is a sci-fi flick and space opera is virtually indistinguishable from soap opera. But the *Star Wars* boom hit every aspect of popular lore, so in next to no time Sarah Brightman was singing "I Lost My Heart to a Starship Trooper" on *Top of the Pops* and regular characters from TV ads like the Milky Bar Kid and the Matey Sailor were suddenly developing rocket technology and having "space" adventures. (Although ironically it wasn't the "space" aspect of *Star Wars* that appealed to the older members of the audience as much as the "tales of derring-do" aspect; see 16.4, "The Androids of Tara".)

Directly or indirectly, this is one of the reasons that *Doctor Who* suffered such a catastrophic ratings drop between the end of Season Seventeen and the first episode of Season Eighteen, and we'll come back to that later.

But for now, let's stick with the visuals. Use of imagery is more crucial in Season Eighteen than ever before. One of the greatest effects that *Star Wars* had on the popular psyche was to introduce the notion of alien objects and ideas casually lounging around in the background of a bigger story, instead of being explained individually in painful detail. Every minor detail of the film seemed to have its own back-story, something that

The John Nathan-Turner Era: What Was the Difference?

...continued from page 13

been hinted, is that with Bidmead as script editor *Doctor Who* started to turn science into folklore. For the most part, it did this visually. It was always part of the series' mandate to "explain" science to the younger viewers, or at least to get them *just* interested enough in scientific theory to make them curious about the way the world fits together, but the application of this varies throughout the series. In the '60s everything's about machinery; rockets and moonbases and gravitrons, perfect for a population which could actually *see* the space-race unfolding. By the late '70s, however, this aspect of the programme had been... not so much "lost" as "hijacked". The later Graham Williams era is full of the kind of science-boffoonery that appeals to university students, not "the kids".

Bidmead, on the other hand, went out of his way to make the science big, charming and fantastical (if not necessarily more accurate...). Those who've mocked him for the technobabble in his work seem to have missed the point that only a pedant would *notice* such a thing, when the big images of Season Eighteen were bigger than ever before. Suddenly it's alchemy rather than chemistry. "Logopolis" (18.7), written by Bidmead himself, is the best example of this style and ties in with the whole "environmental" approach of programme-makers in this period. In "Logopolis", the mechanics of a modern computer are presented as a world full of chanting monks and labyrinthine streets, an entire *landscape* based on popular science instead of just a few throw-away technical references. And in the context of the times, its hardly surprising that many of these visual "hits" seem determined to blur the line between scientific terminology and high mythicism. The Key to Time sequence of Season Sixteen has to spuriously invent time-gods to provide a threat to the universal order; the quest for the Key attempts to set the Doctor an epic Herculean task, but nobody bothers to demonstrate (let alone explain) why this Key is such a thing of power. We're told it's the most important artefact in the universe, yet all we have are some mumbled words about chaos overrunning the universe. Bidmead, on the other hand, turns the equations of the universe's existence and demise into something both tangible and televisual.

So, the new style of the programme is starting to look like an inevitable consequence of the way the writers and directors of the early '80s were responding to the modern media. But John Nathan-Turner's intentions for the programme are also worthy of note. By the end of Williams' run as producer, it was widely felt (even by Williams himself, it seems) that there'd been too great a slide into humour over the previous few years. Still, let's consider the meaning of "humour" here. One of the reasons that the worst of the late '70s stories seem so lightweight isn't just that the writers and / or actors were throwing in too many gags, but that less attention was paid to the "dramatic" parts of this drama series. Even defenders of the later Williams stories, who admire the all-round cleverness and good cheer, have to admit that the programme loses its sense of threat in this era. We've already seen that the first cliffhanger of "The Leisure Hive", with its dismembered and screaming Doctor, came as a bit of a shock. But the second cliffhanger is even more significant. The Doctor comes out of the tachyon machine, and he's horribly, disturbingly *old*.

Bear in mind, by this point a generation had grown up safe in the knowledge that nothing really bad ever happened to the Doctor. He got locked up a lot, sometimes even knocked unconscious, but he never changed, never suffered and hadn't really been shown in a position of weakness since "Pyramids of Mars" (13.3) in 1976. All of a sudden, he was vulnerable. Changeable. *Violable*, even. It's impossible to imagine this cliffhanger in Season Seventeen, or at least, it's impossible to imagine it being presented as something so macabre. By the same tack, Romana's "funny" regeneration scene in "Destiny of the Daleks" (17.1) is impossible to imagine in Season Eighteen. That, in itself, should tell you why the new producership was so welcome in some quarters.

Certainly, at this point the programme begins to re-consider the way that opposition to the Doctor should work, and to understand that drama requires the leading character to actually seem *menaced* sometimes. In fact, the idea of "villainy" becomes more complex after 1980. Every story up until "Meglos" has an obvious, overt bad guy / bad species / bad computer to drive the plot forward, and more often than not these villains are (a) a bit on the limp side and (b) hopelessly overshadowed by the Doctor himself. Baker's insistence on laughing the villains into destruction (his words) became a handicap before long. But after

continued on page 17...

ABOUT TIME 1980–1984

cinema had never achieved before the 1970s. (*Star Wars* wasn't the only movie to do this, of course. But as a story that had to set up an entire universe from scratch, the effect was more noticeable there than anywhere else.)

The most telling moment in "The Leisure Hive" comes when the Doctor and Romana stroll through a zero-gravity squash court, a scene lasting only twenty seconds in which the floating squash-players are treated as a kind of futuristic "period detail" while the lead characters talk about an important plot-point. Zero-gravity sports were standard comic-book fare by 1980, but the idea that the programme could take such things for *granted* was a step into new visual territory. The sequence looks crass and cheaply-made today, yet it's hard to find anything in the series before this point that takes the same approach.

Another great effect of pop-movie SF in the late '70s was, of course, the use of big mythic themes and big mythic images. *Star Wars* was once again the obvious pack leader, although in this case much of the groundwork had already been done by the Erich von Daniken craze of the early '70s (endlessly mentioned in Volumes III and IV of this work), which had made the link in the public consciousness between the idea of "enormous battle-cruisers" and the idea of "ye olde folklore". Before the Nathan-Turner era *Doctor Who* typically approached mythology by taking an old legend and re-making it with spaceships and aliens, a flawed strategy as 15.5, "Underworld" proved. It might have seemed terribly clever at the time, but it missed the mark for those who might have gone to the cinema and come to realise that even *Battlestar Galactica* had more mythic scope than "The Horns of Nimon", despite the fact that *Galactica* was clearly more dreadful.

What's striking about Season Eighteen, at least to those of the younger generation who weren't interested in speculating about the theoretical possibilities of a black hole because you couldn't bloody well *see* it, is the fact that some of its stories feel a lot more fairy-tale than those stories which actively try to be. Christopher H. Bidmead's own script for "Logopolis" (18.7) demonstrates this best (the universe is being held together by something out of Lewis Carroll rather than by an all-powerful mega-computer, and on top of that there are nods towards Jewish mysticism), but "The Leisure Hive" is the first faltering step in that direction. Tachyonics isn't presented as a rational

explanation for events here, it's presented as a *power*, with tangible, visible, nigh-magical effects. And compare this with the Dodecahedron in the next story, which has near-limitless energy purely because it's in tune with the geometry of the universe. Bidmead's stated credo of "less magic, more science" is telling, because there are times in this season when the latter seems to be doing the narrative job of the former.

Enough of all this, though. Let's look at the roots of Fisher's script, rather than the *weltan-scau-ung* of early '80s pop-fantasy. The Doctor - supposedly enfeebled at this stage - hits the nail on the head. The tachyon recreation generator is a 'cabinet of illusions'. Even the technique used by the director to show Pangol coming apart is the same as that used by Victorian illusionists. The central idea of the original version of the story, before all the "protection racket" material, was that this advanced, space-age holiday camp was almost indistinguishable from a traditional British seaside resort. (See also 24.3, "Delta and the Bannermen" and 4.7, "The Macra Terror".) This is decidedly a pre-War, working-class idea of a holiday, far removed from the package deals, time-shares or theme parks that were to come later. All the entertainments are laid on by the staff, and given to you to enjoy whether you like it or not, as much for the purposes of education as "fun". You just sit back and let it happen to you, rather than doing anything yourself. The accommodation - what we see of it - is very much in the form of "chalet"-style rooms.

And then the lizards arrive. As has already been mentioned, Fisher was persuaded to rewrite the story to suggest the Mafia-drama of *The Godfather*, so like "Nightmare of Eden" (17.4) this is about the way the media saw organised crime at the time more than it's about organised crime per se. It's hard to imagine anyone approaching the idea in the same way in the age of *The Sopranos*, but post-Coppola gangster stories seemed far more operatic. (Picture a series called *The Foamasis*, about a family of reptiles who run organised crime across the galaxy but at the same time have to go and watch their hatchlings play Kiddie-League Baseball at the weekend, and you realise what's changed.)

This is also the point when the programme becomes obsessed with nuclear war and dooms-day weapons again, not surprising circa 1980, while this season's obsession with fashionable

The John Nathan-Turner Era: What Was the Difference?

...continued from page 15

"Meglos" things start to change. Occasionally there are no conventional villains, and occasionally the villains have a new kind of relationship with the story. "Full Circle" has no baddies at all. "Logopolis" sees the Master play second-fiddle to entropy. In "Kinda" the Mara is just a distraction, and the real villains are the characters' neuroses. "Black Orchid" presents us with a hurt, confused, emotionally-scarred victim who also happens to be a murderer (and while we're on the subject of madness, Captain Rorvik in "Warriors' Gate" is a very different kind of crazed sadist to the ones we're used to). "Mawdryn Undead" presents the Doctor with an opponent who's just trying to die. "Terminus" ends with the realisation that everybody's being equally exploited... and so on. Tragically, this gets lost as the series goes into decline at the end of Season Twenty-One, after which there's a tendency for the villains to become stomping monsters and leering megalomaniacs again. But in this period there's a tendency for the series to become not just scary, but scary for unexpected reasons.

So Tom Baker is being kept on a leash, at last. The Doctor ceases to be such an overwhelming bore. Barely an episode seemed to go by in the late '70s without him name-checking Einstein as a close friend or being able to hypnotise people in under three seconds, but now he seems more of a troubled creature, less inclined to show off and less insistent on being the unsung hero of everything good that's ever happened. It's hard to imagine the Fifth Doctor claiming to have given Newton the idea for gravity. Not only is he returned to the level of "knowledgeable traveller" rather than "cosmic superhero", he's also *flawed* again. The real test-case is this: a scene was planned for "State of Decay" in which the locals throw spears into the open door of the TARDIS, and the Doctor emerges holding them all, as if he'd caught them with one hand. Nathan-Turner insisted on removing this sequence, on the very sensible grounds that it looked stupid and wasn't funny anyway. One year earlier, Baker would almost certainly have got away with it.

As the Case for the Defence has already mentioned, the bottom line is that by the end of Season Seventeen *Doctor Who* had become wallpaper. It got decent ratings, but only in the same way that a long-running sit-com gets decent ratings; it was something that just happened to be there. Children weren't chanting "I-am-a-Dalek" in playgrounds any longer. The declining "family audience" wasn't being taken to odd new places every four episodes, it was just watching the leading man go through the motions. *Doctor Who* was the Fourth Doctor Goon Show, and the ratings drop for the first episode of Season Eighteen shows how little loyalty there was. Nathan-Turner's decision to "toughen up" the series undoubtedly alienated some viewers, but then, that's what happens if you stop making a programme that's just there to make the audience feel comfortable. We may hate him now for the decisions he made circa 1984, but it comes down to this: if he hadn't done what he did, then it's hugely doubtful that the programme would have survived beyond Tom Baker's departure.

real-world hardware results in the Doctor admiring Argolis' fibre-optics. There's a sense of David Fisher recycling his old material, too, especially "The Creature from the Pit" (17.3). The monsters can't explain that they're nice until they've got translator devices, and the main villain is dealt with at the start of episode four, leaving another threat to become the focus of the story in the last fifteen minutes.

Things That Don't Make Sense As ever in *Doctor Who*, the blithe assumption is that time-technology (in this case involving tachyons) can make people very old or very young in moments, instead of just pushing them forward in time or making them die of starvation in seconds. And as ever, people keep their memories of recent events when their personal timelines are reversed, so their brains apparently aren't "youthened" even though the other parts of their bodies are. This throws up some awkward questions for Pangol, who presumably ends the story as a twenty-year-old mind in a baby's body. The idea that this is a "good" ending, as it allows him to be brought up better this time, looks rather shaky when you consider how bitter he'll be about being swathed in nappies for the next few years. Apart from anything else, it's surprising that he doesn't wee on the Doctor as an act of revenge in the last scene. [Perhaps people *usually* keep their memories after they're made younger - for whatever reason - but don't if their brains get so physically tiny that they can't possibly retain all the old experiences. When making people older, the device obviously makes best-

17

guesses about the subject's future, as the Doctor isn't turned into Christopher Eccleston. So the device's workings would seem to entail some "intelligence".]

Almost as strange, the generator is programmed to produce copies of Pangol in his robe and helmet, but when the Doctor's stuck in the machine it produces duplicate Doctors *also* wearing the robe and helmet. How does the device differentiate between forms of matter so precisely that it knows the difference between Pangol's body and outfit, and knows how to re-dress the Doctor's copies in the clothing? [That settles it, the generator's intelligent. Or magic.] When the "real" Doctor comes out of the tachyon generator he's wearing the same robe-and-helmet ensemble, even though *these* clothes don't vanish like tachyon images and couldn't possibly have been picked up anywhere along the way. What happens to his coat, after he enters the generator? He's apparently not wearing it under his Pangol-robe, as the next time we see it he's picking it up off the floor of a corridor. Then there's Pangol's decision to drag his adopted mother into the regenerator with him, when he's trying to create a new breed of Argolin, which is strange *and* disturbing. And how exactly does the big ending work? The Doctor throws a hat at a TV screen, and a fascist turns into a cute baby. And the "identical" Pangols are all different heights.

Still on the subject of the regenerator... Dr. Science would like a word. The concept of tachyons (from the Greek for "fast") is old hat, but part of the deal with relativity is that although travelling faster-than-light is possible, anything doing so is unable to engage with things moving below light-speed. And even if they can make time go backwards, they can't accelerate its *forward* flow. The whole idea of the Doctor ageing is - aesthetic flaws aside - gibberish. Besides, if FTL technology is so novel, how long does it take for a ship to reach Argolis from Earth? Even with a super-whizzy space-drive, no-one seems to notice that Brock appears to have come from Earth to the Hive in about ten minutes.

Morix, Mena's predecessor as Leisure Hive director, speaks of the 'non-gravity swimming pools' of other holiday-worlds as if they've got Argolis out-classed, but the Leisure Hive has a zero-gravity squash court. And surely, if you take the rackets away then that *is* a non-gravity swimming pool? Unless a proper zero-g swimming

pool involves water, in which case diving would be impossible. (Dr. Science also has some things to say about surface tension, but life really is too short.) Hardin seems quick to accept that the Doctor is a superior being, and therefore Romana too (it's still one of those stories where everyone talks about 'the Doctor and the girl'), because he survived the Ordeal of the Age Makeup. Nevertheless, under Argolin law the Doctor is clearly found guilty of Stimson's murder. If he survives the generator then he still has to be put to death, according to episode two, but this is forgotten once he comes out looking like Fagin from *Oliver Twist*. [Pangol's idea that they test the generator on the Doctor is actually supposed to be a judicial "trial by fire", just like in the good old days of Theron, but it doesn't come across on-screen.]

Episode one sees the Doctor and Romana comment on the hologram of the tachyon rejuvenation experiment even though they only wander into the room after it's finished (you can tell, thanks to the door-opening sound effect). Why do the two nasty Foamasi stand there and let the representative of the Foamasi government rip off their human suits, rather than ganging up to overpower him before he can reveal all? The "nice" Foamasi can't speak English by this stage, so it's not as if it'd be able to tell anybody the truth without a physical demonstration. You also have to wonder why the Foamasi law-enforcer came to the Leisure Hive without a synthesizer of his own, and why the "nasty" Foamasi insist on stripping off their human-suits whenever they're required to kill somebody.

In a desperate attempt to give the story an all-round happy ending it turns out that the "nice" Foamasi wasn't on board the shuttle when it was blown up, and that the West Lodge Foamasi were piloting the ship, so... how did they escape from captivity? [Note, though, that to us all Foamasi look alike. They also sound alike, when using voice synthesizers. It's feasible that the surviving Foamasi at the end of the story is actually the West Lodge "Godfather", and that he's just *pretending* to be the ambassador.] Brock seems to have the legal right to arrest people on Argolis, as well as being *de facto* managing director after Morix dies, so why bother with the sabotage and buy-out if he can just get the contracts rewritten?

Not a problem with this story in itself, but with its place in the *Doctor Who* universe: at the end of the story, Hardin is a hair's-breadth away from perfecting technology that can make anybody twenty years younger. Without side-effects. Or apparent restrictions. Why doesn't this instantly make Argolis the most powerful planet in the universe? Why doesn't it change the entire history of creation, as species from every corner of existence hurry there to effectively gain immortality? Why is Borusa so obsessed with becoming immortal the *hard* way in "The Five Doctors" (20.7), if a device can so easily be created on a world in the twenty-third century that does the job much more efficiently? Why don't the Time Lords step in to stop this happening, when they block a much less drastic form of longevity research in "Mindwarp" (23.2)? [Maybe they *do* stop it. Maybe the Doctor and Romana only help Hardin in his work because they know the Time Lords are bound to notice it and intervene.] In itself, the machine's ability to create people and solid objects out of thin air should make it the most sought-after piece of hardware imaginable; for more of this see the objections to "The Invisible Enemy" (15.2), and **How Do You Transmit Matter?** under "Nightmare of Eden" (17.4)…

Critique (Prosecution) *Imagine the first para-graph narrated by Nigel Lambert (see* **Oh, Isn't That..?***) over footage of lab-coated sadists strap-ping twentysomethings into chairs in front of tel-evisions.*

We took ten minutes of episode two of "Nightmare of Eden" and ten minutes of episode two of "The Leisure Hive", and showed each to our experimental subjects. None of these people had seen any *Doctor Who* before. They were then asked which was the cheap, shoddy, 1970s "comedy" show and which the glossy, scientifically-accurate "serious" 1980s one. The results were conclusive: "The Leisure Hive" drags, but is otherwise indistinguishable from the supposedly "naff" Williams story. Indeed, as the "slow" one has cheap electronic music of the kind most programmes of this type abandon when they can afford real instruments, at least one specimen concluded that "The Leisure Hive" was a pilot for the more accomplished "Nightmare".

So why do we (that is, long-term fans) think otherwise? The answer seems to be because Marvel's *Doctor Who Monthly* told us it was so. Looked at objectively, the title sequence and the lack of any concessions to "mainstream" viewers (like, say, jokes) are the only signs of this supposed "glossiness" and dynamically "new" style.

Williams had aimed for a total family audience, with some things to appeal to adults, some to small children, some to sardonic students and nothing to put off anyone. The stated ambition was to cater for bright fifteen year olds as the median audience, with Baker and Ward pitching their performances to the younger members and a few "cute" younger actors to retain adults.

With the new regime expressing a policy of ignoring the demands of any audience other than paid-up fans or fourteen year old boys with ZX80 computers, they wantonly began the season with the dullest one-hundred seconds of *Doctor Who* ever… compounding the felony by having even the Doctor snoring. It was as though they were drawing a line in the sand to say "if you aren't with us, you're against us" and defying uncommitted viewers to look elsewhere. The ratings show that the public did exactly that. This time, there was an alternative.

When ITV had tried to break the BBC's Saturday Night hold on the public in the past, they had often used family space opera (see 13.1, "Terror of the Zygons"; 6.4, "The Invasion"; 3.1, "Galaxy Four"). But now, with the Glen A. Larson abomination *Buck Rogers in the Twenty-Fifth Century*, they had a serious weapon. Episode one of "The Leisure Hive" got a respectable six-million viewers (for August that's good), but one week later they lost a sixth of this. Of those who persevered with the BBC's offering, the main comment was complaint about the "tacky" new titles and music. It is certainly true that these have aged less well than what they replaced. The starfield titles look unnervingly like those for *The Old Grey Whistle Test*, a '70s "serious" music programme which seemed to have Barclay James Harvest on every week.

And that's the problem with being "up-to-date". Late '70s *Doctor Who* exists in its own timeframe. "The Leisure Hive" exists in August 1980, along with other new, fresh things from that time like digital watches, Pot Noodles and "Eighth Day" by Hazel O'Connor (or, if you're American, anything by Devo).

Anyone who cared enough about the science to prefer things like 'eigenvalues' and 'schrodinger oscillators' to more euphonious and suggestive made-up terms would also be annoyed that they got the science glaringly wrong. Anyone who got off on FIFO stacks and fibre-optics would feel cheated that the TARDIS was now a jumped-up Olivetti, something you could breadboard with a trip to Radio Shack or a Maplins catalogue. A piece of Adams technobabble like 'conceptual geometer' tells you what it is about, and leads the imagination onward to how amazing the TARDIS might be (it's what we in the trade call an "absent paradigm"). An 'anti-baryon shield' simply means a bit of tinfoil, but if you don't know this, it doesn't suggest anything. At least when George Lucas used incorrect technobabble, it was to make a character-point about Han Solo's arrogance. Here it's just something Lalla says to distract us from the horrible music.

Sure, there are little touches which remind us that this is still *Doctor Who*, and no-one who's seen it can resist joining in with the line 'you mentioned... Foamasi?' on later viewings, but the overall impression is that it's all gone flat. The use of the theme tune in the incidental score, like the "I'm dead mysterious, me" question marks on the Doctor's new comic-book costume, seem desperate, much like the imploring tone the producer's catch-phrase 'stay tuned' took on after Longleat. If Tom Baker can't be bothered, why should we?

Critique (Defence)   First, let's get one thing straight here. In 1979, Graham Williams broke the back of *Doctor Who* as a popular series. It was bound to have problems, once the Great Era of Family Television ended - see **What Difference Does a Day Make?** under 19.1, "Castrovalva" - but the Williams regime made the end inevitable.

For all the attempts by Williams' apologists to find a meaningful and significant subtext in "The Creature from the Pit", the truth is that Season Seventeen looked to the non-fan world like tawdry, badly-judged space opera, putting the series closer to *Star Trek* in the public imagination than ever before. (Even though those making it seemed to seriously think they were sending up *Star Trek*, a lot of the time... this is the mindset of people who honestly believe that a parody of "The Devil in the Dark" is in some way a workable starting-point for a story.) So soon after the late '70s Space Opera Explosion, this was just about acceptable and guaranteed to bring in good ratings, but it also set in stone the idea that *Doctor Who* was a "space" series.

And then, suddenly, people could get "space" anywhere. The fact that the first episode of Season Eighteen had *less than half* the ratings for the first episode of Season Seventeen (before anyone had actually seen the new-look series, obviously)

demonstrates that people had just gotten sick of it, and 5.9 million viewers was in no way "respectable" even for August. And the fact that ITV was showing *Buck Rogers* at the same time isn't enough to explain the drop, or rather, if it *were* enough then that should tell you something in itself. Why would any child care about something as slow as "The Horns of Nimon", when BBC1 was showing *Battle for the Planets*? Why would any family audience think that "Destiny of the Daleks" was acceptable intergalactic adventure, when *Star Wars* had already come and gone? Williams and company robbed *Doctor Who* of its unpredictability; turned it into a crass space-based "format"; took out the strangeness, took out the scope, took out the drama, made sure there was no longer anything unique about it except the increasingly tedious antics of the leading man. Suddenly even *Blake's 7* looked more "current". At best, the series was wallpaper, something old and familiar that you had on in the background while you were eating dinner on a Saturday night.

Is "The Leisure Hive" the cure to all that...? Lord, no. It features lizard-people every bit as pulp-sci-fi as the Buck Rogers ones, an alien planet much like those you could find almost anywhere in popular SF at the time. But both Bidmead and Nathan-Turner knew things had to change, and within the year there'd be universes behind magic mirrors, art nouveau gardens and worlds full of chanting wizards. More importantly, there'd be a new sense of *space* within the programme. Stylistically, what we're looking at in this first outing is an attempt - a bold, right-minded but ultimately failed attempt - to pick up on everything that had happened to the visual media while the old production team had been sleeping. Yes, of course a modern viewer is going to think that a piece of '70s slop like "Nightmare of Eden" looks better than this. "Nightmare of Eden" was made by a cast that had grown used to the series' limits (even if the various individuals involved all hated each other), at a time when Tom Baker could breeze through his usual schtick without a moment's thought and make it look reasonably proficient. This is trying harder, so naturally, it gets things wrong. Anyone watching it today wouldn't see the importance of it. Anyone watching it at the time would immediately have noticed the shift, for better or worse.

So as with the last great sea-change in the style of *Doctor Who* (7.1, "Spearhead from Space"), it's… glitched. Basically, there are at least three versions of "The Leisure Hive" going on at once: the story that Fisher wants to tell (essentially a Season Seventeen story), the vision of the programme that as yet only exists in Chris Bidmead's head, and John Nathan-Turner's concept of the way modern television's supposed to look and sound. The result is a compromise, and a rushed compromise. To some extent *all* the stories of Season Eighteen were made under crisis conditions, and this one especially doesn't look as if it's been finished.

One-time-only director Lovett Bickford obviously wants this to be a more dynamic kind of show, but his work seems hurried and uncertain, while the material's such a hybrid of old-style and new-style that it keeps leaving parts of itself behind and forgetting where it left them. There are welcome moments of quiet, brooding sobriety, structural spaces never before seen in this series… yet they're intercut with sci-fi exposition scenes that sound as if the cast aren't following a word of it, not to mention a truly epic list of plot loopholes. Parts of it feel *haunted*, a recurring sensation in this season, and it's a novel feeling to have after what's gone before. But parts of it still just feel silly. And Peter Howell's music, such an important and evocative feature of the series in this era, is completely out of control at this stage.

It's a false start for the series' new style, then; one of two false starts, before "Full Circle" (18.3) gets a grip on where everything's supposed to be going. But it's making a gesture towards a new form of *Doctor Who*, one that tries to make the programme work as a fully-qualified TV programme rather than a theoretical exercise. With hindsight it looks like a pilot, and in a sense that's exactly what it is. Many got fed up with it before episode four, yet it laid the foundations for a season that would end up drawing a new audience to the programme, and begin to redefine it in the mass consciousness at a time when people had less reason than ever to care.

The new coat, incidentally, is quite lovely. Kick anyone who says otherwise.

The Facts

Written by David Fisher. Directed by Lovett Bickford. Viewing figures: 5.9 million, 5.0 million, 5.0 million, 4.5 million.

Supporting Cast Adrienne Corri (Mena), David Haig (Pangol), John Collins (Brock), Nigel Lambert (Hardin), Laurence Payne (Morix), Martin Fisk (Vargos), Ian Talbot (Klout), David Allister (Stimson), Clifford Norgate (Generator Voice), Harriet Reynolds (Tannoy Voice).

Oh, Isn't That..?

• *Adrienne Corri*. As famous for her game-show appearances as any of her many TV and film roles. She's the raped wife in the "Singin' in the Rain" scene from *A Clockwork Orange*, but for every *Dr. Zhivago* there's a skeleton in her cupboard, such as Scottish-based monster flick *Devil Girl from Mars*. Her appearance in this story was the hook for the *Radio Times* coverage.

• *Nigel Lambert*. His *face* isn't that well-known, but as a voice-over artist for educational science programmes he was ideally cast for a story that looks and sounds so much like BBC schools' television. (Recently he parodied this as the narrator of the spoof series *Look Around You*.)

• *Laurence Payne*. Famous as ITV's 1920s sleuth *Sexton Blake* (for a sidelight on this see 3.2, "Mission to the Unknown"), he'd already been in *Doctor Who* as Johnny Ringo (3.8, "The Gunfighters"). This was a return to television acting after losing an eye filming *Sexton Blake*, and he'd whiled away the intervening years writing a series of successful detective novels.

Working Titles "Avalon", "The Argolins".

Cliffhangers On the screen of the tachyon generator, the image of the Doctor is ripped limb from limb; the Doctor emerges from the rejuvenator as a wizened, bearded old man; one of the Foamasi rips away Brock's skin, revealing *another* Foamasi underneath.

The Lore

• First things first. Graham Williams had commissioned a "starfield" title sequence, showing an older Tom Baker, a year earlier. The results had been universally hated.

• As we saw in the last volume, Graham Williams was given *Doctor Who* to produce almost as a sop after having his own project taken away from him. His efforts to put his own stamp on the series in the late '70s were hampered first by the BBC hierarchy's punitive measures against the perceived "excesses" of the previous producer; then by budgetary cuts and double-digit inflation; then by a series of crippling strikes, mainly strategic ploys by EETPU, the electricians' union. Despite all this, Williams knew exactly what he wanted from the series, and he managed to put some of his changes into effect, but the cost to his health and self-esteem (never high, as the rest of his family looked to his cousin - the novelist Emlyn Williams - as the definition of "success") was devastating.

After fighting constant battles against the BBC, the unions and Tom Baker, he finally got to where he believed he should have started with "Shada" (17.6), a story which would have removed the dead wood from the programme once and for all. And it was cancelled. Pausing only to nominate production unit manager John Nathan-Turner as the new producer, Williams resigned and went off to run a computer hire company. His involvement in *Doctor Who*, at least, was renewed when he was invited to contribute to Season Twenty-Three (see under 22.6, "Revelation of the Daleks"). Later he ran a small country hotel. His death in 1990 was the result of a gunshot wound, probably accidental.

• The very first change Nathan-Turner made was to suggest to Graeme McDonald, head of Series and Serials (the two departments had been merged, leaving McDonald unable to micro-manage as he had in the past), a new approach to the music. Nathan-Turner lent McDonald the albums *Oxygene* and *Equinoxe* by Jean-Michel Jarre (as used as background in the original radio incarnation of *The Hitch-Hiker's Guide to the Galaxy*). McDonald thought they actually wanted Jarre to score the new series, and felt the music was a bit too 'trippy'. It turned out that Nathan-Turner was thinking mainly of the budget - Dudley Simpson used a band of about six musicians - but also of his own desire to be seen as "a new broom". Nathan-Turner broke the news to Simpson over dinner.

• Neither Peter Howell (scoring the story and the new rendition of the theme) nor Sid Sutton (making the new titles) felt comfortable about having to follow such iconic, established work by former colleagues. Howell admits that he took most of his inspiration for this score from light-classical pieces, notably Ravel's *Bolero*. The making of the new-style sig tune was the subject of a schools TV programme, aptly.

• As we saw in the last volume (**What Else Wasn't Made?** under 17.6, "Shada"), incoming script editor Christopher H. Bidmead inherited a selection of scripts not to his taste. Among these was "The Tearing of the Veil", a Victorian ghost story which involved the Doctor being prematurely aged and confined to bed for two episodes. Douglas Adams and new producer John Nathan-Turner had liked the idea David Fisher proposed of a "Butlin's in Space", even though Fisher was more keen on another idea about cryogenically-suspended godlike aliens (possibly called "The Castle of Doom").

It appears that Fisher made a joke about mafia lizards running a protection racket; Nathan-Turner and Barry Letts, coming in as executive producer, took his comment seriously and commissioned it. Fisher obviously wasn't averse to the concept, though, as it comes across in his novelisation far more than it does in the finished production. (In fact the novelisation is an interesting one, partly because of the immense amount of back-story it gives to both the Argolin and the Foamasi and partly because of its very un-Target-like, obviously Adams-influenced writing style.)

• Bidmead had got the job by accident. He'd written to Robert Banks Stewart about the series *Shoestring* (Bristol-based private eye shenanigans) and Stewart, a veteran of the Hinchcliffe era, recommended him to Letts. He wasn't their first choice; see 18.6, "The Keeper of Traken". Bidmead refused at first, believing that the Williams / Adams / Read approach had taken the series too far from its "purpose" of educating teenagers about science.

• The new script editor's background was a curious one. He began as an actor (Laertes on stage opposite Alan Bates as Hamlet), tried writing (and worked on a series for Thames in the mid-'70s called *Harriet's Back in Town*, but nobody on Earth seems to know anything more about it, except that Robert Banks Stewart was story editor), worked in radio as both a performer and writer (a regular stint on Radio 2's soap *Wagoners' Walk*) and scripted industrial training films. He also wrote for a few scientific journals, and was a keen advocate of the personal computer. His first act was to get the production office a subscription to *New Scientist*.

• Meanwhile Baker and Ward had been to Australia to shoot adverts for Prime Computers, mixing the technical specs with gabbled references to 'Gallifrey in the constellation Kasterborous' (see the appendix to Volume VI for more on this). Little realising that the series to which they'd return would be similarly obsessed with RAM cartridges and piggyback boards, they even allowed a gag in which the computer advises the Doctor to 'marry the girl'. Filming in Brighton was delayed as Baker, back from a second trip to Australia to promote the series, was severely jet-lagged. It turned out that this wasn't the sole cause of his sluggishness and ill-temper. The next two stories would see him become gravely ill.

• In the meantime Nathan-Turner had decided that the Doctor's "look" needed to be modified, especially with a view to merchandising. He saw the question-mark shirt, in particular, as a commercial possibility (and question-marks will come to haunt all the Doctors from this point on). The coat was based loosely on Tsarist officers' greatcoats, and the socks were especially made by the hosiers to the Prince of Wales. Baker wanted the high boots of earlier years, and eventually got his way.

• As we've seen, the casting of "names" became an important publicity tool, but this came at a price. A special reserve was set up, called the "Knicker-Elastic Fund", to pay well-known actors extra if they asked for it (but the actors weren't always told this, and many - if not most - did it for Equity standard rates as a means of doing something their children could watch). The fund was, apparently, set up *after* Nathan-Turner had assured a director that it existed...

• Director Lovett Bickford, a discovery of Letts' from the "Classic Serial" days, was keen to give the whole production a "comic-strip" look with wipes and mixes straight out of a 1930s musical. His first idea was that the Foamasi should be translucent, with half-visible organs, the analogy being stick-insects or aphids. But this would have required them to have been designated "special effects props" and not costumes, something that would have had budgetary implications. As it was, the costumes cost a lot more than they appear to, as the concept was a two-layer moire-pattern (a fabric called Mousseline had to be imported from Germany) with fibre-optic "scilia" that would coruscate like prisms. However, the lighting was too bright for this to come across on-screen.

• The baby Pangol was played by Alys, the daughter of production assistant Anji Smith. Mum's job involved finding ways to do things

more cheaply (see the next story for some choice examples).

• During Season Seventeen, Graham Williams had objected to the number of self-appointed fan "experts" getting in the way during recording and offering tedious suggestions and criticisms. Nathan-Turner had been taken with Ian Levine, the least obnoxious of these. Levine had been a DJ at "Northern Soul" clubs in Wigan, Lancashire (but apparently not the biggest and most prestigious, the Wigan Casino, as is sometimes reported), then become a record producer and entrepreneur. He's now notorious for the early '90s slew of dreary boy-bands he manufactured. With Season Eighteen he became the semi-official fan opinion, correcting errors of continuity and making suggestions as to what to try next. During the rest of this volume, we'll chart his increasing influence and its effects. 'Stay tuned...'

18.2: "Meglos"

(Serial 5Q, Four Episodes, 27th September - 18th October 1980.)

Which One is This? Tom Baker turns into a giant cactus. And vice versa.

Firsts and Lasts Last appearance of actress Jacqueline Hill, re-appearing for the first time since she left the series in "The Chase" (2.8) and becoming the first former companion to come back to the series as a different character. Here she's the priestess Lexa, and effectively a villain, although she's one of those redeemable "blinkered by her own religion" villains instead of the "wants to conquer everything" type.

The last scene sees Romana receiving a message from Gallifrey, ordering her to leave the Doctor and go back home, a fate she eventually escapes in "Warriors' Gate" (18.5). It's the only occasion on which the departure of a companion is set up so far in advance, rather than the usual technique of making her spontaneously fall in love with somebody at the last moment (although, in the end, her farewell in "Warriors' Gate" is still *fairly* rushed).

Plot-wise, it's the first appearance of those standard-issue 1980s characters, the Rebellious Young Couple. Not wearing jump-suits yet - this will become mandatory by Season Twenty-Two - but with matching Purdey-style hairdos.

First use of Scene-Sync, now an effects mainstay of any programme that uses blue-screen, even the news. The BBC got it on a trial basis, and *Doctor Who* seemed like the best place to put it through its paces. Last use (sob) of the space-jungle sound effects track that's followed us from Kembel to Chloris (see 10.4, "Planet of the Daleks", for one comic side-effect of this). Jungle planets will henceforth sound like synthesizers.

Four Things to Notice About "Meglos"...

1. Get ready for this... it's yet *another* "evil double" story, a sub-genre that pops up at near-regular intervals throughout *Doctor Who*'s history (most recent examples being 13.4, "The Android Invasion" and 16.4, "The Android of Tara"). "Meglos" goes for the big one, having the shape-changing villain spend pretty much the entire story in the shape of the Doctor, and running the full action-serial gamut by convincing the authorities that the Doctor's an evildoer.

But this time, the nature of the villain deserves a mention. Meglos is a cactus. Though unimpressive when he's first discovered, effectively sitting in a planet-pot on Zolfa Thura, the make-up department once again works overtime by covering Tom Baker in vegetable spines whenever he has to look as if his inner cactus is struggling to come to the surface.

2. It takes longer than ever before for the Doctor to get to the planet he's supposed to be saving. Though past stories have frequently required him to hang around a barely-inhabited quarry-world for the first episode until the monsters turn up, this time the TARDIS doesn't even land on the troubled planet of Tigella until halfway through episode two, meaning that an unheard-of amount of time is spent messing around on the TARDIS while Meglos, the Tigellans and the Gaztak mercenaries all get into position. In part the delay is caused by a 'chronic hysteresis' - basically just a posh time-loop - which involves Tom Baker and Lalla Ward going through exactly the same scene over and over again, but even *this* can't pad out the story to its rightful length. (The episodes are definitely getting shorter in this period, and the cliffhanger reprises are getting longer. If you cut out the title sequences then some episodes here are as short as eighteen minutes, and without the reprise there's only fifteen-and-a-half minutes of material in episode four.)

3. Episode one involves one of the most "mixed" special effects sequences the series has yet

seen. The panning shot of the Gaztaks crossing the surface of Zolfa Thura was filmed with the aforementioned Scene-Sync process, a technique based on good old CSO that allows actors and non-existent sets to move together instead of remaining static in the same scene. Which sounds lovely and hi-tech. Except that the large, luminous planet which hangs in Zolfa Thura's sky during this sequence is clearly being held up by a couple of wires, a rather more old-fashioned approach to effects work.

4. In a season that's divided up into trilogies, this story is part of the least well-reported one. With "Meglos" being filmed after (and frantically rewritten during the making of) "State of Decay" and while revisions were being made to "Full Circle", it won't escape your notice that all three have *exactly* the same set-up. "Outsider" scientists try to regain lost knowledge in the face of official obstruction, the planet's single settlement is founded on off-world technology, and the threat from the outside proves to be less harmful than the authorities claim. (Yet "Meglos", it must be said, puts forward less effort than the other two in trying to make itself visually interesting.) It may also occur to you that Chris Bidmead's own "Frontios" (21.3) features the same set-up yet again, although in "Frontios" the oppressive regime turns out to be right about the existence of an alien menace (if 180-degrees wrong about its origins).

The Continuity

The Doctor Here claiming that horticulture isn't his strong point, which contradicts prior claims [13.6, "The Seeds of Doom"].

• *Inventory.* In the Doctor's waistcoat there's a pair of magnetic tweezers, useful when repairing K9, though Romana leaves these on the TARDIS.

• *Background.* The Doctor has been to Tigella before, when he befriended the Tigellans' leader, Zastor. This was 'a long time ago', though Zastor recognises the Doctor's current face. The Doctor claims he wasn't allowed to see the Dodecahedron on his prior visit due to religious objections, but he knows how big it is [he did the reading].

The Supporting Cast

• *Romana.* She's heard of the Screens of Zolfa Thura (see **Planet Notes**), and states that both Zolfa Thura and Tigella are in 'the history books'

Did *Doctor Who Magazine* Change Everything?

When Marvel Comics' UK subsidiary decided to launch a *Doctor Who* title, with a similar format to the popular and TV-advertised *Star Wars Weekly*, they knew who'd be reading it. Children. It stood to reason.

But this was November 1979, and within 44 issues *Doctor Who Weekly* was no more. Instead some of the first generation of hardcore fans were on board, led by the redoubtable Jeremy Bentham[1], someone whose memory went back to Day One. When the Weekly turned into *Doctor Who Monthly*, it was obvious that something odd was going on. Even from the first issue, the magazine hadn't been what you'd call normal kiddie-fodder - *you* try finding another publication that seeks to tell eight-year-olds about black-and-white TV programmes made a decade before their birth - but from this point on it felt more like an ongoing history than a "comic". There were story chronologies, companion profiles, spurious time-lines of the Daleks. There were elements for children, still fondly parodied (letters from the Doctor himself, signing off "happy times and places"... the UNIT codebreaker...), but at heart this was a professional television journal. With a Krazy Kaption competition. Even the obligatory comic-strip was created by stragglers from *2000 AD* - still a potent adolescent force, in those days - and the backup strips that ran until 1982 expanded the *Doctor Who* universe in ways the TV series had never done, by showing us what that universe got up to while the Doctor wasn't around.

For the first time, the fans had a common vocabulary. Bear in mind that until the early '80s, no bookshop in the land could have supplied you with a volume that even told you the names of all the stories. But suddenly we all knew who the producers had been, and what categories of story there were (in the terms the magazine used, not necessarily the terms used by the series makers).

It was possible to make lists: lists of stories you'd seen, or stories you'd read in Target form; lists of which monsters were in which stories; lists of actors in stories; lists of stories set on Earth. You could try to figure out when each story "happened". You could make Top Tens, then you could compare lists with other similarly-minded individuals. And you had the arbiters of the law (or lore), the people who'd actually seen these old stories, telling you what they were like. The reader was told as absolute fact that Season Five was the "monster" season, and it was taken as read that this was the very best the programme had to offer

(such a pity we'd never see it). Season Thirteen was "gothic" and looked like Hammer films. After that came the era of Living Memory. Then came JN-T.

For this was an era when the producer spoke to fans. And he said unto us, 'Stay Tuned'. We had correspondents who actually saw the stories being made, and they were all good because the producer was listening to us, the fans, and giving us what we wanted. John Nathan-Turner created his "personality cult" entirely through his availability to *DWM*. Within the agreed framework of what was good and what should be avoided (and terms like "pseudo-historical" being used without blushing), the readers could ask things. Can we have more old monsters, please? Do Cybermen come from Mondas or Telos? Was what happened at the end of "The Tenth Planet a regeneration or, as *DWM* insisted, just a "rejuvenation"? And we got what we asked for. And it was good.

Well... most people thought so in the letters page. We have no evidence of censorship. Then again, *Doctor Who Monthly* was still aimed at a younger audience than its later reincarnation as *Doctor Who Magazine*; it was still more likely to feature UNIT histories in the style of official military reports than eight-part interviews with minor character actors. Almost by definition, the younger readership was more liable to get over-excited than fans who were already at university and prepared to argue. But *DWM* was more than the in-house journal of JN-T (he began to insist on being called this, and started to appear in more and more of the photos, often pointing at things so that his hand would overlap the actors and the editors couldn't crop him out). It was the official memory of fans. We had photos, and we had story synopses, some less than accurate... "The Time Meddler" notoriously had the Doctor saying: "To think! Another Gallifreyan has done this!" We had sneak previews of forthcoming stories, some astonishingly mendacious: "The King's Demons" is particularly mad. Prior to this only BBC continuity announcers knew what was coming next week. Behind-the-scenes interviews gave us insights into the BBC Archives, and their change of policy about wiping old episodes. We learned words like "Jablite", "Mirrorlon" and "CSO", and what Dick Mills does with fish.

Soon the comparing of lists broke out into fights. The term "fanboy" is an import from comics, and so appropriately began to be used for the list-

continued on page 27...

[meaning, Gallifrey's?]. She even knows about Tigella's bell plants. She says she was a fully-qualified technician when she arrived on the TARDIS.

Trapped in the chronic hysteresis, she reaches the point where she's virtually on the brink of tears. She gets blubbery *again* when the summons comes from Gallifrey [see the next story].

• K9. Not sea-proofed. Repaired after his trip to the seaside [see the previous story], he now needs a battery recharge every two hours, and the Doctor expects problems if they have to re-program 'all his constants'. Completing repairs with the magnetic tweezers, Romana jams K9's probe circuit, but this can be fixed - as the Doctor knows - by waggling his tail. K9 knows of the Prion system, and believes that Zolfa Thura was the only viable civilisation there.

Here K9's said to have a manual, a small black book kept in the console room, which contains post-repair test questions to check his confused circuits. [This "manual" further muddies the question of where K9 Mk. II came from; see 15.6, "The Invasion of Time". A printed manual suggests a mass-produced object. Weird as it seems, the most logical conclusion is simply that K9 is a production-line model, not the work of an individual craftsman. After all, in "The Invisible Enemy" (15.2) Professor Marius only says that he had the "original" K9 'made up', not that he did the design work. It's perfectly feasible that Marius created the dog from an off-the-shelf kit, much like the one the Doctor produces at the end of "The Invasion of Time", and just customised its personality and data-banks for life on the Bi-Al Station. This would certainly explain why the Doctor finds it so easy to acquire *another* one for 18.7-A, *K9 and Company*.]

The TARDIS Using equipment on Zolfa Thura, Meglos puts the TARDIS into a 'chronic hysteretic loop', described by Meglos as a fold in time. This is basically a time-loop, which forces the Doctor and Romana to go through the same actions over and over again, though there's a "gap" of about thirty seconds after each repetition in which they realise they're in a loop and remember what happened in the previous gaps. K9 claims there's no known technological procedure for breaking out of a chronic hysteresis, but the Doctor correctly reasons that the way to escape is to throw it out of phase. Which basically means him and Romana acting out the events of the loop of their own voli-

tion, repeating all their words and actions so that the whole process gets de-synched and the TARDIS can release itself. [See **Things That Don't Make Sense**.]

Mention is made here of the 'time rotor' on the console [this is generally taken to mean the column in the middle of the console, but see 2.8, "The Chase"]. The Ship is said to 'hover' in Prion's planetary system before landing on Tigella, but the rotor still goes up and down as it does so. Zastor claims that when the TARDIS is 'nearby', the Doctor asks to visit Tigella [the only time that the Doctor thinks about asking for clearance before he lands, and the method he uses to contact the planet isn't established]. The TARDIS has trouble taking off from Zolfa Thura, and the Doctor notes that it needs an overhaul [he's certainly doing work by 18.7, "Logopolis"].

The Doctor claims he can get the abducted Earthling back to Earth before the man left [not the kind of thing that's usually supposed to be possible]. The TARDIS ultimately receives a message from Gallifrey, demanding the immediate return of the Doctor and Romana [this is explained in the next story], though it's not clear what form this message takes.

The Non-Humans

• Meglos. The last survivor of Zolfa Thura. He's already sent a message out across space to the Gaztak mercenaries, and when they arrive he's a cactus-like growth in the control room beneath the surface of Zolfa Thura (see **Planet Notes**). In this form Meglos describes himself as a xerophyte [which just means "dry-liking", and is the technical term for cacti and succulents]. But when a male, Caucasian, two-metre-tall human from Earth is brought to him, he uses a cabinet in the control room to meld with the Earthling, taking on the man's appearance even though the skin's covered with cactus-like spines. Having given himself this new body, the cactus "deflates" and Meglos can suddenly change shape, becoming a perfect physical duplicate of the Doctor. Clothes, voice and all. [Meglos may use the Earthling's "mass" to reconstruct himself, but curiously he can remove his coat and there are no bits missing from the Earthling when the man's freed from his power. It's not clear whether he specifically needs an Earthling rather than just a humanoid to shape-shift, but he certainly knows of Earth.]

Meglos seems to be able to do this just by

Did *Doctor Who Magazine* Change Everything?

...continued from page 25

writers who measured a story's success by the inclusion of familiar elements (old monsters, the Master, the Time Lords…). So instead of saying 'I like "The Invasion of Time" because it strikes a balance between tension about the Doctor's motives and amusement at his pricking the pomposity of Borusa and Kelner' - it could happen - or 'I hated "The Invasion of Time" because it was a travesty of "The Deadly Assassin"', you'd hear someone say 'I think "The Invasion of Time" must be a good story because the Sontarans are on Gallifrey'.

And this is the point when another JN-T-ism starts to appear. If anyone said that the series wasn't as good as it had been (and this happened quite a lot from the mid-'80s onwards), he'd pipe up: 'But the memory cheats.' If he'd said it ten years earlier, then few people would have been able to prove him wrong. But he said it in the '80s, when the thoroughly disastrous Season Twenty-Four was on TV and "The Talons of Weng-Chiang" was about to be released on video. Up to a point DWM had been toeing the party line, but before long there were too many dissenting voices to contain, and nothing could stop the letters page getting nasty.

That was a little later, though. Up until Longleat in 1983 (see **What Happened at Longleat?** under 20.6, "The King's Demons"), the magazine was the only indication anyone had of the real potential of the series to shift units. Certainly, the crucible of TV history, fan-obsession and comic-book lore changed the nature of *Doctor Who* in itself. The obsession of certain later fans with the "classic" DWM comic-strips has already been mentioned (see especially **Did Rassilon Know Omega?** under 14.3, "The Deadly Assassin"). It might be a coincidence that the main characters became more identifiable as "costume" figures from this point on, and that from "Earthshock" (19.6) onwards the stories would increasingly resemble "team-up" editions (so by 22.1, "Attack of the Cybermen", you expect Stan Lee himself to narrate and remind us of 'Ish 5.1, "Tomb of the Cybermen", True Believer!'). Or it might not. But see "The Five Doctors" (20.7) for more on this.

DWM has mutated and reinvented itself several times. At its best it's been the most thorough, witty, scholarly, camp and professional Media SF magazine in the world, with sales upwards of 10,000 a month in the UK. *Doctor Who* is the most-researched and most-documented programme in history, bar none. This became possible partly through the development of the fanzine (another subject for another time), but primarily through the consensus and shared vocabulary that were formed during DWM's first two years. Now, as the new TV series brings in new readers - or so everyone hopes - yet another sea-change has come over the magazine, and it's gearing up for a readership which can't be relied on to understand jokes about Chumblies. Yet even here it's slyly inserting sight-gags, rude jokes and a feeling of what it's like to be a fan, without ever quite being "fannish". In fact it's almost come full circle, a fact that was acknowledged when issue #1 was reprinted alongside issue #350, the latter being filled with sardonic updates on the old favourites. Once the new breed start writing in to ask whether Sara Kingdom counts as a companion, it'll be just like the '70s (except for *Doctor Who* being on for six months a year in winter). The programme is now made by the people who bought that first issue. Excelsior!

---

observing records of the Doctor, although he doesn't alter his shape to copy anybody else. In the hours that follow, he occasionally has to struggle to retain his Doctor-shape, and sometimes it looks as if the Earthling is going to break free; the struggle looks like a pair of Siamese twins locked in combat, one of them the Earthling, the other a cactus-skinned version of the Doctor.

Meglos' plan is to steal the Dodecahedron from Tigella, and use it to activate the Screens of Zolfa Thura. Unlike so many megalomaniacs, Meglos at least has a sense of irony [which might explain the name]. He speaks as if he's been under the planet's surface for a thousand years, even though the Screens have been there for ten-thousand, and it's not explained why he's only sent for assistance now. When cornered, he detaches himself from the Earthling and crawls away as a slug-like mass of green slime, but Romana takes one look and says that he must have modulated himself on a particular frequency of light. This apparently makes him virtually indestructible. [In other words, he's made of green. The crawling slug-blob doesn't *look* like "living light", so maybe he's just using the biomass as a carrier. Meglos really is the vaguest of all monsters.]

• *Gaztaks*. A band of ethnically-mixed space-travelling mercenaries, although it's not clear whether "Gaztaks" is the name of their gang, creed or species. They appear human, dress in elaborate, fur-lined clothes and hats [a similar chic to the Graff Vynda-K in 16.1, "The Ribos Operation"… three guesses why], and are familiar with Tigella before Meglos hires them. Only around half a dozen or so are seen here, led by the grumpy General Grugger and Lieutenant Brotodac. When told to bring Meglos a human being, they pick one from contemporary Earth, a bespectacled businessman who has no idea what's going on. [His name's George Morris, according to the novelisation.]

The Gaztak ship is a bulky, block-shaped, metallic sort of vehicle, all brutal edges and no style. It's got heat-shields, but the walls only appear to be a couple of inches thick. The Gaztaks mention a place called Pelagos [their home-world?], believing the trinkets from Meglos' control room might be worth 50,000,000 credits there. Their uniforms don't look consistent, as if they've picked up bits and pieces from all over the place, and their weapons are much the same. They really aren't very bright.

Planet Notes

• *Tigella*. One of two notable planets of the Prion system, the other being Zolfa Thura. Tigella is a world of lush and aggressive vegetation, but the overgrown surface is so hostile that its people have no choice but to live underground [the city seen here is evidently the only city on the planet]. Particularly nasty specimens of the local fauna are the bell plants, which grab hold of passing animals and attack their victims with their red, bell-shaped heads. The planet revolves in an anti-clockwise direction, which is said to be unusual.

The Tigellan underground city is, like so many other similar places in the universe, made up of metallic-looking corridors. There are two leading factions amongst the Tigellans - the Deons and the Savants - both under the leadership of the ageing, purple-robed Zastor. The Savants are scientific types, who like dressing in white and who all have identical white pudding-bowl wigs / haircuts. The red-and-black-robed Deons see things differently, worshipping the great god Ti and believing that the Dodecahedron is a sacred mystery which mustn't be scientifically analysed.

The Dodecahedron - as the name might suggest, a huge, smooth-faced twelve-sided geometrical object, which sits glowing inside the power room at the heart of the city - supplies the Tigellans with all their power, and the Deons believe it came from the heavens. When the Doctor is thought to have stolen the Dodecahedron, the Deons sentence him to be sacrificed, the chosen method being to tie him down underneath a large slab of rock and set light to the ropes that hold it up. They must defy Zastor to do this, planning to put the old man on the lethal planet's surface.

The Tigellans know about the Time Lords [possibly a result of the Doctor's last visit], and they're not surprised by visitors from outer space even though they don't like the idea. Lexa knows about Gaztaks, suggesting that Tigella is frequently visited by intruders. The Savants want their species to re-take the surface, though the Deons see this as sacrilege. There's a debating chamber in which decisions are made, and the armed guards wear the usual clingy black uniforms. The Doctor visited the planet fifty Tigellan years ago, and Zastor knows him as a problem-solver. On this occasion, the Deons want to make the Doctor take the Deon oath before he sees the Dodecahedron. The power source is eventually destroyed here, and with Lexa dead the Tigellans start to think about re-claiming the surface, still under Zastor's leadership.

• *Zolfa Thura*. In the same system as Tigella, Zolfa Thura is a blasted, desert-like place devastated by its people in a global war, its only notable feature now being the Screens. These are five towering pentagonal constructions, hundreds of feet high, arranged in a ring with a central control room that can lower itself into the ground. The Dodecahedron was originally supposed to power the Screens, although it somehow got to Tigella, where the Savants found the device and used it to fuel their civilisation. [The novelisation claims the Zolfa Thuran peace party took it to Tigella, which is typical of a book by Terrance Dicks]. This occurred ten-thousand years ago.

The Dodecahedron uses only a fraction of its power to fuel the whole of Tigella. Meglos claims that its recent fluctuations, which have been alarming the Tigellans so much, are part of its program and that once in re-start mode its output will increase to the power of twelve. [Incidentally, this would probably make it the most powerful artefact in the *Doctor Who* universe.] As far as anyone knows, it works on a process of baryon multiplication. When the Dodecahedron is put in the middle of the Screens, the Screens magnify its power, allowing their user to converge the five beams on any point in the galaxy and blast it to dust. Meglos states, confusingly, that his fellow Zolfa Thurans tried to destroy everything they had to prevent it being activated. In the end the weapon destroys Zolfa Thura, along with Grugger's Gaztaks and apparently Meglos. [Although if Romana is right about him being on a frequency of light, then it's at least possible that he gets away.]

The Zolfa Thurans were obviously a highly-developed people. The gleaming white control room beneath the Screens contains such advanced technology that it can put the TARDIS into a chronic hysteresis / time-loop at long range, before the Ship has even landed on nearby Tigella. Meglos is aware of the Doctor's approach, and there's a file on the Doctor complete with photograph [almost certainly obtained after the Doctor's last visit to Tigella... the records must be remarkably detailed for Meglos to copy his voice so perfectly].

Meglos is also able to shrink the huge Dodecahedron and pocket it thanks to the 're-dimensioner', a hand-held device from the Zolfa Thuran control room which involves mass conversion mechanics.

All signs and computer-screens here seem to use English words [translated for our benefit]. The Tigellans apparently know the planet Zolfa Thura by that name.

History

• *Dating.* Most probably the present day. [The Earthman is contemporary, and there's no indication that the Gaztaks can travel through time, especially as Grugger's never seen anything like Meglos' time-folding trick before. Which means they're not descended from Earth humans, and the Tigellans apparently aren't either. Even so, it's hard to credit that such close matches for humanity might have evolved on a world where the vegetation's so hostile, and where there's no other visible animal life.]

The Analysis

Where Does This Come From? As this story was being rehearsed, BBC television began a series called *The Adventure Game*, in which minor celebrities were supposedly whisked off to another planet and forced to pit their wits against shape-changing aliens led by an irate aspidistra.

We mention this not as a "source", but as an indication of where the BBC thought *Doctor Who* was going.

In space, we can accept familiar faces, lateral-thinking puzzles and whimsy (and *Adventure Game* producer / writer Clive Doig had several connections to *Doctor Who*, not least bringing Sylvester McCoy to our screens; see also 20.7, "The Five Doctors"). "Meglos" is what people had come to think *Doctor Who* was like, and so was *The Adventure Game*. Writers McCulloch and Flanagan admitted in interviews that they were approaching "Meglos" as an adventure story, but one where "anything" could happen. Apart from the notable twist of having a cactus as the villain, "anything" is apparently the pretext for a massive act of recycling.

Maybe it was inevitable that things would start to go in this direction. Unlike previous generations, most of the people who worked on *Doctor Who* in the '80s had grown up in a world that already had *Doctor Who* in it, in a nation that already saw the series as a part of the local folklore. This is why the programme-makers were happy to resurrect the monsters they'd seen on their screens in the '60s, as if those monsters were retro-style executive toys; and why the scripts have a habit of referring to imaginary forms of physics that were made up for old scripts instead of inventing new ones.

"Meglos" is *not* the start of that era - some would say that it really begins in the next story, "Full Circle", which takes it as read that the viewer fully understands what the concept of "Gallifrey" entails - but here, at the very least, the programme's becoming its own principal source. This may be why so much of it feels like an echo of the Graham Williams era. It's made from bits of old *Doctor Who*, but for the most part "old" means "from the last couple of years". There are two planets, supposedly old enemies, one reduced to dust and the other inhabited by people who live in bunkers (16.6, "The Armageddon Factor"). Tigella is a world capable of great scientific progress, held back by Medieval superstition (a standard of the late '70s series, but there's a different spin on it on Bidmead's "watch" and we'll come back to this shortly). It's yet *another* story set on a jungle planet, where there are vicious carnivorous plants, "funny" bandits and only one visible building, which explains why younger viewers kept getting it mixed up with "The Creature from the Pit" (17.3) until they were old enough to know better. And the apocalypse-anxiety comes fitted as standard.

Those parts of "Meglos" which aren't direct lifts from the *Doctor Who* of yore seem to have been soaked up from the overall Zeitgeist of the late '70s pop-SF boom, in all its forms. The Gaztaks are the first fully-fledged "space mercenaries" to appear in the series (note that "space mercenaries" is used here to suggest a whole aesthetic, it *doesn't* just mean people in space doing things for the money), but pretty much every space opera made at the time had something similar. The Earthman, who's dragged onto the surface of Zolfa Thura in his suit and spectacles while people in wigs a la UFO are arguing about the great god Ti on Tigella, is so much like one of the real-world / sci-fi-world contradictions of *The Hitch-Hiker's Guide to the Galaxy* that you'd swear the spirit of the previous season's script editor was still haunting the studio. The completed Zolfa Thuran planet-killer weapon, capable of combining multiple energy-beams to destroy any target in the galaxy, just *is* the Death Star (in a way that earlier doomsday weapons like the one in "Colony in Space", 8.4, just weren't).

Bizarrely, the "evil twin" idea seems almost original here, since this is a one-on-one duel between Tom Bakers rather than the *Stepford-Wives*-fest of "The Android Invasion". It's more like a '60s action serial than anything, and the first time that *Doctor Who* has tried anything similar since "The Enemy of the World" (5.4). Which, in this context, seems like a far-off and obscure source.

And yet… however many disparate, second-or-third hand elements might be on offer here, Bidmead's logic is holding them together. If nothing else, "Meglos" is a good indicator of the way he was thinking, and it's key to understanding his run as script editor. Here's where it gets complicated…

To get a proper handle on Bidmead's version of Season Eighteen, you really need a good working knowledge of Renaissance thought, especially Pythagoreanism. In brief, this was a cult of men living in caves, eating only beans, avoiding the company of women (and on a farinaceous diet we imagine that women would have avoided their company too) and worshipping numbers. By a process of reasoning we'll go into later (18.6, "The Keeper of Traken") the concepts of reincarnation and transmigration of souls, the Music of the Spheres and the various sequences of musical

notes used in different nation-states were intimately bound up with the shapes of conch-shells. And things like that.

Pythagoras held that the ratios between numbers were the key. People who couldn't divide or multiply were "irrational". In the seventeenth century there were attempts made to connect the Five Solids with the Motions of the Planets and the Four Elements (plus the "Quintessence" or Fifth Element, from which the soul and the crystal spheres on which the planets were pushed around the *Primum Mobile* were made). The Pythagorean Solid which represented - or in some mystical way *was* - the soul was…

…go on, guess.

Yup! The dodecahedron. Now, as Season Eighteen unfolds we're going to come across various different versions of the Renaissance in Europe and the idea of re-discovering old science in order to overthrow superstition and repression, just as the Williams-era stories came back to the idea of egocentricity and geocentricity being one and the same (babies, tyrants and the ignorant lack the Big Picture and think the universe revolves around them). Bidmead is trying to suggest that direct, empirical observation is always better than getting it from the books, but seems more comfortable with a world-view that predates Newton.

In fact, although in a smaller way than "The Keeper of Traken" or "Logopolis" (18.7), he's trying to make *Doctor Who*'s science conform with the natural philosophy of Shakespeare's time. We see several worlds where kingship is a semi-divine state and the only thing that stops nature going into revolt, and where material phenomena are a mere reflection of the Eternal Truths of Mathematics. In this case the Dodecahedron's removal causes the decay of all things, from Zolfa Thura (reduced to desert wilderness) to Tigella (rampant, entropic jungle and a stifled society). And Meglos needs an Earthman rather than being content with a mere Gaztak, presumably because Earthmen have souls (see - amongst many others - 6.2, "The Mind Robber"). This idea of corruption due to "de-tuning", causing weeds as its first manifestation, is at the heart of this season.

We might also speculate on oblique possible influences such as cactus-munching mystic Carlos Castenada, the idea of the Shields as analogous to the pyramids (and Meglos as Ozymandias?) and the Renaissance notion of Egypt as the source of all lost knowledge. We might even see the Tigellans' religious disputes as a reference to the rise of fundamentalist Islam in the wake of the Iranian Uprising of 1979, and the Dodecahedron as the Qa'aba (the big black stone in Mecca, the one you have to visit at least once as part of the Hajj).

No, you're right… that might be giving the story too much credit. Because despite all the theoretical underpinning we've just described, the surface layer which McCulloch and Flanagan have added is still a slew of kerr-*razy* regurgitated ideas, which they seem to think are appropriate to *Doctor Who* and which Bidmead was happy to lap up. It's possible, and we'll state it no more strongly than this, that - unbeknownst to the rather serious-minded script editor - the authors of this piece were just taking the piss.

Things That Don't Make Sense The chronic hysteresis. Of all the inane pieces of temporal science in *Doctor Who*, this is perhaps the worst. Leaving aside the question of how *any* time-loop can possibly have "gaps" in it… the way to break the loop is by re-enacting all your movements from that loop, basically so the hysteresis gets "confused". How in God's name is *that* supposed to work? This 'fold in time' is, as far as we're told, some sort of glitch in the space-time continuum. It's not conscious, it doesn't have eyes or ears and it's not monitoring the Doctor and Romana to see what they do. And since the attempts of the TARDIS crew to replicate the loop just result in rough, approximate copies of their actions, there's no way their clowning-around should be able to "resonate" with the real loop at all, unless the loop is sentient and capable of recognising these shoddy pratfalls as representations of the real thing. It's like suggesting that the universe can recognise a picture of an electron *as* an electron, or like suggesting that the space-time continuum can understand instructions in English. In short: it's magic. [Maybe that's it. Maybe the Zolfa Thurans' technology is specially designed to make space-time respond to easy symbols. But if so, then it's a hell of a lot more impressive than anything the Time Lords ever came up with.]

There's apparently only one exit from the Tigellan city, and it's a normal-sized door. Likewise, the entrance to the Gaztak ship looks like a single flimsy piece of hardboard. Why do Meglos' files, which presumably recorded the Doctor's previous visit to Tigella, show him dressed in the new outfit that he only started wearing in the last story? [Throughout Tom Baker's run we're led to believe that this Doctor has had years of unseen adventures. He must have spent some time wearing in the "burgundy" ensemble before we ever saw it on-screen.]

Tigella and Zolfa Thura are twin planets, so if one were destroyed then wouldn't the orbit of the other be seriously affected? Add to that the Dodecahedron's destruction, and they're in for sour times on Tigella. And what possible meaning does 'anti-clockwise rotation' have, when we're talking about a spherical planet? Obviously Romana's explanation as to why navigation is so difficult here is an attempt to confuse the stupid Gaztaks, but this pushes the limits of credulity even for them. Do they actually understand that space travel is different from going somewhere in a van?

Critique (Prosecution) If you sat down and wrote what most people in Britain would think of as the all-purpose *Doctor Who* plot, you'd have either this or "The Visitation" (19.4). Religious cultists sacrificing strangers to a bit of space-hardware… check. Plants more like animals… you got it. Dodgy space-pirates acting like scrap-dealers… present and correct. Ranting megalomaniac alien… uh-huh. Doctor impersonates own doppelganger… but of course. Somehow, it ought to have been more fun than this.

Part of the problem is that the writers don't really want to be doing this, and the director has nothing but contempt for the series. There's a feeling all around that "it's good enough for *Doctor Who*, why put any more effort in?" Fortunately some of the cast defy this. Baker in particular is having fun finding ways to suggest he's a mad cactus pretending to be the Doctor. Even if you don't know what was happening backstage, his enthusiasm is a marked contrast to the stories on either side (as broadcast). Critics of Baker at his height usually claim that he's trying to subordinate the series to his own performance, but here we can see why this was such a key ingredient of the programme's success. When he's not on screen there's barely anything to watch. His example lifts the cast out of apathy. Even the 'chronic hysteresis' scenes are merely silly where they could have been worse (yes, they could!). Another snag is that there's only two episodes' worth of plot here.

And that plot is all old. Even the Dodecahedron looks like a respray of the Conscience of Marinus

(1.5, "The Keys of Marinus"). A couple of stories later they would've had the Doctor comment on the similarity, so maybe it *could* have been more annoying, after all…

Critique (Defence, ish) The second false start for the new regime, with hindsight watching "Meglos" is like watching a testing-ground for some of the techniques that turn up in the stories to follow, but without any of the noose needed to hold it all together. ("The Leisure Hive" is often described as a triumph of style over substance, but it's a description that fits "Meglos" far more snugly. "Hive" was a confused little creature, and here you can see the programme-makers getting to grips with the series without having much to say… yet. This is a much slicker beast than many are prepared to accept; half the props may well be left-overs from other BBC productions, but they're recycled so effectively that you'd never spot it if you hadn't been tipped off.)

The plot is a mean-average plot, though what's striking is that although it lacks the *potential* depth of its twin-story "The Creature from the Pit", it gets a lot of things right that the previous story got terribly wrong. The "funny" bandits here are, occasionally, funny. So is Tom Baker. Thanks to both the direction and the new "mood" of the series, it's better-made than any *Doctor Who* since "Horror of Fang Rock" (15.1), even when the story does something incredibly stupid. The Doctor's late arrival, allowing the script to set up Tigella and Zolfa Thura properly, is a sure sign that the leading man is no longer the end-all of the programme and is exactly what "Creature" so desperately needed. If only the planets in question were more interesting.

It's ironic that the sterile, cod-space-age nature of the Savants is the thing that always sticks in the mind - and it's not just their wigs, their control room's just as bad - because in so many other places there are little touches that seem determined to make this non-event work. The underground city is staged to look as if it's actually *deep*, suggesting that this isn't just a cheap BBC set and that there are catacombs going miles beyond the ones we see. The *geometry* feels right, the Dodecahedron hinting at power in its most Platonic form, echoed by the pentagonal Screens of Zolfa Thura. We're looking at all the old clichés, but this time we're seeing them in 3D. And the new musical style finally settles into its groove,

politely lurking beneath the surface instead of smattering itself across the soundtrack.

None of this changes the fact that it's "one of *those*" stories, full of badly-conceived civilisations and atrocious SF names, the full-colour grand-child of "The Space Museum" (2.7). At heart it's as close as televised *Doctor Who* ever comes to looking like a story from an old *Doctor Who* annual, even down to the Doctor knowing the leader of the alien planet from a previous visit, and talking to him as if he's someone from the local golf club instead of a head of state.

The Facts

Written by John Flanagan and Andrew McCulloch. Directed by Terence Dudley. Viewing figures: 5.0 million, 4.2 million, 4.7 million, 4.7 million.

Supporting Cast Bill Fraser (General Grugger), Frederick Treves (Lieutenant Brotadac), Edward Underdown (Zastor), Jacqueline Hill (Lexa), Colette Gleeson (Caris), Crawford Logan (Deedrix), Christopher Owen (Earthling), Simon Shaw (Tigellan Guard).

Oh, Isn't That..?

• *Bill Fraser.* When William Hartnell left *The Army Game*, Fraser took over as the Sergeant Major, and then appeared in the spin-offs *Bootsy and Snudge* and *Civvie Street*. More importantly, the series *Flesh and Blood* had led to him working with Terence Dudley, who asked him to consider playing Grugger; see also 18.7-A, *K9 and Company*. Famously, Fraser only agreed to do it on the understanding that his character could kick K9.

• *Jacqueline Hill.* Yes, that's the lady who played Barbara for most of the first 77 episodes of this series. After being a mum for a while she wanted to give TV acting another shot, appearing in a BBC production of *Romeo and Juliet* before ending up back on her old "patch". Her husband, Alvin Rakoff, knew Dudley socially.

• *Edward Underdown.* Veteran character actor, whom you'll have seen in at least one episode of any British-made adventure / fantasy series from the '50s onwards. He usually plays genial scientists or civil servants, so here he's both. He's rumoured to have inspired Noel Coward's *Mad About the Boy*, but that was much, much earlier.

Working Titles   "The Golden Pentagon / Pentagram / Pentangle / Star", "The Last Zolfa Thuran", "The Last Sol-Fataran".

Cliffhangers   Meglos turns around to face the Gaztaks in his control room, and has the Doctor's features; in the Tigellan jungle, the Gaztaks surround Romana, and Brotodac gives the order to kill her; the ropes that hold the great big sacrificial rock over the Doctor's body start to burn away.

The Lore

• By this time it was obvious that Baker's lethargy in "The Leisure Hive" was down to more than jet-lag. His hair went lank and needed to be put into curlers. He wore make-up for the first time since getting the part, apparently at Nathan-Turner's insistence, and Lalla Ward had to feed him spoonfuls of baby food. The precise nature of the 'metabolic disorder' has never been divulged, leading to unsavoury rumours among fans; see 17.4, "Nightmare of Eden". (Note that the problem first became obvious during 18.4, "State of Decay", but the stories in this season were shot out of order. Thus, the difference in Baker's appearance between "The Leisure Hive" and "Meglos" is more marked than it otherwise might have been.)

• The illness also seems to have changed Baker and Ward's relationship. Though attempts were made to keep the story away from the press, the two lead actors had begun a romance during the Paris shoot for "City of Death" (17.2). This was called off around the time of "Shada" (17.6), and by all accounts they were at each others' throats during the shooting of "State of Decay", but the spoon-feeding process apparently brought them back together. See 18.5, "Warriors' Gate", for what happened next...

• Christopher Bidmead and Andrew McCulloch were old acquaintances, but as a team the authors had attracted Bidmead's attention by writing a pilot for a sitcom (in a series of six pilots, the most successful was guaranteed a series; the winner was the dire David Jason vehicle *A Sharp Intake of Breath*, so just imagine how bad the building-site-based *Bricks without Straw* must have been). Bidmead found himself giving structure to their wild ideas, which in turn inspired them to try to go further. This eventually resulted in Bidmead, now a strong advocate of their work, giving them the brief to write out the Fourth

Doctor. "Project Zeta-Sigma" was held back to be the Fifth Doctor's debut (for more see **What Else Wasn't Made?** under 17.6, "Shada"), then abandoned totally, after desperate script conferences trying to deal with the logistics of invisible characters having long arguments on-screen... and after Nyssa had been retained and the Master resurrected, requiring Bidmead to write two totally new stories using the majority of the characters and settings.

• Christopher Owen (the Earthling) went uncredited as the voice of Meglos.

• The look of the Gaztaks was deliberately eclectic. The guns were re-used from a number of sources (including *Blake's 7*, with Grugger's the only one especially made; one of the authors of this volume hefted it at the Longleat *Twenty Years of a Time Lord* event, and found it more sturdy than it looked, cast iron components and all). Many items of clothing from "The Ribos Operation" (16.1) were reused, with a few from the BBC production of Verdi's *Macbeth* and occasional trimmings once again from *Blake's 7*. The script had stressed that the Gaztaks shouldn't look "uniform" or "styled", so it wasn't *just* a cost-cutting ploy.

• Director Terence Dudley had worked with John Nathan-Turner on *Flesh and Blood* and *All Creatures Great and Small*. He was a freelance director, but prior to this had been a BBC producer, working on *Doomwatch* (see 7.3, "The Ambassadors of Death" and 6.3, "The Invasion") and Terry Nation's bourgeois eco-catastrophe soap *Survivors* (see 12.4, "Genesis of the Daleks" and 11.2, "Invasion of the Dinosaurs"). He's said to have had a low opinion of *Doctor Who*, but a high regard for its new producer. See "The King's Demons" (20.6) to find out how this went sour...

• As the working titles indicate, the source of Meglos' power was originally to have been a pentagram. Bidmead insisted that a regular solid was more sensible (as far as anything in this story can be). He also renamed the time-loop.

• The closing theme music of episode four has been electronically transposed into a lower key than normal. This means it's a close match for Delia Derbyshire's original arrangement of the theme, in E-minor, but Peter Howell claims this is a coincidence and nobody seems quite sure how it happened. (The *Radio Times* ran complaints about the new theme music at around this time, so many people interpreted it as an attempt to "fix" the problem rather than an accident.)

• The script simply had Lexa realising that the Doctor wasn't so bad after all, and made no further mention of her afterwards. The decision to kill her was largely made to bulk out episode four, although the version screened is still rushed.

• The name "Brotadac" is an anagram of "Bad Actor", as the character was the result of one of the writers engaging in self-parody. Each claims it was the other.

• As *Buck Rogers* carved a swathe through the viewing figures, Nathan-Turner utilised the press with a vigour unseen since Barry Letts' term as producer. The series was rarely out of the papers, not always for the right reasons, but "there's no such thing as bad publicity" seems to have been the motto of the series in the 1980s. Continuing interest in K9 meant that every time it looked as if the tin pooch had been blown up, there was a "save K9" letter in a tabloid or the *Radio Times* (so when the spin-off *K9 and Company* was announced, *The Sun* claimed a victory on behalf of its readers). The casting of stars, often rather against type, usually made a photo-shoot necessary; see 22.1, "Attack of the Cybermen", for an occasion when this went spectacularly wrong. And Nathan-Turner devised various means of keeping himself in the public eye. No previous *Doctor Who* producer starred in a book like *A Day With a TV Producer*, with a photo of himself on every other page. Certainly no other BBC producer would be so recognisable as to be assaulted by fans with baseball bats on the London Underground (see 24.1, "Time and the Rani").

18.3: "Full Circle"

(Serial 5R, Four Episodes, 25th October - 15th November 1980.)

Which One is This? If you were a child of the early '80s, then this is the one with the monsters slowly rising up out of the water and lumbering onto the land. (If you were a child of the '70s then you're thinking of 9.3, "The Sea Devils". If you were a child of the *late* '80s then you're thinking of 26.3, "The Curse of Fenric".) Plus: kids in space-pyjamas alert! The series has gone all "young" again.

Firsts and Lasts Arguably the story where the John Nathan-Turner era really gets into its stride (see **Where Does This Come From?**), "Full

Circle" also marks the point where *Doctor Who* starts to take its own mythology for granted; the script treats Gallifrey as the heart of the Doctor's universe without ever explaining what the planet signifies, and the Doctor talks about meeting Leela and Andred again as if everyone's supposed to remember "The Invasion of Time" (15.6) with clarity. Depending on your point of view, this means that the series either expects far too much fore-knowledge from its viewers or just assumes that the modern audience knows enough about the way TV works to follow everything from the context.

It also demonstrates a new approach to the naming of episodes. Throughout its history, the programme has tended towards titles at the pulp end of the spectrum, from "Colony in Space" and "Revenge of the Cybermen" through to the absolute nadir, "City of Death". From this point on, however, titles become a little more conceptual and often have double meanings attached (though this one, with the "Full Circle" of the title referring to both the shape of the Starliner and the life-cycle that brings the Marshmen back to the seat of their descendants, is hardly subtle). The most telling thing is that after this, Target Books had to re-think their policy and stopped putting the words *Doctor Who and the* at the start of every novelisation title. *Doctor Who and the Full Circle* just wouldn't have cut it.

On a more straightforward note… this story sees the debut of Matthew Waterhouse as Adric, who becomes the first adolescent male on board the TARDIS and at the very least breaks the '70s tradition of the Doctor always being accompanied by a single girl assistant. Mind you, he still fulfils the requirements of the *Who*-girl by spending his first episode twisting his ankle, fainting, getting captured and asking stupid questions. Like K9, Adric divides opinion as to whether he's a workable companion or just an irritation, but it's worth pointing out that he *did* do his job. Snide as the sixteen-year-olds may have been about him (see especially 19.6, "Earthshock"), for once the children of the age had someone they could latch on to. Indeed, for the next few stories the Doctor starts to become an "elder wise man" again, instead of the striding hero-figure of the previous decade.

Paddy Kingsland, another Radiophonic Workshop / schools television veteran, officially joins here (actually he did episode one of

How Does Evolution Work?

If it hasn't already been forgotten as a pointless waste of time, then many of you may recall the "alien autopsy" flap of 1995, when footage was released to the media which purported to be of a genuine extra-terrestrial dissection that the US government performed in 1947. Obviously this was nothing more than a limp-looking hoax, but at least as memorable were the "scientific" arguments immediately put about by the people who fell for it. From *their* point of view the footage was interesting not only because it proved the existence of spacemen, but because it proved that the spacemen looked very nearly human, apart from the black eyes and the bloated heads. That was the term they used, when describing the rubber alien's features: *human*.

None of them seemed to pick up on the curious fact that this alien, built and filmed for the benefit of a US and European audience, didn't simply look "human" but positively *Caucasian*. Its features had far more in common with those of the average white American than with (for instance) those of the average aboriginal Australian, and lo and behold, it had supposedly crashed right in the middle of white America. The oddness of this only became apparent a few months later, when a second alien "corpse" went on display in a museum in Asia. It looked sort of… Chinese.

The *Doctor Who* universe suffers from a similar problem, and then some. Against astronomical odds, the universe we see on-screen is full of people who look remarkably familiar, and not just because they've got the "right" number of limbs. Those who defended the autopsy footage would argue that if you take an Earth-like planet (and *Doctor Who* is full of roughly Earth-like planets) then there's a better chance of it producing simian bipeds than a planet with a different kind of gravity and atmosphere, but one look at the scope of life here in our *own* world shows you how much variation you can expect even when conditions are more or less constant. There are things living in the depths of the ocean which look so bizarre that nobody would believe them if they were used as the template for an alien life-form in an SF movie, yet we're led to believe that it's normal for animals to develop as upright-walking things simply because that's what we're used to seeing around us every day.

And even if we accept that Earth-like worlds *are* prone to producing recognisable "people", then we're still left with that race-problem. The *Doctor Who* continuum is full of Europeans. Even species

like the Argolin (18.1, "The Leisure Hive") have Caucasian features, and they're supposed to be vegetable-people, for Heaven's sake. Some of these - yes all right, let's use the dreadful old word - *humanoids* can be passed off as the survivors of degenerate human colonies, but in a story like "Meglos" (18.2) we're specifically led to believe that we're *not* looking at anybody who might be related to us. (If we were going to be particularly anal, then we could question this at the level of "why does the High Priestess of the Cult of Ti exactly resemble Barbara Wright of London, England, Earth?", but let's draw the line there.) So what's going on?

Let's take a moment to remind ourselves of the way evolution works in the world we know. It's worth dwelling on this, because we're used to sci-fi fodder like (here we go again) *Star Trek* - and, fair enough, *Doctor Who* stories written by Terry Nation - treating evolution as if it were some invisible god-like force that plans the destinies of all living things in advance, and that can turn human beings into lemurs or Kaleds into squid-monsters with one flip of a genetic switch.

But let's concentrate on natural selection. Evolution isn't exactly random, but it is about probable outcomes. In any generation of any species, there'll be unpredictable mutations. If one of those mutations makes it even *slightly* easier for an animal to survive, then the animal will have a *slightly* better chance of living long enough to have offspring of its own, which makes it *slightly* more likely that its genetic features will be more common in the next generation. That's a lot of "slightly"s, and the first animal with the mutation might just get eaten or stepped on, so it's still a matter of chance whether its own quirks become more widespread. However, if you're dealing with a big population and a time-span of thousands or millions of years, then "usefully" mutated animals are going to be more successful than the rest just thanks to the law of averages. Their own genetic features are going to become commonplace, and the others are going to start dying out.

Consider what this means, in the context of a busy SF universe. It means that although better-equipped animals are guaranteed to survive (as long as conditions remain constant… a big if), the *nature* of their special "equipment" is in no way predictable. Human beings, complex as we are, are the result of an inestimable number of flukes. Even

continued on page 37…

35

"Meglos", but this is where he becomes a regular). Providing a rather less blatant story arc than the Key to Time sequence in Season Sixteen, this story marks the start of "The E-Space Trilogy", which sees the TARDIS get stuck in the wrong universe for three stories in a row.

Four Things to Notice About "Full Circle"...

1. Kids, the good monsters are back! This hasn't been any easy time for aliens in *Doctor Who*. Working backwards, the most recent threats encountered by the Doctor have been a cactus, some bean-bag-shaped lizards, a minotaur in platform shoes, awkward-looking dugong-monsters with flares and a big green air-bag. But the first episode of "Full Circle" ends with the arrival of the Marshmen, slippery *Creature from the Black Lagoon*-type creations whose entrance - rising from the mists of Alzarius in slow-motion, to a similarly-rising radiophonic soundtrack - is fondly-remembered by the spawn of the 1980s.

But perhaps what's nicest about the Marshmen is that unlike so many of their predecessors, there's an attention to detail that makes them seem as if they've wandered out of a very strange wildlife documentary. They make credible grunting noises instead of going "raah". Flaps of wet skin stick to their bodies, thanks to the best efforts of the BBC's latex-wranglers, although you'll have to overlook the fact that they seem to be wearing flesh cufflinks. And the Marshmen actually have children, a luxury rarely accorded to non-humanoid species... unless you count the baby Kaled mutants in Davros' incubator rooms, or evil crawling insect-larvae, but that's hardly the same thing.

All of which means that, like monsters from Universal horror movies, these beasts have personality. The Marsh-Child's death-scene, when it electrocutes itself by smashing a video-screen (because it thinks the Doctor, the only person it trusts, is inside), is so much more upsetting than the deaths of any of the series' other supporting characters that you wonder why the BBC ever bothered to hire "proper" actors at all.

2. Sadly, the obligatory rubbish monsters put in an appearance as well, though thankfully only briefly. There aren't just marsh-creatures on Alzarius, but giant black spiders, too. These ones are a lot more active than those seen in "Planet of the Spiders" (11.5), but even more plasticky-looking. Those who remember the TV ads for the late

'70s game *Stop Boris* - which involved shooting at a large battery-powered spider as it crawled in your general direction - may also recall playground arguments about whether the "Full Circle" spiders were actually *Stop Boris* models with some extra markings, or whether they just looked that way.

3. Look away if you don't want to know the score. The plot of "Full Circle", in a nutshell: for generations, the occupants of a crashed Starliner on a hostile, far-flung planet have been trying to repair their vessel so that they can return to their own world of Terradon. Their problem is that every few decades, nigh-legendary monsters come out of the swamps and try to smash their way into the ship. What only the elders of the Starliner realise - until the Doctor turns up, and the occupants suffer a horrible Victorians-meet-Darwin moment of revelation - is that in truth the Marshmen broke into the ship millennia ago, and the Starliner's human inhabitants aren't from the gene-stock they thought. Long-term *Doctor Who* viewers might therefore notice that this story is much like an anti-matter twin of "The Face of Evil" (14.4), in which the surprise twist is that the locals *aren't* descended from the crew of a marooned spaceship.

4. John Nathan-Turner and Chris Bidmead wanted to cut down on the amount of K9 in the series, partly because they felt he was too much of an easy escape-option for the Doctor, partly because Baker was becoming more truculent when having to deal with the prop and seemed threatened by the character's popularity. Having been exploded in "The Leisure Hive", then kicked around and drained of power in "Meglos", K9 sees further abuse in episode two when he gets his head knocked off with a big stick. Since K9 is being incredibly smug at the time, rolling into a cave as if he owns the place and loudly telling everyone that he's in data collection mode, it's very, very hard to watch him get decapitated without going 'hooray'. You get the sense that even the *programme* hates him now.

The Continuity

The Doctor When Romana's recalled to Gallifrey, the Doctor states they 'can't resist' the summons, although he gets K9 to set the co-ordinates [so the recall circuit from "Arc of Infinity" (20.1) isn't used and the Time Lords don't try the same tricks

How Does Evolution Work?

...continued from page 35

if you take a planet that looks exactly like Earth - and planets like Chloris and Tigella blatantly *don't* look exactly like it, even if they're apparently the same size and have the right sort of air - the chances of anything even roughly human evolving there are absurdly small. The chances of anything evolving there that looks like a British character actor are small almost beyond measure. The chances of it happening all over the universe, *and* at roughly the same point in history if "Meglos" or "The Two Doctors" are to be believed, are… well, we're not even capable of imagining numbers that tiny.

Now, it could just be that the sample size isn't very reliable. We have, for obvious reasons, predominantly seen planets with Earth-ish conditions suitable for a humanoid TARDIS crew in their normal clothing. Given the sheer number of potentially life-sustaining worlds in this galaxy alone, and the number of significant galaxies just in the *Doctor Who* cosmos, it's possible that the Ship is selecting places where the Doctor might pass unnoticed. Yet even then, it's spectacularly unlikely that the same happenstances which led to our bipedal, binocular, air-breathing set-up would occur on each world independently, let alone that everyone would end up as a mammal with thumbs. Unless Adric crashed a ship into each and every inhabited planet, of course.

Case proven. Clearly, in the *Doctor Who* universe evolution isn't simply a matter of natural selection. Something else must be messing about with the process, guiding life towards a humanoid norm. Even *Star Trek* has covered itself on this score (note especially *Star Trek: The Next Generation* 6.20, "The Chase"), by suggesting that all the "important" species in the universe were sown by some now-extinct alien super-race. There's never been any indication of anything that crass in *Doctor Who*, though, so who's been peeing in the cosmic gene-pool?

"Full Circle" is interesting, because it simultaneously gets evolution very right and very wrong. On the positive side, this is the one story that actually presents evolution as the way in which species change to suit their environment. The Marshmen become creatures which look entirely human / Terradonian because they spend generations living inside a Terradonian spaceship, so there's a good reason for them to evolve along those particular lines. It's *still* massively unlikely that they

should end up looking exactly like Earth-spawn, but in terms of TV fantasy there's at least a decent rationale here. The trouble is that they make this evolutionary change incredibly quickly. Natural selection should take millions of years to do this sort of work, not thousands. To get around this, the script tells us that the Marshmen are 'highly adaptive', something proven when Adric's wounded leg heals up in super-fast time.

You may have spotted the problem here. Even if the bodies of the Marshmen can grow new cells double-quick, what does that have to do with evolution? Species evolve as their DNA is passed down through generations. It doesn't matter if a creature can heal quickly, it doesn't even matter if it somehow shifts its cells around. Its DNA doesn't change in its own lifetime, and any alteration it makes to its body won't be passed down to its kids. What we're told about the Marshmen only makes sense if - unlike every living thing on Earth - they somehow have the natural-born ability to change their genetic makeup while they live.

There's a name for this idea. Well, actually there are at least two names. One of them is "twaddle", but the technical one is "Lamarckism". Jean Baptiste de Monet Lamarck was an eighteenth-century scientist who, in the days before Darwin had any better ideas, suggested that species change because the things animals experience in their lifetimes can somehow be transferred to their children. This sounds bizarre now, and it's the kind of logic which leads to the belief that the Elephant Man turned out the way he did because his mother was startled by an elephant. (Don't laugh too soon… children in playgrounds were reciting this as a "fact" when the movie came out in the early '80s, and they're probably still doing it.) But let's be fair; Lamarck was writing at a time when it was generally accepted that God had made everything in its finished form, so you've got to give him credit for thinking outside the box. Needless to say, nobody believes a word of it these days, at least not in reality. But are the Marshmen evidence that Lamarckism "works" in *Doctor Who*? If so, then there are any number of possible explanations as to how the evolution of life might have been affected. Stories like "State of Decay" (18.4) insist that when the universe was young, the wars of high-level beings like the Time Lords raged all across the cosmos. The hint is that these wars were profound enough to imprint themselves on the

continued on page 39...

as in "The War Games" (6.7)... perhaps the recall begins with a formal request, and they only force the issue if it isn't obeyed]. He apparently doesn't want to lose Romana any more than she wants to lose him, but he doesn't seem to want to admit it and even has difficulty making eye-contact while telling her it's inevitable. His claim that he's good with children is backed up by his treating Adric as a kind of protégé almost from the moment they meet.

The Earthman kidnapped by the Gaztaks [see the last story] has been returned home in the TARDIS by now.

The Supporting Cast

• *Romana.* Recalled by the Time Lords, she's desperately unhappy and sounds positively bitter about having to live on Gallifrey 'after all this'. The Doctor states she only came on board the TARDIS to help him find the Key to Time [hinting the Time Lords *did* know about the White Guardian's activities; see 16.1, "The Ribos Operation"]. In fact, by now she seems less happy-go-lucky all round, no longer treating a trip to a hostile new planet as a walk in the park but acting as if the environment's a genuine danger. However, she's unfortunately dismissive of the threat posed by the Alzarian spiders. She displays schoolteacher-like concern around young Adric.

• *Adric.* An occasionally sulky but generally rather over-enthusiastic teenager from Alzarius, which means that his ancestry isn't quite what you'd expect - see **Planet Notes** - and a great big gash in his leg heals without a scar in under an hour. Adric is a mathematical prodigy, an 'elite' who's been given a gold-rimmed star-shaped badge for mathematical excellence, but he just wants to rebel and initially tries to join the runaway Outlers. Despite his willingness to steal for them [a tendency he never loses], the Outlers nonetheless feel that he's a bit soft for their gang, and he certainly doesn't look too tough.

Adric eventually stows away on board the TARDIS in order to escape his life on the Starliner, and even before he meets the Doctor he seems to have a premonition that he won't be either on Alzarius or the Starliner when his people's ship lifts off. He's occasionally arrogant about his intellectual abilities, but not too clever in a crisis.

Adric's brother Varsh is seen here, and Adric doesn't shed many tears at the older boy's death. There's no sign of any parents. Adric receives his brother's marsh-reed belt after Varsh's passing, a sign that he's recognised as an Outler. Aww.

• *K9.* The Doctor's letting K9 set co-ordinates, something the dog does by extending his "eye" into the console, and it looks as if the Doctor's using him to make sure the Ship stays on course during the flight. K9 gets his head knocked off by a Marshman here, but the damage is easily fixed. The top of his head can be flipped open, and he can't identify a CVE when he detects one.

The TARDIS   When the TARDIS lands on Alzarius, the scanner displays the wilderness of Gallifrey instead of what's outside. This is because the scanner's image translator reads the absolute values of the co-ordinates, i.e. it looks at the Ship's space-time co-ordinates and shows whatever's at that point in the continuum. But Alzarius confuses it, as Alzarius has the same co-ordinates as Gallifrey but negative, since it's in the universe of E-Space. [So the scanner works a bit like the space-time visualiser in "The Chase" (2.8), though this leaves the question of why the Doctor doesn't use it to snoop around a bit more. At the very least, this might explain how the scanner can apparently see through solid objects (as in 1.8, "The Reign of Terror") and throw new light on the way the Ship occasionally seems to navigate by "looking" (15.1, "Horror of Fang Rock" and possibly 13.4, "The Android Invasion"). E-Space is much smaller than the normal universe, so if Alzarius has the same co-ordinates as Gallifrey then does this imply that Gallifrey is near the centre of the known universe? See also **History**.] A local image translator, i.e. one from the Starliner on Alzarius, fixes the problem. The image translator is immediately compatible with the workings of the TARDIS [as in 15.2, "The Invisible Enemy", it seems reasonable that the TARDIS is designed to accept just about any other form of technology]. Once the new translator's fitted, the Doctor can watch the Starliner taking off from Alzarius even when the TARDIS seems to be in "flight" in E-Space.

Romana claims that the TARDIS weighs 5 times 10^6 kilos in Alzarian gravity, but a group of Marshmen can pick it up anyway. [The Marshmen aren't *that* strong. Possibly Romana's referring to the weight of the entire Ship interior, and doesn't realise that the outside weighs less, although she must surely have noticed that it doesn't cause structural damage to the buildings it lands in. It's

How Does Evolution Work?

...continued from page 37

cultures of species throughout eternity. Imagine, if you will, the Time Lords manifesting on a planet inhabited by life in its early stages. Imagine this contact with "higher creatures" having such a startling effect on the planet that it changed the very nature of existence there. Imagine this experience imprinting itself on the primordial ooze, and changing its DNA forever. It's the Elephant Man scenario on a grand scale. The universe has produced so many humanoid species, Earth-humans included, because the Doctor's own people gave it such a nasty shock.

This leads on to another "theory" that seeks to re-write the rules of evolution, namely the "morphic fields" notion of biologist Rupert Sheldrake, popularised (if that's the word) in Sheldrake's 1981 book *A New Science of Life*. Much caution has to be exercised here, however, as much of the scientific community loathes Sheldrake's ideas and they're generally only accepted by people who want a slightly more God-friendly view of the universe than the one Darwin proposed. In a nutshell, Sheldrake's belief is that underlying the universe is a network of invisible, intangible fields, which act on (and shape) the physical reality around us. Crucially, if an event takes place anywhere in the universe then it imprints itself onto one of these fields, thus making it more likely that a similar

event will happen again. The objections to this are obvious. In the first place, there's no real evidence for it, despite Sheldrake's claim that it's the "only" thing which can explain people's ability to sense when somebody's staring at them from behind (!?!). In the second place, it's not a "theory" which can be reliably tested, which means it's got more to do with rampant philosophical speculation than with science. Needless to say, natural selection doesn't need "fields" of any kind. It's just a side-effect of having genes.

But on the cosmic scale of *Doctor Who*, the morphic fields idea *would* explain an awful lot. By Sheldrake's logic, if the first sentient species in the universe were more or less humanoid then it'd be more likely that all the later sentient species would evolve along similar lines. Those which grew up on similar planets would tend to look nigh-identical, and even those which developed in vastly different environments might end up with familiar features (consider the Ice Warriors, humanoid but reptilian; the Sensorites, humanoid but with candy-floss heads and oversized feet; and so on). When it comes to the mythology of *Doctor Who*, it doesn't take much effort to reach the conclusion that the Time Lords might have been the original root-species, either because they travelled back to the dawn of time and upset the morphic

continued on page 41...

perhaps safe to assume that the weight of the police box exterior can be altered from the console.] Binary co-ordinates for Gallifrey are once again said to be 1001100 by 02 from galactic zero centre, and K9 initiates the 'spatial drive' as the Ship sets off. The journey there takes a little over half an hour.

Romana's room on the Ship turns out to be rather modest, although it's full of clothes and minor effects, including a chess set rather more swish than the one that's sometimes used by the Doctor and K9. The TARDIS homing device is a palm-sized green artefact that goes "bling", and it's kept on the console [a homing device was last seen in "The Chase"]. The Doctor doesn't seem to have a decent microscope on the TARDIS, as he has to use the one in the Starliner when he wants to analyse tissue.

The TARDIS accidentally enters E-Space through a Charged Vacuum Emboitement, described by the Doctor as one of the rarest space-

time events in the universe. [Did it happen while the Ship was in the "real" universe, or do CVEs affect the space-time vortex? We see the Ship spinning through space, but that's possibly just a "dumbed down" version of the process for our benefit. The CVE's origins are revealed in 18.7, "Logopolis".] The Doctor starts searching for another one in order to escape E-Space, as if the TARDIS can't simply re-trace its path to find the point of entry. Time goes strange as the Ship passes through the CVE, but no damage is sustained.

The door control has moved again, which may help to explain why entry into the Ship seems so much easier here. The Doctor sends Adric off to check on Romana, but doesn't even offer a key, and Adric later wanders back in to stow away.

The Time Lords The wilderness of 'outer Gallifrey' has a blue sky, when shown on the TARDIS scanner. [It's obviously the same wilderness seen in 15.6, "The Invasion of Time", but there the sky was orange. Earth's sky is blue but turning orange at sunset, so maybe on Gallifrey it's the other way around.]

Planet Notes

• *E-Space*. Meaning the exo-space-time continuum, outside the normal universe. E-Space is described here as if it were a universe in miniature. Seen on the TARDIS scanner, E-Space looks green-tinted. The planet Alzarius has the same binary co-ordinates in E-Space that Gallifrey has in normal space, which confuses the TARDIS no end. [Funnily enough, the Alzarians have unusual regenerative powers and an oligarchy not unlike that of the Time Lords. Coincidence...?]

• *Alzarius*. An Earth-like world where the only "civilised" inhabitants are the people who live in the crashed Starliner, Alzarius has air, water, plenty of vegetation and is home to some unusually adaptive life-forms.

Every fifty years, the influence of another planet takes Alzarius away from its sun, a time known to the Starliner's inhabitants as 'Mistfall' as the cooling process causes funny-smelling but non-toxic mists to rise from the marshes. [At one point the First Decider speaks of 'suns', but this must be a figure of speech as all later evidence suggests that Alzarius has only one.] At the same time, curious seeds begin to appear in the melon-like river-fruits that the Starliner's people harvest. Eventually the tiny eggs inside the fruits hatch out to reveal large black spiders with glowing yellow eyes, one emerging from each fruit; the Doctor connects the high nitrogen content of the spiders with the environmental process of Mistfall.

These spiders are venomous, though they seem to die once they've used their psycho-chemical bite. When the chemical affects Romana, she forgets her prior identity, goes into a brief coma and takes on the persona of one of the Marshmen, even gaining veiny marks on her skin. While she's in this state the other Marshmen accept her as one of their own, and she feels the pain being experienced by one of the others [so either the Marshmen are somehow linked, or this is a result of Romana's Time Lord telepathy... the latter seems most likely, as there's no apparent empathy between other Marshmen]. It's said that the spiders evolved into the Marshmen, and the Marshmen are now afraid of the spiders. [So the spiders aren't part of the Marshmen's current life-cycle, despite the psycho-chemical's effects on

Romana. There's no evidence of any symbiosis between the species, and the Doctor speaks as if one simply came from the other.]

The Marshmen are humanoid, but inhumanly strong and covered in pale, slippery skins. As they're seen emerging from the water they're clearly amphibious, adapting remarkably quickly as they move onto dry land and breathing air through their gills, as long as the oxygen isn't too rich. They only come to the surface during Mistfall, and as soon as they arrive on land they demonstrate the desperate urge to get into the Starliner. [They home straight in on it, so it doesn't look as if they're just defending their territory. The Marshmen almost certainly realise, on some level, that the Starliner houses their "descendants". Even so, it's not explained why the Marshmen are so hostile to their offspring inside the ship. Maybe the combination of marsh-hormones and apparently alien biologies confuses them. Or maybe they're just jealous.]

The truth, of course, is that the Starliner's inhabitants are descended from the Marshmen who killed the original crew. Analysis of the spiders, the Marshmen and the new Alzarians reveals all their cells to be the same shape, which is why the creatures adapted so quickly once on board the ship and why Alzarians heal at such a rapid rate. They apparently have ape-like intelligence, as they communicate in grunts and can use basic tools. People get dragged into the bubbling swamps when Mistfall comes, which may be the Marshmen's doing. Mistfall lasts for up to ten years.

Romana estimates, loosely, that the Starliner's original occupants were replaced 4,000 generations ago. The Doctor later says 40,000. [*If* we assume that the original crew of the Starliner were entirely human... then on the surface it seems unlikely that the Marshmen could have turned into something near-identical so quickly. But then, life in the *Doctor Who* universe tends to default to human anyway, and at least here there's some *reason* for it. See **How Does Evolution Work?**.]

The Starliner is a large, crystalline-looking colony ship from Terradon, which seems to be a fairly sleek and efficient piece of spacecraft design, apart from the fact that the Alzarians keep removing and replacing perfectly good circuits. The ship was apparently damaged before deviating from its route and crashing here. Over the years the Starliner community has become something like a

How Does Evolution Work?

...continued from page 39

fields or because they really were the first species to evolve; see **Where (and When) is Gallifrey?** under 13.3, "Pyramids of Mars". Indeed, off-screen this is even hinted at in the novel *Lucifer Rising*, where the Doctor goes as far as to give his stamp of approval to the whole Sheldrakian concept.

One odd feature... the title of Lavinia Smith's paper *On the Teleological Response of the Virus* suggests that the '70s Britain of the UNIT stories has respected scientists thinking along these lines (this and Professor Cliff Jones' work on DNA synthesis meet with the Doctor's approval; see 11.1, 'The Time Warrior" and 10.5, "The Green Death"). In the *Doctor Who* world there was at least one previous paper on this, the 1883 work by Josiah Samuel Smith (26.2, "Ghost Light"). The version of "evolution" that Josiah presents strongly resembles the idea that moral character expresses itself somatically. In short, you look more human the "nicer" you are, and outward monstrosity is a reflection of inner wrongness (see 9.5, "The Mutants" and more particularly 19.5, "Black Orchid"). So it might be concluded that anything looking human is morally "right", or at least has the option of being so, whereas "monsters" are just basically bad seeds. Even Davros apparently offers this idea in a cut scene from "Remembrance of the Daleks" (25.1). Maybe the Guardians are responsi-

ble for this part of the cosmic plan, if they don't appear human purely for the Doctor's benefit (see **What Do the Guardians Do?** under 16.1, "The Ribos Operation").

Of course, it may just be that the "truth" about evolution in the *Doctor Who* universe hasn't been revealed yet. We know that this is a continuum full of Guardians, Eternals, demigods and alien interventionists, any number of whom could have been poking around in our DNA. If "Image of the Fendahl" (15.3) can have a stab at explaining the nature of the human beast in only an hour and a half of screen-time, then who's to say that some fifty-minute slice of the *new* TV series won't suddenly drop the bombshell that everything with a face is the offspring of the Ancient Warlords of Xgasarjil? Off-screen, the Big Finish audio *Zagreus* has already claimed that the "humanoforming" of the universe was a deliberate Time Lord strategy devised by (yes, you've guessed it) Rassilon. But the suggestion that *everything* in the universe is descended from one big extra-terrestrial genetic experiment seems unwieldy, even by *Doctor Who* standards. As it's presented to us on-screen, the fact that the universe is populated by some peculiarly British aliens comes across as a law of nature. Not because the programme wants to convince us that we're special but because it wants to demonstrate that we quite categorically aren't.

---

village, with three Deciders acting as its headmen, overseeing law and custom from their Great Book Room inside the ship. Romana says this sounds like a 'type D oligarchy', and Adric is apparently one of the 'elites' even though his brother isn't [elites are measured by distinction, not family].

For years the Deciders have been promising their people that soon they'll begin the great embarkation and return to Terradon, but have been ordering endless unnecessary alterations because... they don't actually know how to pilot the thing, as the pages in the flight manual which cover take-off were damaged in the crash. On top of that there's the problem that the Alzarians aren't native Terradonians anyway, but only the First Decider knows this as he's the Keeper of the System Files. Though the law of the Deciders is reasonably civilised, custom is strict, and only a band of bolshy teenagers called Outlers have left the Starliner to set up their own "gang" in a near-

by cave. Whenever Mistfall comes, the doors of the Starliner must be sealed, whether anyone's still outside or not. The people believe they've only been here for forty generations.

Little is known of Terradon [19.6, "Earthshock", holds that Terradon is also in E-Space]. Other than the Starliner itself, there are few signs of high technology here, and for once the locals don't carry energy weapons. Signs on the Starliner once again appear to be written in English. There are video-screens, and the tools needed for biological research, but that's about all. The end of this affair sees the Starliner take off and head for a new home elsewhere.

History

• *Dating.* No date given. [The name "Terradon" once again suggests that the original Terradonians might have been descended from Earth colonists, which is feasible, since "State of Decay" (18.4) establishes that at least one other Earth ship has ended up in E-Space. "State of Decay" also hints that one other inhabited planet may exist in this mini-universe, at least within K9's scanner range, but "Warriors' Gate" (18.5) clouds the issue. As there's no reason for the Doctor to move the TARDIS through time as well as space while he's looking for an exit from E-Space, it might be fair to suppose that "Full Circle" and the following two stories are all set at around the same point in time. But there's another potential oddity here. From the co-ordinates, the TARDIS scanner believes that it's on Gallifrey in the Doctor's "present". So does this story take place in the same era as modern Gallifrey? Or does the smaller size of E-Space just confuse the Ship's sense of time, what with space and time being interconnected...?]

The Analysis

Where Does This Come From? So, after two false starts (at least if you're watching things in broadcast order), this is where the John Nathan-Turner era really kicks in. And perhaps the biggest change here is who this programme seems to be aimed at.

As script editor before Bidmead, Douglas Adams famously said that his brief was to make the plots simple enough for adults to understand but complicated enough to keep children interested, which is fatuous but hints at something key about the '70s series: it was deliberately pitched at two separate audiences, providing science-trickery for the clever-clogses and monster costumes for the commoners. Graham Williams did, after all, see it as his job to provide "something for everyone". But rather than splitting up the high concept and the crowd-pleasers, the stories made in this period tend to turn the Big Ideas - such as they are - into visual events, so suddenly everything's designed to work on one level. Depending on your perspective, this either gives the storytelling a new sense of purpose or makes the whole programme look as if it's *just* for fourteen-year-old boys (this was certainly Lalla Ward's view, and she still loudly complains about the production team robbing the programme of its 'magic' by getting rid of K9).

The Big Idea here is evolution. The people on Alzarius turn out to be Marshmen. From an SF-geek's point of view, this is no big thing, and anyone taking biology at A-Level would have seen the catastrophic flaws in the plot. But the '80s were a

boom-time for documentaries about evolution vs. creationism, and the question of how one thing turns into another had become an ongoing talking-point after Richard Dawkins' *The Selfish Gene* in 1976 (we could mention who Dawkins eventually married, but if you don't already know then you can look it up).

Given Bidmead's "education, education, education" policy, the plot of "Full Circle" comes across as a primer on the subject, in much the same way that "Logopolis" (18.7) comes across as a primer on entropy. Western culture is still worryingly resistant to the idea of evolution, and even children from non-denominational families tend to stray towards the idea that some great creator made all the animals in the world out of plasticine. Earlier *Doctor Who* seasons dealt with concepts at least as complex as this, yet the Marshmen are designed to make it all seem corporeal. This is typical of the new regime. The monsters aren't just tagged on (although, annoyingly, the spiders are), they're the whole message.

And the early '80s seemed like the opportune time for this sort of thing, because it was the beginning of what we might now call the "hypertext age". We saw in Volume III how the late '60s and early '70s had expanded the vocabulary of fantasy, at least in the imagination of the general public, so that adventures in space and time could be psychological, biological and mythical instead of just concentrating on Martians and moonbases. By 1980, these ideas had become such common currency that they no longer needed to be explained. The bizarre and often-trippy SF movies that had followed in the wake of *2001* were being shown on television, letting the whole family see things which had once appealed only to a minority audience. "The kids" were reading increasingly grim and increasingly SF-literate comic-books, most notably the early, punk-ish issues of *2000 AD*; and even American sci-fi television at its most crass was beginning to draw on a more complex kind of iconography. The mind-tricks that *Doctor Who* had used when Barry Letts and Philip Hinchcliffe had been in charge were now fitted-as-standard in any fantasy production, and soon affordable domestic video would arrive to make the basic, cinematic source material even more accessible.

The influence of '60s and '70s "anthropological SF" comes through loud and clear in "Full Circle". The story resembles nothing so much as *Planet of* the Apes, and even the scene of the supposedly bestial Marsh-child being dragged into the Starliner in a net makes you wonder if it's shrieking 'you stinking humans!' in its own language. The notion of a planet that works as a single ecosystem hints at the Gaia mythology - see 13.2, "Planet of Evil", for a lot more on this - but this is a rather more restrained rendering of the idea than usual, as there's no hint that a single malicious intelligence is controlling everything.

It's also important to realise that this is the first ever script by a paid-up *Doctor Who* fan, as we'll discover in **The Lore**. Thus, despite the presentation, the logic of the story is entirely that of previous tales. In the original draft Alzarius was called "Yerfillag" (geddit?), and the contrasts between the Deciders and the Outlers were precisely the same as those between the Time Lords and the "drop-outs" (15.6, "The Invasion of Time") or the Sevateem and the Tesh (14.4, "The Face of Evil"). Indeed the original idea for the new companion, "Marsha", was that the process of adapting to new circumstances was what "good" characters did. Hence the Deciders scanned people at birth to assess who was "elite", exiling disruptive elements... and everything was bog-standard *Doctor Who*.

Or at least, bog-standard as far as an eighteen-year-old fan knew it. This mean that it was heavily influenced by Terrance Dicks, so obviously the drop-outs had to be right and the grown-ups wrong, as happened all the time in those Heinlein "juvenile" books that Dicks had lapped up. And it was influenced by Robert Holmes, so there were film-buff references and a scepticism about bureaucracy. And it was influenced by Malcolm Hulke, so there was a strong moral case on both sides. We could go on.

The point is that as well as a generational shift in the way that television is presented and "sold" to its audience, at this point there's also a generational shift in the way that TV scripts are made (Andrew Smith had joined the Writers' Guild and submitted sketches to comedy shows) and in what the viewers are expected to accept. It's hard to see clearly, given that this is his only completed script and there's a whole layer of Bidmead to hack through, but Smith doesn't waste time making a case that the audience has already taken on board. We don't have lengthy speeches about the ethics of vivisection, simply an unfortunate consequence and each side reacting according to their lights. We have a speech about procrastination and

bureaucracy, but this is short-circuited when we find out why it's happening. Compare this to the next broadcast story - "State of Decay", by Terrance Dicks himself - and the difference is obvious. Dicks is still fighting battles that Smith assumes have already been won.

As for overt references: Grimwade seems to have decided that the Marshmen not only have to look familiar to film buffs, but to act like well-known sympathetic monsters. So in addition to the blatant *Planet of the Apes* and *Creature from the Black Lagoon* influences, the assault on K9 is straight out of the beginning of *2001*... and so on. The idea of the natives evolving into spacemen isn't too far removed from the first third of Gene Wolfe's *The Fifth Head of Cerberus*, then available in all high streets with a pretty cover (although the rest of the book is less amenable to such treatment), and - a dead giveaway, this - Smith's novelisation of the story opens with a rubbish poem about Mistfall that's almost fingerprint-identical to the rubbish poem about "Threadfall" at the start of Anne McCaffrey's *Dragonfire* (then just being released in paperback, and adapted as the serial in Radio 4's *Woman's Hour* that spring). The use of K9's head as a totem isn't too far from *Lord of the Flies*. Matthew Waterhouse later did a one-man play based on *Huckleberry Finn*, and the riverfruit-stealing seems to have been at least partly inspired by this (the book, not the play).

Things That Don't Make Sense The Marshmen fear the spiders even though the effect of being bitten by one is, um, to turn into a Marshman. Romana's decision to stand in the cave saying 'they're only spiders' as an unidentified, venomous giant arachnid claws at her boots seems... unwise. Having failed to simply run from the cave, she then decides to chuck a marsh-fruit at the spiders instead (ooh, heavy artillery) even though she's already seen the fruits hatching out and must know what's likely to happen.

Marshmen being affected by increased oxygen supply, OK. Romana being similarly affected? Nope. [But then, she's obviously in telepathic contact with the Marshmen and capable of feeling their pain. This is psychosomatic as much as anything.] The climax of the story sees the Doctor and Romana showing the Deciders how to pilot the huge and incredibly complex Starliner in about ten seconds, not even stopping to check whether they've understood the instructions, so it's a miracle the ship gets off the ground safely.

Critique (Prosecution) In the first two minutes of screen-time we have nine continuity references. With a dull thud, the "JN-T Era" has arrived. Up until now it's been new-look *Doctor Who*, almost unchanged but less enjoyable. Now it's a whole new series, with similar characters. Tom Baker's in there, somewhere, under protest.

To give it it's due, the set for the Starliner looks fantastic, and the pacing of the story is always (well, nearly always) just half a step ahead of the average viewer, assuming any average viewers were watching. Corny though they might seem to anyone half-asleep a few weeks earlier when the BBC re-ran *Creature from the Black Lagoon*, the Marshmen were at least recognisably "trad" monsters, if not great. As with "The Visitation" (19.4) or even "The Keeper of Traken" (18.6) it's a really good story with the sound down. The dialogue, though...

It isn't just the obsessive continuity, or the undigested lumps of technobabble, nor even the irritatingly nearly-right (but graceless) science. It's that we have a planet where everyone's speech has the same cadence, the same one they had on Tigella and (sometimes) Argolis. When they differ, it sounds like a different story. The Deciders going into management-speak about 'holistic, real-time responses', jars not because it's badly-written but because they've not sounded like this for three episodes. Sometimes this is an asset, as when the Deciders try to browbeat the Doctor. When experienced actors aren't around, it's excruciating. The fact that the Outlers are supposed to be the Young Rebel Heroes we're rooting for makes it all the more grotesque.

Then there's the music. Occasionally it drowns out the dialogue, so it's not all bad, but it intrudes and grates. Like a bad film-score - say, something by James Horner - it tells you what you should be feeling, rather than underlining it as Dudley Simpson's music would have done (except in Season Eight, when Barry Letts again insisted on wall-to-wall synthesizers).

And... omigod! Romana's possessed! There hasn't been a good possession since "The Invisible Enemy" (15.2), and that was the rather desperate Doctor-infection. She's memorably creepy here, distant and aloof as she used to be but for all the wrong reasons. Alas, when she recovers, they misalign the effect for her eyes and illuminate her teeth. And she talks about something really banal, like gel electrophoresis. When the "proper"

Fourth Doctor recovered consciousness, he said something oblique and witty. Now, had it been him, he would have wittered about chromatographs or something

Adric antagonises audiences from the outset. He's vain, whiney, duplicitous and far less likeable than the other Outlers. On paper he's fantastic; a master-thief with a computer-brain who recovers from serious wounds in hours... give him his own show! Sadly, none of this potential is ever realised, so instead he gets "adopted" by middle-aged men for dubious ends and that's about it. He's "sold" to us as a companion from the outset, not wanting to be there, trusted by the Doctor to go into the Ship unassisted to fetch Romana, being scolded and siding with the Time Lords against the other Outlers, but there's no reason to buy this. In any other story he'd be the foil of the Doctor (and the youthful Seth from "The Horns of Nimon" is the obvious comparison, rather than the student Chris Parsons from "Shada" or the Savant leader Deedrix from "Meglos").

So turn the sound down, fast-forward through the rubber spiders, switch off just before the rather disappointing take-off and that nonsense about green space. Pretend Adric stayed behind. It's not a bad story, seen this way. Just try to avoid thinking of *Spinal Tap* when the Deciders stand up and announce themselves to the Doctor.

Critique (Defence) Volume up, eyes open, forget all this blather about "continuity references" (because the casual audience isn't bothered by back-referencing any more than it's bothered by any other Time-Lord-talk that might come out of the Doctor's mouth... we'll come back to this in 19.1, "Castrovalva").

This isn't about the fans, and it isn't about university types who want to obsess over the scientific terminology. This is what the series *meant* for those who were growing up in the early '80s. The first sign that the rebooted programme understands the techniques of its era, the first sign that *Doctor Who* can still demonstrate some visceral power post-Hinchliffe, and the first sign that it's about to become the best thing on television again.

So, how does this work? Well, at heart "Full Circle" takes the same approach to the construction of modern TV that we mentioned under "The Leisure Hive". But whereas "The Leisure Hive" got stretched in several directions at once, and ended up looking like a shapeless mass of space-putty, this is the story that pulls everything together: plot, theme, direction, design, the works. Alzarius is a world of dark, tactile spaces, where the mists, the blackness of the Starliner interior and the horrible biological secret of the planet's "humans" all feel as if they're part of the same process. The Marshmen's caves echo the ship's internal dimensions in such a way that when they break through the hatch, it looks as if they really *are* just coming home. Romana spends much of the second half of the story possessed, an old SF standard, yet while her mind's under the influence her stately, dream-addled appearance makes her look like a tribal leader of the Marsh-folk instead of the usual zombie mind-slave. (Because this is *Doctor Who* at its most anthropological, reminding us even in its little visual touches that all human beings are pack animals at heart, something that's never clearer than in the scene where the Doctor uses K9's head as a totem-like "mask" to hold off the monsters.) This is a place of *depths*; even the corridors look as if they're part of a much larger, three-dimensional space.

Finally, there's a sense of a programme taking itself seriously again, trying to make us take a deep breath and get involved in what's happening. The "problem" with the dialogue is simply that it's not supposed to be the focus. As the old directors' axiom goes, if you can judge a TV programme by its soundtrack then it's bad TV. The revelation about the Alzarians is a *great* revelation, yet it's not announced with trumpet fanfares but - an irresistible word - evolves from the action.

The death of the Marsh-Child has already been mentioned, but it's easy to see why it seems so striking; this is actually being played as drama, something that also comes across in the Doctor's angry, no-clowning-allowed haranguing of the Deciders and Romana's misery on being told to go home, a world away from Lalla Ward's cod-comedy entrance in "Destiny of the Daleks". Baker's Doctor himself becomes the figure he was always *meant* to be, veering between alien eccentricity and brooding presence, so you finally get to see what a good actor he is when he's not doing a double-act with K9 or hypnotising security guards. If he was miserable while making this, then somebody should have trodden on his toes earlier. At last the programme's found the balance between the Doctor and the world around him, and here - after all the space-bandits, trite megalomaniacs and petty superstitious villains of

recent years - we've finally got a story in which there are no contrived, less-than-threatening "evil" characters and the ecosystem itself is the menace. Even the E-Space theme fits the plot, making this complex environment feel as if it's tangled up in something even more convolute.

This is how you make television. It suggests a universe of layers and textures, something that makes you want to huddle up on a sofa on a winter evening and ask questions about the new world you're being shown. Only the spiders - oh, all right, and maybe a few of the scenes with the Outlers - seem to jar. Overall, the word for this is "cracking".

The Facts

Written by Andrew Smith. Directed by Peter Grimwade. Viewing figures: 5.9 million, 3.7 (disastrous), 5.9 million, 5.5 million. Unusually, episodes two and four got better ratings during the repeat run in August, 4.2 and 6.4 million respectively. But in both cases episode two was the runt of the litter, odd considering the "classic" cliffhanger of episode one.

Supporting Cast George Baker (Login), Richard Willis (Varsh), James Bree (Nefred), Alan Rowe (Garif), Leonard Maguire (Draith), Tony Calvin (Dexeter), Benard Padden (Tylos), June Page (Keara), Andrew Forbes (Omril).

Oh, Isn't That..?

• *George Baker.* Now famous for playing Inspector Wexford in a crime series that no-one will admit to watching, but then best-known as Tiberius in *I, Claudius*. He had also starred in Bowler, a sitcom spin-off from *The Fenn Street Gang* (itself spun off from *Please, Sir!*). Many of the remaining cast had worked on *Doctor Who* before, especially in stories where debutant director Peter Grimwade had been PA.

• *James Bree.* He's one of those vaguely-familiar faces to most British viewers, but to us he's Jimmy Bree, convention regular and known for at least two other significant *Doctor Who* performances (the Security Chief in 6.7, "The War Games" and the Keeper of the Matrix in 23.4, "The Ultimate Foe"). Similarly Alan Rowe (Dr. Evans in 4.6, "The Moonbase"; Edward of Wessex in 11.1, "The Time Warrior"; Colonel Skinsale in 15.1, "Horror of Fang Rock").

ABOUT TIME 1980–1984

Working Titles "The Planet That Slept".

Cliffhangers The Marshmen rise up out of the mist of the swamps; one of the spiders bites on Romana in the cave, and she drops to the ground amidst all the others; the "possessed" Romana opens the hatch that lets the Marshmen into the Starliner.

The Lore

• In order to avoid straightforward alien sounds for the Marshmen, Dick Mills went to a pig farm to record porcine noises under various conditions. The Radiophonic Workshop had small, window-less studios. Imagine how popular he was.

• Adric got his name from an anagram of Dirac, as in Paul Dirac, Nobel Prize-winning physicist and mathematician who - amongst other things - came up with the first version of anti-matter theory. The original idea had been to allocate the Marsh-child most of Adric's plot-functions (possibly, although this is unconfirmed, becoming the new companion "Marsha" and becoming more humanoid / Time Lordly with each story... Marsh-child actor Barney Lawrence certainly thought this was a goer), but the notion of a cosmic "Artful Dodger" caught Nathan-Turner's imagination. Matthew Waterhouse had been in the public school drama *To Serve Them All My Days* (pre-War in setting, but being made as rehearsals for "State of Decay" were ongoing, hence the dodgy wig Waterhouse sometimes wears) and only later revealed himself to be a *Doctor Who* fan. He appeared in the background in *Top of The Pops*, introduced to the viewers by DJ Kid Jensen, in the week that episode one broadcast. That he was wearing his costume and passed un-noticed among the *TotP* audience speaks volumes.

• In order to make Alzarius seem alien, powder-paint was dusted on the fronds of the tropical plants, and multiple lights with different colour-filters shone on the locations. The script speaks of "suns". It's exactly the same location, Black Park in Buckinghamshire, that was used in "The Visitation" (19.4)... but not, it appears, the almost identical-looking location in "State of Decay" (18.4).

• On hearing James Bree, George Baker and Alan Rowe singing in close harmony during the lunch-break while still in costume, Nathan-Turner took to referring to the highest authority on Alzarius as "The Decider Sisters".

• The rehearsals for this and "Castrovalva" (19.1) were visited by the makers of ViewMaster, who shot 3D reels of the story.

• Andrew Smith had been submitting stories since the age of fifteen, and had been determined to become a writer from an early age, joining the Writer's Guild as soon as he was able. His earlier proposal "The Secret of Cassius" had drawn favourable comments. (There's some confusion here... was the story submitted before 15.4, "The Sun Makers"? And if so, is this where the transplutonian planet got its name?) Bidmead's ambition to form a workshop for new writers, stifled by BBC lawyers' comments about possible rights issues, seemed like it had a good start with Smith. He later wrote sketches for Scots comedy series *A Kick Up the Eighties*, possibly the ones about drunks urinating against the TARDIS (yes, plural; it was a running gag). It has recently emerged that Smith is now in the Metropolitan Police.

• Smith travelled with the team on location, allowing him to appear alongside Waterhouse in press features on the "new generation". The fact that Smith had vomited on the costumes wasn't mentioned, and nor was the fact that Waterhouse had already done a whole story before this (the next one broadcast).

18.4: "State of Decay"

(Serial 5P, Four Episodes, 22nd November - 13th December 1980.)

Which One is This? Real bats (on stock footage), rubber bats (on wires), hairy peasants and kohl-eyed aristocrats. A Dark Tower from which no-one ever returns, blood-red walls and... *something*... sleeping below the earth. Yes, it's the *Dracula* one.

Firsts and Lasts First mention of the great pre-historic war between the Time Lords and the Giant Vampires. In fact it's the *only* mention of this in the TV series, although the subsequent novels, audios and fan-guides have never let us forget about it.

First (and as it turns out, last) time we actually *see* K9 leave the TARDIS through the police box doors; first story to be filmed with Adric, though nobody broke the news to Tom and Lalla; and the last speaking role in the series for Stuart Fell.

Four Things to Notice About "State of Decay"...

1. Regarded at the time as "*Doctor Who* at its most gothic", in retrospect it's more accurate to describe it as "*Doctor Who* at its most goth". Made in an era when post-punk fashion was urging the younger generation to dress up in pop-video period costume, "State of Decay" presents us with a planet run by vampires where the witch-lords dress in lush velvets and wear eye make-up that borders on the New Romantic (see 18.5, "Warriors' Gate", for more on this). Traditionally, fans have attempted to interest non-fans in this series by showing them some of the best-loved episodes - "The Talons of Weng-Chiang" and "City of Death" are always favourites - but when introducing the programme to college students who like mascara and black silk gloves, "State of Decay" is the perfect primer.

2. Today's moral from Terrance Dicks: people who suppress learning are evil, with the "nice" rebels objecting to the Lords not letting them read at least as much as they object to their children being eaten. Vamp-queen Camilla insists on melodramatically underlining this, when King Zargo insists that the Doctor is unarmed, with: 'You're wrong. The Doctor is not weaponless. He has the greatest weapon of all... *knowledge!*'

3. Following the reversal of "The Face of Evil" (14.4) in "Full Circle", this story takes for granted that the audience *expects* primitive societies to be descended from crashed colony ships. In episode two, the Doctor reaches the obvious conclusion that the three make-up-smeared witch-lords who rule this Medieval society are the great-great-grandchildren of the officers of the spaceship *Hydrax*. It takes him another episode to get to the surprise twist that they *are* the originals, and that the pale complexions were supposed to be the big clue. Meanwhile Counsellor Aukon sums up the attitude of the entire series, when one of the guards tells him that his men are bound to be killed fighting the rebels: 'Then die. That is the purpose of guards.'

4. Once again, K9's getting short shrift here. In "The Armageddon Factor" (16.6), he was used as a Trojan horse in the Doctor's heroic mini-assault against the Shadow. Here, the Doctor builds up K9's abilities as an armoured war machine in front of the rebels before the dog finally rolls out of the TARDIS, to an overwhelming silence from the locals and a disappointed drooping noise from the incidental music.

The Continuity

The Doctor Still saying 'not now' when K9 tries to tell him something important. Discovering that Adric has stowed away on the TARDIS, he intends to get the boy back to the Starliner [there's no hint in the next story that he's even tried to do this, so something must make him change his mind].

• *Inventory.* He's got a telescope inside his coat [the same one Romana used in 16.2, "The Pirate Planet"?].

• *Background.* The Doctor's familiar with arrow-class scout-ships like the *Hydrax*. He refers to an old hermit who lived in the South Mountains on Gallifrey, and who told him ghost stories when he was young. [Given that this script was written by Terrance Dicks, script editor of the series in the early '70s, this has *got* to be a reference to the Time Lord formerly known as K'anpo; see 9.5, "The Time Monster" and 11.5, "Planet of the Spiders".] Thanks to these stories the Doctor has heard about the swarming of the giant vampires, but it's not common knowledge as Romana doesn't know the same tales [despite referring to herself as a 'historian' in 17.6, "Shada"], and the Doctor himself doesn't know the details until he consults the Record of Rassilon.

The Supporting Cast

• *Romana.* Used to work in the Bureau of Ancient Records [i.e. on Gallifrey], where she once saw a reference to something called the Record of Rassilon on one of the old data-books, so she knows that a copy of the Record is installed on type-forty time vehicles such as the Doctor's TARDIS. There seems to be a genuine tenderness between the Doctor and Romana here, not just the non-stop quipping that marked his relationship with her in the early days [they know they won't be together for much longer]. She's got a good memory for names.

• *Adric.* Confident around strangers, ready to improvise and back-chat when caught by the villagers on a strange planet, but at this point it comes across as haughtiness rather than intelligence. He shows no guilt at all about the fact that the rebel Tarak dies while attempting to rescue him; is cynical enough to think that the Doctor might just run from danger and leave Romana behind; and may well seriously consider joining the vampires, although it's not clear when he's bluffing. He throws a knife well, and has a patch where he tore his PJs at the knee. [In the last story, although his romper-suit is magically restored for every subsequent adventure. So either the TARDIS wardrobe contains replacement clothes from "impossible" universes, or someone's really handy with a needle and thread. It isn't the Doctor, as we saw the sloppy patches on his scarf as early as 15.3, "Image of the Fendahl".]

• *K9.* He's familiar with vampire legends from seventeen inhabited planets [not very impressive, since the Doctor believes that almost every inhabited planet has these legends]. From the TARDIS, he detects the habitable planet in E-Space at the extreme limit of scanner range, and can sense its gravity and rotational period. [His own scanners, or is he in constant touch with the TARDIS now?] His orbital scan can detect the energy-levels, and therefore the level of technology, of the planet before landing on it. He can tap the TARDIS' data core when he's hooked up to the console with two leads, and seems positively curious when the Doctor starts reading from the Record of Rassilon.

Ready for battle, K9 describes himself as 'reconfigured in aggression mode'. The Doctor describes his weapon as a nose-laser.

The TARDIS   There are 18,348 emergency instructions in the TARDIS memory core / data core, as K9 discovers when he taps it. There's nothing in the databanks about vampires. But as K9 knows, somewhere on board the TARDIS is a trolley which contains various books, papers and records on magnetic card, the latter of which can be fed into the console to produce results on ticker-tape. Among these files is the Record of Rassilon, from which the Doctor learns the history of the Time Lords' war with the Giant Vampires. Among this data is the Directive of Rassilon, which states that Time Lords must destroy these creatures even at the cost of their own lives, and describes vampires as 'the enemy of our people, and of all living things'. The Record is a feature of all type-forty TARDISes. [It's not explained who's supposed to use this record, when prior to this the Doctor hasn't even known of its existence.]

The Doctor can now make the TARDIS land in a specific room in a specific building, but only because the relative smallness of E-Space makes these short hops easier.

The Time Lords   Once upon a time, 'when even Rassilon was young', the Giant Vampires came out of nowhere and swarmed all over the universe.

There followed a war between vampires and Time Lords, which the Time Lords won after Rassilon ordered the construction of 'bowships' that fired great bolts of steel through the vampires' hearts. But when the Time Lords came to count the bodies of the vampires [they knew the exact total?], they found that one - the King Vampire, mightiest and most malevolent of all - had vanished. His whereabouts has never been discovered until now.

The war against the vampires was so long and bloody that it supposedly sickened the Time Lords of violence forever, and the Doctor speaks of the vampires being deliberately hunted down. The story isn't well-known among Time Lords, as the Doctor's only heard of it as a ghost story and has no idea of its historical validity.

[The first question that springs to mind: when did this happen? The war seems to have taken place in the days before Time Lords had full mastery over time, so did the vampires attack the universe in Gallifrey's "present"? Indeed, could the Giant Vampires themselves travel through time? If it wasn't a time-travelling war, then this is good evidence that Gallifreyan history is in the ancient past; see **Where (and When) is Gallifrey?** under 13.3, "Pyramids of Mars".

[Outside broadcast *Doctor Who*, the later novels have an awful lot to say on the subject of the vampires, and some of it is worth repeating. *The Pit* claims that they came from outside the normal universe - but not actually from E-Space - and only entered the known continuum when Rassilon's early time-travel experiments punched holes in the fabric of the universe, which explains why the Time Lords have been covering up the affair. There are hints, especially in *Goth Opera*, that Time Lord regenerative powers in some way inspired the vampires' healing abilities. The novels routinely assume that Gallifrey exists / existed in the far-distant past, which means that this war took place billions of years ago.]

The Non-Humans

• *Vampires.* The Giant Vampires were, according to the Record of Rassilon, hundreds of feet tall and capable of sucking whole worlds dry. Energy weapons were useless against them, as the vampires absorbed and transmuted the energy to become stronger. They also had incredibly efficient cardiovascular systems, and could only be killed if their hearts were destroyed, hence the creation of the bowships. The King Vampire

... Or Could It Be Fantasy?

Now, in Volume IV we spend some time dwelling on the question of whether *Doctor Who* really, truly qualifies as a science fiction series; see especially the essay under 14.4, "The Face of Evil", which is a companion piece to what we're going to look at here. This meant that we had to ask ourselves what SF actually is. To recap the scintillating conclusions we reached:

1. If you're talking about *mode*, then SF can be thought of as "the way you read SF". An SF story invites you to take in information about a new world, compare it with the way you see the world you know, and work out how different this world must be in order for it to make sense. (We'll come back to this thought - and look at the way it relates to the idea of "fantasy" - for 25.4, "The Greatest Show in the Galaxy".)

2. But if you're talking about *themes*, then SF can be described as being about the relationship between humanity and its tools; about the way humans externalise themselves through the things they make, from power-over-life-itself being put into human hands in *Frankenstein* / "The Brain of Morbius" to the juxtaposition of space-technology and stone-age weapons in *2001* / "An Unearthly Child".

All fair enough, but the sharp-minded amongst you may notice that this definition's still blurry at the edges. If SF is all about people and their tools, then what about language? Language is a tool. Does SF only cover tools that need fingers, or what?

And this question is important, because it may be key to understanding the difference between "science fiction" and "fantasy", and why *Doctor Who* occasionally seems to have such an odd relationship with the two.

Consider the following storyline. In some other world, there lives a tyrant who's held sway over that world for as long as anyone can remember. However, he knows he's running out of time. In the middle of his realm is a device which takes the form of gigantic clock, and when the clock strikes twelve, the tyrant's life will end. Thus a hundred million slaves work day and night at the clock, straining against the enormous cog-wheels and forcing back the hands of time, ensuring that midnight never comes and that the tyrant lives on.

Is this an SF story, or a fantasy? Well... it could be either. If the great clock is some form of slave-powered "time dam" (much as in 16.2, "The Pirate Planet"), which uses temporal technology to renew the tyrant's body and takes the form of a

clock just so he can keep track of the way the operation's going, then this is SF. But if it really is a clock, which has the power to prevent ageing just by its mythic clock-ness, then this is fantasy. A clock has nothing to do with time, or at least, it has no more to do with time than any other object in the universe; it's just a *symbol* of time, from a human perspective.

And this is the crux of it. SF, like science itself, is a process of figuring out how things actually work. Fantasy takes the symbols of things to be literally true. In fantasy, a clock-face has power simply because it represents something powerful, i.e. the passage of time. Likewise, a magician might claim that the first knife to be plunged into Julius Caesar in 44 BC has a certain totemic power simply because it was the first knife to be plunged into Julius Caesar in 44 BC, whereas a scientist would point out that if you analyse it, it's pretty much indistinguishable from any of the other knives used in the slaughter (and probably not much different to any other knife on Earth[2]).

If fantasy - perhaps we should say "magic" - is based on the notion that symbols are powerful in themselves, then it throws up some interesting questions about language. After all, language *is* just ("just"!) a series of symbols. It's no surprise that many writers over the ages have ended up believing they're performing rituals of some kind while they're writing; from a certain perspective, language is magic, a set of shared symbols that changes the way the world looks. And once again, you can see how SF and fantasy would start to blur together. Science and science fiction try not to take symbols for granted, but to investigate and re-consider, yet to an extent *all* literature demands that we take certain symbols for granted. The word "whale" isn't an actual whale, it's a symbol representing a whale. But read the word "whale" and you immediately think of something big and blue and sea-going, because if you stopped to consider whether you should accept every word at face value then it'd take you hours just to get through a sentence.

In other words, there's a "magic" element in everything that's ever been written. SF in particular seems to demand that certain pieces of "magic thinking" are acceptable, if only because it makes storytelling easier. Almost every disintegrator ray in SF - certainly in SF television - works on the assumption that if you point it at a victim, then the

continued on page 51...

escaped into E-Space [perhaps through a CVE of its own making... see the **History** of 18.7, "Logopolis"]. It somehow brought the Earth vessel *Hydrax* into E-Space by mentally communicating with its Science Officer.

Though the Giant Vampire lies inert beneath the ground, its heartbeat is still audible within the turret of the Tower. For the last few centuries its bidding has been done by the Three Who Rule; the Captain, Navigation Officer and Science Officer of the *Hydrax*, now turned into vampires of a more conventional variety and acting as the King, Queen and Counsellor of the planet. The Great One, when glimpsed by an x-ray scan, is largely humanoid in shape but with a bat-like head and vast wings. Blood is being stored inside the Tower's fuel tanks, deep in the bowls of the ship [we can assume there's *some* mechanism keeping it fresh], and the Time of the Arising is approaching when the Great One will emerge from its sleep and its servants will swarm back into N-Space.

The Great One has regenerated from its wounds after all the 'blood and souls' fed to it over the years, but Counsellor Aukon wants a Time Lord as a sacrifice as it forces its way out of the ground, and claims that it'll be displeased if the proper rituals aren't carried out. An enormous, long-fingernailed hand emerges from the ground as the Great One starts to rise, but it dies when a scout-ship is driven through its heart.

The Three Who Rule still appear human, for the most part, though they can reveal fangs when necessary. Naturally, they thrive on blood. Aukon seems to be the power behind the throne and tells the King and Queen what the Great One wants; using swarms of vampire bats as his eyes and ears, or commanding the animals to attack his enemies at long range. He seems to have mild telepathic powers, detecting that Adric is shielding his mind and later mesmerising the boy. This mesmerism requires eye contact, and is at least powerful enough to petrify the Doctor. Aukon can also make a piece of rock shatter into pieces when it's thrown at him [on-screen it looks as if it just breaks up when it hits him, but the novelisation claims that some kind of psychic power is involved]. The Three age to death and crumble to dust as soon as the Great Vampire is destroyed. [Giant Vampires themselves don't crumble, as the stories of the Time Lords refer to vampire 'bodies'. Though the Three are clearly "night people",

Aukon doesn't seem to have any trouble moving about by day; as the idea that vampires shrivel up in the sun was only invented for the 1922 movie *Nosferatu*, and doesn't have a precedent in folklore despite what the Doctor says, it's possible that the Giant Vampires are quite comfortable in daylight. Which isn't surprising, if they're capable of flying through space.]

The Doctor points out that vampire myths exist on 'almost every' inhabited planet, the suggestion being that these are in some way connected to the Giant Vampires. [Either race memories or signs that "lesser" vampires still thrive in the universe, though really it's easy to see how any culture might develop myths about blood-sucking monsters without help from outer space.] He points out that according to myth they fear sunlight, running water and certain herbs [there's evidence of none of those here, and anyway, he pronounces "herbs" the American way], and can only be killed by a stake through the heart or beheading. [Romana believes that the Three Who Rule can only be killed by a *wooden* stake, but she may be wrong, as the Great One can be destroyed by metal if the blow to the heart is big enough. Although a dagger in the chest doesn't seem to damage one of the lesser vampires.]

Planet Notes The normal universe is described as N-Space, to distinguish it from E-Space. [Barry Letts' radio-play *The Ghosts of N-Space* claims that N-Space is a realm called "Null-Space" rather than just being the normal universe. Perhaps in the Doctor's language, "Normal" and "Null" start with different letters, so it never occurs to him that when translated into English the two sound exactly the same. In real-world terms Barry Letts was working as an adviser on *Doctor Who* in this period, which might suggest that he heard the term "N-Space" but forgot what it meant later on.]

• *The Planet.* Located in E-Space, the world that's now home to the Great One is never named. It's Earth-like, with plenty of woodlands and apparently some animal life, but the humans are apparently all descended from those brought here on the *Hydrax*; see **History**. The sky goes E-Space-green as it goes dark.

For centuries, the locals in the village - the only settlement on the planet [Terrance Dicks' novels *Blood Harvest* and *The Eight Doctors* somewhat expand on this] - have been living in the shadow of the Tower, actually the *Hydrax* itself. Under the

... Or Could It Be Fantasy?

...**continued from page 49**

victim and the victim's clothes will vanish, but that all the molecules *around* the victim will be untouched (see 12.1, "Robot", in which the super-weapon can neatly disintegrate a soldier who's lying on the ground and leave the grass intact). This is scientifically weird, yet makes sense to us on an instinctive level. Why? Because we see things in terms of whole units, not in terms of atoms. We see the victim of the ray as being a single, self-contained "idea", even if the ray itself can't possibly make that distinction. This is magic thinking, and it's nothing to be ashamed of.

Perhaps what we should ask is: what are SF and fantasy *useful* for? If SF is generally about the way we make and use tools - about finding out *how* to make and use tools, as we measure and explore the things around us - then it's the perfect form for a story about humanity's relationship with the outside world. It's a medium of discovering what's beyond our bodies. Whereas if fantasy involves accepting our own personal, private symbols as "true", then it's the perfect form for a story about our *internal* explorations. We'll come back to this, to an extent, when we look at the less-than-scientific "Kinda" (19.3... the menace in "Kinda" is the Mara, which can be driven back into the unconscious by mirrors, something that makes no rational sense but works in terms of symbolism). In recent years the best-known and most successful example of this has been *Buffy the Vampire Slayer*, which in its prime used a variety of demons and mis-fired spells as metaphors for the anxieties of adolescence. You'd be a fool to try to do that in "pure" science fiction.

The trouble is, of course, that if fantasy is done badly then it just becomes an excuse for laziness and ignorance. While SF insists on asking us to constantly question, there's a perpetual risk that fantasy's "take things at face value" approach will lead to an attitude of "believe everything you're told", an idea which should hopefully be abhorrent to anyone who's reading a book about *Doctor Who*. It's telling that the most easily-marketed form of fantasy, the elves-and-halflings variety, is largely based on the assumption that there's a Way Things Should Be and that a natural, God-given order always needs to be re-established. Both the Doctor and elves-and-halflings heroes have a habit of overthrowing evil dictators, but elves-and-halflings heroes also have a tendency to replace the overthrown monarch with a

"Rightful King" or "Rightful Queen" who was cruelly deposed from the throne, whereas the Doctor's more likely to question the wisdom of the entire monarchy. ("The Androids of Tara" is a rare exception to this, although the same season also gives us "The Ribos Operation", in which the "rightful" ruler of Levithia is a war-mongering lunatic and none of his subjects want him back.)

There's another interesting side-effect of the way fantasy works, again connected to the fact that all its symbols are automatically accepted as "true": it's taken for granted that old things have power. The knife that stabbed Caesar is only the beginning. Most fantasy fiction, from the banal to the sublime, acknowledges that there are ancient and terrible forces in the world which have a strength, a knowledge and an authority far beyond that of "younger" beings like ourselves. This is hardly surprising, since all of us grew up in a world where all-powerful giants really *did* walk the Earth (they were called "mum and dad"). The difference between this and SF should be obvious. Why are Martians scary? Because they've got protonic X-missiles that can destroy our planet, and we have to be told about these missiles for the story to make sense. Why is Morgrax the Dark One scary? Because he represents something unknowably *old*, which is terrible by its very nature, whether we know what he's really capable of or not. (A related point: science requires repeatability. You have to be able to repeat an experiment, and achieve the same results, for that experiment to be scientifically valid. Yet in fantasy, magical artefacts are magical because nobody in the modern world is capable of manufacturing them. Certainly, nobody's capable of mass-producing them. They're non-repeatable events.)

It's interesting to note that those things which are most often called "science-fantasy", and seen as hybrids of the two styles, frequently involve confrontations between the scientifically-minded modern world and the unknown past. *Doctor Who* is full of this sort of thing. Sutekh (13.3, "Pyramids of Mars") and Azal (8.5, "The Daemons") are terrifying even before we know the full extent of - or rationale behind - their powers, because they're presented to us as primal evils, i.e. the domain of fantasy. In both cases there are attempts to rationalise them with talk of telepathy, telekinesis, cytronic induction and God-knows-what-else, but the fact that scientific / pseudo-scientific lingo can

continued on page 53...

power of the Three Who Rule, the villagers are kept in a state of ignorance and fear, not being permitted any advanced technology and not being allowed to study science even though they still know the word 'scientists'. The rebels only know the term 'doctor' from the old records.

The penalty for knowledge is death; children work in the fields as soon as they can walk; and reading is prohibited, but the skill is passed down in secret. They don't seem to know what cheese is, either. Food allowances are making the villagers too weak to work, but the head-man states the official line that the Lords protect them from 'the wasting'. The Tower's guards enforce the Law, and every so often young people from the village are selected to be taken to the Three. Most of them end up drained of their blood, though a few become guards and Lord Aukon is looking for 'chosen ones' to become new servants of the Great Vampire when the Time of Arising comes. The interior of the Tower / ship is furnished like a great gothic palace, which the Doctor dubiously describes as 'rococo'. Of the Hydrax's scout-ships, one is still operable enough to skewer the Great One.

The only resistance to the vampires is an underground movement with a secret lair in the woods, whose members wear hooded robes and who possess computer equipment and walkie-talkies from the Hydrax. A mixture of scientists and guerrillas, they want to overthrow the vampire lords and return to Earth [which must be remembered in their folklore as a kind of promised land, as they're desperate to go there even though they've never seen it]. When the Great One dies, it's routinely assumed that these resistance people will be running the planet from now on, as they have enough knowledge in the Hydrax computers to become a technological civilisation.

K9 states that the planet has a day equal to 23.3 Earth hours, and a year equivalent to 350 Earth days. Romana describes it as losing its grip on Level Two development [a similar system to the one used in 16.1, "The Ribos Operation"], and believes that a society which evolves backwards must have a more powerful force restraining it.

History

• *Dating*. The computer screen of the Hydrax suggests that the computer was programmed on "12/12/1998". [But this is ludicrous, given what we know of the rest of human history in the

Doctor Who universe, as humanity doesn't leave the solar system until around 2100. Nevertheless, given that the readout is done in 1980s-style Ceefax lettering (with the date in the top left, as with news bulletins on teletext) and given that the equipment around the 'technocotheka' includes valve amplifiers, this is at least *consistently* stupid. Possibly we can put this odd date down to degeneration in the ship's systems. The novel *Lucifer Rising* suggests a date of 2127, which is far more reasonable, as long as you ignore the rather retro swipe-cards.]

The rebels believe that nothing has changed for 'a thousand years', while Aukon says the Three Who Rule have been breeding the villagers for twenty generations. [The latter would seem more likely, as Aukon was actually there and the villagers only have folklore to draw on. Assuming the 2127 date to be roughly accurate, and assuming a generation to be around twenty years, a date in the 2500s seems a fair estimate It's not clear whether the TARDIS travels through time to get here, but since the Doctor arrives just in time to stop the Great One's rising, you could almost believe that something - TARDIS or Time Lord - steered him here at this particular moment.]

The arrow-class scout-ship *Hydrax* was heading for Beta Two in the Perugellis Sector when the Great One brought it into E-Space. The Doctor states that these ships were designed for local exploration. Judging by the pictures in the computer records, the original officers wore very unflattering Norman-like helmets [compare with 6.6, "The Space Pirates"].

The Analysis

Where Does This Come From?   It's the job of this part of the book to say something about the time in which the story was made, but in the case of "State of Decay" there's an obvious complication: it was, for the most part, written three years before it was filmed. And this makes a difference.

As has already been mentioned (15.1, "Horror of Fang Rock"), the BBC pulled Terrance Dicks' original script in 1977, as the powers-that-be were scared that it might clash with their high-profile adaptation of *Dracula*. But three years later, *Dracula* just didn't seem like the kind of thing that BBC drama *did* any more. Watch Dracula now and it looks like a '70s period piece with Hallowe'enish video effects thrown in, but by the

... Or Could It Be Fantasy?

...continued from page 51

be applied to them doesn't alter the fact that they primarily *are* icons of fantasy. Indeed, much of the programme's technobabble is unnecessary when applied to forces like these. If a Cyberman displayed the ability to make a wall disappear just by gesturing at it, then you'd bloody well want an explanation. Yet when an Egyptian god does the same thing, it seems perfectly valid, and Sarah's line about 'tribophysics' seems surplus to requirements.

Which brings us to "State of Decay", the greatest test-case of them all. There's nothing here that's actually *offensive* to the principles of SF. Once again, we have an ancient horror. A vampire, as we all know, can be killed by a stake through the heart but not by most "normal" means. In fantasy this strange method of execution makes a perfect, symbolic form of sense, especially given the sexual imagery found in so many vamp tales. Terrance Dicks covers this, ish, by explaining why vampires in the *Doctor Who* continuum are immune to anything short of bowships; it's something to do with their cardiovascular systems, but the lines in question are so vague that Tom Baker might as well mumble them.

Does it change anything? No. The Giant Vampire remains, resolutely, a fantasy villain... who's finally dispatched by a scientist, wielding scientific tools and acting in the name of science. Every turn of the script pushes this point home. In "The Daemons", the Doctor already knows that Azal is a thing from another world and can therefore safely rationalise the creature's powers. His is the voice of scientific experience. But in "State of Decay", even the Doctor doesn't know of the existence of the vampires. They're so old that they're a myth even to him, symbols of ancient terror from *his* point-of-view as well as our own. Unlike the Daemons (and unlike the age-old horror in 15.3,

"Image of the Fendahl", which is also a Doctor-frightener from the legends of Gallifrey), the Vampire King isn't even given a point of origin. The Doctor's slaying of the beast is a victory over the darkness of the past, not merely the defeat of an alien which has been *mistaken* for that darkness.

The final thing to notice here is the way this fantasy / SF schism makes us reconsider the Doctor himself. Nobody half-sane can watch *Doctor Who*, particularly its early episodes, without spotting that a lot of the time it's pitched as folklore rather than a product of "hard" science fiction. The Doctor adopts the role of a magician, not of a space-pilot. The TARDIS is a magic cabinet, not purely a space-time vessel even in the H. G. Wells sense. Or at least, this is what the system of symbols is telling us. The very first episode makes it clear that everything within the Ship *can* be explained scientifically - just not to stupid humans like Ian Chesterton - but the science is so hazy, and the presentation so dependent on us recognising the "eccentric old alchemist" figure from the lore of antiquity, that we wouldn't be *too* surprised if the Doctor went along the same road as *Catweazle* and told us that the thirteenth sign of the zodiac powers the TARDIS' time-drive. It may be significant that as the Doctor becomes visibly younger and palpably less mysterious, the series takes a positive shift towards space opera, as if it knows we'll be less willing to accept sorcery when the Doctor isn't such an obvious icon of the old and the unknown.

Equally significant, perhaps, is that when the programme-makers deliberately try to turn the Doctor into something far more enigmatic and with a history far older than that of the Time Lords themselves - see 25.1, "Remembrance of the Daleks", et seq - the programme suddenly takes giant leaps back towards out-and-out fantasy (with crushing inevitability, we'll come back to this for 26.1, "Battlefield").

---

early '80s costume drama was becoming a thing of the past, while effects-based spookiness just wasn't having the same impact. You could see much stranger things in every video on *Top of the Pops*, and anyone who was around at the time will know how very, very hard it is to resist mentioning Bowie's "Ashes to Ashes" at this point. All of which means that "State of Decay" is a one-off hybrid, a story written at a time when this sort of thing seemed perfectly straightforward but filmed in a style that's heading towards the proto-New-

Romantic look of "Warriors' Gate" (18.5). When it tries to look *really* antique, you occasionally get a whiff of BBC1's 1981 historical epic *The Borgias*, which bombed like nothing on Earth and was in many ways the end of an era.

But there's no way of getting through this without mentioning the vampire canon that supplies most of Dicks' source material. As scripted, "State of Decay" has got a damn sight more to do with the Hammer vampire movies than with Bram Stoker's original text, in the same way that "The

Brain of Morbius" (13.5) has got more to do with Universal's *Frankenstein* than with Mary Shelley. The film which springs to mind straight away is *Vampire Circus* (1972), partly because of its vision of vampires as child-snatchers but mostly because *Vampire Circus* has got Lalla Ward in it as well. There's a possible literary reference in the vampire-queen Camilla, obviously a descendant of Sheridan Le Fanu's "Carmilla", although Dicks didn't necessarily have to go all the way back to Le Fanu's novella as Carmilla also received the Hammer treatment (most memorably in 1971's *Lust for a Vampire*, a film which can best be summed up by the sentence "Lesbian Vampire Schoolgirls Meet Ralph Bates").

The idea that these vampires are in some way *alien*, and therefore killable with technology instead of magic, is obviously a staple of mid-'70s *Doctor Who* and another tell-tale sign that the plot was devised during the Philip Hinchcliffe days. As we've already seen, by the '80s people had grown far too used to the idea that extra-terrestrials might have been responsible for old legends; nothing really comparable turns up in the programme again until the very last season, when some more SF vampires arrive and turn out to have a completely different origin to the ones seen here (26.3, "The Curse of Fenric"). See also ...**Or Could It Be Fantasy?**.

Things That Don't Make Sense The bats produce a noise that makes them sound as if they've all been electronically tagged, and the same sound effect is used whenever Aukon displays any kind of paranormal power. For some reason he thinks the bats are required during the ceremony to rouse the Great One, so much so that he refuses to sic them on the attacking rebels, but all we actually see is one of them landing on Romana's neck and flapping a bit. Aukon also believes that the Great One will be angry if there aren't any 'chosen ones' to act as its servants when it rises, yet in the end one mopey teenage boy is the only 'chosen one' he even attempts to provide. And the scout-ship supposedly penetrates the Great One's heart, but after the vampire-slaying it's seen sticking out of the ground as if it's barely scratched the surface.

Ivo states that the Three Who Rule protect the villagers from 'the wasting', and this is heavily underlined by the rebels in episode one, but it's never explained as it's a left-over from an earlier draft of the script. The rebels are spurred into action by the Doctor's parody of the St. Crispin's Day speech - 'he who outlives this day and comes safe home shall stand a-tiptoe when this day is named, and rouse them in the name of E-Space' - even though the locals can't possibly know what "E-Space" is, let alone that they live there [they're caught up in the moment]. Adric also seems to know a surprising amount about E-Space, in the same way that all the rebels know what a "scanner" is when they've never seen one before.

It makes sense that the Three Who Rule might have dumped all the computer equipment that gets snapped up by the rebels, given that the power of the Great Vampire makes human science more or less obsolete (Aukon doesn't *need* a scanner, he's got his bats), but didn't they think about trashing it rather than leaving it lying around the place for the World's Oldest Hacker to find? [Zargo claims that he ordered the records of the *Hydrax* to be destroyed, so possibly the resistance was started by a guard who ignored orders and ran off with all the hardware.]

Critique (Prosecution) Due to the odd nature of the production, it's not really surprising that this story is Tom's Greatest Hits. In rapid succession in episode two we have a near-verbatim reprise of the line when he first twigs that Sutekh is alive ('I've a suspicion, but it's almost too horrible to contemplate') and some low-key clowning with Romana treading on his toes. We have a ghost story from his youth (like the Fendahl), a rousing speech, a "Drake's Drum" invocation of Rassilon and - as he walks back to the TARDIS in episode three - a minor-key reprise of the Dudley Simpson "Fourth Doctor" tune.

But for all that it didn't feel especially special. We have this idea now that the Doctor vs. a Giant Vampire ought to have been iconic and momentous, but it's routine, like the pseudo-mediaeval planet and the rebel outsiders with access to "lost" records telling the truth. Releasing it as a talking book made sense on paper, but only if you hadn't seen the broadcast version. Perhaps the cornyness of the ending, or the "tick-box" approach to vampire lore, makes this seem like contractual obligation.

One or two moments stick in the memory: the dissolve from Aukon to slow-motion film of a bat flying towards us (this is the same director who gave us "The Five Doctors"?); the 'you're wonderful' scene, when the Doctor even gets an indulgent smile from the guard he's about to thump; the crane-shot of the Doctor and K9 in the TARDIS realising that Gallifrey Expects… but for each of these there's a clunker like the model of the spaceship, and the infra-red shot of the vampire (which is so bad that the next shot, of the Doctor looking away from the monitor in horror, seems like a commentary).

And of course, there's the liability of Adric. Matthew Waterhouse can't even walk across the console room convincingly. Making so much of the plot hinge on him being "special" and worth rescuing is a major setback. Of course with hindsight, the brat's siding with the authority-figures is business as usual, but we were supposed to wonder who's side he was on. This involved caring, and this was never easy. Here, at least, the idea of the "Artful Dodger" is being addressed by someone who knows Dickens and makes him at least a clever thief with an oddly East End turn of phrase. But even here we're never allowed to forget that this is the production team's idea of who's supposed to be watching.

Critique (Defence) From the point of view of those whom the production team thought were supposed to be watching (ostensibly)…

Unsurprisingly given its pedigree, it works for exactly the same reason that "The Brain of Morbius" works: this is about family. *Frankenstein* was one of the great-grandparents of *Doctor Who*, so having the Doctor stroll into the middle of a modern-day re-wiring of the story felt almost like a return to the family estate. And the Hammer vampire movies, with their dependence on British character actors and their close ties to the traditions of British theatre (like so much of the BBC's output, many of them look as if they're staged as plays rather than full-blown movies), can safely be considered cousins to this series. Which means that as with "Morbius" there's a cosy, confident feel to all of this, a sense of a programme that knows exactly what the ground-rules are. After the awkwardness of "The Leisure Hive", the new production style has settled down, knowing just how it wants the programme to work and no longer feeling the desperate need to impress; "State of Decay" was the second story made in this season, but you'd never guess it.

The thing that most regularly gets a trouncing from less analytical-minded viewers is the appearance of the Big Vampire, this being a tale which sets up a great unearthly horror and then realises

it doesn't quite have the ability to render such a thing on-screen, a problem that'll raise its head again in 19.3, "Kinda". Yet anyone who grew up with the series should be used to that sort of thing by now. In every other respect this is a finely-practised balancing-act of SF and folklore, a tale which treats the ancientness of the vampires and the Time Lords as if they're all part of the same history, a tale which puts computer-banks into the middle of a Medieval hovel and makes them look as if they belong there. (The scene's actually improved with age, since in our collective imagination the green-screen technology on display immediately makes us think of something hopelessly antiquated.) E-Space wasn't an original feature of the script, but even *that* serves an aesthetic function, making this planet seem like a true backwater… effectively, an Eastern European village in the furthest corner of the universe.

But above all else, this is a demonstration of why *Doctor Who* needed to be shown in the winter. If you want to watch "State of Decay" properly, then it has to be getting dark outside. Not because it's scary - that isn't precisely the point - but because, whether Dicks consciously picked up on it or not, it's a story that understands the connection between *Doctor Who* and a vastly older style of storytelling. This is a "curfew" story. It's about a community surrounded by the dark, about the need to lock yourself indoors when the Bad Thing comes to take the children away. It *demands* that the viewers huddle together in a warm, TV-lit space. The early '80s was the last period when "family" television actually meant something, before politics and technology split the media up into demographic factions; the last period in which certain programmes were treated as if they were definitive parts of the national psyche (and the decline of *Doctor Who* in the years to come has at least as much to do with this loss of community as with the nature of the programme itself). This is, in effect, the last time the series makes us feel as if we're all living in the same village.

The Facts

Written by Terrance Dicks. Directed by Peter Moffatt. Viewing figures: 5.8 million, 5.3 million, 4.4 million, 5.4 million.

Supporting Cast Emrys James (Aukon), Rachel Davies (Camilla), William Lindsay (Zargo),

Clinton Greyn (Ivo), Rhoda Lewis (Marta), Thane Bettany (Tarak), Iain Rattray (Habris), Arthur Hewlett (Kalmar), Stacy Davies (Veros), Stuart Fell (Roga).

Working Titles "The Witch-Lords" (when submitted for Season Fifteen), "The Vampire Mutations", "The Wasting".

Cliffhangers In the forest, the Doctor and Romana are surrounded by some stock footage of a swarm of bats; Aukon welcomes the Doctor and Romana as they enter the Great Vampire's 'resting place' beneath the Tower; the vampire Lord and Lady corner Romana and Adric in their inner sanctum.

The Lore

• Baker believed that, as a Lord of Time, the Doctor should have blue blood. Look closely at his hand at the end of episode one, when the bats bite. Nathan-Turner was understandably appalled, but there was no time for a re-shoot so the scene was edited to remove close-ups.

• Lalla Ward had been concerned when "The Horns of Nimon" (17.5) had shown corpses collapsing into dust. In the studio it had seemed innocuous, but when it appeared on-screen several children had been terrified (this is, amazingly, a matter of record in BBC files). She therefore insisted that the similar scene in "State of Decay" should be dimly-lit. This actually proved a great deal scarier, but was seen - looking at the ratings - by precisely half as many viewers.

• *The Hydrax* had been called the *Hyperion*, but as Ian Levine had established himself as advisor this was changed in order to placate the three people who might have remembered the name from "The Mutants" (9.4, but see 23.3, "Terror of the Vervoids").

• It was also Levine who suggested that three stories might be linked together as a "trilogy", and the E-Space concept was formed by Bidmead early on in 1980. "The Wasting", "The Planet that Slept" and "Sealed Orders" were designed to write out Romana and K9, and Bidmead issued a memo in June about the precise nature of the CVE. In this he notes that the emboitement has no mass, so no gravitational field, and is thus not only rarer than a black hole but less easy to detect until you run into it. He also hints that each CVE may contain

others inside it, like a Russian Doll (see 18.7, "Logopolis" and 17.4, "Nightmare of Eden") or a Klein bottle (which is to three dimensions what a Mobius strip is to two). He states that E-Space has two galaxies within it, and invokes twenty-first century physicists to prove that it may be composed equally of matter and anti-matter.

• Bidmead and director Peter Moffatt clashed, as the first version of the script had seemed like a Hammer Horror movie. More like a Hammer Horror movie than the final version, anyway. This appealed to Moffatt but appalled Bidmead, who wanted more explicitly scientific ideas. The ancient scrolls became punched cards, references to CMOS chips and the vampires hatching from eggs were added (though not all of them stayed)... and Moffatt found the constant alterations tiresome. Many cuts were also made at the behest of Graeme McDonald, Head of Serials, on grounds of "scariness". He'd been responsible for "The Vampire Mutations" being pulled in the first place (see 15.1, "Horror of Fang Rock"). K9 hadn't been in the original, so the minimal use of the prop allowed the drive system and radio-control receiver a further upgrade after the quick botch-up of "The Leisure Hive".

• Although "State of Decay" was made before "Full Circle", that story's director - Peter Grimwade - was involved in the casting of Adric. Matthew Waterhouse, then working in the BBC as a clerk, was chosen by Grimwade, Nathan-Turner and Letts as the best to have auditioned. Bidmead had worked out the character in some detail, and *then* the role was cast, a process which the script editor now concedes was a mistake. Waterhouse was presented to Baker and Ward as a *fait accompli* (see the previous volume for some idea of how Baker would have reacted to this).

• Moffatt had first been approached by Graham Williams three years earlier, and again later on. He'd been keen to have a go at *Doctor Who*, and he had a reputation for getting complex shows done on time. This meant that he was very much in demand, and so was unavailable when Williams had contacted him.

• It was at about this point that a thaw set in with Baker and Ward's complicated relationship. Moffatt had worked with Ward before, and diplomatically arranged for the two stars not to be in close proximity too often. (Waterhouse has mentioned that his first day in rehearsal was marked by someone explaining 'the blue corner' and 'the red corner'.) Nevertheless, eventually Ward lost patience with Moffatt and left the studio - Baker was sent to calm her down, remarkably - and at one point Ward also had to intervene in a row between Waterhouse and costumiere Amy Roberts about taking off the elaborate "sacrifice" costume before going to lunch. Ward and Waterhouse, now off on a bad footing, became more hostile to one another as the season progressed.

Meanwhile Baker's illness was becoming more obvious; Moffatt's concern, plus his experience and helpful suggestions, won over an initially-hostile leading man. The director also lent support to the star's decision to discard parts of the new costume. Baker liked the look of the coat, but not wearing it in a studio in spring.

• The rod-puppet Giant Vampire was proposed to Moffatt early on, but only used when all other options had failed to pan out. You can tell, somehow.

• The use of bats as a threat was the subject of comment in a debate over wildlife in the House of Lords. This was the last time the government would cite the programme as scary.

• The "Agincourt" routine was Baker's idea, and his line about 'Bull's Blood' was an ad-lib; the Hungarian wine was being aggressively marketed in the UK in the winter of 1979. Several sight-gags he proposed were rejected. A scripted reference to Browning's poem "Childe Roland to the Dark Tower Came" was cut, but Dicks re-used the idea in "The Five Doctors" (20.7).

• Waterhouse mistimed the scene with the dummy knife, and ended up scraping a lump off his leg and having the prop fall on his foot.

• It was around this time that attempts to make Pennant Roberts' "Erinella" fit into the new regime's template for the programme fell through (see **What Else Wasn't Made?** under 17.6, "Shada"). Nathan-Turner liked Roberts personally, and was intrigued by what he later described as the '*Midwich Cuckoos* element' of a story about small creatures controlling the minds of humans, but Bidmead was less sure. For Roberts, the "elfin" mind-parasites were a pretext for retelling a story from the *Mabinogion* of Celtic mythology (as Loyd Alexander had done for *The Book of Three*, then being animated by Disney as *The Black Cauldron*). For Bidmead they were an end in themselves, and the dragons and suchlike were "silly". Once it became obvious that Roberts wouldn't budge, the story was dropped.

• As Nathan-Turner had gained an extra two episodes per season from BBC1 controller Bill Cotton, by the time "State of Decay" went into production it was obvious that seven four-part stories would be included in that year's production-run. One of Nathan-Turner's first decisions was to preserve the shot footage from "Shada" with a view to remounting it, and indeed, Douglas Adams found time to prepare a four-part rendering with Bidmead's help. However, Cotton declined to permit this to be part of Season Eighteen, and once Baker and Ward left it became impossible to complete the story.

18.5: "Warriors' Gate"

(Serial 5S, Four Episodes, 3rd January - 24th January 1981.)

Which One is This?   Another story where the TARDIS lands in the middle of nowhere, but this time there's a looking-glass that leads to a place where lion-faced people hold great feasts and goblets can be knocked over with aplomb.

Firsts and Lasts   It's the end of Romana's time on board the TARDIS, and her very last appearance in the series, if you don't count flashbacks, recycled footage or "Dimensions in Time" (see the appendix of Volume VI, sadly). Fittingly for a goodbye, the emphasis is on the companion here, and Romana does most of the "proper" work in the first couple of episodes while the Doctor wanders around being chased by robot suits of armour. A nation's teens breathe a sigh of relief as she takes K9 with her, never to darken the Doctor's door again. (Anyone you ask now swears that they never liked him, but beyond a certain point he *did* seem to be the part of the programme that your mum and your uncle liked, rather than the supposed "children's favourite".) As part of the great Season Eighteen re-fit, the TARDIS console gets a new central column here, although the rest of the console won't be upgraded for another two seasons.

This was the first story ever to have subtitles on Ceefax, the coded system of data-bursts sent as the top three lines of the TV signal. The graphics weren't up to much - as you can see on-screen in 18.4, "State of Decay" and 19.1, "Castrovalva" - but when test transmissions started in 1973, it was amazing. And in 1981, if you were hard of hearing, it was a godsend. The announcers used to mention this before the programme, accompanied by a little graphic of a Dalek zapping something or a computerised picture of the TARDIS, as well as telling us all to rush out and buy the 7" single of the revamped theme tune (it made the Top 150…) or visit the Madam Toussaud's *Doctor Who Experience* and meet Meglos.

Four Things to Notice About "Warriors' Gate"…

1. This is the one that almost nobody "got" at the time. A story that finally shrugs off the series' long-felt need for exposition and fiddly technical explanations, "Warriors' Gate" has a logic all its own, in which linear time becomes as changeable as the weather and characters move from scene to scene / time to time according to what's aesthetically *right* instead of what's rational. Those who'd grown up expecting *Doctor Who* to be about monsters and clever electronics were bemused. The fans were, on the whole, hostile. (Interestingly, the people who liked the story best were the younger viewers who weren't particularly used to the series, who just assumed there was some sort of science-magic at work and went with the flow.) But watching it again now, it's clear that the last twenty-odd years have prepared us for everything "Warriors' Gate" had to offer. In today's non-linear, channel-surfing world, the overlapping time-streams of the story seem so reasonable that you start to wonder what everybody found so puzzling.

2. It's also a very *dirty* story, and quite right too. We've already seen how the 1970s saw stiff-shirted space-marines being replaced by interplanetary pilots who occasionally complained about their jobs (10.4, "Frontier in Space"), and finally by people who got thoroughly sick of each other after being stuck on board mining vessels for too long (14.5, "The Robots of Death"). But by now *Alien* has happened, not only changing the way that "outer space" is directed but also the way that people behave there, and all the industrial unrest in the '70s can't have hurt either.

In "Warriors' Gate", the crew is thoroughly miserable; there's graffiti on the walls; those who work "below decks" don't mind jeopardising the slave cargo, as they're on a different contract to everyone else; people are reluctant to use large-scale hi-tech equipment, for the quite credible reason that they can't be bothered shifting it around; and, most gloriously of all, orders given over the ship's communications system have to be

repeated at least once before the man on duty presses the right buttons. On the downside, the comms link on the wall by the hatch looks exactly like a '70s telephone handset, which may be taking the "down-to-earth" thing a bit too far.

3. The world of the Tharils, which exists on the other side of a magic mirror and is supposed to suggest somewhere terribly old and not-quite-right, is depicted as a series of black-and-white photographs… in which the characters can walk around in full colour. This is typical of the special effects trickiness being employed by the BBC at the time. When CSO had come to the series in 1970, the programme-makers had used it to try to make unlikely things seem *real*, although it hadn't often worked. But by this stage, everybody in the audience is so used to the idea of things being video-superimposed over other things that the effects people have started getting experimental. "Educational" children's programmes of the day would often miniaturise their presenters and let them walk around inside old paintings or etchings, and often they were the only colour parts of a black-and-white world. And since the use of startling monochrome in "Warriors' Gate" is supposed to suggest a fallen empire, and since this story sees the ravages of time eating away at K9's circuits, it also suits the running "decay" theme of this season that's blatantly concluded in "Logopolis" (18.7).

4. How you can *really* tell that *Doctor Who* is going off in strange new directions: the I Ching is used as a storytelling device, with various plot-points depending on characters flipping coins or strategically doing nothing at all. Never has the sonic screwdriver seemed so redundant.

The Continuity

The Doctor Has no problem with the idea of taking Adric out of his own universe, or even to Gallifrey, even though Romana isn't sure they have the right. The Doctor's goodbye to Romana is brief, but he's confident that she'll be able to single-handedly sort out E-Space, and the sense is very much of someone who's seeing a protégé decide to go off on her own.

• *Inventory.* He's carrying small tools for working on robot brains. And a pair of patterned knitted gloves in case of time-winds.

Which are the "Auteur" Directors?

It soon became apparent, as *Doctor Who Monthly* got into its stride, that there were different directors for the different stories. Yes, of course it seems obvious *now*, but we'd never had a reason to think about it before. So we got used to being told who was good, and who was a "stylist". The stylists were the ones who made a difference to the kind of story it was.

There were, the *Monthly* averred, two of them: Douglas Camfield and David Maloney. Christopher Barry was flexible, and could do everything equally well - they assured us - but he wasn't someone whose presence made a story *happen* differently (as witnessed by Richard Martin taking over halfway through the first Dalek story without making much difference, except for more studio noise and possibly a more sluggish climax than anyone else would have managed). We had directors who did certain things regularly - Pennant Roberts always recast at least one character as a woman, Michael Hayes included an ex-girlfriend's photo wherever he could, Peter Grimwade had pert male buttocks in shot as often as possible[3] - but the Stylists' Club had only two members, and its roster was written in stone.

Adapting these criteria, here we suggest a list of five honest-to-goodness *auteur* directors in *Doctor Who*. These are the men (they're all male, oddly) whose approach includes a recognisable style, a readiness to adapt the script to his own ends, a reputation sufficient that producers and script-editors will angle stories specifically for him and a willingness to see working on *Doctor Who* as a challenge rather than a day-job. Moreover, we've taken into account how little they antagonised the crews; indeed, in some cases there were people volunteering to do a show because they heard a particular director was on board. And naturally, a director needs to have made more than one story to qualify for the list. So Lovett Bickford ("The Leisure Hive") and Paul Joyce ("Warriors' Gate"), despite having their admirers, don't make the cut.

Douglas Camfield. His track-record is formidable by any standards. In terms of episodes directed he's right at the top. The latter two(ish) episodes of "Planet of Giants" (2.1), "The Crusade" (2.6), "The Time Meddler" (2.9), then the big one: all twelve-plus-one episodes of "The Daleks' Masterplan" (3.4). That's 23 episodes of Hartnell alone. Add to this "The Web of Fear" (5.5) and another marathon, "The Invasion" (6.3), and in monochrome we're at 37 episodes and six stories

(all right, five-and-a-half).

He also has a claim on the grounds that he was the floor-manager who opened the doors of 76 Totters Lane right at the start of things (1.1, "An Unearthly Child"). In fact he seems to have directed the filmed fight scene in that story, and some of the chases. Going into colour, we have the disputed claim that he wasn't solely in charge of "Inferno" (7.4) and a gap of several years before his final push, "Terror of the Zygons" (13.1) and "The Seeds of Doom" (13.6). As we've seen, his face appears in the series twice, as the *faux*-Jamie in "The Mind Robber" (6.2) and the alleged "early" Doctor in the mind-duel with Morbius (see **Who Are All These Strange Men in Wigs?** under 13.5, "The Brain of Morbius").

That isn't the half of it. For "The Invasion" and "The Daleks' Masterplan" he was de facto producer. That's about as long as Derrick Sherwin's stint. Some accounts claim he was as good as in charge during "The Web of Fear" as well. He certainly added scenes and dialogue to it. Even if he wasn't recognisably more ambitious in his visual approach than the majority of directors in the black-and-white days, this would be enough. But with his pseudo-military style of directing, addressing the crew as "Lieutenant", "Sergeant" and so on, he got the job done. He offered cash to anyone, no matter who, with a possible solution to a technical problem.

So if he's an *auteur*, what features should we be spotting? There's a repertory company, with a handful of actors who keep coming back for his stories (his wife Sheila Dunn, obviously, but also Iain Fairburn, Derek Waring, Nicholas Courtney, Jean Marsh, Tony Beckley…). There's the military detailing. Even in space, we have the appearances and ranking of the British Army. UNIT is, in effect, his creation. There's the stock-footage, reckless on occasion, but flamboyantly used (unless you're watching "The Invasion" in one go, which takes us into Ed Wood territory). There's a cinematic flair even in the BBC studios; on location, on film, he makes something wonderful from the least promising materials. When the second episode of "The Daleks' Masterplan" unexpectedly turned up in 2004, those who'd heard the limp dialogue of the audio recording were amazed to see how coherent it all seems on-screen. He occasionally borrows ideas from other directors, such as Akira Kurosawa's convention that the person nearest

continued on page 61…

The Supporting Cast

• *Romana*. Claims to be fully qualified at fixing K9. When Captain Rorvik tries to get her to navigate his ship - see **History** - she's not 'time-sensitive' enough to pull it off, but isn't killed by the process either. Her decision to stay in E-Space and help the Tharils is a rushed one, and she clearly only makes it because she doesn't want to go back to Gallifrey. She may get on with Biroc quite well, but it's not as if they're going to run off and get married. Biroc believes that the Tharils 'need' a Time Lord; Romana states that they can help her and K9 use the Gateway to go anywhere in E-Space, while she can give them time-technology. [Possibly against the laws of the Time Lords, unless those laws don't count in E-Space. See the Doctor's comments in 18.7, "Logopolis".] She doesn't seem too bothered by the Tharils' slave-owning past, either, and wants to help free them now *they're* in chains.

• *Adric*. Happy-go-lucky enough to press random buttons on the TARDIS console when it's in flight.

• *K9*. Knows the I Ching [specifically in the 1910 Richard Wilhelm translation, if that's important], and again claims that he doesn't feel anything. He detects mass by triangulation, so when he's damaged his readings get more accurate when one of his "ears" is removed and taken further away. He calls Adric 'young master', and he's light enough for a member of Captain Rorvik's crew to hurl him. His memory contains all the necessary schedules for duplication of the TARDIS.

After the time-winds damage K9's circuitry, the Doctor believes there's no way for the metal dog to leave E-Space; see **Planet Notes**. When K9 is given to Romana, the Doctor doesn't even bother to say goodbye, which doesn't suggest that K9 is the Doctor's 'best friend' as he's previously claimed. [Is the Doctor getting sick of the dog? He never produces a K9 Mk. III, at least not for himself. Then again, this Doctor's going to be quite busy for the rest of his short "life".]

In the aftermath of the time-wind damage, at least one of K9's memory wafers crumbles to dust, and his systems are worse than useless until the Tharils' mirrors fix him. Improbably, Gundan memory wafers are compatible with his systems, while his power can be diverted to other robot brains if cables are attached to his eye-stalk [and not his ears, as in 17.4, "Nightmare of Eden"].

The TARDIS The Ship doesn't respond to co-ordinates when it hits a time-rift, and there's turbulence in the console room. Tinkering with the controls doesn't help much, and it begins drifting through E-Space, though the Doctor speculates that this may be the best way out. Taking the I Ching route, he thinks of pressing a random button and goes for the reverse bias, though Romana believes that activating the reverse bias in full flight is suicidal and stops him doing it. It's eventually a random button-press from Adric that halts the TARDIS and makes some of the controls pop. Then the doors open, and time-winds get into the Ship. Though the winds can cause "ageing" in the things they touch, they don't devastate the entire console room, but both K9 and the Doctor's hand are badly-hit.

Romana speaks of the TARDIS as travelling between the timelines, just like Rorvik's vessel, and describes the Gateway area as being a theoretical medium between the striations of the continuum. She claims that when it comes to navigation, the TARDIS knows where its going as it uses a digitally-modelled time-cone isometry parallel-bussed into the image translator, with local motion being mapped over every refresh-cycle [essentially more evidence that the TARDIS "sees" where it's going; q.v. 18.3, "Full Circle"].

The TARDIS' co-ordinates can be checked by twisting a silver handle on the console. Romana states that half the shelves in the Ship's stores are empty, but she brings out some dust-covered cardboard boxes full of odds and ends useful in the repair of K9.

The Non-Humans

• *Tharils*. Elegant, physically powerful humanoids with leonine features and a fair amount of fur on their hands, the Tharils once ruled a wealthy, opulent empire. [Apparently in E-Space, though this is foggy. One of the Gundan robots states that the Gateway is the place from which the Tharils came, which seems to mean that the Tharils originated in N-Space. It's also stated that the Gundans' attack drove the Tharils through the Gateway, and the Gateway leads to E-Space, again indicating that the Tharils started out in N-Space but were driven into slavery outside the normal continuum.]

The Tharils built the fortress at the Gateway; see **Planet Notes**. Though not ruthlessly evil, they enslaved humans from E-Space, treating the uni-

Which are the "Auteur" Directors?

...continued from page 59

the camera knows most, and the end of episode six of "The Invasion" is as flagrant a film-quote as you could hope for. (Oh, all right. For those of you who only watch Jackie Chan, it's the Odessa Steps scene from **Battleship Potemkin** by Eisenstein, as recycled in Brazil and *The Untouchables*.)

The Bottom Line: how many other TV directors got phone calls from Stanley Kubrick asking for advice?

David Maloney. Another film buff. In the three stories he directed in Season Six, he innovated in areas such as the use of animation, the non-use of music and most noticeably his approach to set-design. He created worlds out of the symbols in the stories. In "The Mind Robber" (6.2) this is vouchsafed by the nature of the plot, so he can use enormous books, blank spaces and giant cardboard cut-outs with a brazen-ness not even *The Avengers* would have risked. But then in "The Krotons" (6.4) he does it again, with big crystal monsters (alas, not as practical as the designers said) and a spaceship which is another "void" space. And more trippy cameras. By the time we reach "The War Games" (6.7) the verisimilitude of the separate time-zones is present and correct, but the central control - with another new designer assigned to him - features giant sergeant stripes and op-art brainwashing rooms. Maloney gets away with it, just, by focussing on the actors.

Here we must note that as the production office was in meltdown, Maloney was given the task of supervising the scripts and finding the extra episodes, and asked his son which wars would be fun to see. When faced with plot-holes, he had the Doctor's pockets contain everyday objects with which to improvise an escape or a trap - a strand he continued up to "The Talons of Weng Chiang" (14.6) - and filled out at least one episode with a memorable scene based on this. Here also his interest in gas-masks becomes apparent. By "The

Deadly Assassin" (14.3), the designers are having fun and showing him designs for World War One horse-masks. By this stage the Holmes and Hinchcliffe team have started giving him projects that allow him free reign with his abilities, and including suggestions as to which of his favourite films he might wish to reference (see 12.4, "Genesis of the Daleks"). This extends to set-design in-jokes, such as basing Greel's lair in "Weng-Chiang" on the sewer from Fritz Lang's *Dr Mabuse, der Spieler*.

His first task on *Doctor Who* was the thankless one of helping to make an army of toy Daleks enact the destruction of Skaro after a civil war (4.9, "Evil of the Daleks"). Lumbered with "Planet of Evil" (13.2) he manages to make even the Morestran spaceship set look vaguely interesting, to begin with at least. You might argue that with the budget allowed him, his two Season Fourteen stories could have been made well by anyone, but to get "Planet of Evil" even half-watchable was his real achievement.

The Bottom Line: they gave him *Blake's 7* so he could fill the screen with men in gas-masks.

Derek Martinus. The trouble is, a lot of his stuff has gone missing. He only made one colour story. Mind you, it was the *first* colour story, and the only one entirely on film (7.1, "Spearhead from Space"). In the '80s this added to his cachet as a director, in that those who remembered his work spoke fondly and nobody could gainsay them. Since then, a lot more of the black-and-white material has become available. We have a whole episode of "Evil of the Daleks" to look at, and it's very neatly done. Six minutes of "Galaxy Four" (3.1) is back with us, and while it creaks a bit - being an exposition scene - it has its charm.

The four surviving parts of "The Ice Warriors" proved the turning-point, though. This looks like nothing else. We all knew about Peter Barkworth

continued on page 63...

verse as their garden and claiming that the weak enslave themselves. The tableaux of the Tharil empire seen here has them celebrating in a great banqueting hall, abusing their human servants. Biroc, a Tharil who seems quite civilised and as prone to dress in the "romantic" style as all the others, eventually acknowledges that his people abused their power. Now the Tharils themselves are being enslaved by humans, on 'many worlds'

in E-Space according to Biroc. [This may indicate that Captain Rorvik's slaver ship comes from E-Space, despite its seemingly Earthly origins. See **History** for more.]

Tharils are valuable because they're time-sensitives. They can 'ride the time winds', and are therefore ideal for navigating ships like Rorvik's through hyperspace. At one point Biroc sees the TARDIS while he's navigating [suggesting this process is in some way connected to the space-time vortex], and later enters the Ship, something he can do because he's 'out of phase' and on a different timeline. This means he seems to judder like a bad video effect, even though this would tear most life-forms apart. In this state he can touch the TARDIS controls, and he knows what he's doing as he manipulates the console. A Tharil can apparently walk through walls by crossing the timelines, taking someone else with him. [Biroc's description of himself as 'a shadow of my past, and of your future' when talking to Romana might hint that he already knows her destiny, which is in keeping with what we see of his kind. Their lives don't seem entirely linear. Writer Steve Gallagher's original conception was that the Tharils could see various potential futures and "choose" the one they wanted, but this is muddled in the finished version.] Though the slavers keep their Tharils unconscious, a Tharil can wake up one of his brethren with a touch, and it appears that some form of energy passes between them.

• *Gundan.* Basically robotic suits of armour with axes, created by the Tharils' human slaves as only the robots could survive the time-winds. The slaves discovered the secret of the Tharils' Gateway, and the Gundan walk through the mirrors in the castle without difficulty. Though one of the Gundan is happy to tell its story when the Doctor shoves a screwdriver in its brain, the robots barely seem sentient and never show any desire to communicate. Those at the Gateway simply attempt to kill anyone who enters. They take a while to re-activate when the Doctor arrives, don't seem very certain on their feet and don't have very acute senses. [Degeneration... they wouldn't have been much good against the Tharils if they'd always been this slow.]

Planet Notes

• *The Gateway.* The intersection between N-Space and E-Space is an area which appears to be an absolute white void, but which nonetheless has a floor to walk on and an atmosphere to breathe [this place has been artificially constructed]. It's a micro-universe, with zero co-ordinates as N-Space is positive and E-Space is negative. But it may only be accessible from E-Space, at least unless you're a Tharil.

In this void stands a great arch, set into a crumbling edifice of brick, and within are the halls of a grand, cobweb-covered castle much larger than the facade. The Tharils banqueted here, once, and their skeletons still sit at the table. Also within this structure is a large mirrored wall, which appears perfectly normal to all analysis but which can - according to the whim of a Tharil - act as a portal to... well, elsewhere. One of the Gundan suggests that this realm, the arch and the mirrors are three gateways, but that all three are one.

The Doctor steps through the mirror and finds himself crossing the striations in the timelines, witnessing the Tharil empire at its peak, yet the visit seems curiously dream-like and he later refers to it as a 'reflection'. Though he can interact with the people and objects he sees, Biroc - apparently a "present-day" Tharil - is there to "narrate" the experience, and in the blink of an eye the Doctor can find himself back on the other side of the mirror.

In the past, the Doctor sees the Gundan robots attack the castle in mid-feast, and several dusty Gundans are still there in the present. Things damaged by the time-winds instantly heal if they go through the mirror into E-Space, but non-living matter returns to its damaged state if it goes back [surely a deliberate feature designed by the Tharils, not a side-effect of time-wind physics?]. The mirrors are seemingly indestructible.

The E-Space world of the Tharils, where Romana will be spending so much of her time from now on, is a grandiose place full of stone carvings, stately buildings and elaborate topiaries... but all in mysterious black and white [at least to *our* eyes]. The Doctor states that only the Tharils can get into Captain Rorvik's universe through the mirrors, but doesn't elaborate as to which universe that is. [The implication is that Rorvik's crew are from N-Space and use E-Space as the Europeans used Africa, and the novelisation reinforces this impression, though the dialogue seems contradictory; see **The Lore** for some possible reasons. If Rorvik *does* come from N-Space, then how does his ship normally "commute" to E-Space, when he's obviously never seen the Gateway before?] For anyone else, the Gateway is a cul-de-sac, just a reflection of what's in the real banqueting hall. [Biroc takes Romana through the looking-glass into E-Space, which would again suggest that E-Space is "his" universe.]

The great mass of Rorvik's ship causes a 'mass conversion anomaly' in the micro-universe of the Gateway, making space and time contract; not the objects inside the space, just the distances and

Which are the "Auteur" Directors?

...continued from page 61

(as base leader Clent) in a psychedelic body-stocking from the photos, but the perspex walking stick and the limp were a total surprise. The scene with the bear, missing from the novelisation, is tense even though it's not that exciting. What we dreaded was a whole episode of Debbie Watling fluttering about in polystyrene glaciers; this turns out to be a highlight. Every other Ice Warrior story uses them as Baddies, or supposed Baddies; Martinus turns Varga and Isbur into characters. He cast an actor, not just a tall man who could hiss (this isn't to disparage Alan Bennion, but Bennion was good *despite* his directors). Of course, the horror stories from the set are another thing. Martinus even cheesed off the actors doing Dalek voices. If it turns out that "Evil of the Daleks" still exists somewhere, and that more of "Galaxy Four" is stuffed down the back of someone's sofa, and that the end of "The Tenth Planet" isn't as big a let-down as it sounds, then we'll have to re-evaluate.

The Bottom Line: case not proven.

Alan Wareing. All the things people used to say about "Kinda" (19.3) are true of "Survival" (26.4). This is the first radical feminist critique of *Doctor Who* to be broadcast within the series itself - no, really it is - and the first to explicitly change a companion's entire personality without switching it back at the end. Overtly symbolic and yet presented to us as all equally "real" - even down to Ace's dream-like running with the Hunt - this is both theatrical and Realistic (see **Is "Realism" Enough?** under 19.3, "Kinda").

If this were a one-off then it'd be interesting, but the other two stories he directed can be seen the same way. The difference is that "Survival" did all of this on location, including Perivale High Street. "Ghost Light" had scored some occasional moments of internal states being externalised - the police lights as Ace recalls her career as an arsonist being a prime example, and the only one not necessarily scripted that way - but everything had a dozen levels of significance. The main priority was getting it in the can.

The same can be said of "The Greatest Show in the Galaxy" (25.4), but this is the story where an apparent setback turned into the key to the production's success. Being filmed "for real" in a circus tent, with the cave sets and arena filmed as locations, it was all equally "unreal". Hence when the downright trippy symbolic stuff with kites, eyes and clowns in hearses came along, we were already in a mental space where these things could be presented to us without disruption. If we look at the other symbolism-laden story that year, "The Happiness Patrol", then the difference is obvious. Could Wareing have made a studio-based story with this script work better than Chris Clough did? "Ghost Light" seems to indicate that he could.

The Bottom Line: what the hell is he doing on *Emmerdale*?

Graeme Harper. The view in many parts of fandom is that he was "Camfield-on-a-stick". The use of "real" projectile weapons instead of neat rayguns showed the touch. The fact that he's popularly credited as the real director of "Warriors' Gate" is unsurprising, especially when the crewman Sagan's electrocution is compared to the androids exploding or Davros' apparent assassination (21.6, "The Caves of Androzani" and 22.6, "Revelation of the Daleks").

Nevertheless, he was more than the sum of his parts. Harper's main trade-mark, the almost-accidental use of asides to camera, is a step that Camfield would never have taken even with Kevin Stoney as the villain. The use of digital jiggery-pokery technique Quantel as a narrative ploy, rather than as a way of making "realistic" special effects, is also more daring than anything we've seen before (again, the only parallel is the coin in "Warriors' Gate", but "The Leisure Hive" comes close with the pull back from Brighton to space). What made Harper stand out most at the time - and remember what BBC drama looked like in 1984 - was the foregrounding of the camera almost as a character. This not only allowed pacy scenes of action but, and this was the real Camfield inheritance, occasional slow, lingering, dissolves. We invite you to compare the shots of Sharaz Jek lusting over Peri's image and preparing an android in "Androzani" with the Zygons fondling their controls before we get to see what they really look like in "Terror of the Zygons" (13.1).

The Bottom Line: he's doing *Heartbeat* while Guy Ritchie makes a fortune as a Camfield wannabe? There really is no justice.

periods between them. The realm gets smaller and smaller until Rorvik eventually tries to break the mirrors with a back-blast from his ship's warp motors, which bounces back and blows him up. The TARDIS is able to get back to N-Space when it dematerialises at the same moment that Rorvik's ship explodes. The enslaved Tharils survive the explosion, since they're out of phase, and head for freedom at the Gateway.

History

• *Dating*. The future, surely. [Earth isn't mentioned, but the names and natures of Rorvik's crew suggest Earth ancestry. Biroc's assertion that he and Romana are going to free the other Tharil slaves in E-Space suggests that humans from N-Space are occupying E-Space by now, so Rorvik's people may even be descendants of the Tharils' slaves, brought to E-Space from N-Space in the good old days of the Tharil Empire. For all we know, they're the Terradonians mentioned in "Full Circle" (18.3). Rorvik's ship uses a method of hyperspace navigation that isn't seen at any other point in human history, unsurprising as mainstream humanity doesn't seem to have met the Tharils. The sound of the respirators suggests they were designed in the thirtieth century; c.f. 23.3, "Terror of the Vervoids". Since the programme is so obsessed with continuity in this era, this kind of minor detail may actually mean something.]

Captain Rorvik's bulk freighter is a chunky, unsubtle-looking number with a hull made of dwarf star alloy, the only thing that can hold the Tharils. He describes his crew as 'traders' rather than slavers. Dwarf star alloy is an absurdly dense material, and thus has a greater gravitational impact on the area of the Gateway than any metal should. This makes the ship vastly heavier than the TARDIS, and means that it needs huge warp motors. Though technically advanced, the ship is also in a bad state of repair and manned by an indifferent crew. For the ship to go anywhere, one of the time-sensitive Tharils has to have its head wired up to a control system on the bridge, the Tharil 'navigating' a path through hyperspace. 'Time-pictures' can be seen on a simple screen during this process.

The ship then jumps the timelines with a supra-light warp drive, 'with dampers'. Rorvik's ship apparently loses its warp drive and "crashes" near the Gateway because Biroc deliberately steers it there, although it hits a time-rift first. Tharils are kept in some kind of unconscious state, and the ship doesn't have reliable apparatus for reviving them, but a device can be jury-rigged even though there's a good chance of it killing its subjects. Most of the crew get a commission on each Tharil they bring back alive, but some of the lesser crewmembers have an all-in contract.

Also kept on the ship are a portable mass detector, a bulky piece of hardware that sits on the chest like an accordion; and an MZ, a large, artillery-like device on a wheeled chassis with a business end shaped like a radar dish. The men carry the usual dull energy weapons. Rorvik speaks of 'space-ways', suggesting pre-determined routes [through hyperspace?], while one member of the crew hints that it's bad luck to have a girl on board the ship [an old naval tradition].

The Analysis

Where Does This Come From? For anyone who remembers the '80s even vaguely, one glance at "Warriors' Gate" is enough to fix the style: it looks like a pop video. Specifically, it looks New Romantic. The banqueting hall, full of candles, cobwebs and robot suits of armour, gives you the feeling that it's just waiting for Adam Ant to turn up and dance on the tables. The "time-winds" special effect is so familiar that you can imagine it accompanying anything on *Top of the Pops* in that period. The lion-faced Tharils pre-empt Madonna's "Like a Virgin" by some years. And much of the story takes place in a void, a favourite "venue" for pop music in the days when directors realised they could make rock stars look far more interesting by putting them in the middle of nowhere and making the sky turn day-glo.

And yet "Warriors' Gate" was made in 1980. If it'd been made in 1982 then it would have looked like an obvious attempt to be hip, but at this stage the worst excesses of video mainly involved large, fuzzy patches of colour rather than grandiose historical romances. It'd be nice to imagine that someone in the music business watched this story and got ideas, but it's far more likely that *Doctor Who* was just being more fashion-conscious than it had been since the days of Jo Grant. Even before the New Romantic movement re-discovered the joys of period costume (and just as the BBC was forgetting them…), it was fairly obvious that the hip kids were going to turn into a bunch of mincing fops before long. Punk rock - a trend which sadly never had a direct impact on *Doctor Who*, apart from the Doctor's comment about people wearing safety-pins in "Four to Doomsday" (19.2) - was about kinky fashion sense as much as anything, and however much its proponents might have wanted to look like snarling urban rebels, they were drama queens at heart.

You could see where the culture was going, and many of the design flourishes in "Warriors' Gate" can be seen as extensions of the drama-bound pop culture of the '70s. It may look proto-goth to us now, but the Tharil castle is really just the sort of thing you'd get if you gave Alice Cooper enough money for a big stage set and made him promise not to use decapitation effects. In fact there are moments when the whole set-up looks as if it could have been designed for *The Muppet Show*, a place for rock stars to perform in front of puppet scary monsters. (As in 13.3, "Pyramids of Mars", there's also more than a dash of Cocteau's *La Belle et le Bete* - 1946, better known in the US as *Beauty and the Beast* – here. Admittedly the film was so influential in artistic circles that you can find bits and pieces of it wherever you look, but the Tharil "look" is blatant theft. See **The Lore** for more on Cocteau-plundering.)

Then there's the supporting cast, the below-stairs crew on Rorvik's ship. The shift of focus from "big" characters to "spearholders" had become a trend in the debunking of clichéd situations. One famous example is Tom Stoppard's *Rosencrantz and Guildenstern are Dead*, the story of *Hamlet* from the point of view of two existentialist minor characters, who spend a lot of time tossing coins. We'll come back to this a few times in this volume (in particular **Did Kate Bush Really Write This?** under 20.2, "Snakedance", which also has a lot more on pop-video style circa 1982-83.) The point here is that Rorvik's crew can't see how big a story they're in, nor that it isn't about them.

Oh yes... and "Warriors' Gate" has a plot, as well. As we've seen, this was a replacement for a Christopher Priest's script "Sealed Orders" (see **What Else Wasn't Made?** under 17.6, "Shada"). Steve Gallagher was part of a mood - it wasn't really a "movement", as such - which included the younger SF writers in Britain. Literary, sardonic and down-to-earth, when they dealt with Big Ideas they did so in a characteristic style, looking at the way people would cheapen and exploit the marvellous and the way these things connected to deeper, ancient threads in our culture. Robert

Holdstock's then-recent novel *Where Time Winds Blow* has no actual connection to the 'time winds' of this story, but the approach he takes to archetypal objects materialising out of the collective unconscious is exactly Gallagher's: dismay at how commercialism taints the process. This generation, which also included Ian Watson, David Langford and old pros M. John Harrison, Brian Aldiss and Bob Shaw, had been sceptical of NASA and *2001* and therefore weren't going to take kindly to the gosh-wow sci-fi escapism being peddled in the cinemas. Gallagher's knowledge of commercial radio and television gave him a grandstand view of how something potentially amazing is turned into "product" by people doing it to pay bills (see 20.4, "Terminus", for more on this).

The slavery of the Tharils is historically suggestive, but this isn't a piece about the slave trade, imperialism or man's inhumanity to man. Slavery is just the kind of big, dramatic concept that SF likes to play with all the time. So many other ideas are touched on here that to name all possible sources would read like a bibliography, although *Alien* has already been mentioned and it's worth pointing out that this script's clearly being written by someone with a post-'60s view of the literature. Writing for the series in the '70s, Robert Holmes drew on the '50s "topical satire" school of SF. Writing in the '80s, Gallagher draws on the "doubt and uncertainty" school. This is a universe of alternate states of mind, exotic parallel thought-systems, shifting certainties and crippling neuroses, where time's unreliable and the I Ching is as useful as a spaceship... well, you get the idea. No wonder it seems "trippier" than any other *Doctor Who* since 1969.

The Doctor mentions the Cheshire Cat, and we ought to mention the cut scene in which he quotes the White Queen ('it's a poor sort of memory that only works backwards'). And it's worth remembering the whole *Tao of Physics* school of pot-boiler pop-science - see **What Do the Guardians Do?** under 16.1, "The Ribos Operation" - as well as the other famous cat that's known for choosing between reality-states, in Erwin Schrödinger's *reductio ad absurdum*. Tossing a coin, the I Ching and cats, all in one volume.

Things That Don't Make Sense One of the Gundan axes bounces off the Doctor's back in episode two, and he doesn't even flinch. Romana's "life-or-death struggle" in episode four, limply slapping Rorvik with a clipboard in an attempt to stop him strangling the Doctor, is perhaps the least convincing fight-scene since the Cyber-Leader tried to back-rub the Doctor to death in "Revenge of the Cybermen" (12.5). Biroc goes from being an unapologetic slaver in episode three to being a repentant noble in episode four, convenient as Romana has to run off with him. [Another effect of the Tharils' non-linear lifestyle; Biroc only approves of slavery when he's in the "past" of the Tharil empire, before the Tharils learned their lesson.]

Romana can lift up dwarf star alloy, which is presumably supposed to be neutronium, the "teaspoon weighs a ton" stuff. Adric hefts it about like polystyrene.

Critique   More than any story, this is the one where the Doctor's activities are pointless. The TARDIS forms a life-raft (or simply a landmark in time and space?) for Biroc in episode one, and ultimately Romana and K9 are on hand to help with the real "adventure" just beginning. Everything between these two non-events involves the Doctor working out the story, or being told it, or seeing it happen.

Predestination is antithetical to the whole *Doctor Who* ethos, we always thought, but here it seems entirely appropriate. The programme is about making a difference, resisting the inevitable, or what "they" tell you is inevitable. Even when we know the ultimate historical outcome, there are small victories to be won. But the series is also about having hope, despite all evidence to the contrary. Combining these gives us the pro-active, self-reliant, empirically practical Doctor we'd watched for almost two decades. In a universe that isn't his, he tries his usual tactics and finds that he hasn't made any impression on history at all. In fact, even his being there is apparently down to blind chance. And Adric.

We talk a lot about symbolism in this volume, especially in the early sections. It's obvious what the symbols in the original script are hinting at: faded glory, the mundane imprisoning the imaginative, spiritual emptiness and so on. What's more of a puzzle, as **The Lore** explains, is what the overlay of imagery brought by the director would have amounted to. As soon as we have a clear idea of what kind of story this is, it actively challenges us to rethink it. All the "clever" stuff with the coins, especially the slow-motion close up right at

the start, is telling us "watch out for symbols"… but when we do there are fewer and fewer of them, and they don't seem to represent anything. They're just sitting there saying "I am a symbol". Had the network of images been made as planned, by now we'd just have a straightforward "puzzle" to be "solved" (like the character names in 19.3, "Kinda", and the snake from *My First Freudian Clichés Book*).

Instead we have something more tantalising. As viewers, many people found they preferred this. The ruined feast, with the Doctor righting the cup that we later see him knock down after it runneth over, is a case in point. It could mean a lot of things, but director Paul Joyce, Steve Gallagher and any given viewer would have an explanation apiece. A quarter-century later, this story is better-remembered by the general public than the more obviously "iconic" season finale, "Logopolis". Indeed, it made more "new" fans than any other story of its era. People found it baffling, but in the same way that they found *Top of the Pops* or the increasingly surreal ads on commercial television baffling (this was the early '80s, remember, the golden age of fast-and-loose imagery).

Even relative newcomers to the series ended up being drawn into its chain of thought, and it couldn't have hurt that at the time it seemed like such a hip, video-literate form of SF, a world away from what anybody might have expected from a BBC "standard" struggling towards the end of its second decade. Where it's *unnecessarily* puzzling, it's mainly because constant rewrites have obscured the details. The Gateway's logic is confused; so is the distinction between E-Space and N-Space; so are the relationships between different factions in different universes.

No matter. This is a story of associations. As with most of the best episodes of this era, events are linked by themes instead of plot devices, so synchronicity's on a par with the laws of cause and effect. You're being asked to participate in the story's own aesthetic, to ride the 'time-winds' along with the Tharils, to be led by your impressions rather than trying to work out the mechanisms. In the end, that's both the strength and the weakness of "Warriors' Gate". It takes you from A to B, but to get the most out of the journey you have to make inferences of your own. If you find that the result makes sense, well, then your inferences are probably in synch with the author's (or rather, the *authors'*). For everyone else - and it's curious how often this happens, in *Doctor Who* - the structure of the story resembles the environment in which it's set. There are things hanging in the void, and all of them are worth seeing, in themselves. Often they may *only* seem to exist in themselves, but at least they're never boring.

The Facts

Written by Steve Gallagher. Directed by Paul Joyce. Viewing figures: 7.1 million, 6.7 million, 8.3 million, 7.8 million. The new, post-Christmas slot for the programme was even earlier than before, usually 5.10 pm.

Supporting Cast Clifford Rose (Rorvik), Kenneth Cope (Packard), David Kincaid (Lane), Freddie Earlle (Aldo), Harry Waters (Royce), David Weston (Biroc), Vincent Pickering (Sagan), Robert Vowles (Gundan), Jeremy Gittins (Lazlo).

Oh, Isn't That..?

• *Kenneth Cope.* "The dead one" in *Randall and Hopkirk (Deceased)* - American readers may have seen it broadcast under the rather more obvious title *My Partner the Ghost* - he'd also been in *Coronation Street* and *The Avengers* (and a Carry On or two).

• *Clifford Rose.* The Lead Nazi in French Resistance drama *Secret Army* (see 12.4, "Genesis of the Daleks") and the star of the spin-off, *Kessler*, in which Weisenthal-style investigators hunt him down after he reinvents himself as a wealthy industrialist and humanitarian. This was being broadcast as "Warriors' Gate" was filmed.

Working Titles "The Dream-Time" (punctuation varies).

Cliffhangers While the Doctor's back is turned in the castle, a Gundan robot raises its axe over his head; Romana remains strapped into the navigator's chair of Rorvik's ship as a revived, heavy-breathing Tharil makes his way towards her (Romana's last great chance to scream before she leaves the series); the Doctor and Romana cross the timelines from the "past" of the Tharil empire, only for the Doctor to end up back in the present-day banqueting hall and surrounded by Rorvik's men.

The Lore

• Steve Gallagher's previous work included a radio series, *The Last Rose of Summer*, which was adapted into two different books (one first person, one third person). He'd worked at Manchester's Granada Television, which is where the privateer crew's personalities and attitudes originally came from (with the author as the dreaming, chained lion). Bidmead was also impressed by Gallagher's Radio 4 play *An Alternative to Suicide*.

• Gallagher's script was commissioned as a fall-back if "Sealed Orders" didn't pan out (once again see **What Else Wasn't Made?** under 17.6, "Shada"). He acceded to the changes that were made, knowing that as a novice in television drama, the professionals knew what needed fixing better than he did. Barry Letts added the dialogue on how the I Ching was to be used. (The original breakdown had the five previous random landings of the TARDIS plotted as a hexagram, to determine whether the next one would be "unbroken". Some of this had been used by Gallagher before, in a proposed SF play for radio, but adding the TARDIS and connecting it to events in "Sealed Orders" made it function more fluidly as a plot.)

• Bidmead and director Paul Joyce found the practicalities of filming what Gallagher wrote to be daunting, so various rewrites were requested. Eventually the director and script-editor pieced together their own script using Bidmead's new toy, a computer called the Vectorgraphic MZ (System B). Joyce had various advanced ideas as to how the story should be realised, but time and logistics were against him. Because of the troubles involved in bringing "Warriors' Gate" to the screen, all sorts of rumours have abounded, beginning with the false premise that Joyce quit during shooting. In these versions the stand-in director is production assistant and future "star" director Graeme Harper, or even John Nathan-Turner. Harper admits that various unforeseen snags needed rethinks on the studio floor, but credits the most experienced person on set - Tom Baker - with thinking up ingenious and practical solutions to many of them.

• A big problem came when Joyce proposed using the studio construction as part of the set for the privateer ship (see 19.6, "Earthshock"). The head of lighting, John Dixon - with whom Joyce had been arguing throughout - now stopped the filming when one of the lights appeared in shot. But Dixon's main worry was the safety of the scaffolding for the "upper" section of the ship, and he dragged the production further behind schedule by checking it for over half an hour. Nathan-Turner pondered sacking Joyce, but as Joyce had a better idea of the script than anyone and the cast were behind him, the production limped on.

• Paul Joyce's plan for the story involved references to many classic films, and to this end he arranged showings of the following:

L'Annee Derniere a Marienbad (Alain Resnais, 1961), AKA *Last Year at Marienbad*. A time-slip (or is it "false memory syndrome", or two mutually-exclusive pasts?) in a chateau resort, in stark monochrome and with small, repetitive details becoming increasingly intense.

Orphée (Jean Cocteau, 1949), in which Orpheus goes through a mirror and is buffeted by winds which don't affect his guide. Cryptic messages, and lots of simple tricks like shooting things backwards, make the "dream" world coherent if not comprehensible. (Gallagher has admitted that Cocteau's *La Belle et Le Bête* was a big influence, along with Joe Haldeman's post-Vietnam satire on Heinlein's *Starship Troopers*, 1974's *The Forever War*.)

Kiss Me Deadly (Robert Aldrich, 1955). Late *film noir* with car-boots containing stolen atomic substances - lots of blank white screens as people are vaporised - and severe black and white photography.

Dark Star (John Carpenter / Dan O'Bannon, 1974). Stoner spacemen blow up unstable planets, but just as a day job. They wear rompers and hippy beards, nothing works properly on their ship and their bombs are cleverer than they are. O'Bannen developed this idea in *Alien*, while Carpenter made *Halloween* and plenty of others, but this was their student project.

• However, Joyce delayed blocking out the shooting schedule and the camera positions. Graeme Harper contacted the producer with his concerns. Joyce was held up by the work he had to do on the rewrites (Gallagher was in Manchester, at work on a Granada project in similar difficulties), for which he got £750 but no credit, by his own request. Bidmead removed later I Ching references and conflated two characters into one. Bidmead's computer, the MZ, became the name of the *deus ex machina* allowing the Doctor to escape in episode four. Gallagher, asked about these changes by 'phone, found himself recognising less and less of his story. One idea

Joyce fought for until the last minute was that the passage through the mirrors should have a "howl-round" effect, like the original title sequence, to prevent it looking like some cheesy CSO shot. In the end they used some cheesy CSO shot.

• The rewrites didn't stop when it was in the can. The ending had Romana, K9 and Biroc, the Doctor and Adric going their separate ways, *then* the Gateway exploding. Thereafter the Doctor inserts the N-Space image translator; then Romana and K9 pledge their support to the Tharils; then it's back to the TARDIS. It is unclear whether Joyce or Nathan-Turner authorised the version we see.

• Gallagher tried to reinstate his version of the story in the novelisation. He thanked the production team for the steep learning-curve through which he'd been put, and got permission to overrun the page-count of a normal *Doctor Who* book. Nathan-Turner complained about the deviation from the broadcast version at the eleventh hour, leaving Gallagher to rewrite the book at four days' notice. It was published under the name of a character from *An Alternative to Suicide*, John Lydecker.

• Nathan-Turner apologised to Graeme McDonald, his immediate boss, for the big fat mess. He admitted that the finished result was good, but with the caveat that it was only the cast's goodwill and crew's professionalism that kept it viable. Joyce also apologised. By way of thanks, Nathan-Turner pointed out that this story's ratings were the highest of Season Eighteen. As the recriminations subsided, Bidmead decided to leave, offering Christopher Priest another slot for a new story (but see 19.6, "Earthshock").

• Much of the privateer vessel was the Vogon Constructor ship set from the BBC TV version of *The Hitch-Hiker's Guide to the Galaxy*. It was a co-production deal like the *Doomwatch* / "Ambassadors of Death" spaceship (see 7.3).

• The "Tharks" became "Thars" at Nathan Turner's request. Then these were renamed "Tharls" at Bidmead's request. Then Ian Levine dipped his oar in again and pointed out that it sounded exactly like "Thals" (see 1.2, "The Daleks", etc). Perhaps embarrassed by this basic error, Bidmead proposed 'Tharils'.

• Two of the Tharils in the "feast" scenes are comic actors Steve Frost and Mark Arden. Best known for a series of TV ads with the punchline 'I bet he drinks Carling Black Label', they've worked as a double-act and as part of troupe "The Wow

Show" (see 19.3, "Kinda"). They also toured in a production of Stoppard's *Rosencrantz and Guildenstern are Dead* (see 20.2, "Snakedance").

• Actors considered for the role of Rorvik included John Normington (see 21.6, "The Caves of Androzani"), Frank Windsor (20.6, "The King's Demons"), Stratford Johns (19.2, "Four to Doomsday") and Derek Jacobi. A David Rorvik had written some pop-science books in the late '70s... as had, of course, Dr. Carl Sagan.

• It was during rehearsals for this story that it became clear Tom Baker had had enough. He was ill, tired, bored and frustrated. The new regime had stifled his input, and the ratings confirmed his belief that the series was in decline. The press caught the mood and speculated on whether the series could survive without him. Meanwhile, suggestions for possible replacements abounded (see 19.2, "Four to Doomsday", for those the producer contacted). Martin Jarvis, a serious actor who'd become beached in sitcoms, was a popular suggestion; see "Castrovalva" (19.1) for more on this, plus "The Web Planet" (2.5), "Invasion of the Dinosaurs" (11.2) and "Vengeance on Varos" (22.2) for his actual roles in the series.

• Baker and Ward announced their engagement soon after Ward's departure from the series. Their marriage, in the midst of this story's transmission, was a surprise to Nathan-Turner. He still managed to milk it for publicity.

• Ward complained that her departure was too rushed and uninvolved. Bidmead stressed that this wasn't a soap. John Leeson was similarly querulous: 'They stuck [K9] behind a mirror and forgot about him. That's what you do with the 'phone bill!'

18.6: "The Keeper of Traken"

(Serial 5T, Four Episodes, 31st January - 21st February 1981.)

Which One is This? There's an ominous-looking statue with glowing red eyes, in an Elizabethan garden with art nouveau trimmings. This being a fantasy, it's bound to start walking around the place before long. This being '80s *Doctor Who*, there's bound to be an old enemy living inside it.

Firsts and Lasts See the pieces of the Peter Davison years being put into place. While the Doctor starts to come to terms with life without K9, two new characters quietly slip themselves into the series without immediately being recognisable as regulars. The first is Nyssa, who'll be part of the TARDIS crew for the next two seasons, but whose entrance is decidedly strange; the Doctor doesn't take her with him when he leaves, and she ends up following him across the universe for the next story. (It's fairly typical of this era. As script editor, Bidmead has a habit of making stories bleed into each other in a way that puts even the '60s series to shame.) The second new arrival is the new version of the Master, played by the late Anthony Ainley and giving the arch-villain his old "dark hair and satanic beard" look back. "The Keeper of Traken" is the first act of what we might call "The Master Trilogy", though *this* incarnation will be haunting the series right up until the very end in 1989.

Roger Limb supplies the incidental music for the first time, and some would say that it's a lot less intrusive than much of his future work. And for the first time, a little dinner-gong "boing" in the console room announces that the TARDIS has materialised.

The Fourth Doctor rigs up some unlikely-sounding pieces of equipment for the last time, including a 'binary induction system' that makes invisible TARDISes re-appear. He also takes this one last chance to stun some guards, here using an ion bonder instead of K9.

Four Things to Notice About "The Keeper of Traken"...

1. The problem with describing Season Eighteen is that you start to run out of words for "lush". This is the era of the programme that's got the greatest love for extravagant, velvety design, full of rococo crinkles and architectural flourishes. "The Keeper of Traken" gives us a fairy-tale world where everything's puff-sleeved gowns and brass-rimmed technology, but most striking of all is the Melkur.

Ah, the Melkur. Someone must have figured out that since modern *Doctor Who* was better at architectural spaces than at squidgy alien costumes, the perfect monster would be a living piece of architecture; a spiky, looming, hyper-stylised statue, a beautiful artefact in itself and also pant-wettingly scary when it starts to move. And as children are much more interested in statues that come to life than in boring old things from outer space (or at least, they were in the days when every other TV advert featured someone in a spaceman costume and most robot-monsters were guaranteed to be out-classed by the two-hundred-foot-tall versions you saw in Japanese cartoons), you can see why Melkur was *the* fashionable baddie of 1981.

2. Something unique and disturbing happens here. "The Keeper of Traken" has the usual happy ending, with the Doctor saving the planet and the villain's plans being thwarted, etc. *But* it ends with a stinger, in which the Master steals the body of one of the Consuls of Traken and leaves his puzzled teenage daughter an orphan, making this a decidedly grim sort of fairy-tale. Worse still - and here's the real killer - the next story, "Logopolis", sees the Master wipe out huge swathes of the universe. Including Traken. This, then, is the only time in the series' history when the Doctor successfully saves a planet and then sees it snuffed out just a few episodes later.

3. Those following the trend for over-appropriate names in *Doctor Who* will be delighted to learn that when the Master finally takes over the body of one of the people of Traken in order to kick-start his new life, the victim he chooses is called "Tremas". Parents in the *Doctor Who* universe really should know better than to risk their children's lives with names like that.

4. A big dribble of snot insists on hanging out of the Doctor's nose in episode three (when he's escaping the prison cell). Well, apparently it's supposed to be a "cobweb effect", but it still *looks* like an enormous dangling bogey. Which clashes with the "lush folkloric beauty" angle of the story, to say the least. Other odd facial features on show here include sinister red eyes that seem to have been painted onto Kassia's eyelids, and the skeletal teeth which seem to have been painted onto the Master's lips.

The Continuity

The Doctor   The Doctor claims he's still supposed to be heading for Gallifrey, even though Romana's left him. [In the end he never obeys the summons, but the Time Lords never seem to care, so Romana must have been their main concern.] He claims that 'they' always said he had a sophisticated prose style, though Adric seems to think his handwriting's awful. He's 'dabbled a bit' in bio-electronics.

On this occasion, the Doctor doesn't recognise the Master's TARDIS when he's staring straight at it. [He spots it at once in "Terror of the Autons" (8.1), and is at least a little wary of it in "The

Deadly Assassin" (14.3).] He now seems quite happy to have Adric around in the TARDIS, and seems to enjoy educating the boy, or at least showing off. He mentions empathy and the Second Law of Thermodynamics [almost as if it's a premonition of 18.7, "Logopolis"].

• *Inventory.* At one point Nyssa wields an ion bonder, a little hand-held device that can knock guards unconscious with a short-range beam when its ion rate is increased, but the Doctor pockets it. [He's never seen to use it after this, fortunate as it would have made things so much less interesting.]

• *Background.* He can't remember whether he's been to Traken, but probably not, although he identifies the Mettula Orionsis planetary system just by looking at it on the scanner. He also states that its evil-calcifying nature may be the reason he's never been. [Ooh, that's questionable. Does he mean "I've never had a reason to go there because there's no planet-saving to do", or "I've never risked going there because I'm a bit evil myself"?]

The Supporting Cast

• *Adric.* Believes he's quite good with locks, picking one easily with a brooch. Adric's already familiar enough with the console to identify the planet the TARDIS is heading for, and he knows plenty of science, not just maths. He even feels confident enough to work on the TARDIS circuits. [No time at all has passed since the last story, so the Doctor must have showed him quite a bit between "State of Decay" (18.4) and "Warriors' Gate" (18.5).]

• *Nyssa.* Daughter of Consul Tremas of Traken, a prim, well-educated young lady who's good enough with science to help Adric lash together a device for sabotaging the ultra-hi-tech bio-electronic Source on Traken. She's more of a swot than an aristocrat. Like Adric, she's happy to break the grown-ups' rules and doesn't mind putting herself in danger, though here it's mostly because she doesn't seem to appreciate what "danger" actually entails. Being such a well-brought-up young thing, she treats the Doctor almost like a visiting dignitary, and doesn't show any interest in joining the TARDIS crew here. It's implied that her mother is dead, as Tremas has recently wed Nyssa's "wicked stepmother" Consul Kassia, and he's been married before.

The Supporting Cast (Evil)

• *The Master.* The last time he was seen [14.3, "The Deadly Assassin"] he was a rotting, skull-faced cadaver. Here he's healed somewhat, having a proper human face again, but his skin looks horribly burned and there are still signs of bodily decay. He hasn't changed his shredded old robe, and his original TARDIS is still in the shape of a grandfather clock, although strangely it's a *different* grandfather clock. [So he came to Traken not long after his last run-in with the Doctor. The end of "The Deadly Assassin" saw him attempting to regenerate with the power he absorbed from the Eye of Harmony, but clearly he only had enough power to half-finish the process. The Doctor doesn't recognise his voice, so at least his vocal cords must have re-formed.]

He's explicitly said to be nearing the end of his twelfth regeneration, and he's hoping to gain the power of the Keeper of Traken to renew himself [though, as ever, there's no hint as to how he got through all his lives so quickly]. He believes the power will give him the ability to take over the Doctor's body and steal the Doctor's knowledge, but it's not clear whether he was expecting the Keeper to summon the Doctor here. He dismissively refers to the Doctor as 'Time Lord', as if he isn't one [compare with "The Deadly Assassin", again].

The Master's Melkur - see **The TARDIS(es)** - arrived on Traken some years ago, and he's been stuck inside his vessel all that time. [Putting the pieces in place and waiting for the Keeper to die, though as a time-traveller there must surely be more efficient ways of executing this plan. Perhaps he needed healing-time. As Time Lords always seem to meet each other in the correct order, it's possible that as much time has passed for him since "The Deadly Assassin" as has passed for the Doctor. The Doctor's aged about ten years since Season Fourteen, and ten years is a fair estimate for the amount of time the Master's been on Traken, from what we see here.]

He quickly goes back to using his old tricks, manipulating the weaknesses of others and using the Consul Kassia as his pawn. He gives her a neck-band to wear, which can glow red and cause her pain if she fails him, but which also lets him see through her eyes on the internal screens of the Melkur and seems to allow him to channel the power of the Melkur through her. It glows and gives her a 'gentle irradiation' when she first wears it, which puts her in a sort of trance and confirms her allegiance to him.

And then... when the worst seems to be over, Consul Tremas finds the Master's old TARDIS in its grandfather clock form, and makes the mistake of touching the dial. He's frozen in place, at which point the Master steps out of the clock and weirdly merges with his body. The new, reborn Master has the style and hair-colour of the "original" Master, but keeps Tremas' features. Even his clothes change in this metamorphosis, becoming black and sinister, and he leaves the planet laughing diabolically. [In just the same way that his body must have "stored" some of the power of the Eye of Harmony in order to half-regenerate, here he must have "stored" some of the Keeper's power. The Doctor suggests as much in the next story. After this Tremas' personality never comes to the surface, though the slightly altered persona of the new Master might indicate that Tremas' experiences at least change his behaviour a little.]

The Master's motives here are interplanetary conquest, plus acquisition of the deeper mysteries of time, which he believes the Doctor possesses. [Previously the Master has been described as a great technician who knows a lot about time-travel, so this acknowledgement of the Doctor's superior knowledge is unexpected. The Master may know that the Doctor has certain unique secrets; see 25.1, "Remembrance of the Daleks", etc.]

The TARDIS(es)   Now re-entering N-Space. On board the Doctor's Ship are at least two old 'time-logs', great hardback tomes apparently written by the Doctor, though he states that he doesn't have time to keep them any more. Adric is capable of reading these, but the style's a bit beyond him, never quite deciding whether events did happen, didn't happen or happened a long time ago. Traken must be mentioned in detail, as Adric says he's read about the Keeper and the bio-electronics system. [These books look like the result of years of labour, the Doctor suggesting that they're the accumulated wisdom of centuries. Were they penned by the First Doctor in his early years of travelling? It'd explain the less-than-snappy style.]

From one of the panels on the console - on the opposite side to the one that *used* to supply the co-ordinates - Adric can tell the name of the planet to which the Ship is heading. The TARDIS goes into orbit of Traken before landing there, at the Keeper's behest. The console now chimes gently when the Ship lands. Adric tests the TARDIS' drive, just in case they have to leave in a hurry, but the console makes shuddering noises and Adric describes it as 'blocking'. This is probably a result of the Master's interference, though the Doctor describes the TARDIS as being run-down and needing an overhaul [a thought which carries over into the next story].

The beam from the Melkur's eyes makes the TARDIS vanish, as it's been displaced by the current time-cone. A binary induction system, i.e. a device that can easily be lashed together on Traken, can be used to set up a standing-wave that the auto-systems can home in on. Which makes it reappear. [Alarmingly, this very nearly makes sense.]

The Master's vessel is, of course, disguised as the Melkur "statue" in the Grove of Traken. In this shape it can walk, though somewhat stiffly. [Could a TARDIS disguise itself as a human being, then, or is that too complex for it?] It lands on the planet vertically, glowing red rather than materialising, but later it arrives on the Keeper's throne with the familiar wheezing noise. It can also make its eyes glow, and there's always trouble when that happens. The red eyes invisibly "attack" the Keeper in his chamber, with a form of energy that looks as if it's giving him a heart attack; fire beams that either kill or knock people out; and at one stage even make the Doctor's TARDIS vanish.

The Doctor seems to believe that the beams can't hurt you if you don't make eye-contact. Kassia gains the ability to shoot eye-beams when she's wearing the Master's neck-ring, and when Kassia becomes the new Keeper of Traken, the Master can make his Melkur appear in her place to take the Keeper's power. This is, of course, fatal to Kassia. The technology of Traken can detect the Melkur's plasma fields, which the Doctor states would need great amounts of magnetic containment, while the wave loop patterns of these energy emissions suggest a TARDIS generator even though you don't get shift ratios of that magnitude in a type-forty.

Inside the Melkur is a dark control room, without the usual hexagonal console but with a rather more conventional control bank, and two videoscreens that mirror the Melkur's "eyes" on the outside. There are TARDIS-style roundels, but not many. A device fitted in this room can force the Doctor to remain absolutely still (while he's in there) or be destroyed, as it keys the whole domain to the Master's biological rhythms [meaning, the Master gives one signal and the Doctor

goes boom?]. This isn't the Master's old TARDIS, which is currently inside the Melkur in its grandfather clock form, and which the Master uses to escape when the Melkur is destroyed.

[Note: the implication is that the Melkur is a TARDIS, although it's never referred to as such by the Master, who just calls it his 'new ship'. But as it doesn't have the usual TARDIS console, doesn't materialise on Traken in the usual way and is never seen to travel in time, it may be a much cruder form of hardware that's just been hooked up to his real TARDIS to gain some extra power. Indeed, that may seem more likely, as the Master has no apparent method of getting hold of a new capsule from Gallifrey. Unless he stole it from the late Chancellor Goth. The fact that the scanners inside the Melkur resemble eyes hints that the control room was designed with the exterior "statue" shape in mind.]

When the Doctor sabotages the Source, it destroys the Melkur vessel, filling its control room with flames. The Doctor escapes by crashing through a wall of what looks like glass, and appears right outside the Melkur-ship.

Planet Notes

• *Traken.* Central planet of the Traken Union, an idyllic sort of place full of people in stately Shakespearean dress who obviously have a great love of gardens. But here nothing's really seen of the planet except the precincts of the court, which seem to lie at the heart of Traken's "government". It's said that the atmosphere is so full of goodness that particularly evil beings will just calcify and pass harmlessly into the soil if they set foot there, while the Doctor describes the Union as being an 'empire' held together by people just being terribly nice to each other.

[It's never quite clear whether evil really does shrivel on Traken. The Melkur seems to turn to stone, but that obviously isn't a bench-test as it's probably meant to look like a statue anyway. What's *more* telling is that those who see it land on Traken aren't remotely worried, as if they honestly believe they've got nothing to fear. The Master can leave his TARDIS on Traken without calcifying, though for all we know he's spent years working on a way of letting himself move freely, or he's immune to the atmosphere's effects after absorbing some of the power of the Keeper.]

Nonetheless, evil is attracted to the place by its compassion, so Melkur literally means 'a fly caught by honey'. Some of these evil-doers are redeemed rather than getting rooted to the spot, and young Kassia believes that less evil things than the Melkur can at least move and talk a little.

The centre of power on Traken is a large palace-like complex whose residential quarter is home to the Consuls, members of a five-person council who make the law and take consular vows to serve the state. Sacred law dictates that a Keeper only makes contact through these Consuls. The heart of the palace is the hall where the Keeper traditionally manifests himself, inside a protective chamber of glass. When the Keeper appears from out of nowhere, he appears seated on his throne and seems incapable of moving from it.

In fact the Keeper is dedicated to the Source, a complex bioelectronics system which takes the form of a large, glowing, pearl-like sphere. Kept in the catacombs beneath the chamber, the Source gives the Keeper the power to act as the organising principle of the whole Union and lets him draw on the minds of all the people in that Union. Though he usually only materialises in the chamber when there's a good reason, each Consul wears a ring, and the Keeper can be summoned when the rings are inserted into the chamber's control bank.

Tremas can claim consular privilege to put the Doctor under his protection when the Doctor's given a death sentence, but this means that his life also becomes forfeit if the Doctor steps out of line. If a Consul is accused of some injustice, he must enter rapport with the Source while another Consul keeps vigil, so that the Keeper can judge him. This entails a painful shaft of light, and can apparently be fatal if the Consul is guilty.

The Source has kept this Keeper alive for a thousand years, and he appears horribly old and frail, though he can still make his chair appear on the TARDIS and even change the Ship's co-ordinates in flight. [This sort of TARDIS-penetration demonstrates near-god-like levels of power; see 13.3, "Pyramids of Mars". But then again, see also 25.4, "The Greatest Show in the Galaxy".] Once the Master has the Keeper's power, he can control the movements of the Doctor and Tremas for at least a few minutes. When a Keeper dies, s/he suffers agony before vanishing, and terrible storms rage across Traken as nature reverts to chaos. These storms terrify the locals [who've obviously never seen anything similar]. They abate when the Consul who's been appointed Keeper-Nominate sits in the chair to take the Keeper's place, though

this period of transition is usually difficult.

The bio-electronics only permit a Traken to become Keeper, and there's a period of instability after a new Keeper takes the throne in which the power comes and goes. The Consuls have to ratify this new Keeper by giving him or her access to the Source from the control panel, and all five encoded rings can be used to manipulate the Source from these controls.

The current Keeper has heard of the Doctor's intelligence, and senses all-pervading evil coming even as he senses the time of his own 'dissolution', hence his decision to call on the Doctor. [It's not clear whether he draws the TARDIS into this part of space from long range, or has to wait until it's in the right neighbourhood, but probably the former as the TARDIS arrives at the critical point in time.] There's been restlessness in the Union lately, and superstitions about Melkur are on the rise. Crops have been failing, and floods and droughts have been bothering the planets, normal events when a Keeper is expiring. But Trakens have lived through this sort of thing many times.

Outside the court is the grove, a well-kept garden where the statue of Melkur has been standing for the last few years. The Grove is tended by men called Fosters, under the command of a Proctor, but when there's trouble - which there isn't, usually - the Fosters become a security force. Yet the Consuls consider the idea of arming the Fosters to be controversial, and the Keeper calls them guardians of the spiritual welfare of the capital. Once armed, they carry various energy weapons and *are* permitted to execute "evil" people.

The technology of Traken is obviously highly advanced, especially the Source, but the people obviously aren't interested in showing off. Consul Tremas keeps the plans for the Source manipulator in an 'atmosphere safe', which means that part of the wall mysteriously gives way to a glowing storage-space, though Tremas swore an oath not to let anyone see these secrets. The court has a penal wing, with cells that haven't been used in a long time, and the Trakens don't seem to have cracked teleportation as dematerialisations are new to Nyssa.

When the Doctor interferes with the Source to remove Melkur / the Master from the Keepership, and to cancel out the sabotage device built by Adric and Nyssa, Consul Luvic becomes the new Keeper and Traken can look forward to a fruitful and happy future.

Mmm.

History

• *Dating*. No indication given, and Traken has no known connection to Earth dating. [18.7, "Logopolis", sees Traken's destruction and has Nyssa speak as if the planet dies during her own time. It's therefore usually assumed that "The Keeper of Traken" takes place in 1981, which isn't unreasonable. Certainly, it doesn't take place *after* 1981.]

The Analysis

Where Does This Come From?   It looks (and sounds) more like a fairy-tale than ever before, which underlines one important fact about "The Keeper of Traken": it's staged as if it were a children's programme. This is no bad thing. In the days before commissioning editors reached the conclusion that modern-day children swear like troopers and prefer watching adult programmes to material that's made specially for them, the BBC put an awful lot of time and effort into its children's drama serials, often producing prestige adaptations of "classic" children's fiction.

In particular we could mention the 1976-77 version of *The Phoenix and the Carpet*[4], and the 1979 rendering of *The Enchanted Castle*, which also involved an art nouveau setting and walking statues. (In the same way that Peter Jackson's *Lord of the Rings* movies are taken far more seriously than most other Hollywood special-effects blockbusters purely because they're based on a "proper" book, the general perception was that these programmes were a lot more highbrow than most other series which involved people dressing up as monsters.)

Production-wise *Doctor Who* had never quite seemed on a par with these serials, partly because it had to churn out twenty-six episodes a year and partly because it didn't have that "literary" edge, nor the co-production money that accompanied it. But in "The Keeper of Traken" we see a series that's insisting on being taken as seriously as E. Nesbit, perhaps even as seriously as the version of *A Midsummer Night's Dream* made by the BBC in that same year. This isn't just *Doctor Who* attempting to become a science-fantasy series again, it's *Doctor Who* nicking an entire production style, and modifying it so that the unlikely space-technology seems as opulent and as through-the-looking-glass as the setting. And yet again, it should be noted that this sort of fairy-tale / outer space

hybrid was the height of fashion in the wake of That Film by George Lucas Which We've Mentioned Too Much Already. "The Keeper of Traken" was made in the year of *The Empire Strikes Back*, so things like the great Doctor / Master clash - which, both here and in "Logopolis" (18.7), often looks like a man struggling with his own id - were all the rage again. But as ever, there's something deeper and older going on here.

When World War Two broke out, part of the way in which the British public was "included" was to try to make an issue out of What We Were Fighting to Protect. There were strenuous attempts to force the whole nation to care about all forms of culture, from music-hall to Picasso. We saw in the Hartnell stories how the idea of the National Story is important as a shared touchstone, and how this was the founding principle of BBC television. In 1940, as the bombs were falling, many previously remote and arid academic studies were made as digestible and (to use the current terminology) "accessible" and "relevant" as possible. Key among these, and the biggest single influence on a generation to come, was E. M. W. Tillyard's *The Elizabethan World Picture*. Primarily using Shakespeare, it put forward the point of view that there was a "lost" vision of harmony and mutual respect, and that if you grasp this then all the beauties of "highbrow" art and literature become available to all. So long as Jerry doesn't blow it all up, of course.

So the generation coming into the school system after this were taught all about the Great Chain of Being, as if this were all there was to Shakespeare. And what's the Empire of Traken, but Tillyard's book made flesh? The cosmos is, essentially, music; universal harmony. Everything devolves from a semi-divine power, a king who's attuned to the Heavens and thus no longer merely mortal, one who can "retune" others (curing scrofula with a touch). The "Head" of the Body Politick. The Keeper uses the very term to describe his function, 'organising principle', that's used by Hobbes (see 11.1, "The Time Warrior").

Imbalances cause war, plague, weeds, cellulite and so on. Just as the ratio of the lengths of a plucked string make notes which are proportionate and harmonious, so the distances between the Crystal Spheres and the measurements of Man - think of that Leonardo sketch, of the bloke with lots of arms and legs - are as one. The true celestial harmonies are imperceptible to us, but we can guess what they're like (or half-remember from before being born), because we have souls and can do maths. This half-baked neo-Platonism reaches its peak in *Doctor Who* with "Logopolis" (18.7), but it was familiar to anyone who'd waded through to the end of the Narnia books or those with the patience not to skip the Lothlorien passages of *Lord of the Rings*. Never mind that we'd fought a Civil War to get away from this sort of dictatorial nonsense, a lot of jaded ex-hippies believed it. Bidmead and writer Johnny Byrne were the right age to have inhaled.

And on that note, a word should be said about escapism. In Volume III we saw how early '70s *Doctor Who* was, in its own space-miners-and-giant-maggots way, determined to reflect British politics. The UNIT set-up made it feel as if the government were always looking over the Doctor's shoulder, at a time when it wasn't pushing the narrative *too* far to suggest that blackouts, terrorists and eco-hazards might have had an extra-terrestrial connection. There isn't even a whiff of that in Season Eighteen, and on its surface level "The Keeper of Traken" is as abstract as it gets. In the same way that punk gave way to the poncing-about of New Romanticism and '80s soul, there's a hint here of the series turning its nose up at the nasty, uncouth television of the past and attempting something altogether more swish.

It has to be remembered, of course, that 1981 was *not* a quiet year in politics. Thatcher was in her first term of office as PM, and the specialities of the day were divisive government, crippled communities and rising unemployment. Those who hear the word "1980s" and don't immediately think "yuppies" most likely think of race-riots and the Last Great Miners' Strike instead. Yet none of these things make themselves felt in *Doctor Who*, and in the stories from this batch there's no hint of the existence of human politics at all; the fact that we've somehow managed to get 50,000 words into a book about the '80s *without* mentioning Thatcher is telling in itself. Like some of the (ostensibly) trendier teenagers of the time, *Doctor Who*'s response to Thatcherite Britain is to dress up in flouncey shirts and posh frocks.

Things That Don't Make Sense The Fosters are apparently fully-armed with death-weapons within moments of the Consuls suggesting it, even though the idea of them carrying guns is initially unthinkable and they shouldn't even have an armoury. The dying Keeper names Tremas as his successor at the same time that Tremas marries Kassia, basically guaranteeing that Kassia's going to lose her new husband mere days after the wedding... then people act surprised when she goes berserk and starts conspiring against the court.

Night falls on Traken very, very quickly in episode one, and it's dawn just a few scenes later, suggesting that the Consuls spend hours arguing about the Doctor between the rather more concise arguments we actually see. When they're trapped in the cell, Adric asks the Doctor why the sonic screwdriver can't open the lock even before the Doctor can try it, and then (not for the first time) there's the question of why the Fosters lock him up with the screwdriver to begin with. Also, there's some *very* noticeable off-stage coughing in the same scene.

The Master takes a remarkably long time to figure out that the Doctor must be destroyed rather than captured, given the number of times they've met each other before. It's taken as read that the Melkur can only hurt you if you make eye-contact with it, even though it attacks the Keeper invisibly and from out of sight at the end of episode one. Adric calls Nyssa "Neesa" in episode two, as if nobody's quite sure how to pronounce her name yet. When Adric and Nyssa build the device to make the Source consume itself, they both hope that they won't have to use it, then run straight off and use it.

Why can't the Fosters open the door of the Keeper's chamber in episode four, when there's a control-pad next to them and the Doctor and Tremas don't even bother locking it from the inside? Why does the Master kill one of the Fosters before the Doctor arrives, thus drawing attention to himself within the court? [Is he testing the Melkur's weaponry? Alternatively, he may know that the Doctor's coming and want to set him up right from the start.] With only three Councillors left, is Kassia's election to the Keepership legal? Why does no-one notice when she starts wearing an alien-looking collar over her ceremonial gowns? And doesn't she ever have a shower? How's she ever going to change?

Breakfast at Tremas': an iced bun, a spiky cucumber and a *sma-a-all* aubergine.

Critique (Prosecution) At last, a production that knows the difference between "leisurely" and "slow". This story, for all its faults, is at least one that allows the viewer to get to know the world under threat well enough for this threat to matter.

If during the many *longeurs* you find yourself looking at the scenery, then it's worth a look, even before Geoffrey Beevers starts chewing it.

It has surprising alarm-bells. Everyone seems to be making the effort to make at least a watchable bit of television. But the party's over. Even as we tick off things we've heard already this year (Tremas talks about how he'd like to rediscover the old forgotten sciences of the Empire, Kassia says not to; the Keeper summons the Doctor and then forgets to tell anyone about it, letting him be mistaken for a malefactor like Meglos; large prime numbers as the key to everything…) we're hearing things we'll hear again, soon. The laws of probability, the Second Law of Thermodynamics, 'heh-heh-heh', all will dominate the next round of the programme's slide.

Critique (Defence) It's rare - chronically, depressingly rare - that *Doctor Who* manages to get all the right tabs into all the right slots, and set up a world-space that generates exactly the right mood, tone and texture without letting you see the joins. Usually you have to make excuses for the lapses in the dialogue and the holes in the budget, at the very least. Not here. At this point it hasn't happened since the programme's wanton strip-mining of all things Victorian in "The Talons of Weng-Chiang", and there as here, it's got nothing to do with observed realism and everything to do with the way we think this sort of story's *supposed* to work.

As in the better scripts of Robert Holmes, "The Keeper of Traken" takes an obvious and positive joy in the nature of language, using not only its sense of lyricism but the very act of naming to create expectations and unspoken histories; to suggest traditions far older than this one story, traditions we almost-but-not-quite recognise from the world we know and almost-but-not-quite-recognise from the stories we heard when we were younger. We have a world where the agony of direct knowledge of the Keeper is known as "rapport", where the guardians of Arcadia are "Fosters", where the Master can quote Shakespeare and it's indistinguishable from the natives' speech-patterns. There's a running theme here of science being encased inside works of art, from the Melkur to the Source, from the trinkets of the Trakens to the half-magical, half-technological keepsakes that the Master gives to Kassia. There's more technobabble than in any script

since the early days of Douglas Adams, yet each artefact (and, in parts, each line of dialogue) seems hand-crafted.

Perhaps its grandest achievement, though, is the way it re-establishes *Doctor Who* as a modern myth. This is the story that has the job of re-introducing the Master, and unlike "The Deadly Assassin" it doesn't take the audience's knowledge of the part for granted. From the first episode it's established that this is a universe of elemental forces, where ancient Keepers can call on time-travelling science-magicians in times of crisis. There's no crass, tedious tying-up-and-escaping in the Master's plans this time. The Doctor only comes face-to-scar-tissue with his "other half" in the final episode, and when they confront each other it's clear to everyone in the audience - even those too young to have any memory of the Master's former life - that the feud between these two goes far beyond these four episodes.

This isn't the ham-fisted White Guardian exposition of "The Ribos Operation", but an extension of the mythos that feels perfectly natural. The Keeper's extended "flashback" in the first episode is superbly in keeping with this sense of "Once Upon a Time…", and it doesn't hurt that right from the outset, the Doctor looks as if he's tutoring Adric as an apprentice (we started to forget it after Nyssa and Tegan made life on the TARDIS more soap-like, but the on-screen relationship between Tom Baker and Matthew Waterhouse is inexplicably strong, with none of the adolescent moping we later came to expect from the boy).

And as with the best work of the Brothers Grimm, there's a keen sense of the *dark* here, the supposedly cut-and-dried nature of "evil" constantly being thrown into doubt as people fall foul of their own weaknesses. The shadows cast by the Doctor himself are longer than ever, and it's glorious to behold. If only more of Baker's stories made him seem this… unsettled.

The price for all this majesty? The padding. This is a three-act performance piece, not a four-part adventure story, and the fact that episode three drags so much is clinching proof that the whole dynamic of the series has changed. Just a couple of years earlier, it would have been perfectly normal for a four-parter to be at least *half* an episode too long - at least, from the point of view of younger, snappier viewers - but by 1981 the programme had put on an extra burst of speed, and suddenly the running-up-and-down sequences are painfully obvious. A seventy-minute edit of "Traken" would be much-appreciated, but really, there's too much here that's praiseworthy to complain too loudly.

After so many years of drab second-fiddle characters, how can you object to a story in which every member of the supporting cast is memorable, and each has at least one moment that's funny, touching or just finely-honed? An hour after you've watched it, you'll still be able to remember the names of all the Consuls, and try saying *that* about the supporting cast of "The Power of Kroll". And after so many years of hollow villains, how can you object to a story in which both Master and Melkur generate a proper sense of menace, with Geoffrey Beevers giving a vocal performance of almost Sutekh-like weight (except, tellingly, when he's required to laugh in a sinister way)? This is, let's not forget, a time before the Master got silly. We might have felt differently if we'd known things were heading towards "The King's Demons", but at the time the final scene was genuinely *exciting*, a strange, disturbing twist in what looked like a happy ending; something that made us feel we were moving into an uncomfortable new future, and await Tom Baker's send-off with even more anxiety.

The Facts

Written by Johnny Byrne. Directed by John Black. Viewing figures: 7.6 million, 6.1 million, 5.2 million, 6.1 million.

Supporting Cast Anthony Ainley (Tremas), Geoffrey Beevers (the Master, credited as "Melkur"), Sheila Ruskin (Kassia), Denis Carey (The Keeper), John Woodnutt (Seron), Margot van der Burgh (Katura), Robin Soans (Luvic), Roland Oliver (Neman).

Oh, Isn't That..?

• *Anthony Ainley.* He was the U-Boat commander shooting at pterodactyls in *The Land that Time Forgot*. And the tormented priest in *Blood on Satan's Claw*, although if you've seen it then you may have been distracted by the satanic nude scene involving Wendy Padbury. Before that he'd been the star of brief but memorable espionage spoof *Spyder's Web* in 1972; about a kerjillion films in the '60s, often playing Frenchmen (including opposite Alan Arkin in the *Inspector Clouseau* movie that everyone forgets); and, of

course, *The Pallisers*. He'd been in the Barry Letts version of Nicholas Nickleby, which may also be significant.

• *Sarah Sutton.* Star of fondly-remembered children's series *The Moon Stallion* (written by Brian Hayles... small world, eh?). She'd been at ballet school when her acting career started, aged eleven, playing Baby Roo in a stage *Winnie the Pooh*.

• *John Woodnutt.* Not a household name, but one of the most familiar actors of the era, and we weren't doing this listing when we looked at his other *Doctor Who* appearances: "Spearhead from Space" (7.1), "Frontier in Space" (10.3) or "Terror of the Zygons" (13.1).

• *Denis Carey.* Another actor who was rarely off our screens in the late '70s; the rumour that he was given the title role as a consolation prize for "Shada" (17.6) being abandoned doesn't seem to hold water.

Cliffhangers Believing the Doctor to have attacked the Keeper, the Consuls and the armed Fosters surround him; after the Fosters apprehend the Doctor and company, Kassia tells the Melkur that it's done, and the Melkur informs her that it's only beginning; the Melkur materialises around Kassia's body on the Keeper's throne.

The Lore

• Bidmead tells the story that he met this bloke in a pub who claimed to be a poet, and took the man's number. Several years later this bloke was script-editor for Space: 1999 (see 13.1, "Terror of the Zygons" for the days when this very nearly meant something) and working on *All Creatures Great and Small*. What Bidmead doesn't mention is that Nathan-Turner had approached Byrne to be his script editor, and that Byrne had approached Philip Hinchcliffe and Robert Holmes with proposals, but moving to London with a young family hadn't appealed to the writer.

• Byrne's track-record was varied. He'd co-written the notorious *Groupie*, and shared digs with the Beatles and a stage with Pink Floyd before either band had been famous. Then he'd worked with Gerry Anderson.

• Many rewrites were needed. Quite aside from the inclusion of the Master as the "Mogen" (later "Melkur") the main problem was that the story was a lot like "Meglos" (18.2), with mystical Greys and scientific Blacks, and the Doctor being

77

pressed to death under a slab. Byrne co-operated with these rewrites until August, whereupon he went on holiday to Greece and told Bidmead and Nathan-Turner that they could do whatever they wanted with the script. (Indeed, something suspiciously like the original proposal was submitted to Eric Saward as "Guardians of Prophecy" for the Sixth Doctor and Peri. It wasn't commissioned.) Unusually, the writer later said that he was happy with the result.

- The plan had been to bring back either Louise Jameson as Leela or Elisabeth Sladen as Sarah Jane Smith to "oversee" the regeneration. Neither was keen, although Sladen was still fond of the character (see 18.7-A, *K9 and Company*). Instead, the idea was mooted of getting two female companions to try different "extremes", to see what the public wanted. Byrne had included a character based on a friend called Nerissa: Nyssa was the daughter of a character called "Hellas" in the original draft. (Both names are places in the near east. "Hellas" is what Greeks call Greece, "Nyssa" is a city on the Turkish border, home to Mediaeval scholar Gregory of Nyssa.) She was psychic and technically-minded, so formed a good contrast with the other one, an Australian (see 18.7, "Logopolis"). The contracts needed to be sorted out to ensure that Sarah Sutton was available, and Johnny Byrne got a royalty for his character's further use, initially for three stories.

- Geoffrey Beevers, as Melkur / the Master, had been Private Johnson in "Ambassadors of Death" (7.3) and was married to Caroline John. His vocal talents had led to him doing a great deal of radio, and narrating re-dubbed foreign-language children's television.

- The Source Manipulator is Davros' datasphere from "Destiny of the Daleks" (17.1).

- Director John Black asked for a set which combined the kind of detailing found in the paintings of Gustav Klimt with the angular organic look found in the buildings of architect Antonio Gaudi. The Melkur was based on a bronze statue then in the Tate Gallery ("Unique Forms of Continuity in Space" by Italian modernist Umberto Boccioni, completed 1913).

- The new Master's first line was, originally: 'So… a physical body, at last.' His new costume was based partly on Traken's usual velveteen (but obviously in black as he's a panto villain), and partly on North African formal dress (hence the copper filigree around the collar). The Master costume from "The Deadly Assassin" was about to be junked; when it was retrieved, it was in a cardboard box in a warehouse.

18.7: "Logopolis"

(Serial 5V, Four Episodes, 28th February - 21st March 1981.)

Which One is This?   It's the end… which basically means Tom Baker falling off a big radio-dish.

Firsts and Lasts   For those who insist on believing that the most important thing about *Doctor Who* is the actor playing the Doctor (and that's all of us, when we're eight), it's the end of an era: Tom Baker's last story, and his final "proper" appearance in the series, although he'll be back as a ghost on recycled footage in "The Five Doctors" (20.7). We know he's a dead man walking from the very first episode, so "Logopolis" feels more like a funeral than a final adventure. And just to push home the idea that life goes on after a change of actor, it ends with a sort-of-cliffhanger into the next story, with "Castrovalva" (19.1) picking up exactly where this leaves off (although this wasn't the original intention…).

Obviously Peter Davison makes his silent debut as the Fifth Doctor in the final scene, while both Janet Fielding and Sarah Sutton join the programme as Tegan and Nyssa, giving the TARDIS a "proper" crew-compliment of three for the first time since 1967. It changes the whole shape of the programme. For the next three seasons, this is an ensemble piece (some would argue "soap opera"), not a series about one hero and his shrieking assistant. It's also the start of the programme's obsession with uniforms, since over the next year Adric, Nyssa and Tegan never bother to change their outfits.

For the first time, the device which supposedly makes the TARDIS change shape to suit its surroundings - and which has been broken ever since the start of the series - is referred to as a 'chameleon circuit'; an idea that started with the mention of a "chameleon mechanism" in Terrance Dicks' Target novel *Doctor Who and the Terror of the Autons* (1975) but has never been used on-screen until now.

It's also the last time until 2005 that the protagonist is identified in the end credits as "Doctor Who", a change that comes just in time for the programme's move to weekday evenings from its hallowed Saturday Teatime slot. So maybe it really *is* the end of an era, after all…

Four Things to Notice About "Logopolis"…

1. Let's start with the obvious: the Fourth Doctor's "death" scene. Tom Baker himself hated this, and the story in general, as he wanted to go out with something more 'heroic'. As the visibly aged Doctor lies dying in the shadow of the antenna-dish, accepting his death with Zen-like grace while Paddy Kingsland's score delivers the most memorable musical phrases of the age, we're led to feel as if we're one of the three youngsters who gather around his fallen body and realise that we're meant to be *involved* in this scene. (A loop of this sequence was shown on a video-screen as part of the 1991 *Doctor Who* exhibition at the Museum of the Moving Image, and bystanders were seen to quietly weep.)

2. But then, this is a story full of memorable, curious images. A tale in which the whole universe seems to close in around the Doctor and lead him towards his fate, there are signs and portents all along the way. A seemingly infinite number of TARDISes (actually four, but it *seems* infinite) are stacked inside each other, each one darker than the last; a figure with no face watches the Doctor from the side of a motorway (a bizarre juxtaposition of the real-world and the odd, helped by the fact that the Watcher - who shares a rapport with the Doctor that even we don't - has a role in the story unlike any character we've seen before); the universe is shown to be held together by a community of muttering, Biblical wizards; the TARDIS' depths become haunted, overgrown places where evil things can play hide-and-seek; the Monitor of Logopolis disintegrates before our eyes, patches of emptiness spreading across his body before he vanishes altogether (very *Barbarella*, this); planets die by crumbling to dust instead of exploding dramatically; and for those who weren't around in 1971, even the shrinking of the Master's victims seems shocking and grotesque.

If you saw this at the time and don't remember it, then what on Earth is wrong with you?

3. "Logopolis" has the highest body-count of any *Doctor Who* story. Or at least, that's what we assume. "Inferno" (7.4) may destroy an entire parallel Earth, but in "Logopolis" whole swathes of the universe are brought to dust, overcome by bright green entropy. Why does this happen?

Because the Doctor insists on going to Logopolis, a world which is secretly holding the universe together, even though he knows the Master's hitching a ride on his Ship. We'll go into this in detail later, but just bear that in mind: one little trip in the TARDIS destroys planets, and the man never even apologises. (Since Nyssa loses her homeworld here, it's been suggested that at this point she becomes that classic SF cliché, the Last Survivor of an Extinct Race. But this is never mentioned on-screen, and besides, the idea of a Last Survivor doesn't make much sense in a series about time-travel. After all, we saw the Earth's destruction as early as Season Three, but that doesn't mean it isn't *there*.)

4. It may be the end of this particular phase, but it's determined to go back to its beginnings. The "final" showdown between the Doctor and the Master takes place in the shadow of an enormous aerial dish, the same place their on-screen relationship began in "Terror of the Autons" (8.1). More importantly, though, the story opens with a shot of a policeman and what appears to be a police box… just like "An Unearthly Child" (1.1). But this time, the TARDIS isn't the Doctor's and the policeman dies in agony.

The Continuity

The Doctor He's thinking about skipping the trip to Gallifrey, as there are bound to be official enquiries about Romana [again, the Time Lords never chase him up about this]. The Master believes that if the two of them work together then the Doctor can never return to Gallifrey [which turns out to be quite wrong].

Even before the Watcher turns up - see **The Time Lords** - the Doctor is starting to get broody, and there's the sense of impending collapse in the air. He's starting to miss Romana, and always meant to ask her to help fix the chameleon circuit. He's positively snappish with Adric, and later with his other companions. When he meets with the Watcher, he obviously accepts his fate but refuses to talk about it. No longer close to any of his "crew", he displays a rather grim sense of humour; after the Master shrivels up Tegan's aunt to doll-size, the Doctor tells Tegan he's seen 'a little' of the old woman, and feels no immediate need to break the news to her. His behaviour is also rather erratic, his plan to flush out the Master by landing the TARDIS on the bottom of the Thames and opening the doors deserving special mention.

The Fourth Doctor meets his end when he falls from the aerial dish of the Pharos Project on Earth. Shortly before the regeneration he "hears" a host of old friends and enemies speaking his name: the Master in "degenerate" form, a Dalek, the Captain of Zanak, the Cyberleader, Davros, Stor the Sontaran, Broton the Zygon, the Black Guardian, Sarah Jane Smith, Harry Sullivan, the Brigadier, Leela, K9 and the two faces of Romana. [All fairly recent acquaintances, so if this is his life flashing before his eyes then he sees his life as beginning with this incarnation.] It's possible, as he's lying broken on the ground, that he wouldn't have survived the accident without the Watcher's intervention. When the time comes for his regeneration, he seems positively serene about it, his confident last words being: 'It's the end… but the moment has been prepared for.'

• *Ethics.* As has already been noted, and will be noted again… by taking the Master to Logopolis, the Doctor imperils the entire universe and is responsible for the deaths of whole planets, but shows no guilt about this and acts as if it's destined to happen this way.

• *Inventory.* In the coat for this final outing: an extendable ruler.

• *Background.* The Doctor speaks of Thomas Huxley [1825-95, yet another nineteenth-century connection for the Doctor] as an 'old friend', and has been to Logopolis before, treating the Monitor there as an old friend as well. The Monitor apparently knows the Doctor's face, and says that the Doctor has changed little. The Logopolitans offered to do the chameleon conversion for the TARDIS, and explained the details, but for some reason the work was never done. The Doctor knows of the Pharos Project on Earth, recognising its exact duplicate on Logopolis.

Here the Doctor claims that when he 'borrowed' the TARDIS, it was 'in Gallifrey' for repairs [so it was still in active service despite its age], which explains why the chameleon circuit doesn't work [although it worked prior to 1.1, "An Unearthly Child"]. He says he should have waited for them to do the chameleon conversion, but 'rather pressing reasons' motivated him to leave.

The Supporting Cast

• *Adric.* Still asking far too many questions, but most of them are quite intelligent. He's heard of Earth as the planet with all the oceans. He sounds delighted to see Nyssa when she unexpectedly turns up on Logopolis [puberty], and for now there's at least as close a bond between them as there is between Adric and the Doctor. Adric knows a lot about the TARDIS by now, recognising what'll happen if the co-ordinate sub-system is disconnected and identifying problems like gravity bubbles even before the Doctor does.

He states that the Doctor has taught him to read Earth numbers, but curiously he can read English like a native [see **Does the Universe Really Speak English?** under 14.1, "The Masque of Mandragora"]. He's habitually carrying a notebook and pen around in his Alzarian pyjama-suit.

• *Nyssa.* She unexpectedly turns out to be on Logopolis when the Doctor gets there, and explains that the Watcher brought her there, though she doesn't reveal exactly how. Nyssa seems quite prepared to join in with the Doctor's planet-hopping, universe-saving antics even before her own planet is eradicated.

When Traken is shown to have been destroyed, she obviously tries to keep her dignified composure but can't quite pull it off. Even so, it doesn't take her more than a few hours to recover from the shock of the atrocity and start beaming her head off [nor does she ever blame anyone but the Master for it…]. As on Traken, she feels closer to her father than anyone else, so when the Master turns out to have killed him it hurts her at least as much as the death of her own civilisation.

• *Tegan.* Tegan Jovanka is a mouthy Australian in her twenties who thinks she's about to start her first day as an air hostess at London airport [meaning Heathrow, as "The Visitation" (19.4) establishes]. In fact, she becomes the first person since the 1960s [3.5, "The Massacre"] to stumble on board the TARDIS because she thinks it's a real police box.

Tegan's first reaction, on finding herself lost in a labyrinthine alien spaceship, is one of panic and she's clearly close to tears. However, she's an angry young thing who gets the anxiety out of her system by shouting at people, and she's at least bright enough to work out that the TARDIS is a vehicle of some kind. Though obviously perplexed by much of what she sees as she's dragged across the universe, she can get practical when she needs to [air hostesses are, after all, crisis-trained], so most of her time is spent whining about wanting to go back home rather than running away from things. Favourite swearword: 'Rabbits.'

Tegan's father owned a farm, which she likes to

How Does Regeneration Work?

The straightforward answer is, the way K'anpo says it does at the end of "Planet of the Spiders" (11.5). Every cell in the patient's body renews itself simultaneously. The result is a shake-up of personality and memory, and a variation in bodily form.

Straightforward, but not complete. We now have reason to believe, for instance, that at the point of regeneration a Time Lord can adapt to local conditions (see the TV Movie, 27.0). Even if it's *not* the case that the Doctor only becomes half-human because of his most recent regeneration, his revelation that Time Lords can change into other species is telling. As the Doctor's regenerations in the "proper" series all happened either aboard his own Ship or in the company of at least one other Time Lord (if we count the Watcher and the Master as Time Lords), this potential mutation towards "alien" biological norms wouldn't have happened until now... although see **When Did He Get a Second Heart?** under "The Wheel In Space" (5.7). The Doctor seems to think that the TARDIS is heavily involved in the regenerative process in "Power of the Daleks" (4.3), so the Ship may well be the thing that's been keeping him on an even keel, species-wise. But as the Watcher, Cho-Je, debatably the "weird" Romanas (17.1, "Destiny of the Daleks") and probably the Valeyard (Season Twenty-Three) can be seen as "avatars" rather than actual selves, we have to ask what else - besides DNA - is at work here.

Bearing in mind what we said in **How Does Evolution Work?** (under 18.3, "Full Circle"), it could plausibly be argued that the outward form of a Time Lord is some kind of somatic manifestation of the personality. In "Logopolis" the Doctor speaks as if the forthcoming events are his own, personal death. Even though someone called the Doctor wakes up in the shadow of the radio-dish - with the Doctor's memories, and wearing the Doctor's socks - the consciousness we've been watching since "Robot" (12.1) is no more. It's his "soul" that's changed, and the body merely follows suit. This might help to explain why all the Doctors are described as having different lives and different time-streams in the "reunion" stories. (See **What *is* the Blinovich Limitation Effect?** under 20.3, "Mawdryn Undead". But see also **How Does Time Work?** under 9.1, "Day of the Daleks", and ponder whether Time Lords are the only people in this universe who have souls. The term "regeneration", remember, derives as much from religious parlance as from biologica terminology for growing new limbs like a newt.) New consciousness, new flesh, new face. Perhaps the clothing is affected, too ("Power of the Daleks" and 19.1, "Castrovalva"). Some form of psychic energy? Or something deeper, some side-effect of the relationship between Time Lords and the causal nexus they apparently helped to create?

Following hints in the Target novelisations, it's been suggested that the ability to regenerate is partly a yogic practice and partly technological. The Doctor keeps making a hash of it not because of the state of crisis whenever one of him dies, but because he was such an inattentive student at Prydon Academy. This would make sense of Romana's superior ability, but still leaves awkward questions. How is he able to do it at all, if it's a "skill" and not a genetic birthright? It's certainly not everyone who can do it. Gallifrey seems to be divided into Time Lords and plebians, and we're led to assume that only the elite can regenerate. Indeed, on at least two occasions (14.4, "The Deadly Assassin" and 20.3, "Mawdryn Undead") it's implied that you're no longer a Time Lord if you've used up all your regenerations, though this doesn't seem to apply to Azmael (21.7, "The Twin Dilemma"). There's some confusion as to whether the Castellan and the Captain of the Guard qualify as low-born or high-born, so perhaps "promotion" is possible; this seems to have been the intended fate of both Adric and Ace. In that case, perhaps Leela is no longer an "alien". That's certainly what you'd deduce from "Arc of Infinity" (20.1).

But here's the real crux of it. At least two races have acquired Gallifreyan technology and given themselves extended, ever-regenerating lives (15.5, "Underworld" and "Mawdryn Undead", again), yet it's noticeable that in both cases that technology just refreshes the subject's old body instead of providing a new one. This is telling. It suggests that the agency which rebuilds the body during a regeneration is purely "mechanical", but that the factor which makes a Time Lord change shape during that regeneration might not be. Anybody can be renewed, if they hook themselves up to a machine - though in the case of both the Minyans and Mawdryn, the machine may do strange things to the genes, as nobody in the universe ever risks such a device just to cure the occasional dysfunction - and a similar form of mechanical regeneration must be built-in for Time Lords, or perhaps spliced into their biological makeup when they come of age.

continued on page 83...

pretend was in the outback, and the man was apparently a self-sufficient type. She herself claims to come from Brisbane [despite the accent being completely wrong]. She leaves for work from a house which she seems to share with her similarly Australasian aunt Vanessa. Their sporty red car breaks down near one of the few police boxes left in Britain in the early '80s, and the Master murders Vanessa. [Tegan's relatives are always unlucky. See also 20.1, "Arc of Infinity" and 21.2, "The Awakening".] Tegan's choked when she finds out about her aunt's death, but like Nyssa, events seem to put the thought out of her mind. By the time the Doctor regenerates, she's apparently found her bearings enough to actually care what happens to him.

Tegan's hostess uniform is a starchy purple number, which she insists on wearing for much of her time with the Doctor, hat and all. Clearly not the ignorant antipodean she might sometimes seem, she knows that "Pharos" is ancient Greek for "lighthouse". She can drive.

• Romana. The Doctor states that by joining up with the Tharils, Romana broke the cardinal rule of Gallifrey and became involved. He doesn't think she'll ever be able to return. [Countless novels, audios and works of fan-fiction beg to differ. The books, and later the audios, have her ending up as President of Gallifrey.]

The Supporting Cast (Evil)

• The Master. His original plan is evidently to target the Doctor, now he's got a body to call his own, and in many ways this whole crisis comes across as a duel between them. He may or may not know about Logopolis before the Doctor takes him there. [The Doctor claims that Logopolis was the Master's target all along, but this seems unlikely as the Master could just have gone there on his own without needing to involve the Doctor. Unless the Doctor's the only one who knows where it is?]

Though the Master's prepared to work alongside the Doctor in order to save creation, he can't resist turning the situation to his own ends, using the Pharos Project to send a message to the entire universe and threatening to doom everyone unless they make him their leader. [This plan has often been ridiculed as insane, but it's in character for the Master, who enjoys wielding power. Letting the universe *know* that he can doom it is reason enough for him to do this, even if he can

hardly take over all the planets that receive the message while he's stuck in an antenna-dish control booth on Earth. Besides which, he must surely expect the Time Lords to hear, so this is as good a gloat as any.] The Doctor seems to honestly believe that the Master's mad, and there's some evidence for this, what with the amount of maniacal laughing he does. Ultimately he gets away [but his plan isn't finished yet, as "Castrovalva" (19.1) reveals].

The Master correctly predicts that the Doctor will materialise around a police box on Earth. When Adric asks whether the Master read his mind, the Doctor's reply is: 'He's a Time Lord. In many ways we have the same mind.' [Perhaps best not to take this too literally, as mind-sharing is a common theme in Time Lord culture. See the Doctor's communion with himself in 10.1, "The Three Doctors"; the Matrix in 14.3, "The Deadly Assassin"; and the special features of the Doctor's brain in 15.2, "The Invisible Enemy".] His stated philosophy here: 'Envy is the beginning of all true greatness.' [This may say a lot about his early relationship with the Doctor...]

Once again, the Master is using a weapon which kills by shrinking its victims to doll-size. Here it's revealed to be a stubby black rod, though it isn't referred to by name yet. He gives Nyssa an electro-muscular constrictor, a gold bracelet which crackles with electricity whenever anyone tries to remove it and which turns her into a zombie-slave when activated by the Master's remote-control unit. He says it just gives him control over her hand, but her mind seems to blank out while she's strangling people.

The TARDIS(es) Shown to be in a worse state of repair than ever here, with the time column 'wheezing like a grampus'. A retractable computer screen and keypad in the TARDIS console - which emerge when the Doctor fiddles about under the controls - can be used to program the TARDIS' chameleon circuit and make it change its exterior shape, or at least, it could if the chameleon circuit were working.

Simple computer images of various shapes are shown on the screen, including a pyramid. The Doctor describes this as an 'early version', so instructions have to be punched into the device in machine code. [Other stories see TARDISes change shape without any apparent programming, most notably 22.1, "Attack of the

How Does Regeneration Work?

...continued from page 81

But Time Lords also have the extra "soul" factor, which allows them a form of diversity. If regeneration is their way of compensating for the inability to reproduce naturally, as the New Adventures claim, then this metamorphic change may have been deliberately introduced in order to prevent the race stagnating. After all, Rassilon was clearly distrustful of the idea of longevity in an unchanging state (20.7, "The Five Doctors"). So the yogic practice of the Target books is a way of controlling the change, not of triggering the rebuilding of the body. The bonus element in Time Lord biology may even be the same thing that gives them their "special relationship" with time, their ability to withstand localised temporal phenomena and arguably their ability to demonstrate free will in historical affairs. "The Two Doctors" (22.4) hints at this, although much of what the Doctor says in that story may be bluster. This begs the question of where the Time Lords get their new identities from, but for more on that see **Why Are There So Many Doubles in the Universe?** under "Arc of Infinity".

The most complete explanation for regeneration to have been "officially" published is John Peel's account in *The Gallifrey Chronicles* (1991), which maintains that it's all done with nanotechnology and that the Time Lords acquired the ability when someone walked into Rassilon's office one day and said "look, I've invented nanites that let you regenerate". But since nanotechnology is the all-purpose cop-out answer of '90s sci-fi, this is a bit like a writer in 1969 claiming that the TARDIS runs on moon-dust collected by the Apollo missions and then expecting later generations to stick with it.

Cybermen". The suggestion here might be that there's a "bank" of set shapes, and new models have to be added if a TARDIS pilot wants something specific.] The Doctor believes that the best way of getting this facility working again is to have the Ship reconfigured on Logopolis, and for some reason he thinks he'll need exact measurements of the TARDIS' police box exterior. [So he's planning on letting the Logopolitans re-tailor the whole dimensional make-up of the TARDIS, rather than fixing the circuit as he tries to do in "Attack of the Cybermen".]

The outer plasmic shell is, of course, mathematically modelled on a British police box. For this reason, he materialises the Ship around a police box on Earth, so it appears in the middle of the console room [the only time the TARDIS attempts to materialise around an object, apart from another TARDIS]. Only the exterior of the TARDIS exists as a real space-time event, but 'mapped on to one of the interior continua'.

However, the police box turns out to be a TARDIS shaped like a police box. Entering the second TARDIS, the Doctor finds himself inside an exact copy of his own console room, with another police box in the middle of it. Entering *that* police box leads to another console room… each console room being slightly darker than the previous one. The nested boxes are apparently caused by a 'gravity bubble', something that leads to an instrumentation failure and some gurgling

from the original TARDIS console, but the Doctor describes the whole thing as a dimensional anomaly. It's evidently a side-effect of two TARDISes locking together, and when the Doctor enters the *next* police box, he finds himself outside the Ship. [This is different to the TARDIS-inside-TARDIS procedure seen in 9.5, "The Time Monster". There, only two console rooms were in evidence, one inside the other. Here, the interlock of two TARDISes is just causing weird space-time effects.]

While the Doctor and Adric are caught up in all of this, the police box in the original console room - apparently the Master's TARDIS - dematerialises and arrives at another point inside the Doctor's Ship. [But there's nobody working the controls in the police box's console room, and the console rotor doesn't go up and down when it moves, again suggesting that this is a "warped" version of the Doctor's TARDIS rather than part of the Master's.] The doors of the Doctor's TARDIS shut soon thereafter, trapping Tegan inside [as if somebody's closing them by remote control after she enters, but this is never explained and it may be the Watcher's work].

The anomaly prevents the TARDIS taking off [it makes the same noises as when it was "blocked" in the previous story], but on the console there are controls for architectural configuration, which handle interior allocation of space. The Doctor uses these to jettison Romana's room from the

Ship, giving it an extra boost of power that lets it break free. [The same systems come into play again for 19.1, "Castrovalva". It seems odd, though, that the TARDIS should need such a boost when it can draw on all the power of the Eye of Harmony and / or the 'power of a sun'. Perhaps there's a limit to the amount of power it can run through its systems at any one time, and only the jettisoning can add to the energy being used. There are any number of rooms that the Doctor could jettison, many containing less useful items than Romana's, so this looks an awful lot like "closure" on the Doctor's part.]

Before it's lost, Romana's bedside table has a photo of K9 on it... bless.

The TARDIS has cloisters, wrought out of what looks like stone and wrapped in ivy, a good place for pacing or sitting pensively on a bench. [A cloister is usually a covered walkway in an open area; we never see the ceiling here, so does this part of the TARDIS have a "sky" overhead? That's certainly what Bidmead's novelisation suggests.] It also has a deep, tolling bell, the cloister bell, which the Doctor describes as a communications device reserved for 'wild catastrophes and sudden calls to man the battlestations'. [Meaning, it's the Ship's way of communicating in a crisis? It sounds long before the Master actually threatens the universe, hinting that the TARDIS predicts the crisis. Perhaps the Watcher gives it a clue.] He also says that Adric can sound the bell if it's terribly urgent, so it's not just an automatic process.

There are plenty of white, roundel-indented corridors between the console room and the cloisters. And either the corridors don't all lead where they logically should [q.v. what Borusa says about the Ship's 'pedestrian infrastructure' in 15.6, "The Invasion of Time"], or Tegan's just got a bad sense of direction. Here the Ship's seen in "hover mode", floating above Logopolis before it lands there, and the console hums during this procedure. [The Ship's seen to hover several times over the next few years, usually accompanied by an exotic sound effect. The Logopolitans are expecting the Doctor when he arrives, and according to the novelisation he contacts them while the TARDIS is hovering, politely asking them for "clearance" to land.]

At one point the Watcher takes the TARDIS out of space and time altogether, disconnecting the entire co-ordinate sub-system and letting it 'hover'. [This doesn't just take it into the vortex, but somewhere else - or nowhere else - entirely. A similar thing happens in "The Mind Robber" (6.2), so it's likely that the TARDIS ends up in the same sort of no-place here, but obviously there are no nasty super-computers waiting outside the universe on this occasion.] The Watcher's reasons for doing this seem to be to keep Adric and Nyssa out of harm's way until the time's right. From outside, the whole universe can be seen on the TARDIS scanner.

Somehow, Traken sends a message to the Doctor telling him that Tremas has disappeared [see the previous story], and it arrives via the TARDIS console. The Doctor has to put his ear to a speaker to hear it, and later states that Nyssa sent the message, begging him to help her find her father. [This would seem to indicate that Traken's "present" is 1981. Alternatively the message might be sent via the vortex, like the space-time telegraph in "Revenge of the Cybermen" (12.5), but the Traken Union has never shown any sign of possessing time-travel technology. Since it's the Watcher who takes Nyssa to Logopolis, he may also play a part in the delivery of the SOS.]

When preparing to land the Ship underwater and open the doors, the Doctor and Adric shut down everything on the console, and Adric knows how to follow the Doctor's instructions to fold back the Omega configuration; halt the exponential cross-field; close the pathways to conditional states seven to seventeen; and end the main and auxiliary drive. Most of this is done by fiddling around with the underside of the console, and the Doctor states that afterwards they're 'partially materialised', so there's a jolt as they land in full. Various buttons on the console can apparently be used to open the doors, but they can be held shut by the Doctor and Adric pushing against them. [From Season Nineteen onwards, the door control is always a big red knob.] Earth is in sector 8023 of the third quadrant [of the galaxy], according to Adric's co-ordinates.

The Master's TARDIS obviously has a fully-functional chameleon circuit [which makes you wonder why he let it stay as a grandfather clock on Gallifrey in 14.3, "The Deadly Assassin"], here taking the forms of a tree and an ionic column as well as the police box. Its navigation is faultless. When entropy starts to collapse the universe, the Master suggests reconfiguring the two TARDISes into time-cone inverters, then creating a stable safe zone by applying temporal inversion isometry to as much of space-time as they can isolate. They never actually seem to get round to this. The light-speed overdrive from the Master's TARDIS can evidently get a signal to the CVE in the constellation of Cassiopeia instantaneously, and his Ship can't move while it's disconnected.

The Time Lords

• *The Watcher.* A figure dressed all in white, with blurred, half-moulded features that make him look as if his face hasn't been finished, the Watcher first appears by the side of the road as the TARDIS materialises on Earth. For a while he's just seen hovering in the distance, and seems to go wherever the Doctor goes. Then the Doctor spots him, and insists on going over to talk, refusing to let Adric listen in on the conversation. The Doctor refers to this meeting as dipping into the future.

The Doctor doesn't reveal who the Watcher is, but seems to know him. It's the Watcher who convinces the Doctor to go to Logopolis, even though the Master's hiding on board the TARDIS, something the Doctor considered unthinkable before the conversation. It's also the Watcher who removes Nyssa from Traken before its destruction, who takes both Nyssa and Adric out of the space-time continuum when it's threatened and who makes sure they're around when the Doctor regenerates. [He seems to be putting all the pieces in place, as if he somehow knows that Nyssa should rightfully be part of the TARDIS crew. Perhaps Tegan too, if he's the one who closes the TARDIS doors on her.]

Only when the Doctor suffers a fatal fall from the Pharos Project, and lies dying on the ground, does the Watcher step forward. His body and the Doctor's merge together, in a haze of light, so that the Watcher's half-finished face appears to be a "chrysalis" around the Doctor. The Fourth Doctor regenerates, and becomes the Fifth. Nyssa instinctively seems to know that the Watcher was the Doctor 'all the time'.

[This isn't a new idea, of course; Cho-Je "blends" with K'anpo in much the same way in 11.5, "Planet of the Spiders". The Watcher doesn't seem as fully-formed a creature as Cho-Je did, perhaps because the Doctor hasn't been anticipating his death for as long as K'anpo. Arguably, the Valeyard (23.4, "The Ultimate Foe") is the same kind of entity, a projection of a Time Lord's future self. Naturally, no proper explanation has ever been given as to what these beings really are. In "Logopolis" the process is particularly hard to get

a grip on, as the Watcher is the one who tells the Doctor to go to Logopolis and ultimately sets him on a course for his own death. Though this might make the Watcher a harbinger of destiny, making sure that the Doctor meets his end in the "right" circumstances, here the intervention also leads to the deaths of millions, billions or trillions of people. See also **The Lore**.]

Perhaps the most telling thing the Doctor says, when he's speaking of the future catastrophe described by the Watcher: 'A chain of circumstances that fragments the law that holds the universe together.'

Planet Notes

• *Logopolis.* A community on an unspecified planet, though it's possible that Logopolis may be the name of the world as well as the settlement. A labyrinth of streets made up of identical sandstone hovels, from the air the "street-plan" of Logopolis looks like a web of cracks in the earth, a human brain or - to complete the metaphor - a circuit-board.

The settlement is exclusively inhabited by robed, grey-haired old men, who seem to fall somewhere between monks and scientists. One Logopolitan occupies each hovel, and mutters sequences of pure mathematics. As all of the men are working to the same plan, the whole of Logopolis thus functions as an enormous computer. So advanced are the mathematics of Logopolis that these old men can alter the structure of the universe with their numbers, a process known as block transfer computation, technically described as a way of 'transcendentally' modelling space-time events - solid objects - through pure calculation.

The Monitor speaks to his people over a PA system, intoning the numbers in a non-human language. The Doctor believes that this can fix his chameleon circuit; after the Logopolitans do the calculations, he's given a single piece of paper which contains the relevant data to feed into the TARDIS console. The Monitor believes there's a chance of a transfer instability, but that very little can go wrong, though when the Master changes the numbers by killing some of the old men in their hovels it reduces the dimensions of the TARDIS with the Doctor still inside. Sonic projectors, black speaker-like pieces of hardware, are put around the miniaturised TARDIS in order to 'create a temporary zone of stasis' which arrests the dimensional spiral and lets the Doctor move properly in the console room. Entering the correct code into the console restores the Ship to normal. The Master later uses these sonic projectors to create a sound-cancelling wave and make all the people of Logopolis cease their work.

In charge of Logopolis is the Monitor, who knows the Doctor of old and is more than happy to help out. The Monitor states that computers aren't subtle enough to perform the block transfer computations, and that only the living mind will do the job; their mathematics affect the physical world, so the computations would change a computer's nature and cause it to malfunction. But when the Doctor arrives he immediately notices a new feature on the planet: an exact replica of the Pharos Project on Earth, modelled by block transfer computation, fitted out with computers and capable of beaming signals across the universe. Even the Doctor's surprised that the Logopolitans can model the whole project mathematically and supply the energy [which potentially makes Logopolis the most powerful force in existence, at least until its fall]. One key section of Logopolis, the 'central register' of Logopolitans, is housed in the Pharos copy.

There's a good reason for this copy. As the Monitor explains, the universe is naturally a closed system, and in any closed system entropy will increase. What only the Logopolitans know, and what even the Doctor doesn't suspect, is that the universe long ago passed the point of total collapse. The Logopolitans have fixed this problem by opening "voids" into other universes, to make it an open system. These are the CVEs [see 18.3, "Full Circle" et seq]. The Logopolitans have to keep chanting to stop the universe collapsing, while the advanced research unit works on a long-term plan. They've been working on a computer program that can make the CVE stay open permanently, and intend to send this via the aerial dish of the Pharos Project once the program's complete. When the Master interferes with the work of Logopolis, by briefly freezing the settlement and allowing the CVEs to close, entropy instantly takes its toll on the universe and things start to fall apart. It's said that this unravels the causal nexus, so the Master's interfering with the law of cause and effect.

Logopolis is affected by the entropy first, its buildings rotting and its people turning to dust, but the effect soon works its way outwards. It's implied that whole star systems vanish, certainly Mettula Orionsis and therefore Traken. To open the CVE again, the Doctor and the Master have to take the Logopolitans' program to the real Pharos Project on Earth and transmit it to the location of the nearest CVE in the constellation of Cassiopeia. From outside the universe, the 'entropy field' appears to be a great dark shadow sweeping across the universe [though it can't possibly remove as much as it seems to on the screen, or the universe would end up about half its former size]. Earth's galaxy only has hours left, according to Adric.

Before their deaths the Logopolitans never seem to talk or smile, except for the Monitor. He claims they're a people driven by mathematical necessity, not individual need. [There's no hint as to where they come from, since they surely can't be a *species* of old men. Unless they replicate by block transfer mathematics. Are they recruited from another culture, or from several? Though the Monitor states that the universe 'long ago' passed the natural point of collapse, it's unclear whether the Logopolitans have been keeping the CVEs open for millions of years or whether their calculations have somehow been "beamed" back in time to an earlier point in the universe's history. The former seems unlikely, as Logopolis has only recently created the Pharos Project to help with the workload. The latter seems odd, as the story seems to suggest all of this is happening "now".]

History

• *Dating.* No date given, but on Earth it's apparently the present day. [The exact present day, in fact. "Four to Doomsday" (19.2) establishes that Tegan leaves Earth on the 28th of February, 1981, the day that the first episode of this story was broadcast. Season Nineteen also reveals that she boarded the TARDIS by the side of the Barnet bypass, which is where the location-work was filmed. It's virtually certain that the sequences on Logopolis happen at the same time as those on Earth, as the Doctor has to hurry to install the Logopolitans' software at the Pharos Project. Besides, it's doubtful that the laws of time would let him nip back into the past and save the universe ahead of time. Such a thing would be too easy.] Police boxes are more or less obsolete in this period, though the Doctor believes a few in the north are still in use.

The Pharos Project is a large antenna-dish on Earth, apparently in England, manned by a single technician but surrounded by uniformed guards. It sends signals out into the universe in the hope of contacting alien life. [Easy to believe that money might be spent on this sort of thing in a world where everyone must at least *suspect* the existence of aliens. Harder to believe that UNIT wouldn't step in and ask whether this isn't just begging for more invasion attempts. Still, there are no "conventional" attempts to overrun the planet after this - at least until 2005, when it turns out that aliens are attracted to *any* big round metal thing, not just transmitter-dishes - so Pharos doesn't appear to cause any trouble.]

The Analysis

Where Does This Come From? First the history lesson...

In 1492, when Ferdinand and Isabella united Spain, they expelled both the Moors and the Arabic-educated Jews. Both groups settled in large numbers in Venice, where they made a notable contribution to the economic and cultural life of the city. The "Ghetto" - a local term, adopted more widely afterwards - provided Western Europe's introduction to the idea of the Kabbalah. Put crudely, this is the notion that the universe is the Word of God, naturally in Hebrew. So learn the values of letters, try different combinations, and you can "hack" the Master Control Program of the cosmos. (These days, of course, computers have conditioned most people in the western hemisphere to perceive the world as a series of computer systems and the younger generation tends to "know" this sort of thing instinctively. *The Matrix* is a bad sign.)

As this idea filtered across the continent, coinciding neatly with the Lutheran Reformation and the Renaissance generally, it became the "secret" source of much of the mainstream. We saw under "The Keeper of Traken" how the version of Elizabethan culture propagated in War-time Britain fed into the hippies and genre fantasy; now we're seeing a numerological twist. A jocular version of it, very influential on this story by all accounts, is found in "The Nine Billion Names of God" by Arthur C. Clarke. In this, monks get a computer to accelerate the iterations of all the possible names of the divinities. As they complete the task, the universe fades away, since it's now unnecessary. But in late '70s pop-culture the Kabbalah was never far from the surface, in heavy metal, SF, fantasy or the popular-science text-

books. It was often cited as the "ancient" version of mathematician Kurt Gödel's incompleteness theorem.

And in 1979 an American academic named Douglas Hofstadter wrote the immensely trendy *Godel, Escher, Bach: An Eternal Golden Braid*, which made connections between the kind of scientific concepts that make you go "hmmm" and the works of the logician, artist and musician of the title. The influence of this in *Doctor Who* is most obvious in 19.1, "Castrovalva", but there's been a subtle effect on the series ever since Season Seventeen. Indeed, Hofstadter later lamented the fact that a lot of people had been distracted by all the "cool stuff" in his book and missed the whole point of it, although at least he got a Pulitzer Prize for his trouble.

You have to put the success of this book into the context of the time. While the bright young things were dressing up as highwaymen in order to escape the grimness of post-punk Britain, the reasonably-educated grown-ups were getting abstract as well, spending more and more of their disposable income on "interesting" pieces of theoretical science. Things that had seemed terribly urgent in the '60s and '70s were now conversation-pieces. When "The Ambassadors of Death" talked about the search for extra-terrestrial life in 1970, it was an age when NASA was still going to the moon and these things looked as if they were part of our future. Whereas in 1980 the BBC was showing Carl Sagan's *Cosmos*, which described the immensity of the universe in the television equivalent of a full-colour coffee-table book, something to make the educated audience go "well, gosh" instead of something palpably real (it helped that in the special effects boom that came after 1977, it was *possible* for documentary programmes to give you casual trips to Alpha Centauri).

If it gives you some idea of the way that science and science fiction were seen by the masses, then this was a time when various SF novels were actually advertised *on television*, making them consumer objects in a way they'd never been before.

In short, this was the age of the executive toy, when the reasonably-well-off could buy all sorts of trinkets that seemed like little crystallised pieces of the scientific future-world the '60s had promised them. Everyone should remember *Newton's Cradle*, a wholly useless artefact which "demonstrated" the laws of motion with five little silver balls and some string. Note the name, though: Newton's Cradle, as if it were a little birthday-present from the world of science. Naturally this trend had its place in publishing, and *Godel, Escher, Bach* was just the tip of the iceberg. At the same time logician / magician Raymond Smullyan was publishing books full of logic puzzles for adults, with titles like *What is the Name of This Book?*, often drawing on the nonsense-logic of Lewis Carroll and inadvertently chiming with *The Hitch-Hiker's Guide to the Galaxy* at the same time. "Logopolis" is, in the nicest possible way, *Doctor Who's* answer to Newton's Cradle. Turning entropy into a tangible, elemental force makes perfect sense in a culture which was already being shown TV "reconstructions" of the creation of the universe. Entropy was "in", even for those who weren't of a scientific bent.

And self-organising structures were the way to resist entropy. We've seen how this is the theme of later Tom Baker stories (see especially 17.6, "Shada"), but now it's practically a character. The central conceit in this story is that a colony of chanting monks, arranged into "registers", can work like a computer and effectively re-program the cosmos. Rather than describing this in technical terms, here an entire *planet* is turned into the computer in question, making it fashionably visual instead of theoretical. Most significantly, it's a story that feels comfortable wiping out whole worlds, not as dramatically as the Death Star (see 18.2, "Meglos") but still demonstrating the kind of scope that people were expecting by this time.

The rise of the home computer is also worth mentioning here. Prior to this, nobody owned such devices apart from geeks - or, as they were called then, "enthusiasts" - who liked building their own machines out of kits, but in 1981 things were changing. People like Bidmead were already taking their computers apart to learn the architecture of the processors, and the rest of the world caught up that summer. (Bidmead's trusty Vectorgraphic MZ had a function by which the screen showed where the memory was "at" while a program ran, a function which provided him with the term "block transfer"... as script editor anecdotes go, it's not really up to the standard of the one about Douglas Adams and the mammoth transcontinental drinking binge.) The year before, Sinclair had brought out the ZX-80, the first ready-made computer that was anything like affordable. In 1981 they topped it with the ZX-81.

Nobody who wasn't there at the time can possibly imagine the impact this had on the psyche of the boy-spawn of Britain. A cheap, tacky little plastic box in dashing black and red, it had 1K of memory and even in *those* days everybody knew how appallingly primitive it was. But it also brought computers to the masses in a way that nothing else ever had, not only because it was cheaper than anything before it but because even those who didn't have one could play with one. ZX-81s were regularly set up in electrical shops and branches of W. H. Smith's, letting teenagers with nothing better to do write their very first programs in BASIC (10 PRINT "KNOCKERS"... 20 GOTO 10).

But here's the key thing. Backed up by a technology-obsessed government, the BBC itself embarked on a crusade to bring computer literacy to the masses - almost unthinkable, today - and eventually produced its own brand of microcomputer, largely aimed at schools and schoolchildren. In future years, the BBC Micro would be used to provide the pictures on the TARDIS screen. In episode one of "Logopolis" the graphics are done on an Acorn computer, but Acorn was the company that eventually designed the BBC machine, so the look's the same.

Almost all computers in '60s and '70s tele-SF involve banks of tape-spools, so much so that even the Daleks ended up joining in (17.1, "Destiny of the Daleks"). But this marks the start of the era in which all the technology in the universe *is* based on home computing, and a very British form of home computing, too. After all the cyclotrons of yesteryear, suddenly we're being treated to mentions of 'subroutines' and 'hexadecimal'. Perhaps the most charming moment in "Logopolis" comes when the Doctor discovers that the computers at the Pharos Project have bubble memory, a kind of memory which means that programs stay around even after the machine's switched off, and insists on explaining this idea to the audience. In the days before PCs with hard drives, this was a revelation indeed.

Things That Don't Make Sense Let us assume, first of all, that the Master's scheme to blackmail the universe is just his way of gloating over those few who can understand him and not a serious plan of conquest...

Conveniently, the cloister bell rings for the first time (as far as we've ever heard) mere minutes after the Doctor explains it to someone for the first time (as far as we've ever heard). The Master's

TARDIS arrives on the vegetation-free outskirts of Logopolis, mere feet away from a crowd of Logopolitans, disguised as a tree... and nobody notices it appear, or sees anything funny about its presence. [Maybe things pop out of nowhere on Logopolis all the time, as the locals get their sums wrong and model random space-time events.]

What does the Master actually want to *do* with Logopolis? His motivation is dubious at the best of times, but in this story he seems motiveless and erratic. He kills Auntie Vanessa, but decides that confusing Tegan by moving his TARDIS to the cloisters and laughing at her a lot is a better idea than simply shrinking her. Rather than make a break for it, he stays stock still when the Doctor's on the gantry (because it's a photo of Anthony Ainley). In episode three he doesn't bother to arm himself when he's gloating about bringing Logopolis to a standstill, but instead of rushing him everybody else just stands there warning him of what'll happen if he doesn't listen. In the same scene the Doctor figures out that Logopolis is crucial to the survival of the universe, yet later on he's surprised to hear the details, as if he just guessed that the universe was at stake [he may have got a hint from the Watcher].

The Logopolitans have apparently been working on their home computer project for years, but it takes no time at all to finish the program once it becomes vitally important to the survival of everything in existence. [Obviously the Logopolitans are perfectionists, and have just been tinkering with it for the last few months.] Why does entropy spread out from Logopolis, specifically? Or, indeed, from any one point? Why don't the visitors to Logopolis suffer the same fate as the natives, as entropy can hardly be choosy about people's planet of origin? Why does the Master's bracelet crumble, when nothing else he owns does? Why does the Master abruptly sod off from Logopolis when he sees the Monitor die, even though he's already agreed to help the Doctor and even though he must know he's doomed if he doesn't? If the TARDIS leaves space *and* time to escape the entropy, then how can Adric and Nyssa watch what's happening in the universe "now" and see the entropy spreading? Even accepting that the best way of stopping the universe's collapse is by using a radio signal from Earth, if the 'light-speed overdrive' device is any use then it must have some kind of magic decelerator attachment for when the signal gets to the CVE.

Dispatching the policeman in the opening scene, the Master's unusual tactic is to bodily drag the man into the police box *before* hitting him with the handy shrinking-weapon. The officers who later apprehend the Doctor by the roadside want to speak to him about the two doll-sized corpses found in Aunt Vanessa's car, rather than just assuming that the bodies are action figures. [This is so often cited as a flaw that it's worth repeating, but actually it makes sense. If a policeman goes missing on duty, and his fellow officers then find a doll-sized likeness of that policeman in an unattended car, then they're well within their rights to think something funny's going on even if they don't realise it's a corpse.]

On the subject of things which may or may not be feasible... the Doctor's plan to flush out the Master isn't that unreasonable, but what *is* bizarre is that after supposedly landing the TARDIS at the bottom of a river, he's prepared to open the doors without giving himself and Adric (a) any defence against the rushing water apart from 'brace yourself' and (b) any way of breathing. [If nothing else, this sequence proves that the TARDIS interior can't be infinite, or it'd drain the entire river and probably much of the water supply of England at the same time. Even so, the TARDIS interior is so massive that this ploy would have had *some* serious effect on the local environment, had the Doctor seen it through.] Besides, doesn't the Doctor realise that the Master's TARDIS is on board? Surely the Master could escape the flushing-out just by staying inside it and waiting?

Even harder to avoid is the mass planetary destruction that follows the Master's interference on Logopolis. Leaving aside the obvious "why does the Watcher think this is acceptable?" question... even if it makes sense, it doesn't sit well with the rest of *Doctor Who* as we know it. Since huge numbers of planets must die along with Traken, isn't this the single greatest alteration to the history of the universe that we've ever seen? Doesn't this cause such a massive timeline upset that *all* future history should change beyond this point, one way or another? Traken aside, surely a lot of the worlds caught up in this must be worlds the Doctor helped to "save" before now.

And what about the Time Lords? Don't they notice? Don't they step in to sort things out? Indeed, why doesn't the Doctor just ask them for assistance as soon as the crisis starts, instead of teaming up with the Master? If all he needs is a machine that can run the Logopolitan's CVE-opening program, then surely there's something a lot more reliable on Gallifrey than the Pharos computer? [You could argue that all this is *meant* to happen, and that the Watcher is just making sure history runs its course, or even that it's just the Watcher's "brief" to ensure the Fourth Doctor's death. But it seems strange in this context.]

Even in the most continuity-heavy days of the John Nathan-Turner era, it's not the place of this series to produce wanton sequels following up old stories, but this devastation seems so cataclysmic that it's odd nobody mentions it at any point. [Possible cop-out: we only actually see Traken and Logopolis suffer, and it's merely *implied* that entropy is damaging the rest of the universe as well. Perhaps these two worlds are the only inhabited parts of the universe to perish; though it's massively coincidental that the recently-visited Traken should be first on the entropic hit-list.] And for much of this story to make sense, you have to assume that the Master is capable of predicting the Doctor's actions through some form of telepathy - hence 'in many ways, we have the same mind' - which is a nice idea and might have made the Master interesting again, but it's never touched on after this.

In "The Keeper of Traken" it was obvious that Nyssa had no idea about TARDISes. Now she's able to contact the Doctor and, apparently, in such a way as to activate the cloister bell. [Close analysis of the data she picked up during the Doctor's visit, possibly?] When the Master's TARDIS materialises around the police box in the opening scene, why does the telephone inside the box somehow switch to the outside of the TARDIS instead of being swallowed up like the rest of the box? Why can't the policemen get into the TARDIS at the start of episode two, when the Doctor doesn't bother shutting the "real" TARDIS door and the only thing keeping them out are the exterior police box doors, which aren't locked? Same goes for Adric and Tegan later on.

Just before the Monitor dies in episode four, Anthony Ainley shamelessly gives Janet Fielding a nod to remind her to look in the right direction. There's a "Please Take Your Litter Home" sign by the side of the motorway, and it's right next to a litter-bin (and the sign is a prop, brought to the location by the BBC).

Vision is subjective: Nyssa sees the Doctor hit the ground a second before the others.

Critique (Prosecution)   The Second Law of Thermodynamics, the Doctor's most implacable foe. The return of the ultimate force of evil. 'A chain of event that shatter the laws that hold the Universe together.' So why does it look so crummy? The release of runaway entropy should be more impressive than a few bits of polystyrene and the lights dimming on the worst planet-model not hanging from a kindergarten ceiling. But it's more than that. The programme has lost its grandeur.

Perhaps reducing the cosmos to an Amiga graphics package wasn't the smartest move. In trying to suggest a cosmic order, as had been evident through "The Keeper of Traken" and even "Meglos", there was a quite honourable attempt to make a self-consistent world-view for the new version of the series. The cornerstone, though, needed to be big. There had to be a feeling that whatever ended this season, even if there was no climactic end for the Doctor, had to change everything. We heard rumours of an opening-out of the format into parallel universes or whatever, but what we have is lumpy security guards chasing irritating kids around in a field, as Paddy Kingsland's overheated music tries to make up the deficit.

And once again, the dialogue does nobody any favours. Adric claims that the Doctor calls the Pharos project 'a reiterated invitation to alien intelligences in deep space'. The Doctor from the late '70s would never have said anything so… pompous. But then, he would never have tolerated these kids in the first place, nor let the Master escape Traken. We've been sold a pup.

Any attempt to make the Watcher mysterious is doomed as soon as he gets his tootly music. He's supposed to be Fate, Destiny, Doom personified, and plausibly the Master's new form (see **The Lore**). You need *Omen*-type music and more cryptic photography. In the *Radio Times*, he's called the "Distant Stranger". Bidmead couldn't bring himself to suggest anything supernatural, and that's exactly what this concept needed. Similarly the Master. Reducing the motivation of any character to "I want to kill the Doctor" is bad enough, but having the Man in the Black Hat (which is all he is) coming back specifically for this story is a cop-out. Unless you're going to make him significantly more powerful, and remove the need for gloating explanations of his every move - and Bidmead's version has the tendency to give

Victorian-style brand-names to things like the Neuro-Muscular Constrictor, the Tissue Compression Eliminator and Poly-Directrix lenses, in the novelisation - why not simply have Entropy as an abstract, unbeatable force and the race-against-time plot running smoothly?

So much else is frustrating. The dim policemen. The Doctor's dim response to the dim policemen, acting like some nutter who's been watching *Doctor Who* rather than the Doctor himself. The stumblebum analogy of the universe to the faulty old TARDIS, and that to Vanessa's car. The universe has a flat and there's no repairman. And this is from a man who calls Douglas Adams 'silly'.

Critique (Defence) Some people, of course, have no sense of subtlety.

The first point that needs to be made is the most obvious one: this simply wasn't what we'd been expecting. Whether we'd been watching *Doctor Who* for years and had grown up not being scared of the Mandrels, or been occasional passers-by who knew the series was there but usually only saw it when we were waiting for *The Generation Game*, we'd all heard there was going to be a new *Doctor Who* and we all thought we knew how it'd end. This was Big Tom's last story, so it was obviously going to be a colossal showdown of some kind. There'd be explosions, there'd be spectacle, there'd be a heroic last stand (which is, as it turns out, what the leading man wanted) and there'd quite possibly be a mass attack by millions of Daleks. And yes, there'd probably be chronic *Omen*-style music. What we got instead...

...what we got instead was a work of near-crystalline silence. From the first episode it feels like a wake, and in episode three the entire universe comes to a stop, with absolute quiet reigning over Logopolis and creation itself slowly coming to dust in front of our eyes. *Quiet:* we'd been trained to think that the end of the universe would be a colossal *boom*, that at the very least there'd be spaceships involved.

The criticism from some quarters of fandom - the bizarre assessment that you could tell the same story in two episodes - misses the point horribly. It's written by Bidmead, and directed by Grimwade, with a sense of untouchable, unembraceable *space*. To say that we'd never seen this in *Doctor Who* before would be a thwacking great understatement. We'd never seen anything like this, not on television, not in the cinema.

Logopolis itself is the ultimate expression of Bidmead's science-as-environment approach, a conundrum given flesh, but more importantly given flesh as a world we really hadn't imagined. Apart from anything else, try seeing it through the eyes of the under-twelves. This is no dry, pseudo-scientific crossword-puzzle, but a whole new kind of playground, closer to the logic-expanding nature of Lewis Carroll than anything else on TV. The message was clear. This series was no longer in competition with *Buck Rogers*.

Nor does it end with Logopolis. The TARDIS, for so long misused as nothing more than a conveniently effects-free spaceship, is re-invented as a nigh-mystical puzzle-box. This is the way it always *should* have been, the sense of an apparently-magical artefact than can still be uncovered and understood by a rational mind, implicit in "An Unearthly Child" but so often ignored in the years since. For those who'd grown up taking it for granted, this was "An Unearthly Child" all over again. It starts with the cloisters, and our sudden, shocking understanding that the Ship - like the universe itself - is a system perpetually on the brink of falling apart. It develops a presence, a character, that we always *knew* it had but that we'd never seen put into effect.

Indeed, what's interesting is how much of the later lore of the *Doctor Who* universe has its roots here, not simply in terms of crass continuity (although the use of the TARDIS as an "imaginary space" will re-emerge over the next few years) but in terms of the way a whole generation would understand things. The better stories of the late '80s, the better New Adventures and the better slices of fan-lore all owe more to this story than anyone has consciously acknowledged; the notion that the mythos of *Doctor Who* isn't simply something that can be added to (e.g. all the Gallifreyan lore in "The Invasion of Time") but something that can be *unravelled*, something that can have interior depths and dimensions. In this, "Logopolis" is closer to the conscience of the programme than any story since... well... since when? Discussions of the "continuity" generally harp on about the way that it ends where the Doctor / Master relationship began, but this is as much about the future as the past.

Yes, much of it seems a little peculiar now. Yes, there are many, many logical flaws. The science isn't terribly good either, but it at least taught we-the-minors that entropy might genuinely be something worth thinking about, which is more than "Planet of Evil" ever did for anti-matter. This is more like a walk through an art gallery than an adventure, an exploration of imagery, concept and storytelling in which the array of icons - the Watcher, the silent planet, the stacked TARDISes (something which, unlike the "Time Monster" version, is used here to suggest a palpable doom) - makes absolute aesthetic sense even when the details are left unexplained. All this and the most evocative, most glittering musical score of any *Doctor Who* story, bar none.

All that needs to be said, now, is this: the departure of Doctor Number Four was always going to be the talking-point, but the greatness of this story lies in the fact that it makes the departure an event in itself, *not* a side-effect of the way television works. If you'd never seen Tom Baker's version of the Doctor before, or if you'd never had any affection for the man, then you'd still watch "Logopolis" and realise you were being told that there was something profoundly wrong with the order of things. Those who were "with" it came away understanding what we'd suspected all season, that we were suddenly being presented with a deeply unsettling universe. *On top of* that, there was the hit of sentimentality from knowing that this was 'the end', but as the new Doctor sat up in the old man's clothes we weren't exactly in floods of tears. We came away emotional, but fascinated. This is, was and always shall be how things are supposed to work.

The Facts

Written by Christopher H. Bidmead. Directed by Peter Grimwade. Viewing figures: 7.1 million, 7.7 million, 5.8 million, 6.1 million (for such a "historic" moment, this is dire).

Supporting Cast Anthony Ainley (The Master), John Fraser (The Monitor), Dolore Whiteman (Aunt Vanessa), Tom Georgeson (Detective Inspector).

Oh, Isn't That..?

• *Tom Georgeson.* He was in hit cop-show *Between the Lines*, and is now the sort of actor whose name attracts audiences to projects even when viewers forget the title. At this stage, though, he was the Kaled named Kavell from "Genesis of the Daleks" (12.4) and not a lot else.

• *Jodrell Bank.* The radio telescope used in

establishing shots of the Pharos project was as recognisable as any actor. The administrators decided not to allow filming there, but granted use of the one shot.

Cliffhangers The police show the Doctor the two shrunken corpses in Aunt Vanessa's car; on Logopolis, the block transfer calculations start to make the TARDIS shrink, with the Doctor still inside; agreeing that they have to work together to save the universe, the Doctor and the Master shake hands.

The Lore

• Tom Baker's illness and general disgruntlement with the grim new regime had made it seemingly inevitable that he'd leave at the end of the season. John Nathan-Turner had planned that the stories "The Keeper of Traken", "Project 4G" (AKA "Project Zeta-Sigma") and "Day of Wrath" would see in the replacement, and had devised a new companion to "smooth" the transition. This girl was to be a nineteen-year-old Australian air stewardess called either "Jovanka" or "Tegan". Due to a misunderstanding the character ended up as "Tegan Jovanka", suggesting mixed Cornish / Yugoslav ancestry, and had to be made 21 when the regulations governing hostesses were checked.

Then Nyssa was retained from "The Keeper of Traken", and the Master was reintroduced to kill off the Fourth Doctor. It emerged that "Project 4G" needed tuning, so this was rescheduled as the debut of the next Doctor (with "Day of Wrath" coming second; see 19.2, "Four to Doomsday"). The Australian Broadcasting Commission had approached the BBC with a view to co-production, so an Australian character and possible overseas filming seemed like a good move.

• Bidmead took on the task himself, and planned a story relating to the core concepts of the series: the TARDIS, the Master and instilling the youth of Britain with the Love of Science. It was his idea that something so fundamentally bad was to happen to the universe that nature would go into revolt, sending a "fetch" version of the Doctor's future self into the past to supervise. As this was "mystical" it had to be shown as unnatural, and the camera script was adamant that the Watcher wasn't to be dwelt upon. Indeed, to maximise the impact it was to be hinted that this was the Master's new form. (Hence the fact that the

Master doesn't appear on-screen for the first half of the story, and the 'heh-heh-heh'; Ainley's voice got a credit, while Adrian Gibbs - Rysik from "Full Circle" - was in a non-speaking role as the Watcher. So the end credits would include the Master, but Ainley wouldn't be seen… a brilliant strategy, almost thoroughly ruined by the last scene of "The Keeper of Traken".)

• Janet Fielding, recommended as a "real live" bolshy Australian, was auditioned after over a hundred others had been seen. She was challenged about her height, and improvised a story about Australasian airlines reducing the minimum height to cater for Indonesian stewardesses.

• The need for a real police box led to the Barnet bypass, only for the crew to discover that it had been knocked down a few weeks earlier due to vandalism. The old TARDIS prop used from "The Masque of Mandragora" (14.1) to "Shada" (17.6) was pressed into service.

• On location in Battersea, the original house for Aunt Vanessa turned out to be unavailable, so they used one nearby; the home of "Meglos" co-defendant Andrew McCulloch. Dolore Whiteman (Aunt Vanessa herself) is the mother of the backing-singers in "Delta and the Bannermen" (24.3).

• The music used when the TARDIS scanner shows the Thames from space, and again when the Ship lands on the dredger, is the "Reinfahrt" from Wagner's *Siegfried* (see 20.3, "Mawdryn Undead", for more Grimwade operatics).

• The story was re-shown as part of the first ever "themed" series of repeats, *The Five Faces of Doctor Who*, starting with "An Unearthly Child" around the time of the series' eighteenth birthday. By default, Davison had to be represented by the three seconds or so of the regeneration. Despite being so recent, and despite having received mediocre ratings on its first transmission, "Logopolis" inherited good ratings from the four previous stories. Nevertheless, reviews compared it unfavourably to Hartnell and Troughton (being re-evaluated for the first time as the Equity regulations were revoked; see **What Was the BBC Thinking?** under 3.1, "Galaxy Four"). And the Troughton story in question was "The Krotons" (6.4), which shows you how harsh a judgement this was. Episode three of "Logopolis" actually got higher ratings the second time round, even though it was shown on BBC2.

• The Logopolitan costumes, if you hadn't guessed, were redyed Argolin robes from "The Leisure Hive" (18.1).

• The set on which the regeneration took place was recycled from *Top of the Pops*. The scene was shot on a supposedly closed set for secrecy, but fans still managed to infiltrate the editing suite.

18.7-A: K9 and Company, "A Girl's Best Friend"

(Pilot, One 50-Minute Episode, 28th December 1981.)

Which One is This? It's the only mutant offspring of the original run of *Doctor Who*, the pilot for a spin-off series in which K9 teams up with Sarah Jane Smith and they investigate satanic goings-on in rural England. (If you've forgotten it, then don't worry; even hard-core fans tend to do that.)

Firsts and Lasts In addition to being the first and only spin-off… it's the first Doctor-Who-related piece of fodder to be script-edited by Eric Saward, future script editor of *Doctor Who* proper. Co-script-editing is Antony Root, who'll also pop up in Season Nineteen.

It's worth mentioning that the only casualty here is the local policeman, one of the very, very few people in the *Doctor Who* universe to die of natural causes and the only one to die of something as straightforward as a heart attack.

The Continuity

The Supporting Cast

• *Sarah Jane Smith.* Back in England after being abroad for a fortnight and working for Reuters, Sarah has come to Morton Harwood to write a novel. The village is home to her scientist aunt Lavinia [mentioned in 11.1, "The Time Warrior"]. She's given the keys to Lavinia's place, 'phone number Morton Harwood 778, and it's a rather substantial estate. Commander Pollock, secretly the leader of the local Hecate-worshipping coven, has been renting the east wing of the house and helping with Lavinia's market-gardening business. Sarah doesn't seem to have told anyone about the Doctor, and doesn't want to tell her relatives the truth. She's got a car, and here she's very nearly involved in a collision with a tractor, again [see 11.5, "Planet of the Spiders"].

Aunt Lavinia is briefly seen here, but goes back to America to lecture before Sarah arrives, and has an agent at Cornell University Press in New York.

Lavinia's a relative newcomer to these parts, and Sarah first met Pollock two years ago, evidently during another visit. Lavinia has a ward, Brendan Richards, who treats Sarah like a cousin. He's a well-read but sullen boy, who goes to Wellington boarding school and is taking O-Levels [so he's most likely fifteen or sixteen]. He knows far too much about computers and agriculture.

• K9. The crate containing the new K9 has been in Lavinia's possession for some time, and Sarah has never come to collect it. It's been crammed in the attic at Croydon for years [the Croydon address is Sarah's, but Lavinia - as her legal guardian - looked after things while Sarah was in space, apparently]. K9 is inactive when he's removed from the package, but comes to life as soon as one of the buttons on his back is pressed and instantly recognises Sarah as 'mistress'. He describes himself as K9 Mk. III, and says he was sent as a gift by the Doctor. [This might suggest that he's only the third K9, but see the note on the mass-production of K9s under 18.2, "Meglos".] K9's predictable response to the 'who is the Doctor?' question: 'Affirmative.'

K9 has a tri-state bus-driver and a U-ART, both components that Brendan recognises from computing c. 1981 [suggesting that the Doctor has re-designed this version of K9 to use "contemporary" pieces, thus making maintenance easier]. He has a self-charging nuclear battery and a holographic memory, and Brendan isn't surprised by these things. [Once again, science is more advanced in this world than in ours. That said, "holographic memory" was the sort of thing being bandied about in magazines like Omni at the time, so it's not too speculative.] He also has five heuristic interfaces, and can rely on his memory and his logic gates, so he doesn't need updating from a piggy-back board. He's as much a smartalec as the other two K9s, knowing plenty about horticulture and happily analysing the local soil, printing out the data on paper. But he doesn't know what a garden gnome is, and has to learn about witchcraft here. He sounds positively offended when told to 'stay'.

The stun-weapon comes fitted as standard, but this K9 is a little clumsy, knocking over ladders and breaking greenhouses. He's bossier than previous versions, forming strategies rather than just following orders. His attempt to sing is horribly flawed, and he even gets the words in the wrong order [why???].

History

• Dating. Sarah arrives in Morton Harwood on Friday the 18th of December, 1981, just in time for Christmas. K9 has been in the attic at Croydon for some time, and states that the Doctor gave Sarah his best wishes in 1978. [Sarah has obviously grown older since her last appearance in 14.2, "The Hand of Fear", and every indication is that it's been a while. The Doctor wouldn't leave K9 Mk. III on Earth before he parted company with her, so this pretty much proves that the '70s Earth-bound stories end around 1977; see **When Are the UNIT Stories Set?** under 7.1, "Spearhead from Space".]

There's still a Hecate-worshipping cult in Morton Harwood, for once not affiliated with any ancient extra-terrestrial powers, but the locals are sensitive about that sort of thing. Ram's-skull masks are involved in their ceremonies. One of the locals claims there hasn't been a human sacrifice since 1891, but they're working up to it again before Sarah and K9 expose several of the villagers as cultists. It's suggested that there must be other cults like this one all over the country.

The closest train station to the village is Chipping Norton [Gloucester].

The Analysis

Where Does This Come From? The BBC was having a great deal of success with its format for light-weight detective shows. They were fifty minutes long, made entirely on film, shot in picturesque locations and with a small cast of regulars whose involvement in the caper was often spurious. Usually the writers and producers were names familiar to Doctor Who credit-watchers (Robert Holmes, Bob Baker, Chris Boucher, George Gallaccio, Pennant Roberts, Douglas Camfield…). The model for this format was the more blokish Euston Films productions like The Sweeney, shown on ITV. BBC's first effort at this, Target - with optional exclamation mark - has been discussed in an earlier volume (see 14.5, "The Robots of Death"). "Terror of the Zygons" author Robert Banks Stewart offered lighter, character-led dramas like Shoestring. Christopher Bidmead was a huge fan and wrote to Stewart, which is what led to him getting the Doctor Who gig.

Looked at coldly, K9 and Company is a pilot for just such a series, but aimed at a younger audience and without the "made entirely on film" fea-

What *Other* Spin-Offs Were Planned?

For the purposes of this piece we're taking "planned" to mean "proposed by someone in a position to be listened to by the people in charge", not seriously timetabled or budgeted. Some of these may perhaps have been exaggerated as a result of interviews and convention panels. Some are documented, though, as serious options (and in some cases, escape-plans for production staff keen to get away from the career-killing influence of *Doctor Who*).

Son of Doctor Who. William Hartnell proposed a twist on the format as early as Season Two. In this, the Doctor's estranged son (also to be played by Hartnell) has a better-equipped TARDIS and sets about trying to rewrite history. The real Doctor therefore has to set things to rights and avoid being mistaken for the malefactor, as well as handling whatever caused the division.

As you may already have noticed, this idea crops up in various forms throughout the programme's run, particularly in Hartnell's period. It can't be coincidence that episode five of "The Chase" (2.8) is called "The Death of Doctor Who" and features an android duplicate, in order to test the logistics of Billy-on-Billy action. Nor is the plot of the next story, "The Time Meddler", entirely dissimilar. Six months later the Abbot of Amboise in "The Massacre" (3.5) allows Hartnell to play a different character, and to the casual viewer is either the Doctor in "up to something" mode or a sinister doppelganger trying to sabotage history. It must also be said that the experience of having Edmund Warwick play the Doctor's evil twin in "The Chase" was less than satisfactory, and was probably the means by which Hartnell was persuaded to drop the idea. Also, by this time the notion of the Doctor having a family somewhere was seen as something of a blind alley, and Susan was pretty much hushed-up.

Jago and Litefoot Investigate. For years this was thought to have been a fan rumour, but paperwork has been found showing that at least one of the BBC hierarchy thought it had "legs". In the late '70s the Victoriana boom was fading, although period-piece soaps like *The Duchess of Duke Street* persisted. The huge impact of "The Talons of Weng Chiang" (14.6) made a series set in 1890s London, with fantasy overtones and singalong set-pieces in the style of *The Good Old Days*, look possible. Certainly Granada Television could see the potential of Victorian romps, and optioned the *Sergeant Cribb* novels as a series of hour-long filmed episodes. Some years earlier Thames had produced a short series of adaptations of "Penny Dreadfuls" and "Shilling Shockers" called *The Rivals of Sherlock Holmes*, compiled and presented by the BBC's former Director General Sir Hugh Greene, and many of these had involved mad scientists. There was clearly an audience for this sort of thing, but it would appear that reports of *Cribb* (which, being on film, had a longer lead-in time and only reached our screens in 1980) made it seem impractical. Also, Christopher "Jago" Benjamin was committed to the Thames sitcom *It Takes A Worried Man* at the time this is said to have been planned. One report, unsubstantiated as yet, has the BBC rethinking the idea when the Granada *Sherlock Holmes* series ran out of steam; but this would have been during Michael Grade's reign as BBC1 supremo, so it seems unlikely.

UNIT. Everyone reading this can see that there's a possible series here. The trouble is, which one? It could have been something like early '70s hit *Doomwatch*, and involved a small team of undercover investigators tackling environmental hazards and sinister schemes. It could have been a proto-*X-Files* set-up, as *The Omega Factor* later became. It could conceivably, with the success of episode one of "The Ambassadors of Death" (7.3), have been "Yeti-in-the-loo"-formula *Doctor Who* without the foppish Time Lord. UNIT even had its own theme-tune (see also 8.2, "The Mind of Evil").

The title is the problem here. "United Nations Intelligence Taskforce" sounds good, but what does it mean? There's nothing in this to suggest that "they're here to save the world" in a *Man from UNCLE* sort of way, let alone that they're the paramilitary wing of scientific investigators like Quatermass or Quist in *Doomwatch*. A series based on the UNIT of "The Invasion" (6.3) would be prohibitively expensive. A show like the UNIT of "The Time Monster" (9.6) was redundant while *Dad's Army* was being made. Another snag, of course, is the production team. There was arguably only one person who could have made this show a hit: Douglas Camfield. And his wife and doctors had advised him to avoid the stress of making *Doctor Who*.

It was also a standard BBC ploy to take a popular character and relocate that person in a new job or setting. When Stratford Johns and Frank

continued on page 97...

ture. The overseas sales of *Shoestring*, and the residual interest in both Sarah and K9 among British viewers, made it worth a shot. Nor should we forget that by this stage, "cute" robots were everywhere. K9 predated Twiki from *Buck Rogers* by some years, but there was at least a precedent for internationally-distributed programmes that used (excuse us) "droids" as a way of drawing in the kids.

The specifics of the script, however, were from another tradition. The interest in Paganism amongst thriller-writers far outweighed its popularity in rural Britain. A few bored teens may have left goats' heads around when off their faces on mushrooms and snakebite (the tipple of choice for Goths), but films like *The Wicker Man* (1971), *Psychomania* (1972) and groundbreaking TV play "Robin Redbreast" (1970) would leave you convinced that it was a bucolic epidemic. There's also a hint of *Rosemary's Baby* here, though on this occasion the people who are creepily polite and welcoming to Sarah turn out to be among the few who *aren't* involved in the cult (Sarah insists on doing a "just think, I thought you were evil Satanists, too" line, to try to underline what a clever twist this is).

Deliverance it ain't, but the suspicion of outsiders is a familiar strain in stories set in the back of beyond…

Things That Don't Make Sense (Note that this was originally planned as a ninety-minute pilot, so a lot of the elisions make no sense as the reasons for things aren't set up properly. Nevertheless…)

What possible reason could farmer George Tracy and his son Peter have to break into the Smith household the first time round, especially as Peter then warns Brendan to leave? Even with George Tracy being in the coven, Peter would never risk his probation officer finding out, surely? Brendan clearly sees George as well as we do, but fails to recognise him - dressed the same way - the next morning. He's asked 'would you recognise them again?' and answers no, while standing three feet away from the guilty party (and George is so flagrantly acting in a "I hope he doesn't say yes" way that even a dim cop like Sergeant Wilson should be able to spot it).

Commander Pollock introduces himself to someone he's already met, and screams before K9 zaps him from behind. The production team's decision to turn Lavinia Smith into a best-selling

author rather than a writer of obscure scientific papers leads to the unusual phenomenon of an 'eminent virologist' with an agent. Brendan claims that the plant he's got in his hand, and the soil with it, are pH 7; the soil over yonder is pH 11. Aside from being physically impossible, the fact that so many alkaline levels in one acre hasn't got the local lawyers investigating chemical dumping or a big claim for compensation from the EU agriculture commission is rather odd. Oh, and Brendan can assess soil acidity by smell.

Lavinia's friend Juno Baker talks of herself and her quiet husband as 'locals'. This might be a very subtle joke, but draws attention to the depressingly familiar '70s *Doctor Who* syndrome of a village where no two residents have the same accent (even George and Peter Tracy). This is specified as a short drive from either Chipping Norton or Cirencester, but many of the residents seem to be from somewhere nearer Norwich. Bill Pollock meanders around the North of England. (American readers may like to imagine a redubbed *Dallas* with Woody Allen as JR, Salma Hayek as Sue-Ellen, Woody Harrelson as Bobby, Vincent Price as Jock and Bjork as Miss Ellie.)

It's still light at 4.15 pm on the 20th of December. The Solstice is said to be the 22nd, when it's really the night of the 20th and 21st (or it was that year). It's specified that the 20th is a Sunday in 1981 - so obviously someone looked at a calendar when making this - and there's a full moon that night. But there wasn't.

Critique If ever there was an example of a "project" falling between two stools, then this is it. Wherever we have one scene looking like a spooky adventure series, there's another looking like a "mainstream" one-off play about market gardening. So while we have some fairly solid - if dull - performances, one or two cast-members are indulging in children's television acting. Does it want to be an action-packed spectacle, or a comedy of manners? It's obvious why Brendan (of all people) should be the sacrifice, but they can't say it on a kiddy show. The look of the thing is as much a mess as the truncated script. There's a lot to be said for the filmed work, and the general ambience of the rural backwater; there's something to be said for the studio work's sense of a few snug cottages, cut off from urban civilisation with the nights drawing in. But the two don't gel, and we don't have any reason to care about either.

What *Other* Spin-Offs Were Planned?

...continued from page 95

Windsor left *Z Cars*, they got a spin-off series (*Softly, Softly*) which was left to its own devices and had spin-offs of its own. Similarly, cop-shows like *Rockcliffe's Babies* were spawned by one character leaving and getting on with something else (see the essay under 2.1, "Planet of Giants", for more). So a Brigadier Lethbridge-Stewart solo project, or maybe a post-Season-Eleven Mike Yates project, could certainly have happened.

Of course the other possibility is that this wasn't initially proposed as a Pertwee-UNIT spin-off, but a replacement for *Doctor Who* after 1969 (see 6.7, "The War Games"). "The Invasion" could have been the pilot for the new Saturday Teatime adventure series. And in a sense, it was exactly that.

Mr. Oak and Mr. Quill. Every time someone interviews Victor Pemberton about "Fury from the Deep" (5.6), he brings up the plan which he claims was seriously proposed for the story's seaweed-possessed double-act to get their own show. And the audience nods sympathetically, then retires to the bar to avoid laughing at him. But ponder the way things were, c. 1968; the Production Office had a revolving door, with script-editors finding themselves producing for a week or so, directors making up the stories as they went along and everyone trying to jump what seemed like a sinking ship.

It's got to be said, though… Oak and Quill don't have a lot of potential. Only one of them speaks, and they were menacing partly because of the make-up and partly because of the intrusion of the alien weed into domestic kitchens. Very little of their impact was due to the dialogue, characterisation, acting or music (an odd amalgam of "Pink Elephants on Parade" and the "Cuckoo" music from Laurel and Hardy shorts accompanied them on their malefaction). Perhaps they would have tried different jobs each week. Insurance salesmen, scoutmasters, bus-driver and conductor, pop stars (anyone who remembers Sparks will have fun with this)… it could have been the *Mr. Bean* of the late '60s. Of course, today the notion of a camp, northern, middle-aged Jay and Silent Bob would be commissioned straight away.

The Daleks. Before the "Dalek Empire" audio series was even a glint in Big Finish's eye, Terry Nation spent about fifteen years trying to get a big company interested in his project of a Dalek Wars series. After the BBC and commercial companies rejected his idea, he moved to America. But no-one unaware of the pepperpots' impact in '60s Britain could see any potential in what was basically just a standard "Space Rangers" scenario.

It's possible to imagine that Nation stayed in his trailer, ranting - this is certainly the impression one gets from some accounts - but let's not forget that he was very secure. Aside from his rights to the Daleks, there were residuals from franchised TV shows he made for ITC (*The Baron* alone would have kept him afloat, and financially if not creatively the Tara King *Avengers* episodes he'd script-edited and occasionally written were the high point of the series). When he went back to the BBC after seven years, he had *Survivors* and *Blake's 7* up his sleeve. But most financially rewarding of all, even if not one British viewer in a hundred would have heard of it if it hadn't been repeatedly mentioned in *The Simpsons*, was *MacGyver*. For American TV bosses, Terry Nation was an established writer and producer, a Somebody. And he had an agent, Roger Hancock, who took no prisoners.

Let's face it, far worse projects have made it onto American television because the creator's reputation is enough to get a green light. People like Irwin Allen, Glen A. Larson or Donald P. Bellisarius would get any amount of high-concept piffle onto prime-time with reputations about as powerful as Nation's was after *MacGyver*. (Gene Roddenberry still gets back-of-an-envelope doodles made into shows, a dozen years after his death.) With the groundswell of interest in *Doctor Who* in some parts of the States around 1982, it was certainly worth another try. The reason it didn't happen has been a mystery to fans, but anyone who wasn't a child in Britain at any point between 1963 and 1979 can explain it. Frankly, all too often, the Daleks just aren't very interesting.

It starts with Lavinia talking about villagers we don't know and discussing her gardening business, and doesn't get any more interesting, not even when it frantically attempts to drum up tension by dressing a pallid teenage boy in a skimpy robe and trying to get K9 to sound urgent when counting down the time until he's sacrificed. Even as a "younger viewers" programme, it just underlines K9's silliness, especially when one of the superstitious villagers sees the big tin toy in action and starts ranting insanely about 'the goddess Hecate's familiar… a dog belching fire!'.

97

Sarah and K9 might actually have worked in a spin-off series. Just not *this* one. Juno Baker might have been a better foil for Lavinia Smith in a weird *Mapp and Lucia* kind of way (and indeed, Mary Wimbush is now playing almost exactly that role in *The Archers*, BBC Radio's social comedy masquerading as a soap opera about farmers). But Sarah and K9 need a big city and international conspiracies, not a bunch of hicks and goat-fearing bobbies. Like the *Doctor Who* TV Movie (27.0), its failure as a pilot is even greater than its failure as a piece of television in its own right. The last scene has Sarah hinting that there are satanic covens all over the country, apparently in an attempt to lead in to a possible "episode one", but it's difficult to imagine what episode one might actually be like... except for the suspicion that it'd be virtually identical to the fifty minutes you've already seen.

Fan humour can be cruel, but when it was discovered that the title sequence synchs *exactly* with the original theme to *Scooby Doo*, all reviews became redundant.

The Facts

Written by Terence Dudley. Directed by John Black. Viewing figures: 8.4 million (a power-cut affected the transmitter for the Liverpool / Manchester area).

Supporting Cast Elisabeth Sladen (Sarah Jane Smith), John Leeson (Voice of K9), Mary Wimbush (Aunt Lavinia), Colin Jeavons (George Tracey), Bill Fraser (Bill Pollock), Nigel Gregory (Vince Wilson), Sean Chapman (Peter Tracey), Ian Sears (Brendan), Linda Polan (Juno Baker), Neville Barber (Howard Baker), John Quarmby (Henry Tobias), Gillian Martell (Lilly Gregson), Stephen Oxley (P.C. Carter).

Working Titles *Sarah and K9*, "One Girl and Her Dog".

The Lore

• The first draft had a twist: this version of K9 was built by the Master as a trap (because he's always had such a grudge against Sarah...?), but then rebuilt by Brendan. Sarah's background was collated and refined in a document - for the first time ever, as it turns out - by Nathan-Turner and

Antony Root. In this, she's revealed to have been orphaned when young and raised on the proceeds of Aunt Lavinia's book *Teleological Response of the Virus* (it was a paper when the Doctor mentioned it, in 11.1, "The Time Warrior"). She got a First at University, after setting up the college paper. She was made redundant when the London paper for which she was diary editor and columnist was merged, and retired to Moreton Harewood to write a novel. And not, as is often surmised in fan-fiction, an exposé of UNIT.

• It was in the final re-writes that Eric Saward took over the script-editing duties from Antony Root. His requests for clarifications and amendments led to terse comments from writer Terence Dudley, which had a negative effect on their relations when working together later. Nathan-Turner's insistence on using his old colleague's scripts was the first source of friction between producer and script editor (see 20.6, "The King's Demons").

• For Season Nineteen, Nathan-Turner was given the budget for another 28-episode season. He decided to make 26 episodes instead, and use the left-over time and resources to produce this spin-off. The studio work was shot in November 1981 at Birmingham's Pebble Mill studios (as used for 15.1, "Horror of Fang Rock"), as the "real" programme was filming "Earthshock" (19.6) in London.

• The theme music was written by Ian Levine and Fianchra Trench. In addition to being the programme's self-appointed continuity expert, Levine's "day-job" was head of disco label Record Shack, where Trench was an employee. Trench has since been active in scoring and arranging film music, but this was one of his first gigs. This remains Levine's only accredited contribution to anything officially *Doctor-Who*-related (but see 22.6, "Revelation of the Daleks" for his semi-official charity "protest" record *Doctor In Distress*, which we suspect was mentioned in Nostradamus somewhere).

• In 2004, Jon Ronson's book *The Men Who Stare at Goats* - and the accompanying TV series on Channel 4 - uncovered the odd fact that certain cliques within US Special Forces repeatedly performed experiments with the aim of telekinetically stopping the hearts of goats, just by staring at them. In light of this, Sarah's discovery of the dead policeman in "A Girl's Best Friend" looks much like the same process with the roles reversed...

19.1: "Castrovalva"

(Serial 5Z, Four Episodes, 4th - 12th January 1982.)

Which One is This?   The new boy does impressions of his forebears, Nyssa and Tegan leave a pram in the river, Adric gets stapled to a climbing-frame (and finds out that "hadron" is an anagram), and the Master disappears up his own existence in a city that's inside itself.

Firsts and Lasts   First full appearance of Peter Davison as the Fifth Doctor, although by this point he's already getting into the swing of things, as most of this season's stories were filmed out of sequence and this was the fourth one he'd done (the first and only time, as it happens, that an incoming Doctor got the chance to "practice" before making his debut). Now that all the characters are in place, here we see the start of the "soap opera" TARDIS line-up, with Adric, Nyssa and Tegan all digging in for the next six stories and the Master firmly establishing himself as lead recurring baddie. And just as the companions seem intent on wearing "uniforms" in this era, the new Doctor immediately takes to wearing the cricketing costume that he'll keep right until the end of his run, sticking a sprig of celery to the lapel for no good reason whatsoever.

It's also the first time that Eric Saward does the script-editing duties, the first time that the end credits conceal the Master's appearance with a contrived anagram ("Neil Toynay"), and the first time the Doctor uses "Master" as a proper noun with no article.

But perhaps most significantly of all, this was the point when *Doctor Who* moved days, from its traditional place (and since it had been going for eighteen years, it really *did* feel like a tradition) at Saturday tea-time to a twice-weekly evening slot on Mondays and Tuesdays. Or Mondays and Wednesdays, if you were living in Wales. Those who weren't around at the time may find it hard to believe how disconcerting this was, but we'll come to that later...

Four Things to Notice About "Castrovalva"...

1. Castrovalva itself, a pleasingly three-dimensional arrangement of archways, stairways, bal-

Season 19 Cast/Crew

- • Peter Davison (the Doctor)
- • Matthew Waterhouse (Adric, 19.1 to 19.6)
- • Sarah Sutton (Nyssa)
- • Janet Fielding (Tegan)

- • John Nathan-Turner (Producer)
- • Eric Saward (Script Editor, 19.1, 19.3, 19.5, 19.6 uncredited, 19.7)
- • Antony Root (Script Editor, 19.2, 19.4, 19.6)

conies and peculiar angles, is - as the name might suggest - based on the designs of Dutch artist M. C. Escher (much, much more of this in **Where Does This Come From?**). This is a novelty in *Doctor Who*, a planet that's based on the catalogue of one particular artist instead of a terrain type. We used to have desert-planets, volcano-planets and no end of quarry-planets, but now we're moving up in the world.

What's most striking is that it manages to turn Escher's impossible architecture into solid reality on a BBC budget, although as per usual, the sets are more impressive than the visual effects and things go a bit wrong when the script requires the town's dimensions to collapse in on themselves. Nonetheless, the best moment here comes when the Doctor forces one of the native Castrovalvans to see what's wrong with this world by getting the man to draw a map, at which point the poor bewildered soul (played by Michael Sheard, for extra sympathy value) has to confront the fact that his home seems to be in four different places at once.

2. This brings us on to Peter Davison himself. At the time, many had difficulty believing that anyone could fill Tom Baker's big boots, and Davison solves the problem by going to the opposite extreme; by being perpetually puzzled, vulnerable and unsure of himself, quite specifically trying *not* to dominate every scene. Pretty much the first thing he's required to do as the Doctor is fall over, which is a nice start. (At one point he has to giggle in the style of William Hartnell, and does it more convincingly than Richard Hurndall; see 20.7, 'The Five Doctors'.) But the essence of the Fifth Doctor is best-defined when, during his post-regenerative state of bewilderment and

amnesia, a small child in Castrovalva has to teach him how to count. Suddenly, this youngest of all Doctors is one of the kids instead of *with* the kids.

3. Oh, and while we're on the subject of Tom Baker's boots… "Castrovalva" follows directly on from "Logopolis", but was made some time later, so spot the continuity glitches. The aforementioned boots have regenerated into shoes between seasons; the TARDIS has unexpectedly moved into a new field; and the security guards at the Pharos Project have all got new faces, just like the Doctor has. Perhaps this is why nobody asks whether the universe is still doomed, as it appeared to be the last time we were all here.

4. Episode one opens with the first pre-credits sequence since "The Ambassadors of Death" in 1970 (7.3), a recap of the last moments of the Fourth Doctor that leads into the new, Davison-faced title sequence with an almighty whoosh. It should be pointed out that just two months earlier, BBC2 had begun the *Five Faces of Doctor Who* season, the very first time that "old" Doctor Who stories had been screened on the BBC and therefore the very first time that those of the younger generation had seen Hartnell, Troughton or Pertwee in action (for the record, the repeated stories were "An Unearthly Child"; "The Krotons"; "The Three Doctors"; "Carnival of Monsters"; and finally a reprise of "Logopolis"). In the days before anything was available on video, this was quite unbearably exciting, and made us feel as if we were working up to the beginning of a whole new age. With "Castrovalva" picking up the baton where "Logopolis" left off, there was a real sense of *impetus* here, a real buzz in the air as Davison took over. Were we disappointed? Well, let's see…

The Continuity

The Doctor Behold the new Doctor. Younger, fitter, blonder and - there's no other word - more "boyish" than his predecessor, here he's deeply unstable after his metamorphosis, but even so it's already clear that he's a lot more "human" than he was. Whereas the previous version had no problem alienating any mere mortals who got in his way, the new model seems far more vulnerable, and is at least *trying* to talk to the people around him as if he were on their level.

He describes this regeneration as 'difficult', and seems muddled, distracted and physically weak while he's in Castrovalva, only really pulling himself together at the end of the affair. By that point he's ready to take the lead again, confidently striding back to the TARDIS with his companions in tow. Though he appears rather disappointed the first time he sees his new face in a mirror, ultimately he seems convinced that everything's going to work out splendidly.

While recovering his wits, the Doctor states that Tegan has it in her to be a 'fine co-ordinator'; that Nyssa has the technical skill to pull them all through this time of crisis; and that Adric 'knows' him. [This might imply that the Watcher in "Logopolis" was rounding up the necessary crew for what was to follow.] As in earlier regenerations, his fashion sense is dictated by the first clothes he comes across while he's recovering; an ensemble which involves a yellow jacket, a shirt with question-marks on its lapels and striped trousers, the clothes of a cricketing man. [See the next story, and 19.5, "Black Orchid". Indeed, as with the Third Doctor - see 7.1, "Spearhead from Space" - these props may help him define his new personality, since there's quite a *Boy's Own* feel to this Doctor once he stabilises.]

While his mind's scrambled he repeatedly quotes the dialogue of his earlier incarnations, as well as mistaking his companions for previous members of the TARDIS crew. When the TARDIS hurtles backwards in time towards the beginning of the galaxy, the heat and excitement temporarily affect the bewildered Doctor's biochemistry and seem to make his brain work faster.

The Doctor can identify the common-or-garden herbal ingredients of Castrovalvan medicine by tasting it, but nonetheless claims that he doesn't know as much about medicinal matters as the town's Master of Physic.

• *Ethics.* The Doctor acts as if the "artificial" people of Castrovalva are "real", and is prepared to bargain for their lives with the Master. He's happy to hope that the Master is dead, and doesn't act as if he has any sentimental attachment to his old nemesis at all. [Unlike the Third Doctor. Still, the Third Doctor seemed to relish the challenge of an arch-enemy, whereas the new version is much less brash and has recently been through a painful rebirth thanks to the villain in question.]

• *Inventory.* He's got a pad and a pencil in his new jacket, plus a pair of spectacles, which he initially seems to need for reading and writing [see also the next story]. He's already transferred the sonic screwdriver to his new clothes. He equates

What Difference Does a Day Make?

It seems almost impossible, now. These days, if a TV station moves a programme from one day to another then it's a purely pragmatic, no-nonsense decision, and all anyone can ask is whether its new position will maximise the viewing share of the target demographic. Yet when *Doctor Who* changed days in 1982, from the Saturday tea-time slot it had held since 1963 to a twice-weekly evening slot on Mondays and Tuesdays, it was *news*. The story got its own column on the front page of *The Times*, supposedly Britain's most "serious" newspaper: TIME-SLIP FOR DOCTOR WHO.

It's already been said in previous volumes of this work, but it's difficult to explain the way Britain saw television before the 1980s. The modern world likes to think of TV as an idiot-box by definition, an unhealthy influence on the minds of the young that's bleached society's brains and caused a catastrophic decline in levels of literacy... but it's a view that largely comes from the *American* media, and America has never had anything like the BBC.

Ah, the BBC. A body which traditionally thought of itself as a lynchpin of the national community as much as a company that made light entertainment programmes. A body which pioneered some of the most revolutionary techniques in television simply because it had a mandate to. Even when the BBC was in competition with commercial television, there was always that sense of Britain being one big village. We've already mentioned that in the 1970s, Saturday Night was *the* big night on TV, not because the two major UK stations broadcast all their audience-grabbing shows on that evening (although they did) but because the Saturday TV-fest was an event in itself. It was the night when the entire family watched as one. *Doctor Who* and *Basil Brush* were of the greatest interest to the children, but at the heart of the process was *The Generation Game*, which at one stage was watched by a third of the total population.

Everybody, *everybody*, knew these programmes. Even if you didn't watch them every week, everyone watched them sometimes. The erratic viewing figures for *Doctor Who* in that period demonstrate that the audience was big-but-fickle. Circa 1977, the Saturday evening BBC line-up was a focal-point of the whole nation. It's tempting to try to think of a modern equivalent, but the fact is, there isn't one.

So when *Doctor Who* moved days, it wasn't just about *Doctor Who*, and it wasn't just the end of an eighteen-year tradition for one single programme. It was a change to a much bigger order of things.

It was also the best move the series could possibly have made. Because by 1982, the Saturday Night line-up was dying.

The problem was this: the 1980s was the decade in which family TV ceased to exist. In part, this was due to a shift in technology. As the '80s wore on, hardware became so disposable that individual members of the household could afford to have their own TV sets, and no surly teenager with a colour portable would ever sink to the level of watching the same programmes as his or her parents. Remote-control units made people less likely to stick with a single channel for an entire evening. Video was on the rise, making the public's viewing habits go non-linear; there was no longer one single point when everybody *had* to watch.

But more important than the technology, there was the politics. You know all the clichés about the 1980s, about a generation that grew up wanting to be "career professionals" instead of astronauts, about a decade in which designer goods and crippling self-involvement were the height of fashion. The very idea of TV as part of the community - indeed, the very idea of "community" - was out of vogue (c.f. Margaret Thatcher's famous statement that 'there's no such thing as society'). In Britain, there was a time when a "Corporation" was the municipal body that made sure all the public amenities were in working order. Now the meaning of the word had changed, and the British Broadcasting Corporation was about to become truly *corporate*, in the modern and more depressing sense. This was the era of the audience demographic. This was the era when we all went American.

Let's sum it up like this: when the Director-General of the BBC said in 2004 that he considered the institution to be the greatest cultural force for good in the world, everyone sniggered. If he'd said it twenty-five years earlier, nobody would have found it remotely strange.

There was a massive ratings drop in *Doctor Who* between Season Seventeen and Season Eighteen. The first episode of "Destiny of the Daleks" had thirteen-million viewers; the first episode of "The Leisure Hive" had less than six-million. This had nothing to do with the content of the series; ratings were poor even from the first week, before

continued on page 103...

celery with civilisation, and eventually sticks a sprig of it to the lapel of his jacket. [Which is curious for a number of reasons. The celery's usefulness is finally explained in 21.6, "The Caves of Androzani", but *this* celery would seem to come from Castrovalva and therefore isn't "real"; by rights, it should cease to exist when the rest of the settlement does. Nor is it explained why his jacket is capable of holding the celery in place. The sprig is seen to be replaced in 20.5, "Enlightenment".]

• *Background*. During his post-regenerative crisis, the Doctor exclaims 'not far now, Brigadier, if the Ice Warriors don't get there first'. [He could just be gabbling, but since virtually everything else he says in his confusion sounds like a direct quote from one of his earlier selves, this *could* indicate that at some point he and the Brigadier met the Ice Warriors and we never got to hear about it. He also seems to think that a description of the events of "Day of the Daleks" (9.1) is a suitable after-dinner anecdote for the timid Castrovalvans.]

The Supporting Cast

• *Adric*. Kidnapped by the Master and used to create the Castrovalva space-time trap for the Doctor - see **The Supporting Cast (Evil)** - Adric nonetheless remains crafty, and does everything he can to resist [a far cry from his behaviour in the next story]. Not for the first time, he pretends to side with the villain. It's Adric, or at least a projection of Adric, who sets the TARDIS co-ordinates for Castrovalva. [The Master may tell him how to do this, but he's already getting the hang of the co-ordinates in 18.6, "The Keeper of Traken".]

Judging by the state of his clothing when he's hooked up to the Master's block transfer web, Adric dresses to the right.

• *Nyssa*. Clued-up enough to make guesses as to what the TARDIS console instruments are, although initially she only knows how to work the door control and the instruments are too complex for her to attempt to fly it. The Doctor recalls that bioelectronics is her strong point, and thus expects her to understand the TARDIS zero room. She describes the Doctor's period of regeneration with the word 'telebiogenesis', but says she knows little about such things. She's still got her ion bonder [from "The Keeper of Traken"], which she uses to make a zero cabinet for the Doctor, but it gets water-logged and rendered useless here.

• *Tegan*. Not whining about wanting to get back home, surprisingly. She's unusually quick to accept the new Doctor as *the* Doctor, and the fact that she helps him escape from the security guards at the Pharos Project - rather than, say, giving up in the hope of getting back home - suggests she already thinks of herself as part of the team. Indeed, Tegan, Nyssa and Adric are already working well together [it won't last]. Tegan apparently learns how to set TARDIS co-ordinates here, but the successful landing turns out to be part of the Master's scheme [and she's apparently clueless when she tries to use the Ship again in the next story]. She's still got her handbag, and she's brought lipstick with her, a different shade to the one she's wearing. 'Rabbits' is still her favourite swearword.

Tegan's dad used to say that "if" was the most powerful word in the English language. She considers Brisbane to be cut off from the rest of the universe. [It's worth pondering whether her use of the past tense whenever she talks about her father is significant. See **Who Went to Aunt Vanessa's Funeral?** under 21.2, "The Awakening".]

The Supporting Cast (Evil)

• *The Master*. Yet again, the Master's insistence on setting elaborate and humiliating traps for the Doctor beggars belief, and he's wholly motivated by spite on this occasion. He sounds downright unhinged when his plans are thwarted. He displays a modicum of what appears to be telepathic power, sensing it when Adric's plotting against him [but he shows no sign of being able to instantly hypnotise his victims, as he so often did in his old body].

It's the Master who devises the Castrovalva trap for the Doctor [suggesting that the Master knows the work of Escher, not the first time he's had a passing interest in human culture], and he's creative enough to pose as the Portreeve on Castrovalva, an achievement as the people of Castrovalva use a far more poetic form of language than the Master's usual "nyah-hah-hah" mode of speech. His weapon, apparently the same thing he uses to shrink people, has no effect on the Doctor's zero cabinet.

The Master has set up a painful-looking metal web which is either inside his own TARDIS or on a planet in the Andromedan Phylox Series, into which Adric is firmly strapped after the Master kidnaps him. Funnily enough, the room which

What Difference Does a Day Make?

...continued from page 101

anybody had really seen the programme's new look. It's notable that whereas most *Doctor Who* seasons suffered a ratings slump after the first couple of stories, ratings held more or less steady throughout Season Eighteen and actually increased towards the end (partly due to the publicity surrounding Tom Baker's departure, but partly because the decline in family viewing saw a loyal, regular audience replacing the big-but-fickle one).

The truth is that *all* the Saturday Night ratings-winners suffered from dwindling audiences around this time. As has been mentioned elsewhere, *Doctor Who* was particularly hard-hit because it was perceived as an SF show - Season Seventeen had been quite spaceship-heavy, remember - at a time when a lot of people were getting sick of SF and a lot of others were getting their spaceship-fix from other programmes. Old-style *Doctor Who* fans still have a fetishistic love of the Saturday Night slot, which is why the makers of the new, 2005 series insisted on it even though Saturday is now the day which gets the lowest TV audiences. This may, in fact, be one of the reasons that the BBC is making a new series at all; to try to regain this "lost" time-slot.

But the truth is that if *Doctor Who* had stayed where it was in 1982, then it almost certainly would have been cancelled before 1989. Indeed, it was only when it moved *back* to Saturdays (for Season Twenty-Two, in 1985) that the trouble really started. Saturday was the day for an audience that no longer existed. Is it really any surprise that the '80s episodes seem less fondly-remembered by the general public than the '70s episodes? The content of the stories is almost irrelevant. The '70s episodes were watched by children in an atmosphere of actual *excitement*, when everybody sat down and expected to be presented with something shiny and new. The '80s episodes were watched by an audience so casual that it really wasn't too bothered *what* it saw, an audience that was quite happy to channel-surf if it got bored after the first two minutes.

Besides, there was simply more "stuff" in the world than there had been. Why would a teenager in the mid-'80s stay home with his family and watch a programme like *Doctor Who* when he could go round his friend's house and play computer games instead?

(A small point, but a telling one: there was a new generation of TV sets. Even apart from the affordability, the portability and the potential for channel-zapping, the new sets took mere moments to warm up. Which meant that there was less reason to have the television switched on, if nothing you specifically wanted to watch was being shown. '60s and '70s television was the golden age of accidental hits, with people finding that they enjoyed things which hadn't looked promising in the published schedules. *Mastermind*: a quiz based on minutiae, in a format devised by the producer after being interrogated by the Nazis. *Pot Black*: a speed-snooker tournament designed specifically to let TV engineers test the new colour transmission system. *Monty Python's Flying Circus*: well, you probably know that one. But now, if you weren't that bothered then there was no reason to keep watching.)

There were other considerations, though. The slot into which *Doctor Who* was now placed had its own constituency. It was the home of *Angels* (about trendy young nurses), of *District Nurse* (about a mumsy middle-aged nurse in rural Wales in the 1950s), and above all of the spectacularly dire *Triangle*. (That show was about... dear God... about a North Sea ferry and its glamorous crew and passengers, written in the main by Pip and Jane Baker. The very first episode opened with Kate O'Mara sunbathing topless on the deck, a desperate attempt to be "sexy" like the US soaps even though O'Mara was apparently trying to soak up the rays on a drizzly, overcast, painfully English-sea-side sort of day.) These were all soap operas, and had enough redundancy that you could miss alternate episodes if - say - you were out on Wednesdays.

When they made bi-weekly *Doctor Who*, they had to try to make it comprehensible to anyone who might have had Scouts or piano lessons for half the screen-time, usually in the form of info-dump dialogue and scenes beginning 'surely you remember, Tegan...'. As we've seen, the series' production team was more concerned with boys' things, but this was a broadly "feminine" timeslot. It was after a current affairs series - the hallowed institution *Nationwide* went all serious at around this time, for more on which see 20.6, "The King's Demons" - and before a sitcom. After that came *Dallas*.

continued on page 105...

contains this climbing-frame of evil looks much like the zero room on the Doctor's TARDIS, only painted matt black. The web lets the Master draw on Adric's computational powers and model entire towns using block transfer computation [see 18.7, "Logopolis"], creating the whole of Castrovalva and its people out of thin air. [The Logopolitans believe that only the subtlety of the mind can manage block transfer, which is why the Master needs the mathematically-gifted Alzarian instead of using a computer. As this set-up is already in place at the start of the story, he must have known about the power of Logopolis before the Doctor took him there, something which is rather unclear in "Logopolis" itself. Did he know about Adric, as well?]

The process even makes a copy of Adric, who can interact with everyone else without anybody noticing that something funny's going on. The Master has a remote-control unit to make Adric do his bidding, and Adric can also be used to 'receive' images from beyond the Master's scanner-range. The lash-up is fuelled by hadron power-lines, lethal to the touch, while the Castrovalvans can be made to disappear without trace on the Master's command... apparently when the Master touches a switch on the side of his TARDIS, strangely. The Master believes the simulator projections to be real enough to have a will of their own, 'almost', something that's proven when the Castrovalvans turn against him.

The Master is stuck inside Castrovalva when it folds in on itself, so it's believed that he ceases to exist. [He'll be back for 18.7, "Time-Flight", though it's never explained how he gets out of this particular fix.]

The TARDIS(es) On the console is a computer screen which, when operated by a keypad, can give the travellers details of interesting planets and TARDIS systems. [It tells Nyssa and Tegan about Castrovalva, obviously part of the Master's trap, so nothing in the databank can be taken at face value here.] Tegan finds an entry in the databank marked "TARDIS Flight Procedures Stage 387", which states that on zeroing the co-ordinate differential, the automatic systems reactivate the real-world interface and the doors can be opened. But the Doctor later claims there aren't any such instructions in the computer, and that it was just one of the Master's projections. Nevertheless, the databank would seem to have an index file, acces-

sible just by typing "IF". Inspecting the rest of the console, Nyssa concludes that it has a mean-free path-tracker and a referential differencer, while two different controls seem to be able to open and close the shutter on the scanner screen. The cloister bell rings again here, this time indicating a threat to the TARDIS itself rather than a threat to the universe, and the Doctor instinctively seems to know that the Ship's in trouble.

Thanks to the Master, a course is set on the TARDIS console for the hydrogen inrush known as Event One; see **History**. As the Ship continues on this course, the databank starts chirruping and warns that the environment takes the TARDIS 'beyond engineering tolerances'; the air in the TARDIS becomes insufferably hot, and the atmosphere gets steamy. [Events outside the TARDIS don't normally affect the interior in this way, a sure sign that the structure's cracking up. Compare with 21.3, "Frontios"; 6.2, "The Mind Robber"; and primarily 1.3, "The Edge of Destruction". Then again, see the bizarre claims made in 10.4, "Planet of the Daleks".]

Nyssa states that the TARDIS is caught in the 'field' of Event One, drawn towards it by a 'time-force' many times greater than gravity, and the TARDIS is seen spinning through space as it heads for this so-called biggest explosion in history. [The implication is that it's spinning through space *and* time, but it apparently isn't travelling through the vortex, as if Event One itself is capable of dragging it back through history in real-space. This is, at least, how it's shown on-screen.]

The heat defeats the automatic controls, but the Doctor shows Nyssa how to use the manual override by venting the thermo-buffer. This appears to be a simple metal handle, hidden behind a roundel somewhere outside the console room. The Doctor claims that using the override will be easier if the Ship is put into 'hover' mode first, always remembering not to reverse the polarity of the neutron flow [but this last phrase, a supposed "catchphrase" of the Third Doctor, might just be a confused post-regenerative rant]. Once the Ship's on manual, the temperature levels start falling and the console functions are restored, though the Doctor indicates that it's harder to fly the Ship in this state.

Once again, it's indicated that the TARDIS interior can be reconfigured from the main console [see "Logopolis" and arguably 17.6, "Shada"]. And once again, parts of the Ship are deleted in order

What Difference Does a Day Make?

...continued from page 103

So how did the "time-slip" from Saturday to Monday change the way the public saw *Doctor Who*? Answer: instead of being part of the dying "big event" breed of television, the series now wanted to be seen as something familiar, something you could depend on. Not in terms of content, which if anything was less predictable than it had been, but in terms of format. Three years later the BBC would launch *EastEnders*, one of the first soap operas to be watched by young people as well as old women and your middle-aged aunt who had nothing better to do with her life. Also shown twice a week, *EastEnders* became the very essence of BBC programming in the '80s, a home-made, inexpensive little production that said "permanence" instead of "spectacle". This was the league that *Doctor Who* was in now. When the series' budget was cut in the mid-'80s, and it gave up location shooting on film in favour of cheaper all-video work, the illusion was complete. *Doctor Who* even *looked* like the space-borne cousin of *EastEnders*, so the hideous collision of the two programmes in "Dimensions in Time" - see the appendix in Volume VI - seemed rather more natural than anyone might have liked.

These days digital technology allows the BBC to shoot programmes on cheap video but process them to look as glossy as film, as the new series of *Doctor Who* will demonstrate. However, the Corporation chooses *not* to use this "film-look" process on *EastEnders*, because the audience still associates the soap opera's video-only style with something homely, familiar and down-to-earth. For those who grew up with British television of the '70s and '80s, film puts a sense of distance between the viewer and the programme, which is why many of those who grew up with later *Doctor Who* find the all-film "Spearhead from Space" (7.1) so difficult to get into even though all the pieces are in the right place. (Mind you... the generation born in the '90s grew up in a world where most of the "realistic" TV programmes were shot on film and, apart from *EastEnders*, only spaced-out children's programmes like *Teletubbies* were shot wholly on video. So maybe *they'll* grow up thinking that video is the "weird" medium and film is the "normal" one.)

And at the end of the day, that's what the move to Mondays and Tuesdays was all about. Narrowing the distance between the viewer and the world inside the box, at a time when the various bits of society were growing further and further apart.

---

to escape an imminent disaster. In this case, the mass of deleted rooms is converted into momentum so that the Ship can escape the pull of Event One. It takes 17,000 tons of thrust, a quarter of the TARDIS' interior, to do the trick. As the Ship's on manual override [meaning, the automatic safeguards aren't active], the crew have no control over which 25% they lose, so even the console room's in jeopardy. A small green LED on the console counts down the seconds to destruction as the TARDIS heads for Event One. In the end, the procedure gets rid of the TARDIS' zero room, and afterwards the door of the room leads to a blank wall. Earlier the Doctor states that 'ordinary spaces' show up on the architectural configuration indicators, whereas a zero room is balanced to have 'zero energy' within its walls.

The zero room is - at least until it's jettisoned - a chamber where the usual white-walled TARDIS surfaces are tinted pinkish-grey. The Doctor speaks of 'neutral interfaces', while Nyssa concludes that it's a neutral space cut off from the rest of the universe. [More so than the rest of the TARDIS? Nyssa's hardly reliable on this score.] This means it can help the Doctor stabilise after his regeneration, cancelling out the 'ambient complexity' which can cause problems for a Time Lord in a post-regenerative state. It smells like roses, although the Doctor's never worked out why. Nyssa thinks it feels like Traken. Even the gravity's local, so not only does it let the Doctor's dendrites heal, it also lets him levitate. His coat-tails don't dangle while he does this, as if he's lying on an invisible bed. When asked whether anybody can levitate in the room, he says 'you don't do it, it just sort of comes to you... like sleep'.

After the room is lost, Nyssa is able to unscrew the hinges of the doors with the sonic screwdriver and use her ionic bonder to construct a 'zero cabinet', in which the Doctor can lie and recuperate. Strong-force interaction fuses the internal interfaces together, which means it can only be opened from the inside. The Doctor's capable of levitating even inside the cabinet, but apparently needs to keep concentrating to do it. This handy item eventually falls apart [possibly due to the

Master's abuse of it] in Castrovalva. [Strong-force interaction or not, Nyssa finds it remarkably easy to assemble the cabinet; it even has a convenient automatic sliding lid. Do separated bits of the TARDIS like joining themselves together? Does it work like Lego?] The TARDIS databank suggests that some places in the universe have properties similar to, and sometimes more effective than, zero environments… but of course, nothing in the TARDIS databank can be considered reliable on this occasion.

Here the TARDIS is shown to have more roundelled white corridors than ever before. In one of them is a full-length mirror, next to which is a hat-stand that bears the hat and jacket appropriated by the new Doctor, with a recorder [hinting at the Second Doctor] lying on top of the mirror's frame and a cricket bat lying nearby. There's also a pair of green wellies, which thankfully the Doctor doesn't adopt as part of his costume. Close to this is a room full of cricketing memorabilia [bringing to mind the Fourth Doctor's obsession with cricket], which is where he gets the rest of his outfit.

In a nearby corridor Nyssa and Tegan find a store-room full of crates marked "Handle with Care", and sense that they're going 'downwards' into the Ship. A roundel in another of these corridors contains a first aid kit, full of ampoules and such [it conveniently pops open just as the sick Doctor's passing, as if the Ship "knows" he's in trouble]. Some of the ampoules have labels marking them out as "the ointment", "the potion" and "the solution". A motorised wheelchair is waiting in the passage close by, but it eventually gets left behind on the Castrovalva planet.

The Doctor, while he's still confused, states that there are 'strong dimensional forces' close to the centre of the TARDIS and is worried about getting too near to the 'main TARDIS drive'. [His obvious anxiety here hints at the existence of something nasty at the centre of the Ship. This may well be a reference to a story that never got made; see the essay under 17.6, "Shada", for more.] In the same puzzled state, he believes that Tegan's lipstick on the walls might be 'seepage', and wonders whether it's the TARDIS' auto-systems playing up again.

Nyssa obviously believes the TARDIS drifts in real-space, as she states that without the Doctor at the controls it'll inevitably crash into something, given the star-densities in this galaxy [a bit of a

stretch, and an outright contradiction of "The Edge of Destruction"]. Earth can be seen on the scanner after it takes off, getting further and further away. Tegan's landing on the planet in Andromeda puts the TARDIS down at an angle, and everything inside the Ship tilts at an angle as well. The scanner shows both Earth receding and the pinkish planet in the Phylox cluster as though the TARDIS were travelling between galaxies like the Starship *Enterprise*.

The Master's TARDIS, meanwhile, is still defaulting to the shape of an ionic column but eventually becomes a fireplace. It can't take off from the collapsing space-time trap of Castrovalva, as space is squeezing in on itself too tightly. The Master can make great big crackling energy-lines come out of his vehicle that cause everyone in the vicinity to fall unconscious. When the block transfer web is installed in the Master's "evil" zero room, the room's little escalator is operated by the same all-purpose handset that's used to turn up the power.

Planet Notes

• *Castrovalva*. According to the TARDIS databank, Castrovalva is the central habitation on a small planet of the Phylox Series in Andromeda, also known as "Dwellings of Simplicity". Although pinkish-purple when seen from space, the planet appears to have plenty of lush forests and flowing rivers, and has a pleasantly Earth-like ambience. The only sign of civilisation is the stone-walled town that's noted in the databank for its "Classic Plainness", and it's believed that the Doctor can start to recover there after his regeneration, as this place has properties even more powerful than those of a zero room.

Castrovalva is a place of elegant architecture and tall, white towers. Its people aren't technologically advanced, dressing in clothes that make them look almost Medieval - despite the plastic head-dresses and bustles - and having no technical books in their library. Some wear small gems in their foreheads, and they're generally civil to strangers, not being surprised by outsiders at all. Prominent locals include Shardovan the librarian; the Master of Physic, who specialises in herbal remedies; and the Portreeve, a wise old man who rarely grants audiences. The pharmacy of the Master of Physic is stocked with herbal ingredients familiar from Earth.

The TARDIS crew are found by spear-wielding hunters from Castrovalva, who dress in colourful, ceremonial costumes and masks that are said to be relics of the present Castrovalvans' ancestors, as Castrovalva supposedly arose out of an alliance of warring hunters 1,200 years earlier. They hunt what appear to be Earth-like pigs [despite the true nature of Castrovalva, this planet may well have its own genuine wildlife], and birds can be heard in the area. A tapestry in Castrovalva, which the Portreeve claims was created using the forgotten skills of the community's forebears, can show images of far-off events as if it were a scanner; the Doctor believes it's done with fast-particle projection [rather contradicting the claim of avoiding all technological complexity].

In fact, Castrovalva is a fraud. The settlement has only just come into existence, created by the Master using block transfer computation. None of its inhabitants are aware of the fact that they're not "real". The librarian Shardovan has begun to suspect that something's wrong [was he created with these suspicions already in mind, perhaps as a result of Adric's input into the town's creation?] as the thirty-volume history of Castrovalva was supposedly written five-hundred years ago but details Castrovalva's history up to the present day. The Portreeve is none other than the Master himself, with a white beard and an elaborate headpiece that simply vanish when he reveals himself. [It's likely that the disguise is generated by the same computations that hold the whole of Castrovalva together, as the Master's usual style is to wear rubber masks.]

The settlement has been designed as an elaborate trap for the Doctor, its architecture folding in on itself and making escape impossible. The Doctor calls this 'recursive occlusion'. The natives don't perceive the spatial anomalies, and oddly the Doctor believes that a silver-backed mirror can hold the occlusion out of his quarters in the town. The tapestry conceals the Master's block transfer web. Castrovalva is held in balance by the web, and collapses in on itself completely when the web's destroyed, entirely ceasing to exist.

• *Gallifrey.* According to the Doctor, there was a very good polygonal zero room under the Junior Senate Block on Gallifrey, known for its healing properties.

History

• *Dating.* The present day, ish. [The story begins where "Logopolis" leaves off, so it's still 1981. It's not clear whether the events of Castrovalva are set in the same period.]

Event One, the 'hydrogen inrush', is a point in space and time where hydrogen is the predominant element and even the TARDIS is in jeopardy. It's explicitly said to be the beginning of the galaxy [*not* the beginning of the universe, but see 20.4, "Terminus"]. Nyssa speaks of the TARDIS going through a 'boundary layer' about forty seconds before reaching the inrush itself, while the Doctor speaks of a 'starfield'. [The word "starfield" is often used to describe the programme's title sequence in the early '80s, although the special effect isn't the same. So are the opening credits supposed to represent a journey back to Event One, in the same way that the early '70s credits apparently represented the inside of the Doctor's mind (see 9.1, "Day of the Daleks") and the late '70s credits represented either the Matrix (14.3, "The Deadly Assassin") or the vortex (17.6, "Shada")?]

The Analysis

Where Does This Come From? Self-conscious fictionality was big in "serious" '70s literature, and writing about writing seemed to be all that ever won the Booker Prize. So the obvious next step after a story about infinite regression was to ask how it would feel to discover that you were a character in someone else's story.

Like all bright kids, Bidmead was - by his own confession - scared and excited by this Lewis Carroll-ish idea. And as someone learning to program, he was attracted to the notion of recursive loops, especially the "strange loops" which take the operation somewhere new each time; once again, we're into the realms of mathematicians Kurt Godel and David Hilbert (see 18.7, "Logopolis"). And in early '80s *Omni*-reading circles, where you have Godel, you have Escher...

We've already mentioned the influence of Douglas Hofstadter's pop-science epic *Godel, Escher, Bach* on *Doctor Who*, but here it's more explicit than ever. Once again, we have to remind ourselves that this was the early '80s, when logic puzzles and visual riddles were tragically hip. This was the age of the Rubik's Cube. Anything with odd angles was in vogue, and by the middle of the decade Escher's works were everywhere, proving especially popular with the kind of people who owned home computers. In 1979 the illustrations had been franchised by Athena Prints, who throughout the '70s had supplied the nation with

The Lord of the Rings posters and prog-rock album covers. Pretty soon the prints were even turning up in the offices of the BBC's Head of Serials, where they annoyed John Nathan-Turner, who stated a belief that 'art should exist to soothe, not distract'.

(For those who don't know... M. C. Escher was an early twentieth-century Dutch artist who specialised in illustrating the impossible. His works are full of twisted geometry and recursive architecture, with buildings folding in on themselves and tricks of perspective being used to create entire landscapes. No wonder Chris Bidmead was interested. Escher's illustration "Castrovalva" - no, it's *not* very subtle, is it? - depicts a high-towered town much like the Castrovalvan exterior we see here, although the interior sets are lifted directly from the dimensionally-confusing "Ascending and Descending". Various film-makers have attempted to put Escher on the screen since *Doctor Who*, with mixed results but usually with higher budgets. In an '80s context, perhaps the best-known is the scene with David Bowie and the impossible staircases in the movie *Labyrinth*, a film which demonstrates many of the same trends as Seasons Eighteen and Nineteen but with added Muppets. In *Doctor Who*'s version, even the costumes suggest the figures in Escher's work.)

The other noticeable thing about "Castrovalva" is that it's far more serial-like than any *Doctor Who* since the '60s. A story like "The Daleks" (1.2) is as loose in its structure as a 1930's *Flash Gordon*, but by the '70s four-part stories were much more inclined to have definite beginnings, middles and endings, like hour-and-a-half-long tele-movies that just happened to be spread over the course of a month. Yet at times it feels as if "Castrovalva" isn't actually a single, discrete story at all. The first episode concentrates on the aftermath of the Doctor's regeneration, and doesn't even mention - or hint at - the Castrovalva of the title. The second episode is about various crises on the TARDIS, so the actual *plot* is confined to episodes three and four. Today we should be used to this sort of format from programmes like *Buffy the Vampire Slayer*, but it still feels odd to watch all four episodes on video as if they're a single entity. (It's also notable that the story seems to be split down the middle, the first half set on the TARDIS and the second half in Castrovalva. In this period, remember, *Doctor Who* was shown twice-weekly and episodes arrived in pairs... was this structure

a deliberate attempt to get to grips with the new schedule, presenting viewers with a two-part "TARDIS story" one week and a two-part "planet story" the next?)

This serial-like approach is one of the reasons that many people have compared this period in the programme's history with soap opera, and it doesn't help that "Castrovalva" was the first story to be shown in *Doctor Who*'s new weekday evening slot, traditionally the place where soap operas go. See **What Difference Does a Day Make?** for more on this.

The more literate among you might have spotted a possible parallel between events in the non-existent city and another highbrow best-seller of the era, *One-Hundred Years of Solitude* (1967) by Columbian novelist Gabriel Garcia Marquez. Events in Macondo, "the City of Mirrors, or Mirages", are told in a history book detailing everything up to the day when somebody reads it (at which point the city fades into dust). A more direct South American influence is Argentine writer Jorge Luis Borges - if you'd read Hofstadter, then this was often the next step - especially the story "Tlon, Uqbar, Orbis Tertius".

And yet, the most obvious influences are once again right under our noses. This era saw people watching old episodes of *Doctor Who* while making new ones. Aside from Davison's impressions, we get a wholesale recycling of "The Edge of Destruction" and a location whose logic isn't unlike that of "The Mind Robber". But more obviously, the story Bidmead had just been editing - "Kinda" (19.3) - features a culture rejecting (but not wholly abandoning) technology in favour of a safer lifestyle, and the use of mirrors to reflect badness in on itself.

More prosaically, the zero room is obviously a bathroom metaphor, in the screamingly-fashionable Habitat colour-scheme of that year.

Things That Don't Make Sense Many plot oddities here. You have to ask why the Master goes to all the trouble of making the TARDIS go back to Event One when there are a million simpler ways of killing the Doctor through block transfer computation (making a bowling ball appear in his throat, for example), why he doesn't have more control over the structure of Castrovalva than he evidently does, and so on. Most of these can be brushed under the carpet with that old stand-by excuse "he wants to take his revenge in the most elaborate way possible and isn't exactly stable", but we also have to ponder why he has a contingency plan for the Doctor surviving the fall from the radio-telescope, and another in case *that* failed. [But then, it turns out that the Doctor did survive both of these things, so by now the Master must realise that it's always best to go for overkill.] Not to mention why he has such elaborate plans for a boy he only briefly glimpsed on Traken. And once again, you've got to wonder why block transfer computation isn't more widely sought-after in this universe if it's capable of creating whole settlements out of thin air. The strangest thing is that even the Master never thinks about using it again. Surely, Adric can't be the *only* mathematical genius in the universe who's up to scratch?

On reading about Castrovalva in the TARDIS databank, Nyssa asks Tegan 'where's that?', even though the answer is right in front of her on the screen. In big letters. Thanks to the magic of video effects, the question-marks on the Doctor's shirt are reversed when he's levitating in the zero room, while Tegan's bag spontaneously moves from the cloister (where she left it in "Logopolis") to the main console. Has Adric been using it to practice modelling space-time events? The Master muses that 'these simulated projections have a will of their own' after the real Adric sends a message into the zero room, but if Adric can do this then the zero room's not really very 'cut off', surely?

Oh yes, and our chief scientific adviser would like to query the use of 'galaxy' in episode two. If Event One is the Big Bang, as "Terminus" (20.4) suggests, then it's the *universe* that's created by a hydrogen inrush. A galaxy isn't "created" that way, and certainly not by an inrush of anything. If the analogy with "The Edge of Destruction" (1.3) is deliberate, on the other hand, then it's a solar system which is being created with sufficient force to damage the TARDIS. Dr. Science would also wish to have a quiet word with whoever thought a 'mean-free path tracker' was a sensible idea (but will only say why to anyone patient enough to listen to the explanation without fidgeting).

Critique (Prosecution) When people parodied *Doctor Who* in the '80s, they didn't bother with jokes about washing-up-liquid bottles, they made sport with the hammy thesps declaiming technobabble in cod-Shakespearean metre and making incomprehensible references to past stories. This story, and the ones either side of it, demonstrate what they had in mind.

Everyone talks like a Chris Bidmead character, even Tegan, supposedly the "viewer identification" character these days. The experienced former child-actor Sarah Sutton has difficulty making lines like 'I know so little about telebiogenesis' work as dialogue that anyone would ever say. As for her yelping 'you've got to stop him, he's the Master!', all you can say is, worse was to come. If even Michael Sheard (as the physician Mergrave) and Derek Waring (as the librarian Shardovan) are struggling against the writing, then what chance does Matthew Waterhouse have?

Once again, the production team have mistaken "pace" for "speed", so we have people running around a lot but the viewers have already guessed what's coming next. The most egregious example is in episode four: the protracted shot of the cloister which is obviously a mirror-image of the one above it. They could have had one person running left to right *whilst* someone ran, upside-down, right-to-left, but no, we have to wait thirty seconds before *everyone* has left the top shot before starting the bottom one. This is supposed to be the exciting climax, and after episode two spent fifteen minutes of prime-time with two girls pushing a pram around the woods it does seem comparatively energetic, but childrens' television of the time was so much brisker.

The world and her mum had guessed that the zero room would be in the 25% of the Ship that would be jettisoned, and watching Nyssa doing DIY was no substitute for having enough plot to fill the slot. The production team seem to have spent a lot of time watching Hartnell stories; if they'd focussed on having as much happening as took place in those, rather than making sure they name-checked all of the TARDIS features 'accurately', things might have been better. At seven episodes long "The Daleks" (1.2) seems less long-drawn-out than this "adventure", because there's seven episodes'-worth of things happening. At times it seems that more thought was put into what to have on the readout screens for a split-second than what to have in the story for ninety minutes.

More damningly, the ten-million viewers who tuned in to see what the new Doctor was going to be like still didn't know by the end of part four. This contempt for the average viewer is typical of the early '80s travesty of the series. Davison does his impressions, but never gets the chance to say '...and this is me!'. There's a Doctor-shaped hole in this story, and the three kids aren't enough to fill it. It might just as well have been Martin Jarvis, or anyone.

None of this would matter if this story wasn't at heart, quintessentially what *Doctor Who* should be doing. The central conceit is wonderful. We have a city where space and time have gone wrong, and the locals are unaware of this. It's obliquely like a Flemish master and overtly (if you spot it) taken from a well-known engraver. If you don't know Escher, it doesn't matter. The possible consequences of this should be enough for a well-paced four-parter. The focus should have been on the city throughout, and reconciling mutually-exclusive views on a topic as basic as geometry should have had echoes of other conflicts without being didactic.

But no, this is the finale of a story about a bearded man going 'heh-heh-heh' and gloating that soon he will finally kill the Doctor, because the Doctor is good and he is (nyarr harr harr) evil. The city of Castrovalva (when they finally get there) is a nasty horrid booby-trap, and everyone can see the "surprise" coming a mile off. If Bidmead had done what he asked other writers to do, to think out how this world works and then throw the Doctor at it, we'd have a masterpiece on our hands. Instead, it's a comic-strip and a rather dull one.

It's not all bad, though. The "made-up" city seems more real than the supposedly solid worlds like Tigella or Alzarius from the previous year. Even though this is Planet Smug, and - like Traken - everyone finds everyone else's over-written dialogue hilarious, there are enough rough edges to make it seem lived-in. Children, breakfast and gossip seem to be the Bidmead tricks for this (see 18.6, "The Keeper of Traken" and 21.3, "Frontios"), but they work well here. Like those early '80s text-based computer games, the characters have things to do off-screen which aren't necessarily important to the plot (although even laundry is significant in this story). There's even more of a pop-video look to the last episode than ever; see **Did Kate Bush Really Write This?** under 20.2, "Snakedance".

And it *is* nice scenery.

Critique (Defence) Actually, when people parodied *Doctor Who* in the '80s they rarely made jokes about anything *except* washing-up-liquid bottles. It was the fans (if we can safely consider them to be something other than "people") who whined

on about "incomprehensible references to past stories", simply because they were the only ones who noticed. The general public didn't care one way or another, and to them hearing Peter Davison reference a "real" story by saying something like 'of course, the Cybermen came from the planet Mondas originally...' was no different to hearing Tom Baker reference an "unseen" story by saying something like 'well, the Droge of the Gabrielides once put a whole star-system on my head...'. And anyone who seriously believes that there's more technobabble in the Nathan-Turner / Bidmead era must have watched Season Seventeen with their fingers in their ears and going 'laah laah laah'. But that aside...

The keystone of *Doctor Who* in the early '80s - indeed, the keystone of all film-making that had learned the lessons of the '70s, consciously or otherwise - is its use of space. In film there's a school of thought that all great cinema (and, by association, TV) forms relationships between the spaces we see on-screen and our own *internal* spaces, making us feel as if the things we're looking at and the environments we're putting together in our heads are both parts of a complete spatial structure, rather than just two causally-linked events. Modern film is a medium of these spatial relationships, creating worlds not by dialogue or exposition but by giving us a sense of "where" we are in the story. It's more like architecture than literature.

And this, above all the other things mentioned under "The Leisure Hive", is what *Doctor Who* inevitably picked up from films like *Star Wars*. The script for "Castrovalva" has its flaws, yet in both its conception and its execution it's a top-of-the-line demonstration of how to use three-dimensional space to give the audience a sense of the elsewhere.

This is apt, given that it's about a town where dimensions collapse in on itself, but it's obvious even *before* Castrovalva folds together at the end of episode three. It's there even in episode one, when Bidmead goes one step beyond even "Logopolis" in turning the TARDIS into a near-unknowable, often-intimidating *environment* again. The story, the direction and the set design (none of your shoddy "Invasion of Time" nonsense here) all act together to present the Ship as a bona fide labyrinth, the perfect setting for (or reflection of) the TARDIS crew's hysteria. This is a place that's worth exploring, a place potentially as menacing as anywhere it might visit, which means that we feel just as lost as the new Doctor. This time we're not one of the puzzled humans, trying to cope with his post-regenerative antics; this time we're growing up with him.

And Castrovalava itself, once we get there, is perhaps the single most impressive "world" created by the series up to this point. This is a setting that feels as if it exists from every angle, where the shape of the story can be defined with nothing more than a change of perspective. (The central square of the town is "just" a central square when we're at ground-level, but whenever one of the characters looks on it from above we're being invited to think about it as an enclosed, inescapable *system*.)

Anywhere else in the universe the "spatial anomaly" idea wouldn't work, purely because we wouldn't be able to believe that this was a world in which we could lose ourselves. But here we get an instinctive feel for the geometry. The "wholeness" of it is obviously helped by the fact that the set and costume designs are spectacularly great, but also by the fact that the dialogue given to the Castrovalvans fits them like a bodkin. As in "The Keeper of Traken", here there's a love of both language and the way language can shape our expectations of fantasy. Newly-made Castrovalva feels older than most thousand-year space-empires. Even the names of the characters have their own poetry, and imply their own histories: "Shardovan", "Mergrave", a local wise man called a "Portreeve". This is what Great British Character Actors were *made* for.

The flaws in the script? Some shocking gibberish from the *non*-Castrovalvans, and both Sarah Sutton and Janet Fielding are really struggling to sound convincing in the first act. Castrovalva is obviously bound to be more interesting than Event One, making you suspect that the TARDIS should have got there sooner, but in its original two-episodes-every-week format this set-up makes perfect sense. And like its sister-production "Logopolis", none of this can spoil the quiet, understated beauty of its "visual rhetoric".

More importantly, it did its job better than most commentators now recognise. As the first *Doctor Who* story to be broadcast in a new slot and on a new day, it brought the series back to the attention of people who'd lost track of it on Saturdays, and - at least in its latter half - gave them something they simply weren't expecting. It demonstrated that this really *wasn't* just about spaceships and cute robots anymore, that the series could still be serenely surprising. It fulfilled Bidmead's own brief, by expanding the minds of a generation a little further. And isn't that the main thing?

The Facts

Written by Christopher H. Bidmead. Directed by Fiona Cumming. Viewing figures: 9.1 million, 8.6 million, 10.2 million and a very healthy 10.4 million.

Supporting Cast Anthony Ainley (The Master), Micheal Sheard (Mergrave), Frank Wylie (Ruther), Derek Waring (Shardovan).

Oh, Isn't That..?

• *Michael Sheard.* In the fifth of six appearances in the series, here he becomes a "guest star" rather than just a distinguished character actor. One of three well-known *Doctor Who* faces to have played Imperial officers in *The Empire Strikes Back*, after this he'll be even more famous as the stuffy, wig-wearing deputy headmaster Mr. Bronson in *Grange Hill*, a series which regularly beat *Doctor Who* into second place when "Best Children's Programme" polls were taken in the early '80s. Here he wears a pink dress and a tupperware hat with the dignity that comes of having worn a shower-curtain (in 3.6, "The Ark") and played Hitler as a space-being (in *The Tomorrow People*).

Working Titles "The Visitor".

Cliffhangers As Nyssa and Tegan realise that the TARDIS is hurtling towards the biggest explosion in history, the Master appears on the scanner to have a good gloat; in the forests of Castrovalva, Nyssa and Tegan return to the Doctor's zero cabinet to find it empty; the Doctor realises he's trapped as Castrovalva collapses into a kaleidoscope of odd angles.

The Lore

• Young Adric's bleary look at the end of episode four isn't acting (no jokes, please). The location filming on the estate of Lord de la Warr apparently involved a night of boozy excess, and Matthew Waterhouse became a bit ill the following morning. Some reports have him puking in the TARDIS prop[5]. Lord de la Warr is said to have given permission to film in return for a charity donation and a photo of himself outside the

TARDIS. Unfortunately he didn't announce himself, and on the crew's arrival Nathan-Turner believed his lordship to be the gardener. The estate was nevertheless used for the next story to be filmed, "Black Orchid" (19.5).

• As we've already seen, this was a last-minute replacement for the much-rewritten John Flanagan / Andrew McCulloch offering "Project 4G", and was made fourth in the production block. And as we've already seen, Head of Serials Graeme McDonald was one of those people who had Escher prints in his office, suggesting that Bidmead came up with the idea as a way of winding up the producer. Especially annoying to Nathan-Turner was the etching *Klimmen en Dalen*, the one with the never-ending staircase.

• The small child who teaches the Doctor to count was the niece of Caroline John, Liz Shaw in Season Seven. Patrick Troughton also popped in, and stood in for Davison during the setting-up of one scene in episode three (perhaps significantly, it seems to have been the 'where is he?' scene, when the Doctor finally regains his marbles).

• Fiona Cumming, like many of the production staff and guest artists employed by Nathan-Turner in the early years, had worked on *The Pallisers*. Adapted from Anthony Trollope's vast sequence of political novels, this was to have been the big BBC2 period drama blockbuster, but a strike meant the last few episodes weren't ready in time (they started again from the top, and nobody seemed to notice). Nathan-Turner cut his teeth there, and met people like Anthony Ainley, Barbara Murray (Lady Cranleigh in 19.5, "Black Orchid"), Phililp Latham (Borusa in 20.7, "The Five Doctors") and Peter Sallis (who nearly played Striker in 20.5, "Enlightenment").

Cumming watched "Logopolis" several times, although it made less and less sense to her, in order to get the continuity right. She also worked on removing the on-screen rapport between Janet Fielding and Sarah Sutton, who in terms of screen-time had only just met. Cumming's previous work on *Doctor Who* had been in the '60s historical yarns "The Massacre" (3.5) and "The Highlanders" (4.4) and 1972 kitschfest "The Mutants" (9.4), as production assistant and (in the first instance) assistant floor manager.

• The decision to allow Davison three stories before filming his debut was taken very early on. Once his casting had been confirmed, the round of interviews included *Pebble Mill at One*, where a

"design a costume" contest had been run. It was here that a child's letter was read out suggesting that Davison should play the Doctor like Tristan (i.e. Davison's character in *All Creatures Great and Small*) 'but brave'. Davison had been playing in sitcoms, and was keen to "age" into a character actor. His drama teacher had suggested that he wouldn't come into his own until his forties. Many were surprised by the casting, but those who'd suggested Martin Jarvis - whose career Davison seemed to be re-enacting - were less so.

19.2: "Four to Doomsday"

(Serial 5W, Four Episodes, 18th - 26th January 1982.)

Which One is This?   Mayans and Australian Aborigines celebrate Chinese New Year on a spaceship, while Stratford Johns plays the incredible shrinking frog-god.

Firsts and Lasts It's the first story of this season, and thus the first story of Peter Davison's run, to have been filmed. It's also the first of three stories in this season to have been script-edited by Antony Root (who fills in for this and "The Visitation" before Eric Saward takes over as full-time script editor, then steps in again for "Earthshock" - officially, at least - so that Saward can write the story himself).

It's the first of three occasions on which Nyssa will get excited about android design whilst thinking up nifty ways to smash them to bits, and it's the first and last time that Adric gets close to a lady. Two ladies, in fact. Admittedly one's an android who's trying to kill him, and the other's a fellow companion who's trying to beat him up, but it's as close to copping a feel as he ever gets.

Four Things to Notice About "Four to Doomsday"...

1. Today's moral: 'In a civilised world, there is no substitute for democracy.' The villain of "Four to Doomsday" is a tyrannical, autocratic and literally soul-less ruler who wants to invade Earth and claims it's for the planet's own good, since the place is rife with disease and most of the people there are starving (he's called "Monarch"... see, the clue is in the name). Hence, the moral question here is whether despotism is justified even when "freedom" means suffering and hunger.

Since this is *Doctor Who*, it's not much of a spoiler to say that the Doctor's answer is "no", while Adric briefly becomes a naïve young fascist idealist who wrongly believes that tyranny can solve things. Sadly, this argument breaks down when the story tries to "prove" how evil Monarch is by revealing that he destroyed his own world after depleting the ozone layer and greedily burning up all its mineral wealth. Yeah, 'cos democratic societies *never* do that kind of thing, do they?

2. Mind you, around here you get a better class of megalomaniac. This frog-like would-be destroyer of humanity may like to involve himself in the usual sort of villainy, but has two things in his favour. One: he believes that he's God, and thus wants to meet himself at the beginning of time, which is a much more promising motivation than usual. Two: he's played by distinguished old thespian Stratford Johns, who somehow maintains his dignity even though he's got green skin and a gungy head. Even so, it's Monarch's Minister of Persuasion who gets the best "bad guy" moment here, proving that even humourless alien conquerors are capable of comic timing. After Nyssa discovers a way of deactivating androids with a pencil and the sonic screwdriver, Persuasion confiscates the screwdriver and tells her (imperiously, and as if he expects her to be grateful): 'You may keep the pencil.'

3. Considering this was his first shot at playing the Doctor, Peter Davison puts in a more-than-acceptable performance here, although you can tell he's not 100% sure how to play it (he seems to have a particular problem working out how much he should shout at his stupid companions) and you can tell the writers aren't 100% sure either. This becomes obvious when the recently-rescued Nyssa tells the Doctor about the terrible things the Urbankans have been trying to do to her, and he responds with the exclamation: 'The devils!' And Peter sounds as if he can't work out whether it's meant to be sarcastic or not. But the most memorable line of all is the Doctor's protestation to Monarch: 'I wouldn't dream of interfering with your monopticons.' ("Monopticons" being mobile spy-cameras, because as per usual, the totalitarian villains are obsessed with surveillance.)

4. Not for the first time under this regime, there's only three episodes' worth of story here. But this time the programme-makers have made this a virtue by allowing a break every so often for a musical item. We have what the choreographer thinks is authentic Mayan dancing in episodes two and four, as well as an Aboriginal korroborree (even if most of the dancers are from the West Indies), Chinese dragon-dances and the sort of gladiatorial fight to the "death" that Athenians didn't actually go for much. It looks - to anyone who saw it at the time - like an edition of *The Generation Game*, with all these spectacular events taking place on-stage and then members of the public having a go... especially the swordfight, which isn't exactly snappy. If ever there was a *Doctor Who* story designed for your mum or your gran to watch, then this is it. (See **What Difference Does a Day Make?** under the last story.)

The Continuity

The Doctor Short-sighted in his right eye. [Hence the spectacles in the last story. The First Doctor occasionally wore a monocle in his right eye, but the intervening incarnations all seem to have been 20-20.] He can withstand sub-zero temperatures, even in space, for six minutes. Once again he's calling himself a Doctor of everything, and he claims that travelling through time by moving faster than light is 'impossible' [and sure enough, there's no indication that any time machine in the series works that way].

• *Ethics.* The Doctor apparently has no qualms about condemning the entire population of Urbanka to destruction [not only assuming that they're all as bad as Monarch - even though Monarch's an autocratic dictator - but, we assume, concluding that the Urbankans don't "count" as people if they're all stored on microchip], though fortunately he never gets the chance to actually commit genocide.

• *Inventory.* He's now carrying an eyeglass of the Sherlock Holmes variety [even though the script seems to indicate a monocle], and gives Tegan a spare TARDIS key. He's also got some string and a cricket ball, though his pockets obviously aren't as voluminous as those of his last incarnation / coat and a search reveals nothing else. The sonic screwdriver can reverse magnetic fields, or give off a signal that blocks listening devices.

Nyssa, not the Doctor, works out that conducting the sonic screwdriver's power through ordinary pencil graphite can immobilise the Urbankan androids. [He may not be at his best yet.]

• *Background.* The Doctor states that only his 'professor' at the Academy really understood artron energy [probably not Borusa this time, as

ABOUT TIME 1980–1984

TARDIS engineering doesn't seem to be Borusa's sort of field]. He claims to have been a friend of Drake [1540-96, a rare name-drop for this Doctor] and says that the last time he was at Heathrow Airport, strange things were being done to Terminal Three. He tries to demonstrate his cricketing credentials by claiming that he once took five wickets for New South Wales, and he used to bowl a good Chinaman. [Compare this with his claimed cricketing prowess in 16.1, "The Ribos Operation" or the demonstration in 14.2, "The Hand of Fear". A Chinaman is bowled with the left hand, hinting that the Doctor's ambidextrous.]

The Doctor claims that the Mayan civilisation flourished eight-thousand years ago [actually, *one-thousand* years is a better estimate... see **History**]. Though he knows nothing of Urbankans, he finds the design of their monopticons familiar.

The Supporting Cast

• *Adric*. He doesn't seem to be getting on with the rest of the TARDIS crew at all, and claims that women are mindless, impatient and bossy, though he could be just trying to annoy Tegan. He gets particularly irritated when the Doctor goes off to explore with Tegan and leaves him behind. [When he was alone with the old Doctor, Adric seemed quite chirpy and willing to listen, but now he's got competition from two girls he's becoming increasingly petty and mean.]

He's gullible enough to be taken in by Monarch, and this time isn't faking his allegiance to the villain, as he and Tegan get into a particularly nasty physical fight. The Doctor describes the boy's belief in a "correct" tyranny as 'idealism'. [Adric really is *very* stupid here, and it's massively out-of-character with what we see in - say - "State of Decay" (18.4). Maybe it's just a teenage, hormonal thing.] He believes the Doctor always gets in trouble because it 'amuses him'.

• *Nyssa*. Traken's sole surviving girly swot is here said to be skilled in bioengineering and cybernetics. By now she knows enough of the TARDIS to know all about its time-curve circuits [even though these are apparently quite obscure systems].

• *Tegan*. Getting snippy and impatient now the Doctor's failing to get her back to Earth, here she's also prone to panic, breaking down into tears when she's scared and her planet's in jeopardy [the stress is finally getting to her]. But she's unexpectedly artistic, and good at sketching people. She can also speak at least one Australian aboriginal language. [Coincidentally, the same one the aborigine named Kurkurtji speaks. As there are thousands of aboriginal dialects, and as Kurkurtji's tongue is thousands of years old, it seems likely that some sort of automatic translation is in effect here. All of the other captured "humans" on Monarch's ship speak English, possibly thanks to the Doctor's 'Time Lord gift' but possibly thanks to the Urbankans' own methods. Is aboriginal language too "difficult" for these techniques to translate into English? If so, then is the process at least capable of translating one aboriginal dialect into another?]

The flight Tegan was trying to catch when the Doctor hijacked her was AA-778, due to depart from Heathrow at 17:30. Like every good Australian stereotype, she sees anything that's too advanced for her as Pommy mumbo-jumbo. Here she has a new U-Certificate expletive, 'cripes!', which she uses at least three times.

The TARDIS   Adric describes the TARDIS passengers as being 'fifth-dimensional' while they're on board [q.v. "The Hand of Fear" and 1.1, "An Unearthly Child"], and also states that the Ship's interior is in another dimension. According to the Doctor, Artron energy powers TARDISes, though when questioned by Monarch he claims that even *he* doesn't understand it. [He may be lying. Also, "The Deadly Assassin" (14.3) describes the Doctor himself as having high levels of artron energy. This, like so much else, hints at some symbiotic link between TARDIS and pilot.]

There are navigational problems with the Ship again, as the Doctor's aiming to get Tegan back to Earth but doesn't even manage to hit the planet. He states that the dense magnetic fields of Monarch's ship may have caused a fluctuation of the artron energy.

Adric mentions the TARDIS' power room and bathroom. On board the Ship are 'space-packs', helmets which provide the crew with a limited air supply and allow the Doctor to space-walk. The space-packs have visors, though these don't seem to be necessary, and the air comes from three canisters at the back of each helmet. There are at least four packs on board. [They stop the user decompressing in space as well as supplying air, so some sort of force-field seems likely, though they don't

Four *Whats* to Doomsday?

Impressive as Urbankan technology may be, Monarch has never mastered faster-than-light travel. This is hardly surprising as it's probably impossible, but in *Doctor Who* terms it's the next step after electricity for every single species (even the Mutts from "The Mutants" can do it, apparently, if we're to believe "The Brain of Morbius"). So the Urbankan ship has been doing the Inokshi-Sol run at relativistic speeds and halving the time taken with each go around.

There are two ways to account for this. One, apparently the simple one, is that the android crew and megalomaniac frog skipper have come up with increasingly ingenious ways to squeeze more speed out of the engines. All well and good, but top whack is always going to be around 300,000 km per second. Even leaving aside Einstein, the faster they go, the more energy they'll need to slow down again at the other end and the more G-force they'll pull in the process. Even Monarch would be unable to survive. Besides, his is a huge ship, as everyone spends five minutes per episode pointing out. Which means that manoeuvring is going to be a worse problem than steering an oil tanker. So maybe we should accept what Bigon seems to offer as an explanation, that the ship never slows down and the journey is one long circle, halving the time taken with every circuit.

Constant acceleration brings its own problems. The last leg of the journey started 1,250 years ago (the implication is *Earth* years), the first lasted 20,000. Assume - for the moment, as it's probably wrong - that they've almost got to light-speed, hereinafter *c*. That puts the distance to Urbanka at a *maximum* of 1,250 light-years, very much more local than the galactic distances they claim to have traversed, unless the word 'galaxy' is being used as loosely as *Doctor Who* writers tend to use the word 'constellation'. However, the closer you get to *c*, the more mass you have; the slower time passes for you, compared to everyone else (it seems to go one second per second wherever *you* are, even if you're watching "Underworld"); and the more your dimensions contract, even if - again - you don't notice and think everyone *else* is warped. Anything with mass would reach *c* and become a one-dimensional point with infinite mass, and the rest of the universe would fall into this singularity. A ship this big would have the mass of a planet even at a tenth of *c*. For the passengers this isn't a problem, unless one of them steps out of the ship... as the Doctor does in episode four, when he shunts himself through space by lobbing his cricket-ball at the ship and then catching it again.

(Dr. Science undergoes a *Hulk*-like metamorphosis into a wrathful beast when this scene is mentioned. There'd be problems doing it even in Earth orbit at sensible speeds. The mass of a cricket-ball is such a tiny fraction of the mass of a Time Lord that no discernible effect would follow hurl-

continued on page 117...

appear to keep the user warm as the Doctor's innate ability to withstand the cold comes into play when he's space-walking. Compare with the space-gear used in 2.5, "The Web Planet" and 4.6, "The Moonbase".]

Also found on the Ship are at least two volumes of the *Principia Mathematica*, which Adric states is by someone called Bert Russell [actually it's by philosophers / mathematicians Bertand Russell and Alfred North Whitehead, with Whitehead getting top billing]. Tegan looks through a volume identified as the type-forty TARDIS handbook [not the same manual seen in 16.2, "The Pirate Planet"]. The Urbankans' analysis of the TARDIS exterior reveal it to have a molecular structure consistent with Earth, although the lock can't be opened either by the Urbankans' laser-key or their directional cobalt flux, both of which are hefty-looking pieces of hardware that fire beams at it.

A pop-up control can be raised from the TARDIS console [the same one used to program the chameleon circuit in 18.7, "Logopolis", though its function is very different here] which allows Adric to examine various circuit diagrams on the TARDIS screen. Nyssa mentions 'time-curve circuits', and the suggestion is that she must fix them before the TARDIS can try getting back to Earth again, but this is foggy. The co-ordinates that the Doctor tells Adric to set, in order to get Tegan back home, are 6309 in the inner spiral arm of Galaxia Kyklos. [The Greek name for Earth's galaxy. Again, four-digit co-ordinates are used, as in "The Ribos Operation" (16.1). These are presumably just "rough" co-ordinates for the planet, not exact co-ordinates for Heathrow in 1981.]

Tegan thwaps some buttons on the console and the Ship moves from Monarch's ship to the void outside, apparently a sheer fluke.

The Non-Humans

• *Urbankans.* Get ready for this, it's going to be complicated...

Approaching the Earth in 1981 is an enormous, bulky, grey metal spacecraft, created by the Urbankans and owned by their autocratic ruler Monarch. In their natural form, the Urbankans are - or were - roughly humanoid, with bloated heads and green, frog-like skins. But then they left behind the 'flesh-time', apparently at the instigation of Monarch himself; the three-billion-strong Urbankan population dispensed with their original bodies, and had their identities stored on silicon microchips. These chips are now inserted into android Urbankan bodies when they're needed, though Monarch objects to the word "android" as the Urbankans are supposedly fully-integrated personalities with a racial memory. Speaking of the flesh-time is now blasphemy, as is talk of the soul. Even culture is considered to be primitive.

On the ship are Monarch himself and his two ministers, the female Minister of Enlightenment and the male Minister of Persuasion. Once Tegan supplies them with some "contemporary" fashion designs, these two can change their forms within minutes to appear human, and the pictures eliminate the need for - and may be more reliable than - telemicrographics. [The change happens off-screen, but the implication is that their microchips have been inserted into newly-made human bodies, not that they've shape-changed in the usual sense. Enlightenment says that anyone can change form, but that Adric doesn't need to 'yet'.]

The three Urbankans seen here wear green, puffed-up robes, and like sitting on thrones. In their natural form they used to secrete a lethal poison from a neck-gland, and the poison is now being reproduced and stored in the ship's mobilliary chamber, although it's also said that the poison comes from the Earth-like frogs kept in the flora chamber [the Urbankans' relatives?]. Bigon describes the poison as the deadliest in the known universe, as it causes matter to shrink in on itself and one-trillionth of a gram could reduce a human being to the size of a grain of salt.

Monarch himself is partly biological, though he keeps this quiet and still maintains that the 'flesh-time' was a time of weakness. His aim is to travel faster than the speed of light, as he believes this will allow him to travel backwards in time, and he wants to visit the creation of the universe so that he can meet himself as God. [Urbanka is in a different galaxy, but it takes mere centuries for Monarch to reach Earth, which implies faster-than-light speed. Presumably, then, the Urbankans have some sort of hyperspace or transmat technology and can't move faster than light in the "normal" space-time continuum. But we'll come back to this...]

Enlightenment claims that Monarch led his people out of the Urbankan slime [is he really *that* old, or is this the typical dictator habit of rewriting history so that nothing prior to the current regime exists?] to conquer the land and the elements. He's eventually shrunk down to a couple of inches in height by a canister of the poison, and the Doctor acts as if he's still alive [which makes Bigon's 'one trillionth of a gram...' claim look a bit exaggerated, though presumably Urbankans have some natural immunity to it].

It's stated that Monarch's ship has been visiting Earth for a long, long time, going backwards and forwards between Earth and Urbanka [or maybe not; see **Four Whats to Doomsday?**] and establishing its suitability for invasion. Monarch wants the planet's silicon and carbon, and plans to approach the Earth in friendship before shrink-poisoning the population and replacing them with Urbankans. Bigon, an "abducted" human, believes that the speed of the journey doubles each time [as far as he can tell].

The ship first visited Earth over 30,000 years ago, and on every trip it's picked up groups of humans for analysis. The more talented of these humans have all been stored on microchip and inserted into android bodies, meaning that they still survive after thousands of years, and on Monarch's ship they regularly perform displays of their native cultural rites known as 'recreationals'. Some androids have silver discs on the backs of their hands, and spend their time working on Monarch's technical projects as mindless drones. It's suggested that these 'slaves' might have Urbankan, rather than human, chips inside them. The cold of space makes their lubrication freeze and their joints seize up.

Many of the slaves are working on power formulae to try to achieve Monarch's faster-than-light dream, while another of the android-attended areas is a mobilliary chamber with an induction furnace, where damaged androids are repaired in automated transparent cabinets. Bigon describes his android body as a polymer stretched over a non-corrodable steel frame, his mind being stored

Four *Whats* to Doomsday?

...continued from page 115

ing the ball. Even catching it again, assuming that -270° C ambient temperature doesn't make the ball turn to powder on impact with the ship, hardly makes a difference. Certainly, to cross the 200 metres or so to the TARDIS would take well over six minutes with this as a means of propulsion. And we have to assume either that the Doctor has a built-in engine keeping him accelerating along with the ship, or that the ship's gravitational pull keeps him in line, in which case jumping off the vessel is as easy as jumping off Earth. The ship's velocity, if it's decelerating toward Earth or if it's constantly accelerating as stated, isn't going to be that of the Doctor as he leaves it. We have the old problem that as soon as the airlock door is opened, the gravity seems to "leak out". And why don't his fingers shatter when he catches the frozen ball at three degrees absolute? Plus, the music's rubbish.)

So. The dates given for Monarch's visitations are "local" time. Without more information it's impossible to come up with absolute, authoritative durations, distances or accelerations. We can make a guess that the acceleration is 9.81 metres per second per second, as this saves the passengers the bother of generating gravity (but of course monopticons can float, so it's entirely possible that

the gravity is enhanced or "relaxed"). At this acceleration (1g), you can get to 97% of light-speed (0.97c) in about ten years - eight to the passengers - after chucking out as much energy as the USA has used in the 225 years since it formed. Moreover, as something this massive approaches Earth, surely the tidal effects would be noticeable? Maybe they are; Bigon's era was the last 'dropping-time', and the sixth century BC is full of odd events that got turned into legends.

You can never accelerate to c, but as you get closer the numbers get weird. At 99.49% of light-speed time passes at 10% of the rate it does at rest, then at 99.87% it's only 5%. If they're going that fast, then Bigon's ETA of 'four days' is over two months as far as the Earth is concerned. But after thousands of years the mass of the ship would be about that of a neutron star, if it were accelerating at 1g. At a less breakneck acceleration, after all this time the ship would still be on course for 0.9949c but with a more realistic energy-use (perhaps using interstellar gas in what's called a Bussard Ramjet, and this would also protect the ship from dust, which would hit like a nuke at those speeds).

Either way, Bigon's estimate of how long Earth has until doomsday is meaningless unless we know how far they've travelled, how fast they're accelerating and how good their brakes are.

on three chips; one for memory, one for reason, one for motor power, though the slaves only have the motor chip. The reasoning chip contains more circuits than there are synapses in a brain, linked by lines a hundred nanometres thick. Even the Doctor finds this impressive [by twenty-first century standards, it isn't, particularly].

Though Bigon has free will, built into him is a failsafe mechanism which signals any aggressive intent. The lesser androids have failsafes that stop them revolting by causing them to jam up if they engage in any collective activity. Bigon's only attempt to rebel was punished by putting his chip in the mobilliary chamber's filing-cabinets for a hundred years, alongside the entire Urbankan species. When humans are turned into androids, they're put under hypnosis and made to recall every part of their lives, these memories being stored on chip before the body is disposed of. Enlightenment can easily hypnotise Nyssa [perhaps using technology… it begins off-screen], after which she's put in an alcove where a hi-tech helmet starts to work on her brain. It apparently

only takes five minutes to finish reading her.

The ship is cluttered with exotic alien technology, including a device that increases density and reduces matter. Nyssa calls this a resonant stroboscope, while the Doctor says it's worthy of Gallifrey. There's also an interferometer for measuring gravity-waves, and a graviton crystal detector. Nyssa points out that the interferometer superseded the crystal on Traken. [The importance of this, and of the stroboscope, is never explained. It's feasible that the matter-reducing device has in some way helped to perfect the Urbankans' posion, since it's doubtful that a poison with the properties Bigon describes could have evolved naturally.]

Air is supplied by a flora chamber, containing all the plants that survive from Urbanka, although the atmosphere isn't quite Earth-normal until Monarch tells the ship's computer to provide a better atmosphere for the guests. Monopticons, floating spherical surveillance devices with magnetic shields, monitor the ship's many halls, galleries and laboratories. They can also relay

Monarch's orders in what sounds like a form of machine-code. The Urbankans would seem to be able to understand any language, and carry small but powerful energy weapons when needed. The beams from these weapons go right through the Urbankan androids themselves, although in other respects the Urbankans aren't physically powerful.

Monarch refers to his landings on Earth as 'dropping times', and doesn't seem surprised by the thought of an astral plane. The ship's computer claims that Gallifrey isn't in the Urbankan memory banks, but believes the Doctor must have access to 'fifth-dimensional' travel. Yet Enlightenment knows there's a galactic legend about Rassilon, he who found the Eye of Harmony [possibly a race-memory of the vampire wars, as mentioned in "State of Decay", likely to be found on many planets]. But Monarch refuses to believe that anybody's science is better than his.

Ultimately, the ship heads off into space with Monarch defeated and the "human" androids in charge. [What happens to the Urbankans in the filing-cabinets is unknown. The Doctor initially aims the ship back towards Urbanka in order to thwart Monarch, but it's doubtful that the androids are planning on going there.]

Planet Notes

• *Urbanka.* The homeworld of the Urbankans orbits the star of Inokshi in galaxy RE-1489. Monarch wrecked the place in his attempts to develop faster-than-light technology, exhausting the minerals and destroying the ozone layer so that ultra-violet rays ravaged the planet, although the official story is that Inokshi collapsed into a black hole a thousand years ago.

History

• *Dating.* The Doctor arrives on the 28th of February, 1981, at 4:15 p.m. This is, apparently, the point at which he hijacked Tegan [and therefore the date of 18.7, "Logopolis"].

The Urbankans first visited Earth around 30,000 years ago, when they snatched some Australian Aboriginals. The other humans they captured on their visits include Mayans like Princess Villagra, Orientals of the Futu dynasty that the Doctor believes flourished four-thousand years ago [not a "real" dynasty, as far as recorded history goes] and various Athenian Greeks. The visit to Greece was the last of the visits until now, and the ship left Urbanka for Earth 1,250 years

ago. [Bigon's claim that Monarch's speed doubles with each journey between Earth and Urbanka suggests that the ship arrived on Earth around 35500 BC, 15500 BC, 5500 BC and 500 BC. 35500 BC isn't an unreasonable date for the Aboriginals, although none of these dates fits the Mayans, so possibly they're not really Mayans - even though Bigon describes them as such - but from some older, pre-Mayan civilisation. The Doctor's way-out estimate of the Mayans flourishing around 5000 BC might hint at some knowledge of this similar-but-unknown culture. The "abductees" from the Futu dynasty don't match Monarch's flight-plan at all, of course, although it's feasible that this kind of Chinese civilisation might have existed in 5500 BC. See also **Four Whats to Doomsday?**.]

The visit to Greece was 'one-hundred generations ago' [so 500 BC fits]. The ship's been picking up signals from Earth for the last fifty years.

The Analysis

Where Does This Come From? As many people have pointed out, this one just looks *peculiar*. It seemed odd at the time, and seems odd when you watch it again in the context of the rest of Season Nineteen. It's a story full of strange pacing and awkward spaces, laden with often-disjointed imagery and often-surreal dialogue. It's so out-of-character that some have wondered whether Terence Dudley had ever seen *Doctor Who* before he wrote it.

What's wrong here? Why does "Four to Doomsday" feel so off-kilter, so much like a weird cross-breeding of different styles, themes and ideas?

Here's a clue. Try watching it again with the colour turned off.

This is, above all else, a '60s *Doctor Who* story. Try to imagine William Hartnell in the lead role, and it all starts to make sense. The trouble is that the programme (and television itself) had changed so much in the '70s that by 1982, "traditional" *Doctor Who* meant "Pyramids of Mars", not "The Daleks". The story begins with the TARDIS arriving in an unfamiliar, seemingly-uninhabited environment, and the four-person crew trying to work out - for their sake and for ours - where they are and what's going on. The Doctor's even trying to get one of his companions back to Earth, just like old times. When the aliens and the travellers meet, they meet in the style of a "formal introduction"; the scene in Monarch's throneroom is even *staged* like a '60s production, with the two sides explaining their customs to each other in painful detail (this is very much a feature of early Doctor-meets-other-cultures stories, but not of the series in the '70s, when the Doctor's far more likely to barge into the middle of the action and act as if he belongs there).

The seemingly-bizarre plot, which insists on piling faster-than-light technology, people stored on microfiche and shape-changing alien frogs on top of one another, seems a lot more reasonable in the context of the slightly manic, slightly trippy sort of story you got when the world was black-and-white. "The Ark" (3.6), especially, springs to mind. Even the Doctor's space-walk is more reminiscent of "The Space Pirates" (6.6) than the spaceship-antics of "Frontier in Space" (10.3).

But the biggest giveaways are the recreationals, specially-choreographed displays of "historical" human culture, complete with Chinese dragons and Greek swordfights. There's nothing comparable in any Pertwee story, and precious little like it in the Tom Baker run. It's easy to be reminded of a story like "Marco Polo" (1.4), in which the script will occasionally launch into "interludes", explaining other places and other times to the younger viewers in the hope that they'll take an interest in history.

As we've already seen, by the 1980s *Doctor Who* was being made by people who'd watched *Doctor Who* when they were younger and who took its mythology for granted. Terence Dudley, on the other hand, had already been at the BBC in 1963 and had very nearly ended up working on the programme in its early days. Far from being a story written by someone who'd never seen the series, "Four to Doomsday" has the ring of a story written by someone who remembered a much earlier brief.

The most "modern" thing here, in fact, is the notion that the Urbankans are storing people's identities electronically. Minds-on-computer are (and were) by no means a new concept, but here the script describes the whole thing in terms of consumer electronics. If this story *had* been made in the '60s, then the personalities of the "humans" on Monarch's ship would almost certainly have been stored in one big research-lab-sized computer bank. (On the other hand, both "The Ark" and "The Faceless Ones" take the view that the best way to store people is by shrinking them.) But

now the word "microchip" is being bandied around. In a world that was just getting to grips with the idea that information could be stored digitally, not just in labs but in digital watches and on home computers, even the human soul potentially becomes something you might be able to run on a ZX-81. Anyone trying to mount a defence of this story on the grounds of deeper significance may also like to know that Lenin had a Ministry of Enlightenment and a Ministry of Persuasion, the latter being the people who gave the director Sergey Eisenstein his big break, but also his biggest worries.

And oh look, another *Star Wars* opening (the huge space-cruiser passing overhead) with *Alien* overtones (the throbbing, seemingly-deserted ship interior). As in "The Android Invasion" (13.4), the androids are straight out of *Westworld* (1973), especially when required to pull their faces off or dress up in period costume and fight.

Plus one final thought: this was the first Davison story to be made. His first public appearance, in costume, was on a float at the Lord Mayor's Show in November 1981. Anyone who's seen one of these processions will make the connection easily enough; Chinese dragon-dancers, carnival costumes, bands playing music from around the world...

Things That Don't Make Sense Monarch is four days away from Earth when the Doctor arrives on his ship, hence the title of the story. In the first place, if Monarch can move between galaxies in mere thousands of years then he must be travelling so fast that "four days from Earth" would put him light-years away. Which means that the Doctor's attempt to land the TARDIS on Earth is a massive, chronic misfire, not the small error we're led to believe.

Moreover, there's no way that a ship travelling slower than light in real-space can travel between galaxies in a mere millennia (the nearest galaxy is Andromeda, two-million light years away; see **Four Whats to Doomsday?**). And if Monarch wants to invade Earth to get his hands on the planet's silicon, then wouldn't grabbing the moon be a lot easier? A better source, and without all those irritating oceans.

The Chinese community on the ship has been there for four-thousand years, yet somehow the dragon costume has "Tsang Kung Fu Club" written on it in English. The Athenians wear Corinthian battle-dress, which is rather like Italian troops in World War Two wearing Soviet uniforms. Bigon is supposed to believe in democracy, but claims to have been on the ship for 2555 years, and 564 BC is rather too early for the Athenians to be experimenting with that sort of idea. All the history-bots have kept their cultural diversity, yet the food's remarkably cosmopolitan, unless Herodotus neglected to tell us that the Athenians sailed to Mexico to pick up avocados. Any 'collective activity' causes the slave androids to become uncontrollable, so they become uncontrollable when all the recreationals are performed at once, but if *any* collective activity jams them then how can teams of them perform things like the dragon-dance? Why are the androids primed to perform 'recreationals' anyway, when in every other respect they're just drones and Urbankans consider culture to be worthless?

The Doctor carefully briefs his new TARDIS crew on safety procedures before they leave the Ship, and even gives Tegan the spare key, but he never locks the door as Adric can wander back on board whenever he feels like it. He also tells Tegan that nobody on Earth will believe them if they try to warn the authorities about the Urbankan invasion, so he's completely forgotten about the numerous military organisations who've helped him hold off alien invasions before [is he worried they won't recognise him?].

In fact, everyone's memory is faulty here. Adric talks about this new Doctor as if they've been in lots of scrapes together, and what he says about his mentor is clearly wrong: 'I've never known him to hurry anything' and 'he knows I'm no good with my hands' are prime examples. Adric, who used to help make microscope slides, also needs to have photosynthesis explained to him. Monarch's scan of the TARDIS indicates a molecular patina 'consistent with Earth and its solar system'... because they have wooden boxes on Jupiter, don't they? [Do the Ice Warriors cultivate trees on Mars?]

When Tegan dematerialises the TARDIS, Monarch just sits there looking pleased that any idiot can operate the controls, as if he somehow knows that she's only going to move it a few yards and isn't going to stop him stealing it. The Urbankans are said to have been receiving messages from Earth for fifty years, presumably rather blue-shifted and garbled. The interferometer and electron microscope are products of a culture that's allegedly 'worthy of Gallifrey', but they were available at a provincial hospital in "The Hand of Fear" (14.2). Likewise, the screens used in the mobiliary are the standard-issue microfilm readers found in any good library.

The magic frog-juice that shrinks all organic matter (somehow) is secreted by Urbankans, but affects Monarch, which isn't evolutionarily sensible. And if he's 'partly' organic, despite his great age, then why does all of him shrink?

Critique (Prosecution)   It's very pretty, isn't it? Hardly the most incisive comment you'll find in this book, but the one thing to bear in mind when talking about "Four to Doomsday" is how little the actual story matters. It's an exercise in filling four weekday evening half-hour slots with nice things to look at and just enough matter to keep them coming back. Watched all in one go, with a critical eye on plot inconsistencies, acting ability or the felicity of the dialogue it falls apart like tissue paper.

If we wanted to try to defend it, we could say that there's a lot in here that one feels is "typical *Doctor Who*" but hasn't been done before, or not like this. You have the feeling that it was always Stratford Johns saying things like 'this will eliminate the need for telemicrographics' or 'directional cobalt flux!'. Peter Davison was always using his cricket ball, and sinister aliens all dressed like people in early '80s pop videos. As the 1980s unfold this idea of a "folk-memory" of the series overrides everything else, until we get to a stage where the only things that ever change are cosmetic, like which bit of English history the Master will pop up in next, which old monster is going to threaten the Time Lords and which clips will be used in the "flashback" scene this year. Then a new generation applies a different, later "folk-memory" and things perk up a bit. Then the whole series becomes a memory, and as Nathan-Turner kept telling us when we compared his product unfavourably to the glory days, 'the memory cheats'.

All that lies ahead. Here we have a desperate attempt to fit in with the Bidmead model ('would you pass the sodium chloride?'), the Ian Levine-inspired insertion of continuity-references, here "inserted" like an enema ('it's got a bathroom, and cloisters') and the strictures of the new twice-weekly timeslot. All the dialogue is geared towards pleasing one of these constituencies, and nothing is left for wit or characterisation. Visually it still delivers, mainly because of the 'recreation-als' and John Black's direction. The sets in partic-ular give a sense of scale to the yarn which was missing in previous studio-bound stories. When you're looking at the sets and not the cast, things are getting bad.

There are three performances to relieve the monotony, one way or another. Stratford Johns basically plays the same part he always plays, and lifts the whole thing. Paul Shelley as Persuasion says some odd things, but does so with such a sneer that it's hard to avoid siding with him against these irritating kids, especially the one who's playing at being *Doctor Who*. And Philip Locke… by Zeus! Philip Locke. Watch his mis-timed fists of fury. His reacting late to everything. His over-emoting on lines like 'it's an avocado pear', let alone the second cliffhanger.

It would be a shame if such things were all the story is remembered for, but if we're honest, the fans barely remember this story at all. Mind, there are other things *worth* forgetting… the Doctor's "joke" reply to the line 'I'm Lin Futu' is excruciat-ing, and Bert Kwouk is criminally under-used. At least his simpering to Locke as the TARDIS dema-terialises is a hoot. You rather expect them to burst into a duet.

But even *this* is too forgettable to be really worth saying anything about. All things considered, this story is rather like watching a work in progress.

Critique (Defence) To precis. A story that doesn't seem to know how much the audience has already seen or how best to get its point across, a script that sounds as if it's changing its mind about the details with every other scene and throws in twice as much exposition as anybody really needs, and yet still "Four to Doomsday" manages to reach to the end of its four-episode lifespan without getting on the nerves of anybody but the pedants.

Its linear, no-frills nature makes it feel like a connecting corridor between the far more emi-nent stories on either side of it, but for all its weird twists of logic it remains distinctly likeable. Even when Bigon rips off his skin and shows us his cir-cuits, in theory an inexcusable cliché by this point, we're inclined to find it "cute" rather than "annoying".

Everybody here, on-screen and off, seems com-fortable with what they're doing. The interaction between the TARDIS crew members has rarely been better, assuming you're not the type who's offended by companions under the age of twenty-

five. We may mock Adric for being a nauseating adolescent, Nyssa for being terminally wet and Tegan for being a shrieking Australasian, but there is a real sense of something dynamic behind the regular cast here, with Peter Davison at the core of the process even if he hasn't quite figured out who the incoming Doctor's going to be. Despite its obvious '60s roots and its shamelessly '80s appearance, in its execution much of this feels like a story from the Graham Williams era, with the principle actors (Davison and Stratford Johns, in this case) confidently breezing through a light-weight plot and instinctively keeping up the pace. Unlike the Graham Williams era, the cast and pro-duction team aren't killing each other behind the scenes, so these look like Good Times on board the TARDIS.

The other reason this comes off is that by now, the new-look series has got into its stride so well that it feels as if *any* story can be made to work (although this will, before long, prove to be a false hope). Monarch's ship is the kind of environment that the early Doctors were just *gagging* to explore, a cosmic playroom of labs, gantries and throne-rooms that uses space almost-but-not-quite as well as "Castrovalva" did. The sight of the frog-emperor on his throne, flanked by sinister, slinky human advisors, gets far closer to the joy of "pulp" SF than any other space-opera of its day.

Since this was the first Davison story to be filmed, you could even see it as an experimental space in itself, with a structure simple enough to let the programme toy with new sights, sounds, quirks and foibles. If "Four to Doomsday" seems insubstantial, as if various elements have been bolted on to the story by mistake and certain sub-plots are heading down dead-ends, then it's at least fulfilling the programme's duty to investigate strange places and make the audience either go "ooh" or "eh?".

Undoubtedly, it's a mediocre story for this peri-od, but by this stage even mediocre stories can be pleasingly weird-looking and bring us Chinese dragons dancing with Aboriginals on enormous alien battleships.

The Facts

Written by Terence Dudley. Directed by John Black. Viewing figures: 8.4 million, 8.8 million, 8.9 million, 9.4 million.

Supporting Cast Stratford Johns (Monarch), Paul Shelley (Persuasion), Annie Lambert (Enlightenment), Philip Locke (Bigon), Burt Kwouk (Lin Futu), Illarrio Bisi Pedro (Kurkutji), Nadia Hammam (Princess Villagra).

Oh, Isn't That..?

• *Stratford Johns.* As mentioned in Volume I (see 2.1, "Planet of Giants"), Detective Chief Inspector Barlow in Z Cars was a groundbreaking figure in British popular culture. After twenty years in the role, Johns wanted as big a change as possible. A mad frog in a bathrobe seemed like just the ticket. After this he was seen being tied up naked and tortured by a dominatrix with a cattle-prod in Channel 4's rather alarming *Brond*.

• *Bert Kwouk.* Aside from pouncing on Inspector Clouseau at unexpected intervals, Kwouk was the BBC's resident "Ah-So" voice-over artist for series like *The Water Margin*. (What are we saying? There's never been a series exactly like *The Water Margin*.) More importantly he played the commandant of the women's prison camp in *Tenko*, a series in which Louise Jameson broke the "curse" of *Doctor Who* by becoming more famous for her new role than for playing Leela.

• *Philip Locke.* Anyone can play a mad scientist in *The Avengers*, but how many mad optometrists have there been, let alone ones who got to kill Jon Pertwee? (It's the episode "From Venus with Love", and Pertwee plays a Brigadier.) More recently he'd been in ATV's *Antony and Cleopatra* and an advert for Refreshers ("may the Fizz be with you"… you can imagine the vibe).

Working Titles "Day of Wrath".

Cliffhangers Enlightenment and Persuasion arrive in the "dining room" of Monarch's ship, looking exactly like Tegan's drawings; Bigon reveals his android nature by pulling the skin off his chest and face; the Chinese android-people force the Doctor's head down, and the Greeks prepare to chop it off. The last episode ends with Nyssa collapsing in the TARDIS console room without explanation, a lead-in to the next story.

The Lore

• The Doctor's costume was still being made up as rehearsals began. One idea, which got as far as being included in scripts for "Project 4G", was a grey morning-coat and collapsible top-hat. The Doctor's monocle / eye-glass in this story seems to be a legacy of this. Colin Lavers, who'd worked on "The Power of Kroll" (16.5) and will return several times throughout the 1980s, designed the new "uniform". The buttons on the back of Davison's jacket kept getting caught on the metal chairs.

• A company called Unit 22, recommended by Dee Robson (who'd been asked to do the costumes for this story, but who'd been otherwise engaged), made the spacesuit. The Unit 22 people were rehired several times, making the "Earthshock" Cybermen (19.6), the new-look Omega (20.1, "Arc of Infinity"), the revamped Silurians and Sea Devils (21.1, "Warriors of the Deep") and others.

• The shooting schedule for this and the next two years were determined by Davison's prior commitments to two (yes, *two*) sitcoms he was making at the time: *Sink or Swim*, about two brothers trying to make it in London after moving south (see 21.6, "The Caves of Androzani"); and *Holding the Fort*, about the husband of a high-ranking military officer staying at home to raise the children, with hilarious consequences (it says here).

• At least two other actors were approached to play the Doctor before Davison was cast. Richard Griffiths had to refuse as he was committed to comic-strip *I, Claudius* knock-off *The Cleopatras*, and after that appeared as the brilliantly unlikely hero of the brilliantly unlikely techno-thriller *Bird of Prey*. He's rumoured to have been the contender to replace Sylvester McCoy, had Season Twenty-Seven ended with a regeneration (see **What Would Have Happened Next?** under 26.4, "Survival"). Griffiths may be best-known to overseas readers as Uncle Monty in *Withnail and I*… opposite Paul McGann and Richard E. Grant. It appears that Iain Cuthbertson was also asked (see 16.1, "The Ribos Operation").

• Davison had grown up with the programme, and would have loved to have been in it as a guest villain. He claimed that his fondest memory was of being scared by soldiers coming to life out of some ice (probably 1.5, "The Keys of Marinus"; possibly 5.3, "The Ice Warriors"; almost certainly not 5.1, "Tomb of the Cybermen"). His previous reputation had been based on his role as Tristan Farnon, well-meaning Yorkshire vet in the seemingly eternal Saturday Night series *All Creatures Great and Small*. He was, in short, TV's Mr. Nice Guy. He and his wife Sandra Dickinson had appeared in "A Man for Emily", a story in ITV's *Doctor Who* clone *The Tomorrow People* which was bizarre and homoerotic even by *that* show's standards (the opening shot was a long pan up Davison's near-naked body to his Harpo Marx wig).

Dickinson was at that stage playing Trillian in the TV version of *The Hitch-Hiker's Guide to the Galaxy*, so Davison tagged along, eventually playing a small but memorable part as "Dish of the Day". Both Tom Baker and Patrick Troughton congratulated him on becoming the Doctor, but Christopher Barry (see - for instance - 17.3, "The Creature from the Pit" or 9.4, "The Mutants") told him that he was wrong for the role. Davison had also just filmed a series of beer commercials for Greene King IPA, based around the idea of "The Beer Vets Like", which had to be scrapped as his *Doctor Who* contract specified that he couldn't be seen drinking or smoking outside the programme.

• Terence Dudley had submitted ideas to the programme before. One "pet" project, entitled "The Beast", was based on his historical drama experience but with a bit of SF malarkey thrown in. Bidmead rejected it, so Dudley sent it in again to incoming script editor Antony Root, whereupon it became "Black Orchid" (19.5). Root had been a floor manager on *Blake's 7* and other series (he'd worked on 17.1, "Destiny of the Daleks"), and had been placed with the *Doctor Who* office on a three-month contract. (If the sequence of events here is a bit confusing, then we'll try to sort it all out under 19.4, "The Visitation".)

Many Bidmead-commissioned scripts came unstuck at around this point. One of these was by Rod Beacham, author of what some experts reckon is the worst *Blake's 7* episode ("Assassin") not written by Ben Steed; one by Jim Follett, author of the third-worst ("Stardrive"); and one by Tanith Lee, who arguably wrote the fifty-first and fifty-second worst. (We can't bring ourselves to call any episode "best" but "Sarcophagus" and "Sand" are as good as it got.) Bidmead's often-repeated claim that he didn't want to make *Doctor Who* stories that were in any way like *Blake's 7* looks rather shaky.

• It appears from some sources that Nyssa was originally going to be killed off at the end of this story. Davison, with whom Sutton had immediately established a rapport, interceded. (Like Tom Baker before him, Davison has said that he never felt anyone really listened to his opinions, but there is evidence that Nathan-Turner went to some trouble to keep him happy.) As the character of Nyssa was copyright of Johnny Byrne, all sorts of complications arose in the contracts. Life really is too short to go into all the intricacies, but one of the immediate consequences was giving her at least a token presence for two episodes of "Kinda"(19.3) and barely acknowledging her existence in the other two.

• Most of the lab equipment was recycled from "The Leisure Hive" (18.1).

• Although *The Stage* ran ads for Aborigine actors, only one showed up. The Chinese dancers were all staff at the restaurant favoured by the production team. One of the two "Mayan" dances used music from the National Theatre production of the Aztec-based play *The Royal Hunt of the Sun* by Peter Shaffer (see 1.6, "The Aztecs"). Other stock music came from a series set in Australia's outback, *Quest Under Capricorn*, filmed in 1962.

• The original plan was to slow down the space-walk using the disc system used for action replays in sports coverage, but this would have made the episode about five minutes too long. This may be why Adric looks such a tool doing his little jig when the Doctor reaches the TARDIS.

19.3: "Kinda"

(Serial 5Y, Four Episodes, 1st - 9th February 1982.)

Which One is This? A complex meditation on the divisions between individuals and the externalisation of self, touching on the nature of the colonial mind-set and the importance of the jungle as a physical reflection of the human subconscious… oh, all right. It's the one with the big pink snake and all the people in hula skirts.

Firsts and Lasts First of two appearances by the Mara, the wobbly psychic serpent from the dark places of the inside. For the first time since the 1960s (when the series put out forty-odd episodes a year, and actors would frequently take holidays in the middle of a story), one of the TARDIS crew gets a "day off", with Nyssa staying put inside the

Ship while everybody else is busy with the adventure. In terms of production - though not broadcast order - this is actually the start of Eric Saward's tenure as script editor, and for better or worse he's going to be in the role for the next four years.

Barney Lawrence and Mike Mungarven, who've been under latex several times in the last eighteen months, show their faces as the two Kinda "hostages" (Lawrence also was the Marsh-Child in 18.3, "Full Circle").

Four Things to Notice About "Kinda"...

1. *Doctor Who* is getting trippy again. The series has often flirted with nightmare sequences and visual-effects-ridden dreamscapes over the years (6.2, "The Mind Robber"; 9.5, "The Time Monster"; 14.3, "The Deadly Assassin"...), but "Kinda" sees the Doctor get involved in shamanic practices on a planet full of Noble Savages, using CSO rather than LSD to expand his mind. This time the dream-imagery's more heavily symbolic than ever, both when the Doctor's having visions of the Great Wheel of History and when Tegan's exploring the black hole of her own head-space, but what's really noticeable - as in "Warriors' Gate" (18.5) - is that the nature of the hallucinations are more like pop video than hippy culture. The figures in Tegan's bad dream once again have more than a splash of the New Romantic about them, while the Doctor's premonition of the apocalypse is smeared with the kind of effects you'd expect from every single video made by every single electro-pop band between 1979 and 1983 (see **Did Kate Bush Really Write This?** under 20.2, "Snakedance" and **Is "Realism" Enough?**).

2. The series' flirtation with eccentric and oddly-motivated villains continues. The closest thing to a "proper" villain here is Hindle, a twitchy young security officer on a survey mission to the jungle-world of Deva Loka, who also happens to be having a nervous breakdown and gets the last word in insane imperialism. One minute he's pouring the mute, telepathic local tribesmen into military uniforms and criticising them for not having straight ties, the next he's reaching exactly the *wrong* sci-fi conclusion and claiming that the plants on the planet are conspiring against him. (As with Rorvik in "Warriors' Gate", mad people in this series actually seem mad these days... see **The Lore** for more on why Hindle loses it.) Experienced viewers may find themselves tempt-

ed to scream along with Hindle's choicest rants, including '*I have the power of life and death over all of you!*'; '*you can't mend people!*'; and, of course, '*mummy!*'.

3. Very well. We'll mention the snake. Obviously there are many, many unconvincing monsters in this series, but as in "State of Decay" (18.4) the problem here is that the monster is only required to put in an appearance at the climax of the story. If a dreadful alien costume is seen shambling around the place for most of the plot, then you can get used to it and concentrate on the story instead of the visible zip up its back. But if the manifestation of the beast is supposed to be the *piece de resistance*, then you can feel somewhat... cheated.

So when we finally see the Mara - an entity which supposedly represents all our fears and repressed impulses, and is supposedly so terrible that it can't bear to face its own reflection - we just find ourselves asking who in the world could feel gut-wrenching anxiety about a big pink plastic snake with lockjaw. Unless it's supposed to be a Freudian thing? And ironically, Adric's reaction to it is to exclaim: 'It's fantastic!'

4. Aris, one of the "primitive" tribespeople living in a post-technological Eden, is possessed by the Mara in episode two and required to scream in horror. Later, he's required to throw his head back while laughing demonically. Which is unfortunate, as on both occasions he just ends up revealing how many fillings he's got. (As the Doctor points out, the Kinda are obviously more sophisticated than they look.)

The Continuity

The Doctor When Adric shows him a basic sleight-of-hand trick, the Doctor seems positively fascinated, as if he's never seen such a thing before [even though he pulls off a similar trick himself in 8.4, "Colony in Space"]. However, he's soon copying Adric's style, although it takes him a while to get it right. Repeatedly called an 'idiot' by Panna the wise-woman, he readily accepts the abuse [it's hard to imagine most Doctors putting up with this kind of stick].

• *Inventory.* He ends up running off with Adric's coin. The sonic screwdriver is otherwise engaged, on the logical surmise that a jungle won't have any electronic equipment.

• *Background*. The Doctor knows of the Mara as a legend, but has no idea why such creatures exist. [It's not surprising he's heard of them. "Mara" is the name given to a ruling evil spirit in Hindu lore, but the word also suggests a demon in both Norse and Old English, hence the word "nightmare".]

The Supporting Cast

• *Adric*. Yet again, he's in the position of pretending to side with the bad guys, on this occasion snapping out of his recent sulkiness and showing his crafty side again. At least, until he starts grouching at Tegan and telling her that the release of the Mara is all her fault [he *really* doesn't seem to like Tegan]. He is, as has already been mentioned, good with sleight-of-hand trickery and would seem to have at least one coin on his person. [See "Warrior's Gate" for more of his tossing. There didn't seem to be an economy on Alzarius, so why he has them is a mystery.]

• *Nyssa*. Her recent collapse [at the end of the last story] was due to 'mild mental disorientation'. [Not surprising, considering that she's recently seen her homeworld destroyed and been hypnotised twice in one episode. Alternatively, the Big Finish audio "Primeval" puts down Nyssa's collapse to telepathic interference by the demi-god Kwundaar, who strangely enough hails from Traken's past.] Still suffering headaches and lapses in concentration, she sits out most of this adventure to recover in the TARDIS.

• *Tegan*. Unusually susceptible to the wind-chimes on Deva Loka, looking as if she's going to faint as soon as she hears them, while the Doctor doesn't seem affected by the noise at all. It is, of course, through Tegan that the Mara manifests itself; see **The Non-Humans**. [A particular psychological weakness?]

In the dreams she experiences while under the influence of the wind-chimes, she sees two rather unpleasant games-players who treat her as if she doesn't exist, significant as she previously saw Adric and Nyssa playing draughts. Likewise, the hostile-looking metal structure in the dream seems to represent the TARDIS. [The obvious suggestion here is that she feels intimidated and alienated by her two "smart" fellow companions on the Ship. It's quite possible that Dukkha, the figure in the dream who seems to know how this whole hallucinatory universe works, is an "evil" reflection of the Doctor. The word "Dukkha" is used in Buddhism to mean the state of suffering that

results from the material world, although it also sounds enough like "Doctor" to be suggestive. To our eyes the TARDIS is something cosy and familiar, but the dream-version looks spiky and threatening. See **The Lore** for what the cut scenes from this story tell us about "the Wherever" (as the dream-zone's called in the script).]

Tegan has a memory of not liking the taste of ice cream when she was three. After events here, she's obviously terrified by the thought that the Mara might still be inside her, although the Doctor believes she's safe. [See 20.2, "Snakedance"...]

The TARDIS The Doctor rigs up a delta-wave augmentor, using equipment from the TARDIS and employing the sonic screwdriver as its delta waveform generator. This puts Nyssa into 'D-sleep' and helps her recover. There's also a set of draughts on board the Ship.

The Non-Humans

• *The Mara*. An entity that inhabits the 'dark places of the inside', although it isn't restricted to a single form, so it's hard to tell whether it should be seen as a single thing or a "species"; Panna says both 'he' and 'they', claiming that they thrive on suffering and madness.

A being that seems to lurk in the unconscious, the Mara seen here can only cross over into physical reality through 'the dreaming of an unshared mind'. When Tegan falls into a trance, she finds herself in a scary dream-world, a black void inhabited by sinister, pale-faced figures who bear tattoos of red snakes on their arms. One of these - Dukkha - taunts, terrifies and disorientates her, claiming that all the dream-people are the same as each other [i.e. all the Mara] and slowly driving her mad until she agrees to let him borrow her form. [The fact that he claims she'll be 'entertained' by the experience says a lot about the nasty urges the Mara represents.] At this point, Dukkha's snake tattoo wriggles off his arm and onto Tegan's. When she awakes, she has the tattoo on her *real* arm. She appears paler, her gums are redder and she acts in a way that veers between "malicious" and "over-sexed". In this state she "tempts" Aris, one of the Kinda males; when the tattoo moves to *his* arm, Tegan falls unconscious, and she remembers these events as a mere dream when she wakes.

Under the Mara's influence, Aris leads an attack on the off-worlders' base. Panna believes the Mara will set the great wheel of history turning, starting off the cycle of civilisations rising and falling; Karuna refers to the Mara's influence as 'the curse of time'. Wherever the wheel turns, there's suffering, delusion and death. However, the Mara can't bear its own reflection - because evil can't face itself - and when Aris is surrounded with mirrors, the snake falls off his arm. It becomes three-dimensional and begins to grow, ultimately becoming the Mara in its true form; an enormous pink serpent. Even Adric has to wonder where it draws its energy from. Surrounded by reflections and reflections of reflections, it's repelled, forced back to the dark places of the inside 'or wherever'. [But compare this with the Mara's later manifestation in "Snakedance".]

Planet Notes

• *Deva Loka*. A lush, jungle-covered world with birds in the trees and flowers in constant bloom, much like the Garden of Eden and with apples to match. There are no predatory animals or diseases, the temperature is constant and the trees are in fruit all the year round, which means the natives don't need shelter and don't have to worry about food.

Deva Loka is home to the 'culturally non-hostile' Kinda, a tribal people who seem to be primitives but whose necklaces bear a design uncannily suggestive of a DNA double-helix. In fact, the Kinda are mutually telepathic; only the wisewoman and her girl apprentice seem able to speak, at least until Aris develops the gift of voice under the Mara's influence. Panna indicates that voice is a mark of wisdom, but her teenage apprentice Karuna seems to suggest that it's a gender issue [it may be a mixture of both, as there are no wise *men* here]. Physical contact would seem to make it easier for the Kinda to communicate, and Karuna suffers pain when she reads the thoughts of those under Aris' control.

Telepathy isn't their only strange feature, either. Panna dies here, and her knowledge and experience are transferred to Karuna. This means that Karuna inherits her special walking-staff, and she states that the two of them are now one.

Panna also uses the Box of Jhana, seemingly just a small wooden box with a little figurine inside it, which once opened can induce "hallucinations" in all those present and let them [telepathically] share the Kinda's perceptions. The opening of the Box also disrupts the power supply

of the dome, and causes the door of the Doctor's cell to miraculously open [the implication is that there's a purpose behind this, most likely that Panna is responsible]. Panna claims the off-worlders have to understand the Kinda through the Box, but at first only a woman can open it without going mad. The male off-worlder Sanders is initially reduced to a child-like state by it, and Panna believes that if the Doctor wasn't affected then he must be a fool.

But the Doctor also describes the Box as a healing device, designed to bring the mind back into phase with Deva Loka, speculating that it generates sound at a frequency beyond his ears and that the Kinda are very sophisticated people indeed [even so, it's hard to guess how they'd make something like this]. The more out-of-phase the mind is, the more dramatic its effect, so ultimately it cures both Sanders and the already-crazed Hindle. Panna's meditations can bring on visions similar to those caused by the Box, and it's from these that the Doctor learns the Mara's nature, though it's hazy whether what he sees represents the past, the future or both. He and the off-world scientist Todd seem to "materialise" back in the real world after experiencing such a vision, as if they've actually been on another plane.

Mental "therapy" is obviously a priority for the Kinda, as there's a set of wind-chimes in the jungle at the Place of Great Dreaming, with a chromatic scale in an eccentric sequence - at least, to human ears - designed to allow shared dreaming between the Kinda when the wind blows. However, it's these chimes which send Tegan into a trance that eventually allows the Mara to manifest itself. The Kinda are aware of the Mara's existence, and know that only the dreaming of an unshared mind can bring it forth. They also believe that mirrors can capture their innocence, as the two tribesmen who are shown their reflections by Hindle are willing to follow his orders even when it comes close to destroying them. They walk off, looking bored, as soon as the mirror's broken.

The Kinda refer to the off-worlders as the Not-We. There's a prophecy that when the Not We come to Deva Loka, a man will arise with the gift of voice, and must be obeyed. The Kinda believe Aris to be this man. [This prophecy is never explained. The Kinda *do* have the potential to glimpse the future, but Aris brings them nothing but destruction. Did the Mara somehow plant this

Is "Realism" Enough?

Now we're going to have to be rigorous in our definitions.

"Realism" doesn't simply mean being "realistic", in the sense that Trekkies mean it when discussing model shots. What we're talking about here is the entire process of mimesis, "copying", an aspect of reality. This can be on several levels, often at once. If what's being shown looks like news-footage, CCTV feed or some other non-fictional or allegedly unmediated image, then that's one thing. However, if we have a manifestly untrue situation but the characters behave the way you or someone you know might under those circumstances, then that's altogether a different kind of "real".

For instance, if what you're looking at is blatantly false - such as actors on stage performing a mime of walking in a strong wind - but the symbols make a coherent whole and the emotions ring true, then an audience can accept some things and not others. For clarity this can be termed "naturalism". Precise judgement is needed to get the audience's threshold right, so that they "buy" (just to take the present example) aliens speaking English but not necessarily a big rubber snake being made from guilt.

Finally, if what you're seeing conforms closely to what you expect to see - if it follows conventions of genre or style or mode - we've got a third kind of "real". There's an argument that for most audiences "real" amounts to "closely resembling what you've been taught to see", so unmediated raw footage is less comprehensible than material which has been processed into a narrative form.

It's almost impossible to do all three kinds of "real" at once. Peter Grimwade was anxious to make the jungle set in "Kinda" look real (in the first, basic mimetic, sense), whilst making sure that Adrian Mills and Nerys Hughes had Received Pronunciation accents (because for some reason people from Liverpool never make it to alien planets... actually it works for Todd, just because the human intruders are supposed to suggest a sense of British imperialism that's unconsciously linked to BBC English). And, as in all but a handful of Doctor Who stories, there's music throughout. Yet when filming the "Wherever" scenes he made sure that everyone knew it was all in Tegan's head, and in the "Beyond" scenes all sorts of digital trickery were used to demark this as "not-real".

But it was, nonetheless, "true". Here we move from plot-logic to narrative aesthetics, and this is always going to be a matter of judgement. For the most part, Doctor Who has been presented to us as "really happening", in the sense that we never have a Bobby-Ewing-in-the-shower moment (at least not unless it's clearly labelled "this bit is a dream"; see 23.3, "Terror of the Vervoids" and 6.2, "The Mind Robber"). There have been occasional moments, such as the Graf's death scene in "The Ribos Operation" (16.1) or Ace's flashback in "Ghost Light" (26.2), where a non-real, subjective effect over-rides the more-or-less objective storytelling. But these are rare.

The overall sense is that if you pointed a camera at the events, then what you'd see is what the story more or less gives you, allowing for music, cliffhangers and dysfunctional props. Where obvious non-mimetic incidents have also occurred, they've been stylistic flourishes to aid the storytelling or mood-setting, such as wipes and dissolves (Chancellor Aukon summoning the bats in "State of Decay", the irising of the image in "The Leisure Hive", and so on). Occasional subjective shots, dream-sequences and other odd narrative ploys - up to and including a song commenting on what's happening, in 3.8, "The Gunfighters" - have been admitted into the storytelling, but usually claimed to take place within a wider "realism". There's an overall assumption that the Doctor's travels are being presented to us in the clearest way (see **Who's Telling the Story?** Under 23.1, "The Mysterious Planet"), as if these were "reconstructions" of real events.

What's become known in media and theatre terminology as "Realism" is a set of assumptions and connections. We see it in many guises. In the theatre, the convention of the "Fourth Wall"; ignoring the audience, and behaving as if we were "eavesdropping" on one ordinary-but-significant two-hour stretch of real life, when everything of note happens in one room and between the start and end of the play. In cinema, the fact that we cut from one shot to another as if there were a narrative connection; there's the "30° Rule" of eyelines between people in conversation, even when one is shown in close-up... it even extends to people in different cities talking by 'phone. Early moviegoers weren't as startled by close-ups or trains approaching the camera as is often claimed, but it took a while for the new "grammar" of film to become "automatic", let alone as rigid as it was by 1970. It's sometimes claimed that children today process images differently, or at least faster, than earlier generations. Research conducted by neu-

continued on page 129...

prophecy?] Karuna states that she has seven fathers, including Aris, and is surprised that the Not-We only have one each. Like many societies, the Kinda have a trickster-figure to defuse conflict. ["Snakedance" might lead us to believe that Deva Loka was once part of the Sumaran Empire, which might mean that the Kinda are themselves descended from off-worlders, but it's not an idea that's explored. Bailey, in interviews given to Tulloch and Alvorado (see **The Lore**), suggests that his starting point was the idea that the planet is an "ashram" for refugees from another, techno-cratic, culture.]

History

• *Dating.* It's implied that the expedition on Deva Loka is made up of Earth-born humans, though it's never explicitly stated and they only refer to an overcrowded 'homeworld' a couple of dozen parsecs away. [It sounds an awful lot like the time of the Earth Empire, after "Colony in Space" (8.4) but before "The Mutants" (9.4). The twenty-seventh or twenty-eighth century is a fair bet, although a couple of dozen parsecs means about seventy light-years, not *that* far from Earth in galactic terms. From the way Todd speaks, the implication may be that the expedition's 'mother-world' is in itself an Earth colony. And there's a hymn that sounds a lot like "Abide with Me". All that said, compare with the dating of "Snakedance".]

The off-worlders who've come to Deva Loka have named the planet S14. This is the fourteenth world on which the commander, Sanders, has done an 'ex and rec' [so one assumes he put the "S" in "S14"]. Their base, a dome in the middle of the jungle, originally had a crew of six [three of them have already vanished by the start of the story, though we never find out the men's fate]. The humans are pompous, imperialistic and nar-row-minded, except for the scientist Todd. They even wear pith helmets. It's standard procedure to take "hostages" from native cultures, according to the manual, which comes in book form and also forbids eating local food rather than the standard rations. Hindle, the designated SR security, insists on keeping a log. A mothership is due to arrive in six seasons, at which point a report will be made on this world's suitability for colonisation.

After events reach their conclusion here, the two butch, procedure-minded members of the expedition are "cured" and Sanders is thinking of staying on Deva Loka, though the report con-cludes that the planet is unsuitable for humans. Before this, the off-worlders only leave the dome and explore the jungle in their Total Survival Suit, a metal box with robotic arms which prevents its user coming into direct contact with the environ-ment outside. The TSS operates on the brain-waves of its operator, so it goes berserk if the user starts to panic. Naturally, it's fitted with an energy weapon. It's also programmed to return to base, and "escort" anyone in the area back with it, if the door's shut while nobody's inside. [The design isn't unlike that of the IMC robot in "Colony in Space", funnily enough.] The colonials' hand-held weapons are chunky guns, covered in buttons that make them look programmable.

The dome is also equipped with mine-like explosives capable of reducing it to its base chem-ical constituents, and the manual states that in extreme emergencies the SR security officer can order this rather extreme self-destruction. The solar generator panels in the dome's storeroom are large mirrors, useful for repelling giant psychic snakes.

The Analysis

Where Does This Come From? Visually it's suspi-ciously like several pop videos of the era, notably Visage's hilariously dour 'Fade to Grey" and Genesis' "Mama", and we'll come back to this later on (see **Did Kate Bush Really Write This?** under 20.2, "Snakedance").

But it's the religious icons that tend to stick out here. Deva Loka is presented to us as a corruptible Eden, and the Mara blatantly suggests the serpent in paradise. The names of the figures in Tegan's dream - Dukkha, Anicca and Anatta - are the names of the three "marks" of existence in Buddhism (although they're only named in the credits, not on-screen). The Kinda themselves hint at all sorts of shamanic and pre-Christian practices; the wheel of history suggests the wheel of karma.

But this isn't a work *about* religion, which in itself tells you something. When "The Face of Evil" (14.4) was made in the '70s, religion wasn't a big issue in Britain, and Christianity was seen as a rather harmless and ineffectual thing on the mainland (excuse Ireland). In the 1980s, Britain was more secular than ever. As *Life of Brian* proved in 1979, you had to go to extremes like turning

Is "Realism" Enough?

...continued from page 127

rologists contradicts this, but it's definitely true that the number of possible interpretations made by anyone born after 1990 is drastically smaller than for those raised in the 1960s. "Realism" is the level of unthinking interpretation, and anything made to avoid disturbing this process.

It's not as if audiences for mainstream television were unenthusiastic or scared when it came to disruptions of conventional realism in drama. Most 1970s series used some sort of "device". Many went out of their way to do something new, especially when people like dramatist Dennis Potter were involved (and you can't say that *I, Claudius*, with its overt television trickery, multiple timescales and playing to camera, was a minority show). Yet since 1980 BBC drama has fallen into definite categories, so that anyone doing what was once fairly routine "internal" narrative is hailed as "experimental". When music that doesn't come from a jukebox appears in *EastEnders*, it seems odd. No other country's soaps have this hair-shirt approach. The dream-sequences in *Sunset Beach* were the highlights, in a series where supernatural events happened daily.

Is this why the bulk of *Doctor Who* has been so conservative when it comes to "realistic" story-telling? Is it, at the end of the day, a soap opera in time and space? We think otherwise.

Doctor Who has developed out of a number of narrative traditions, the pseudo-documentary "gritty realism" celebrated by advocates of the early Pertwee stories merely being the last to have been grafted on (why realism should come in "gritty" form, like peanut butter, is a mystery). Forty years prior to this, there was expressionism. The sets, lighting, music and acting were all there to represent a single, subjective view of the world. It might not be how *you* see it, but it was logically and aesthetically self-consistent. If the world seems like an intimidatingly large and dehumanising place, full of faceless bureaucrats and zombie office employees, then show that to be literally true. Don't provide a rational "back-story" explaining why it's changed from what we all "know" is true, just do it. If you feel that people with disabilities of whatever kind are shunned unfairly, even though they don't necessarily *feel* different, then use an average-looking able-bodied actor with a sign around his / her neck and have everyone treat this person *as if* different. You're telling an emotional truth at the expense of literal, objective "truth".

(The idea being that there are things in the "outside" world which are true, but "truth" - an account linking them together - is a purely subjective set of associations, albeit one usually dictated from outside by opinion-formers. These same opinion-formers had sent the young men of Europe off to blow each other to bits for four years, so fewer people trusted them in the 1920s than in the 1890s.)

Expressionism had been part of television drama since the Alexandra Palace days before the Second World War. It was, before vision-mixers and easy lens-changes, the only practical form of dramatic presentation. Director Rudolf Cartier came to British television in the 1950s and opened out the vocabulary of the form from pointing a camera at a play, and as *Quatermass* and *1984* were among his projects we can't ignore the impact of this. The Special Effects department of the BBC was set up for this sort of thing, not for making spaceships out of squeezy bottles (see 1.2, "The Daleks" and 5.1, "Tomb of the Cybermen").

On the other hand, you have the playwright-director Berthold Brecht and his *Verfremdungseffekt*. This is literally translatable as "en-strange-ness-ing-effect", but those of us with theatrical backgrounds usually say "alienation technique". In this, the biggest riddle is why people pay good money to see stories about people like themselves. If you know it's fiction, then why not say so on stage? You can have the actors in their usual clothes, holding the scripts and prefacing each line with "and then my character says…". You can have characters suffering from their mistakes and then making the same ones in the next scene, so members of the audience feel like yelling "haven't you learned anything?" before realising that it's something they themselves have been doing. (Like, say, not objecting to all the new laws Hitler's been passing or buying from big corporations who support oppressive regimes.) In this style of theatre, you're supposed to apply what you've been seeing to your life, not escape for two hours into someone else's world. You still get attempts at Brechtian staging these days, but they look like cobwebbed oddities, not a living, vibrant challenge to orthodoxy. Quite a few of the BBC's late '70s / early '80s "serious" dramas were done in a quasi-Brechtian style (the easiest to find would probably be the production of Brecht's *Baal*,

continued on page 131...

the crucifixion into a song-and-dance number before anyone really noticed.

By this stage the programme can use religious symbolism in a way that's almost casual, as if the Bible's just another literary reference instead of the foundation for the country's official faith. "Kinda" is about anthropology rather than religion per se, so these symbols become case studies. At a time when the media were so keen on Jung, Campbell and other such popular dissectors of mythology, this uses the Book of Genesis as wantonly as *Battlestar Galactica* used the Book of Exodus (except that, unlike *Galactica*, "Kinda" clearly doesn't believe a word of it). The author of this piece is usually referred to as "chain-smoking Buddhist university lecturer Chris Bailey", which tells us less than it seems, though we'll come to that in **The Lore**.

And religion isn't the only thing that can be safely satirised in this secular '80s world. There's also the matter of the British Empire. As we saw in Volume III (notably 9.4, "The Mutants"), the generation of writers who worked on *Doctor Who* in the '70s was a generation growing up after the Decline and Fall. By that point, programme-makers were happy to send up Britain's former dominion over large chunks of the world and prepared to suggest that it might not have been such a great idea. But the generation after that, making TV in an age when Britain was firmly established as a minor-league power, took the stupidity of Empire for granted. Sanders, the shouty, pith-helmet-wearing leader of the Deva Loka expedition, isn't just a parody of the kind of figure you used to see in colonial fiction (although he is) but a parody of an entire age.

This is no longer news. It's taken as read that our grandparents were pompous and daft-looking, and the imperial days seem quaint when they don't seem immoral. Many viewers at the time might have seen Sanders going through his "grumpy sergeant major" routine and been reminded of BBC sit-com *It Ain't Half Hot Mum*, also about ridiculous military Englishmen being stuck in the middle of a jungle and using natives as servants. Even the Kinda themselves, typical SF savages-who-turn-out-to-be-less-than-savage, are used as archetypal ingredients instead of being a "comment" on the plight of the native in colonial times (again, compare with both "The Mutants" and "Colony in Space").

Onto the psychology. The belief that dreams were as important as waking had - from a mental heath viewpoint - become commonplace, especially after the publication of the paper on the Senoi tribe by adventurer / anthropologist Kilton A. Stewart. Even though this was later found to be either total fabrication or erroneous, it had a significant impact on those researching REM sleep and "altered states". We're entering the golden age of "biofeedback kits", advertised even in the *New Scientist*. And since in *Doctor Who* terms Buddhism is the one belief-system that you can't really knock, there's a connection being made here between the idea of the sleeping, undifferentiated self and the Buddhist notion that the whole being (or "uncarved block") is a lot bigger than the identity you're aware of.

In earlier drafts, the Kinda are just as bad as the colonists because they cut off parts of their psyches and make walls between self and other, hence the term 'Not-We'. In the primary sources for this story, this is the cause of trouble on both sides. (Those sources, we'd better mention, are Conrad's *Heart of Darkness*; Achebe's *Things Fall Apart*; and LeGuin's *The Word for World is Forest*, all good staples of any university course on colonialism and its discontents. We might also include that old **Where Does This Come From?** favourite, *Dune*, especially when Panna and Karuna are playing at being the Bene Gesserit from that book.)

Talking of *Heart of Darkness*, the first draft of this story was written in 1979, when *Apocolypse Now* was on at the cinemas. Make of that what you will.

Things That Don't Make Sense If the Kinda *know* that the dreaming of an unshared mind can summon the Mara, then why don't they think about waking Tegan up when they find her dozing next to the wind-chimes in episode one, rather than putting garlands of flowers around her neck? Or at least have someone watch her, in case she wakes up evil? More dubiously still, Sanders instantly agrees with Adric that a malfunctioning Total Survival Suit may have caused the missing colonials' disappearance, then immediately gets into the suit and toddles off into the jungle anyway. Even by Sanders' pig-headed standards, this is pushing it.

The draughts board is the wrong way round in episode one, as Adric makes his move with a

Is "Realism" Enough?

...continued from page 129

because they cast David Bowie in it) and "Kinda" resembles these in many ways.

What happened was that someone let the expressionists loose in the UFA studios in Germany in the 1920s. To begin with, they simply got on with what they'd been doing on stage, but with edits, lighting, close-ups and distorted camera-angles added to their repertoire of "aren't-we-weird" effects. *The Cabinet of Dr. Caligari* is often held up as a prime example, but mainly because it still exists in the archive. (Many of these pioneering films were lost either to Nazi / Soviet censorship or Allied bombing. Nice to know we aren't the only ones...) *Der Golem*, though, is held up as a precursor to the 1931 *Frankenstein*. The next stage was to show these "internal" worlds as though they were "external" and "real", and that's how things like *Metropolis* happened. Yet even then, dream-sequences were given as much prominence as dream-like things "really" happening, so the whole shebang was larded with symbolism. In America, especially after the arrival of sound, the boundaries were more rigidly maintained. The one area of film where the difference was erased, if only temporarily, was the musical. Whilst the increasingly popular horror and monster films stayed as close to "realism" as the audience could take, the musical was emphatically anti-realism.

This idea of the story-world as a space "other" than that found in the usual kinds of stories is taken to its logical extreme in the 1930s *Flash Gordon* serials. The music, sets and props were taken from Universal's horror cycle (the music in particular is almost shockingly familiar when you see the original films whence it came... *Bride of Frankenstein* is the primary source for *Flash Gordon's Trip to Mars*). The costumes, as in the original comic-strip, are a collage of "other" places and genres; Robin Hood, Fu Manchu and Ruritania in particular. The "punctuation" of these serials is taken from musicals, in particular wipes, dissolves and title-sequences (what George Lucas took for *Star Wars*, and as a consequence what director Lovett Bickford wanted for "The Leisure Hive"). The planets Mars and Mongo were made of other movies, knitted together with the flimsy pretext that "that's how things are here". Audiences bought into it, because they were mostly young and had never known a time before film...

Doctor Who inhabits a strange halfway state between realism and expressionism. It never quite draws attention to itself as fiction - although it flirts with the idea, as we'll see - but it has music, and highly symbolic events and items are treated as though real. All the oddness is presented to us as having a logical cause, not just representing something in someone's head as in *The Singing Detective* or *Brazil*.

However, in Media Studies terms it might be just as useful to think of *Doctor Who* as a musical where no-one ever sings. Like a musical, the set-designs, costumes and other elements are just that little bit more... well, *more*. Things happen in a musical in a way that's less likely in "straight" drama, and aesthetics over-ride orthodox causality of plotting. In a musical, characterisation is largely established through the genre of song that each person gets to do; in *Doctor Who* it's often down to whether they have green skin or metallic voices.

Along the way, as the grammar of television became more flexible (or the viewers less so), the shift towards an unthinking realism became irreconcilable with the original aims of the programme. The Daleks were, initially, as much rhetorical devices as a viable attempt to present how alien life might be. The Cybermen were an existential threat, rather than simply a foe who couldn't be stopped. When *Doctor Who* attempted to return to its dramatic roots in stories like "Kinda" and "Survival" (26.4), it was bound to have problems.

Try to imagine how different the average episode of 1960s *Doctor Who* was from anything else on screen. No matter how much the bulk of each episode resembled the mainstream (so that most of the two remaining episodes of 4.8, "The Faceless Ones", look like *Compact* or *Dixon of Dock Green*), there are moments of pure aesthetic oddness. The sound wasn't just sound-effects, it was a sensual experience in itself, free from its narrative function. The late '60s took this to extremes; in stories like "The Krotons" (6.4), "The Dominators" (6.1) and "The Wheel In Space" (5.7) the boundary between music, sound and speech breaks down. For anyone watching in 1968, the experience was midway between the more esoteric pop of the era (the first two Pink Floyd albums are borderline Radiophonic Workshop) and a Busby Berkeley routine where the human form and the sense of scale are distorted. Plot was almost a side-issue, just as the plots of Fred Astaire or Gene Kelly

continued on page 133...

white piece but seems to be sitting in front of the ranks of the black ones [being the "clever" members of the crew, he and Nyssa play the game this way in an attempt to make things harder].

And the Doctor is surprised when Adric appears to go over to Hindle's side. Does he *never* learn?

You could also quibble with the 'seven fathers' idea (actually we will, in a moment), but for all we know it's metaphorical rather than biological. Indeed, since the Kinda have a culture that's all about overlapping identities, this is actually a lot more likely.

Critique (Prosecution)   Watched in sequence, this stands head and shoulders above the rest of Season Nineteen. Watched in isolation, it is slow, preachy, crassly literal-minded and self-consciously "tricksy".

Laden with club-footed "symbols" - including names of characters we only discover in the end-credits - there's never any doubt that we are being given a lecture, just not what the lecture is about. With hindsight, and a bit of background information, we can figure out that the recognition of our repressed desires and fears as part of ourselves is only possible through admitting that the "self" is a transient illusory thing (multiple Tegans) which leads to desire and dissatisfaction (Anicca and Anatta... they're the bods playing chess, remember) which causes suffering (Dukkha). The way out is through wisdom and compassion (Panna and Karuna) and meditation (Jhana). Got that? Good. So all that business about isolation and quarantine, which both the Not-We and the Kinda have fallen into, is symbolic of our rigidly holding on to self-hood and privacy (and the Greek for this is "idios", so you get the idea).

How many kids watching on weekdays at 7.30 figured that out, do you think?

Paradoxically, the real trouble starts with the idea that this is a parable and should therefore behave like one. Grimwade's decisions in this case burden the story with too much heavy-handed figuration. He imposes onto the story a literal monster, a big pink snake, instead of a largely-unseen threat made almost-tangible *Forbidden Planet* style (and the reference to this film will become obvious when we look at "Snakedance"). He has a "dream sequence" which is clearly labelled "this is not really happening" rather than being shown to be on the same narrative plane as

the rest of the story, then a "prophecy" sequence which is green and with the camera slanted, like in *Batman*. He has pith helmets. He has Todd wear blue stockings and a lab-coat (and glasses, and hair in a bun: "but... Professor Todd, you're beautiful!").

Underneath all the "look at me" pop-video digital jiggery-pokery is a solid piece of theatre. As would be the case with many Sylvester McCoy stories, there is a great deal of vital information in the scenes trimmed to make the running-time, not least the reasons for Hindle's breakdown, which reveal a clearly-thought-out character study within an SF context. Even the minor figures have depth to them (again, in the cut scenes the chess-players are real people, in a Samuel Beckett kind of way). This is - with the possible exceptions of "The Caves of Androzani" and "Snakedance" - the best script for a Davison story, but those are definitely better pieces of television.

It's not like the metaphor hadn't been done before. Although he was ridiculed in the press for saying it, Christopher Eccleston immediately picked up on the idea that the Daleks were scared, isolated children hiding in their tough casings inside walled cities. That's only one similarity between "Kinda" and "The Daleks" (1.2). The Kinda themselves are ex-civilised, reformed warriors, advanced, beautiful people living in the jungle, just like the original Thals. The Doctor and his friends bring the two races into conflict but end a cycle of history. No-one's seriously suggested that Terry Nation was writing Buddhist homilies, but symbolism doesn't have to draw attention to itself.

When this was first broadcast, some reviews believed that the Mara was the name of a race of alien mind-parasites (Dukkha, Anicca and Anatta), reviewing this as though it were *Blake's-7*-style space-opera. The point is, and "Snakedance" reinforces it, that this is specifically *Tegan's* Mara; anyone else would have different symptoms (although Bailey picked up the notion of the pink snake and tried to salvage something from it). Yet at the story's end she hasn't changed. They could film the start of the next story six weeks earlier for all the difference this experience has made to her. In effect, she's been raped, but next morning she wants to get to her job and carry on as if Aunt Vanessa were still at home waiting.

Symbolically, the more coherent way to resolve this story - the one closest to Buddhist thinking,

Is "Realism" Enough?

...continued from page 131

movies were irrelevant when you've got dances on the ceiling or cameos from Tom and Jerry.

Doctor Who was a place you went for twenty-five minutes. After all, why should a story so obviously silly as the average *Doctor Who* set-up interest anyone? Simply because the ideas being enacted - concepts made flesh, as it were - represent ideas and feelings which wouldn't be articulated anywhere else. In creating a "zone" between narrative realism and outright symbolism, our mental dirty linen can be washed in public. That "zone" might be appealing in its own right, but what's important is what can happen there and nowhere else. The connectivity between half-understood fears and desires, and Stuart Fell in a rubber suit, is what makes these things worthwhile. Otherwise, why not make "Timelash" (22.5)?

Later on, we have a definite shift towards commentary on the programme's nature and status. Eric Saward, not everyone's immediate first choice as a symbolist writer, begins to insert "Greek Chorus" characters into otherwise straightforward stories to speak for - and indeed to - the viewers. The DJ on Necros in 22.6, "Remembrance of the Daleks, is only the most obvious. The Doctor does it throughout "The Trial of a Time Lord" (23.1-4), and characters like the officious Mr. Popplewick represent the BBC's attitude to the series. This is flagged up by characters like the ruthless Morgus (21.6, "The Caves of Androzani") and the TV watchers Arak and Etta (22.2, "Vengeance on Varos"). On

paper this should only really have been of importance to him, but with the siege mentality of anyone still watching the series by that stage it seemed charged and resonant. If it matters enough to the writer, then it'll generally come across.

So if symbolism is "allowed", and the connections between items in a story can be subjective and aesthetically-motivated rather than simply a case of "that's what would have happened", then why isn't more *Doctor Who* like this? Simply, it seems, because these effects are best achieved within what appears to be a conventional linear narrative.

Just as all three types of realism can't be achieved at once (short of having every story appear to be "found" footage, like *The Blair Witch Project*), so at least one of the three is needed to "ground" symbolism for the general public. "Kinda" gets away with such symbolism as is retained because, for the most part, the actors perform "naturalistically" (as opposed to "realistic" acting, which was a set of conventions from the 1880s[6]). Even though his costume is almost a neon sign saying "this is a metaphor", Simon Rouse elects to play Hindle as someone responding as anybody reasonably unstable would under those circumstances. The UNIT / invasion / Yeti-in-the-loo-in-Tooting-Bec format works because it has a toehold in everyday experience; even when the Loch Ness Monster is badly CSO'd onto the Thames Embankment, we already know what one of these two items looks like.

as well - would have been to have Tegan accept this aspect of herself, rather than have it (to all intents and purposes) removed surgically. This would have meant the character developing, and in the production-line conditions under which it was made it was deemed better to have a series that "flowed" than risk having a good story which wrecked everything else in the pipeline. We like to pretend that *Doctor Who* is invariably superior to *Star Trek*, but if ever there were a "character re-set button" in the script department it's in Season Nineteen, for all its contrived conversations at the start of each story. We can have two or ten Tegans occupying our screens because the one Tegan is no more "solid" than a digital trick herself. "Snakedance" goes some way to rectify this, but after a dozen episodes she's no more "known" to us than Todd is after four. Bailey's skill shows up how, even when judged against Season Seventeen,

the general level of characterisation in the programme has weakened to the point where Bigon supposedly shocks everyone by being revealed to be a machine.

The Kinda, as Bailey himself noted, look like they've 'just stepped out of a salon'. Deftly though he has sketched in a culture, the whole thing falls apart when they hallucinate alarm-clocks and then Karuna says she has seven fathers. This is almost, but not quite, as crass as "The Sensorites" (1.7) and smacks rather of 'tell me of this Earth thing you call "kissing"'. Having seven fathers is too big a thing to not have other knock-on (so to speak) effects. In presenting a culture that has sufficient in common with those we know for Todd to become K9 and deliver background information, Bailey has painted himself into a corner when it comes to suddenly throwing things like their reproductive cycle into the mix.

The other three stories directed by Peter Grimwade are, to a certain extent, improved by his additions and choices ("Logopolis" is almost saved by these). "Kinda" has greatness in it, but despite Grimwade's efforts, not because of them.

Critique (Defence) Most crucially, this is where it all comes together; the sense of space and *scale*, the use of detail and fable, an instinct for the way "bad guys" are supposed to work and the way the modern audience "receives" television. It's the still-point between the theatrical and the cinematic, everything the series has been aiming at since the great sea-change of Season Eighteen. Its philosophy brings home everything the series was always meant to be, and yet it's not like anything we've seen before.

As we saw in Volume IV (see **Is This Really an SF Series?** under 14.4, "The Face of Evil"), one of the definitions of science fiction is that it's about the way human beings externalise themselves… in which case this isn't SF at all, because this is all about our internal spaces. Ah, yes: here, this era's ongoing "space" theme is turned inside-out, and we're forced to ask ourselves where the lines are drawn between our own head-scapes and other people's. A big concern here is the divisions between selves, and this provides a visual "rhyme" which touches everything from the TSS machine (the humans can only relate to the Kinda by putting on a reinforced metal suit first) to the moment when Karuna talks like Panna and you realise that this is a place where there are no barriers between identities; from the woop of Tegans (yes, that's the collective noun) to the playful, off-handed 'seven fathers' comment.

Throughout Bidmead's run as script editor, *Doctor Who* sought to turn high-concept into tactile experience, and - though Bidmead has now left the building, and probably would have quibbled with the apparent "mysticism" anyway - here the approach is in full effect. This isn't an outer-space crossword puzzle, this isn't a story that feels the need to drop "clues" in at every opportunity. It's a world where the themes are expressed in every visual aspect, in image and sound and movement, in actual character rather than *dialogue* (there's a difference).

In this, it's one of the most sophisticated *Doctor Who* stories of them all. The Buddhist symbolism, so derided by those who focus more on the end credits than on the dynamic of the story, is very nearly an irrelevance.

Yet despite being a thing of its times, its use of the canon of "old" *Doctor Who* is exceptional. On the surface, so many of the characters *might* be familiar from the humans-under-threat stories of yesteryear, but the psychology that drives them is as troubling as you'll ever find (we'll come back to this in a moment). The Doctor finally becomes the character we've always expected him to be, the "fool" who understands everything by accepting nothing. For the first time in so very, very long, he actually *investigates* this planet, coming to accept his role in it even though he knows he'll never be a part of it.

If you don't understand the philosophy that's being put forward here, about the relationship between self / other and known / unknown, then you've missed something key about the series' philosophy. The Mara "possesses" Tegan, but it's nothing like any possession we've seen in the programme so far; as she turns into a debauched, self-involved monster, we're left in no doubt as to what's really going on here. Unlike every other possession-monster in *Doctor Who* history, this one really *is* us, so in itself it comes across as the ultimate evolutionary form of every "invisible invader" in the series' history. (This programme's always at its best when it demonstrates instead of explaining. The nightmare monster in "Image of the Fendahl" is apparently supposed to be death incarnate, but we only know that because the Doctor mentions it. From what it does, it could be any other super-powerful monster doing the usual super-powerful monster things. By contrast, we know the Mara comes straight from our own urges not because we're constantly told it, but because of how it operates on the characters. And *that's* how you tell stories.)

The big flaw with all of this, of course, is that it isn't child-friendly and therefore fails in at least one of its *Doctor Who* duties. Though nine-year-olds may have drawn snakes on their arms in felt-tip in the days that followed, just for a laugh, younger viewers found this… puzzling. And not simply because of the shifting frames of reference. This is, frankly, a story that you can only appreciate once you've been through puberty. As the thing from 'the dark places of the inside', the Mara is the most Freudian monster of them all, even without the big pink snake-prop. There's a sense of sticky fingers being run through our thoughts, and it's going to be lost on anyone who doesn't have fully-functioning hormones.

Even apart from the obvious sexuality that the Mara's victims demonstrate, "Kinda" is virtually unique in that the characters aren't being driven by the usual 2D *Doctor Who* motives - greed, megalomania, revenge - but by the assorted messy anxieties which lie at the root of those motives. Hindle isn't ambitious, he's impotent. Aris isn't vengeful, he's trying to be a big, sweaty, powerful man. The scene in which he presents himself before the "wise" teenage she-shaman Karuna, is forced to face up to the fact that he's utterly bewildered and dependent on her, then *after* this goes berserk in a rush of testosterone, is as acute a piece of characterisation as you'll ever see and is done without Aris saying a single word. The male Kinda are mute. These things have to remain unspoken. This jungle is a place of desire, and the characters who can't face that are the characters who insist on fresh-sealing themselves inside containers (even Aris forsakes the forest by building himself a "protective" box just like the TSS).

So it leaves the kids behind. A shame, but never mind. This was the dawning of the video age, and it was fast becoming clear that we could go back to this when we were post-pubescent and have another crack at it. We did, and it worked. Its analysts have tried to point out its similarities to SF literature, but this is a miserable dead end because it doesn't *work* like literature. They've tried to "make sense" of the symbolism, but the symbolism is the story's environment, not a "puzzle" on which we're supposed to focus. They've tried to underline the obvious religious imagery, but it's a pointless exercise, because "Kinda" uses those images as parts of a coherent, self-contained syntax of its own. It understands what television can do, but never forgets its roots in stagecraft and never tries to over-stretch itself. If only it weren't for that bloody snake, it'd be a world-beater.

Right, that's thirty-two straight episodes in a row without any major cock-ups. Something's got to give.

The Facts

Written by Christopher Bailey. Directed by Peter Grimwade. Viewing figures: 8.4 million, 9.4 million, 8.5 million, 8.9 million. The following summer's repeats got between 3.9 and 5 million (oddly, they showed "The Visitation" and *then* "Kinda" in August 1983).

Supporting Cast Richard Todd (Sanders), Nerys Hughes (Todd), Simon Rouse (Hindle), Mary Morris (Panna), Sarah Prince (Karuna), Adrian Mills (Aris), Jeffrey Stewart (Dukkha), Anna Wing (Anatta), Roger Milner (Annica), Lee Cornes (Trickster).

Oh, Isn't That..?

It's got an all-star cast, at least as much as *Doctor Who* ever has, so…

• *Nerys Hughes.* A household name thanks to massively successful sitcom *The Liver Birds* (see also 4.8, "The Faceless Ones" and 21.2, "The Awakening") and the rural Welsh soap *District Nurse*, as well as a higher-brow adaptation of *How Green Was My Valley* (where she'd worked with Nathan-Turner). Immortalised by Half-Man Half-Biscuit's rather unflattering track "I Hate Nerys Hughes".

• *Adrian Mills.* Later went on to be one of Esther Rantzen's straight-men in *That's Life*, and host a few game-shows. If anyone born in Britain after 1980 wants to imagine how strange his role as Aris now seems to the rest of us, then try to imagine Alan Partridge playing Tarzan.

• *Mary Morris.* Had been an *ingenue* in a few films of the '50s, but came into her own as one of the Number Twos in *The Prisoner* (she's the best bit in the otherwise dull episode "Dance of the Dead").

• *Richard Todd.* A leading man of the 1940s, appearing in such films as *The Hasty Heart* (opposite Ronald Reagan) and *The Dambusters*. In *The Yangste Incident* he'd worked with William Hartnell, though he hadn't been seen as much since growing too old to convincingly hop out of a Spitfire cockpit.

• *Anna Wing.* Became famous as Albert Square matriarch Lou Beale in the first few years of *EastEnders*.

• *Lee Cornes.* Part of comedy troupe "The Wow Show" (see also 18.5, "Warriors' Gate"), but better-known as the science teacher in *Grange Hill*.

• *Simon Rouse.* A stalwart - and at the time of writing, one of the few remaining original cast members - of *The Bill*, where his co-stars include Jeff Stewart (Dukkha) and Graham Cole (seen in 18.1 "The Leisure Hive").

Working Titles "*The* Kinda".

Cliffhangers Hindle, now in charge of the dome and using the Kinda as "soldiers", screeches that he has the power of life and death over everyone; Hindle forces the Doctor to open the Box of Jhana, and Todd screams as the lid comes off; coming down from his hallucinatory history-trip, the Doctor finds Panna the wise-woman dead in her cave.

The Lore

• Matthew Waterhouse caused a mixture of exasperation and amusement when he tried to teach Richard Todd how to act. Todd received an Oscar nomination for *The Hasty Heart*, but had incautiously said that he wasn't too experienced in television. He'd been in *A for Andromeda* (much more about this ancestor of *Doctor Who* in Volume I), but not much else.

• The script refers to the TARDIS-like object in the Wherever as "the Caravan". The vision / altered state / timeslip (the script is more ambiguous than the broadcast version) is designated "the Beyond".

• About ten minutes of unscreened footage exists from episodes one and two.

In the first episode, Hindle is repeatedly shouted down or ignored when he stresses that the disappearances should be taken more seriously. He's ridiculed in front of the Doctor and Adric for causing a state of emergency to be declared, thus - according to the manual - forbidding the consumption of local produce, hence the unappetising emergency rations for the visitors. Sanders reads the relevant passage of the manual sneeringly (you can see how the Doctor eating an apple as Todd explains "secret" plans is the final straw for Hindle).

Between Tegan sitting beneath the chimes and the "zoom" into her eye, Sanders makes Hindle stir the Doctor's porridge. Tegan's exchanges with the chessplayers are longer, and include her making a move (as she does for Nyssa in episode one). As they discuss whether she's real, she slaps their faces Eric Morecambe style. Before he sets it in motion, the TSS shoots at Adric. As the Doctor and Adric are escorted to the dome, a spherical red camera on a stalk (not unlike a Monopticon from 19.2, "Four to Doomsday") surveys them, relaying the Doctor's and Adric's beaming faces to the occupants.

In episode two the "punishment" scene is different. Tegan's awakening as Dukkha-Tegan is longer, and sees her find a bag of apples at her feet. A returning Sanders asks if he can sit down as his legs are tired, and just before the episode two cliffhanger Adric is pinned down by the Kinda hostage; Hindle asks 'what are you doing here?', then says 'come on, you're missing the fun'. Other small trims were made, but these are the most significant ones.

• However, as the "duel" between Adric in the TSS and Aris in his bamboo model took less screen-time than anticipated, some "filler" scenes were added to episode four by Saward (mainly Adric and Tegan arguing) and shot during the making of "Earthshock" (19.6). Bailey read these and offered to re-do the job himself, complaining that the 'clunky' dialogue was unrealistic and that the way people stopped in the middle of running for their lives to explain plot-points was too bad to go out with his name on it. Forty-eight hours later he had a new draft. Saward, in his defence, said that Bailey thinks a cliff is something with a view and a hanger is something you put a coat on. A great deal of rewriting was done to make the episodes end rather than just stopping.

• During the filming of this story, the studio was visited by John Tulloch and Manuel Alvorado. These two were academics who'd written extensively on British television, and were at work on *Doctor Who: The Unfolding Text*. Chapter six of this is about "Kinda", and is partly responsible for this story's reputation among fans with degrees.

As we saw with "The Creature from the Pit" (17.3), Australian structuralist John Fiske had already written a risibly blinkered piece on the series which was widely circulated. Now, with a whole volume attempting to try every possible analytical approach, it was open season. There's much to commend this book, but the most immediate impact it had was on Eric Saward, who rethought his whole approach in the light of comments from Robert Holmes, Douglas Adams and Verity Lambert cited in the earlier chapters. (The full effect of the media studies boom on the series' practitioners, and some of the other wild theories in print, will be delved into later; see **Does the Semiotic Thickness of a Performed Text Vary According to the Redundancy of Auxiliary Performance Codes, or What?** under 24.4, "Dragonfire").

One element of the book's treatment of this story was to find Buddhist students learning English in Australia, and show them the story on video. As they weren't used to BBC drama, or the language, they failed to notice any religious overtones in the script. Indeed, Bailey now admits that whilst he was interested in Buddhism, he hardly qualifies as one himself; he's now embarrassed at naming characters after core concepts (one wonders whether he's aware of how brazenly George Lucas has done this).

• Effects designer Peter Logan spent a great deal of time making the pillar on which the alarm-clock rests collapse impressively. However, the studio hands insisted on stopping filming at ten PM on the dot. Another stiffly-worded memo about the time allotted for effects flew in the direction of the Sixth Floor.

• The Kinda child choked on an apple and spent ages crying, causing yet another delay and another memo about safety. No-one pondered the symbolism.

• Mary Morris drove in from her home in Switzerland to do the filming in one day. This was the final day in the first block of filming, the 31st of July, 1981. Two days earlier filming had been punctuated by the cast and crew watching Prince Charles marry Lady Diana Spencer, whenever there was a telly available.

• When he finally broke his silence after eighteen years, Bailey claimed not to remember having read LeGuin's *The Word for World is Forest*, though the parallels are too clear to ignore. The terminology alone ('ILFs', 'Not-We'), never mind the story's plot and themes, are manifestly there. After the editorial mauling Saward gave this script, "Snakedance" (20.2) was almost a consolation prize. But despite submitting two further script proposals, Bailey all but vanished from view for over a decade, adding weight to several juicy rumours involving Tom Stoppard and others (see **Did Kate Bush Really Write This?** under "Snakedance").

• Another persistent rumour is that Adric was to have been spanked in a scene which never made it to the screen. This got as far as *The Unfolding Text*, but may have been a result of Waterhouse winding up a fan colleague.

19.4: "The Visitation"

(Serial 5X, Four Episodes, 15th - 23rd February 1982.)

Which One is This? It's the one where London burns down in 1666, after 85 minutes of trying to pretend that something else might happen in a story set in 1660s England. It's also got the dinkiest android ever, and lizard-like aliens who nevertheless seem to be twirling moustaches for much of the story.

Firsts and Lasts The first "historical" story (or at least, "historical with aliens" story) since "Horror of Fang Rock" in 1977, and the first story written by incoming script editor Eric Saward. Being the first Saward script, it's the first time in this era that a cliffhanger is resolved by someone holding a hand up and shouting 'wait!' just before the baddies kill the Doctor. At least it's not the Doctor who's doing the shouting this time (c.f. practically every sodding Colin Baker story). It's the last time Stuart Fell and Alan Chuntz do the stunt duties, and most noticeably of all it's the death of the sonic screwdriver.

A small point: the escape-hatch of the Terileptil ship makes a little "tink" noise, like a genuine product of early '80s technology. From around this time the use of "special sound" to suggests alien-ness is less important than the attempt to make everything sound like something you'd buy from an electrical retail outlet.

Four Things to Notice About "The Visitation"...

1. One could argue that this is the very first "trad" *Doctor Who* story... or at least, that the first story which actually *tries* to be like a traditional *Doctor Who* story (because even in the alien-invasion-of-the-month days of the early '70s, nobody was consciously attempting to remind the audience of the *Doctor Who* of yore). Even "Meglos" wasn't this shameless a looting of the series' own mythology. This one's got everything you expect from a *Doctor Who* story, and that may well be its biggest problem. Aliens on Earth who plan to wipe out humanity and change history... a scene where a companion gets "possessed" and turned into a mind-slave... a world-threatening virus... the now-obligatory token android...

2. Also, it ends with the Doctor and company "inadvertently" causing a famous historical event, which is almost as big a *Doctor Who* cliché as you can get (although see virtually the entire plot of 22.5, "Timelash"). It's worth mentioning this now, because Eric Saward's going to do exactly the same thing in his *next* script, "Earthshock" (19.6). There, he at least goes the whole hog and wipes out the dinosaurs. Here, the best he can do is to burn down Pudding Lane.

3. In one respect, however, "The Visitation" is unusual: it's one of the most *people-free* stories of the whole series. It's normal in this programme for the Doctor and friends to split up and have separate mini-adventures with different groups of supporting characters, but "The Visitation" only has one real supporting character, seventeenth century actor-turned-highwayman Richard Mace (played by Michael Robbins from *On the Buses*, who does his best but really doesn't stand a chance of carrying so much of the plot). Everybody else is either an alien villain of the "boo, hiss" variety or a blank-faced villager under alien mind control. The locals don't even have names; the man with the scythe is called 'scytheman' even by his fellow villagers.

4. This fortnight's bunch of personality-free alien warmongers: the Terileptils, reptiles who cleverly have a name that sounds a bit like "reptiles". These creatures are even more desperate than most, and dress their pet android up as the Grim Reaper in order to scare the locals away from their secret headquarters. As the Doctor saves the day with the help of Adric, Nyssa and Tegan, it's thus very hard to see the Terileptils' plans being foiled without thinking: 'And they would have got away with it, too, if it weren't for you meddling kids.'

The Continuity

The Doctor Hasn't finished telling Adric off for messing about in the TSS [in the previous story, so very little time has passed]. He claims that he never misses when firing a gun, not that he's ever seen to get much practice.

• *Inventory.* After years of good service, the sonic screwdriver is destroyed by the Terileptils. The Doctor notes that it feels like they've killed an old friend [he doesn't seem to think about getting a replacement, at least not until the TV Movie (27.0), although see the notes on the "Missing Season" after Season Twenty-Two]. The screwdriver's "corpse" is one of the many pieces of alien technology left on Earth here. Other than that, he's got a safety-pin and some string.

• *Background.* He knows a fair amount about Terileptils, identifying the species from the design of their escape pod. Even so, he's surprised how advanced their technology is.

The Supporting Cast

• *Adric.* Relations with the Doctor are getting strained, as this new incarnation's telling him off all the time. It's here that his great sulking phase really kicks in, and even Nyssa [who he used to fancy, judging by 18.7, "Logopolis"] isn't taking him seriously any more. 'And I try so hard!' He's also convinced that Tegan doesn't like him much. [No wonder he's getting so awkward by the time of 19.6, "Earthshock".] Yet when escaping from the Terilpetils, he's still prepared to ask Tegan 'but what about you?' when it looks like she's not going to get away.

Adric's still carrying the TARDIS homing device [from 18.3, "Full Circle"], although it gets dropped in the 1600s. He can now pilot the TARDIS with surprising efficiency.

• *Nyssa.* Sometimes forgets to check the scanner before letting people into the Ship. Nyssa's familiar with the various bits and pieces of hardware that are available on board the TARDIS. [Hinting that some considerable time passes between 19.1, "Castrovalva" and 19.2, "Four to Doomsday". All the other stories since "Logopolis" have led directly on from each other.] She seems a bit upset at the destruction of the Terileptil android [even though she spends most of episode three arranging it, making this the second story in a row where she's left alone in her bedroom with a vibrating mechanism of some kind].

• *Tegan.* Her possession by the Mara is just starting to sink in, and she appears to be slightly in shock. She's also sad at the thought of leaving the TARDIS, finding it harder to go than anyone might have expected. Then she gets it out of her system by shouting at the Doctor, and eventually ends up getting possessed again.

This is the only occasion on which she says 'g'day', as Australians are supposed to do all the time.

The TARDIS Still having navigational problems, as the Doctor succeeds in getting Tegan to Heathrow but arrives over three-hundred years too early. [This is the second time that the TARDIS has missed the destination and put the Doctor close to a world-threatening alien menace, and see also 19.7, "Time-Flight". Does the Ship "know" about the threats from the Urbankans and the Terileptils, and has it been taking these opportunities to drop the Doctor into the trouble-zones?] The Doctor believes it's due to a temperamental

What Happened to All the Stuff Under Heathrow?

If Season Nineteen is to be believed, there are several unusual items buried in the vicinity of Heathrow Airport. One of these is Speedbird Concorde 192, which we're told is located beneath the sewage farm across the road (19.7, "Time-Flight"). Assuming that the planes kept their relative positions when travelling 140 million years back in time - a questionable assumption, as most of what's now Southern England was underwater and on a tectonic plate which shifted and was in the Bahamas back then - we should consider whether an aluminium-titanium airframe would even last that long. There may be fragments of plastic, but not much else to show. Hopefully these odd prehistoric specimens are buried too deep to ever be uncovered by human researchers, "hopefully" because finding them also entails finding a Xeraphin citadel and matching spacecraft.

A more disturbing proposition is the Terileptil escape pod, left abandoned at the end of "The Visitation". Adric confirms that the TARDIS lands plumb on the future site of the aerodrome. The pod and the manor house are nearby, but far enough away for Adric and Nyssa to try a short-cut with the TARDIS, so it's unlikely that the pod is right underneath a runway.

According to the Parish records of the Hundred of Elthorn (site of the present-day Heathrow), there was a hamlet called Dawley which was enclosed around 1550, i.e. the land was bought and the village became part of someone's estate. The most likely site of the manor-house was at the junction of Dawley Road and North Hyde Road. This was close to the main route west, just as the M4 is today. The house was demolished in 1772. Twenty years later the Grand Junction Canal was dug, and in the 1830s the Great Western railway main-line was laid over the land. Neither set of navvies reported any cosmic ice-cream parlours embedded in the ground.

It might have been broken up for parts or souvenirs; this is just before the great age of the Cabinet of Curiosities, after all. It's possible that Richard Mace might make a living flogging vintaric crystals to the many eminent natural philosophers in the fledgeling Royal Society, or using the energy cells in a production of Doctor Faustus. Samuel Pepys (whose diary, as many of you wil remember, gives a first-hand account of the Great Fire) paid a lot of money for far less remarkable contrivances. This, however, assumes that he could find a way to break up whichever astonishingly tough metal was used to make this pod (the Terileptils and exotic metallurgy go together like Leela and weapons).

More plausible is the notion that after London was refined and rebuilt, the architect Sir Christopher Wren and his ilk would study this famed Dawley marvel, the arrival of which was marked by shooting stars and visions of the Grim Reaper. The inquiring architect would gain much from close observation of a self-illuminating ceiling, automatic sliding doors and a vaulted roof in pepto-bismol pink. Had such an event taken place, St. Paul's would have resembled a Restoration Arndale Centre, so we can reluctantly conclude that word of the ship never reached London.

As an aside: as every schoolchild knows, or used to, the main reason plague and fire were more notable that year than any other was that 1666 was calculated as being the most likely date for the Second Coming and / or the Antichrist. There'd been cometary sightings in 1665, just as this latest and worst plague had been setting in. Such reasoning had already indirectly led to the Civil War and was "proved" by reference to the Book of Daniel, and the fall of four empires before the execution of the previous monarch. In Vienna, an unlikely chain of events followed the announcement by one Sabbatai Tzevi that he was the Messiah and would convert the Jews (look it up, it's weirder than anything in Doctor Who).

So if Mace or anyone else had used stolen Terileptil technology then it would have been remarked upon, to say the least. In fact, the absence from our history of anything more alarming than London being extensively redeveloped is an indication that nobody touched the pod (well, that and it being in a made-up story for television). One option is that secretive cliques who already knew more about otherworldly "visitations" than they were letting on - one of the New Adventures even hints at Terileptil artefacts in the Vatican's possession - might have recovered and concealed such objects. But given the sheer weight of matter available, it's still hard to believe that the pod and its contents would have had no visible impact on the local culture.

So it wasn't broken up by human agency, and wasn't around for long enough to become a tourist attraction, then what about a self-destruct mechanism? If so then it must have been automatic, unless one of the villagers wandered into the ship and pressed the wrong buttons. But why

continued on page 141...

solenoid on the lateral balance cones, and something beeps on the console to indicate the fault. One of the controls comes off in his hand when he touches it. Adric manages to steer the TARDIS across short distances, but the Ship seems unwilling to fully materialise, and it only lands when he gives it a Doctor-style thump to the console.

Getting ready to leave the TARDIS crew, Tegan applies her make-up in a room with a mirror, various furnishings, some pot-plants and plenty of fragile-looking ornaments on shelves. [How did the ornaments survive the bumpy landing in "Castrovalva" (19.1), among others? Both this room and Nyssa's are obviously the same set, but it's unclear whether they're meant to be the same location.] Nyssa's bedroom is just one short corridor away from the console room, and just outside her room is a stack of plastic boxes containing a fire extinguisher.

On board the Ship she's able to construct a large and not-very-portable weapon from a sonic booster and a frequency accelerator, using heavy-duty cable and an adapter to connect it to a power supply [probably the console]. It shakes apart the Terilpetil android on board the TARDIS, and the android fires blaster-beams in return. [So the 'temporal grace' mentioned in 14.2, "The Hand of Fear" either isn't working or doesn't cover robots. Mind you, it may require the doors to be shut.] At one point Nyssa pulls a trolley with a hefty-looking toolkit into the console room, and Adric hands her extra spare parts for the device in a small cardboard box.

The Doctor uses the TARDIS scanner to detect the location of the Terileptils' base in London, and the map which appears on the screen is a genuine seventeenth century map of the area rather than a direct image of the city [from the TARDIS databanks, though this still seems curious]. Radar-like lines sweep across the image, as the TARDIS searches for an electrical emission from the Terileptils' equipment

There's at least one glossy magazine on board the Ship for Nyssa to flip through. It's a copy of *Woman's Journal* [so maybe her Season Twenty makeover isn't a sudden whim].

The Non-Humans

• *Terileptils*. The Doctor describes the Terileptils as warlike but notes their great love of art and beauty. They're upright-walking reptile-creatures, with gills, scales and "carapaces" of lizard-skin around their shoulders. Their skins are a variety of colours, with the reds, greens and blues varying between different members of the species. They're also the type who consider war to be 'honourable'.

The four Terileptils who land on Earth in the seventeenth century are escaped criminals, sentenced to life imprisonment in the tinclavic mines of Raaga [mentioned again in 21.2, "The Awakening"], as indicated by the leader's horribly scarred face. They have a crashed and half-buried escape pod, which is all white and shiny on the inside [and the Doctor never deals with it, so it might give future archaeologists something to think about; see **What Happened to All That Stuff Under Heathrow?**]. The pod's lit with vintaric crystals, which according to the Doctor is a common method of lighting. The ship from which the pod came was damaged in an asteroid storm and drawn into Earth's gravity, breaking up on entry.

The Terileptils carry high-energy beam weapons capable of blowing up sonic screwdrivers, and which can explode if mishandled, potentially leading to Great Fires. The Terileptils are also capable of genetically re-engineering the plague, and are planning on wiping out humanity with plague-bearing rats, their leader having a neat little hand-held device that can infect a rat with the touch of a button.

Meanwhile several human beings have been turned into their slaves with control bracelets, normally used to control prisoners. These turn the wearers into obedient zombies when activated from a control panel, and can relay the wearers' thoughts back to the Terileptils. The Doctor's mind would be strong enough to override these effects, naturally. The bracelets require power-packs of a common design [do the Tereleptils trade with other cultures a lot?] and are made of polygrite, found in many parts of the universe. Nyssa certainly recognises it. The Terileptils still write on paper, and their script looks like mathematical formulae to Tegan [nothing seems to be automatically translating it on this occasion].

The Terileptil android [where did these escaped felons *get* all this stuff???] is, as one might expect from such a beauty-loving species, quite pretty. It has a chiselled, surprisingly human-like face and a body inset with what look like jewels, although the Terileptils have been dressing it up as the Grim Reaper. It's bulletproof and physically powerful, although prone to being shaken apart, and

What Happened to All the Stuff Under Heathrow?

...continued from page 139

would an escape pod have a self-destruct mechanism anyway? Well, it *was* a pod from a prison ship. Earth's enough of a backwater for a Malus probe to have been sent there and not followed up (21.2, "The Awakening"), and the Malus' creators had known links with the Terileptils, so the prison ship probably wasn't sent to this area deliberately (it may even have been ensnared by Kalid's time-contour in "Time-Flight", or is that too cute?). It's possible that the penal authorities came to investigate and, on finding no survivors, removed the

pod in case it fell into the wrong hands.

And the TARDIS homing device, dropped in the woods in 1666? Either Adric found it again before its reappearance in "Mawdryn Undead" (20.3) or, like one of the Yeti spheres (5.2, "The Abominable Snowmen" and 5.5, "The Web of Fear"), it found its way back to the Ship and returned to its niche. Or if the one used by Tegan in "Mawdryn Undead" is a replacement, then the lost device might not have been found when the area was redeveloped for apple-growing.

It may even still be there, but the TARDIS would have been able to home in on it, surely?

can fire blaster-beams from its fingers. Its hands look a lot like cricket gloves. The Terileptils defend their territory with an energy barrier, disguised as a brick wall, and when the Doctor picks the "lock" the wall can be walked through.

The creatures seem to need occasional whiffs of soliton gas, and they've got a device that pumps it out into the air, although it's volatile when mixed freely with oxygen.

The existence of time-travel doesn't seem to surprise the Terileptils very much. [As their escape pod is so much larger inside than the exterior we see (and not just because it's part-buried, as the Doctor tells Mace), this may indicate a higher culture than we're led to believe from the dialogue.] Being criminals, they're worried about being found by Terileptil scout-parties. [See 23.2, "Mindwarp", for a surprise appearance by the Terileptils' midget cousins.]

History

• *Dating.* The seventeenth century. [According to the history books, the final showdown with the Terileptils takes place on the 2nd of September, 1666.] The Terileptils landed on Earth some weeks earlier, and began taking over various individuals in a village near the future site of Heathrow Airport.

At this stage plague is already abroad in the land, especially in these parts. The Terileptils' base in London is at Pudding Lane, and when one of their weapons explodes it starts a fire that the Doctor believes should be allowed to run its course [because, historically, the Great Fire of London did so much to end the contamination]. The Doctor leaves a component from the Terileptil control panel in the possession of out-of-work

actor and highwayman Richard Mace, another thing to puzzle the archaeologists.

The Analysis

Where Does This Come From? Not for the last time this season, what we're seeing here is *Doctor Who* trying to re-invent its "standards" for the 1980s; in this case it's an attempt to resurrect the pseudo-historical for the benefit of the *Star Wars* generation. A story like "The Time Warrior" (11.1, another prime example of an aliens-fiddling-about-in-history plot) is effectively BBC costume drama with extra added monsters and robots, but this wasn't a good time for BBC costume drama.

Since 1974, cinema had taught the audience to swashbuckle again. "The Visitation" isn't full of meaty period dialogue and theatrical set-pieces, a la *Elizabeth R*. It's full of fights, escapes and elaborate technological weapons. It's trying to stage itself as a motion-picture extravaganza, and a cynic would say "no wonder it seems so ruddy shallow". Lynx's robot servant in "The Time Warrior" is basically just a suit of armour which serves a specific plot function, whereas the sparkly Terileptil android is supposed to be an exciting event in itself, even getting a "dramatic" show-down with Nyssa on board the TARDIS.

It seems like a small thing, but the title's a dead giveaway. *Really* traditional *Doctor Who* would had given this story a title like "Curse of the Terileptils", but "The Visitation" is the kind of name you'd expect from one of the straight-to-video SF movies that flooded the market in the early days of the home VCR.

This is also as good a time as any to talk about the "soap opera" side of this season. At this point the TARDIS has a crew of four, and they spend much of their screen-time urgently shrieking at each other. This "full house" approach obviously isn't new, given that it's how the programme started back in 1963. But the four-person central cast in Season One suggested a family, reflecting the programme's family audience; the old Doctor as the ultimate grandparent, Ian and Barbara as conventional dramatic leads, Susan as a way of giving the younger viewers a stake in things. Yet as we've already seen, by the early '80s the idea of "family television" was disintegrating. Suddenly everyone on board the TARDIS is young.

A few years later *EastEnders* would make its debut on BBC1, and become one of the first soap operas that under-eighteens actively watched (see **What Difference Does a Day Make?** under 19.1, "Castrovalva", for a longer version of the story). What's notable is that although *Doctor Who*'s structure would become increasingly soap-like throughout the early '80s, in 1982 Tegan, Nyssa and Adric looked much too young to be real soap stars… although it wouldn't be long before argumentative teenagers became the order of the day.

Things That Don't Make Sense   When the Terileptil android locks the TARDIS crew into the cellar at the end of episode one, the camera does the usual "suspense-building" thing of focusing on its hand and not showing us its face. Except that we saw its face right at the start of the episode. So it's a bit late for mystery now.

Even given that the Terileptils have a surprising amount of hardware with them, it's hard to imagine why they'd have a Grim Reaper mask for their android, or a handy means of making one. It's hard watching the "disguised" android's entrance in episode two, as it creeps up on Mace and Adric, without shouting 'behind youuuu!!!' It's harder still to swallow the subsequent "fight" scene, in which the robot stands there trying to look menacing while most of the cast shuffle right past it and escape.

On the outside the crashed escape pod is buried in the ground at an odd angle, yet on the inside the floor's perfectly even. And the rear hatch of the pod, which leads out onto the surface, should clearly be buried below ground level. In episode three the Terileptils prove to be among those many, many villains who never bother searching their prisoners for hi-tech pieces of hardware or explosive power-packs. They're also

among those many, many villains who arrange a complicated death for the Doctor, then walk out before he's actually dead and give him a chance to wriggle out of it.

Mace seems to understand the term 'refresher course' with surprisingly little difficulty. And his costume's thirty years out of date, as well; as he only has the one outfit, and would've been sleeping in these clothes, it's no wonder that nobody wants him in their theatres. The Doctor already knows that the TARDIS has landed on the site of Heathrow, not far from London, so why on Earth does he have to ask Mace what the nearest large city is? Then again, if this really is the site of the future Heathrow then there shouldn't be any trees more than twenty years old (the area was used as heath-land for the Parliamentarian New Model Army in the 1640s).

Critique   Imagine, if you will, what it was like watching this story as a ten-year-old. It had been seven years since the TARDIS had "properly" gone back in time, longer than living memory, from a child's point of view. It'd be another half-decade before stories like "The Time Warrior" and "The Talons of Weng-Chiang" turned up on video. All of a sudden the Doctor wasn't on another planet, or on a space-cruiser, or hanging around in modern-day Surrey. All of a sudden he was in *history*.

You know? History? That place where everyone rides horses and talks funny. That place from, well, history books. This was exciting in itself. And on top of that there was a new species of monster, a glitzy android, plenty of urgent running-about and a big fire at the end. Oh, and the sonic screwdriver got twatted.

Because that's the thing about *Doctor Who*; if you grew up with it, then a lot of your opinions are going to be biased by your ten-year-old mind, and to most people it always *was* a children's programme above all else. But when you watch the same episodes years later, you realise that there was more to it than you thought, that there were subtleties behind the latex masks and implications in the technoblather. You realise that it really was as good as you thought, if not necessarily for the same reasons.

"The Visitation" is the exception. This is the one story that looked bloody fantastic to the child-mind, but has now revealed itself to be incredibly shallow and really very annoying. You have to give Eric Saward a *little* slack here; he was trying to redefine this particular thread of *Doctor Who*, and in terms of how the programme was supposed to work *visually* in the early '80s, he succeeded. But this doesn't excuse his decision - if, indeed, the decision was conscious - to do this by making the plot as straightforward, and as banal, as it could possibly get.

"The Time Warrior" tried to present the audience with a new style of pseudo-historical too, and Robert Holmes still managed to shove a cart-load of his own ideas and obsessions into it. But there are no surprises here, no subtexts. The aliens do what they're supposed to, the one supporting character tries to prop up the entire seventeenth century ethos (Saward was reportedly unhappy with Michael Robbins' performance, but for Heaven's sake, what was he *expecting*?), and the production relies on the period sets and costumes to carry everything through.

And as ever in this season, they're perfectly lovely sets and costumes, but this is a story so lacking in dramatic thrust that halfway through episode one Adric has to fall over in the middle of the woods and go "argh, I've sprained my ankle" to try to add some tension to proceedings.

Only the opening scene looks promising, and even *that's* just like "The Time Warrior" minus the comedy bandits. The TARDIS scenes which follow feature some of the worst companion dialogue you'll ever hear, while Nyssa spends half the story sitting in her bedroom and talking about how hard it is to build an android-killing weapon without the Doctor. The only really memorable thing is the incredibly weary way the lead Terileptil delivers the line, 'drop the sonic device'.

Aliens started the Great Fire of London? Who would have guessed it? Bleeding everybody, that's who.

The Facts

Written by Eric Saward. Directed by Peter Moffatt. Viewing figures: 9.1 million, 9.3 million, 9.9 million, 10.1 million. The repeat in summer 1983 averaged out at around 4.4 million.

Supporting Cast   Michael Robbins (Richard Mace), Peter Van Dissel (Android), Michael Melia (Terileptil), John Savident (The Squire), Richard Hampton (Villager), James Charlton (Miller), Neil West (Poacher), Eric Dodson (Headman), Anthony Calf (Charles), John Baker (Ralph), Valerie Fyfer (Elizabeth).

Oh, Isn't That..?

• *Michael Robbins*. He'd been in *On the Buses*, one of those sitcoms that make British TV's claim to have been the best in the world in the 1970s look a bit suspect. (Still, since then it's become bewilderingly popular in certain parts of the US.) He then went on to play dim coppers in comedy shows with lower ratings but higher standards. At around this time he was most often seen on TV advertising oven chips.

• *John Savident*. In those days well-known as a character-actor, playing "plummy" aristocrats. Now he's Fred Elliott from *Coronation Street*, a pork butcher with a Lancastrian accent and Foghorn Leghorn's, ah say Foghorn Leghorn's style of delivery.

• *Michael Melia*. The lead Terileptil is another future *EastEnders* regular, not that you'd know it without looking at the credits.

Working Titles   "Invasion of the Plague Men" (a bit of a giveaway), "The Plague Rats" (at a time when Richard Adams' book *The Plague Dogs* was still reasonably fresh in the public consciousness).

Cliffhangers   The TARDIS crew descend into the cellar where Nyssa left the Doctor, to find him missing as someone bolts the door behind them; the zombie-villagers force the Doctor's head down, and the man with the scythe prepares to chop it off, prompting the comment 'not again' from the Doctor (see 19.2, "Four to Doomsday"); locked in a cell with the Doctor, a zombified Tegan prepares to open a cage full of plague-rats.

The Lore

• The behind-the-scenes story of Seasons Eighteen and Nineteen can get unpleasantly muddled, so here's a reminder of the production order so far...

March - April 1980: "The Leisure Hive"

May: "State of Decay"

June - July: "Meglos"

July - August: "Full Circle"

September - October: "Warriors' Gate". Baker announces intention to retire.

November: "The Keeper of Traken" (barring one day's work remounted after a strike, 17th December). Baker and Ward announce engagement, rehearsals besieged by press.

16th - 22nd December 1980, 8th - 9th, 21st, 24th January 1981: "Logopolis"

April: "Four to Doomsday"

May: "The Visitation"

29th - 31st July, 12th - 14th August (remount 11th November): "Kinda"

September: "Castrovalva".

• Christopher Bidmead commissioned the first version of this script early in 1980 when "The Leisure Hive" (18.1) was being filmed. Nathan-Turner thought it was too comical. As the crisis over that year's scripts and commissions grew worse, the story was revised to accommodate new line-up and format requirements. Saward was asked if he wanted Bidmead's job; then Antony Root was given the three-month placement. Then "Project 4G" fell through, and "The Visitation" was brought forward, just as Root left to edit *Juliet Bravo*.

• Many press reviews at the time were puzzled at the Squire's early demise. John Savident was - Davison aside - the most prominent cast-member, and it appeared from the publicity that he was to be a "guest star". He and the Squire's family disappear four minutes into episode one. We assume that they all die.

• The making of this story was the subject of a hardback book for children on the production of a TV series. In this we learned of: the crew's weariness of hearing every local constabulary they met on location jocularly asking for their police box back; Davison's excuses for late appearances on site; the length of time it took to blow up the android; and the precise function of all the oddly-designated posts in the end credits.

But Alan Road's *Doctor Who: The Making of a Television Series* was just one of the books released in this period. Others include: *A Day with a Television Producer*, in which John Nathan-Turner walks his dog, interviews Matthew Waterhouse for the role of Adric, plans to cast the new Doctor and fools us all into thinking they planned a story called "The Doctor's Wife"… all in six hours; *The Doctor Who Technical Manual*, in which - due to a crass misprint - we find that the sonic screwdriver is the size of a street-lamp; *Knit a TARDIS*, which is self-explanatory; and *The Doctor Who Cookbook* by Gary Downie. We shall doubtless return to this masterwork.

• Aside from noise from the *real* Heathrow, and the occasional mower, the main problem on location was curious schoolchildren. However, Waterhouse was the only cast-member that any of them recognised.

• One significant cut: in the first episode, when the Doctor beats up a posse of villagers, he was seen to inadvertently tread on the chest of one. This was thought to give the wrong impression (whereas knocking lumps out of them was perfectly acceptable?).

• Some ten years earlier Eric Saward had written a few radio plays about a Victorian actor and amateur sleuth called Richard Mace, the last being broadcast a few months before "The Talons of Weng-Chiang" (14.6), which they strongly resemble. This Mace was also fond of his tipple, but less cowardly.

• Filming the "execution" scene (which, as Antony Root noticed just hours before, was the same cliffhanger they'd used in "Four to Doomsday"… hence the 'not again' gag), Robbins got Housemaid's Knee - a recurrence of an old injury - and the nurse had to be sent for.

• Michael Melia got so hot in the Terileptil costume that his socks changed colour.

• The establishing shot of the scene outside the bakery was mainly a glass-shot. This may be why this impressive footage isn't used as often as most viewers might have liked.

• The Target novelisation of "The Visitation" was the first to feature the Fifth Doctor, and the first to use a photograph on the cover instead of a "proper" piece of art, in part because Peter Davison objected to the portrait of himself which had originally been submitted. The new photographic style was universally hated, and it didn't help that almost every book seemed to use a staggeringly drab publicity shot of Davison rather than the wide array of monsters, machines and special effects familiar to readers from the 1970s. The cover of "Earthshock", which features no Cybermen (were they trying to retain the surprise?) and shows the Doctor packing a blaster, is so wrong that it's almost evil.

19.5: "Black Orchid"

(Serial 6A, Two Episodes, 15th - 23rd February 1982.)

Which One is This? They do the Charleston, play cricket, order cocktails, change into fancy dress, wander into secret passageways and flirt outrageously with the chief constable. Which leaves a good fifteen minutes or so for the plot.

Firsts and Lasts For the first time since 1966, the TARDIS goes back in time for an adventure which doesn't involve history being put in jeopardy by aliens, time-travellers or alien time-travellers. This means it's often regarded as the last-ever "straight" historical story, although "historical" suggests that the Doctor's going to meet someone famous or get involved in a major historical event (just look at the previous story…), whereas "Black Orchid" is more like a '20s murder-mystery than anything.

Finally, after years of boasting, the Doctor gets to prove that he can play cricket. And finally, after years of seeing people casually slaughtered all around them, the TARDIS crewmembers actually attend the funeral of a dead character (see also 25.1, "Remembrance of the Daleks").

Two debuts here. This is the start of Gary Downie's full-time association with the series; as floor manager, choreographer (as he is here) or production assistant, he'll be around until the end, and then some. His previous form includes choreographing the orgies in *I, Claudius*. (Strictly speaking his work on the programme began at a lowly level with 15.5, "Underworld", but this is where he becomes a fixture.) Meanwhile, Gareth Milne will be the regular stunt arranger for the next five years or so.

Two Things to Notice About "Black Orchid"…

1. A constant problem for *Doctor Who* in this period is that with the audience taking so much for granted, it's just a nuisance when characters have to learn things the viewers already know. In "An Unearthly Child" (1.1), the Doctor spends the best part of an episode explaining the TARDIS' nature to Ian Chesterton before the man even comes close to accepting it. In "Pyramids of Mars" (13.3), the Doctor and Sarah do their best to ignore Laurence Scarman as he wanders around the console room pointing out that this is just like something from H. G. Wells. But by now TARDIS-shock is so passé that the reaction of the average British policeman, on seeing the Ship's interior in 1925, is boiled down to a single line: 'Strike me pink!' Then he gets on with his job without passing any further comment.

2. Viewers who are familiar with "doubles" stories from the TV adventure genre might want to keep themselves amused by ticking off the requisite camera-tricks as Nyssa meets her doppelganger. The first time they come face-to-face, the actors carefully arrange themselves in two groups, one standing behind Nyssa and the other standing behind Ann Talbot but definitely *not* touching each other. (This means that you know exactly where the split-screen line is, even though you can't see it. Compare with Count Grendel's vanishing hand in 16.4, "The Androids of Tara".)

And when the two Sarah Suttons shake hands, it's shot from two angles, the camera making sure - as is traditional - that we're always looking at the back of one of the girls' heads and that only one face is visible at a time. Things get a little more strained at the masquerade ball, when Ann spends most of her time hanging around in the background in a mask, although in long-shot she and Nyssa appear to be different heights.

The Continuity

The Doctor The TARDIS crew have only just come from the seventeenth century when the Ship arrives in 1925, and here - uniquely - the Doctor insists that what happened in London would have happened whether they'd been there or not, 'all part of Earth's history'. [This is questionable. See **Can You Change History, Even One Line?** under 1.6, "The Aztecs".]

This Doctor's already acknowledging that he lets curiosity get the better of him [two seasons on, he'll acknowledge it again just before it kills him]. Asked for his name, he replies that it's 'a very difficult question'. His cricketing skills as both batsman and fast-bowler are good enough to win his team the match at Cranleigh Hall. He's now perfectly happy to let humans from the twentieth century wander on board the TARDIS and have a good look around [so much has changed since "An Unearthly Child"].

• *Ethics*. He's also happy to let Tegan drink alcohol, but steps in to stop Nyssa getting boozed up. [Possibly because he knows that Nyssa will have no alcohol resistance, although Lord Cranleigh assumes it's because Nyssa and Adric are 'children' while Tegan's a grown-up.]

• *Background*. The Doctor claims that he always wanted to drive a steam engine 'as a boy'. [Are there steam trains on Gallifrey, and what exactly does he mean by 'boy'…? The nightmare sequence in 14.3, "The Deadly Assassin", might suggest that trains are indeed a deep-rooted part of his psyche.]

The Supporting Cast

• *Adric*. Doesn't know what a railway is. When required to dance up close with a less-dressed-

ABOUT TIME 1980-1984

than-usual Nyssa, he looks slightly terrified, and claims that he'd much rather eat. He still can't help stuffing his face at every opportunity [he probably needs to eat more to keep doing his "rapid Alzarian healing" trick], and he's used to Nyssa nagging him by now.

• *Nyssa.* By some extraordinary coincidence, it turns out that Nyssa is the exact double of bright young society thing Ann Talbot in 1925. [Compare with 3.5, "The Massacre"; 5.4, "The Enemy of the World"; and most particularly 16.4, "The Androids of Tara". There's something *very* funny about the way this keeps happening, and perhaps what's most remarkable isn't that Nyssa has a doppelganger but that the TARDIS brings her to the right location on Earth at exactly the right point in Ann's life. See **Why Are There So Many Doubles in the Universe?** under 20.1, "Arc of Infinity".] Unlike Ann, she doesn't have a mole on her left shoulder.

Nyssa has been trained to dance, and believes she's quite good, although on Traken dancing is far more formalised and complex. This means she can convincingly do the Charleston after the bare minimum of training. She refers to her place of origin as 'the Empire of Traken'.

• *Tegan.* She too can Charleston, having learned it for a play at school. Her tipple of choice is a screwdriver, and being a good Australian she likes watching cricket.

Tegan has decided to stay on board the TARDIS for a while, and is no longer asking the Doctor to get her to Heathrow [the events of the last story seem to have been a bonding experience for her, weird as she was brainwashed and very nearly exposed to bubonic plague]. In a dramatic turnabout, she's now the one asking to go and look at what's outside the Ship.

The TARDIS The Ship's having worse navigational troubles than ever, insisting on bringing the Doctor back to Earth, and the Doctor can't understand why. Still, short hops across town are no problem. The console can now give the Doctor an exact time and date once the TARDIS lands [this has been variable over the years].

After the death of George Cranleigh, his family give the Doctor a copy of Cranleigh's book *Black Orchid* [which will turn up on board the TARDIS in future]. The TARDIS crewmembers also get to keep their '20s fancy dress costumes.

History

• *Dating.* It's the 11th of June, 1925, according to the TARDIS console.

George Cranleigh, brother of Lord Cranleigh, stole the sacred black orchid from the Kajabi Indians while exploring the region of the Orinoco. For this crime his tongue was removed and he was horribly disfigured, and he's officially believed dead. In truth he was rescued by another tribe, whose chief befriended him and brought him home. Now Cranleigh is homicidally insane, and is being kept at Cranleigh Hall by members of his family, although his name's famous enough for '80s girl Tegan to recognise it [see **Things That Don't Make Sense**]. Cranleigh dies at the climax of events here, and the Doctor and company attend his funeral [so the TARDIS crew stick around for a few days after their arrival].

The nearest station to Cranleigh Hall is Cranleigh Halt [England, obviously, though not actually a real place].

The Analysis

Where Does This Come From? When it comes to historicals and pretend-historicals, *Doctor Who* has a long and noble tradition of taking another form of BBC drama and dropping the Doctor into the middle of it to see what happens (see, especially, the three past-based stories in Seasons Fourteen and Fifteen).

"Black Orchid" follows this tradition, in its own pocket-sized way. Although "serious" costume drama had ceased to be a BBC staple, there was a rising fashion for semi-historical whimsy, for cutesy little early-twentieth-century set-pieces. Nobody seemed to want to make programmes about the Fall of the Roman Empire or the Six Wives of Henry VIII, but in a time as fashion-conscious - some would say "vacuous" - as the 1980s, it's easy to see how the 1920s might have had a certain escapist charm. (After *Doctor Who*, Peter Davison would go on to star in *Campion*, based on the books by Margery Allingham about a bespectacled '20s detective. This is almost a dry run, especially since the same house would later be used for some of *Campion*'s location work.)

Among the prime literary sources for "Black Orchid" are mystery authors like Agatha Christie or Dorothy L. Sayers, and both the BBC and ITV heavily-plundered this oeuvre during this decade. We might also mention E. W. Hornung's *Raffles*,

Do Mutilation and Entertainment Mix?

At a convention in the mid-'80s, a raffle was held with prizes given out by Colin Baker and Nicola Bryant. One lucky chap won twice in five minutes, and collected his booty along with handshakes from the Doctor and a kiss from Peri. What made this awkward was that it was just after "Timelash" (22.5) had been broadcast, and the raffle winner had a facial deformity not entirely unlike that of the "monstrous" Borad in that story. He didn't seem at all embarrassed, neither did Ms. Bryant. This being the mid-'80s, in the bar afterwards many discussions followed in which people vied to see who could be most "right-on" about the ethics of exploiting such things to scare kiddies.

What's interesting is that these discussions never would have happened before. The Victorian freakshows, the Medieval / Renaissance depictions of injury and mutilation as the inevitable consequences of sinful living and the 1930s horror movie cycle all relished using physical abnormality for entertainment. As we saw in How Does Evolution Work? (under 18.3, "Full Circle"), the assumption in Doctor Who is that anything which looks human is "evolved". The corollary of this, a view espoused by the Greeks, is that physical beauty equates to moral worth. Stories such as "Galaxy Four" (3.1) gain their effect from "surprisingly" inverting this connection. In fact, in many cases - and Doctor Who is not exempt - looking unusual is considered an adequate motivation for doing nasty things.

Those early horror films, especially the ones made by Universal, had their own agenda. Not only was mutilation a more common sight then, after World War I casualties returned to their small towns or major cities, but the eugenics movement was in full flower. Injury and suffering were ennobling, and a sign of someone making a sacrifice for the good of all; if their behaviour was inexplicable, it was at least motivated by something we should be thankful we couldn't comprehend. Above all, to have survived showed a stoicism and willpower far above the common herd.

Birth defects, on the other hand, were as much a sign of evil as they had been in the middle ages. Instead of witchcraft, they were a mark of genetic inferiority, often through in-breeding. This was to be weeded out for the good of future generations. Note how in John Steinbeck's Of Mice and Men, George tells his friend Lennie never to tell anyone that Lennie's simplicity was innate, but to claim that a horse kicked him in the head. George, who's

less physically imposing and thus less employable, tells everyone that Lennie is his cousin. The implication of any "taint" was to be avoided at all costs. Birth defects could also result from poor diet, bad housing or environmental toxins, but it was unthinkable that the aristocracy should acknowledge any blame. The proletariat were, simply, inferior.

So those of us looking at the freaks were superior. There's always an implication of a power-relationship in anything presented as a spectacle. In the same way that looking at pretty girls wearing not-a-lot allowed the viewer to feel that he or she (especially he) was in control, so the visual presence of someone / something "outlandish" was patronising in the most literal sense of the word. We were the patrons, and they were the merchandise. Treating people like objects may be what bad characters do in Doctor Who, but it's also how viewers respond.

Janet Fielding in a lace teddie was there to "get the dads watching" (a crass move even today, so in the early '80s it was outrageous... only a gay man would believe that this was what dads thought was "sexy"). Kalid oozing snot in "Time-Flight" (18.7) was there to keep the kids watching. This was the age of the video nasty, and excessive bodily seepage was considered to be quite "now". A ravaged face or body was like seeing a city being trashed or a minor character being killed in a pretty effects-shot; this is discussed in more detail in **How Important Was the Blitz?** under 2.2, "The Dalek Invasion of Earth". Until 1980, the first appearance of a monstrous face came at the cliffhanger, usually the first (as in 11.1, "The Time Warrior") but sometimes the last (14.6, "Talons of Weng Chiang"). From "Meglos" (18.2) onwards, the monster was introduced in mid-episode and the cliffhanger was the Doctor's face (whether or not it really was the Doctor... see both "Meglos" and 21.6, "The Caves of Androzani"). Sharaz Jek is "unveiled" ten minutes before the end of "Androzani", George Cranleigh fairly early on in "Black Orchid", and so on. It doesn't signify a change in the situation, as with most cliffhangers, but is simply there to shock.

So is this proof that Doctor Who exploits disability or disfigurement? Not exactly. The majority of these cases use the disfigurement as proof that the stakes for the (literally) injured party are higher than usual. In a great many stories in the gothic

continued on page 149...

successfully adapted for television in 1977, in which a jewel-thief gains access to country houses by virtue of being a gentleman and a good cricketer. In fact, with hindsight the only thing about this story that looks odd is that the interior scenes are shot on video. By the mid-'80s this sort of period production was almost always film-based, making "Black Orchid" look like a weird halfway-house between two eras.

Thematically, in many ways this is a straight re-tread of *Jane Eyre*, with George as Bertha and his mother as Mr. Rochester. Certainly, the main thrust of the second episode is the sense of duty which leads to an almighty cover-up (and this goes right back to the origins of both the detective novel and the gothic horror, uncovering a family secret that's caused sinister side-effects). We even have the secret passages of a late eighteenth-century chiller. As we'll see in "Mawdryn Undead" (20.3), the misunderstandings and near-misses of farce sit well inside this format of *Doctor Who*. The entire set-up of mistaken identity and double-takes - especially when the viewer temporarily becomes convinced that something *Doctor Who*-ish is afoot, as soon as W. G. Grace is referred to as 'the Master' - sets up an expectation that things are going to go wrong at any moment. We even have a quotation from the cross-dressing play *Charley's Aunt* ('Brazil... where the nuts come from').

On top of that there's George Cranleigh himself. A madman in a mask, whose persona is summed up by the blank expression of a harlequin costume... does it really need to be pointed out that this was the golden age of the "modern" horror movie, the age of *Halloween*, *Friday the Thirteenth* and their many, many imitators / sequels? Audiences were less and less impressed by supernatural nasties, more and more anxious about faceless, unidentifiable threats in the human world (in Cranleigh's case the "monster" seems almost sympathetic, which smacks of the old Universal movie-monsters as well). This being *Doctor Who*, the killer here is far classier than the villain from any slasher movie, and Cranleigh's harlequin guise has a kind of grace that you never used to see in the video nasties. If anything, this sort of masked horror looks more at home here than in Hollywood. *Doctor Who* may not have a tradition of psychotic murderers, but we are used to Cybermen, Voc robots and Terilpetil androids, just as expressionless and with equally inhuman/e

intentions.

But we have admit, the real early-'80s sources are *Chariots of Fire*, with "Britishness" being equated to sporting prowess and nice pullovers; and *Brideshead Revisited*, protractedly dramatised at around the time this was commissioned. It was, as is well-recorded, the 1930s-based cricket-match episode of *All Creatures Great and Small* which inspired the Fifth Doctor's look.

Things That Don't Make Sense Let's see if we've got this straight. George Cranleigh went up the Orinoco, was captured and mutilated, went mad, was rescued by a friendly chief, then was secretly brought back to England and kept locked up in a hidden room. Bound hand and foot, a lot of the time. Precisely when did he write his book? Before he actually found the flower, presumably. In which case, isn't it a bit of a giveaway that the Cranleigh family now keeps a specimen of it proudly on display at the Hall? And if Tegan's heard of him, then wouldn't she know what ghastly fate befell him? And wouldn't the Doctor already have a copy of *Black Orchid*? [Maybe he does, and he's too polite to say so when he gets one as a gift.] And when did Tegan become an expert on 1920s botanists, anyway? Unless Cranleigh's pitiable exploits were the subject of a film, in which case the previous questions still arise.

Lord Cranleigh invites the Doctor and chums (never has the word "chums" been more apt) to his cricket match and masquerade ball because he thinks the Doctor is a friend-of-a-friend he's never actually met, but he doesn't even know this *other* doctor's name. Nor does he bother asking why his mysterious guest has brought three uninvited youngsters along, or who these weirdly-dressed interlopers might actually be. Honestly, these upper classes.

When George Cranleigh kidnaps Nyssa in the belief that she's Ann, the Doctor's terrified of what he might do if he finds out he's got the wrong girl. So the Doctor promptly chases George up to the roof of Cranleigh Hall and... tells him he's got the wrong girl. Perhaps most bizarrely, though; this one moment, when George abducts Nyssa, is the *only* point when the "doppelganger" subplot has any impact on the story at all. Why does the script spend all that time emphasising how identical Nyssa and Ann are, if it just comes down to George having the wrong hostage on the roof?

Do Mutilation and Entertainment Mix?

...continued from page 147

mode, the 'hate kept me alive' line crops up. Aside from making sense of otherwise poorly-motivated characters, it can instil sympathy. We're right back to Frankenstein and Quasimodo. *Doctor Who* frequently sides with outcasts against the mainstream and with heroic, romantic rebels defying the restrictions of society. The Doctor is one himself, after all. A visible sign of having crossed some kind of boundary allows the inattentive viewer to follow the story.

Yet in Season Nineteen we have a more sinister trend. The Terileptils, and more crucially George Cranleigh, are depicted as being bad because they've been mutilated. The Lead Terileptil's scar is the mark of a criminal, not so much a way of establishing that he's guilty as establishing that he's got a violent history, in the same way that British war stories tend to give distinctive duelling-scars to evil German officers. Cranleigh is criminally insane, deranged after his capture and injury by the Kajabi. We know nothing about this tribe except that the Black Orchid is sacred to them and George blasphemed by stealing it. Many cultures in the Amazon basin use scarification as a coming-of-age rite, like tattoos; perhaps, as a Caucasian adult male with no cuts in his face, Cranleigh looked monstrous to them and was made "normal". It's not the ordeal that's blamed for the insanity, but the drastic assault to the subject's self-image. Sharaz Jek is just a more articulate version of the same idea. We can only guess at why the

Master dresses up as a deformed, oriental(ish) wizard in "Time-Flight", but even the Cybermen in "Earthshock" (19.6) are once again shown as surgically transgressive, not just tin men. After Season Nineteen this became untenable, as the Falklands War resulted in a change in the public mood. Simon Weston, who was injured in the conflict and facially reconstructed, campaigned against the tendency to hide people with disfigurement from public view.

Today, we're more accepting of unconventional appearances. Piercings, tattoos and a backlash against the botox culture have reinforced the shift in attitudes. Whilst the available repertoire of body-images is contracting, and dysmorphia is being diagnosed more readily (anorexia, bulimia and self-harm being only the headline-grabbing manifestations), a story where someone goes on a killing-spree because he thinks he's ugly simply wouldn't be broadcast today. At least, not unless an awful lot of textbook psychology was introduced to justify it, along the lines of "he was bad because he was abused by an unforgiving society" (in cinema, Red Dragon is the most recent big-budget version of this). As we stated at the start, many were uncomfortable with the bad-because-he-looks-bad idea even in the mid-'80s. If "Black Orchid" were made today, then the motivation of the well-meaning family - keeping George imprisoned and telling everyone that he's dead, rather than live with the shame - would be examined, and face the full force of the Doctor's wrath.

Wouldn't the story work just as well if he was putting Ann's life in jeopardy instead of Nyssa's?

The Doctor claims to be a fast bowler. We don't see any evidence of this. As is well-documented, the police box - or at least the blue, specially-designated version - was launched in 1929 and confined to cities until rather later, but the local policemen still recognise it in 1925.

Lord Cranleigh makes a big mystery of what his costume's going to be. When we see it, it's apparently just his usual hunting reds. Party-pooper.

Critique (Prosecution) The knee-jerk thing to say is that there's no science-fictional content here, but that's baloney. There are no rockets, aliens or parallel universes, but the viewers at home are constantly being teased with mysteries that look like having "conventional" *Doctor Who* explana-

tions. Someone's expecting the Doctor when the TARDIS arrives by accident; Nyssa has a near-twin; there's a reference to 'the *other* doctor… the Master'; the odd-looking silent figure bound up; the secret passages; Lady Cranleigh's strange behaviour… we're invited to speculate on what's going on, and the context shapes our expectations. While we try to work out what's happened, we get some pretty costumes, girls in silk floaty dresses and satisfyingly "period" touches.

Then a few minutes into episode two, it all comes crashing down. All *Doctor Who* stories of this era will suffer the same fault. They set up something intriguing, then the rest is business-as-usual with the "novelty" features as a backdrop but the same old storyline (usually the Master or an old monster that's somehow learned all about Time Lords). And the Doctor will just herd everyone into the TARDIS and resolve things by double-talk, or make speeches until everyone else is dead. As Sir Robert points out in a cut scene, simply having a time machine isn't proof of innocence, but everyone acts as though it were.

This story would make sense if the Doctor had as little experience of Earth as Adric or Nyssa, but we know that's not true. Instead even small children watching wondered what was wrong with him. The other regulars seem to have had personality transplants too; Tegan is now really enthusiastic about time travel (despite having just been brainwashed and exposed to plague and filth in 1666), Nyssa is now a party animal and Adric is regressing to eight years old. All their tension and bickering has stopped, and they get on like the Teletubbies. Was there an unscreened episode where they got blitzed on tequila slammers? (It *would* explain the beginning of "Earthshock", though.)

Critique (Defence) Once again, it doesn't make any sense unless you can see it through the eyes of the first-time audience. Preferably through the eyes of the young 'uns.

"The Visitation" had reminded the nation that history had a history in *Doctor Who*, had shown the under-twelves aliens-versus-highwaymen and made us all go "mmm" at the period detail. Now it was time for the programme to show that it knew how to add some glitter to proceedings. As with so much in this period, the most important thing to remember is that a whole generation had never seen anything like this before; indeed, in a lot of ways this is new territory even for pre-'70s *Doctor Who*, despite the straight-line plot. The TARDIS, in the middle of a '20s mystery romp? A sympathetic "monster" who isn't an alien? How terribly novel, Mater.

In the end, of course, it's less than satisfying. The biggest part of the problem (and this is almost inevitable, for a two-parter) is that the Doctor never really solves anything, never has any reason to get involved in the details of this world. He turns up, gets arrested, spends some time protesting his innocence - and to be fair, these "Doctor insists he's not guilty of murder" scenes are the best we've ever seen, Peter Davison once again stealing the show without getting in the way of the other characters - but in the final analysis all he actually does is… go up on a roof and say a couple of lines to a madman. By the time he gets back

to Cranleigh Hall to face Mad George, the Cranleighs have already decided to come clean about the family secret, leaving us in no doubt that if he hadn't been there then much the same thing would have happened.

Yet at this stage, the programme's encouraging us to think of *Doctor Who* as an ongoing serial, not as a series of epics that just happen to be split up into episodes. Even at the time, there was the sense that "Black Orchid" was only an interlude, a quiet stopover with cricket and a masquerade ball before we moved on to something meatier. Twenty years on it looks perfectly shallow, but shown over two consecutive evenings in the days when this sort of thing was just becoming fashionable, it made sense. In a time when we were still half-expecting every story to feature laser-guns, it gave us alien companions getting confused by cocktails and a dancing villain in a scary fancy-dress outfit. It may even have given the children in the audience some interest in 1920s pizzazz. (It certainly seemed to be more popular with the girls than the boys… this is about dressing-up, not about toy soldiers.) Which means that it does, at least, fulfil *one* of the functions of good *Doctor Who*.

The Facts

Written by Terence Dudley. Directed by Ron Jones. Viewing figures: 9.9 million, 10.1 million. The summer '83 repeat got 4.4 and 5.0 million.

Supporting Cast Michael Cochrane (Lord Cranleigh), Barbara Murray (Lady Cranleigh), Moray Watson (Sir Robert Muir), Brian Hawksley (Brewster), Ahmed Khalil (Latoni), Gareth Milne (The Unknown / George Cranleigh), Ivor Salter (Sergeant Markham), Andrew Tourell (Constable Cummings).

Oh, Isn't That..?

• *Michael Cochrane.* Appeared in *Wings*, a period drama about the founding of the Royal Flying Corps, playing a character called Gaylion (no, really).

• *Barbara Murray.* She was in *The Pallisers*, *The Power Game* and many, many more.

• *Moray Watson.* A veteran of the '60s BBC soap *Compact*. More recently he'd been in *Rumpole of the Bailey*, like almost everyone else with an Equity card.

Working Titles "The Beast".

Cliffhangers The escaped madman, disguised by the harlequin costume, extends a sinister gloved hand towards the throat of the unconscious Ann Talbot. (Or is it Nyssa…? No.)

The Lore

• This was filmed at the same estate as "Castrovalva", in the following month. (Yes, October. It looks cold, doesn't it?) John Nathan-Turner's future partner Gary Downie was an experienced choreographer, and the producer had intended to direct this story himself. As it turned out, the problems with "K9 & Company" (18.7-A) got in the way. Chris Bidmead rejected the first version of this story, and he insists the finished product vindicates his decision.

• As the weather deteriorated, the scenes which didn't *have* to be set outside were redrafted to work in the drawing room. Fortunately the cold weather had at least been sunny when the dancing had taken place, but as drizzle set in it was decided to have the Doctor introduced to Lady Talbot separately from the others (whom he meets at the cricket match).

• When the story was broadcast, Davison was delighted to see that the flukey ball with which he'd clean-bowled the batsman had been filmed and used. He hadn't been enthusiastic about this story in rehearsals, and whilst he enjoyed much of the location-work he felt it to be out-of-key with the rest of the season.

• Yet again, a walkout by the electricians' union delayed studio shooting. A few sequences in Ann Talbot's room were scrapped, but the cast and crew rehearsed for the first two hours in available light. (The recording was scheduled for the evening anyway, by which time much of what director Ron Jones wanted was blocked out and only two hours' recording time wasted.) Latoni's efforts to restrain George were also lost.

• Gareth Milne had been hired purely for stunt-work, but Jones thought he could handle the grunting and whimpering which constituted George Cranleigh's role. Milne was slightly injured in the "fall" sequence, but continued filming. Nevertheless, they decided to abandon the idea of the Doctor (played by Milne) scaling the outer wall. He still did the drainpipe climb as Lord Cranleigh, though.

19.6: "Earthshock"

(Serial 6B, Four Episodes, 8th - 16th March 1982.)

Which One is This? After a six-year absence from the programme, the Cybermen return to wreak vengeance on the planet that caused their downfall in the Cyber-Wars, first by planting a bomb on it and then by trying to smash a great big spaceship into it (q.v. 12.5, "Revenge of the Cybermen"). This time, Adric dies.

Firsts and Lasts Ah, yes, Adric. Here he becomes the first "proper" companion to die while in the Doctor's service. (For years fan-lore has claimed that Adric was the *third* companion to die, after Katarina and Sara Kingdom in 3.4, "The Daleks' Masterplan". But see **Who Decides What Makes a Companion?** under 21.5, "Planet of Fire". Adric's death is genuinely unique, although as we saw in Volume IV Sarah Jane Smith, the Brigadier and Leela all narrowly escaped the same fate.)

Post-mortem, the credits of episode four roll in silence over a close-up of Adric's crumbled badge, the only occasion that an episode doesn't end with the theme music. Nathan-Turner, ever the TV-obsessive, apparently picked this trick up from *Coronation Street*.

On an "up" note / on even more of an "up" note (delete according to preference): making their first appearance here are the new, improved, '80s-style Cybermen, the first of their kind to have visibly organic facial features and the first to have long-standing Cyber-Leader David Banks as one of their number. Like the "Revenge" models, the actors inside the costumes speak the lines, which are then electronically distorted to sound either "butch" or like Denis Healey[7]… though this also affects any actor delivering lines too close to the Cybermen, as we learn in episode three. We have also the debut of the "Earthshock" space-trooper helmets, with little lights built-in. These are going to crop up at least once a year between now and 1986.

The Doctor says 'brave heart, Tegan' for the first time.

Four Things to Notice About "Earthshock"…

1. Despite all the Doctor's claims, it's at this point that we really have to forget the original brief of the Cybermen being creatures devoid of emotion, because the new Cyber-Leader insists on

hamming it up at every opportunity. He sounds as if he's positively relishing the occasion when he orders his minions to activate his world-shattering bomb, and when he works out that he can manipulate the Doctor by threatening Tegan, mere sadistic menace just isn't enough and he's forced to resort to smugness. But his best moment is one of Cyber-machismo, when he clenches his fist in a furious manner and demands '*more powerrrrr!*'.

2. The Cyber-fun doesn't end there. Episode two features a scene in which the renovated Cybermen use their holographic VCR to watch clips of old Cyberman stories, giving the youngsters in the audience another chance to see what those William Hartnell and Patrick Troughton people used to look like. Sharp-minded fans watched this sequence and noticed that while the Cyber-Leader's describing the events of "Tomb of the Cybermen", the screen is showing him a clip from "The Wheel in Space", as if there's something very wrong with the Cyber-filing-system. (And the clips didn't end there. To celebrate the Cybermen's return, that week the BBC's TV-programme-about-TV-programmes *Did You See?* ran a special feature on the monsters of *Doctor Who*, allowing the newborn generation to see old-fashioned Cybermen, Sea Devils and God-knows-what-others for the very first time. We thought we had it good, in those days.)

3. There's an awful lot of sloppy editing and camera-work going on here, with various stage-hands (and hands of stage-hands) getting into shot, the most famous of them being the woman who sits in the corner reading the script while Tegan's on the stairwell of the space-freighter. Then there's the inept trooper in episode one, who blatantly sees the shadow of one of the Cyber-androids but pretends he doesn't, and the soldiers who keep changing gender between TARDIS and freighter scenes in episode four.

But the fans' favourite has to be the moment when the humans, taking cover in the foreground, nervously spy on two Cyber-sentries in the background. It's notable because despite the supposed emotionlessness of the Cybermen, and despite the fact that none of them except the Cyber-Leader are usually seen to speak unless it's to say 'humans detected in sector four', the two sentries are making elaborate hand-gestures at each other and look as if they're discussing Playstation tactics. Maybe this is what they're *always* like, when they think nobody's watching.

4. And what was the reaction to Adric's death, at the time? Weeeeeeeell… depends who you ask. There's one school which holds that since Adric was an annoying, miserable whelp, his demise was greeted with the kind of approval that would only be matched today by the death of Jar Jar Binks. There's another school which holds that if you happened to be below the age of puberty, then "your" companion had bitten the dust and you might actually have got a bit sniffly. Certainly, the public response proved that *Doctor Who* hadn't lost its ability to get people to write to the *Radio Times*. (Well, some did. Others just complained about the cellophane-wrapped Cybermen.)

Perhaps the most important thing to note, though, is this: since Season Three, a generation of viewers had grown up believing that the Doctor and his associates were *guaranteed* to be okay. They were put in peril with almost every cliffhanger, but you always knew they'd find an escape route somehow. Adric is the only "proper" companion to have been demonstrably slain, but really, one companion *had* to die. To prove that it was at least possible. To prove that the final score wasn't entirely a foregone conclusion. Let's just treat him as a sacrifice, and say no more about it.

The Continuity

The Doctor Doesn't know what hit the Earth and killed the dinosaurs, although he's about to find out. Here he's just been reading the book *Black Orchid* [from the previous story], finding it 'fascinating'. He gets petulant, even child-like, when Adric starts arguing with him, though they make up before the tragic finale. His reaction to Adric's demise is one of silent, bewildered disbelief.

The military scanner in the twenty-sixth century identifies the Doctor as 'ectopic'. [Meaning he's got organs in the wrong places… almost certainly just a reference to his "stray" second heart, as no medical examination he's ever had on Earth has shown jumbled organs to be among his traits. The device is also primed to detect mammals, which is presumably what Time Lords are.]

The Supporting Cast
• *Adric*. The doomed Alzarian youngster is getting moody again, talking about going "home" to Terradon and insisting that he can work out a course for E-Space. Which he does, although he later admits that he doesn't really want to go back

What's Wrong with Cyber-History?

It starts with a simple, trivial continuity error, made by a writer under pressure who was just trying to tell a decent story rather than write a consistent history (although some would say that's a generous view of "Earthshock"). As with so much else in *Doctor Who* continuity, however, the mistake turns out to have ramifications which make some kind of sense.

In episode two of "Earthshock", the Cyber-Leader watches clips from a variety of previous encounters between the Doctor and the Cyber-race, revealing in the process that Cyberman monitoring equipment always chooses exactly the same camera-angles as the BBC. The last of the three clips is taken from "Revenge of the Cybermen" (12.5), with the Cyber-Leader describing the Fourth Doctor's interference in their plan to blow up Voga.

Except that "Earthshock" is supposed to be set in 2526. And "Revenge of the Cybermen", though slightly harder to date, is set in the twenty-ninth century at the earliest.

So, a simple mistake. But if you're *trying* to make sense of it... then short of writing an entire "missing adventure" to deal with the discrepancy, there's only one explanation that adds up. These Cybermen are time-travellers.

Which would explain a lot. At the climax of "Earthshock" the Cybermen attach an override device to the freighter and try to smash it into the Earth, but Adric's tinkering causes the equipment to send the ship sixty-five million years back in time. Now, unless you assume Adric's mathematical skills to be so great that he can create a time machine out of any old piece of fluff he comes across (and they're not), then you have to conclude that the Cyberman device has some built-in time-travel capability of its own. Perhaps it only

has enough power to shift a freighter sixty-five million years when it's hooked up to the ship's anti-matter engines, but even so... is it really feasible that the Cybermen might have the secret of time-travel right under their noses[8], and never even realise it?

When "Earthshock" was first broadcast, to suggest that Cybermen might have time-travel capability would have been a bit of a stretch. In the '60s they didn't even seem to have faster-than-light space travel (see 5.7, "The Wheel in Space"). But the next Cyberman story to turn up was "Attack of the Cybermen" (22.1), in which they *do* get their hands on a working time-vessel. "Attack" ends with the craft's destruction, and the Doctor acts as if that's the end of the matter, but does this really make sense? The fact that they can watch video recordings of "The Tenth Planet" (4.2) suggests that Cybermen have some kind of "Cyber-internet" for storing information; they can apparently transmit data between units without any special equipment; and it's even hinted that Cyber-personas can be moved from one body to another. If the thoroughly-methodical Cybermen found a crashed time-ship, then what would they do? Start gallivanting around history straight away, or strip it down, find out how it worked and give the information to as many Cyber-units as possible?

This volume would suggest that from the Cybermen's point of view, "Attack of the Cybermen" takes place before "Earthshock". On gaining time-travel, their first assault on history is an attempt to prevent Mondas' destruction. Failing to do this - and presumably not being allowed to try again, thanks to the Blinovitch Limitation Effect, etc - they use the same technol-

continued on page 155...

at all, and just wants the Doctor to take him seriously. [Once again, he seems to want attention now there's a risk of him not being the Doctor's "favourite". The way he asks the Doctor to spend more time with him suggests that he sees the Doctor as a father-figure, although this doesn't last and before long he's calling the Doctor 'immature'. He was obviously happier with the Fourth Doctor.]

Proving that he has savant-like mathematical powers, Adric can instantly estimate the square root of 3.69873. As it turns out, it's this cleverness that gets him killed, as he insists on staying

aboard the hijacked freighter and trying to crack the codes on the Cyberman's override device as the ship hurtles towards Earth. He very nearly manages it, too, but a shot across the controls from a Cyberman dooms him, the freighter and the dinosaurs. [Ironically, if the Cyberman *hadn't* fired then the dinosaurs wouldn't have died, and humanity would almost certainly never have evolved.] Adric's mopey final words, before the impact: 'Now I'll never know if I was right.'

The Doctor uses Adric's gold-rimmed badge to kill the Cyber-Leader, and it's last seen lying in pieces on the TARDIS floor.

• *Nyssa*. Can't really pilot the TARDIS, although she understands certain principles. She's seen using pencil and paper to work out settings on the TARDIS console, something that's beyond Tegan. She's the first one to turn away when the scanner shows them Adric's death.

• *Tegan*. Describes herself as a 'mouth on legs', but she seems comfortable with a gun. Like Nyssa, she's massively shocked at Adric's death, and she's the one who starts blubbing first. Tegan also seems to need more comforting than Nyssa and her "stiff upper lip" attitude.

The TARDIS   Both Cyberman and human weapons function within the TARDIS [again blowing holes in the 'temporal grace' idea]. The androids on Earth contact their Cybermen masters with a powerful ultrasonic signal, and the TARDIS console picks it up as a constant chirping, without any member of the crew asking to hear it. The Doctor can detect the source of the Cybermen's signals and jam the command that activates their bomb on Earth, if he fiddles around under the console. But the signal gets through when the Cybermen increase the power, as the TARDIS has unlimited power but its transmitter doesn't. The bomb is defused with the help of a toolkit from the TARDIS, including a magnetic clamp, a probe, a laser-cutter and a magnetic drone.

The freighter from which the Cybermen send their signal is in 'sector sixteen', by the Doctor's reckoning, and Nyssa recognises this as deep space ['sector' perhaps indicating a position relative to the planet on which the TARDIS has landed]. When the freighter starts spiralling backwards in time, the TARDIS can't lock onto it until it's arrived at its destination.

Adric's room on the Ship is full of clutter. Visible here are plenty of books, a Kinda necklace, the Grim Reaper mask from the Terileptil android and an unidentified tribal mask on a stand. Unlike the Nyssa / Tegan room, it has no roundels [instead it's got the "hexagon" mouldings of most BBC SF of the era, first seen in 9.4, "The Mutants"]. Adric uses the console computer to help him work out the course into E-Space.

The Non-Humans
• *Cybermen*. A brand new model of Cyberman is at large here. Though they have the ever-familiar blank expressions and handle-like "ears", the lower part of each Cyberman's faceplate is transparent, revealing an organic, silver-skinned jaw underneath [they may have got this idea from the Ice Warriors].

They also speak with near-human voices, and not for the first time they don't seem anywhere near as emotionless as they should. They even use contractions in their speech. Their leader seems positively riled by the Doctor's taunting, and also frustrated by his underlings' lack of initiative. [The implication may be that these Cybermen are running out of mechanical "parts", so they're more dependent on their organic bits. This makes sense if they come from the future, but we'll come to that. Perhaps tellingly, before now the only other Cybermen who've spoken with near-human voices were the ones in "Revenge of the Cybermen" (12.5), desperate survivors of the Cyber-Wars.]

These Cybermen are aware of an alliance being made on Earth which will threaten their species - see **History** - and have come to wipe out the planet, seeing this as 'war' and also believing that the conference's destruction will be a great psychological triumph. Their first attempt is a computer-controlled bomb, planted in a cave system on Earth itself, capable of killing most of the population and making life intolerable for the survivors. [The Cyber-Leader states that it's Cyber-technology, but it's apparently not one of the Cyber-bombs seen in "Revenge of the Cybermen" as the Doctor doesn't recognise it. It may be something even worse.]

When the bomb fails, they plan to smash a space-freighter into the planet instead. The device they attach to the computers on the freighter, a small box designed to override the ship's controls, unexpectedly time-warps the vessel when Adric starts solving its three logic codes. Even before they come up with this emergency plan, the freighter is already important to the Cybermen. An army of them is secretly in storage there, kept in plastic wrapping [much as in 6.3, "The Invasion"] or in cargo compartments. Reactivating the Cybermen drains power from the freighter and creates a powerful electromagnetic field that the TARDIS can detect.

The Cybermen are under the control of a Cyber-Leader, identifiable as he has black handles

What's Wrong with Cyber-History?

...continued from page 153

ogy to go for the *second* big historical target and try to prevent the Cyber-Wars. It's certainly the easiest way to make sense of the time-travelling override gadget.

So really we have to conclude that the Cybermen in "Silver Nemesis" (25.3) are also time-travellers, which neatly explains the way they behave. "Silver Nemesis" is set in 1988, not long after "The Tenth Planet" and only a decade or so after "The Invasion" (6.3), but somehow there's a complete Cyber-fleet assembled near Earth. The Cybermen are the same "desperate-looking" units (with human voices and humanoid jaws visible under their faceplates) we see in "Earthshock" and "Attack". And not only do they know all about the Doctor, they also know about his past, about his heritage and about the Nemesis statue. This is so far removed from the native twentieth-century Cybermen we see in "The Invasion" or "The Tenth Planet", who talk like computers and can't even shamble from planet to planet properly without help, that it's impossible to fathom without time-travel being involved. The "Silver Nemesis" Cyberman is a far more knowledgeable, sophisticated breed of marauder than those who attack Earth between the 1970s and the late 2000s, and without time-technology it's hard to see how they'd even know about Time Lords in that era. The Cyber-Leader's notoriously puzzling line in "Earthshock", "so, we meet again", is as telling as it is mysterious.

It's certainly suggestive that while the Cyber-Leader in "Earthshock" talks of Time Lords and TARDISes as if they were known but rarely-seen phenomena, the Cyber-Leader in "Silver Nemesis" takes them for granted. This is, in short, a race that's been researching.

on his head instead of silver ones. He has a Cyber-Lieutenant under him, as well as a personal guard of regular-looking Cybermen, and they monitor operations from a hidden area on board the freighter that's designated Cyber-Control. From here the 'main fleet' can be informed of the mission's progress. The Cyber-Leader says his task was to lead the squad to eliminate the survivors of the bomb, but with the freighter replacing the bomb he aims to join up with a secondary force to complete this task.

This time the Cybermen have no built-in weapons, and carry chunky silver guns. They also have a rifle-like thermal lance for cutting through spaceship doors, and use powerful conventional explosives. Cybermen are again said to be susceptible to gold, as just a little of the substance suffocates them when it's rubbed into their chest-units, but they don't need to breathe and normal blasters don't harm them unless several beams are concentrated on a single Cyber-target. Their own weapons can blow them up.

Defending the bomb on Earth are never-before-seen pieces of Cyber-technology: two dark, smooth-bodied androids, human in form but without any features. These seem to be little more than walking weapons, capable of firing beams from their hands which reduce human targets to a green sludge. The Cybermen can "see" through these androids, their perceptions being relayed to a holographic projector in Cyber-Control. The androids are painfully logical and show little sign of intelligence, though as with their masters, blasters don't kill them unless several beams are concentrated on them. Mention is also made of the Cybermen's deep-space probes, which can sense the TARDIS heading for the freighter. [When the TARDIS is in the vortex, or does it emerge to "hover" in space and get its bearings before materialising, as it seems to do in so many other stories?]

These Cybermen are far more knowledgeable than expected. The Cyber-Leader recognises the TARDIS' police box exterior, and even his Lieutenant knows of the Time Lords, stating that they're forbidden to interfere. They also know that the TARDIS only requires one operator. Extracts from three previous encounters with the Doctor are shown on the holographic display. [From "The Tenth Planet" (4.2), "The Wheel in Space" (5.7) and "Revenge of the Cybermen", although the Cyber-Leader mentions the events of "Tomb of the Cybermen" (5.1). "Revenge of the Cybermen" is set at a point in time *after* this story, more evidence that these Cybermen are time-travellers. See **What's Wrong with Cyber-History?**.]

The Cyber-Leader says 'we meet again' on encountering the Doctor. [If he's not speaking figuratively - and Cybermen aren't really ones for flowery speech - then this might indicate that the Leader has "downloaded" memories of other, doomed, Cyber-Leaders. Which could explain why most Cyber-Leaders from this point on have the same voice.]

The Cyber-Leader is prepared to leave guards on the bridge of the doomed freighter to watch the reactions of the captured humans, just for research purposes [and because he's obviously a sadist], although the guards expect to evacuate at the last minute. A ship is sent from main fleet to pick up the Cyber-Leader's squad, but the fleet is some distance away, which is why the Cyber-Leader uses the TARDIS. The secondary force is due to arrive when the freighter hits the planet.

History
• *Dating.* 2526, according to the TARDIS instruments.

At this point, a major interstellar peace conference is being held on Earth involving the heads of many powerful planets, its goal being to sign a pact to unify their military forces and wipe out the Cybermen. [Every indication is that the Cybermen have been menacing the spaceways up until now, but that this is the beginning of the Cyber-Wars mentioned in "Revenge of the Cybermen". Earth is in contact with Draconia at around this time - see 10.3, "Frontier in Space" - so are the Draconians invited to the party?]

However, though the Cybermen are clearly a major concern, the members of the Earth military seen here don't seem to know them that well. Earth's on red alert, and incoming freighters are being subjected to intense scrutiny, which is why the Cybermen use the cleared freighter as a weapon instead of a conventional missile. [Their original bomb was planted weeks ago, maybe months ago, before the security precautions were put in place. We can assume the Cybermen wouldn't be able to reach the planet to plant another bomb now the conference is on.]

The caves where the Cybermen hide their bomb appear to be in the middle of a quarry-like, uninhabited area of Earth, which isn't identified. Humans have only recently discovered the caves [because the Cybermen opened them up?], which are full of strikingly impressive dinosaur skeletons. A survey in the caves was wiped out by the Cybermen's androids after being there for four weeks, which is why the military are sent in, led by a lieutenant. The soldiers are professional, well-equipped and fairly ruthless, with protective helmets, visored face-masks fitted as part of the uniform and great big stun-or-kill blaster-rifles

that run on power-packs. Their scanning device is described as 'ancient' and seems rather primitive, a radar-like screen that shows the presence of heartbeats inside the caves but nothing else. It's tuned only to detect electrical signals from mammalian life-forms [they're not worried about Draconians, then], and lead can block it. Wrist-computers are obviously all the rage for both military and civilians.

The freighter that's on its way to Earth is carrying an unspecified cargo, and huge amounts of it, using warp drive to get to its destination. It's one of those operations where everybody's worried about losing their bonuses and getting fined for late deliveries. It seems to have miles of corridors and galleries, although the ship's mostly automated, and only the captain and two officers are ever seen on the bridge. Security officer Ringway indicates that murderers can be executed on board, and other members of the small crew patrol the vessel, packing blasters. [The Cybermen mention a crew of ten, but this seems to mean ten *after* the occasional "vanishings" of crewmembers.]

Piracy is evidently a problem in this era. The freighter has anti-matter engines. When the Cybermen burn their way onto the bridge, the Doctor cleverly rigs things up so that the systems which stabilise the molecular structure of the anti-matter's containment vessels "regenerate" the door. This kills the Cyberman who's coming through the door by instantly re-solidifying it. The freighter has at least one escape craft, and stops off at a station in deep space en route.

Lastly, but most significantly: it's revealed that 65,000,000 years ago, the dinosaurs were wiped out when the anti-matter-powered freighter spiralled backwards through time and hit the planet. Judging from the picture on the TARDIS scanner, it explodes before impact, taking Adric with it. [See **What's the Origin of the Silurians?** under 7.2, "Doctor Who and the Silurians", for more of this prehistoric larking-about.]

The Analysis

Where Does This Come From? With Ian Levine now firmly entrenched as *Doctor Who's* unpaid critic-advisor, and with Eric Saward involved, it was inevitable that a Cyberman story would turn up. However, there's been a change. The Cybermen, as Kit Pedler and Gerry Davis conceived them, were emotionless Valium-zombies with power-steering. Saward's version of the race does away with hypnosis, infiltration, stealth, or cunning and focuses on raw machismo. These aren't walking life-support systems out for recruits, these are Ultimate Warriors going to kick Earth's sorry butt.

The American turn of phrase is deliberate. Instead of representing a sterile future for humanity, these Cybermen are shown to be *potent*, and in some ways even admirable; it's the same borderline homoeroticism found in early Schwarzenegger flicks and body-popping (and the mechanical / macho overlap is common to both of these). Now, to our eyes the idea that an all-out terrorist assault on Earth would destroy the unity of those fighting the culprits might seem odd, but looked at in the context of earlier hijackings the bomb-planting and commandeering of the freighter are what fanatical (i.e. sketchily-motivated) villains *do*. We're still in the era of Beirut, and the Black September organisation. The one thing that can't be risked in a story like this is the let-down of such formidable creatures being beaten by stumbling amateurs - see for instance the UNIT vs. Daleks "rumble in the bramble" in 9.1, "Day of the Daleks" - so there has to be serious firepower on both sides.

Which means that on the human side, all of a sudden the nature of the military seems very, very different. This time soldiers actually seem *dangerous*, at least when they're not being out-flanked by androids. This being *Doctor Who*, nobody packing a gun in the series has ever proved to be particularly competent, but compare this with the UNIT era of the early '70s. The Brigadier of the Pertwee years is exactly what you'd expect a soldier to be in post-war British culture, exactly what you'd expect from a country coming down from a time of Empire; he's bluff, old-fashioned, stiff as a board and under the delusion that Great Britain still rules the world, but he's still basically a Good Man at heart. Those under him are also Good Men at heart, although they're not terribly efficient and - typical of the English, whose national characteristics include a deep-rooted love of the amateur - there's the impression that these soldier-boys are just muddling through. Certainly, they're easy to distract with cocoa and rugby.

But by 1982, a huge shift in the military was already in effect. Which is to say, a huge shift in the *culture* of the military. In Britain, the Thatcher government was trying to appeal to some Great British ideal that largely seemed to involve stuffing the foreigners and executing the Irish without trial. In part this trend had begun in the '70s (see 13.6, "The Seeds of Doom"), but by this stage the army was being reclassified as something proud, aggressive and *professional*. The SAS had become prominent when it had busted the Iranian Embassy siege, and taken on the mystique of the French Foreign Legion. From hereon in, and especially when Eric Saward's writing the scripts, there's barely a trace of amateurish UNIT good-naturedness and the universe is full of space-marines who have no compunction about shooting bystanders on sight.

In the case of "Earthshock", what's alarming is that the soldiers still ultimately end up being portrayed as the good guys, firmly on the Doctor's side in a crisis even though they've got nothing to offer but brute firepower. In a way, it was prescient. Two weeks after the story was broadcast, Argentina invaded the Falklands, and the subsequent war would define the new military culture better than any other single event. Soon Harrier jump-jets would be among the Great British icons of the age. Saward obviously enjoyed writing "war" stories, but there's no evidence that he was keen on the real thing, which might explain why his space-mercenaries had become a shade more sociopathic by the time he wrote his next epic of military bloodshed (21.4, "Resurrection of the Daleks").

And yet again, we have to mention the influence of cinema on this story. If "The Visitation" was an attempt to remake semi-historical *Doctor Who* in a world after New Hollywood, then "Earthshock" is an attempt to give the Cybermen the same treatment. It's fairly clear that Saward is *deliberately* cashing in on "traditional" elements from Cyber-tales of old, but - let's come out and say it - trying to bring in some of the darkness and dynamism of *Alien*. By the same token, "Earthshock" is the first *Doctor Who* story to try to do space-age gunfights the way the audience had seen them done in the *Star Wars* oeuvre. In previous seasons, stories like "The Invisible Enemy" (15.2) had featured laser-gun battles (a) because they were necessary "filler" material in the plot and (b) because they livened things up a bit. But these battles were slow, hesitant, largely unconvincing and often filmed as if they were afterthoughts (the ones in "The Invisible Enemy", especially, were more or less cobbled together during editing). Whereas the battles in "Earthshock" are staged, filmed and cut as if they're "cinematic" events in themselves, although whether you see this as a way of distracting people from the script or an actual step forward in terms of televisual film-making is another matter.

It's also worth pointing out that like "Castrovalva", this almost comes across as two two-part stories - one in the caves, and one on the freighter - as if the programme's deliberately shaping itself to its twice-weekly format.

Things That Don't Make Sense   As ever, the Cyber-scheme is full of holes. No reason is given for the Cybermen planting the bomb in those particular caves, and even the Doctor wonders about it. Surely, just burying the bomb in a hole and then covering it over is a better way of ensuring that it's not found? Nor is it *quite* clear how most of the Cybermen get off the freighter before it starts its suicide run towards Earth, as there's no mention of them having a ship of their own, nor any mention of the freighter having that many escape pods. Surely, the Cyber-Leader doesn't wake them all up just so they can die? Even if the Leader doesn't care whether his troops suffer when they're smashed into tinfoil, there's always the risk that as the newly-awoken Cybermen aren't aware of the change of plan, one of them might de-activate the logic codes and save the freighter in order to achieve the old mission objective.

Adric insists on reminding the Doctor what a CVE is in episode two, for the benefit of those who haven't been paying attention. The troops in the caves repeatedly state that it's 'impossible' for their enemies to fail to show up on the scanner, even though the scanner only picks up mammals and in this era they *must* know about aliens, robots and such [military lack of imagination]. Why does it take a whole minute for the signal from the Cyber-Leader to detonate the bomb on Earth? Not only does the time-delay seem inconvenient, but it's a nice round figure like a *minute*, as well.

It's never explained why the Cybermen are drawing attention to themselves by dispensing with crewmembers aboard the freighter [did the missing men discover too much?], and when accused of the crime the Doctor never suggests that the freighter crew should verify his story with the military officer who's come with him on the TARDIS. Still, he's given a surprising amount of freedom to move around and look over people's

shoulders, with all of the bridge crew happy to turn their backs on him even when they think he's a murdering pirate. Ringway never answers the Doctor's point, i.e. why on Earth he's working for the Cybermen when they can hardly pay well. Why does the Cyberman in episode four capture Tegan and reunite her with the Doctor, instead of just shooting her like everyone else, since the Cybermen have no way of knowing that she might be an important bargaining-chip?

The Cyber-Leader announces himself with the words 'so, we meet again… Doctor', yet we've rarely seen a Cyberman, let alone a Leader, who manages to survive an encounter with the Doctor. It's possible that this Leader has only recently been "promoted", and had his ear-handles painted black accordingly, but if so then it's a mystifying gloat. [Did the Doctor meet this Leader on Planet 14…? See 6.3, "The Invasion".] Another possibility is that the Cyber-Leader met the Doctor later on in the Doctor's timeline, but in that case he's trying to cause a logical paradox by killing the Time Lord *now*, and Cybermen really should hate logical paradoxes.

Leaving aside the convenient fact that Earth is in the same position in the past as in the present (and not, for example, elsewhere on its orbit around the sun; this is a problem with all time-travel, but it's more noticeable when the time-travel's accidental and you can't assume the ship's computers are deliberately plotting a course)… Earth, circa 65,000,000 BC, looks exactly the same as it does now. No continental shift at all, then. Also, the Doctor describes dinosaurs as a 'species' rather than a group.

For that final shot, the TARDIS floor magically turns funeral-black. Professor Kyle seems to be wearing one boiler-suit on top of another, just in case anyone wants to go on a military expedition. Handy that Tegan shares her shoe-size too, isn't it? Especially as the boots have stack-heels, so practical when you've just been caving.

Plus, an aesthetic problem with the gunfights. The humans' blasters, which are shown to be relatively weedy, fire great big noisy glowing laserbeams. The androids' weapons, which can reduce people to mush with a single shot, just go "bang" as if they've got cap-guns in their hands. Obviously you shouldn't judge a weapon by its video effects.

Critique (Prosecution) Watched again that summer, the story didn't seem so pacy or ground-breaking. When you know how it ends, and what the monsters are, the remaining story is a bit flat. But it's not badly-made, there aren't any real embarrassments and the episodes have about an episode's-worth of events and developments. Even Matthew Waterhouse gets his act together, a little too late. In many ways the Doctor / Adric tiff is scripted as a married couple rowing (which - when seen with Saward's other Adric / Doctor script, "The Visitation" (19.4) - has raised eyebrows). Then we have guns that sound unlike any others, androids that move smoothly and enough that isn't quite like any story which has gone before to keep it going.

The problem is exactly the same as the breakthrough. Using the programme's past, not only by treating old episodes as a source for references but by re-doing old types of story with modern techniques, seemed like a good idea at the time. When it aired, this story settled a lot of long-running debates in *DWM*'s letters page about whether the Cybermen came from Mondas or Telos. It looks suspiciously as though whole lines were introduced specifically for this purpose. It's just about plausible, in a crisis, that the harried First Officer would casually ask 'where do these Cybermen come from?'. Yet the answer isn't exactly natural. It was exciting to get a connection with the programme's "glorious" past; then the new look was genuinely new; then after all that tension, there was the blessed relief at the end. It was, in every way, daring. But it was also, in every way, "safe". Short of doing a Dalek story with an all-star cast, explosions every three minutes and some connection with the Time Lords, there's not much else you could do to make *Doctor-Who*-by-numbers.

That isn't necessarily a bad thing: a lot of people like "The Talons of Weng-Chiang", and that's as obvious a set-up as you can get. Some even enjoy "The Brain of Morbius". In Yeti-in-the-loo mode, "The Green Death" is a slam-dunk. What "Earthshock" lacks is any ambition beyond this. It's a "greatest hits" compilation of Cyberman moments of the past, not putting them in a new situation to see what happens. Bidmead's approach, dogmatic as it was, is being discarded as a bad mistake.

If we're looking for specific faults, comedienne Beryl Reid and everything connected with her character is a good place to start. The tipsy auntie performance isn't what the story calls for, yet everyone around her reacts as though she were playing the part as written. The result is even more camp than Scott's arrival on the bridge, with fanfare and "determined" look; watch it again, it's straight out of *Doc Savage*. Reid unbalances the whole production, making it a Beryl Reid show with space-monsters (and those of us who recall her children's series *Mooncat* will shudder at the thought).

Then there's the recurrent fault that Davison's Doctor, as written by Saward, is out of his depth in most things not involving cucumber sandwiches. 'I wish to announce my *presence*' he proclaims at one point… but when Beryl Reid and a Cyber-Leader are in the same scene, he has barely any.

Critique (Defence) In Volume III, we described "Terror of the Autons" (8.1) as being like a packet of Skittles. In which case "Earthshock" logically has to be seen as a big pile of sugary cakes on a plate made of raw sugar with extra sugar coating, served by waitresses made of giant pancakes. It has, as everyone knows, a plot which makes the bare minimum of sense. From the whopping great holes in the logic of the Cyber-plan to the sudden and bizarre "anything's possible when you've got an alien computer on board, even time-travel!" moment, the writer / regular script editor blatantly needs a much bigger script editor standing behind him to make him do another draft. Can we ever forgive it?

Well… it's a funny thing. It's full of holes, but they're the kind of holes that could be covered over with just a few scant lines. It's worth considering this for a moment. A story like "The Time Monster" (9.5) looks awkward because it's so transparently made up of bits and pieces that the programme-makers just liked the sound of, many of which don't seem to belong in the same plot. If it doesn't make sense, then it doesn't make sense for big, aesthetic reasons. But all the parts of "Earthshock" mesh. The bit about the freighter travelling backwards though time is perfectly in keeping with the rest of the story; it just needs someone to mention the fact that the Cyber-device *might* make it travel backwards through time about an episode earlier. The Cybermen's decision to smash a ship into Earth after they fail to detonate a bomb on the planet is, dramatically and dynamically, not only workable but actually very good; it just needs a little extra something to underline the fact that the planet's on red alert.

After all the stick this story has received, and after all our worst suspicions about Eric Saward, what's surprising is that so much of "Earthshock" is actually coherent. It has a drive, a sense of how stories should *move*, that makes sense even when the soldiers are delivering macho dialogue and Professor Kyle's overplaying every line. There's a genuine sense of menace building throughout the last couple of episodes, as the Cyberman slowly force the Doctor into a corner, so their entry into the TARDIS seems like an actual defeat and the last scene comes across as a finale rather than a twist.

And that coherency seems an achievement in itself, given how many "crowd-pleaser" elements are being thrown to us here. The return of the Cybermen; caves done properly in *Doctor Who* for the first time; post-*Star-Wars* gun-battles that looked really, really good in the early '80s; the fantastic moment when a Cyberman gets melded into the bulkhead door; and finally, shockingly, *unimaginably*, the death of Adric. Are these things distracting us from a lack of substance? Perhaps they are, but the way in which they're presented to us - as a fluid, almost *chic* work of television - is in no way artless.

In more recent times, one TV critic summed up the US series *24* by pointing out that it works because the relentless, hysterical ticking of the clock stops you noticing how ridiculous it all is. "Earthshock" is what we had instead, in 1982. It was, and remains, a guilty pleasure.

The Facts

Written by Eric Saward. Directed by Peter Grimwade. Viewing figures: 9.1 million, 8.8 million, 9.8 million, 9.6 million. (As with "Full Circle", the biggest drop in ratings comes after episode one, the episode with the "memorable" cliffhanger…)

Supporting Cast James Warwick (Scott), Beryl Reid (Briggs), David Banks (Cyber Leader), Clare Clifford (Kyle), June Bland (Berger), Alec Sabin (Ringway), Mark Hardy (Cyber Lieutenant), Steve Morley (Walters), Suzi Arden (Snyder), Ann Holloway (Mitchell).

Oh, Isn't That..?
• *Beryl Reid.* Beloved radio comedienne of the '40s and '50s, later known for some "straight"

roles (notably *The Killing of Sister George* in the late '60s and *Tinker, Tailor, Soldier, Spy* in the '70s). Almost, but not quite, the last person anyone half-sane would have hired to play the Sigourney Weaver role in this version of *Alien*. The near-kinky spacesuit doesn't help.

• *James Warwick.* Had played the lead in the Robert Holmes / Douglas Camfield 1980 thriller series *The Nightmare Man*. Prior to this he'd been the voice of "Vidar" in freakish early-'70s Saturday morning series *Outa-Space!*. He's one of three actors to have been in both *Doctor Who* and *Babylon 5* ("Exogenesis", if you're interested).

Working Titles "Sentinel".

Cliffhangers While the androids in the caverns attack the Doctor's party, their controllers watch from their HQ and are revealed to be *Cybermen!!!*; having found the Doctor and Adric hovering over the corpse of a dead crewmember, Ringway points a gun at them and tells them that 'on this ship we execute murderers'; the Cyberman army awakens in the bowels of the freighter (accompanied by a rather curious video effect, but never mind).

The Lore

• As we've already established, the clip of the Second Doctor in episode two isn't really from "Tomb of the Cybermen", as this had been wiped and didn't reappear until 1992 (and therein lies a tale, but not just yet). It's from episode six of "The Wheel in Space" (5.7).

• The music was composed by Malcolm Clarke, whose previous score was for "The Sea Devils" (9.3). This score was, in its own way, just as remarkable. Asked to provide a "theme" akin to the "Space Adventures" track used for the first three Cyberman stories in the '60s, he did exactly that. The score used a palate of quasi-"real" instruments, including bass clarinet and a gamelan, while the film cans used by the BBC were sampled for the clanging noises.

Peter Grimwade hated it. Nevertheless, when the Radiophonic Workshop's *Doctor Who: The Music* was re-issued on CD, it was with the title *Earthshock*. The theme when Scott and Tegan are creeping around the freighter seems to be a deliberate "quote" from Mahler's Symphony No. 3 (see also 18.7, "Logopolis" and 20.3, "Mawdryn Undead"), which - as Grimwade may well have known - includes a setting of a passage from Nietzsche. On a lighter note, the plinkety-plonk tune that plays when Nyssa discovers the dinosaur bones in the cave is based on "The Fossils" from Saint-Saens' *The Carnival of the Animals.*

• As with "Warriors' Gate" (18.5), the studio itself was used as the basis for the freighter set. This time, however, it was cleared with the lighting crew and stage-hands beforehand.

• Alec Sabin (Ringway) had worked with Grimwade on *Tinker, Tailor, Soldier, Spy.* He now reads the news on the BBC World Service. Amazingly, Beryl Reid wasn't the first choice to play Briggs; soap legend Pat Phoenix had been approached (when we say "legend", bear in mind that her stepdaughter is now married to the Prime Minister and that her real life - to say nothing of her role as Elsie Tanner in *Coronation Street* - was the sort of thing Country and Western songwriters dream of inventing).

• The helmets with lights were, like the Cyberman heads, made by Unit 22; a small company (basically just Richard Gregory) specialising in props of this kind. During filming David Banks and others got a bad case of "Cyber-nose", an irritation caused by their schnozzles rubbing against the glass-fibre. As the helmets were bolted on by technicians, they had to wait until there was a long enough recording-break before applying ointment. Apparently the Lieutenant's death caused concerns on the set, as the explosion was unexpectedly big and the fire went on just a little too long.

• As mentioned above, the letters page of the *Radio Times* carried several complaints. Most of these were about the fact that the "dormant" Cybermen were shown with cellophane wrapping, looking as though they had plastic bags over their heads, and that young children might try to copy this. The BBC took note, and it hasn't happened since (some reports claim that the July 1982 repeat was trimmed, but we've been unable to confirm this... certainly the complaints again surfaced in the *Radio Times*). One letter was upset at the handling of Adric's death, but more followed the lack of explanation as to why the Doctor refused to help (see 19.7, "Time-Flight").

• And also as mentioned above, the occasion of the Cybermen's return elicited a feature on BBC2's *Did You See..?* in which presenter Gavin Scott believed himself hilarious in pointing out that the Sea Devils wore string vests. This is one of the

"bonus" features on the "Earthshock" DVD, alongside the claymation "Episode Five".

• The entire plot and setting of this story are – and our lawyers have advised us on the phrasing of this - echoed to a remarkable extent by the 1997 film *Space Truckers*, except with Dennis Hopper in the Beryl Reid role. (Though disappointingly the *Space Truckers* novelisation, written by former New Adventures author Jim Mortimore, doesn't play up this similarity much.)

• When the BBC showed the 1982 World Cup, ITV retaliated with a season of vintage television episodes called *Best of British* (including *The Prisoner* and *On The Buses*, both of which were repeated in full by Channel 4 when it began six months later). So when the imported western *Bret Maverick* (the oft-forgotten 1980s version, not the original series that propelled James Garner's career) stiffed on BBC1 on Monday evenings, a season called *Doctor Who and the Monsters* was aired. A savagely-trimmed "Genesis of the Daleks" (hacked to two fifty-minute episodes, see 12.4) and the newly-rediscovered colour version of "The Curse of Peladon" (9.2, adapted from a Canadian 525-line copy) were shown alongside "Earthshock". It averaged five-million viewers, and this was when most people were watching the coverage of the Falklands conflict or *Coronation Street*. In all, four of the seven Season Nineteen stories were re-shown within eighteen months.

19.7: "Time-Flight"

(Serial 6C, Four Episodes, 22nd - 30th March 1982.)

Which One is This? Concorde gets dragged back in time to a stark, low-budget prehistoric landscape, while an old enemy becomes an Arabian magician and says "size of Orson Welles!". And ends up with a longer moustache to twirl than ever before…

Firsts and Lasts Tegan becomes the first companion to *apparently* leave both the series and the TARDIS, but then fool everyone by turning up again and rejoining the crew in the next story. Her horrible stewardess' uniform is worn for the last time here. Pat Gorman, as one of the policemen in episode four, is finally given his gold watch (see 4.6, "The Moonbase"; 16.6, 'The Armageddon Factor"; and many others).

Having already directed "Full Circle",

"Logopolis", "Kinda" and "Earthshock", Peter Grimwade tries his hand at writing a script for the first time. (Actually, he wrote the first draft before he was asked to direct any of these. It's a long story, so see **The Lore**.) Kalid's "death" is the first of many to involve green slimy snot gushing out of every facial orifice, one of the trademarks of Davison's run on the series. And after thirteen years, the Master's trademark shrinking-gun is finally given a name.

But most importantly, this was the first time that British Airways and the British Airports Authority had ever allowed Concorde and Heathrow Airport to be used in a drama production. Of course, they set certain conditions…

Four Things to Notice About "Time-Flight"…

1. This is where the Master starts to lose it. Once again disguising himself in order to fool both the Doctor and the viewers, here he plays the part of an Arabian sorcerer with a Chinese accent called Kalid, who's got a false tummy and an "ancient-looking" latex face. All well and good… except that he has no stated reason to disguise himself in this way at all. He seems to be doing it for a laugh, or maybe just to get on the audience's nerves. The actor playing Kalid is listed on the end credits of episode one as "Leon Ny Taiy", so nothing spoils this wholly baffling surprise. (And once again, this story seems to have two "acts" spread across the two weeks of transmission, with lots of Arabian sorcery going on in the first two episodes and lots of typical Master-style gloating going on in the last two.)

2. It's a story set in that most cosmopolitan of modern settings, Heathrow Airport. Heathrow being the busiest and best-known airport in Britain. Imagine our surprise, then, on finding out that the Air Traffic Control section - which we always imagined was a huge, bustling area full of operators and ultra-hi-tech equipment - seems to be one man sitting at a display screen in front of some filing cabinets.

3. It's got Adric in it. Or rather, it's got Matthew Waterhouse in it for a single scene, playing an illusion of Adric that's generated by the Master in the hope of distracting Nyssa and Tegan. Since a companion had never died before, and since the Master had already used the *real* Adric in one of his previous schemes, *just for a moment* the viewer might have found him-or-herself wondering if this was the big twist and the events of "Earthshock" were all a bluff. (In fact, Adric was only included so that his name could appear in the *Radio Times* cast list, to stop anyone realising that he was going to bite the dust a week earlier. The production team really is paying far too much attention to the cast lists in this period.)

4. Peter Davison, whose Doctor once told Monarch that he wouldn't dream of interfering with monopticons, is now required to tell the villain that he's always found domination to be an unattractive prospect. By now you get the feeling that the writers are doing this deliberately.

The Continuity

The Doctor   Only a little time has passed since Adric's death, as the TARDIS has only just finished taking home the humans [from the last story], and the Doctor looks as if he's trying not to think about it too much. His response to this period of crisis is "let's take a holiday and try to forget about it", and soon he's lamenting the state of English cricket instead. He doesn't wish Tegan goodbye when he leaves her at Heathrow Airport, and there's no real discussion about whether they should part company [he evidently feels this is the right place for her to be].

Establishing his UNIT credentials at Heathrow, the Doctor mentions Brigadier Lethbridge-Stewart, adding 'unless he's a General by now' [which means the Doctor hasn't been keeping track of the Brigadier's career, and doesn't know about the man's retirement; see 20.3, "Mawdryn Undead"].

• *Ethics*. He steadfastly refuses to try to go back in time and save Adric, insisting that there are some rules which can't be broken even in the TARDIS. Talking about it just seems to make him angry [and there's a hint that he doesn't do it because it's morally wrong, not because the TARDIS isn't capable of it].

• *Inventory*. He's still flipping a coin to decide which corridor to take, but often ignoring the result.

• *Background*. The Doctor knows of the Xeraphin as a legendary race, and knows something of their history, recognising the shrunken corpses in their sanctum.

The Supporting Cast

• *Nyssa*. Fairly numb after Adric's demise. However, it doesn't take long for her to forget the "death in the family" when the Doctor takes her somewhere distracting. When the Master brainwashes everyone on prehistoric Earth into seeing Heathrow Airport, Nyssa is the first to notice that anything's wrong, briefly glimpsing the true nature of the world around her. Nyssa also "hears" the mind of the Xeraphin nucleus, and it's occasionally able to speak through her as if she were a medium. [Either some personal affinity with the nucleus - they are, after all, both survivors of destroyed worlds - or a sign of some telepathic ability in the people of Traken, though it's odd that the obviously telepathic Doctor doesn't hear anything. Although as with Nyssa fainting at the end of "Four to Doomsday," the Big Finish audio "Primeval" offers a more complicated explanation.]

By now, she knows enough TARDIS instruments by name to check the various malfunctions suggested by the Doctor. She's now less uptight than she has been, and even starts screaming.

• *Tegan*. Particularly insistent that the Doctor try to go back and save Adric, and here she's more agitated than grieving. But like Nyssa, she's strikingly quick to forget about the dead when the Doctor tells her they're going on holiday. Before now Tegan has only ever seen Concorde on the tarmac at Melbourne. [Possibly on her flight to England, as we've no evidence of her ever leaving Brisbane before. It's odd that she didn't arrive at Heathrow, nor see Concorde when having her interview or training.]

Here she finally gets to do some proper stewardessing, albeit in unusual circumstances. When the Doctor leaves her in her own place and time, it's immediately obvious that Tegan doesn't *want* to stay on Earth, and she's clearly disappointed that the TARDIS departs without her. Even so, you can tell she's tempted by the sight of aeroplanes at the airport.

Tegan knows enough history to know that Hyde Park, 1851, was the venue of the Great Exhibition [see also 18.7, "Logopolis" and 19.5, "Black Orchid" for more unexpected book-learning from the mouth on legs]. At some point either the Doctor or Adric must have told her what happens when one TARDIS materialises around another.

The Supporting Cast (Evil)

• *The Master*. It's stated that he escaped Castrovalva, though he never reveals how.

Now stranded on Earth during the Jurassic period, he's set himself up in the citadel of the Xeraphin - see **The Non-Humans** - and is disguised as Kalid, a fat *Arabian-Nights*-like magician with a bald head, greenish skin and an elaborate moustache. In fact the face of Kalid is a rubbery mask, though when the Master fakes Kalid's "death", weird ooze bubbles up out of his mouth.

Master-Kalid's control room within the citadel contains a glowing white sphere, which has properties that resemble magic, being able to spy on anything in the realm and acting as a focus for the Master's telepathic connection with the Xeraphin. The Doctor wrongly assumes it's done with psychotronics. [The Master definitely *isn't* dressing up as Kalid for the sake of the kidnapped humans from the twentieth century, and he's got no apparent reason for fooling the Doctor. Since the forces being tapped by the Master here verge on the mystical, and he uses incantations to invoke the Xeraphin's power, it's possible that he's adopted the Kalid persona as part of some kind of ritual process. Does posing as a sorcerer make it easier to wield the power? This may be the implication, but it's never stated.]

It is, of course, the Master who's responsible for the 'time contour' that carries two aeroplanes into the Jurassic from the twentieth century. The crew and passengers of these 'planes are used as slave labour, to penetrate the sanctum of the citadel and reach the Xeraphin nucleus, and all of them have been brainwashed by 'perceptual induction' to believe they're still in the present day. This illusion, another result of the Xeraphin's power, can only be broken if a lot of people try to see through it at the same time. The Master's still packing a rod-like device to shrink his opponents, here referred to by Nyssa as the tissue compression eliminator. Its victims are, surprisingly, as light as dolls [so the device must remove mass rather than just compressing it, despite its name].

According to the Doctor, the Master ends up being transported to the planet Xeraphas, which isn't likely to be very hospitable. [The Doctor feels no overwhelming need to go to Xeraphas himself and make sure the Master's stuck there. The exile on Xeraphas is mentioned in the Master's next appearance, 20.6, "The King's Demons".]

The TARDIS(es) The Doctor is aiming to take his companions to the Great Exhibition of 1851, but they get caught up in a time contour and end up at Heathrow Airport [exactly where they've been aiming for all season... contour or not, perhaps the TARDIS has a sense of comic timing]. When the Ship encounters turbulence from the contour, the Doctor suspects that it might be because somebody's fiddled with the dimensional stabilisers; because the relative drift compensator's malfunctioning; or because of feedback from the solar comparator. He thinks the TARDIS could be destroyed if it doesn't materialise immediately, and ducks under the console to trigger the co-ordinate override, a 'sort of anti-collision device' which takes the TARDIS out of Heathrow airspace and lands it nearby. Ever-smart Nyssa later suggests that 'cross-tracing on the space-time axis' could be responsible for the disappearance of Concorde during this period of turbulence.

When the Ship is on board Concorde, one instrument on the console makes a "woop" noise as it starts travelling through time. The Master can operate the Doctor's TARDIS without difficulty, but the co-ordinate override returns it to its starting-point after a few minutes. The Master then takes an element salvaged from his own TARDIS, and adds it to the Doctor's console, apparently to get around the override [he doesn't know how to switch it off?]. But it makes the console lose power, and the Ship can't dematerialise properly. He eventually just steals some of the circuitboards from under the console for his own vessel. The TARDIS is still capable of moving after this, even though the Master has taken the time-lapse compressor; he thought it was the temporal limiter, but one of the Concorde crew switched the parts, and the Doctor believes this exchange could have been catastrophic [if he'd tried moving through time]. The Master also takes a quantum accelerator, though the Doctor eventually gets all his parts back.

When the Ship's exterior is on its side, the interior space is on its side too, but one switch on the console can be used to "tilt" the interior so that it's the right way up. Various objects in the console room tip over when this happens. [Many, many breakable objects on board the TARDIS must have been lost in this season.] It doesn't take more than a dozen people to carry the Ship.

The Master's TARDIS is in bad shape, and stuck on Earth c. 140,000,000 BC. It's inoperative because its dynomorphic generator is exhausted, although the Master knows the Xeraphin nucleus can be used as a replacement and give him the power to... well... conquer the universe. Stranded on prehistoric Earth, the Master generated an 'exponential time corridor', which only drew in Concorde by mistake. The time contour was created by an induction loop, which basically involves hooking up his TARDIS to the Xeraphin sanctum with big red jump-leads. Stolen parts from the Doctor's TARDIS let him perfect the loop, dematerialising the Xeraphin nucleus from within the sanctum and installing it at the centre of his own TARDIS. He's also planning on using molecular disintegration to melt the Concorde passengers down into a neat little store of protoplasm [to "feed" the nucleus].

Once he's got the nucleus as a new energy source, the Master's TARDIS still has a limited range and can't leave prehistoric Earth without a temporal limiter. The Doctor would seem to have a spare one on board his own Ship, which he gives to the Master as part of a trade. When the vessel's operative, the Doctor points out that the Master's virtually 'running in' a new TARDIS, so he has to steer it along the time contour to 'check out the temporal dimensions'. This means the Master's heading for Heathrow, but the Doctor has programmed the temporal limiter with an inhibition factor to make sure that *he'll* get there first. [He can't just set the co-ordinates for "five minutes before the Master arrives". This suggests that the Doctor's timeline and the Master's are linked, so the same time that passes for one in the Jurassic must pass for the other in the vortex before they meet again. See also **Do Time Lords Always Meet in Sequence?** under 22.3, "The Mark of the Rani".]

Arriving at the end of the contour, the Master's TARDIS tries to land at the same co-ordinates as the Doctor's, and is sent spinning back into timespace as a result. The Doctor believes that he's sent the vessel back to Xeraphas [how?], and that the temporal limiter on the Master's TARDIS will need replacing with all that extra energy on board, stranding the Master there.

Though the Master's TARDIS is still defaulting to the form of an ionic column, here it disguises itself as a Concorde and can materialise around a real Concorde without difficulty.

The Non-Humans

• *Xeraphin.* According to the Doctor, the planet Xeraphas was devastated by the crossfire of the Vardon-Kosnax war, at least 140,000,000 years ago [Vardon is sort-of-mentioned again in 21.5, "Planet of Fire"]. The Xeraphin escaped the war and landed on Jurassic Earth, where they apparently built an impressive stone citadel somewhere in the region that's now Heathrow Airport. Still affected by radiation sickness, they elected to use their psychic power to amalgamate into a single bioplasmic entity, and wait for the contamination to pass before attempting to regenerate. But the Master arrived at the moment of regeneration, and killed the first few of the reborn Xeraphin. The Xeraphin neuronic nucleus lies in the sanctum at the heart of the citadel, a lump of living matter in its open sarcophagus, described by the Doctor as an immeasurable, all-seeing, all-knowing intelligence at the centre of a psychic vortex.

The Xeraphin [rather pompously] believe themselves to carry 'the wisdom of the universe'. Professor Hayter - one of the kidnapped Concorde passengers - agrees to be absorbed by the Xeraphin life-force in order to allow it to communicate with the Doctor, and two ghostly apparitions manifest themselves; humanoid, but silver-skinned and with jagged black marks on their heads and shoulders. Known as Anithon and Zarak, these represent the "good" and "evil" sides of the Xeraphin consciousness. The Master has been communicating with the "evil" side in order to gain its power, tempting it with dreams of conquest. Zarak calls on the power of other bad Xeraphin to fight Anithon, and the Doctor attempts to add his own mind-power to the "good" side. Later, a solid manifestation of the Professor briefly appears on the TARDIS to steer it to the Doctor [on behalf of the "good" Xeraphin].

Tapping the power of the Xeraphin in his guise as Kalid, the Master is able to create and control Plasmatons; make those who arrive in his realm perceive it as modern Heathrow; throw up force-barriers with a gesture; and create insubstantial-yet-talkative illusions within the citadel. Ultimately the nucleus is sent back to Xeraphas on the Master's TARDIS, apparently in the twentieth century, and the Doctor believes the Xeraphin will be able to regenerate there now as the radiation was millions of years ago [we can safely conclude that the Xeraphin couldn't time-travel].

• *Plasmatons.* Protein agglomerations, random particles assembled from the atmosphere by psy-chokinesis and bonded together by psychic energy. The Plasmatons can manifest themselves as a frothing grey "ectoplasm" that imprisons their targets, or as rather more stable-looking grey blobs with rock-like skins. In either form, they can appear out of nowhere and teleport away with anybody they surround, taking their victims into the Xeraphin citadel. Some are controlled by Kalid / the Master, but some are controlled by the "nice" side of the Xeraphin, and when they surround the Doctor he can hear the voice of the Xeraphin asking for help. He returns from the experience knowing exactly what the Plasmatons are and what they're called [if he didn't know already], though they evidently aren't intelligent in themselves.

When the Master draws on deeper reserves of power, the particles combine into something much worse than a Plasmaton, a floating two-headed serpent-monster that's said to be capable of doing real damage instead of just teleporting people around.

History

• *Dating.* The TARDIS arrives at Heathrow Airport in what seems to be the present day. [Possibly 1981, as that's when Tegan was "abducted" by the TARDIS and the Doctor acts as if this is where she belongs. This may not be true, though, and if not then it might explain her discomfort with Earth in the next story.] The Master's time contour drags two Concords back into the Jurassic, 140,000,000 BC.

Oddly, the Doctor believes that the aircraft pass through centuries of 'cosmic radiation' as they travel back in time. Nyssa briefly glimpses humanoid corpses on Jurassic Earth [probably of the Xeraphin who died of radiation sickness before the rest amalgamated into the nucleus]. The wreckage of the Xeraphin spaceship can still be found close to the citadel, and the Doctor believes it's been there for a long time even in the Jurassic. One of the Concordes is also left on pre-historic Earth.

Confronted by the authorities in modern-day England, the Doctor uses his UNIT credentials. He suggests calling Sir John Sudbury at department C19, a man who immediately orders the airport authorities to let him investigate the first missing Concorde. The Cold War is apparently still on in the present day, as Professor Hayter from the University of Darlington believes that Concorde's been hijacked by Russians and taken behind the Iron Curtain. ['70s stories like "Invasion of the Dinosaurs" (11.2) seem to be set in a world where the Cold War is over, but obviously things have worsened since then.]

The Analysis

Where Does This Come From? Five years on from the first passenger flights, Concorde still had the cachet of being transportation for the elite. It was then only just being allowed into US airspace, so it was something high-tech and British (well, Anglo-French, but BA played that down as much as possible). In what we'd now call "cross-promotion", British Airways and *Doctor Who* are dovetailed; two things the Yanks couldn't do and would never think to try, both suddenly very popular Stateside for their "Britishness".

And so, the series gets back to the airport. We've been here before, of course. In the '60s, when air travel still seemed glamorous, the Doctor thwarted a dastardly alien scheme at Gatwick (4.8, "The Faceless Ones"). In the '70s, when package holidays were becoming commonplace and disaster movies like *Airport* were already getting stale, space-monsters started eating the passengers in economy class (17.4, "Nightmare of Eden").

By the '80s, the vibe had changed again. There was a time when international travel seemed exotic, but by now the fact that you were travelling was a bigger status symbol than actually going anywhere interesting. It was about being "cosmopolitan", not "well-travelled".

Nobody had heard the word "yuppie" in 1982, but you get the idea. The airport was a common setting for TV drama in this period, just because it was such a good symbol for energetic middle-class success.

Doctor Who's response to this? A story in which a bunch of camp stewards slouch around on prehistoric Earth and the Doctor reads a newspaper in Terminal One. So much for the upwardly-mobile. What's most ironic is that in this attempt to look sleek and modern, the series actually ends up taking the SF-and-aeroplanes genre back to its TV roots. Nobody well-read ("well-viewed"?) in television can watch this story of passenger flights and time contours without thinking of the 1961 *Twilight Zone* episode "The Odyssey of Flight 33", in which an aircraft finds itself inexplicably drawn backwards in time and buzzes a brontosaur. As

the BBC started a highly-publicised repeat run of *The Twilight Zone* in the early '80s, the similarities were fairly obvious before long. And as in "The Leisure Hive" (18.1), radiation sickness is obviously in vogue again. Well, it was the '80s. We all knew what the four-minute warning siren sounded like.

The big influence, though, is the one we'll see again in "Mawdryn Undead" (20.3): the operas of Wagner, and in particular *Parsifal*. Peter Grimwade was irked that the "epic" quests in his scripts, which were symbolically the journeys "within" to confront inner demons (in this case Nyssa and Tegan confronting hallucinations to penetrate the core of the citadel), were reduced to bad effects and a quick wander through a studio. As an enthusiast for the "mythic" aspects of Wagner's work, Grimwade obviously found appealing the concept of the "pure" hero taking the advice of an older man who sacrifices himself so that the hero can return the "grail" to the world. As we've seen in "Kinda" (19.3) and will see again in "Snakedance" (20.2), in this period the production team members often had to deal with people spouting Jung at them. This is going to get ridiculous eventually (see Season Twenty-Three, "The Trial of a Time Lord").

And collectors of "urban myths" will be delighted to hear - once again - the old chestnut about the girl who's saved by a truck driver, but who then tells the other drivers at the truck stop about it and is told 'that musta bin Ol' Pete, but he died in a horrible crash, ten years ago this very night…'. Here, Ol' Pete is Professor Hayter and the truck is the TARDIS.

Things That Don't Make Sense Getting the dating wrong yet again (see 19.2, "Four to Doomsday"), the Doctor seems to believe that the late Jurassic isn't far off the Pleistocene era. In the first place, it's supposed to be the Pleistocene *epoch*. In the second place, the Pleistocene only began 2,000,000 years ago, so the nip in the air he feels certainly *isn't* an impending ice age. [This Doctor's still very confused, or just likes bluffing.] Stock footage of Concorde means that there's a very anachronistic bird flapping its way across the flight-path of prehistoric Earth [fan-lore says 'err… maybe it's a pterodactyl', but isn't fooling anybody], and that the sky wobbles while the ground stays perfectly still.

Even if the Master has a good but unspecified

reason for dressing up as Ali Bongo[9], neither Flight Engineer Scobie nor Hayter seems to notice that the man they've just seen die in a gush of snot has got up, stripped off and is pointing a gun at them while going 'heh-heh-heh'. Weirdly, the Master - a Time Lord, i.e. one of the most powerful and knowledgeable beings in creation - expects to gain the 'wisdom of the universe' from the nucleus of a species which couldn't even escape somebody else's nuclear war and ended up crash-landing on a backwater planet like Earth. The implication seems to be that since the Xeraphin nucleus is an ancient artefact, it must have some sort of all-knowing mystical power. Which raises the question of why the Xeraphin, with all their apparent abilities of telekinesis and mind-warping, let their planet get nuked to begin with. Did they not see Vardon or Kosnax coming?

Arriving at an illusory Heathrow Airport, the Doctor quotes poetry about the nature of perceived reality before he has any inkling that they're seeing a hallucination [instinct?]. Making a point about mass delusion, he also describes the Indian rope trick as 'real', which it probably wasn't. [Research indicates that it's never actually been performed… at least not in *our* world. Our old chum John Nevil Maskelyne (see 16.1, "The Ribos Operation") offered £2,000 - allowing for inflation, millions now - for anyone who could do it in the open air.]

In episode three, the airline staff have such a good time hiding on board the TARDIS while the Master's hijacking it that they never think about bringing the story to hasty conclusion by jumping out while his back's turned and piling on top of him [but then, pilots used to be trained to co-operate with hijackers…]. If the Master's been struggling to break into the Xeraphin sanctum, then why are the shrunken corpses of his victims already lying around the place? [He must have got in before the Xeraphin realised he was a menace, and been shut out afterwards, but once again you have to question the 'all-knowing' nature of the Xeraphin nucleus.]

The Master's plan seems to be based on slave labour. If he summoned Concorde deliberately, then why didn't he pick a planeload of healthy, young, able-bodied specimens (and thus get everyone suspecting Chameleon Tours)? If he snared Concorde by accident, then what was he originally planning to do without any slaves to assist in the demolition work? [He's just hoping for the best.] However Nyssa and Tegan get into

the Xeraphin chamber while Nyssa's "under the influence", they must have come past a load of hypnotised VIPs and flight-crew, but there's no sign of this. Nor is there any indication as to how such people, with no training in bricklaying, manage to quickly and silently seal the Doctor in so thoroughly at the end of episode three.

In order to get on or off the plane, the passengers should need a ladder of some description. Even if they use a ladder for all subsequent entries and exits, they still walk down a non-existent stair-truck on arrival at the fake Heathrow. Do they actually climb down a camouflaged brontosaur, like in *The Flintstones*? The "prop" aircraft tyres are much too small to come from Concorde, too. When the Doctor deduces that the spaceship has been on prehistoric Earth for a long time, his evidence is apparently the eight-track cartridge he picks up. Nyssa says 'I'm getting cold' as if this proves they're not at modern-day Heathrow, even though Heathrow was covered in snow when they left. Why, given Tegan's distaste for all things scientific, does the prospect of seeing 'all the wonders of Victorian technology' make her suddenly perk up?

Not actually a flaw as such, but mention of Tegan rouses First Officer Bilton from hypnosis. The idea that he fancies her is somewhat weakened both by Michael Cashman's performance in itself, and - with hindsight - by his campaigning on gay rights issues after playing the first "out" gay character in *EastEnders*. And why did BBC Video go to such lengths to avoid the back-cover blurb giving away the Master's involvement in the story, when the only people buying it must surely have known? They plastered Cybermen all over "Earthshock"…

Critique (Prosecution) Nobody has a good word for this story, it seems. The director didn't understand the script. The writer hated the way it looked. The cast ridiculed it, the production team was disappointed and the viewing public switched off despite the publicity blitz and inherited "buzz" from "Earthshock".

In theory, though, it should all have worked. Grimwade, unlike Saward or Bidmead or those writers whose scripts they'd amended to a pulp, can make characters speak the way those characters would speak under the circumstances. No two people have exactly the same patterns or vocabulary. He took his time learning the jargon of Concorde flight. In the cut scenes we can see that he's thinking about why Concorde (of all air-craft) would make a diplomatic incident inevitable, and justifies the controller's acquiescence with UNIT. The Xeraphin citadel ought to have been forbidding and alien, and their plight - explained in the script as a schism between "ego" and "id" - ought to have been as big a crisis for the TARDIS crew on a personal level as on a "how will we escape?" one. Adric is known to be dead, but this time the girls have to "kill" him themselves (a scenario recycled in "The Five Doctors", but in this context more reminiscent of the cliffhanger to "Frontier in Space" episode five, with its run-through of recent monsters).

The set-up is clearly explained by Captain Stapley in episode two: there are two opposing Xeraphin forces, one aiding the good guys and one aiding Kalid. If a character understands this, then why not the director? Well, in his defence, Ron Jones was a last-minute replacement and his biggest worry was avoiding prehistory looking like a bunch of people standing around arguing on a small set with a painted cyclorama of "marsh-land". He said that it ought to have been done on film, but that he was overruled on budget and time considerations. And there we have it; the producer who got the job on the grounds that he knew how to avoid these worries arising has fall-en victim to them himself. He blew the budget on pretty androids. This was the season when the new deal with BBC Enterprises to get £2,000 an episode had fallen through, then been sort-of-arranged anyway. This was the year when every-thing was shot out of sequence, to hell with character development or motivation, to avoid all the cheap shows coming at the end of the season.

One aspect of the storytelling not commented upon recently, but obvious at the time: cliffhanger reprises. We've seen how, this year, the scripts have been amended so that anyone away on one of the two days it's broadcast can pick up the thread (to the point where amazingly arch info-dump dialogue is laid on with a trowel). This story makes no such concessions. It's written as though for Season Eighteen, with the episodes starting as if we all need a quick reminder, not a synopsis. On video, seen in one go, this is a relief. This also affects the story positively, as the Nyssa written by Grimwade is the one that Johnny Byrne and Christopher Bidmead created, not the one who's been reading glossy mags and doing the Charleston.

The final sign that this is a series on borrowed time is the cliffhanger into the next season. Did anyone really want to see Tegan back? Did anyone really think that giving her the ending the character had been after for over a year in screen-time wasn't right and proper? After inheriting the timeslot from *Triangle*, and making a story that resembles it in so many ways (well, not in plot terms exactly, but the location-work and the boardroom scenes are point-for-point the same… just without Kate O'Mara making eyes at the old men, and one of *these* is in the cast!), we finally admit that *Doctor Who* is a soap.

Critique (Defence) Yes indeed, it certainly gets a rough ride. Considered an embarrassment by those who usually smile on the early Nathan-Turner era, grumbled-about even in 1982 and cited by Peter Davison himself as one of the reasons he came to think of *Doctor Who* as 'crap', tradition holds that "Time-Flight" is a tawdry-look-ing piece of end-of-season filler and little else. What needs to be underlined, though, is that the bits everyone hates are the bits that got bolted onto the storyline in spite of Grimwade's original intentions.

The typical response at the time was to take note of the modern-day starting-point, and the Doctor's brief mention of the Brigadier, and con-clude that this was an out-of-date UNIT-style "contemporary" story; but this is nothing like a Pertwee action-piece, and the twentieth-century sequences are pure gloss coating. It's been heavily criticised for its supporting cast, because it's hard to take something seriously if it features a bunch of bewildered air stewards camping around on prehistoric Earth (although to be fair, the script is aware of how bizarre it all is and plays on that a lot of the time, especially during the debriefing back at Heathrow); but all the nonsense about Concorde is just a gimmick, not the focus of the story at all. It's derided for its sloppy use of the Master; but the Master was, again, never meant to be at the heart of things.

Strip away all the superfluous extras, and what's left… has interest value, or potential at the very least. This is supposed to be a sci-fi *Arabian Nights* tale, a quasi-mystical bedtime story about a scary eastern sorcerer who calls on the powers of a schizophrenic "demon" in order to gain pseudo-magical powers. Except that the demon is really a psychic alien intelligence, which means that this is squarely in the tradition of "The Daemons" and "Pyramids of Mars", but this time Persian-style. It could have been, and should have been, *Doctor Who* at its most legendary. It could have done for the "ancient powers" strand of the series what "Earthshock" did for the Cybermen.

As with "The Leisure Hive", Nathan-Turner's production style ("here are the things I want to see, now get them all into the story") gets in the way, but even so there are glimpses of genuine High Fantasy here. Kalid *does* look like he's going to be a villain worth watching, at least until the mask comes off. Contrary to the claims of many, there's plenty that makes an impact in terms of both design and direction. Prehistory is barren in the *right* way, while the citadel looks like an ancient monument in a way that the City of the Exxilons just didn't. The reputation for poor visuals mostly comes from a handful of shaky CSO moments and last-minute video effects (the washing-up-liquid-on-the-lens manifestation of the Plasmatons springs to mind), but these are brief glitches, and for the most part there's actually a half-decent sense of atmosphere-building going on here.

What's worth mentioning is that given the job of integrating Concorde and a tedious old arch-villain into the plot, Grimwade takes the more serial-like flavour of this season to heart and at least *tries* to do something with it, turning each episode into a distinct "act". The first part is *Doctor Who* in investigation mode. The second is a more-than-competent piece of adventure fiction, complete with necromantic powers, strange subterranean spaces and a token disbelieving Professor. The third, the part that should have been the guts of the plot, is the story of the Xeraphin. And the fourth is a simple face-off between Doctor and Master. Taken individually, each episode works, but once again it's hard to see what it's all aiming at unless you can see through the muddle of BA uniforms and standard-issue villainy.

Still, it's hard to justify treating the story like a leper for its quaint, no-nonsense good-versus-evil approach when nobody seems to have much of a problem with "Terror of the Zygons". And despite his reservations - not to mention Anthony Ainley's best efforts (see **The Lore**) - by this point Peter Davison sounds as if he believes every word he has to say.

The Facts

Written by Peter Grimwade. Directed by Ron Jones. Viewing figures: 10.0 million, 8.5 million, 8.9 million, 8.1 million. Obviously the nation had better things to do on Tuesdays.

Supporting Cast Anthony Ainley (The Master), Richard Easton (Captain Stapley), Nigel Stock (Professor Hayter), Keith Drinkel (Flight Engineer Scobie), Michael Cashman (First Officer Bilton), John Flint (Captain Urquhart), Judith Byfield (Angela Clifford), Hugh Hayes (Anithon), André Winterton (Zarak), Matthew Waterhouse (Adric).

Oh, Isn't That..?

• *Michael Cashman.* Not famous at this point, but he'll become a familiar face; first in *EastEnders*, then as a spokesman on gay rights, then as a full-time politician and Member of the European Parliament.

• *Nigel Stock.* Another of John Nathan-Turner's contacts from *Flesh and Blood*, he'd been Dr. Watson to Peter Cushing's Sherlock Holmes in the '60s BBC version. He'd also been in a medical soap, *The Practice*, and gone "solo" with the spin-off series *Owen MD*. More recently he'd been the foil of Kate O'Mara in the dreaded *Triangle*.

Working Titles "Zanadin" (nothing got changed faster), "Xeraphin".

Cliffhangers On prehistoric Earth, a couple of Plasmatons materialise on either side of the Doctor and envelop him in their grey ooze; in his sanctum, the supposedly dying Kalid gets to his feet and rips off his mask, to reveal… well, you know; sealed inside the Xeraphin sanctum, the Doctor tells his companions that the Master has finally won.

The Lore

• The first version of this story was submitted for Season Eighteen, before Peter Grimwade was asked to direct "Full Circle". It had been moved further and further back as events surrounding the regeneration and the collapse of planned scripts "Sealed Orders" and "Project 4G" (relax, this is the last time we'll be mentioning it) grew more complex. Once it had been decided that this was to be the season-closer - after yet another effort at resuscitating the Flanagan / McCulloch turkey, in some accounts - Grimwade was asked to include the Master in order to complete the three-story contract Ainley had signed. The notion of using the Xeraphin as a 'dynomorphic generator' to power the Master's TARDIS seems to have been a continuity reference to the contentious Christopher Priest script "The Enemy Within" (still planned as the previous story, and conceived to kill Adric off even more finally than "Earthshock" had). During the delays Grimwade undertook to learn, on simulators, how a Concorde would be flown and what the technical crew might really say.

• The design for the Plasmatons was intended to look less human than any previous "mobile" alien, without just being a lumbering lump (like, say, the Ogri from "The Stones of Blood"). To this end legs were included, but not arms. And nor was there any way for the actors to see, so in the studio they were just lumbering lumps (like, say, the gel-guards from "The Three Doctors"). Richard Gregory's Unit 22 team was again responsible, and Gregory himself operated the rather more effective two-headed snake manifestation, which the producer let him keep in gratitude for the "Earthshock" Cybermen.

• Director Ron Jones, who'd coped with the problems of "Black Orchid" well enough to be entrusted with such a complex production, was actually the second choice. Andrew Morgan had been approached, but instead took on a more orthodox production called *Squadron* (see if you can guess what that was about). Morgan would eventually direct two Sylvester McCoy stories, both at the very least flamboyantly-made: "Time and the Rani" (24.1) and "Remembrance of the Daleks" (25.1).

Shooting on the story was conducted as Season Nineteen reached the screens, and post-production - including Roger Limb's score - was finished less than a week before broadcast. The final block of studio recording was attended by staff from Marvel's *Doctor Who Monthly*, one of whom claims credit for the Master's re-use of Delgado's catchphrase 'I am the Master, and you will obey me' in episode three. The final day's recording was taken up with the Kalid scenes. Ainley attempted to make Davison "corpse", and very nearly succeeded; there's one shot, after the girls have penetrated the sanctum, where the star's visibly having trouble keeping a straight face. Mrs. Who, Sandra Dickinson, had started attending filming and

aggravated many of the crew by knitting loudly in the gallery. A U-Matic copy of this recording block exists and is widely-circulated in certain circles, but unlike the ones for "The Claws of Axos" (8.3) or 'Mindwarp' (23.2) it's not terribly illuminating.

• The extras have some odd listings. Even though none of the passengers speaks, they've been given titles like "Photographer's Girlfriend", "Americans" and "Businessman Passengers". One of these is Val McCrimmon, the long-time production assistant, and others include regular walk-ons Leslie Weekes and Barney Lawrence. Some of the male passengers double as Plasmatons. Graham Cole was the one inside the Melkur suit, as in "The Keeper of Traken" (18.6), when the Melkur's here "brought forth" as an illusion. About now he starts thinking about getting a proper job, and will leave for Sun Hill Police Station soon.

• The British Airways jingle "We'll Take More Care of You" cropped up in the fourth episode, although it was carefully removed from the video release. It had been played in the studio as a gag when the scenes involving the Concorde wheel had finally been completed. The deal with Concorde was that British Airways got as much free publicity as possible, as long as the BBC got to use the real thing and not a mock-up. After all the script-checking (and removal of character names because of their similarity to BA staff), they were granted one take-off and landing.

• The limerick recited by the Doctor in episode one, on arrival at prehistoric Heathrow, is an anonymous rejoinder to one by Monsignor Ronald Knox (who, as the originator of the Sherlock Holmes society, qualifies as the very first fanboy and is basically the reason books like this exist... sir, we salute you!). He was commenting on the philosophical ideas of Bishop Berkeley (1685-1753), that we're all ideas in the Mind of God and nothing exists outside our sensory delusions; see **What is the Blinovich Limitation Effect?** under 20.3, "Mawdryn Undead", for more of this sort of malarkey. A variation on this idea of celestial virtual reality would be the basis for one of the rejected stories from Season Twenty-One, Steve Gallagher's "Nightmare Country" (see 20.5, "Terminus").

• The novelisation of "Time-Flight" included the following deathless prose: "The Plasmaton accumulation entered his chamber. '*Eevanaragh!*' he cried." (Page 65, if you don't believe us.)

20.1: "Arc of Infinity"

(Serial 6E, Four Episodes, 3rd January - 11th January 1983.)

Which One is This?   The Doctor chases himself around Amsterdam, Nyssa pulls a gun on the High Council of Time Lords and Tegan's menaced by the anti-matter poultry-monster.

Firsts and Lasts   Second and last appearance of Omega, supposed First of the Time Lords and lynchpin of much future fan-fiction (including the kind that actually got onto the screen in Seasons Twenty-Five and Twenty-Six). This marks the start of Season Twenty's running theme, the return of any number of old villains, monsters and supporting characters to "celebrate" the series' twentieth year on television.

Here we also see the start of a new John Nathan-Turner tradition: the annual Staff Holiday. For the next three years he'll try to make sure that one *Doctor Who* story every season involves filming overseas, although this practice ends after the BBC starts to slash the budget (see also 21.5, "Planet of Fire" and 22.4, "The Two Doctors"). Tegan gets a new outfit for the year here, but Nyssa's still in her Traken clothes and won't be getting the makeover until the next story.

But perhaps the most striking first, at least with hindsight… "Arc of Infinity" sees the first appearance in the programme of Colin Baker, more than a year before his debut in the leading role. It's the only occasion when a Doctor-to-be appears in the series playing a different character, in this case Commander Maxil, who's even less genial than the Sixth Doctor turns out to be.

Four Things to Notice About "Arc of Infinity"...

1. So Omega's back, but this time he's got help, because - well, who would have thought it? - it turns out there's a traitor among the Time Lords. At the risk of spoiling things for newcomers, this month's serpent in the bosom of the High Council is Hedin, but that isn't giving much away as he's the world's most obvious villain. Though the "mysterious" plotter keeps to the shadows while he's talking to Omega, it's nonetheless clear from the start that the traitor is on the High Council, which means there are only five sus-

- Peter Davison (the Doctor)
- Janet Fielding (Tegan)
- Sarah Sutton (Nyssa, 20.1 to 20.4)
- Mark Strickson (Turlough, 20.3 to 20.7)

- John Nathan-Turner (Producer)
- Eric Saward (Script Editor)

pects. One of whom is female, and three of whom don't have the Michael-Gough-like voice which belongs to the character played by Michael Gough. Just to make it *really* clear who's the baddie, Hedin is the only Council member who's sympathetic to the Doctor and comes across as "nice", which is as big a giveaway as you'll ever see. Omega's surprise return at the end of episode three isn't very subtle either, as before this point the series' fans will have been wracking their brains to work out which returning villain might possibly have a grudge against the Time Lords and come from an anti-matter universe.

2. In fact, the first time round a much bigger surprise is / was Tegan's return, who turns up in episode two despite the Doctor ditching her in the previous story. Actually the whole plot hangs on the idea that while Omega's making plans to hijack the Doctor's body, one of the three humans who *purely by chance* wander into his Amsterdam lair turns out to be the woman who left the TARDIS crew just a few months previously. The assumption here is that the Doctor's companions are like Jessica Fletcher in *Murder She Wrote*. Wherever they go in the world, they'll not only find trouble but exactly the right *kind* of trouble.

3. Ah, Amsterdam. The reason for a story set in Holland, of course, is that… well, the production-team wants to get out more. "City of Death" (17.2) could at least justify its Paris footage with a plot involving the Mona Lisa, but here the Dutch location filming doesn't really serve any purpose other than allowing the programme to show you its holiday videos. Nonetheless, during episode four's "chase" sequence Peter Davison does his best to make running through Amsterdam look urgent, playing both the Doctor and Omega's carbon-copy Doctor-body. He gets bonus points for those quiet and rather affecting moments when Omega,

given corporeal form at last, takes in the sights around him and makes you realise that he'd much rather mellow out here than blow up the universe.

4. Omega's always had a problem with his hench-creatures. Following on from the gel-monsters in "The Three Doctors", his servant here is the Ergon, and your heart really has to go out to the costume designers. A skeletal, bio-mechanical construction in the *Alien* mould, the Ergon on paper must have looked sleek, stylish and reasonably terrifying. But there's no way *anyone* can walk around in the costume without its head wobbling from side to side and its feet looking like big rubber slippers, and nobody has yet been able to describe it without using the words "enormous chicken".

The Continuity

The Doctor   Doesn't look at all pleased when faced with the current President of Gallifrey, his old tutor and sometimes-friend Borusa. But he *does* recognise the old Time Lord on sight, despite the President's regeneration. [Either the Doctor can instantly "see through" the change, or he's just heard on the grapevine that Borusa is now the President. The latter seems most likely, judging by his comments on the President in 16.1, "The Ribos Operation".] The Doctor still remembers the Presidential code that can open doors on Gallifrey [despite the fact that his memory of events in "The Invasion of Time" (15.6) was supposedly wiped at the end of that story... what else might he remember that he's not supposed to?]. He positively grimaces when Tegan announces that she's rejoining the TARDIS crew, though he might just mean it in a "friendly" way.

[It's not clear how much time has passed for the Doctor and Nyssa since the end of Season Nineteen. The implication is that it hasn't been long, as the repairs to the TARDIS make it sound as if they've said to themselves "well, now Tegan's gone, let's do some maintenance". But as the Doctor's age jumps from 700-odd to 900-odd between "The Leisure Hive" (18.1) and "Revelation of the Daleks" (23.6), and as most of the stories in that period lead directly on from each other, it's been suggested that the Doctor and Nyssa spend *ages* travelling together in this period and that Nyssa's lifespan might be much longer than a human's. This is a huge leap to make, although Nyssa's statement that the Ship never

seems to land in the right place *since* the damage done by the Cybermen might indicate a few unseen landings after 19.6, "Earthshock". See also **The Obvious Question: How Old is He?** under 16.5, "The Power of Kroll".]

• *Ethics*. Condemned to death by the Time Lords, on the grounds that it's the only way to stop Omega, the Doctor is apparently willing to submit to the High Council's judgement and go to the vaporisation chamber. However, he already suspects that he's going to be saved, even telling Nyssa 'I know what I'm doing'. He's still keen on keeping Omega alive, if he can.

• *Inventory*. Still carrying string, a cricket ball and very little else.

• *Background*. On Gallifrey he knows both Councillor Hedin and the technician Damon, and recognises High Council member Thalia on sight. [He's more willing to fraternise with mere technicians than most Time Lords would be, and it's unlikely that he and Damon knew each other before he first left Gallifrey. The Doctor speaks of the events of "The Invasion of Time", perhaps implying that he met Damon at around that time, though it's hard to imagine how and we certainly never saw it on-screen. He also expects Damon to know Leela. It's not the deliberate implication of the script, but this would all make sense if there were an unseen trip to Gallifrey before Leela's wedding. This would explain how he knows so many High Council members, and doesn't act surprised that they're now *on* the Council when they weren't in "The Invasion of Time".]

The Supporting Cast

• *Nyssa*. Busy little thing that she is, she's more determined to finish repairs on the TARDIS than the Doctor. She doesn't know what a Q-star is, so even she needs to have the technobabble explained to her sometimes. She says she's missed Tegan [so at least a few *days* must have passed since the end of "Time-Flight", if not whole years]. Nyssa's prepared to break several rules, including those of basic hospitality, to pull a gun on her hosts in order to save the Doctor.

• *Tegan*. She's recently been sacked from her job as an airline stewardess and has got herself a decent haircut. When she inadvertently stumbles back into the Doctor's life, she's not only willing to re-join the TARDIS crew but positively insists on it. [She treats it as if it's all a bit of a laugh, although over the next couple of years she's not

Why Are There So Many Doubles in the Universe?

Given this is a universe rife with shape-changing species, where androids seem to be as easy to put together as Ikea tables and where most self-respecting cultures consider holographic technology primitive, you would have thought that there were more than enough "legitimate" reasons for the Doctor to keep running into people who look exactly like him and his close acquaintances.

And yet, the continuum seems to be lightly peppered with lookalikes who have no known connection to the original article. It begins with "The Massacre" (3.5), in which it turns out that the Doctor looks exactly like the Abbot of Amboise c. 1572. And just one regeneration later there's an identical twin for his *new* self, namely Salamander in "The Enemy of the World" (5.4). Just to prove that the Doctor doesn't have a monopoly on this sort of thing, it later transpires that Romana has a carbon-copy as well, the Princess Strella in "The Androids of Tara" (16.4).

What's going on here? It seems inconceivable that it's all just a big coincidence. It's *possible* that in a universe stocked with a googolplex of humanoid cultures, everyone might turn out to have a doppelganger somewhere if they want to go looking for it, but even given the Doctor's wandering lifestyle it's hard to credit that he's just stumbling across his own counterparts by accident. And two of them are found on the same planet anyway, i.e. Earth. Probability is already taking quite a beating. Not only that, but all three of the individuals named above are figures of influence and importance, at least on the local scale.

The most obvious point to make here is that the Doctor and Romana are both Time Lords. Time Lords are, of course, figures of influence and importance themselves. This leads us to two obvious possibilities:

1. People around the universe are somehow modelling themselves on Time Lords. This is by no means as strange as it may sound. Indeed, you could argue that it's the logical conclusion of a trend we've already mentioned. As we saw in **How Does Evolution Work?** (under 18.3, "Full Circle"), it's quite feasible that humanoid species are so common in this continuum because the Time Lords "imprinted" themselves on the biology of the universe when everything was still in a formative state. Did they imprint themselves so hard that even apart from the general two arms / two legs / one head arrangement, other species ended up more likely to acquire specific Time Lord *faces*? For that matter, if Sheldrake's scientifically-dubi-

ous but aesthetically-useful "morphic fields" theory is true then even newly-created Time Lords could be creatures of such significance that they immediately alter the morphic templates of the cosmos, and cause other people across space and time to be born with their features. In which case every incarnation of the Doctor might have six-million "twins" around the universe *somewhere*, and running into one isn't really a big deal at all (although it might be construed as odd that, for example, the Seventh Doctor never runs into anybody who looks exactly like Jon Pertwee).

2. The clear alternative. People aren't modelling themselves on Time Lords; Time Lords are modelling themselves on people.

In many ways, this seems more likely. We know that each Time Lord can supposedly regenerate twelve times, so each has a grand total of thirteen faces and thirteen bodies to get through. Leaving aside the oddity of Romana's regeneration in "Destiny of the Daleks" (17.1)… nothing we see leads us to believe that the Doctor picks up "blueprints" for his extra bodies anywhere, and Time Lords don't *generally* browse through catalogues to pre-order their next incarnation. So, where do their back-up faces come from? The obvious answer would seem to be that their bodies somehow contain thirteen sets of DNA - and almost certainly other, non-genetic, material besides - but that only one set of genes is "active" at any given time. All well and good, but where do Time Lords get all these spare DNA patterns? Are they based on random mutations, woven into a Gallifreyan's body at birth (or at "looming", if you're a New Adventures reader)? It's hard to imagine that the powers-that-be on Gallifrey, as staid and over-cautious as they are, would risk such randomness. Nor do the Time Lords have a great deal of imagination, and it's just as hard to imagine "baby artists" in the Gallifreyan Maternity Service (see 17.3, "The Creature from the Pit") hand-crafting thirteen distinct DNA combinations for every child.

Now, we've said that Time Lords don't generally browse through catalogues before they regenerate. But such a catalogue of new faces does exist; we see it in "The War Games" (6.7), when the Doctor is given his choice of bodies before being exiled to Earth. In this case we might assume that the shape of the Third Doctor, which is eventually chosen *for* him, overrides the "natural" third body he might otherwise have taken on. (Although *why*

continued on page 175...

ABOUT TIME 1980–1984

going to see the funny side quite so much. Given what happens in the next story, it's not impossible that the Mara plays some part in getting her to go back on board the TARDIS.]

Tegan's cousin, Colin Frazer, is a young Australian who just happens across Omega's TARDIS while hitch-hiking in Amsterdam. He comes from Brisbane [note Tegan's description of the city in 19.1, "Castrovalva"]. Tegan was planning on meeting up with him in the hope that it'd cheer her up, now she's unemployed and miserable [and, clearly, bored].

Tegan's visiting Amsterdam, with its reputation, confirms the impression that she isn't *quite* as straight-laced as previous companions [see "Time-Flight" and 19.5, "Black Orchid"].

The TARDIS(es) The Doctor doesn't have any problems steering it at the moment, although Nyssa believes that the navigation system needs some repairs and there's been trouble ever since a Cyberman blaster inflicted some damage on it. [The Cyber-Leader did indeed hit the console in "Earthshock", but the navigation actually seems to improve from this point on, so maybe the blast knocked the circuits back into line instead of damaging them. Much like a big thump.] The TARDIS databank is consulted again, and yields information on the area of space known as Rondel. The typeface has changed since the last time it was seen ["Castrovalva"]. Nyssa brings up the subject of temporal grace, and reminds the Doctor that guns shouldn't work in the TARDIS, to which the Doctor only says 'nobody's perfect'. [This suggests that the events of "Earthshock" are at least *reasonably* recent, as Nyssa's obviously never brought the subject up before.]

The TARDIS has a recall circuit, used by the Time Lords to drag it back to Gallifrey. A crystal on the console starts to chime when this happens, and the Doctor immediately understands its significance. On Gallifrey, the TARDIS' main space-time element is removed from under the console, rendering the Ship incapable of going anywhere. This element is a palm-sized little piece of technology, and obviously the recall circuit is built into it, as when the element's replaced the Doctor asks for one without such a circuit. [In 24.1, "The Mysterious Planet", the method used to drag the TARDIS back to the Time Lords looks a lot more elaborate. The Time Lords never used the recall circuit to bring the Doctor home before "The War Games" (6.7), so it may have been added to the Ship - or a new space-time element may have been installed - at the time of the Doctor's exile on Earth.] When assembling a new element, Damon first has to check his files for the coding of a type-forty time rotor. The console room's dimmer when the element's removed. Once this is replaced with a new one, the Ship proves far easier to handle.

Nyssa's room on the Ship is said to be the closest to the console room [as in 19.4, "The Visitation"], but there are a lot more odds and ends in it than before. So she hasn't learned the lesson of not keeping fragile ornaments on shelves. The Doctor performs a 'simple' repair job with the help of Nyssa and a screwdriver, fiddling around with the technology behind a roundel in one of the TARDIS corridors so that the Ship has audio link-up on the scanner 'again'. [When did it stop working? We weren't informed.]

The Doctor tells Nyssa to fetch the indent-kit from his workbench in the TARDIS, which he believes might be able to open the security locks on Gallifrey. It's revealed to be a tiny set of tools [possibly the ones he uses in 18.5, "Warriors' Gate"]. Using the TARDIS toolkit [seen in "Earthshock"], the Doctor is able to rig up a small piece of circuitry to short-circuit Omega's fusion booster, while Nyssa calibrates a hand-held meter to detect changes in anti-matter.

The TARDIS used by Omega has some rooms that glow in eerie green, but is otherwise unremarkable. The noise it makes when it materialises is similar to the wheezing noise of the Doctor's Ship, only with extra "vworp"ing. The vessel has a working chameleon circuit. After Hedin sends him the Doctor's biodata extract, Omega somehow takes control of the Doctor's TARDIS from within his own vessel and steers it [through real-space, not the vortex] towards the Arc of Infinity. The Doctor can't override the controls, and space-time is distorted once the Ship reaches its destination, where a ball of 'extra-dimensional' light is seen approaching on the scanner before coming through the wall of the console room. The glowing image of Omega then manifests and attempts to bond with the Doctor's body, and the TARDIS sensors register that the intruder was made of anti-matter.

The Time Lords Here the High Council is made up of five members, each in a different colour of robe. Borusa, as Lord President, wears white;

Why Are There So Many Doubles in the Universe?

...continued from page 173

the Time Lords give him a choice on this occasion is another question. Is a regenerating Time Lord always given the catalogue on Gallifrey, and is the Doctor the only one who lets his haphazard "natural" forms rule his life?) The important point here is that we know there must be a "body-bank" on Gallifrey, a definite, finite pool of - to use a Zygon phrase - body-prints, from which a selection can be made. From this we might conclude that Romana's regeneration in "Destiny of the Daleks" involved an attempt to put together a catalogue of her own, hence the rather erratic natures of some of her test-bodies. See also **How Does Regeneration Work?** under 18.7, "Logopolis".

This brings us to Commander Maxil in "Arc of Infinity", who's got the same face as the Sixth Doctor. Here we might have reason to be cautious, because the programme never explicitly states that the two are *supposed* to look the same, and it could just be what we'd call a "dramatic convention" (which is to say, nobody's suggesting that Professor Whitaker in "Invasion of the Dinosaurs" and Nyder in "Genesis of the Daleks" are genetically linked just because they both happen to look like Peter Miles). But it's not unreasonable to suppose that both Maxil and the Sixth Doctor have been built to the same body-print. Being Commander of the Guard, Maxil might well be a lower-caste Gallifreyan rather than an actual Time Lord, though it's safe to suppose that there's *no* natural childbirth on Gallifrey and that even the working classes use the same designs. So even unregenerated Time Lords wear bodies straight from the bank.

Where, then, did the bodies in this bank come from? Even a culture as drab as that of the Time Lords must have realised that if they just kept reusing old Time Lord patterns, then their society would end up going down a bit of a biological cul-de-sac. In fact, off-screen some of the novels have hinted that Rassilon and company deliberately introduced the idea of shape-changing between regenerations (rather than just renewing the old body, as the Minyans do in 15.5, "Underworld") in an attempt to introduce some diversity to the race. So it's feasible, even likely, that many of the body-bank patterns might come from other worlds. Earth would presumably be a prime source, since it seems so terribly important in the history of the universe for some reason.

The meaning of all this is becoming clear. The First Doctor's body really *was* based on that of sixteenth-century arch-plotter the Abbot of Amboise. The Second Doctor's really *was* based on that of twenty-first-century global dictator Salamander.

You can tell the Time Lords are drawn to powerful figures.

On the surface this still leaves one extraordinary coincidence to be explained, to wit: the TARDIS just happens to take the Doctor straight to his doppelgangers. But this may not be down to pure chance at all. It's interesting to note that the TARDIS occasionally demonstrates the ability to "home in" on its owner, the most obvious examples being "Full Circle" and "The King's Demons" (20.6), both of which see the Ship landing in the same room as the Doctor once it's steered in the right general direction. Though we're never told of a scanning device on the TARDIS that can pinpoint the location of *any* given life-form, in "The Five Doctors" (20.7) we *are* shown that the Ship can zero in on the Doctor's brain-patterns, evidently because it's so familiar with him.

And if it knows the Doctor's brain that well, then surely it knows his body-print too? Both "The Massacre" and "The Enemy of the World" take place in a period when the Doctor has no control over the TARDIS' direction, so doesn't it seem likely that with no other navigational system to stop it, the Ship is homing in on biological signatures it recognises? And with its usual flair for dramatic timing, on both occasions it arrives just when the lookalikes are on the point of doing something overwhelmingly evil. This homing system might also help to explain the events of "Black Orchid" (19.5). As Nyssa isn't a Time Lord, for the time being we have to assume that her resemblance to Ann Talbot is coincidental (then again, the people of Traken are good with bio-science and recognise regeneration in terms of 'telebiogenesis', so is there a Trakenite body-bank?), yet the malfunctioning TARDIS delivers her straight to Ann's local train station.

Romana's resemblance to Princess Strella follows the same pattern, but this time the meeting of the two might be more than chance or TARDIS intervention. The events on Tara are part of the Quest for the Key to Time. We already know that the Key is capable of manipulating people's histories, and that it altered the DNA of the Sixth House of Atrios in order to manifest its sixth segment in

continued on page 177...

ABOUT TIME 1980–1984

Cardinal Zorac wears heliotrope; Thalia, the technical expert, wears pinkish-brown; Hedin wears orange; the new Castellan wears greenish-yellow. [See both "The Deadly Assassin" and "The Invasion of Time" for the colour-coding of Time Lord chapters.] The high-ranking Time Lords are happy to lounge around in their elaborate ceremonial robes and collars [although "The Deadly Assassin" indicates they're for special occasions, so it's just the High Council who like to dress up all the time]. Councillor Hedin, a stately old Time Lord who treats the Doctor as a long-time friend, is a historian and aware of his people's debt to Omega. This is why he's secretly Omega's agent within Time Lord society, knocking off the opposition with an impulse laser and ultimately sacrificing himself to the scheme.

The new Castellan's name isn't given, but he knows - and resents - the Doctor. [You could try arguing that it's a regenerated Castellan Kelner from "The Invasion of Time", who'd certainly have reason to hate the Doctor. Though it may seem unlikely that Kelner could keep his position after events in "The Invasion of Time", this is Gallifrey, and it's already been demonstrated that the Time Lords' political system is utterly bizarre. But this Castellan wears robes of a different colour, and see also 20.7, "The Five Doctors".] Hedin states that the Castellan is sensitive to 'public opinion'.

Fearing that an anti-matter creature will be let loose on the universe if it fully bonds with the Doctor, the High Council is prepared to execute him to dispense with the threat. It's said that although capital punishment was abolished long ago [possibly when the Time Lords first became Time Lords], there's one single precedent for termination. [Most probably meaning Morbius (see "The Brain of Morbius", 13.5), but compare with the Doctor's near-execution in "The Deadly Assassin" (14.3). Morbius was executed on Karn rather than Gallifrey, so may not "count".]

Vaporisation is, as ever, the chosen method. A warrant of termination is required, but the Castellan has to check the Matrix for the exact wording. This wording speaks of 'cruel but unavoidable necessity', suggesting the last time was also a case of one [innocent?] life for billions. Charmingly, they write the warrant on a scroll.

The current Commander of the Guard is Maxil, a domineering oaf who's prepared to arrest anyone who stands in the way of his orders. [And he looks exactly like the Sixth Doctor, of course. See **Why**

Are There So Many Doubles in the Universe?.] Time Lord sidearms can, predictably, stun as well as kill. Even Time Lords who never show any interest in alien culture use phrases like 'what the devil' [there's a devil in Gallifreyan mythology?].

• *Borusa.* Borusa, the new Lord President, has regenerated again. [So soon? It surely can't have been *that* long since "The Invasion of Time", so behind the scenes these may be perilous times on Gallifrey.] He's nowhere near as majestic as he was, and comes across as rather confused, warmly welcoming the Doctor and then condemning his old student to death a few minutes later. [It is typical of Borusa to sanction someone's death out of necessity, but he's remarkably unconcerned about the Doctor, and overall his personality doesn't seem too stable. It'll be worse, of course, by "The Five Doctors".] He's also quite slow in this body, not twigging that Hedin's the traitor in the High Council even when Hedin starts threatening him.

• *Omega.* It's not explained exactly how Omega escaped his anti-matter universe after its collapse [in 10.1, "The Three Doctors"], but he got out through Rondel; see **Planet Notes**. Now he has a TARDIS, but he's still made of anti-matter so he can't exist in the normal universe unless he reverses his polarity by 'bonding' with another Time Lord. And Hedin has picked the Doctor, due to time, current location and personality. [We might assume that Hedin provides the TARDIS as soon as Omega arrives through the Arc of Infinity. Even so, you have to wonder how Omega got in touch with Hedin. The fact that *personality* is a factor in Omega's bonding with the Doctor once again underlines the idea that they're both tearaways, as hinted in "The Three Doctors".] Omega describes himself as being of another dimension, and can only exist on board his TARDIS because rapidly-decaying quad magnetism is shielding the anti-matter. This stops the Time Lords locating him, as well as making sure he doesn't explode.

Omega has a snazzy new costume, an ornate and almost organic-looking mask with matching robes, his breastplate marked with what looks like an "R" [and in the credits he's just called "The Renegade", but let's gloss over that]. His voice has changed, too. As before, his motives are a mixture of revenge and just wanting to exist again. Though he's ruthless in his aims, once he's on Earth he displays traces of humanity, and appears fascinated by local culture after being stuck in another dimension for so long. He genuinely seems to care

Why Are There So Many Doubles in the Universe?

...continued from page 175

the form of Princess Astra (16.6, "The Armageddon Factor"). It's Romana's resemblance to Strella that allows her to help the Doctor restore the rightful monarchy of Tara - which is, if you take the "Quest-as-initiation" idea seriously, as much a part of the process as finding the Key itself - before escaping with the fourth segment. Did the Key arrange this? Did it make sure that Romana was born into this particular Princess-body, knowing that one day she'd be a necessary part of the Quest? It's not far beyond the boundaries of what we already know.

Which raises another interesting possibility. When Romana regenerates into a form exactly like that of Princess Astra, i.e. the sixth segment of the Key, it's taken as read that she's just copying Astra's style. But what if it's the other way around? If the Key can (to some degree) see into the future, copy any pattern it wishes and mess around with Time Lord biology to boot, then what if the Princess Astra body is one of Romana's "natural" regenerative forms and the Key just copied it? If anything, this makes more sense than assuming that Romana can exactly mimic any body she likes, as no other Time Lord on TV ever displays this remarkable gift during a regeneration. Or even hints at it, come to that.

Either way, though, the idea of a Time Lord body-bank seems difficult to shake. This may throw new light on the Doctor's comments in "Horror of Fang Rock" (15.1), in which he explicitly compares Time Lord regeneration with the shape-altering techniques of the Rutans... and the Rutans, of course, need to examine a human body-print before they can change form. This leads on to one final question: does the body-bank only contain humanoid patterns, or are there a few alien designs in there as well, perhaps for Time Lord agents who might have to go "undercover" among other species? If the latter then it'd certainly explain the Eighth Doctor's comment in the TV Movie (27.0) that he can change his species, but only when he regenerates. Even though every Time Lord we've ever met has resolutely insisted on turning into another British character actor.

about the death of Hedin, his agent on Gallifrey and 'friend'. Still, he's ready to kill a man on Earth for the local clothing, and eventually he's prepared to cause a massive anti-matter explosion on the planet just because *he* can't have a nice new life there. He believes that the Time Lords wouldn't have helped him to enter the universe of matter if he'd asked them. [Partly because he gave them such trouble the last time he turned up, but it's possible that the High Council's keeping guilty secrets about the way he met his fate. See "The Three Doctors" for more.]

The Doctor describes the bonding process as a 'temporal bonding', the molecular realignment of two basically incompatible life-forms. In order to bond with the Doctor, Omega has to steal the Doctor's biodata extracts from Gallifrey and then move the TARDIS to the vicinity of Rondel. After Omega merges with the Doctor's body it takes time and power for the bonding to be complete, so if the Doctor dies then he won't be able to survive in this universe, at least once the quad magnetism wears off. Through the Doctor, Omega is somehow capable of penetrating the Matrix on Gallifrey, possibly because the Doctor has already become one with it [in "The Invasion of Time", though this is all very muddy]. Borusa states that Omega has invaded the Matrix's 'space-time

parameters'.

Omega is hiding in a crypt in Amsterdam because it's on the curve of the Arc of Infinity, and below sea-level to maintain pressure for fusion conversion. [He must, surely, also have picked Earth because he knows it's a key planet for the Doctor after "The Three Doctors"? That taken into account, it's *still* a bizarre coincidence that Tegan runs into him by accident. Maybe the Arc of Infinity has strange quantum effects that mess around with probability, or something.] He seems to believe he can build himself a new TARDIS on Earth [either he's thinking of accelerating the locals' technological know-how, or he really is an engineer of near-miraculous ability]. Omega refers to Hedin as 'Time Lord' as if he himself isn't one, but later Hedin calls Omega both a Time Lord and 'the first and greatest of our people'. Omega refers to his vessel as a TARDIS [compare with 1.1, "An Unearthly Child", though he might have picked up the term from Hedin].

Eventually Omega generates enough power with his fusion booster to complete 'transfer' and become matter, but the booster explodes as the Arc of Infinity shifts, and Omega's TARDIS is wracked with explosions which render it useless. But the bonding is apparently complete, and - once black ooze has finished pouring out of his mask - Omega removes his garb to reveal the Doctor's face underneath. He believes he can safely exist on Earth, though the Doctor knows the transition isn't permanent and that the body will revert to anti-matter. This means Omega starts to degenerate within minutes, with horrible pustules erupting all over his skin, the Doctor stating that once the magnetic shielding fails there'll be a colossal explosion. The Doctor eventually makes Omega disappear with the Ergon's matter converter, and when asked whether Omega's been destroyed the Doctor merely states that everyone assumed he was dead once before. [Not a direct answer to the question, and before using the converter the Doctor claims he can use it to destroy *or dispel* Omega. Did the Doctor chicken out of killing his old hero, and send him elsewhere instead? Omega finally does return, not on TV but in the Big Finish audio "Omega", only to *again* get hurled into a black hole.]

Oh, and as well as having the Ergon as a servant, Omega can somehow turn prisoners into mindless zombie-slaves.

The Non-Humans

• *The Ergon.* The Doctor recognises it as 'one of Omega's less successful attempts at psychosynthesis' [meaning, Omega was originally trying to recreate *himself*?], and refers to it as *an* Ergon, indicating that Omega made lots of these [in the ancient past of Gallifrey]. The Ergon is humanoid in shape, but has the same skeletal, part-sculpted look as Omega's armour, while its head is mostly made up of a big sharp beak. [The Ergon can interact with the universe of matter, and it's apparently not an anti-matter being that can convert itself like the gel-creatures in "The Three Doctors". The name suggests a being made of energy, of course. It's worth noting that the Ergon seems to be waiting for Omega as soon as Omega manifests himself in the universe of matter, which might suggest that Hedin created it on Omega's behalf. Or is this one of the original batch from ancient Gallifrey? If so, then where's it been all this time?]

Omega is using the Ergon as a guard-dog and manual labourer, and it's armed with a ray-gun-like matter converter, which makes its victims vanish [the implication is that it transports them onto Omega's TARDIS]. The Doctor appropriates this and uses it to make Omega disappear, claiming he can use it to destroy or dispel Omega [as Omega's reverting to anti-matter, the converter

can't just teleport him elsewhere in the universe, but where he goes is never explained]. On Omega's behalf the Ergon also scans the minds of his captives, by putting its hands on their heads and making them glow, useful information being transmitted straight into Omega's mind.

Despite its obvious talents, the Ergon never speaks and doesn't appear to be very independent. Nor is it good at keeping its head still.

Planet (and Q-Star) Notes

• *Gallifrey.* Now looking a lot more bland and a lot more spartan than it once did [but then, in "The Deadly Assassin" and "The Invasion of Time" we saw it while there were important ceremonies in progress, and here it's just business as usual]. The Council Chamber is a large but unremarkable room, from which the President can access the Matrix's knowledge through a levitating circlet [the same one seen in "The Invasion of Time", but not the Coronet of Rassilon… see "The Five Doctors"]. En route to this chamber there's a foyer-like space where robed Time Lords lounge around on sofas as if they're waiting at an airport. There's also said to be a residential wing in the area.

Also seen here is a computer room, run by the technician Damon, a friend of the Doctor's. Damon only seems to have one staff member working with him. [He apparently has similar duties to those of Co-Ordinator Engin in "The Deadly Assassin". Has there been a change in procedures, what with all the recent crises in the planet's history?]

The room is full of consoles and such, and when the 'security circuit' makes a warning light flash on one of these panels, Damon learns that somebody's transmitting the Doctor's biodata extracts to Omega. On the nearby computer screen the biodata scrolls past as a series of letters, numbers and symbols [translated for our benefit, as per usual?]. This transmission of information is apparently 'treason', but only a High Council member could have done it, and the Doctor describes the information as being stored within the Matrix. His location in space and time, i.e. the co-ordinates of the TARDIS, also seem to be found in the Matrix. [Biodata would seem to be the same as the 'biog-data' mentioned by Spandrell in "The Deadly Assassin", although there the biog-data was stored on the Time Lord equivalent of microfilm rather than in the Matrix. Biog-data suggests biographical data, whereas the biodata here is described as detailed biological data, but even in "The Deadly Assassin" there seemed to be an overlap... as if Time Lords' personal histories are somehow bound into their bodies.] Items from Gallifrey, e.g. Omega's fusion booster, can be 'sent' to Earth without the use of a TARDIS [compare with the Time Lord messenger who appears out of nowhere in 8.1, "Terror of the Autons"].

When the recall circuit is used to bring the TARDIS back to Gallifrey, the Doctor states that 'only twice before in our history' has the recall circuit been used. ["Our" history meaning the Time Lords, or meaning the Doctor and his Ship? It's the first time the Doctor's recall circuit has come into effect, as far as we know. The circuit isn't what draws the Doctor to Gallifrey in "The Deadly Assassin" (14.3) and "The War Games" (6.7), and the summons sent in "Meglos" (18.2) is never answered, so a recall is evidently only ordered in times of dire crisis.] The recall is carried out in the Gallifreyan computer room by feeding a small square "disc", bearing the President's seal, into the Matrix itself. The Commander of the Guard orders the TARDIS to be set down inside the security compound in the heart of the Citadel, which the Doctor knows by sight. The Doctor finds that his palm-print no longer opens doors on Gallifrey, and expects it to have been long-cancelled [the suggestion being that the palm-print of any registered Time Lord can open the doors], but he makes his escape by typing the Presidential code - 4553916592 - into the keypad.

The Doctor asks Damon how Leela is ["The Invasion of Time", again], and Damon says she's well. The Doctor also claims she had a wedding, which he missed. [Several things to notice here. One: the implication is that Leela has, at the very least, somehow been in touch with the Doctor since leaving him. Two: weddings exist on Gallifrey. Three: assuming that Leela and Andred live outside the Citadel, the Doctor expects a technician to have seen them lately, as if Gallifreyans are now much more likely to venture outside than they used to be. Either that or Leela's visa allows her residency in the Capitol, and Damon hangs out with the Chancellery Guard and their wives. Four: any amount of time could have passed on Gallifrey since the Doctor was last here, arguably even centuries, so has Leela been given the power of regeneration? Or can Time Lord technology keep her alive some other way?]

When the Doctor is to be executed, an 'alert' sounds in the Citadel which isn't unlike the TARDIS cloister bell. He's led to a vaporisation device in a chamber designated the 'place of termination', where he's seemingly destroyed. However, thanks to Omega and Hedin's machinations he's concealed by a force-screen, and his mind finds itself floating around inside the Matrix [meaning that the second Time Lord to face execution may also be the second Time Lord to survive it].

In the "refectory" area, one of the female Time Lords [the one wearing Rodan's "outdoors" cloak from "The Invasion of Time"] holds her hands on her abdomen as though pregnant. This has led to a great deal of speculation, though it may just be that she lacks pockets.

• *The Matrix.* Referred to by the Doctor as the 'space-time Matrix'. Here the Matrix [or at least, the part of it which Omega controls] is a peculiar void-like space which only seems to contain a web of shimmering light, where the minds of Omega's prisoners can be made to suffer. The Doctor can enter this same area by wearing the President's circlet. The 'space-time dimensions' of the Matrix, the same web of lines, can be monitored on various screens around the Capitol on Gallifrey.

The President can isolate the Matrix, and stop anyone using the master controls, something which requires him to 'charge the transduction field'. Once Omega's in full control of the Matrix, TARDISes can't leave Gallifrey undetected until a pulse loop - a photon-pulse device usually used for tracing faults on the master circuits of the computer room - distracts him for long enough to let the Doctor escape.

• *Rondel.* An 'intergalactic' region of space rather than a planet, Rondel was known to 'the ancients' as the Arc of Infinity, and the Doctor calls it 'the gateway to the dimensions' [implying that *some* people know more about other dimensions than the Time Lords]. Though devoid of stellar activity, in former times it was the location of a collapsed Q-star, a rare phenomenon which on burn-out emits quad-magnetism. Quad-magnetism is the only known shield for anti-matter [meaning the only known *natural* shield, as anti-matter can be safely contained by future-humans in 19.6, "Earthshock"], but it decays quickly. The colloquial name for this region is the Arc of Infinity, and it's through Rondel that Omega arrives in the "normal" universe of matter, though Rondel would seem to be only one part of the arc as the curve of it is said to be in Amsterdam. The Doctor states that Omega controls the 'shift' of the

Arc, while the Castellan believes he wants to relocate it to Gallifrey and link it to the Matrix, thus gaining enormous power.

History

• *Dating.* Obviously sometime in the 1980s, from Earth's point of view. [Tegan says that she got the sack from her hostess job, but doesn't say whether she lost it by default (by never turning up) or spent some time working for the airline and *then* got fired. Either way, months seem to have passed for her rather than years. If "Time-Flight" was set in the same year the TARDIS snatched her up - 1981, and there's never any indication that anyone noticed she was missing - then it's probably no later than 1982.]

The Analysis

Where Does This Come From? As we saw in "The Keeper of Traken" (18.6), Byrne's background is in the more hippyish areas of pop culture, even if he eventually ended up writing for police dramas and rurally-based nostalgia shows. So what have we here? Fairly standard Jung, much like that produced by all the other people who'd read Joseph Campbell's *Hero with a Thousand Faces* and Ursula K. Le Guin's *A Wizard of Earthsea*. The hero and the villain are linked, and each needs the other to stay alive.

Also, we have the all-purpose Byrne moral dilemma: the idea of torturing one person to maintain a utopia. (See both "The Keeper of Traken" and 21.1, "Warriors of the Deep". And compare with 12.4, "Genesis of the Daleks".) On top of this we get teenagers in trouble in a foreign location, while Tegan's line about having 'a friend' who investigates 'this kind of thing' might easily be from a *Hart to Hart* episode, or any British-made romp of that period. It's all very familiar, as regards "ingredients".

Because if Season Eighteen marked the point where *Doctor Who* started playing fast-and-loose with its references, mixing together elements of TV and SF lore safe in the knowledge that the audience didn't need too many explanations, then this is the point where the process arguably goes berserk. The series has always raided other genres, but until now it's only tried poaching one style at a time (as ever, "The Talons of Weng-Chiang" is the most obvious example, although even a rather more subtle story like "The Ribos Operation"

chooses one pseudo-historical oeuvre and sticks with it). But in "Arc of Infinity" we see video nasties, soap opera and pulp SF collide.

In the context of the times, the first of these is the most obvious. As in "Black Orchid", the influence of the horror renaissance is really making itself felt on the series. Perhaps that's no more than you'd expect, considering that *Doctor Who* was traditionally supposed to be frightening and that by 1983 an increasing number of ten-year-old boys had somehow managed to see *I Spit on Your Grave*. The two-young-backpackers-in-a-foreign-land subplot in "Arc of Infinity" comes straight out of *An American Werewolf in London*, while the idea of something nasty and extra-dimensional lurking in the church crypt comes straight out of every video-rental SF / horror movie of the period. It seems almost too obvious to point out that both Omega and the Ergon's designs suggest H. R. Giger's classic bio-mechanical work for *Alien*, but then again, at the time *everybody* was ripping off Giger. And everybody seemed to be obsessed with oozing bodies, with films like John Carpenter's *The Thing* (some would say a more effective re-make of *The Thing from Another World* than "The Seeds of Doom" had been) showing that oddly-coloured internal fluids could be more disgusting than blood. Omega's metamorphosis in episode four sees black sludge pouring out of his head as if he's melting into bile, and is possibly the most early '80s scene of all the early '80s stories.

There's also, it must be said, a sense that the programme's cannibalising its own mythology as much as anybody else's. But despite this story's reckless assumptions that everybody watching will remember what Gallifrey's supposed to be like and what the Matrix does, Omega's reappearance at least makes *some* sense in TV terms. Just over a year earlier, BBC2 had repeated "The Three Doctors" as part of its *The Five Faces of Doctor Who* season, a season that had pulled in surprisingly good ratings. Despite being shown on a "minority" channel, "Logopolis" episode three got a bigger audience than on its original transmission, which should give you some idea of what was happening to Saturdays. Though Omega's return is obviously designed to appease the hard-core fans, a large chunk of the audience would have *vaguely* recognised him as an old enemy. If not, then the reprise of the last cliffhanger would have made less sense than any other in the programme's history.

The last thing that needs to be mentioned here,

if only as an aside, is the series' relationship with technology. In the late '70s the machinery of space-time travel seemed to mirror the rise of consumer electronics, with the Doctor's jury-rigging of exotic technology looking as faux-complex as setting up a stereo. But by this stage cables and connecting-wires are going out of fashion (Omega's the only one here using such unhip-looking lash-ups), and most civilised people in the universe are carrying hand-held gizmos to detect anti-matter or convert particles. Classic *Star Trek* made this sort of pocket-sized sci-fi technology trendy in the '60s, but now it's the age of the cheap digital watch and the portable video game, and suddenly it's taken as read that hand-held gadgets can do *anything*. At least the sonic screwdriver looked like a tool for the working boffin in the field. The devices on show here all look as if they should have LED displays and be able to tell you the time in Tokyo.

Things That Don't Make Sense The plot remains puzzling even now, and the absurd amounts of technobabble aren't helping. Much of the story involves Omega taking over the Matrix, but it's not clear why he has to, since his main aim doesn't seem to be the conquest of Gallifrey (although that's what the Castellan believes) but just the acquisition of a new body.

In which case… why doesn't the Doctor *let* him get a new body? He hurries after Omega on Earth because he thinks Omega's going to revert to anti-matter and go pop, but Omega's fully-bonded form is apparently only unstable because the Doctor interferes in the operation and makes the fusion booster explode prematurely, so everyone would have been much better off just sitting back and letting the alleged bad guy get on with it. Unless the Doctor has nothing to do with the booster's explosion - even *this* is unclear - but if that's the case then why doesn't Omega the great engineer realise that it's going to blow, and that the plan is doomed to failure, even before he starts work on it? Why does he even need such a booster, rather than drawing on the supposedly immense power that fuels TARDISes? And why do the Time Lords notice the theft of the booster, but not the absence of a TARDIS, which Hedin must surely have stolen for Omega's sake?

The booster's explosion is also said to have something to do with the Arc of Infinity shifting, though this is as hazy as everything else and just underlines the fact that the Arc becomes a useless

add-on to the story after the first episode. In which Hedin and Omega discuss their choice of "bondee", and believe the Doctor's location to be a big issue… except that Omega's supposed to be able to shift the business end of the Arc, thus making the subject's location irrelevant. Then there's the whole "anti-matter" question. It's never clear when things are made of anti-matter and when they're not, or what the Ergon's gun actually does, let alone how Omega got out of his realm in "The Three Doctors" and ended up hanging around Rondel.

Despite being a powerful and much-respected member of Time Lord society, Hedin can't think of a less conspicuous way of sabotaging the equipment in the control room on Gallifrey than bursting into the place with an impulse laser, murdering the technician on duty there and shooting up the hardware. He apparently hopes this will be put down to an 'accident', though it's hard to see how, as he blasts the control panels to bits and it's hard to imagine even Commander Maxil being fooled into thinking that the hardware just short-circuited. Still, Hedin can't be particularly stable. He's cool, calm and collected when dealing with the High Council, but whenever he's communicating with Omega he starts maniacally waving small implements around in order to give the camera something to focus on during the "mysterious" talky scenes. Though the CCTV system works improbably well when the plot requires it, Hedin can saunter into the computer room in full High Council drag without being noticed. And he seems to need to cast a big-collared shadow whenever he's doing any other skullduggery.

Other security problems abound. The guards can't hide very well, and even breathing makes them clatter; there are stasers in the computer room for some reason; Maxil's search for the Doctor doesn't include the place where he was last seen (and as he's only 'shielded', not transmatted, Maxil must have walked right through him); they no longer bother using force-fields in the security compound, a routine precaution in "The War Games" (6.7). Oddly, the route from the compound to the Council and vaporisation chambers passes through the Gallifrey branch of Haagen Das, where the same four Time Lords are seen nattering for several hours (in plot terms). Even more oddly, when a former Lord President is frog-marched off to be the first person vaporised in centuries, nobody stops chatting.

On returning to Gallifrey, the Doctor immediately tries to escape custody and nobody's expecting it. Not only is he forgiven for failing to return Romana (and *they* call her that... see 16.1, "The Ribos Operation", for why this is weird), but the small matter of allowing one-third of the universe to be destroyed (18.7, "Logopolis") slips everyone's mind. Zorac's presence on the supreme executive of the cosmos is a touch puzzling, as he not only says incredibly stupid things - 'what the divil's going on ite there?' and 'demneble businness', as if he's trying to cover the fact that he's really the Scarlet Pimpernel - but gets to fill in for Tegan asking inane info-dump questions. Meanwhile the real Tegan's happy to rejoin the TARDIS crew after being mentally violated, zapped by Big Bird and parted from her favourite cousin, whom she leaves behind in hospital despite specifically coming to Amsterdam to see him [unless the TARDIS crew hang around in Holland for a while after the end of the story?]. One sniff of a mystery and she turns into Angela Lansbury.

Robin is terrified by the sight of a Dutch policeman in episode one, and Colin has to reassure him that he's not going to be arrested just for losing his passport, but by the time they reach the crypt they've swapped personalities so that Colin's got cold feet and Robin's the one saying things like "hey, the worst that could happen is we might get arrested". Losing a passport is serious. In a country like Holland, it's usually the work of international drugs rings or terrorist cells trying to create fake IDs; the police wouldn't ignore it, and nor would a report of a foreign national looking like a zonked-out corpse and not recognising his friends be overlooked by the narcotics agency. In fact the crypt's lack of panhandling junkies, discarded needles or people fencing Colin's boots and sleeping bag is curious in itself.

Back on the streets, the Doctor has to turn out his pockets to see whether he's got any change that might let him use a Dutch telephone box, which is surely a bit of a long-shot? If this were the Fourth Doctor then it *might* be worth checking, but this incarnation's only got half a dozen things in his pockets and European coinage really isn't likely to be among them.

Then there's the magic bicycle. When Omega runs down a Dutch side-street, there's what looks like a small phone-exchange relay with two "Venus" symbols interlinked in blue spray-paint (the internationally-recognised symbol for "les-

bian"). Seconds later Nyssa and Tegan arrive, and the next time we get a long-shot there's a bicycle there, covering up the graffiti. Can it be that the programme-makers were fearful of anyone even *subconsciously* getting the idea that Nyssa's enthusiasm for having Tegan back on board was in any way suspect? If so, then why not give them separate rooms?

Why does the TARDIS databank refer to things happening in 'former times', when it's the information system for a time machine? [Does the text rewrite itself according to the era the Ship happens to be visiting?] And why has Nyssa started collecting novelty teapots in her quarters?

Critique   So they've decided what they want: a script that sets the tone for the series' twentieth birthday celebrations, that re-introduces Gallifrey for new viewers, that brings Omega back from the grave, that puts Tegan back on board the TARDIS and that includes the opportunity for location larking-about in Amsterdam. And they give the brief to Johnny Byrne, whose last effort was rewritten so extensively that he managed to resubmit it without anyone complaining.

Worse, you get the feeling he doesn't care about *any* of these things. It's been (rightly) pointed out that all the blather about the Arc of Infinity doesn't make sense, and is that surprising? It's barely part of the story at all, but just a way of using non-science and non-explanation to try to cover the joins when the plot isn't up to the task. In the past, pseudo-science was at least a means of defining the characters through their *attitude* to science; when Leonard Sachs (as Borusa) and Elspet Grey (as Thalia) clearly can't get a handle on what's supposed to be happening, we aren't as inclined to take on trust that the writers know either. Like the story that immediately precedes it across the Season Nineteen / Season Twenty divide, it's a prime case of Nathan-Turner's production style getting in the way of the story, but at least you can see what "Time-Flight" was *trying* to get at if you squint at it hard enough. This isn't getting at anything at all.

But perhaps what's hardest to take is what it does to Gallifrey. "The Deadly Assassin" was always controversial, and as we've already demonstrated, whether it "does" the Doctor's homeworld properly or not is something that's still open to debate. Surely, though, nobody could argue that *this* works? The planet is now just one big '80s-style office block, even down to the foyers where Time Lords hang around on coffee breaks. The Matrix becomes a plot convenience, and a "background" special effect, instead of a tangible nightmare. Borusa's personality vanishes without trace. If you're a newcomer to the series then it's just drab sci-fi, and if you're a long-term viewer then it's *offensively* drab sci-fi, doing for the Ultimate Seat of Power in the Universe what "The Invisible Enemy" did for space-stations. (It's possible the script was aiming for something a bit more majestic, but if exclamations like Nyssa's 'Time Lords, I beg of you, think what you're doing!' are trying to recapture the stately court drama of "Traken", nobody's bothered telling the director.)

Therein lies the big problem. This is an exercise in mediocrity, in blanding-out the programme's format. Other than the Ergon costume… other than a few "notable" performances… other than the music, if we're going to be honest… there's little here that's overwhelmingly *awful*. There are certain stories from the series' later years that can only be thought of as unwatchable embarrassments, but this isn't one of them, simply because it isn't memorable enough. As in "The Three Doctors", the Doctor himself is the subject of the programme; fitting for an anniversary tale, yet the story's sense of purpose ends there, and even on first viewing it's hard to keep asking questions or to keep caring about the answers.

The Facts

Written by Johnny Byrne. Directed by Ron Jones. Viewing figures: 7.2 million, 7.3 million, 6.9 million, 7.2 million.

Supporting Cast Leonard Sachs (Lord President Borusa), Michael Gough (Councillor Hedin), Colin Baker (Commander Maxil), Ian Collier (The Renegade / Omega), Paul Jerricho (The Castellan), Neil Daglish (Damon), Elspet Gray (Chancellor Thalia), Max Harvey (Cardinal Zorac), Alastair Cumming (Colin Frazer), Andrew Boxer (Robin Stuart), Malcolm Harvey (The Ergon).

Oh, Isn't That..?
• *Colin Baker.* "The man they love to hate". As Paul Merrony in *The Brothers*, he'd been the J. R. Ewing of the west midlands haulage industry (see 12.1, "Robot"). Since then he'd been rather typecast as "a bit of a bruiser", and his highest-profile part had been Bayban the Butcher in the nearly-

tolerable *Blake's 7* episode "City on the Edge of the World".

• *Michael Gough.* See 3.7, "The Celestial Toymaker". Now best-known for playing Alfred the Butler against a selection of Batmen, Gough had become a distinguished actor by this point. So it's easy to forget how much crud he'd made, especially around the early 1960s. As the star of *Konga!* (a cheap horror flick involving a man in a gorilla suit climbing a mock-up of Big Ben, also starring Leonard Sachs, funnily enough) and *Doctor Terror's House of Horrors* (see 2.2, "The Dalek Invasion of Earth", for more on producer Milton Subostky's crimes against cinema), he's used to dignity in the line of piffle.

• *Elspet Grey.* Soon to be seen in the original series of *The Black Adder* as Prince Edward's clueless mother, she'd been in *Catweazle* and the musical version of *Goodbye, Mr Chips*, and had played the mother in Felicity Kendal vehicle *Solo*.

• *Paul Jerricho.* Like so many others, he'd been in *Triangle* opposite Kate O'Mara. He'll return at the end of this season, memorably.

• *Leonard Sachs.* Although he was a long-time character actor (see 3.5, "The Massacre"), it's for his two-decade run as the impresario-like host of *The Good Old Days* that Sachs is best-remembered. Both Henry Gordon Jago (14.6, "The Talons of Weng Chiang") and Jim Broadbent's character in *Moulin Rouge* derive from this preposterous performance of absurd and annoying alliterations.

Working Titles "The Time of Neman", "The Time of Omega".

Cliffhangers The Commander of the Guard shoots down the Doctor in the corridors of Gallifrey; the Doctor vanishes in the vaporisation chamber, and the Commander (boo, hiss) announces that judgement has been carried out; as the ghost-like form of "the Renegade" appears on the monitor screens of Gallifrey, the Doctor announces that Omega now controls the Matrix.

The Lore

• John Nathan-Turner wanted to do a foreign location-shoot, and Amsterdam was one of the regular ports-of-call of the floating-TV-studio-cum-ferry in *Triangle*. The story's location-work made it better suited for late spring, so the all-interior "Snakedance" was filmed first but broadcast second.

ABOUT TIME 1980-1984

• Saward approached Johnny Byrne, then working in America, to write the script as "The Keeper of Traken" had appealed to him (and he was unaware that, after rewrites, barely one line in five had been Byrne's work). Byrne was interested mainly because he thought his character Nyssa was being badly used; he'd been in complex negotiations to get a credit for Nyssa in any story he didn't write himself. Saward gave Byrne a lengthy list of subjects that the production team wanted to avoid in an Amsterdam-based story, including drugs, diamond-smuggling and thefts of Old Masters. Byrne had proposed an idea about a time-slippage in London caused by something called the Arc of Infinity, but by the time the story reached the screen this title was just about all that remained of the idea.

• In some parallel dimension, there's a version of this story with the following cast: Borusa, Peter Cushing; Castellan, Patrick Stewart; Maxil, Pierce Brosnan; Thalia, Honor Blackman; Hedin, William Lucas. Yes, all of these people were seriously approached. Colin Frazer is played by the son of Fiona Cumming, director of the next story and a couple of others. Nothing at all suspicious about that…

• Ron Jones had only stepped in to direct "Time-Flight" at the last moment, and according to some sources *this* was the story he'd been assigned to do. He found filming at Schipol airport remarkably unstressful after the bureaucracy to which he'd been subjected at Heathrow. Although the script contains a reference to Victor Caroon - the hapless, mutating astronaut who's chased through London at the end of *The Quatermass Experiment* - the precise details of the chase sequence were left vague, to be determined after a recce on location. Jones claimed that most of what we see was improvised to suit the relatively small area of "Dutch"-looking buildings in central Amsterdam.

Location work was also where the press would be most welcome, and the wily producer let slip that the girls would be showing more leg (the "Chinese whispers" surrounding this report made it seem that Tegan was going to be significantly more raunchy than she actually was). As Holland can receive BBC1 on most days, many came to see "Mr. Tristan" save the world. His appearance as Omega, with latex and breakfast cereal on his face, was commented upon by the local media. One resident, unaware of the filming, tried to use the 'phone booth during a take; look closely in episodes one and four, and you'll see that the man in the sheepskin jacket is John Nathan-Turner himself, trying to deter onlookers from approaching the actors or making calls.

• Ian Collier (Stuart Hyde in 9.5, "The Time Monster") played Omega in the final stages of degeneration, with the same odd mix on his face, extending over his moustache; later an amalgam of green hair-gel and KY Jelly was used. The explosives in his clothing were the work of a new effects designer, Christopher Lawson, who "protected" Collier with metal plates instead of the usual thick rubber or leather to prevent heat being conducted.

• Several cuts were made to prevent the episodes overrunning. In episode one, Damon insists that Talor was murdered (a point referred to in episodes two and three, but never introduced). Maxil is the one who first points out that the Doctor and the "alien" are bonded. In episode four, both the Castellan's offer of resignation and Omega's threat of reprisals for the death of Hedin were cut, and there were various less significant trims.

• The 'space-time element' was introduced when it was pointed out by fanboy-in-supreme Ian Levine that removing the time rotor (the originally-scripted method of wheel-clamping the TARDIS) was impossible according to 1.3, "The Edge of Destruction". How did we ever get by without him?

• The studio recording was tight, and all the vaporisation chamber, Council chamber and Castellan's office sequences were completed on the last day, as well as the delayed pump-house and corridor scenes. Nevertheless, things were good-humoured, with Colin Baker in particular keeping spirits up. He'd been reluctant to take the role of Maxil, as he thought it ruled him out as a future Doctor…

20.2: "Snakedance"

(Serial 6D, Four Episodes, 18th January - 26th January 1983.)

Which One is This? It's the other one with the Mara. A snake's skull fills a crystal ball, which then explodes (a minor detail, but it's the thing that people tend to remember).

Firsts and Lasts Christopher Bailey's last broadcast story for the series, and he takes his big rubbery mind-snake with him when he goes (see 19.3, "Kinda").

Four Things to Notice About "Snakedance"...

1. It's the one where the Doctor looks mental. For years, *Doctor Who* has invited us to laugh at the stupid humans the Doctor encounters on his travels. When he tells the people of Earth that they're about to be invaded, and gets pooh-pooh'd by disbelieving military types, he's so clearly the one who's talking sense that you can't believe *anyone* would dispute the existence of aliens. But on Manussa, the Mara's a creature from legend and only New Agers believe in it. So for once we're invited to see the Doctor through everybody *else's* eyes, as some idiot with a stick of celery on his lapel who insists that the planet's under threat from an age-old horror while everyone else is just trying to arrange parties and get on with their lives. (The story gets away with this because Manussa's rather *better-defined* than most alien worlds. Its people actually seem to have their own history, and - always a good sign, given that so much SF television can be so po-faced - are even capable of sarcasm. Which means the locals can say: 'Yes, of *course* we'll change our age-old traditions just because the ranting celery-man says so...')

2. For a British audience, though, perhaps the most noticeable feature of "Snakedance" is Martin Clunes in the role of the Federator's son Lon. Though many, many now-famous faces from British television have appeared in *Doctor Who* over the years, Clunes has become so well-known (from the BBC sitcom *Men Behaving Badly*, and more comedy-dramas on ITV than anyone can comfortably name) that in recent years clips from the story have occasionally been shown on chat-shows in an attempt to embarrass him. The costume he wears in episode four is particularly amusing, in light of his later work; American readers might like to imagine the impact of seeing a young Matt Le Blanc in a sky-blue tunic and lipstick, if it gives them any idea. But what's striking about Clunes' performance is that it's really, really good, and was an obvious show-stealer even before anyone knew who he was. (As the nominal bad guy here, Lon has one of the best motives that *any* villain can have: sheer boredom. See 17.2, "City of Death" and 20.5, "Enlightenment".)

3. Taking on board the bad public reaction to the big pink Mara prop at the end of "Kinda", here the programme-makers desperately replace it with a new version. It's... a bit better. Strangely, though, the worst part isn't the giant snake at the end of the story but the equally rubbery normal-sized snake that crawls along Tegan's hand earlier in the episode. Once again, prepare to raise your "suspension of disbelief" threshold.

4. This is a story in which a perfect blue crystal is used as a meditation aid, but turns out to have the power to make people's inner demons manifest themselves and ends up creating horrible creepy-crawly things out of thin air as part of a Buddhist parable. We could direct your attention to "Planet of the Spiders" (11.5), but it'd seem almost gauche.

The Continuity

The Doctor He's more manic than usual even before he lands on Manussa to deal with the Mara, and is so urgent while investigating Tegan's snake-dreams that Nyssa has to step in to tell him to go easy on her. Once on Manussa it never seems to occur to him that he sounds like a gibbering lunatic to the natives. [To be generous, he's anxious about Tegan's welfare. But the previous Doctor also tended to get stroppy when he thought there was a serious threat in the air; see especially 13.3, "Pyramids of Mars".] Perhaps significantly, when *en rapport* with the snakedancer Dojjen his over-riding thought is 'all my fault', and saving Tegan is at least as important as saving a planet.

Once again displaying his contempt for fashion sense, the Doctor doesn't even seem to notice Nyssa's nice new outfit, however hard she tries to show it off. He's been teaching the companions more about the functioning of the Ship, a sensible precaution as they both seem to want to fly it themselves.

Background. He doesn't appear to know anything about the Sumaran Empire before landing there, though obviously the "Mara" part of the name is enough to give him a clue.

The Supporting Cast

• *Nyssa.* She finally gets around to raiding the TARDIS wardrobe, ditching her Traken velvets and changing into a rather more feminine multi-coloured number [and two stories from now, she'll be flouncing around in her undergarments]. She gets a bit miffed when the Doctor doesn't notice, and again when he treats her like a child later on. She's apparently sharing a room with Tegan again, and is concerned about her friend's dreams.

• *Tegan.* The Mara, it seems, never really left her [see 19.3, "Kinda"]. On board the TARDIS she's been experiencing dreams of Manussa and giving the Doctor strange co-ordinates, and admits that she's been having these problems for a while. She ends up sobbing once the Mara's out of her system, so life back on board the TARDIS isn't as much fun as she might have thought.

Under hypnosis, it's revealed that she felt safe in her garden when she was six. ['People always come back,' she says. We'll consider this later; see **Who Went to Aunt Vanessa's Funeral?** under 21.2, "The Awakening".]

The TARDIS The Doctor's been trying to teach Nyssa and Tegan to read the star-charts, and the Ship seems able to navigate properly again, although there are [never-explained] traces of anti-matter as it heads for Manussa. At one point Nyssa reads from a large silver hardback volume which contains data on Manussa [the paper equivalent of the TARDIS databank, but obviously not one of the Doctor's diaries as the style's too technical].

From parts on board the Ship, the Doctor rigs up a hearing-aid-like device which puts Tegan into a state of simple hypnosis, then fiddles with it to make it inhibit the brainwaves associated with dreaming. He uses a portable workbench in the TARDIS console room when adjusting the device [the one mentioned in 20.1, "Arc of Infinity].

The Non-Humans

• *The Mara.* Here the Mara's treated as a single, unique entity. It wants to get back to Manussa, the planet of its creation, and influences Tegan so that she unwittingly gives the Doctor the right co-ordinates. It's still in her subconscious, though her mind fights it when she's awake. The Mara's influence evidently grows when she arrives on Manussa, ultimately taking her over, although she spends a while being malicious and child-like before the creature takes complete control.

On Manussa the Mara no longer has its fear of mirrors, and indeed positively relishes looking at its own reflection, as here it's not trapped in a circle [yeees... see **Things That Don't Make Sense**]. While possessing Tegan, it has the power to dis-tort reflected images, making snake-skulls appear in crystal balls and looking-glasses. The trade-mark snake tattoo appears on her arm before long, and she shares it with the nobleman Lon just by taking his hand [so it can spread itself between minds, which explains why there's so much confusion about it being one entity or lots]. Even so, Tegan seems to be "superior" in the relationship. She can make her eyes glow red, turning anyone she stares at into a blank-faced zombie, and the snake is capable of becoming three-dimensional on her arm. This time it's yellow and black rather than red. The Mara thrives on fear, despair and greed, and Tegan experiences a constant sense of destructive anger while possessed by it.

According to Manussan legend, the source of the Mara's power was the Great Crystal. A big blue man-made object, the Crystal focuses thought into energy or even matter, which is how the Mara was created in the first place. The creature then rose to rule the Manussan Empire, which mutated into the cruel and barbarous Sumaran Empire ["Su-Maran", suggesting "of the Mara"]. The Sumaran Empire lasted six-hundred years before the Mara's defeat, five-hundred years ago, at which point Manussa became part of a Federation and written records began.

Though most Manussans believe the Mara to have been destroyed, one legend holds that it was merely banished to the dark places of the inside. [Which is where we found it in "Kinda", though there's no explanation as to how it got all the way to Deva Loka. Or is it capable of manifesting itself *anywhere* in the universe where the right mental techniques, such as those of the Kinda, happen to exist?]

When the Great Crystal is finally returned to its socket in the Chamber of the Mara - see **Planet Notes** - the snake-carving on the chamber's wall begins to glow, and all those present fall to their knees in agony as a great hissing fills the area. Their fear is focused on Tegan, and the snake from her arm starts to grow as a result. [In "Kinda" it could grow without a crystal, but it doesn't do that here. This might suggest that its physical form on Deva Loka was just a fraction of its true self, and that on Manussa it's trying to manifest itself in all its world-conquering glory.]

To face the Mara, the Doctor has to find the 'still point' within; he interrupts the 'becoming' of the Mara by focusing on one of the smaller crystals of the snakedancers, refusing to submit to fear. The face of the snakedancer Dojjen appears in the crystal as this happens, as if the Doctor's drawing on the power of other crystal-bearers, and the Mara's mind-slaves get a nasty shock when they try to seize the item from him. This interruption allows the Doctor to remove the Great Crystal from the wall, something which destroys the Mara, as it's in mid-manifestation and 'trapped between modes of being'. It leaves a gooey-looking corpse.

[Recovering from these events in the next story, the Doctor states that the Mara could *only* be killed at this point, which is why Dojjen didn't just smash the Great Crystal when he had the chance. The implication is that the Mara usually just returns to its "mental" state if its body is destroyed, and that this is what happened when it was defeated by the Federator. The Doctor also tells Tegan 'for you, the Mara is dead forever', which makes its destruction seem less than final.]

Planet Notes

• *Manussa.* Planet G139901KB in the Scrampus system, type 314S, atmosphere 98% terra-normal, gravity 96% terra-normal. Manussa is the third planet of a three-world Federation in this system, with an economy of subsistence agriculture and trade. It was originally a colony; see also **History**. The people obviously have access to interplanetary travel, but their culture shows few signs of highly-advanced technology, the lifestyles of the population often verging on the archaic. Nonetheless, this is a cultured, organised society, not a place of barbarians. The guards dress in menacing-looking armour, yet don't carry energy weapons and favour swords. Most of the buildings seen in the [capital] city are full of plastics, though there's no sign of any heavy machinery.

This civilisation has a nobility, with a great deal of respect paid to the lady Tanha and her spoiled, bored son Lon, respectively the wife and heir of the Federator who rules the three worlds. Lon is deputising for his aged father [the implication is that the Federator is off-world], and Lon isn't native to the settlement seen here but just visiting. He's said to be a direct descendant of the founder of the Federation who banished the Mara and brought an end to the Sumaran Empire five-hundred years ago. There's a legend about the Mara returning in a dream, though like most people the current Director of the Research Institute believes this to be bunk. The Director's predecessor, Dojjen, had other ideas. The people of the old

Manussan Empire are said to have been highly civilised, their technology greater than that of the current Manussans in some respects.

Only one settlement is seen here. [The only city on this colony planet…? It seems fairly small.] There's a natural series of caves, its opening carved to resemble the mouth of a snake. Its walls are full of primitive-looking pictograms from the Sumaran era, and there are secret chambers, which only the Mara can open, full of broken relics. The largest area within these caves is the Chamber of the Mara, where there's another snake-like carving with an ominous gap in its mouth. The Great Crystal used to fill that hole, but it was removed at the time of the Mara's "destruction" and is traditionally kept by the Director, who has to swear an oath not to let anyone - not even the Federator - get hold of it.

Miles outside the city, up in the hills, are the snakedancers. These people live in the wilds and handle live snakes as part of their 'religion'. It's said that they know the truth about the Mara, which is why Dojjen has become one of them. They meditate using small blue crystals known as Little Mind's Eye, as the Great Crystal is known in the legends as the Great Mind's Eye. Concentrating on one of these crystals makes it glow, if you can cut out external distractions. The crystals have a perfect molecular structure, tuned to the wavelengths of the human mind, and were molecularly engineered by the ancient Manussans in zero-gravity conditions. Someone holding one of the crystals can call another individual with a similar crystal, thanks to 'sympathetic resonance'. [They're strikingly similar to the crystals on Metebelis 3 in "Planet of the Spiders" (11.5), though the Metebelis crystals seem to have been naturally-occurring. Chela claims that the crystal he gives to the Doctor is eight-hundred years old, meaning it was manufactured during the barbaric Sumaran Empire, not the Manussan. The technology to create the crystals shouldn't have existed then, so this is probably a dating error, although it's possible that the first Federator wasn't the first to try to "depose" the Mara.]

The snakedance is a dance of purification in readiness for the Mara's return, as only a perfectly clear mind can resist the entity, but the Federation outlawed the dance nearly a hundred years ago. Dojjen now lurks outside the main settlement in what look like the ruins of an earlier civilisation. Dojjen and the Doctor engage in telepathic communication by allowing a small snake to bite them, and in this venom-induced state the snakedancer shares the understanding that *everything* is the snakedance.

The Manussans believe the Mara was destroyed five-hundred years ago, and once every ten years a ceremony is held to celebrate it. There's a sense of carnival in the streets during this period, and there's obviously a lot of "snake" imagery around, including a Punch-and-Judy show involving the Mara instead of a crocodile. The ceremony itself involves a highly-ritualised reconstruction of the Federation's founder defeating the Mara, in which a large rubber snake [even less convincing than the one in "Kinda"] is paraded through the streets towards the caves. The ceremony seems to suggest that the founder was a stranger to the locals [from another planet]. On the day of the ceremony, Manussans dressed as 'attendant demons' roam the streets, touching people with their rattles; it's traditional for those touched to forfeit a coin [particularly reminiscent of the trickster-figure on the Kinda world].

History

• *Dating*. No date given. [It's fair to assume that the Doctor takes Tegan back to Manussa *after* the events of "Kinda", so the twenty-seventh or twenty-eighth century might seem an obvious estimate. The big question, though, is whether the Manussans are descended from Earth-born humans. If they are then it suggests a much, much later date for both "Snakedance" and "Kinda", as the Manussan Empire fell to the Mara 1,100 years ago. The Punch-and-Judy show is *very* similar to an Earth-style one. Indeed, much of the style and incidental detail of this city resembles that of India. So this could well be a time when Earth's descendants are scattered across the universe and no longer have any connection with their ancestral home, much as in 16.5, "The Power of Kroll".]

The Analysis

Where Does This Come From? Having already toyed with Buddhist ideas (or at least Buddhist names) in "Kinda", here Chris Bailey sets about being rather more varied in his philosophy. Some of the ideas here are explicitly zen, but there's a lorryload of Hindu concepts and buckets of T. S. Eliot.

The Snakedancers are described as resembling Sadhus - the holy men of India - living on bark and roots and wearing ashes, and the idea of the material world as a "dance" is inherent in the god Shiva in his aspect as Nataraja the Cosmic Dancer. The Hindu god Krishna is called "Ruler over Three Worlds", as is the Federator.

And as we can see, the costume designers clearly thought Indian. But this isn't modern India, this is the Raj, the period of direct colonial rule by the British Empire (1858-1947). Specifically it's the Raj through the eyes of novelist E. M. Forster, in *A Passage to India*, with the visit to the caves (originally just "something to do") leading to confusion and conflict... and the source of this is reflections and echoes, leading a young woman to doubt her sanity. The English in India are prone to exactly the same disdain, ennui and mannered pedantry we see here. Over the next few years we'd get sick of seeing this sort of thing on our screens, and if we're talking about "heritage" TV then we might point out how much Martin Clunes resembles Anthony Andrews' performance in *Brideshead Revisited*.

What's ironic is that in a season so determined to reintroduce elements from the series' past, Bailey seems to arrive back at "Planet of the Spiders" purely by accident. Here he's got a certain advantage, though. When Barry Letts tried to turn the programme into a series of Buddhist folk-tales back in the mid-'70s, *Doctor Who* was more closely-linked to two-fisted action TV than at any other point in its history. Really, it's hard to tell a story about inner calm when your leading man insists on as many car chases as possible.

But the '80s series is a much more laid-back kind of affair. Let's remember, the Nathan-Turner era began with ninety seconds of deckchairs, and "Logopolis" showed the universe ending with a whimper rather than a bang. So the Doctor defeats the Mara by going into its chamber and meditating at it, ultimately killing it by closing his eyes and ignoring its influence. Consider how many times the '70s programme gets rid of a threat or an inconvenient loose end by blowing it up (some of the more blatant examples being "The Seeds of Doom", "Doctor Who and the Silurians" and "The Pirate Planet"), and you realise what's changed.

One of the themes that's incredibly explicit here is the problem of knowing too much. "Knowledge" has always been a difficult area in *Doctor Who*. Humanity's need for scientific investigation frequently results in people creating monsters or releasing primordial slime from the Earth's

Did Kate Bush Really Write This?

One of the most bizarre urban myths surrounding *Doctor Who* concerns the true identity of "Christopher Bailey". Nobody, it seems, could accept that the author of two of the most literate and - effects aside - satisfying stories of the early '80s could then vanish without trace. Thus, when two fans came up with a weird hoax to explain it, the joke took on the status of fact. When further (genuine) facts came to light, the theorists got busy and provided "watertight" reasons that "Bailey" was someone far more famous.

Before we look at the evidence provided, and how it all got out of hand, here are the two other popular candidates…

Sir Tom Stoppard. Well, all right, this was a while before his knighthood. Douglas Adams approached Stoppard to write for the series in 1978, and the reply was more "I'm a bit tied up right now" than "get lost". Stoppard was very active in the late '70s. Aside from his two stage plays of this period (*Day and Night* and *Every Good Boy Deserves Favour*), he was writing the TV film *Professional Foul* and episodes of the odd drama series *The Eleventh Hour*, which was broadcast live one week from the start of writing. He was also active in setting up Charter 77, a human rights watchdog organisation keeping up the pressure on his native Czechoslovakia. And - it now emerges - he was writing for several long-running series under a number of pen-names, more for the sake of learning new styles than for the money. He'd already 'fessed up to scripting *Mrs. Dale's Diary* in the '60s, after winning awards and critical respect.

In an interview in 1992, Stoppard admitted that in this period he was particularly concerned about Britain's imperial legacy, and confessed that his interest got a little out of hand in one episode of a popular BBC drama he'd written pseudonymously in the late '70s. It all got a bit comic-strippy, he said.

Could it have been…? The first script by "Bailey" was written in 1979, even if it didn't reach the screen until 1982. The "frog dreaming he was a man" material in "Snakedance" is phrased much like the similar discussion in *Rosencrantz and Guildenstern are Dead*, as is the by-play between Anicca and Anatta in "Kinda", especially in the cut scenes. Then there's the similarity between Hindle and moral philosopher George Moore in *Jumpers*, as well as the vaudevillian Henry Carr in *Travesties* (to say nothing of Albert in *Albert's Bridge*, although his quasi-incestuous relationship with his mother is closer to Lon in "Snakedance"). These people are all trying to impose order on a world which seems to actively resist their efforts to make it fit their measurements.

Stoppard is known for attempting to "road-test" belief-systems, so the application of a book-learned Buddhism to the material would seem consistent. "Bailey's" knowledge of the practices is a touch theoretical. Finally, Stoppard is given to adapting and reclaiming known, existing sources rather than plotting anything new, so the recycling of Ursula LeGuin's *The Word for World is Forest* is entirely in keeping. Similarly the resemblance between Manussa and Madras, in an era when all things Raj were fashionable, is interesting.

The bottom line is that if Tom Stoppard had ever written for *Doctor Who*, then he would've come up with something very much like the work of "Bailey".

Barry Letts. Well, the blue crystals were the giveaway, but the evidence was there from "Kinda" onwards.

There was the fact that in *Doctor Who: The Unfolding Text*, "Bailey" and Letts seemed to be in complete accord. "Bailey" derided the use of technobabble; "Bailey" criticised the Doctor's apparent diminution from Wise Old Man to Boy Hero on Jungian grounds; Letts spoke about the use of metaphor in his time as producer, especially in more personal stories like "The Green Death" (10.5) and "Planet of the Spiders" (11.5). In these, greed - including greed for knowledge - was represented by inflated creepy-crawlies (maggots, then spiders). A big pink snake is just the same idea again. The original concept of the Mara, that which is repressed or unfaceable, is there right from the start of "Terror of the Autons" (8.1) with the Doctor's "evil twin" the Master… and we might also remember that the plan had been for the Master to be "reunited" with the Doctor at the end of the Pertwee run, forcing a regeneration into a "new man".

In their final forms, the teleplays for "Kinda" and "Snakedance" are both very efficient in their use of sets, cast and effects, and show an understanding of *Doctor Who*'s specific problems. Saward may have criticised the lack of cliffhangers in "Bailey's" work, but for all we know he was asked to say those things just to maintain the cover story (and anyway, Letts isn't exactly the best at cliffhangers;

continued on page 191…

core, but at the same time the series has traditionally depended on the Doctor methodically figuring out how the worlds he visits are supposed to work (though this idea occasionally gets lost in the '70s, when he knows about almost every planet in the universe before he even arrives). Again, the script of "Snakedance" seems to gel with certain ongoing concerns of the series without apparently meaning to. We're told the Mara was released into the physical universe because of the Manussans' greed for knowledge, mirroring the greed for knowledge which the Doctor himself faces up to in "Planet of the Spiders", as well as the death-by-curiosity which eventually sees off the Fifth Doctor a year later.

What's important to note, though, is that it's the Manussans' desire for self-knowledge which gives rise to the Mara. This is no *Frankenstein* scenario, where science gets its back broken by human curiosity. This is more like the Garden of Eden - another fable referenced in "Kinda", natch - where the Manussans doom themselves simply by coming to understand what lives in the Dark Places of the Inside. But as this is closer to Buddhism than Christianity, the Mara's darkness is an initiation rather than a curse, something you have to get through by finding inner balance rather than something that forces you to live in Original Sin. The message here isn't that it's bad to explore because it might release monsters, but that it's necessary to "realise" monsters in order to become whole.

And not all the mythologies being raided here are so ancient. Parts of the legend of the Mara, especially the beliefs and rituals that have attached themselves to the memory of Lon's ancestor, don't suggest ancient folklore as much as the kind of Von Daniken material we've seen so many times before in this series. The use of technology to manifest "dark" impulses is straight out of *Forbidden Planet*. The showman in the hall of mirrors has been transplanted straight from Tom Stoppard's *Rosencrantz and Guildenstern are Dead* (although much of this could owe to Brian Miller's performance... played another way he could almost sound like Henry Gordon Jago), while the cave-mouth shaped like a snake's head is so reminiscent of the *Star Trek* episode "The Apple" - the one where David Soul actually says 'show me this Earth thing you call "kissing"' - that it's amazing they thought they could get away with it.

There is (again) a lot of "book" SF slopping

around in this story, and if you're looking for major sources then a good case could be made for Vonda McIntyre's *Dreamsnake*, not just for the use of venom as a spur to mental gifts but for the attempt to create a culture around it. And the name "LeGuin", never far from this sort of discussion, has to be mentioned again here... although, like so much in this story, the influence is less to do with specific references than with the whole approach that Bailey seems to be taking. It's the details that most TV writers wouldn't have bothered to include, like the Punch-and-Judy stall.

A lot of people became very heated over the quotations from Eliot's *Four Quartets* when this was broadcast. Bailey is dismissive of this. He's now affecting an "aw, shucks" stance over the impact of his eight broadcast episodes, and claiming that the stories he couldn't quite get to cohere would have been better. In fact, the primary "source" for "Snakedance" is quite simply that: the changes that were made to "Kinda" inspired refinements, and a keenness to make things more televisual (although, in the end, "Snakedance" actually comes across as a lot more *theatrical*).

Things That Don't Make Sense The Mara's claim that it's not repelled by mirrors because it's not trapped in a circle of them is frankly nonsensical; "Kinda" made it clear that the Mara doesn't like reflections because evil can't face itself, so even *one* mirror should make it look away.

Why does Nyssa believe it's 'impossible' for the Doctor's thoughts to make one of the crystals glow, when she's from a planet where the biotechnology makes that sort of thing look humdrum? Why does Chela believe the Doctor's wild tale of the Mara's return, when even to *us* he looks like a raving lunatic? [Chela's a bit of a nutter.] In the Director's collection of antiquities is a headpiece which supposedly represents the Six Faces of Delusion, and he mocks the legends as unreliable as only five faces are visible, so the Doctor has to explain that the sixth face is the face of the wearer. But has *no* historian on the planet noticed this fairly obvious point? Because most of the viewers have spotted it even before the Director's finished his sentence. And why does Lon, son of the Federator, need to have the Great Crystal explained to him?

The Doctor's gizmo shuts out all sound, despite only having one earpiece. Episode four reveals that Manussa has the same standard-issue guards-

Did Kate Bush Really Write This?

...continued from page 189

see "Planet of the Spiders" episode four, "The Daemons" episode three and the whole of the radio dramas "The Paradise of Death" or "The Ghosts of N-Space"). And we also note how each interviewee in the book is cited as supporting the other, conveniently enough.

Everybody knew that Barry Letts was a Buddhist. If they didn't, then they only had to check out his interviews - where he goes on about how he doesn't like to go on about it - or the fan-jokes about "Barry's Buddha Biscuits" (not, as is sometimes reported, his contribution to *The Doctor Who Cookbook*... though naturally, what he *did* submit was in the vegetarian section).

What were the odds that two sincere, practising Buddhists able to write *Doctor-Who*-ish scripts would be involved in the production of the series at roughly the same time? The elements of "Snakedance" most closely resembling "Planet of the Spiders" are less to do with the content than the approach, the use of detailed sound-cues and folklore (as in "The Daemons"), and especially the repeated "sample" mentioned in the **Critique**. This story has Letts' dabs all over it.

Kate Bush. Then at the height of her fame and influence, singer, songwriter and style-icon Bush had reached the point where record companies gave her leeway on the grounds that she was a capital-A "Artist", whose apparent whims all seemed to pan out in sales terms.

After Kate's first single got to number one while she was eighteen, and after she produced a string of hits each apparently less "commercial" than the last, by 1982 it seemed there was nothing she couldn't get away with. Her music videos had gone from straightforward performances with lots of leotard-shots to mini-films, directed or at least conceived by herself, in which she showed off her training in mime under Lindsay Kemp (whose previous rock protégé was David Bowie, so you can see the kind of clout she had).

The videos from the album *The Dreaming* were cryptic and effects-laden, and more by luck than judgement resembled early '80s *Doctor Who*. The title track put her in a lattice of wires and laser-beams (like the hadron web in 19.1, "Castrovalva"), wearing a pressure suit of the exact same make used in the new Cyber-costumes (19.6, "Earthshock"), for a song about colonialism and Australian Aborigines (19.2, "Four to Doomsday",

and of course "Kinda"). This video might explain why no Aborigine dancers were available to film "Four to Doomsday"; she'd grabbed them all. The same video showed what the Plasmatons could have looked like with time, money and a bit of thought (19.7, "Time-Flight").

This isn't saying much that's new. Many videos at the time, and let's remember that most videos were on video at this stage, used the available effects technology. Specifically, Quantel (the image processing system used to "flip" pictures), pixellation (breaking things up into "blocks", as used at the end of "Castrovalva" and to disguise faces on programmes like Cops), front-axial projection (bouncing light straight back at the camera to make a brilliant light appear from something, usually used for "Warriors' Gate"-style blank white voids) and blue-screen.

At that stage everyone was keen to use whatever was new and available, and the cost of this technology came down rapidly, much as morphing and CGI did in later years. However, the connections between odd images were the same in Bush videos as in *Doctor Who*, and presented as a narrative - rather than effects-for-the-sake-of-effects, as in most promos - of the kind her songs had. And the subject matter of her songs isn't exactly "I Wanna Hold Your Hand". Early hits included "Hammer Horror" (guess what that's about), "Breathing" (a foetus contemplates a nuclear war) and debut smasheroo "Wuthering Heights" (again, the clue is in the title). Later on she got a little more left-field. "Certifiably" in the opinion of many.

Exhibit A in this account is Kate's video for "Sat In Your Lap". In this we see a series of extreme close-ups of her right eye, with inserted shots of trickster-figures in jester garb, minotaurs and Klansman-style figures wearing dunce's caps. (These also accompany her while roller-skating on parquet floor, but that isn't really like "Kinda".) The minotaurs later brandish poles wrapped in leaves, like the ones used by Aris and Panna. Kate is trying to get information from a manual, which then flies away from her. There are lots of shots of over-lit figures against a black background, which in many cases are only seen after one of those eye-zooms. The lyrics refer to 'my dome of ivory', things ending and just beginning, having all 'the answers and the quest for knowledge' as a possibly bad thing. 'Empty boxes' and the like are hinted at.

As with most of the videos made in Britain at

continued on page 193...

ABOUT TIME 1980-1984

who-can't-run-after-escaping-prisoners as most other planets these days. The celebration at the cave is the biggest thing happening on the planet and, as the locals apparently rely on tourism to stay solvent, the whole town must have been preparing it for months... so how can Lon suddenly decide that not only is he going to play the Sky Hero, but that he's going to take the morning off and show Ambril some relics, with less than four hours to go? True, Lon's an important aristocrat, but if Prince Charles tried something like that at the State Opening of Parliament then he'd be politely reminded of what happened to his seventeenth-century namesake.

Critique (Prosecution, ish) Okay, there's a dodgy rubber snake involved, but it isn't the crux of the story this time. All right, episode three is mainly the Doctor in a cell, but while he's there he discovers things of interest and doesn't try any stupid time-wasting escapes with Honda trikes. Yes, Nyssa is even more dopey than usual and starts screaming because she knows it's the end of the episode.

But in principle, this is what 1980s-style *Doctor Who* was supposed to be... witty, professional-looking, exciting for kids, intriguing for everyone else and above all thoughtful. Everyone is doing this because they like the script, it seems, and even the set-designers - with a thankless task and no money (see **The Lore**) - put in a bit of thought and effort. None of the characters does quite what you expect, even the regulars, and the locals seem present because it's where they live rather than for plot function purposes. It's customary at this point to single out Martin Clunes, but that's pointless as the story is an ensemble piece throughout. If anyone gets extra credit it's Jonathon Morris, for the thankless task of making Chela more than info-dump boy. His "ooh, you'll cop it when she gets you home" look, when Nyssa rebukes the Doctor in episode four, is priceless.

Surprisingly, there's really only *one* flaw, but it's inherent in the way the Doctor has to learn things he already knew. Bailey was less than happy when a younger, "vulnerable" Doctor replaced Tom Baker. In his view, the Doctor was regressing through Jung's archetypes. Taking this as a starting-point rather than adjusting his script to suit, he wrote the Doctor in "Snakedance" as someone like Todd in 'Kinda", all book-learning and no insight. On its own terms, this works. Had

"Snakedance" been Davison's only story as the Doctor, this would have been just about acceptable. In the context of the other stories, especially those either side where we're supposed to believe that this man is the same person who fought Yeti and was President of the Time Lords, it's awkward. Other stories, especially in the next year, often hint that the baddies can't believe this lad is the all-powerful Doctor. Here, the Doctor doesn't believe it. But Davison himself takes this redefinition of his role as a challenge, and is the dynamo driving the story on. Even in a prison-cell he's vibrant, energetic and driven.

The other odd thing about this production is how the "old-fashioned" elements seem experimental. The use of sound is confident and at times borders on the sort of thing being done in records then. (The repeated sample of Tegan screaming is unlike anything in the series since Tommy's flashbacks in "Planet of the Spiders"... see **Did Kate Bush Really Write This?**). The "ambient" noise of the Janissary Band and stallholders replaces the more conventional music, mercifully. Similarly the main set for the market is so detailed and seen from so many angles that it seems a lot bigger than it must have been (unlike, say, "Castrovalva" or "Terminus"). The fact that the TARDIS is there already and hidden among crates adds a feel of a Hartnell historical to this setting.

It's damning with faint praise to say that this story isn't like "Arc of Infinity" or "Terminus", but it doesn't seem to belong in the same series, let alone the same year. This is "proper" *Doctor Who*. All it needs is the Doctor.

Critique (Defence) Forget the details for a moment. Let's look at what we might call "the big picture".

The very worst of *Doctor Who* fails because it assumes that the stage ends where the studio does, that nobody watching is going to care how the characters got to be where they are or how any world could have ended up looking like the one on the screen. The very best of *Doctor Who* succeeds because you can't quite remember whether you were actually told about the society beyond the edges of the set, or whether you just imagined it. Robert Holmes, for many people the "definitive" *Doctor Who* writer, was a master at suggesting worlds and histories that you never actually got to see. Had he stuck with the programme, Chris Bailey could well have stolen the honours.

Did Kate Bush Really Write This?

...continued from page 191

the time, it has the look of a sixth-form project now, but so does most *Doctor Who* material not shot on location. It also emerged that the costume worn (or nearly worn) for Bush's "Baboushka" video was based on a design by Chris Achilleos, Target cover artist of yore and designer of the "tubular" logo from the early '80s title sequence.

That's about it. The similarities are there, but they're *just* similarities. The lyrics of Bush's album tracks hint at similar concerns to those of "Bailey", but only hint (we're not dealing with the most straightforward songwriter here). Female wisdom is different from male knowledge. Ho-hum. The Vietnam war was a bad thing. You don't say. The joke did the rounds at a convention that Kate Bush wrote "Kinda", and that was an end to it.

Except that a couple of years later Bush delivered her magnum opus, *Hounds of Love*, with a whole side given over to a mini-concept-album and four of the five tracks on side one being singles (the remaining one, "Mother Stands for Comfort", is a bit Hindle-ish… maybe). The title track uses a sample from Jacques Tournier's film *Night of the Demon* - or *Curse of the Demon*, if you're American - a séance featuring the line 'it's in the trees… it's coming!'. But "Cloudbusting" seems to begin with the line 'I still dream of Organon' (see 17.3, "The Creature from the Pit"). The video features Donald Sutherland as a mad scientist and Bush as the child-like daughter, looking uncannily like Carole Ann Ford as Susan (she normally looks like Lucille Ball playing Morticia Addams). The

other tracks were less overt, but there was a lot of UNIT-like material in the "Experiment Four" video.

Then came a report in the *New Musical Express* that Kate's 1989 album was to be called "An Unearthly Child". (It wasn't. It was called *The Sensual World* after the first track, a mazurka based on the end of Joyce's *Ulysses*. Let's see Britney cover *that*.) Meanwhile, it was revealed that the casting of witch-queen Morgaine in "Battlefield" (26.1) had included phone calls to Bush's agent. And then there was the surname chosen for Bonnie Langford's character in Season Twenty-Three.

It all seemed to fit, better than "some bloke at Brighton Polytechnic wrote eight episodes to pay the rent and then disappeared". Kate Bush herself was increasingly reclusive, leading to speculation about what she was up to and the "hidden" meanings in her work. Her fan club easily beats *Doctor Who* fandom for sad obsessiveness, but also rivals it for infiltration into positions of influence, so we'll say no more. The silence only fuelled rumours, and now this one has been the subject of a BBC radio documentary, along with similarly unlikely modern legends like the one about Howard Hughes in a gas depot.

The two fans who started all of this? One fled the country and now pursues a career in a former Soviet nation, while the other has been known to work for Big Finish and was - until recently - *Doctor Who Magazine*'s curious columnist "The Watcher". No wonder he doesn't want anyone finding out who he is.

The trouble is that since 1980, this world-building process has been as much about visual technique as about dialogue. What's remarkable about "Snakedance", with hindsight, is how badly-staged so much of it is. In an era when directors were trying to make every new environment seem sensurround-deep and cinema-dynamic (though not Ron Jones, obviously), Manussa comes across as an awkward pile-up of BBC design work, with internal spaces made out of mismatched left-overs and costumes that occasionally verge on the stylish but more often suggest fashion-victims from another galaxy.

No, wait. That's not entirely fair. This production has been put together like theatre, and to those who'd objected to the overall style of early '80s *Doctor Who*, it must have seemed more "televisual" than anything since the '70s. The market-

place is a poor film-set, but it's an effective stage-set. And this series used to be about stagecraft, not film-making.

So there's a contradiction here, and yet you forget this, utterly. Looking back on it after the fact, Manussa feels like one of the best-developed worlds in the series' history, through the sheer strength of the script and - as a consequence - the sheer strength of performance. For perhaps the very first time, *Doctor Who* gives us the sense that we're looking at a society which has emerged from an ongoing culture, a sense that other civilisations have archaeological layers and there's actually social evolution in this universe. We're looking at a world that's still a work in progress, not a selection of set-pieces. Manussan history has its own eras and empires, and they're not just funny-sounding outer-space names but logically, aesthetically consistent… no, more than that, they're *interesting*. As has already been mentioned, the locals' boredom, sarcasm and forced decorum makes the Doctor seem like a manic, unsettling force even to our eyes, so this time we're made to feel like outsiders rather than casual spectators.

This means the script can pull off the ultimate *Doctor Who* trick. For years, this series has been taking familiar monsters from mythology and making them part of the *Doctor Who* universe. "Snakedance" takes a familiar monster from the *Doctor Who* universe and makes it feel like mythology. Somebody *else's* mythology, as it happens. In doing this, it gets closer to the series' brief of showing its audience the Other Man's Point of View than just about any other story. Bailey's "controversial" use of Davison's Doctor is ideal for this. To say that it clashes with the other stories of the era, because the Doctor "knows nothing", misses the point; he knows nothing about *Manussa*. This version of the character has to start with a blank slate on every world he visits. Unlike every other version since the '60s, he has no central "databank" to put him in a position of authority, nothing to fall back on except basic principles. And quite right too.

Of course, this kind of story should be too big for "cheap" TV. It obviously wants to show us huge, bustling, carnival-time bazaars, but a BBC studio with a few extras is the best it can manage. The boring old corridors are, once again, *just* boring old corridors. Wisely, both Bailey and director Fiona Cumming deal with this by playing up the aforementioned "theatre" angle, and fortunately almost all the actors are up to Shakesperian standard. In fact, if you're looking for a noticeable flaw then it's that this is clearly a three-act play, not a four-part adventure. As with "The Keeper of Traken", it's prone to drag while all the pieces are being assembled for the last episode, and as with "Traken" you're reminded that the programme really has changed since the days when an episode or two of padding was all part of the process.

Yet it seems almost rude to point this out. The story's trying to present us with the rise and fall of the Manussan and Sumaran empires on a limited budget and in a limiting format, to give us the *I, Claudius* of a parallel universe. Throughout there's the sense of a writer who's already "got it" after only two scripts, a writer who just wants to tell an intelligent, engaging story and doesn't feel the desperate need to impress anyone. The result is

another reinvention of the *Doctor Who* of the past, but this time turning the programme's "standards" inside-out instead of going for something wilfully traditional. Leaving aside the obvious similarities to "Planet of the Spiders", perhaps the best way of thinking of "Snakedance" - as Tegan finds herself possessed by a worryingly masculine entity, one that's determined to give itself form again and return to the planet it very nearly destroyed - is to imagine what "The Hand of Fear" would have been like had it done everything *right*.

The Facts

Written by Christopher Bailey. Directed by Fiona Cumming. Viewing figures: 6.7 million, 7.7 million, 6.6 million, 7.4 million.

Supporting Cast Martin Clunes (Lon), Collete O'Neil (Tanha), John Carson (Ambril), Jonathon Morris (Chela), Preston Lockwood (Dojjen), Brian Miller (Dugdale), Hilary Sesta (Fortune Teller), Barry Smith (Puppeteer).

Oh, Isn't That..?
• *Martin Clunes.* Well, we've already dealt with him.
• *Brian Miller.* He used to be "that bloke who hangs about in the bar at conventions", but Elisabeth Sladen's husband finally gets a speaking part here. Later on, he'll do Dalek voices as well.
• *Jonathon Morris.* A child actor in the very odd sitcom *That Beryl Marston* (featuring Gareth Hunt from *The New Avengers* and 11.5, "Planet of the Spiders"). Later he'd be a regular in whinging Liverpudlian sitcom *Bread*, and appear on umpteen game-shows.

Working Titles "Snake-Dance", "Snake Dance". To be pedantic.

Cliffhangers The Mara finally takes hold of Tegan in the fortune-teller's tent, and the crystal ball reveals the image of a snake's skull before exploding; down in the caves, evil Tegan forces the showman to look into her glowing red eyes; cornering the Doctor and party in a corridor, Lon orders the guards to kill them (this involves the ominous drawing of swords).

The Lore

• Once again, the names are significant. Dojjen is based on Dogen (see 5.2, "The Abominable Snowmen"), the monk who advocated a "right-to-die" policy for boddhisattvas. *Manussa* is Pali, and refers to the everyday, material realm (we hesitate to say "The Sensual World", but see the essay). *Duggati*, the dissatisfaction with direction of life, becomes "Dugdale"; one report claims he was originally called "Duchan", which is a Hebrew pulpit, but this makes less sense. *Chela* means "apprentice", and is the term the Old Man uses to refer to the young protagonist in Kipling's novel about India, Kim. Keeping it multi-faith, *Tanha* is another term for the desperate need for fulfilment, this time Aramaic.

• A third script, "The Children of Seth", was submitted by Bailey and commissioned for the Sixth Doctor before the author gave up on the idea. It was Mara-free and set in a society based on the Byzantine court. This time, the writer had trouble figuring out how to get a monster into it. Or a plot, characters or themes. Saward was still very enthusiastic. (Incidentally, this isn't the same as Bailey's reported rejected script, variously called "May Time" and "Man-Watch".)

• The set for Lon's room was based around a staircase reclaimed from *A Song for Europe*. (We could explain what this is for non-European readers, but you'd lose any respect for the UK you might still have left.) The same source supplied much of Ambril's office. As this had been envisioned as the "cheap" story of the season, much of the rest was based around three main sets and the TARDIS interior.

• Jonathon Morris (Chela) had caught Nathan-Turner's eye when co-starring with Tom Baker in the play *Feasting with Panthers*, about Oscar Wilde. Another future almost-star is Bob Mills, who's made two separate attempts at cloning *Larry Sanders* for British TV as well as fronting the ITV show *In Bed with Me Dinner*. Here he's Lon's bodyguard, but he's added some weight since then.

• A lot of juicy stuff went missing when this story was edited for broadcast. Unlike "Kinda" it's not really important to the plot, but it would have been nice. Tanha's comment, on hearing that Ambril never married (there's a surprise!), is that children can be a let-down. Tegan asks why they couldn't have destroyed the Mara earlier (this conversation eventually takes place in the console room at the start of the next story, where it seems

terribly out of place). The ceremony has a more elaborate build-up, with a longer scene for the megaphone man.

Above all, the story carries on beyond its conclusion with everyone apologising to the Doctor and asking his advice. Terrance Dicks re-integrated much of this into his novelisation, but not all. However, the scene featuring the 'attendant demon' was amalgamated out of two separate scenes, and seems to work better as broadcast.

20.3: "Mawdryn Undead"

(Serial 6F, Four Episodes, 1st February - 9th February 1983.)

Which One is This? Men in robes glide around the outer-space *Queen Mary* with their brains hanging out; the Doctor picks up a nice public school boy; and there's on-screen confirmation of what we've suspected for years, when the Brigadier arrives and an alien scientist proclaims: 'This one is a deviant!'

Firsts and Lasts The beginning of yet another trilogy, this one about the Black Guardian placing his agent on board the TARDIS and repeatedly failing to kill the Doctor. This means it's the first appearance of Mark Strickson as Turlough, and after this brief period as a would-be assassin he's destined to spend another year on board the TARDIS.

This is also Nicholas Courtney's first outing as the "old" Brigadier Lethbridge-Stewart, now retired after the UNIT days of the '70s and working as a teacher at a boarding school for boys. (If this seems an unlikely career move, then there's a reason for it. The story was originally written with ageing schoolteacher Ian Chesterton as the token returning companion, but in the end the Brigadier got dragged back into the fray instead. He turns up again in 20.7, "The Five Doctors" and 26.1, "Battlefield".) Actually, this is the first and only story to credit him as just "The Brigadier".

It's explicitly, irrevocably, categorically stated that the Brigadier retired from UNIT before 1977, finally proving that the UNIT stories are set in the 1970s. No, really.

Four Things to Notice About "Mawdryn Undead"...

1. As with "Arc of Infinity", you have to wonder if this era's reliance on "old" *Doctor Who* continuity is starting to affect the writers' judgement. Here

the audience is expected to understand the nuances of regeneration, remember who the Brigadier is and accept the Black Guardian as the black-hat wants-to-kill-the-Doctor figure without a proper re-introduction. To make things even more complicated for casual viewers, the story's split over two interconnected time-zones, there's a big montage of old black-and-white clips in episode two and Turlough is introduced as an alien staying at an English public school as if such a thing were a perfectly normal part of television drama. The third cliffhanger, in which the Doctor broadly exclaims 'it'll be the end of me as a Time Lord!' if he helps the degenerated Mawdryn (without explaining why), would presumably be of no interest to non-fans whatsoever and may rank as one of the least dramatic in the programme's history. Surely, no newcomer to the series would understand a word of this…?[10]

2. Still, this use of the *Doctor Who* canon provides at least one interesting twist: this is the only story to feature a mis-identified regeneration, apt in an era when *everybody's* supposed to take the "standards" of the series for granted. When Tegan and Nyssa find a horribly burned figure in the transmat capsule used by the Doctor, they assume it *is* the Doctor, and when the man heals himself (and looks like a complete stranger) they assume the Doctor must just have changed form again. Sadly, this is rather brought down by the limits of BBC make-up, as the features of the horribly burned Mawdryn are still quite visible and don't look anything at all like those of Peter Davison.

3. The Black Guardian tries to convince Turlough to kill the Doctor by claiming that the *Doctor's* the evil one, but then enjoys shouting things like 'in the name of all that is evil, the Black Guardian orders you to destroy him now!' when Turlough's close to his target. Some people just can't hold it in.

4. Just to get across the point that this is a return to the good old days, Tegan gets to call the Brigadier a chauvinist. Spirit of '74. (Not that running into an all-male environment in a basque and lace shorts was such a "right-on" move in the first place.)

The Continuity

The Doctor Reasons, correctly, that some cosmic force must be behind the extraordinary chain of coincidences going on here. [Although it's funny how he only notices this when there *is* a cosmic force behind the coincidences, as he never objected to the events of 20.1, "Arc of Infinity".] The Doctor confirms that he can only regenerate twelve times, and overtly states that he's done it four times already. Both he and Mawdryn believe that he'll cease being a Time Lord if he uses up all his regenerations. [Meaning, a Time Lord ceases to be a Time Lord when he or she reaches the thirteenth and final body? If so, it might explain why the Master is always confused about whether he qualifies as a Time Lord or not.]

The Doctor doesn't need much convincing to allow Turlough to join the TARDIS crew, even though he's obviously suspicious of the lad from the outset, noting the schoolboy's knowledge of alien technology but regrettably not questioning Turlough's "evil" communications crystal. [The Doctor may be suffering Adric-guilt of some description.] At the start of events, very little time has passed since the Doctor left Manussa as Tegan's still whining about the Mara.

• *Ethics.* He's unwilling to give up his future regenerations in order to end the suffering of Mawdryn and the other mutants, although typically he agrees to do it when Tegan and Nyssa need help as well.

The Supporting Cast

• *Nyssa.* She's changed her outfit again [months spent in one costume, and suddenly she's got fashion sense]. She thinks Turlough seems 'rather nice', so her instincts aren't the best.

• *Tegan.* Still having terrible dreams about the Mara, although it's just her mind's way of dealing with events. She already wants to go back to Earth, but only for a rest. Strangely, she says she hates transmats, even though she's never been seen to encounter one in her travels with the Doctor. [An unseen adventure, possibly. Lance Parkin's novel *Cold Fusion* is set during Season Nineteen and has Tegan using transmats, although this volume wouldn't dare to suggest that Parkin devised the entire plot simply to justify one line in a TV script.] Unlike Nyssa, she immediately distrusts Turlough.

• *Turlough.* A student at Brendon boys' school, and apparently supposed to be in his late teens, Turlough is selfish, weasely, cunning and has no apparent concern for anyone else. In fact, he's just in a perpetually bad mood because he hates it here, "here" meaning Earth. Turlough's planet of origin isn't disclosed here [for that we have to wait until 21.5, "Planet of Fire"], and nor is it clear how he ended up in England.

Officially his parents are dead, and the school deals with a 'very strange' solicitor in London [this also comes up in "Planet of Fire"]. He can drive, but doesn't have a license and doesn't even like cars. He knows an awful lot about transmats, time differentials and other such odd science, though he can't work out how to steer the TARDIS. [Later we learn that his first name is "Vislor", but it's doubtful whether he's using this at the school.]

Agreeing to help the Black Guardian - after some coercion, it's got to be said - he agrees to kill the Doctor, though he's not sure he can do it and he obviously fails in his mission here [later events suggest that his conscience might be holding him back]. He seems to believe the Guardian's claim that the Doctor is one of the most evil creatures in the universe, at least for now. He boards the Ship with nothing more than his school uniform [which he keeps wearing throughout his travels, improbably].

• *The Brigadier.* Brigadier Alistair Gordon Lethbridge-Stewart is seen here in two time-zones. In 1977, still sporting his moustache, he's retired from UNIT and has recently found a job as a mathematics teacher at Brendon School. Getting mixed up in the Doctor's adventures again, he ultimately makes contact with his future-self, and the resulting burst of energy makes him black out. He's returned to Earth, but the shock causes a state of amnesia that blots out his memory of the Doctor and the TARDIS even though he remembers UNIT. By the 1980s he believes this to have been a nervous breakdown. [So he may just have "forgotten" the hard-to-accept parts of his life like aliens and time-travellers, and probably remembers UNIT as being a fairly standard security organisation.]

This means that when the Brigadier meets the Doctor in 1983, he has no idea who the Doctor is, even apart from the regeneration. By this point the Brigadier doesn't have the moustache, and is less likely to dress in formal blazers. He remembers Sergeant Benton and Harry Sullivan, but mention of the Doctor's companions starts to bring it all flooding back, even if memories of the events which caused the amnesia remain hazy. The suggestion that he might need treatment still makes him angry and paranoid. After he touches his past-self, though, he comes round feeling better than he's felt for six years.

In 1983, the Brigadier states that he left UNIT seven years earlier [he was still in service in "The Android Invasion" (13.5), which most probably took place in 1976, but there's no indication as to what made him quit]. He claims that he's seen regeneration happen twice before [meaning that he's seen the *effects* of regeneration twice before, as he wasn't around when the Second Doctor became the Third]. He speaks of 'thirty years' of soldiering [1946-76?], and still has a photo of himself in UNIT uniform [by the look of it from 8.3, "The Claws of Axos", an action shot rather than a portrait]. He also owns a vintage car from the '20s, which Turlough writes off. He likes teaching, and he's CO in the school corps.

• *Harry Sullivan.* According to the Brigadier's reminiscences, the Doctor's old part-time companion was seconded to NATO and is now doing something hush-hush at Porton Down. [This is a real place, the MoD's biological research station. These days it's mainly used for researching possible antidotes to biological and chemical weapons, they tell us.]

• *Sergeant Benton.* Another Brigadier recollection… Benton left the army in 1979, and started selling second-hand cars for a living. The Brigadier's amnesia apparently covers Benton's first name and promotion [12.1, "Robot", et seq].

The TARDIS Heading for Earth, the TARDIS suffers a nasty jolt which the Doctor attributes to the 'warp ellipse cut-out', meaning that the TARDIS is near an object in a fixed orbit in both time and space. Nyssa thinks the odds of this [occurring naturally] are several billion to one against.

Materialising in space, the TARDIS is nearly hit by Mawdryn's vessel, and it can't escape because of the warp ellipse. It's all the Doctor can do to materialise on board the ship. The Black Guardian implies he's responsible for the Doctor running into the ellipse, though it's not clear how. [The Guardian seems to suggest that he can affect probability in some way, and a naturally-occurring ellipse is described as *unlikely* rather than impossible, so he may be responsible for the ellipse's existence.]

The TARDIS can't dematerialise from the ship when the vessel's transmat beam is active, as the interior of the capsule is 'dimensionally very similar' to the TARDIS. Coming out of the warp ellipse, the Ship tries to land in 1983 but ends up in 1977 instead, which has something to do with the transmat's beam transmitter blowing up and the Doctor miscalculating the offset. Later the TARDIS can't get away from the ellipse without moving backwards or forwards through time, the Doctor pointing out that it takes cunning navigation and a temporal deviation to get away. An alarm sounds on the TARDIS console whenever anyone tries to use the transmat beam on Mawdryn's ship.

As Mawdryn knows, activating 'sequential regression' on the TARDIS console takes the Ship back to his vessel in orbit, so there's no need to enter new co-ordinates. [In other words, there's a switch on the console that makes the TARDIS return to the last place it came from. This must be a reasonably new or recently-repaired feature, or the Doctor would have had no trouble getting Ian and Barbara home in Season One. See "The Edge of Destruction" (1.3) for the nearest thing to this in the 1960s.] Tegan takes a homing device with her when she leaves the Ship. [Adric apparently lost his in 19.4, "The Visitation", so the Doctor may have a spare.] It's apparently in the possession of the Brigadier by the end of the story [but see **Things That Don't Make Sense**]. The atmosphere inside the TARDIS helps Mawdryn to stabilise after his regeneration, even though the Ship no longer has a zero room, and the Fourth Doctor's coat is still somewhere around the console room as Mawdryn briefly tries it on.

More rules of time-travel: when two versions of the same person meet, e.g. the Brigadier from 1977 and the Brigadier from 1983, there's a massive burst of energy as they short out the 'time differential'. No further explanation is given, though the Doctor describes this as the Blinovitch Limitation Effect. [Comparison with 9.1, "Day of the Daleks", suggests this is just *part* of the Blinovitch Limitation Effect. See the essay.] The Doctor claims, with maddening vagueness, that when Brigadiers clash the energy released comes from the TARDIS. [As the agency of time-travel which created the 'time differential' in the first place? Apparently by chance, the Brigadiers meet at exactly the right millisecond to save the Doctor. Given the Black Guardian's "arrangement" of probability here, is this really blind luck? Or is the White Guardian getting involved as well, as he does in "Enlightenment" (20.5)?]

The Black Guardian describes the co-existence of the Brigadiers as 'forbidden' [so it breaks rules that even *he* has to obey]. The Doctor believes that as the Brigadier is safe in 1983, nothing bad could

have happened to his 1977 self [an optimistic view, at odds with what we learn in stories like 13.3, "Pyramids of Mars"].

The Guardians

• *The Black Guardian.* Proud to call himself evil. After a car crash knocks Turlough unconscious, the boy has an out-of-body experience, his mind encountering the Black Guardian somewhere strange and hallucinatory. The Black Guardian hasn't changed much since he last bothered the Doctor [16.6, "The Armageddon Factor"], but he's now wearing a crow on his head as part of his costume.

It's naturally the Guardian's aim to kill the Doctor or at the very least to humiliate him by robbing him of his Time Lord status, so he promises Turlough a way of escaping Earth if the boy acts as his agent. [It's strange, perhaps, that he hasn't acted before now. Presumably he's been keeping track of the Doctor ever since the randomiser was removed from the TARDIS in 18.1, "The Leisure Hive".] The Black Guardian uses Turlough as a potential assassin because he personally can't be seen to have a hand in the Doctor's death. [So somebody's watching, but doesn't spot the Black Guardian's obvious influence over Turlough?]

When Turlough's mind returns to Earth after his encounter with the Guardian, a transparent crystal is found in his pocket, which glows when it's held in his hands and allows him to hear the Guardian's voice. Sometimes the Guardian even appears next to him, and the crystal can stick to Turlough's hand to stop him getting rid of it. The Guardian appears to have mild mesmeric powers when convincing Turlough to do his bidding, as well as the ability to enter Turlough's dreams. The crystal is eventually cracked, so Turlough believes he's free of the Guardian's influence [he's proved wrong in the next story].

The Non-Humans

• *Mawdryn.* Orbiting Earth in both 1977 and 1983 is a spaceship of unknown origin, a plushly-furnished but seemingly-deserted craft with an elegant crimson exterior, all smooth arcs and sharp edges. The interior has apparently been designed for pleasure, but nobody's enjoying themselves here, because sleeping the years away on board are Mawdryn and his seven colleagues. They're basically humanoid, but appear old and

What *is* the Blinovitch Limitation Effect?

The obvious answer is "a really convenient plot device", but let's try to be more specific.

The Blinovitch Limitation Effect - just "Blinovitch" for short - is first mentioned in "Day of the Daleks" (9.1), where it immediately gains a reputation for covering awkward time-travel problems with the minimum of actual logic. Discovering that guerrillas from the future have come back to the present to change their past, Jo Grant asks the Doctor why these people don't just use their time machines to change the outcome of every bad day they ever have. As producer Barry Letts pointed out, this is a good question as it blows a hole in every *Doctor Who* story ever written, or at least every story where the Doctor has a properly-functioning TARDIS at his disposal. But the Doctor replies that the guerrillas can't do that, because of the Blinovitch Limitation Effect. Then one of the goons interrupts him before he can explain the details.

The key word here is "Limitation". Contrary to what fan-lore has claimed since "Mawdryn Undead", there's *no* suggestion in the "Day of the Daleks" scene that Blinovitch is something that stops people meeting themselves. Indeed, the Doctor meets himself in "Day of the Daleks" and has no problems at all. The Limitation Effect, in this version of things, is something which *limits* interference in the past... apparently one's *own* past. In the case of "Day of the Daleks" the suggestion seems to be that the guerrillas can only have one shot at changing their history, and can't keep messing around with the details. (Which might explain why time-travelling types like the Daleks and the Cybermen will occasionally make a token effort to change history, but won't take a second crack at it once they fail.)

This is backed up by Barry Letts' later radio script "The Paradise of Death", in which the Doctor explicitly tells the Brigadier that he can easily take the TARDIS to another planet and make it land ten minutes before it took off, because the Blinovitch Limitation Effect only stops you interfering in your own past. How this is supposed to work remains vague. The suggestion may be that it's possible to push history, a little, but that if you push too hard then it'll blow up in your face. This at least chimes with what the Doctor says in "Time-Flight" (19.7), about not being able to go back in time and save Adric because there are some rules he can't break even with the TARDIS.

It's not until "Mawdryn Undead", more than a decade after "Day of the Daleks", that the idea

emerges of Blinovitch being something which stops you encountering yourself. The two Brigadiers touch each other, and the result is a massive burst of energy, described by the Doctor as a shorting-out of the time differential. Weird in itself, if aesthetically fitting, but it also seems to contradict the "Day of the Daleks" version. Jo, remember, asked what was to stop the guerrillas going twenty-four hours back in time and altering anything that might have gone wrong. The "Mawdryn" version of Blinovitch wouldn't stop this sort of interference, since a time-travelling guerrilla wouldn't have to touch him- or herself in order to change things, but just issue a verbal warning along the lines of 'no, back Greece in Euro 2004'. Ergo, we have to conclude that the problem with manhandling other versions of yourself is just *part* of the Effect, not the entirety of it.

But both of these aspects of Blinovitch, the one about not changing your own past and the one about not touching yourself - no sniggering at the back, Atkins - have one thing in common. They both seem to imply that the universe is in some way *conscious*. Or at least, that consciousness is an important part of its structure. This may mean that the idea of history being somehow "active" (as in Season One... see **Can You Change History, Even One Line?** under 1.6, "The Aztecs") isn't as far out of line with current thinking as it may seem.

When the Brigadier touches his former self, time reacts badly and there's a big bang. Why? It *can't* be a simple, physical law of nature that causes this. Consider for a moment. Every cell in the human body dies and is replaced after nine years, and in most cases sooner than that. No human being is the same individual s/he was a day ago, but a completely different selection of atoms which just happens to have the same shape and similar memories. Even having breakfast changes us molecularly; that is, after all, what "life" is. We can recognise people we haven't seen in years, just because of the way our brains are wired, but can the universe "identify" any given person? Can it look at a face and know what (or who) that face is supposed to represent? Can it even distinguish between a lump of atoms that we perceive as a human being, and a lump of atoms that we perceive as a big rock? No, of course it can't. To us, the two Brigadiers are clearly the same individual. To the laws of physics, they're no different from any other particles. Yet the continuum itself objects

continued on page 201...

199

grizzled, and seem to have their brains bulging out of the tops of their heads. Their robes are at the more extreme end of alien fashions, and they describe themselves as scientists, with no weapons. [The script calls them "Kastrons", while the credits just call them "mutants".]

Mawdryn possesses a metamorphic symbiosis regenerator, stolen from Gallifrey. The Time Lords use the regenerator in times of acute regenerative crisis, and the device features a central control section surrounded by seats for its users. [Time Lords are obviously paranoid about regenerative crises. They could also use a zero room (19.1, "Castrovalva") or the elixir of Karn (13.5, "The Brain of Morbius").] Mawdryn and his cronies tinkered with the regenerator in order to extend their lifespans, but it just induced a perpetual mutation. This means they can't die, and are doomed to spend their endless lives in agony, the Doctor describing them as 'undead'.

Exiled by the elders of their homeworld due to their horribleness, they feel as if they've been abandoned by the Time Lords and are now looking for help. Mawdryn even has dreams of becoming a Time Lord himself. [Their world isn't named on screen, but it seems to be a planet that's had "official" relations with the Time Lords. At a stretch, it could be Minyos (15.5, "Underworld"), as the Minyans also had access to regenerative equipment. But if it's a world we've heard of before then it's much more likely to be Drornid (17.6, "Shada"). Again, the script calls their world "Kastron".]

After his regeneration Mawdryn hooks himself up to the machine to stabilise his shape, which is liable to change otherwise. The mutants soon degenerate after a regeneration anyway, becoming old and mutated even within the beneficial atmosphere of the TARDIS, and centuries of research have failed to find a remedy for their condition.

Every seventy years the 'beacon' [on board the vessel?] guides the ship to within transmat distance of a planet, and - drawing on the mental energy of the other seven - one of the mutants takes on the appearance of a native of that planet, then goes looking for help [compare with **How Does Regeneration Work?** under 18.7, "Logopolis"]. Their ship is presently in a warp ellipse around Earth. [There's a hint that the ellipse is a "natural" phenomenon, or at least, one engineered by the Black Guardian's juggling of probability. It *could* feasibly be part of the ship's navigational system, as it waits for Mawdryn to return from Earth, but there's no other indication that the ship has built-in time-travel capability.]

By now the ship's been in flight for 3,000 years, and help hasn't turned up so far. It's equipped with a transmat terminal that can send a spherical capsule down to Earth and bring it back again, and in 1983 Turlough finds the pod hidden behind a camouflage screen in the woods not far from Brendon school. It's next to a monument, and the camouflage vanishes when Turlough presses the base of an urn, where there's a beam transmitter device that sends the transmat signal to the spaceship [see **Things That Don't Make Sense**]. The ship's orbit in the warp ellipse takes it within transmat range of Earth every six years, and when Mawdryn uses it to get to Earth in 1977 he's horribly blackened and burned by some kind of transmat fault. 'Perpetual regeneration' soon turns him back into his usual mutant self. The transmat capsule is bigger on the inside than on the outside [more technology nicked from the Time Lords?].

While in Mawdryn's company, Nyssa and Tegan become contaminated by his mutational pattern, a viral side-effect of the mutants' experiments. It's stated as happening when they pull him from the transmat capsule, unconscious, but Mawdryn expects it. This seems unavoidable, even though he claims it's not deliberate. This prevents them travelling through time in the TARDIS, as the virus advances the degeneration and they instantly become old and diseased, much like Mawdryn himself. After the Doctor reverses the polarity of the neutron flow on board the TARDIS, the same procedure turns Nyssa and Tegan into children instead. [Compare with the suspect time-tricks in "The Time Monster" (9.5), "City of Death" (17.2), "The Leisure Hive" (18.1) and many, many more.] Travelling back to the starting-point restores them, although there's no easy cure.

When the Doctor finally agrees to help them, Mawdryn's gang hook themselves up to the regenerator and prepare to use the Doctor's bodily energies to allow them to die. Each mutant cured by this method will "use up" one of the Doctor's eight remaining regenerations. [The Black Guardian wants to humiliate the Doctor, and there *happens* to be the right number of mutants on board to drain all the Doctor's regenerations. Again, this suggests that the Guardian may be playing with probability, arranging coincidences rather than

What *is* the Blinovitch Limitation Effect?

...continued from page 199

when they touch. How does it know?

Well, it's the same consciousness in each Brigadier. Which is to say, there's a *continuity* of consciousness between the two, at least from his own point of view. We should by now be familiar with the idea that teeny-tiny quantum effects are, to an extent, shaped by the presence of a conscious observer. When we observe an event, all the possible outcomes are collapsed down into one *definite* version of that event. Let's gloss over the question of where you draw the line between one consciousness and another, because that's a big question even for the experts.

The point is that if this quantum version of the universe is "true", then putting the same consciousness in two places at once is obviously going to cause trouble. There may be some form of energy release associated with the possibilities collapsing into a certainty, but not in a way that Earth's present science can identify. Maybe, and we'll put this no more strongly, this is the mysterious 'artron' energy which seems to be connected with consciousness (14.3, "The Deadly Assassin"), magnetism (19.2, "Four to Doomsday"), regeneration and the TARDIS itself (see also **How Does Regeneration Work?** under 18.7, "Logopolis" and **What Makes TARDISes Work?** under 1.3, "The Edge of Destruction"). This could explain why K'anpo closely associates regenerating and leaving Gallifrey without a TARDIS (11.5, "Planet of the Spiders"), and why the Doctor's three "unplanned" jaunts without the Ship seem to wind up in odd

extra-dimensional places (7.4, "Inferno"; 9.5, "The Time Monster"; and debatably 6.2, "The Mind Robber").

The same kind of problem applies to the idea that Blinovitch can prevent somebody interfering in their own timeline. How does the universe "know"? When it comes down to it, where's the line drawn? Any event in the universe can, ultimately, affect any other event. Mess around in the history of a world on the other side of the galaxy, and sooner or later you're likely to impact on your own past. It's as if there's supposed to be some great eye looking down on creation, making value-judgements as to which interventions are acceptable and which are breaking the rules.

An "eye", did we say? Oh dear. You can see where this is going. Since there's no clear indication of a definitive God in the *Doctor Who* universe (let alone one who takes an interest in temporal theory), and since there's no indication that the universe is one big thinking, feeling entity in itself, we have to bring in the usual suspects. In these volumes we've already suggested that the Time Lords might be responsible for the nature of evolution throughout the universe, and for the fact that there's such a proliferation of English-like languages. But if the structure of time implies some form of sentience, then the Time Lords obviously look like the guilty ones... although see **What Do the Guardians Do?** under 16.1, "The Ribos Operation", for some ideas about even higher orders of creation.

continued on page 203...

acting overtly.] In the end, however, the meeting of the Brigadier's two selves provides the energy that completes the process. Even though the Brigadier isn't hooked up to anything. The mutants die in peace, and the ship dies with them, coming out of orbit and auto-destructing [it depends on their mental energies]. Nyssa and Tegan are cured by the same procedure, sharing in the Doctor's 'life-force'. [If the mutants need the Doctor's personal energy rather than any other kind, but the zap from the two Brigadiers works just as well, it suggests some organic aspect to the energy from the time differential.]

History

• *Dating*. The 7th of June, 1977; and early 1983, 'almost' six years later. In 1977, bunting

and flags are being put up at Brendon school to mark the Queen's Silver Jubilee.

The Brigadier believes that if the Doctor's aware of UNIT's existence, then he must have signed the Official Secrets Act. [His amnesia's really playing tricks on him. In the '70s *everyone* knew about UNIT, even if few people knew what it really did.]

The Analysis

Where Does This Come From? Like "Arc of Infinity", it's another script that comes out of a specific brief. The producers needed an introduction for Turlough, to replace "Space Whale" (see **The Lore**, and **What Else Wasn't Made?** under 17.6, "Shada"). Grimwade took elements of his own unhappy schooldays and recycled a bit from

ABOUT TIME 1980-1984

novelist John Le Carré, and put it into a story intended to explain whatever happened to Ian Chesterton. The public school material is pretty much off-the-shelf[11].

Continuity issues aside, two main sources are coming through here. The first is the legend of the *Flying Dutchman*, and more specifically Wagner's opera on the subject. The story, of a ghost-ship that's doomed to sail around the Cape of Good Hope for all eternity after its captain swears a blasphemous oath, has been understandably popular with SF authors over the years and has been recycled by other *Doctor Who* writers on at least two occasions (firstly for a comic strip in *Doctor Who Weekly* in 1980, in more recent years for the BBC novel *Vanderdeken's Children*).

Certain people involved with early '80s *Doctor Who* had an interest in introducing these grandiose operatic themes to the series - see **The Lore**, but more importantly see the next story, "Terminus" - and here the *Dutchman* myth manifests in exactly the way you'd expect it. This is SF, so obviously the ship has to be a spaceship. This is *Doctor Who*, so obviously its never-ending voyage has to involve some sort of time-warp effect. It's the 1980s, so obviously the ship is a luxury cruise-liner and not a lost colony vessel... which is what it inevitably would have been if this script had been written in 1977. Just to push home the point that this is a thoroughly modern retelling of the story, video games are shown among the in-flight entertainments, the first time such things have made their presence felt in the *Doctor Who* universe. But at least "Mawdryn Undead" is closer to the spirit of the original than most outer-space renderings, with Mawdryn's people committing the closest thing to blasphemy in *Doctor Who* by profaning the ways of the Time Lords.

Yet one strand a lot of people miss is the idea Wagner took from gloomy nineteenth-century philosopher Arthur Schopenhauer, that the "kernel" of the soul - the Will - is eternal and has no interaction with the outside universe. The mind may experience time passing, the body may get old, but the Will is just along for the ride. The path is pre-determined; the Will experiences it as a journey. Seen in this light, the oddities of the script start to fall into place. Mawdryn needs to be re-joined to time in order to die. Nyssa and Tegan, imprisoned by the viral infection, have their bodies mutated or made childish whilst still knowing where they are and who the Doctor is (c.f. 18.1

"The Leisure Hive"). Randomness exists, yet it can be controlled by cosmic forces like the Black Guardian and turned into a kind of "fate", so nothing's really a coincidence. It may contradict much of the rest of the series, but it's at least consistent with the vision of an "immutable" history in Season One.

The other source, and one that almost as many people miss, is farce. These days, comedy writers tend to see farce as something of an embarrassment - although Steven Moffat, one of the script-writers on the 2005 series of *Doctor Who*, seems determined to keep the form alive - but there was a time when stories about hiding prostitutes from visiting vicars were a staple of both comic theatre and British sitcom. And it's a law of farce that there are always at least two characters who absolutely mustn't be allowed to meet, or hilarious social awkwardness will ensue. See where this is going? Much of episode four of "Mawdryn Undead" is written and staged as a farce, in which various characters wander around the ship's corridors and nearly-but-not-quite bump into each other. This being a sci-fi production, of course, things are taken to extremes and the two characters who mustn't meet turn out to be the same person. In parts it looks like the time-travelling version of *'Allo 'Allo*.

But in other ways "Mawdryn Undead" sees *Doctor Who* becoming more serial-like / soap-like than ever. The Black Guardian isn't a proper villain here, but an ongoing concern. Then there's Turlough, who's introduced in episode one as an alien schoolboy stranded on Earth, but whose nature or origin is never explained. More than that, it isn't even treated as a mystery; it's taken for granted that if the audience is introduced to a new character with a complex origin (well, a more complex origin than most of the regulars, anyway) then the viewers will just accept it as part of a long-term plan and won't find it at all strange. These days we're more familiar with this sort of thing from programmes like *Buffy the Vampire Slayer*, but even by *Buffy* standards Turlough's arrival is remarkably casual. He's set up as an extra-terrestrial with a single bleated line ('I hate Earth!'), and even the Doctor never bothers to ask probing questions.

We mentioned elements of Le Carré, and the reason's simple. In any Grimwade story, the most immediate sources are likely to be anything else he'd ever worked on as a director or a PA. And in

What *is* the Blinovitch Limitation Effect?

...continued from page 201

The Blinovitch Limitation Effect starts to look like a safeguard, a defence mechanism bound into the nature of things by the Gallifreyans of ye olden days, a way to stop people tampering with causality so severely that the whole structure of history becomes untenable. And the explosion of Brigadiers starts to look like one of the quirks of the process, a side-effect of making consciousness such a big part of the continuum's make-up. Some have argued that the Gallifreyan "noosphere" suggested in "Frontios" (21.3) is connected to the fact that Rassilon appears to have been dead but conscious since the Dawn of Time, and that he'll remain conscious until some point in the distant future of the Time Lords, meaning that his continuous observation is the only thing binding the cosmic order together (see 20.7, "The Five Doctors"). But as we all know, at the centre of Time Lord society is the *Eye* of Harmony, and just to underline the point it's buried in a chamber called the Panopticon. The implication that this is the eye which sees all things, which does the duty of an ever-watchful God and keeps space-time in check just by observing it, is difficult to avoid. If nothing else then this at least begins to explain the otherwise-baffling chronic hysteresis in "Meglos" (18.2), a time-loop which seems to watch what people are doing in order to check whether it's been broken or not.

The other question raised by all of this is who the hell Blinovitch was. On-screen, no details of his career have been forthcoming. The New Adventures have insisted on giving him a Christian name ("Aaron", for obvious and hopelessly unfunny reasons). The "Invasion of the Dinosaurs" novelisation reveals that he was a 'great bear of a man from Russia', who threw his own life-stream into reverse. 'Last I heard of him he was reaching babyhood...' *Whatever* the true nature of his Limitation Effect, it seems strange that the Time Lords - or just the Doctor? - would bandy his name around as if he were the first one to discover it. Surely the thinkers on Gallifrey figured out / fixed the laws governing time-travel long before any Earth-born theorist? Maybe an understanding of such matters is instinctive for the Time Lords; maybe they never bothered coming up with their own specific name for the Effect, in much the same way that humans don't have a proper name for their sense of gravity, i.e. it's too obvious for us to consciously notice. The Doctor only speaks of Blinovitch when he's trying to explain complicated things to humans, so he may just be using the easy(ish) human name for the phenomenon, even though he knows it's not going to make things much clearer for them. At least it's got a nice ring to it.

1978, he was involved with the BBC's adaptation of *Tinker, Tailor, Solider, Spy*. As well as being the production which introduced him to Alec Sabin and Beryl Reid (respectively Ringway and Captain Briggs in 19.1, "Earthshock"), this features a whole episode about a former agent who's working as a teacher and living in reduced circumstances at a minor public school. The agent has a vintage car, his one remaining joy, and a relationship with another outcast; the plump, bespectacled boy "Jumbo" Roach. "Jumbo" being one size up from "Hippo", presumably.

Things That Don't Make Sense   Given that they've got access to space travel, can the mutants *really* not find a way of killing themselves without the Doctor's help? Fair enough, they probably regenerate if they're shot, stabbed or garrotted, but can they honestly heal themselves if - to pick an obvious example - they transmat into a sun? If all their constituent atoms are scattered through space? How about using common-or-garden anti-

matter? Perhaps Mawdryn's just confused, since he seems to want to be a Time Lord in episode two but has decided that he just wants to die by episode three.

It's also revealed that there's a massive burst of energy whenever a time-traveller meets himself, and even Mawdryn's bunch expect it, so has nobody ever thought of using this as a power-source? Haven't the mutants considered abducting "matching" humans from different parts of the warp ellipse, in order to meet their energy requirements?

The TARDIS homing device becomes a great big temporal glitch, too. In 1977, Tegan gives it to the Brigadier. In 1983, the Brigadier remembers Tegan giving it to him and passes it on to the Doctor. Then the Doctor leaves it in the transmat capsule... after which, the 1977 Brigadier finds it and pockets it. Meaning that by the time he's returned to Earth at the end of the story, the 1977 Brigadier has *two* TARDIS homing devices in his possession [unless the Doctor thinks to search the Brig's unconscious body before leaving him back on Earth, and confiscates one of them]. Has he been letting them rattle around in the same drawer for the last six years, and if so then do they go "zap" when they touch? It would've been a hell of a paradox if he'd given the wrong one to the Doctor.

The never-explained 'beacon' on Mawdryn's ship is described as taking the mutants to a new planet every seventy years, as if there are regular distances between inhabitable planets in this universe. Where does Mawdryn get his outfit from on the TARDIS? Is there something in the TARDIS wardrobe that looks exactly like the robes of his own people, or do his clothes regenerate too? More mysterious still is the transmat beam transmitter on Earth, which is apparently vital in order for the transmat to work. How did it get there? It apparently wasn't put there by Mawdryn, who's horribly mutilated by the transmat process and can't leave the capsule on his own. [It must get "dropped" onto the planet from the ship, but it's an impressive feat, considering that it's disguised as part of a monument when the Doctor finds it.]

Right at the start of things, when the Doctor and Tegan are having their terribly realistic chat about the end of "Snakedance", we might assume that we've only been away for a few hours at most. But Tegan's hair has grown even more than the Doctor's. Have they been discussing this for two months?

And what kind of public school is this? The headmaster has never met anyone who doesn't like sports or the CCF (officer training), yet one of the boys is carrying a copy of Das Kapital. Nor are the uniforms very uniform. In his dream, Turlough talks to the head about his moral dilemma and seems unaware that the head is taking his story of time-travel, personifications of evil, Faustian pacts and transmat pods rather seriously [well, it is a dream]. 'Haven't I done enough to separate the Doctor from his TARDIS?" he wails, expecting a sensible answer.

If associations with all things Gallifreyan and Doctorish trigger the Brigadier's breakdown, then isn't owning a vintage car going to give him the shakes? It's not really a textbook fugue-state, either, and it should've taken more than a few name-drops to bring it all flooding back. Has Sarah never been in touch? Doesn't Jo send him Christmas cards? Of course, if we wanted to be

really pedantic… then we could point out that when the Brigadier starts to have "flashbacks" of his UNIT days, some of the things we see on-screen are clips from scenes which didn't feature the Brigadier. Or that some of the background sounds of the TARDIS are wrong, with Dick Mills mixing up the "stationary" and "in-flight" noises.

Perhaps strangest of all… the Doctor's remarkably quick to give up his lives to the mutants when Nyssa and Tegan are in danger, instead of doing his usual thing of trying to improvise a cure. Even if he doesn't have the resources to tackle the virus on the space-liner, couldn't he leave his passengers behind, zip off to find a solution and then come back when he's ready? Or even ask the Time Lords for help, given they must owe him a favour or two after the Omega debacle? He never tries getting the girls off the ship by fixing up the transmat, either.

Critique (Prosecution)   Contrary to what's been said in **Things to Notice**, this story didn't seem to alienate the Viewing Public as badly as "Terminus" or (perhaps surprisingly) "The King's Demons". Despite the cast's misgivings, the story as broadcast makes some kind of sense to even the most casual viewer, and even when it looks like it's about to fall apart the first-time audience had the confidence that it would all make sense. And yet, whilst the bulk of the story does the job well enough, the opening few minutes would have made a lot of people switch over had there been anything better on.

There seems to have been no thought at all as to how anyone watching this would react. It's as though everyone making it assumed that public-school hi-jinks, naff electronic effects, the most irritating music ever used in the series (not just incompetent, but inappropriate to every single scene), then a conversation about last week's story was simple family fare. The big surprise - the Brigadier's amnesia - was flagged up months in advance in DWM and Celestial Toyroom, so even fans weren't necessarily that patient. But still the public watched. And what they got looked rather good, all told. The Kastron ship set is full of interest, with secret panels that really are secret. The cast all say lines that their characters would say - yes, even the Black Guardian - and there's a genuine friction, like an early Hartnell or a David Whitaker Troughton story. The two Brigadiers talk in subtly different ways, with the '83 model using post-Falklands words like "yomp" whilst his younger self takes command and is quicker on the uptake.

What's missing, however, is any real feeling. Sure, Mawdryn keeps on about his suffering and the '80s-style Brig may get a bit shirty when the Doctor suggests he's unwell, but it passes us by. For drama to function - even farce, which they say is "tragedy speeded up" - something has to be at stake. However much Mawdryn's crew are tormented, they glide around sedately, and the threat to the Doctor is so ill-defined that it's simply something to say and thereby end an episode. Only Janet Fielding and one version of Nicholas Courtney really give any sense of urgency or dread to proceedings.

As with "Snakedance", the use of sound to give a sense of disorientation (in the 'one lump or two' scene and a few others) is a welcome change from strict mimetic storytelling, but where the sound really falls flat is the school sets. They sound like a TV studio. Acoustically, everything is wrong about all the spaces in this story, with no echoes or variations in the different rooms at Brendon (if anyone has been to a building like this, especially a school, then the difference is obvious) nor aboard the plush spaceship. It might sound like a trivial point, but in between "Snakedance" and "Terminus" - both of which seemed more interested in this story than in making it look "right" - it's noticeable. The hallway, the Brig's hut, the dormer and the spaceship should define one another. Even if the viewer has never been aboard a ship full of mutants, s/he can tell it's bigger than the shed where Lethbridge-Stewart is billeted, which is in turn not like a corridor in a big old house converted into a school.

If this critique has concentrated on silly details, it's because the whole production did. Things are at a pretty pass when the nearest the series comes to "recognisable" and "everyday" is a public school, and a character who ten years earlier was the symbol of how "futuristic" the UNIT stories were. Remember UNIT? This was the era when Britain flew to Mars once a week, cabinet ministers used dinosaurs to evacuate London and Earth kept getting invaded... and still the Brigadier needed Benton to explain 'interstitial time' (9.5, "The Time Monster"). When the public are intended to use a man who fires disintegrator guns at giant robots as their benchmark for "normal", something has gone very wrong.

It's been argued that this is the heart of the story,

that the Brigadier's loss is also our lost innocence, and that the mundane and petty life he leads - electric kettle and A-Level maths - is a prison for his soul. In this reading all the "repressed" memories amount to an early version of the "retro" ironic affection for the future we were promised in the 1950s, jet-packs and Esperanto. If you were a child in the early '70s, then you would have been watching this on a set with a remote control, and this ache for a future that was "cancelled" isn't really a factor. Watch this story that way if you want to, but it's a long way from what the public thought in 1983.

Critique (Defence) The last critique raises an interesting point, one that's at the heart of any argument about what *Doctor Who* "should" be like: is it supposed to *surprise* the audience, or give the audience exactly what it wants? This is a big issue, when you're dealing with a series that's both populist *and* progressive. Or if not progressive, then certainly a little on the odd side.

"Mawdryn Undead" is a case in point. It opens... strangely. It expects the viewers to accept that various peculiar, disjointed events are all part of the process. It runs the risk of driving those viewers away in their hordes (though, as it happens, they didn't go). But if a story opens with "simple family fare" instead, then isn't that *just* as big a problem, when unpredictability's part of the mandate?

The '70s answer to this dilemma was to say that the series worked on two levels, so that each story should look reasonably "exciting" for a mainstream audience but feature "ingenious" things for hardcore viewers. Yet this style of programme-making only works if you can be sure the programme already has the viewers' complete attention, so that specific groups can start to pick up on specific details. In the 1980s, this was an assumption which nobody working in television could make. The importance of the remote control has already been mentioned, although that's just the beginning of it. Brought up in a synaesthesic, media-saturated, choose-your-own adventure culture, the up-and-coming generation was full of people who tended to think in impressions rather than details. (This isn't necessarily a bad thing, but that's an argument for another time.)

Now, one thing needs to be reiterated here. "Mawdryn Undead" *is*, quite unashamedly, part of a serial rather than a fully-formed story. Like many of the earlier works of *Doctor Who* - and, noticeably, like Grimwade's two other scripts for the series - it's not built to be a self-contained plot with one beginning, one middle and one end. This is a series of episodes, a catalogue of incidents. Mawdryn and the mutants, supposedly at the story's core, barely even make their presence felt until episode three. Call it soap opera if you will, but if anything each episode is more like an edition of *The Amazing Spider-Man* (and we'll come back to this comic-book connection for 20.7, "The Five Doctors"), bringing in new characters and setting up new relationships against a backdrop of casual fantasy.

Can "casual" ever be good, though? Doesn't this suggest that the viewer is expected to sit there and vegetate, rather than becoming an active participant...? Well, perhaps. Or perhaps it's just a different way of creating world-states around the audience. "Impressions" rather than "details", remember. "Mawdryn Undead" isn't presenting the viewers with a plot, it's presenting them with the world of *Doctor Who*.

That borne in mind, it's hard to find serious fault with *anything* here, with the exception of the spurious and irritating "infection" sequences in the last episode (series' writers have a habit of introducing surprise viruses if the story's underrunning... q.v. 7.2, "Doctor Who and the Silurians"). Moreso, many of the story-strands are hugely undervalued. Turlough, a new companion who arrives with the intention of killing the Doctor and has a back-story we're asked to take as read, is an *astonishingly* great conceit. These days we'd call it a story-arc, but here it's just part of the package of what this series can do, and commendably the script gets us to accept it as part of the overall picture without "priming" us first. The Black Guardian, now he's been established as a fully-functional part of the *Doctor Who* universe, is free to act as an arch-manipulator / long-term story-engine and doesn't have to take up too much screen-time with what would otherwise be very dull black-hat villainy. The narrative device in episode two, switching between Tegan in 1977 and the Doctor's reactions to the Brigadier *remembering* Tegan in 1977, works beautifully.

And then there's the Brigadier himself, whose reappearance is carried off with affection and goodwill without any painful "in-jokes" for hardcore fans. The idea of splitting the story up into two time-zones, showing us the world we knew *then* and the series we know *now*, underlines the

fact that this is a return to a rose-tinted past (the Queen's Silver Jubilee, of all things...) which nonetheless doesn't want to get stuck there. The story's smart enough to know that whereas UNIT used to represent the future, it now represents something in our heritage. The explosion of touching Brigadiers feels symbolically *right*, even if you're going to quibble about whether it actually makes sense.

No, it was never going to look like an all-time classic. The story's lightweight almost by its own admission, and there's no serious threat to the natural order of things, so it's bound to feel like a brief encounter rather than an epic struggle. But as a deliberate attempt to remind us of the importance of *Doctor Who*'s mythology, rather than to expand on it, that's no bad thing. And it's *still* not like any other programme on television. If this is soap, then it's a curious, unpredictable kind of soap that aims to leave the viewer slightly disorientated. Let's see any *other* fantasy series play it that way.

The Facts

Written by Peter Grimwade. Directed by Peter Moffatt. Viewing figures: 6.5 million, 7.5 million, 6.5 million, 7.4 million.

Supporting Cast Nicholas Courtney (The Brigadier), David Collings (Mawdryn), Valentine Dyall (Black Guardian), Angus MacKay (Headmaster), Stephen Garlick (Ibbotson), Roger Hammond (Doctor Runciman), Sheila Gill (Matron).

Oh, Isn't That..?
• *David Collings*. Now seemingly a permanent resident on BBC Radio 4, in those days he was best known for *Sapphire and Steel*, where he played semi-regular scene-stealing character "Silver". He'd already been Poul in "The Robots of Death" (14.5) and Vorus in "Revenge of the Cybermen" (12.5).
• *Lucy Benjamin, AKA Lucy Baker*. The "youthened" version of Nyssa grew up to be a regular in *EastEnders*, which meant that for a short while the clip of her in "Mawdryn Undead" was nearly as popular as the one of Martin Clunes in "Snakedance". In-between she was also in BSB's doomed outer-space soap opera *Jupiter Moon* (occasionally written by Ben Aaronovitch) and in

ITV's award-winning children's series *Press Gang* (written by Steven Moffat, and often featuring David Collings as the headmaster, funnily enough).

Cliffhangers While the Doctor's fiddling with the transmat device on Earth, Turlough creeps up behind him and prepares to smash his head open with a rock; Mawdryn reveals himself to the Doctor's companions on board the TARDIS, exposed brain and all; with the mutants surrounding him on board the ship, the Doctor explains that if he helps them then it'll be the end of him as a Time Lord.

The Lore

• The young version of Tegan, Sian Pattenden, is now a style journalist and used to write for *Smash Hits* and *The Guardian*. Neither she nor li'l Nyssa was credited, despite having dialogue. Janet Fielding got married shortly after this story was filmed, and the press were given photos of her in wedding dress and "aged" make-up. (The fall-out from the end of this marriage is a story in itself and involves a major financial scandal, a press tycoon and the Israeli secret service. Ms. Fielding now refuses to talk about it.)

• Mark Strickson had auditioned for hospital soap *Angels*. That show's producer (Julia Smith… see 4.1, "The Smugglers" and 4.5, "The Underwater Menace") told him it was a choice between doing real acting with her or getting more money on *Doctor Who*. Nathan-Turner replied that it was a choice between being one of twelve regular cast or one of four.

Strickson, being blond, needed to be made less Davison-like. The first thought was to shave his head, but Strickson said he'd only do it if six months' loss-of-earnings money was added to his fee after he left (and he regrew it). The "ginger" dye offset his eyes, and was shown to be practicable in a short time each day of filming. He and his girlfriend Julie Brennan (see 24.2, "Paradise Towers") selected the uniform, choosing a size of trousers too short to make him seem younger.

• Saward's idea of an ambiguous companion had originally been part of the abortive Pat Mills script "The Song of the Space Whale" (see **What Else Wasn't Made?** under 17.6, "Shada"). This was to have been about a colony cut off from the rest of the universe, eventually revealed to be inside a giant creature's stomach. Mills had origi-

nally submitted this as a comic-strip for *DWM*, where he'd already written (or co-written) classic works of comic-book *Doctor Who*-ness like "The Iron Legion" and "Star Beast".

The original Turlough seems to have been rather like the conniving Steerpike in Mervyn Peake's *Gormenghast* trilogy, who's determined to rise from being a humble kitchen worker to ruling the House of Groan. As BBC Radio had recently produced a well-publicised version of the first story in the series, *Titus Groan*, with Sting as Steerpike and Stratford Johns as his grotesque master, this wouldn't have been far from people's minds at the time. Charming, aggressive and self-serving, Turlough would ingratiate himself with the Doctor (and any other authority figure) but act capriciously. Nathan-Turner decided that he'd be revealed as an agent of the Black Guardian, presumably in the last story of that "arc".

• Nicholas Courtney was actually the third choice as "guest star" for this story. Other commitments prevented both William Russell (Ian Chesterton) and Ian Marter (Harry Sullivan) appearing in their old roles, so the return of Lethbridge-Stewart - planned for a while, as Courtney had been asked at Tom Baker's leaving party whether he'd be willing - was brought forward into this script.

• The obelisk is a real feature of the location, Trent Park, part of the grounds of the University of Middlesex. This is usually open to the public, and is about five minutes' walk from Cockfosters tube station. This meant that the crew and cast could commute from home for the location work, using the BBC's usual coach or public transport.

20.4: "Terminus"

(Serial 6G, Four Episodes, 15th February - 23rd February 1983.)

Which One is This? Lepers in space, the entire universe endangered by a single vessel, and: who's afraid of the Big Bang dog, the Big Bang dog, the Big Bang dog…?

Firsts and Lasts Final appearance of Nyssa, who proves to be a companion of the "I'm unexpectedly staying behind in this completely alien society in order to help the natives" type. It's the first and, as it turned out, last story directed by Mary Ridge (see **The Lore**). On paper, she was *exactly* the right director for the series as it was then…

ABOUT TIME 1980-1984

Four Things to Notice About "Terminus"...

1. As is so often the way in this era, the "opponents" in this story aren't your usual villains with blasters and big plans. (Remember, this comes right after a story where the supposedly-bad-guys just want to commit suicide and right before a story where the villains are just trying to keep themselves occupied throughout eternity.) Here the Doctor and company find themselves sandwiched between hordes of shambling, half-crazed lepers - so much more scary than any "real" monsters of the age - and the money-grubbing company that handles them, a company whose agents are never seen and which makes its presence felt only through the desperate, abusive conditions it's created. The plot ends with a compromise rather than with a big bang, and most tellingly of all, this is the first *Doctor Who* story since the 1960s in which absolutely nobody seems to die. (For more on this see **Which Stories Have the Best Body-Counts?** under 21.4, "Resurrection of the Daleks".)

2. The Doctor saves the universe. Although once again, it's his presence which puts the universe in jeopardy in the first place (a la 18.7, "Logopolis"). On this occasion the continuum can be saved by pulling one lever on a control panel, but at the very least the Doctor finally gets a cliffhanger in which he can dramatically announce that if he doesn't act then absolutely everything will blow up. To find out the reasons for this dramatic overstatement, see **Where Does This Come From?...**

3. The other thing everybody (well, everybody male and heterosexual) notices about "Terminus" is the amount of companion-skin on display. Having spent most of her time on the TARDIS swaddled in Trakenite velvet, Nyssa finally gets to loosen up, dealing with her feverishly high temperature by removing articles of clothing and dropping them all over the Terminus station. Many lingering petticoat-shots follow. Meanwhile Turlough's telling Tegan that she's sweet when she's angry, "sweet" apparently meaning that her bad temper repeatedly threatens to make her tube-top burst (again, see **The Lore**). And then she has to crawl around a maintenance tunnel on all fours. And get fondled by lepers.

4. The exact centre of the universe turns out to be a drab, empty access shaft in the middle of a space station. Even the Doctor looks as if he's not sure how to react to this.

The Continuity

The Doctor Insists on giving Turlough the benefit of the doubt, despite Tegan's belief that the new companion's up to something [this explains much of the Doctor's reputation as "the naïve one"]. He looks as if he has to reign in his emotions on Nyssa's departure, far more so than on most prior occasions when someone leaves his company. He doesn't try to argue with her decision, but just asks her if she's thought of everything before she sets out on her new career as a miracle-worker.

This Doctor doesn't seem great in physical fights, defeating one of the weakened Vanir in combat but without much finesse [he's better with a sword, as we'll see in 20.6, "The King's Demons"]. He prefers dodging the blows to responding with martial arts. He also seems impervious to radiation again [see 11.5, "Planet of the Spiders"; 9.4, "The Mutants"; 1.2, "The Daleks"... and many others where his apparent susceptibility varies from planet to planet].

The Supporting Cast

• *Nyssa.* Elects to stay behind on the disease-ridden Terminus station, helping to cure the Lazars with the skills she learned on Traken. [In part this is obviously an ethical decision, and it's fair to assume that Nyssa had this sort of "help the needy" approach drilled into her back in the Traken Union. But in part, it looks almost as if she's doing this because it's a challenge. It's the first time she's landed in a society where her skills with bio-science are really *essential*, and she seems to want to prove she can make a difference.] She claims that she's enjoyed 'every moment' of her time on board the TARDIS, hard as it is to believe. Her farewell - 'please, let us part in good faith' - is as formal as you'd expect from one of her caste, but she blubs when saying goodbye to Tegan.

On the TARDIS, Nyssa's been synthesising an enzyme in her spare time and evidently prefers to use an abacus to a calculator. Tegan says she's done this before, although Adric did the calculations then and Nyssa believes her figures aren't as good. [Most of the Season Nineteen stories lead on from one another, but more time must have passed between adventures than we might have guessed.]

• *Tegan.* Does her best to talk Nyssa out of the decision to leave. Tegan considers Turlough to be an ill-mannered brat, and she's still the only one on the TARDIS who's figured out how shifty he is. Being nice, she doesn't think she could kill anyone unless it was to save a friend, while…

• *Turlough.* …isn't sure he can kill anyone either [even though he came within a hair's breadth in the last story]. He's still under the Guardian's influence, despite the cracking of the Guardian's crystal. [He's not surprised by this, so the Guardian must have been in touch since "Mawdryn Undead".] When the Guardian instructs him to sabotage the TARDIS and kill all of those on board, Turlough's quicker to do it than he was to try to kill the Doctor with his own two hands. He wastes no time in trying to smarm his way around the crew, but he's clearly scared in the Guardian's presence. While messing around with the switches on Terminus, he puts the entire universe in jeopardy and never even realises it.

The TARDIS The Black Guardian gets Turlough to sabotage the TARDIS by opening one of the roundels in the corridors, and operating 'the blue switches' on the circuitry inside. [The roundel pops open again when Tegan's passing, which might just be a result of Turlough not shutting it properly, but *might* be the TARDIS' attempt at a warning. Compare with the similarly handy roundel-popping in 19.1, "Castrovalva".] After this Turlough is able to remove the space-time element from beneath the console, described by the Guardian as the 'heart' of the TARDIS. [As in 20.1, "Arc of Infinity", although there the Time Lords didn't seem to need to operate the blue switches before removing the element. Maybe the switches override the safeguard that stops it being removed in flight.]

Turlough doesn't quite get the element free, but it *nearly* comes out. The result of this sabotage is that a siren sounds from the console, the central column jams, and there's dimensional instability within the Ship which causes parts of the structure to give way to grey, blurry space. The Doctor tries using the console's safety cut-out, but it doesn't work. With the Ship on the brink of breaking up and letting in the outside universe, the TARDIS' failsafe seeks out and locks onto the nearest spacecraft. The Doctor's never mentioned this failsafe before, as it's never worked before [has it had any reason to?]. The Ship and the spacecraft seem to merge together, so that one of the spacecraft's doors appears in the lab on the TARDIS and leads into the craft's corridors, and once the door closes it keeps vanishing and re-appearing in the

corridor wall [as if the door isn't really one of the spacecraft's doors at all, but a temporary part of the TARDIS that's based on the local design].

Prompted by the Black Guardian, Turlough uses an emergency bypass switch on the spaceship to make the door stabilise [whether it does is a moot point, but the effect is - apparently - to re-initiate Terminus' computer and start the countdown to the end of everything].

Turlough is given Adric's old room, which is still full of the clutter [it contains many of the props that were there the last time we saw it, in 19.6, "Earthshock", plus a lot more books]. Tegan takes the Kinda double-helix necklace for herself. Nyssa's quarters are now equipped with all sorts of test-tubes and beakers for her scientific research, as well as a microscope and an abacus. The scanner in the console room can be re-focused to look at the Ship's interior spaces, and when this happens the Doctor can communicate with Nyssa's room from the console.

The Guardians

• *The Black Guardian.* Claims that if Turlough sabotages the TARDIS and causes its destruction, then he can safely spirit Turlough away to safety [do we believe him…?]. The crystal he gave Turlough has now repaired itself after being cracked, and at one stage the Guardian punishes Turlough by making it glow with a blazing light, causing him to pass out in some discomfort.

It's the Black Guardian who gives Turlough instructions to mess around with the workings of Terminus, something which very nearly destroys the universe, although the Guardian's apparently just *trying* to show Turlough how to make the door to the TARDIS re-appear. [Does the Black Guardian really not know what the consequences will be, or is he prepared to blow up the whole continuum just to kill the Doctor? What we've seen of the Black Guardian so far suggests that he wants to make the universe break down into chaos, not that he wants to make it cease to exist. In episode one the plan seems to be to destroy the TARDIS rather than to force it to head for Terminus, so it's not another elaborate long-term scheme.]

The Non-Humans

• *The Garm.* The shaggy guardian of the forbidden zone of Terminus (see **Planet Notes**). A seven-foot-tall biped with the head of a dog, glowing red eyes and armoured clothing, the Garm is actually quite genial and has the job of escorting the Lazars into the radiation-soaked parts of the station. It - or possibly "he", judging by the voice - is blaster-proof, physically powerful and capable of speech, but generally morose as he has to obey the instructions of whoever holds his control unit.

The Garm is being used to tend the Lazars, so he obviously isn't affected by the radiation in the forbidden zone, and the Doctor eventually frees him by destroying the control box. Nyssa believes that it'll take the Garm's help to run Terminus as a proper hospital, and indeed, the Garm seems to have a genuine sense of responsibility when it comes to the patients.

[The Garm's origins aren't explained here. It's possible that the creature was specifically brought to the station by Terminus Inc, but then again, Terminus was originally built by a race of physically-powerful (if humanoid) people. Was the Garm originally their pet, and is Terminus Inc just using him because he's there? If so then he could be aeons old, but that's in keeping with the giants-from-the-dawn-of-time flavour of the story, and would explain why he's so miserable.]

Planet Notes

Terminus. A vast spacecraft currently being used as a station by Terminus Incorporated, full of cavernous spaces and metallic gantries, which from the outside looks like a great lattice of metal tubing.

Terminus is what Olvir describes as a 'leper ship', where the human victims of the Lazars' disease are supposedly treated. Hordes of moaning, mumbling, sickly-looking Lazars are unloaded from the automated craft that dock at Terminus, where they're herded into the station's depths. [Few of the Lazars are heard to speak, and at one stage they attack as a groaning, thoughtless mob, which might just mean they're desperate but might suggest that brain damage is among the symptoms of the disease.]

Definite symptoms include pallid skin, facial sores and physical weakness. One by one the Lazars are taken into an area of Terminus known as the forbidden zone, where the Garm exposes them to the massive doses of radiation from the leaking engine. When Nyssa is infected by the disease, exposure to this radiation cures her, but it's hit-or-miss and many of the "cured" develop lethal side-effects. The Vanir believe that no Lazars have ever come back from the zone, although the Garm

knows there's a pick-up ship that comes to take away "cured" patients, as most of the Lazars are successfully treated in the short-term. The radiation apparently comes from the ship's leaking engines, and is merely being exploited by the company. The space pirate Olvir believes that Terminus Inc is only interested in profit, and acts as if the disease is airborne, but only Nyssa contracts it here.

The Vanir are the permanent crew of Terminus, though they have the minimum possible contact with the Lazars. Dressing in elaborate armour and face-masks to protect them from the radiation levels near the forbidden zone, they never enter the zone itself. They're armed only with staves, and are understandably aggressive after being stuck on this station for so long, as they're technically slaves of Terminus Inc. The company supplies them with a drug called hydromel, a glowing green substance that comes in little glass tubes which fit into slots in their armour. The drug relaxes the Vanir and supposedly keeps them alive, which is how the company controls them. And at least part of the latest shipment of hydromel turns out to be coloured water. [Is it too expensive for the company to keep providing? The cutback might suggest that rather than *literally* keeping them alive, the drug is just a form of narcotic, something on which the Vanir have become dependent. It may also prevent them being contaminated by the Lazar disease, as they're not particularly worried about becoming infected.] The hydromel arrives on transport ships along with the Lazars, and the Vanir's leader dishes out the drug.

But Terminus has a secret. Within the forbidden zone is a control room where its original pilot can still be found, a skeleton of a powerful-looking humanoid in a spacesuit. [It's suggested, though not overtly stated, that the station wasn't built by humans but found and re-fitted by them much later.] Not only that, but the station's at the exact centre of the known universe. [The implication is that it's at the exact centre of the universe, "known" or otherwise. Unless by "known" the Doctor just means "the bit of this universe we already know", and not one of the more exotic alternatives.]

And it was once capable of time-travel. When the pilot jettisoned some of its unstable fuel at the dawn of time, the explosion started a chain reaction, causing the big bang in a 'chance combination of circumstances' and bringing the universe

How Can the Universe Have a Centre?

A spectrograph is a device which allows you to tell what something is made of by looking at the colour of the light it gives off when heated; or rather, the bits of the light that aren't there. Every element absorbs some of that energy in a different section of the spectrum. So even though helium is hard to find on Earth, people knew it existed by looking - carefully - at the sun (hence "helium", as in the Greek sun-god bloke with the chariot). When people look at other galaxies, they can tell that the hydrogen and helium which make up most of our stars are present there too. And that's as "technical" as this essay gets, except for one thing.

Yes, there's hydrogen and helium, but their absorption lines are in the wrong place. The entire spectrum is out of whack. The whole of the universe, except for this bit, is moving away from us at such a big proportion of the speed of light that the colours are Doppler-shifted (the same way a fast-moving car or plane or train or bullet makes a note that lowers in pitch as it recedes into the distance). Everywhere else is leaving us, equally fast in all directions. Anyone would think that we smell.

Two obvious explanations present themselves. Either we're at the exact centre of everything (flattering but unlikely), or the space between galaxies is expanding. If all of space were expanding evenly then we wouldn't notice, because our frame of reference would expand at the same rate. But, it seems, the expansion isn't as even as it could be.

In Volume IV we discussed the idea of the "edge" of the universe, and pretty much concluded that There Ain't No Such Animal. We entertained the idea, mentioned in stories like "Planet of Evil" (13.2), that the matter in the universe might run out even if the space in which it could be located is boundless. An expanding universe, all expanding evenly, could be "rewound" mathematically to determine a start-date (the current estimate for the beginning of everything is 13.8 billion years ago, so the Arar-Jacks of Hierardy might be *seriously* not from around here… see 21.3, "Frontios"). Matter and energy affect space-time, so a pre-existing continuum into which matter and energy emerged is as meaningless as matter and energy existing without space and time in which to exist. Expansion is space expanding, not matter expanding into empty space.

One possibility is that the universe is four-dimensional, spatially, and something we can't perceive is happening in the mysterious number four (or five, if you insist on counting "time" as four). The usual analogy is a piece of paper with dots on it. If the paper expanded, then the dot in the top left would be receding from the dot in the bottom right twice as fast as from the top right or bottom left. But if the dots are painted on a balloon, which is then inflated, all dots will part company from their near-neighbours at the same rate. The distance between two adjacent dots on the balloon expands less than the distance between one dot and another a quarter of the way around. (Oh, go on then. Try it yourself with a balloon and a marker-pen.)

Applying the two-dimensional surfaces and their behaviour to a three-dimensional space, with the "air" as the fourth dimension, we get a good enough match for what's observed as one could hope for. The presence of a fourth, fifth or even eleventh dimension is a given for any series involving a time machine, let alone one which dematerialises and is dimensionally transcendental. Even the "loop quantum gravity' theory we mentioned in connection with TOMTIT (see 9.5, "The Time Monster") is in need of more than three-plus-time. Eleven dimensions were the prerequisite of the mid-1980s' best available theory, but even this needed an edge-less, de-centred universe. So, any universe with an "edge" and a "centre" shouldn't allow TARDISes.

This doesn't even allow us the get-out clause that everyone in "Terminus" is talking about the *known* universe. It's the known universe that's the problem. If there's anything much further away than the furthest objects we can see, then either it must have been around before the Big Bang or the rate of expansion has changed. The furthest-away objects, i.e. the ones we see as they were a very, very long time ago (because it takes so long for the light to reach us), are as basic as anything can be and still exist visibly. The Time Lord in "Genesis of the Daleks" (12.4) uses size rather than age to "pull rank" on transmat technology; he speaks of his people transcending such devices when the universe was 'less than half' its present size. This is relativistically plausible as a different way of saying "half its present age", though it could mean that the expansion has been tampered with. The obvious candidates for such tinkering are the Time Lords themselves, but if they can do this then why are the Logopolitans left to handle Heat Death alone (18.7, "Logopolis")? Adding

continued on page 213…

into existence. [A paradox, as the universe was created by something that was the result of the universe. Unless, of course, Terminus came from a universe before the present one...? Gallagher's original storyline seems to suggest this.]

The Doctor speculates that the pilot time-jumped the ship before realising just how unstable the craft was, but the shockwave caught up with it, boosting the ship billions of years forward in time, killing the pilot and damaging the engine. Terminus is certainly an old vessel, and the Doctor describes the technology as 'phenomenal'.

Turlough's sabotage of the ship's systems makes the computer begin an automatic sequence to jettison the unstable fuel again. This explosion at the centre of everything would cause a chain reaction and *destroy* the universe, but this can be averted by pulling the great big "stop" lever on the console. The control's so heavy that it takes the Garm to pull it, and the space pirate Kari points out that the pilot must have had the strength of a giant to operate the controls. [Another hint that the Garm might be related to the station's original crew, although the novelisation claims that the lever is so hard to move because it's at odds with the timestream of the rest of the universe.]

Staying behind on Terminus, Nyssa believes she can improve things by properly controlling the radiation given to the Lazars and synthesising hydromel for the Vanir, freeing them of company control. Nyssa claims the company won't send in the troops to quash this "revolution", as no soldier would agree to set foot on a leper ship. Terminus' engines are shut down, preventing any future universe-threatening calamity.

History

• *Dating.* Unspecified. [Once again, it's never stated that the humans seen here originated on Earth, although the feel is very much "Earth-people in the far, far future". Olvir speaks of 'the old plagues' before the Lazar disease as if he's talking about the Black Death. If Terminus is at the exact centre of the universe then it's unlikely to be in Earth's galaxy, so these people may be a long way from home. See **How Can the Universe Have a Centre?**. Predictably, signs on Terminus look like English to us.]

As ever in this era, pirates plague the spaceways. The raiding-ship that attacks Terminus' transport liner is sleek, silver and unremarkable, its two-person advance party dressing in bubble-headed spacesuits and melodramatic capes. They carry stun-or-kill energy weapons with limited power-packs, and don't know the nature of the liner before they attack it [people would seem to be widely spread across the galaxies, and communications aren't great]. The raiding-ship abandons them when things aren't going well.

One of the Vanir - Valgard - realises that Olvir has a raider's combat training, and concludes that he's working for Colonel Periera, 'the one they call the Chief'. Valgard himself went on five tours with Periera, and claims raiders were better-trained in his day, but Periera eventually turned him in for the reward money. [As the Vanir are the slaves of Terminus Inc, this would imply that slavery is a common fate for convicts.] Terminus' nature is well-known, and the public are apparently terrified of the Lazars' disease.

The craft that takes the Lazars to Terminus is described as a big liner from a rich sector, and its internal doors are marked with a highly stylised image of a skull [probably meaning "warning, lepers"]. The décor is as harsh and metallic as that of Terminus itself. When the raiders blow a hole in the wall to enter, they seal it behind them with an instant air-seal of yellow gunge. The transport liner runs on automatic, but it's tended by at least one mute and rather mindless robot, a drone with a single camera for an eye and lots of spindly arms. It's the robot who initiates the procedure to sterilise the ship with gas.

The Doctor describes the explosion caused by Terminus' jettisoned fuel as the biggest explosion of all time. Kari calls it the Big Bang, and the Doctor refers to it as Event One. [This contradicts "Castrovalva" (19.1), in which Event One is just the beginning of the *galaxy*, not the universe. Yet, as we saw, the "Castrovalva" account of a 'hydrogen inrush' is closer to the usual description of the start of the universe than the aeons-long accretion of matter that leads to galaxy-formation. Both Nyssa and the TARDIS computer obviously have Robert Holmes' casual touch when it comes to cosmology. Again, see the essay.]

The Analysis

Where Does This Come From? So, let's see. Terminus' armoured caretakers are called the Vanir, like the "lesser" race of gods in Norse mythology who go to war with Odin; the guardian of the station's forbidden zone is called the Garm,

How Can the Universe Have a Centre?

...continued from page 211

"extra" mass and energy from another universe would slow down the expansion, making the oldest known objects younger than we think by possibly a billion years or more, but not too much or else life wouldn't have been able to develop. The universe would already have begun to contract.

But to recap. Either everywhere is both edge and centre, or the known universe is receding away from us because we *are* the centre and time travel can't happen. And if our galaxy is at the "geographical" centre, then why isn't it blown out of whack by whatever's sending everything else away so fast?

There's a possible way out. Assuming - as the original script and novelisation make more clear - that the ship which becomes Terminus is from an earlier universe, and assuming that the fuel isn't just kerosene but some sort of time-travel quantum mojo-juice (artron energy or suchlike), Terminus could be a "rupture" in n-dimensional space-time. In this case, we might tentatively propose a still higher dimension in which this is the exact "centre", whilst to ordinary, everyday time-travellers it's one of an infinite number of centres and edges. Yet Kari, the Doctor and even Tegan recognise it from the star-charts, without recourse to exotic Klein-bottle holograms. Using our balloon analogy again, the place where the person blowing it up is puffing is the one breach in an otherwise even surface, but that's where the analogy fails because the "air" is coming from within the balloon's skin.

Suppose we have a lot of "Russian Doll" universes (as suggested by Romana in 17.4, "Nightmare of Eden"), the difference being that each new one is "outside" the previous one, not within. The "centre" would be the location of the "earlier" universe, and no edge is needed. All very hazy cosmic, but hard to draw on a map. It would be "in" our universe but not "inside" (rather like the way TARDIS dimensions are continuous but not contiguous with wherever the Ship happens to be located). It makes as much sense as any other account of "Terminus", and fits the Nordic creation myth hinted at in Gallagher's script.

This idea does allow the threat in the story to be viable, if a touch abstract. A "pocket" universe created "inside" one already functioning quite nicely could alter the dimensions of the "outer" one (although this rather contradicts the precise meaning of "universe"). This would be different to what occurred at Event One, apparently, because it's happening to this universe and not creating it. If this is what made the 'shock-wave' that sent Terminus to historic time, then another might well distort our dimensions, collapsing the cosmos in a matter of an aeon or so. Time would go wonky. This prospect genuinely unsettles the Sixth Doctor on Station Chimaera (22.4, "The Two Doctors"). However, as at least two CVEs have been opened "recently" - in cosmic terms - with no apparent ill-effects on the stability of the created order (see "Logopolis" again), it seems a touch melodramatic.

Of course, if we're talking about faster-than-light travel and time machines, then we're implying that Einstein was right and space and time are the same thing looked at from different angles. In which case, maybe Terminus was hurled forward to the "centre" of time, the apex of the universe's expansion, after which it'll start to contract and all of history will go into reverse. If this were true, then the Time Lords couldn't be occupying that niche as well; see **Where (and When) is Gallifrey?** under 13.3, "Pyramids of Mars" and **What Do the Guardians Do?** under 16.1, "The Ribos Operation". The Doctor would have known all about it before the story started.

[Note: as stated in the comments on those stories, in "Planet of Evil" and "Underworld" (15.5) the evidence suggests that when the writers talk about the edge of the universe, they actually mean the edge of the *galaxy*. Whereas in "Castrovalva" (19.1) and 'Terminus', Event One is clearly meant to be the beginning of the universe, even when Nyssa talks about 'the galaxy' being created in a hydrogen inrush. As far as is known, galaxies form from gravitationally agglomerated hydrogen concentrating into supermassive black holes, so Terminus certainly isn't at the centre of one.]

after the enormous dog who guards the Norse underworld; and all the characters have mythic-sounding Nordic names (Valgard, Olvir, and more blatantly Bor and Sigurd).

As was so often the way in the '70s, *Doctor Who* is once again tapping conventional mythology, although - inevitably - in this case a lot of it comes via Wagner. Wagner's *Ring* cycle is guaranteed to be a prime influence on anyone attempting to "stage" this kind of thundering Teutonic drama, in much the same way that it's hard for anyone born after the '60s to think about Jason and the

Argonuats without thinking about the 1963 film with the Ray Harryhausen-animated skeletons. Parts of "Terminus" look like pure opera, or at least, look as if they were *meant* to be pure opera.

But in terms of its back-story, this is a straightforward raiding of the Norse creation myth from the Elder Edda (also called the "Poetic Edda"), a collection of Norse mythology. Curiously, many of the pop-science books of the time - especially *The First Three Minutes* by Steven Weinberg - invoke the Norse version as an example of how creation-myths generally kick the big questions into the long grass. In this account the cosmos was made from the spilt milk of a god-like cow; like many northern European versions, it suggests the cow was in turn the left-over from a previous age, and the original "Terminus" storyline is more explicit in stating that the ship which kick-started the cosmos came from a previous universe.

As we saw in "The Ribos Operation" (16.1), this cyclic version of decline and re-kindling is at the heart of Nazi mythology. It crops up in things like the Von Daniken "Just-So" story (see - for example - 11.3, "Death to the Daleks") and the philosophies of Schopenhauer (see the previous story, "Mawdryn Undead"). The difference here is that whereas for something like "The Horns of Nimon" (17.5) the audience had a pretty good idea where the story came from and which mythology was being ripped off, here not even the director really knows what the "source" is about. A story like "Underworld" (15.5) cannibalises Greek mythology and gives all the important characters outerspace counterparts, yet in "Terminus" the connection's more thematic. There's a Norse "feel" to the script, but nobody's fulfilling any pre-determined roles in the story.

The idea that Terminus has the power to blow up the universe seems faintly ridiculous if you pretend this is "orthodox" sci-fi, but the key moment comes when the chart of the known universe - note the way that's phrased - is described as looking like an old map of creation with Earth at its centre. In part this ties in with the Medieval idea of pilgrimage that's suggested elsewhere in the story, specifically pilgrimage to Jerusalem, depicted on the maps of the time as the centre of the world. But in part it's supposed to be as broad and as overstated as all things Wagnerian, and on top of that there's the way the story uses the idea of "giants". The Ring cycle assumes that a bigger, stronger race of men once inhabited the world,

and that these giants will one day rise again to overthrow the gods (for the Nazi overtones of this, see De Flores' speech to the Cyber-Leader in 25.3, "Silver Nemesis").

It comes as no surprise, then, that the long-dead pilot of Terminus is described as having the strength of a giant. Gallagher's novelisation of the story goes further, making the corpse larger than the one seen on TV and describing it as if he's imagining the gigantic extra-terrestrial skeleton from *Alien*. The idea that this story's aiming at something hugely mythic is underlined by the fact that when Terminus is about to destroy the universe, matters are put right not by the Doctor's scientific cleverness but by the Garm, who's the only one capable of pulling the "do not destroy universe" lever on the console.

This time it's not about reprogramming computers. Only the Old Race has the power to avert the end of the natural order.

In "Terminus" the gods themselves don't put in an appearance, although there is an evil corporation, and that *does* get overthrown. But even this isn't business as usual for *Doctor Who*. When ruthless, money-grubbing companies have appeared in the series before now they've been decidedly corporeal, often behaving like well-drilled military organisations and frequently being run by petty, fallible, very *human* bureaucrats. Yet in "Terminus", The Man remains invisible. The company doesn't have a face; it's just assumed that some divine executive order has to exist, and that by definition it has to be bad. This is a particularly '80s view of things, although you only realise how much has changed if you compare it to an earlier story like "Colony in Space" (8.4). This was a decade in which the mass of the population became aware, as never before, that the world was run by unseen corporate forces moving insubstantial currencies around via undisclosed channels. Stories like "The Green Death" (10.5) and "The Sun Makers" (15.4) see the Doctor personally facing off against the ultimate head of the company, and on both occasions The Man turns out to be something other than human, but from this point on - both in *Doctor Who* and in other, more cynical, dramas that grew up out of the world of the '80s - corporate concerns tend not to *have* heads. And the organisation certainly can't be brought down just by disposing of one high-rolling company employee. This is, again, in keeping with Gallagher's background (see 18.5,

"Warriors' Gate").

In fact, the thing this most closely resembles is *The Boys from the Black Stuff*[12], a series in which unemployed Liverpool labourers struggle to get by in the face of intransigent government agencies. The Vanir would have been instantly recognisable to anyone signing on for benefits, or anyone trying to negotiate with housing officers, or anyone with relatives in care. The novelisation has the Vanir named Valgard thinking along the same lines as NHS interns, trying to keep things moving by not getting involved. A couple of years later US television would have *St. Elsewhere* occupying this sort of territory. (We might posit *Hill Street Blues* as being a non-SF source for Saward's obsession with big organisations running down and making do with shoddy equipment, but (a) it wasn't broadcast in Britain until he'd already started down this path and (b) the BBC itself is a much clearer model… see 23.4, "The Ultimate Foe".)

Since we've been keeping track of the way the series has been getting more and more serial-like over the last couple of seasons, it's worth mentioning that "Terminus" comes closer (note: closer) than any other story to properly balancing soap and space-opera. As in a lot of the '60s stories, the first episode is pretty much a mood-setter, requiring the TARDIS crew to nose around a mysterious and seemingly-derelict spaceship until the first cliffhanger arrives. This means there's a decent venue for Turlough to re-establish his relationship with the Black Guardian, and for Tegan to get her bile out of her system, before most of the supporting characters - and, indeed, the plot - turn up in episode two. Gallagher wanted to write something closer to the stories he'd enjoyed as a child, and to take advantage of Davison's version of the Doctor. The result is something very like a Troughton story, most noticeably "The Wheel in Space" (5.7) in episode one, though with more angst from the regular cast.

Things That Don't Make Sense Anyone keeping count of how many "last final chances" the Black Guardian has given Turlough up to this point?

For now, let's accept all the business about Terminus being the centre of the universe, because it makes sense within the context of the story even if it's several dimensions removed from reality (again, see **How Can the Universe Have a Centre?**). But… isn't the existence of this space-station a bit of a liability, even with the engines shut down? Doesn't the Doctor even *think* about

dragging Terminus away from the middle of things, or at least getting rid of the unstable fuel on board? Surely the station must be destroyed one day, and what happens then?

As ever when something universe-imperilling comes into play, you also have to ask why no passing megalomaniac has decided to use Terminus to hold the entire cosmos at ransom. And why nobody, not even the ever-curious, space-time-travelling Doctor, has bothered finding out what's at the universe's centre before this. And why none of the humans in this era have noticed the significance of the station, which is visibly at the centre of the universe even on the charts of the transport ship. Fair enough, Terminus Inc has decided to save money by refitting an "ancient" vessel rather than building its own, but has the company really not conducted a full survey? Didn't it find the original pilot's body, or think about clearing him out of the old control section? Didn't it *notice* the unfamiliar time-travel technology on board, or try to deduce what all the defunct mechanisms did?

The power-pack on Kari's blaster is exhausted after a single shot, so she's not exactly the galaxy's most threatening space-raider. Nyssa knows an awful lot about the Garm's lifestyle in episode four, considering they've never had a proper conversation. Why is Turlough given Adric's old room, thus necessitating the throwing-out of all Adric's things, rather than being given one of the x-thousand other rooms on board? [A bed shortage? Or maybe it's closure. Compare with what happens to Romana's old room in 18.7, "Logopolis".] It's hard to believe the Vanir have never noticed a pick-up ship coming to take away cured Lazars [the company presumably keeps its existence secret to stop the Vanir trying to escape on it]; hard to imagine that there *would* be a pick-up ship, since all the Lazars seem too poor to afford better health-care and it'd be cheaper to let them rot on Terminus; and hard to understand why Olvir thinks the disease is incurable, if 'most' of the sufferers are cured on Terminus and then head back into civilised space. [People must be fairly ignorant of galactic affairs in this era, although the novelisation claims that social shame stops people discussing the truth too openly.]

And: Nyssa's belief that Terminus Incorporated won't sent in troops after the Vanir revolt, as no soldier would dare to board a leper ship, is bizarrely optimistic. Don't soldiers have disease-proof clothing? Don't they have automated weapons? Ways of forcing out the Vanir by shutting down the life-support? Or robots, like the one that sterilises the liner? Let's not forget, though… the Vanir never *wanted* to work on Terminus. In fact, they positively hate the place. So Nyssa's going to be lucky if these hormonally-active ex-criminals don't just kidnap her, force her to manufacture their hydromel and shoot off across the galaxy the next time a pick-up ship comes. Or is that overly cynical?

Critique (Prosecution)   It should be apparent to anyone reading this who hasn't seen Season Twenty that the stories therein are wildly uneven. One week we may be in a weird hybrid of *Scooby Doo* and costume-drama set in Amsterdam, the next we're in a complex, allusive, philosophical treatise directed like a pop video. What no book can convey is how this seemed in the context of *A Question of Sport* and *Open All Hours*, the other evening highlights of Wednesday nights.

"Terminus" is the story least like anything else on BBC1 in March 1983. Where the rest of that year's *Doctor Who* was either baffling to non-fans or richly-woven fantasy-drama purposely aimed at being "like *Doctor Who* used to be", this is neither. It has a number of elements which no other series would have touched - even other programmes in that vein - and a whole episode deliberately written to evoke the feel of the black-and-white days, but it doesn't quite "fit". It's out of key with both the style of the series as it was in 1983 and the general "feel" of the series that the public had. While there are parts that are almost *Blake's 7* (the whole "Norse" thing, and the "centre of the universe" concept in particular), it has an equal number of things that are utterly unlike that show (the whole "Company" idea for one, the Garm's response to simple good manners and the saving the-universe theme).

In its new format and slot, *Doctor Who* wasn't "behind the sofa" any more, nor was it lateral-thinking fun. It was a soap about these people who live in a time-machine, and how they cope with their emotional problems and the occasional killer android. "Terminus" is mainly about how the TARDIS kids handle their 'issues"; Nyssa's sense of aimlessness and an incurable illness, Tegan's inability to get "closure" over Adric, Turlough's… well, when we joked about the Foamasi (18.1, "The Leisure Hive"), we said that a *Doctor Who* version of *The Sopranos* was ludicrous. Here's the proof.

When the novelisation came out, this was suddenly hailed as a neglected gem; when the preview in *DWM* said the story was "not for the squeamish", everyone anticipated a gorefest. Neither of these things is true. The version as broadcast is at least an episode too long, it's shoddier-looking than anything in the Williams era and has the worst Saward-style "filler" lines ever. (Everyone has their favourite. 'The bitter-sweet taste of life' makes many people cringe, but the author's own choice is the way that 'do they think we're stupid or something?' became 'they must think us fools'.) From this point of view, the fact that soundtrack composer Roger Limb drowns out a lot of the dialogue with excruciating music is almost a blessing.

While Gallagher has finally grasped that television is a visual medium, Saward and Ridge seem to have other ideas. Nevertheless, there's just enough going on here to keep the patient viewer from feeling short-changed. Most of it is Peter Benson (as Bor) amiably whittering on; like K9 in "Warriors' Gate", he knows what the disaster is but can't get anyone to listen long enough to figure it out. Some of it is when things that seem like cornball riffs from old movies are turned on their heads, such as when Sigurd appears to fall for Olvir's useless disguise.

Season Twenty has a "theme-ette" of boredom and the futility of existence. It would be a cheap shot to say that this story exemplifies it, but it's true that there's less to distinguish "Terminus" from all the others than any other story. (You might, perversely, see that as its distinctive feature.) In a lot of ways this story's status as the one from Season Twenty everyone forgets is an advantage. It means that the single crappiest robot of all time is overlooked when the jokey lists are made, the dullest fight (at the end of episode two) is overlooked in *any* resumé of lowlights, and the miscasting of Lisa Goddard as Kari is a mistake which has been forgiven. While the tape's running - or on those occasions when it's rerun on television somewhere - it's a scandal that such things were allowed, just as it was a cause for celebration that Bor was there and Nyssa soon wouldn't be. But as soon as it's over, it's as though it had never happened.

Critique (Defence, ish)   It's also the greatest single waste of potential in the whole of *Doctor Who*.

As written, Gallagher's script is based on a spectacular principle: this is space opera, but it's *Wagnerian* space opera. It's *Doctor Who* staged as if it were the *Ring des Nibelung*, an opus of sweeping gestures and bold, overstated characters which sees the universe itself put in jeopardy and the day saved by giants. The influence of the '60s ethos is obvious, because this is a story that's aiming for the kind of glaring, aggressive contrasts - both visual and conceptual - that you only used to get when the universe was black-and-white. There are hints of this throughout the design. The Vanir masks look as if they've been made for the Royal Opera House; the Lazars are presented as a huge, oppressed mass, an entire peasant-class ready to reach up out of the underworld; Olvir and Kari's costumes, with their overblown bubble-helmets and ostentatious capes, are exaggerated parodies of every cover of every space opera in every SF magazine you ever saw. The Nordic imagery's there to make the end of creation feel like Gotterdammerung.

What goes *wrong* is that nobody seems to have explained this to the director. Certainly, nobody's bothered telling the actors. When the space-raiders burst their way through the hull of the ship in the first episode, it's meant to be a big, explosive entrance accompanied by "The Ride of the Valkyries", but instead it looks like exactly what it is: two bit-part actors wandering onto the set in funny costumes. This is the one production where everybody's *supposed* to overact, or at least play it "large", and instead they're all mumbling. Much of the sci-fi dialogue has been ridiculed, especially when Kara has to say things like 'freeeeze!', but in context these brash, overcooked lines make perfect sense (and even Saward's rewrites would have been passable, if delivered "properly").

The trouble is that in this story, every single character is supposed to be played by Brain Blessed, including the women. Without the sound and fury to back it up, things that are supposed to be grandiose and majestic simply look like set-pieces, like long sequences of people running around gallery sets. There's a worrying lack of urgency in the second half, even when the universe is supposed to be on the brink of ending, and needless to say the music isn't "operatic" at all. In fact it sounds more like Limb's trying to mimic the "dan-dan-*dannn*!" style of the '70s scores, but this time using '80s synthesisers, so it's even worse.

And yet, all that said... at this point even failed *Doctor Who* isn't gut-wrenchingly awful. There are moments - surprisingly, quite a few of them - when you get glimpses of what "Terminus" might have been. Its very environment, of disease, despair, damnation and drug-popsicles, is enough to make an impression. Arguably, the shambling hordes of lepers make the first cliffhanger the scariest thing seen in the series since "The Talons of Weng-Chiang". A lot of the little details are right, including the decision to shoot the service-tunnel sequences on film, giving you the sense that these are "real" claustrophobic spaces and that something lethal's going to be pumped into the system at any moment. Granted, like the other flawed stories from this period, "Terminus" feels empty even in spite of its apocalyptic storyline, but if it degenerates into "some people running around" then at least it avoids the worst of the genre's clichés. In themselves, the absence of a story-book villain, the absence of a typical violent "solution", the paranoiac set-up of Terminus Inc and the Lazar-colony background are all worthy of praise. No wonder people started liking it after they'd read the book.

The Facts

Written by Steve Gallagher. Directed by Mary Ridge. Viewing figures: 6.8 million, 7.5 million, 6.5 million, 7.4 million.

Supporting Cast Liza Goddard (Kari), Dominic Guard (Olvir), Valentine Dyall (Black Guardian), Andrew Burt (Valgard), Martin Potter (Eirak), Tim Munro (Sigurd), Peter Benson (Bor), R.J. Bell (The Garm), Martin Mulcaster (Tannoy Voice).

Oh, Isn't That..?

• *Andrew Burt.* Had mainly been involved in prestige projects, costume dramas and the like (playing Captain Fitzroy, commander of HMS Beagle and founder of the Met Office, and later King Arthur). But he'd also found time to appear in arguably the all-time *Blake's 7* bummer – Ben Steed's "Harvest of Kairos" - and to co-star with Elisabeth Sladen in Granada's *Play School* clone *Stepping Stones*.

• *Lisa Goddard.* Made a name for herself in *The Brothers*, and married co-star Colin Baker. She then did the sitcom Yes, Honestly for LWT, where she became chummy with the company's planning guru Michael Grade. After that she married Alvin Stardust (we *could* explain who he is for the sake of non-British readers, but you wouldn't believe it). Of course, her greatest claim to fame had been as a child, when she'd been acted off the screen by *Skippy: The Bush Kangaroo*.

And look carefully at the extras in episode three; keeping an eye out for a young Kathy Burke may relieve the boredom.

Cliffhangers As the space-lepers emerge from the cargo hold by the dozen, Olvir shrieks that this is a leper ship and they're all going to dieeeee; having half-throttled Kari the space-pirate, one of the Vanir lunges at the Doctor with a hearty 'you, I'm going to kill!'; with Terminus' computer preparing to jettison its unstable fuel, the Doctor informs Kari that if they don't do something then the whole universe will be destroyed. (As with "Four to Doomsday" and "Time-Flight", this story ends with an unresolved issue, in this case the Black Guardian giving Turlough one final chance. Again.)

The Lore

• The basic idea of the story involved what Gallagher called a "Pandora Device", a space-drive for a ship from another universe which penetrated this dimension, creating our cosmos. An idea like this had been the basis of Michael Swanwick's award-winning story "Ginnungagap" (and that title reminds us again of Norse creation myths). After being messed about with "Warriors' Gate", Gallagher wanted to write a very traditional *Doctor Who* story, and was pleased with the finished product. Saward's main concern was giving Nyssa the lion's share of the activity. This annoyed Strickson, in particular, who lost the skin from his hands and the knees of his trousers crawling around the tunnel set in lieu of any real part in the story. He was also uncomfortable with the idea of leprosy being used for entertainment.

• The voice of "Terminus Incorporated" is the same person who tells tube passengers to 'mind the gap'. Martin Mulcaster was then an announcer on the BBC World Service, and has since appeared on several quiz shows. He was credited as "Tannoy Voice", getting the BBC a stiff letter from the Tannoy company[13].

• It appears that Kari was originally called Yoni, but Saward spotted the source of the name (look it up; if it's not in your dictionary then try the *Karma Sutra*). The raiders were supposed to have

costumes in blue, but then the decision was made to do the CSO for this story in a similar shade. New director Mary Ridge was angry at this, and much else. Kari's "Barbarella" helmet was unperforated and misted up quickly.

• John Waller, who'd later choreograph the swordfight in "The King's Demons" (20.6), was brought in to handle the two main fights. Andrew Burt (Valgard) had recently had a cartilage operation, and was reluctant. Waller was hired despite Mark Strickson being a qualified fight arranger (it was in his contract that he'd handle his own stunts), as the use of staves moved it into a different "genre"; Waller is an expert in Medieval combat, and had arranged the fights in the 1980 disco-fantasy epic *Hawk the Slayer*.

• Dee Robson, costumier for "Arc of Infinity" and originally scheduled to work on "Earthshock", took Gallagher's hints about Westminster Abbey's mediaeval *memento mori* sculptures when designing the Vanir's masks. Valgard's appears to be the Sutton Hoo helmet (see 8.5, "The Daemons"). The basic idea of a "sackcloth and ashes" pilgrimage was overlaid with Norse elements, as in the story itself.

• Stop us if you've heard this one before... during filming of the cliffhanger to episode one, Janet Fielding "popped out" from her top. According to convention anecdotes of ages past, Davison had previously engineered similar events.

• Mary Ridge was a seasoned BBC veteran, and her credits include the kind of programmes we've mentioned a lot in this volume (*The Brothers*, *Owen MD*, *Blake's 7*, *Z-Cars*, *Angels*...), but she'd also been an associate producer on costume soap *The Duchess of Duke Street* (see 14.1, "The Masque of Mandragora"). Moreover, it had been her job to train directors for Open University broadcasts.

Ridge, who'd never had any trouble getting a production in on time or on budget, ran into huge difficulties here. The impending industrial action which would later affect "Enlightenment" meant that a remount was needed a month later for the twenty-five shots not in the can. In the interval Sarah Sutton had left, the sets had been badly damaged and everyone had become dispirited. The delay did, at least, allow Saward to fill out the under-running episode one with the scenes in the TARDIS corridor (Gallagher had misinterpreted a request for an extra two minutes and made all the extant scenes a shade longer), and resolved a piddling point of continuity; they'd included a reference to the 'space-time element' from "Arc of Infinity", but the precise piece of plastic used in that story was now being exhibited in Blackpool. The re-mount took place during the filming of "The King's Demons" (20.6), on the 16th - 18th of December, narrowly getting Sutton for one more day before her contract ran out.

• In the original shooting session, most of the footage was completed before the deadline, and Ridge had been assured that the necessary extra time would be allotted on the final day. It wasn't, but Ridge only found this out at the last moment. Ridge and Nathan-Turner became estranged as the situation worsened, and Sutton's leaving "do" was affected. In the longer term, the knock-on effect of this story's woes was to be disastrous, and much of the rest of this volume - and the next - will prove to be the result...

20.5: "Enlightenment"

(Serial 6H, Four Episodes, 1st March - 9th March 1983.)

Which One is This? Lots of "yo-ho-ho" music as Edwardian sailors hoist topsails and splice mainbraces, whilst seemingly unaware that they're in orbit around Saturn.

Firsts and Lasts The end of the "evil Turlough" trilogy, the last appearance of the two Guardians and the last visit to our solar system except for Earth-based larks. Unbelievably, after nearly twenty years it's also the first *Doctor Who* story to be written by a woman (although see 3.6, "The Ark").

Four Things to Notice About "Enlightenment"...

1. Sailing-ships in space; hardly a breathtaking new idea, but so firmly within *Doctor Who*'s space-time-fantasy territory that it's hard to believe it's never been used before. What's really noticeable, though, is how much the revelation feels like "actual" *Doctor Who*. At a time when first-episode cliffhangers were increasingly inclined to involve the re-appearance of an old enemy or the first whiff of a life-or-death situation for the Doctor, this feels a lot like the '60s programme in its heyday. First you think you're on a ship, then you start to suspect that something isn't right, then the shutters in the wheelhouse open and... with one simple image, all the children are going "ooh" and

"oh, I see" simultaneously. Even the Eternals, as ageless, amoral games-players, suggest the days of Season Three and "The Celestial Toymaker" (3.7). More on this later...

2. One of the Eternals (Marriner) eventually develops a crush on Tegan, for some reason finding himself fascinated by her cluttered and none-too-deep mind, and this results in some of the strangest pseudo-romantic, boy-alien-meets-girl-human dialogue to be heard in the programme since "The Curse of Peladon" (9.2). His ultimate chat-up line: 'You're not like any ephemeral I've ever met before.'

3. Throughout the Nathan-Turner era, the programme has a habit of drafting in "guest stars". This is a trend that reaches crisis proportions when people like Ken Dodd and Bonnie Langford start turning up in the late '80s. "Enlightenment" gives us Leee John, vowel-loving vocalist of top ten pop act Imagination. Though John is by no means the first pop person to appear in the series, he stands out partly because Imagination had been on *Top of the Pops* just the previous summer, and partly because his performance here is so much worse than that of all the proper actors. (See **The Lore**.)

4. Interesting things we're told during this story: a pig can never be a sailor, because he can't look aloft. No, it's probably best not to ask.

The Continuity

The Doctor Has started to work out that he can't trust Turlough, although he's really quite forgiving when he finds out the boy's been trying to kill him all this time. He doesn't look happy about being mistaken for the ship's cook, and here he stops Tegan drinking champagne [possibly just because he wants her to have a clear head, as he didn't stop her boozing up in 19.5, "Black Orchid"]. The Doctor refuses Enlightenment when it's offered to him, claiming that he's not ready for it, and that he doubts anybody is. [He has a long, long history of refusing this sort of power...]

• *Inventory.* After more than a year of service, the celery on his lapel is exchanged for a fresh stick from Wrack's ship. [So it may be just as "unreal" as the one from Castrovalva (19.1), although for all we know the Eternals have been abducting vegetables from Earth as well as sailors.]

• *Background.* He knows something of Eternals, enough to realise that none of them should be

ABOUT TIME 1980-1984

allowed to claim the prize of Enlightenment. Even before he knows what Enlightenment actually is.

The Supporting Cast

• *Tegan.* Less forgiving of Turlough than the Doctor. Gets sea-sick easily, but enjoys dressing up in a nice period frock even when she's in a dangerous situation. Judging by her "reconstructed" quarters on Captain Striker's ship, back in Brisbane she's got a cuddly koala and a framed photo of Auntie Vanessa in her bedroom. She doesn't have much trouble "shutting out" mental intruders these days [she's used to this sort of thing, after all that business with the Mara].

When the Doctor appears to die, she's noted as having less 'life' in her head, and Wrack also points out that Tegan's mental image of the Doctor is 'intriguing'. Here she's a better chess-player than Turlough, bizarrely [see 21.3, "Frontios" and 19.3, "Kinda"].

• *Turlough.* A self-confessed coward, he doesn't yet trust the Doctor enough to follow orders that might jeopardise the TARDIS. Desperate to escape the clutches of the Black Guardian, his first reaction is to panic and try to sell everyone out, but he's prepared to go to the lengths of jumping off the deck of a space-going ship in order to escape the Guardian's influence. Even so, the next time he's about to die he's ready to beg the bad guy for help. But when Turlough finally has a straight choice between a valuable slice of Enlightenment and letting the Black Guardian have the Doctor, he does the decent thing [and from this point on he's definitively "good", but only as far as Adric was].

This chapter in his life over, he immediately asks to be taken back to his own planet. [21.5, "Planet of Fire", suggests he desperately wants to avoid the world of his birth. This might mean that he sees his home as being somewhere else, though we never find out where it might be.] When Wrack destroys one of the Eternal ships, he claims that he's never seen a spaceship break up 'like that' before, so he may have seen it happen in other ways. He finds the idea of the Doctor cooking hilarious. [If "The Five Doctors" (20.7) is to be believed, the TARDIS crewmembers live on grapes, aubergines and yoghurt.]

The TARDIS Turlough seems to have dug the Ship's chess set out from somewhere. The TARDIS is half-lit at the start of events here, as if something's draining the power. When the energy output's increased to "full" from the console, the White Guardian just about manages to manifest himself in the TARDIS with a warning, but when the power's kept at full for too long there are explosions on the console and the room gets even darker. Still, the damage has obviously repaired itself by the end of the adventure [or been repaired by whatever happens to the Ship when it's "hidden" in the Doctor's mind]. The scanner "camera" is, judging by Marriner's examination, inside the lamp on top of the police box exterior.

The co-ordinates given by the White Guardian, 'galactic north six degrees, 9077', put the TARDIS on board the ship of one of the Eternals inside Earth's solar system. There's turbulence on landing, which the Doctor attributes to 'time override'.

The Guardians The Black and White Guardians both seem to be involved with the Eternals in some way, as they're the ones who wait at the end of the Eternals' great race; see **The Non-Humans**. The Eternals refer to them as 'the Enlighteners'. Here the White Guardian tells the Black that he'll never destroy the light, and the Black responds that others will do it for him, but ultimately they both acknowledge that light and dark can't exist without each other. The White Guardian states that while he exists, the Black Guardian exists also, until they're 'no longer needed'.

The race ends in a shimmering city-like harbour somewhere in Earth's solar system, where both Guardians manifest themselves in a suitably historical-looking room. On the table between them is the prize for the Eternals' race, a glowing diamond within a sphere which is called - or which represents - Enlightenment. Interestingly, it's the Black Guardian who produces the sphere from his robe and puts it on the table. The Eternals believe this is the 'wisdom which knows all things' and will allow them to achieve what they desire most, while the Black Guardian believes that as the Eternals don't know good or evil the power will let them invade time itself. Chaos will come again, and the universe will dissolve. [So whichever Eternal wins the race, the Black Guardian wins? Probably not, as he's backed Wrack. His belief that *any* Eternal will dissolve the universe is probably just bluster. See also **What Do the Guardians Do?** under 16.1, "The Ribos Operation", for how the White Guardian is also potentially an agent of destruction.]

But the Doctor ultimately wins the race, and the White Guardian agrees with the Doctor's assessment that nobody's ready for it, although he allocates a share to Turlough as the Doctor's second-in-command. The Black Guardian claims the prize under the terms of his agreement with Turlough, but offers to give Turlough everything he wants if he gives up the Doctor instead. Turlough elects to let the Black Guardian have his slice of Enlightenment [it's useless to the Guardian anyway], and the Guardian vanishes in agonising flames when Turlough chucks it at him. *Real* enlightenment, at least for Turlough, turns out to be the choice itself.

[What rules of the cosmos demand that this race be held, and who decided that the Eternals should be able to vie for Enlightenment? Why does Enlightenment even exist as a physical object, and is it made of the same stuff as the Key to Time? No answers are given. But it's possible - probable, even - that the Black Guardian has been so desperate to kill the Doctor because he wants to stop the White Guardian calling on the Doctor to influence the race. Which begs the question of why the Doctor, and nobody else, can be called on. Since the Doctor claims that Enlightenment is the choice rather than diamond, it's possible that it's meant literally and the diamond is a worthless bauble, a trap for those who don't get the point.]

• *The White Guardian.* Manages to appear on the TARDIS to send the Doctor a message, but only when the Doctor boosts the power, and he can barely be seen or heard. Then a much more corporeal Black Guardian appears before the Doctor to gloat, claiming that he controls 'the game'. [The White Guardian never had trouble sending messages to the Doctor before; see especially "The Ribos Operation". Whatever rules apply to the Guardians, the Black one seems to have the upper hand here. Even after the apparent victory, the White Guardian points out that the Black Guardian's power 'does not diminish'.] The White Guardian's powers are said to be waning, though he believes that others will recharge them for him. He's now wearing a dove on his head to match the Black Guardian's crow.

• *The Black Guardian.* His sinister laugh is getting increasingly duck-like. When he manifests himself next to Turlough, he can physically attack the boy and is strong enough to render his victim unconscious with one hand. When his "contract" with Turlough is terminated, Turlough's crystal turns black. The White Guardian states that after

this and the Key to Time incident, the Black Guardian will be waiting for a third encounter for the Doctor [it never comes, as far as we ever see].

The Non-Humans

• *Eternals.* Powerful and seemingly-immortal entities with no explained origin, the Eternals have no purpose in their endless lives other than avoiding boredom. Seeing themselves as superior beings, they have no concern for the lives of short-lived mortals, display a limited capacity for human emotion and have no apparent moral code other than the rules they make for their "games".

All the Eternals seen here take human form, but this is all part of their latest diversion, a race across Earth's solar system in sailing-ships abducted from various periods in human history. Planets are used as marker-buoys, the route taking the ships around Venus and through a perilous asteroid storm. The crews of these ships have been brainwashed so that they don't remember how they got there and don't see anything strange about their superior officers, although this changes when they have to put on spacesuits to go up on deck. Even so, they soon stop panicking and set about their work, apparently due to something in their rum. The ships are surrounded by vacuum shields, powered by solar winds and ion drives, and evidently the Eternals don't mind using anachronistic electronic computers or scanners on their ships as long as everything *looks* right. It's possible to breathe on the deck, thanks to an energy barrier that maintains the atmosphere.

Eternals taking part in the race include Striker, captain of the Edwardian racing yacht *The Shadow*; Marriner, his first mate; Critus the Greek, whom Striker considers to be the only serious competition, but whose ship is destroyed by the villainous Captain Wrack; Davey, whose ship Wrack also removes from the competition; and Mansell, Wrack's leering first mate. [The very fact that ships carry more than one Eternal suggests a hierarchy among these beings.]

Wrack herself is captain of the pirate ship *The Buccaneer*, and seems to have a greater capacity for laughter and merriment than the others, but unfortunately she gets her kicks from acts of sadistic cruelty and is secretly working for the Black Guardian. [It's possible that the Eternals are caricatures of the "people" they're supposed to be. The officers of the *Shadow* are English and reserved, while Wrack is a hot-blooded pirate-queen.] She gives her rivals precious gems as gifts, but these are used as focusing devices for the power amplifier in her ship's ion chamber. When Wrack stands in the chamber and wills it, a ship bearing one of these gems explodes into fragments, killing the human crew. The Doctor speaks of this as 'the power of darkness', and the Black Guardian's voice comes out of Wrack's mouth when she calls on this power. Sabotage is within the rules of the race [within limits], but the Eternals find it less diverting [the fact that only Wrack uses sabotage hints that she's the only one who cares about winning more than she cares about the game].

Eternals would appear to have god-like powers, and they display new abilities all the time. [It's safe to assume that they deliberately limit themselves according to the rules.] Marriner looks into Tegan's mind, not understanding why she objects, and is intrigued by the image of the Doctor he finds there. Tegan's room on the ship is a mix of her room on the TARDIS and her room back in Brisbane, and it's ready for her in no time at all; Eternals can make anything they can see in someone's mind, which is how the ships were created. Marriner acts as if he's in love with Tegan and claims that he needs her to exist, but he doesn't know what love is, nor grief either.

Eternals can seemingly teleport over short distances [and undoubtedly long distances, but it'd break the human illusion too much], although it takes them a moment or two to read people's thoughts. They can do this at long range when adrenaline boosts the subject's mind, but Turlough's capable of muddying his 'mind-vibrations' when he meets Captain Wrack. At one stage the Eternals hide the TARDIS from the Doctor by placing it in his own mind, while Wrack freezes Tegan in time with a gesture. [Not *literally* in time, as Tegan wobbles around a bit and her eyelids move.]

Eternals refer to ordinary mortals as 'ephemerals' or 'dwellers in time', but aren't familiar with Time Lords and aren't sure whether to treat time-travellers as ephemeral or not. Marriner refers to the officers on the destroyed ship transferring 'home', and Striker states that the endless wastes of eternity are his domain. Eternals forced to walk Wrack's plank simply vanish. The Doctor believes that the Eternals depend on ephemerals for all their diverting ideas and technologies, describing their minds as empty and used-up. They do at least have private desires, though Wrack's desire is

nothing more than to be amused.

Ultimately the White Guardian sends all the Eternals back to their 'echoing void', despite Marriner's desire to stay with Tegan. [Again, it's not clear what the rules are for them being let loose on the universe.]

History

• *Dating*. Could be any point in the history of the solar system.

The crewmen on Striker's ship were taken from Edwardian England, and there's a newspaper on board dated 1904 which reports the launch of the first British submarine. Cretus the Greek's crew comes from the Athens of Pericles [c. 430 BC]; the *Buccaneer* crew comes from the seventeenth century, and may be Spanish if Wrack's jewellery is anything to go by; Davey's clipper appears to be nineteenth century; and the Doctor recognises one ship as coming from the Ch'in dynasty [c. 210 BC]. All the surviving crewmembers vanish [back to their own times] once the race is over.

The Analysis

Where Does This Come From? The story's roots in children's fiction show in every detail. As in "The Mind Robber" (6.2), "The Celestial Toymaker" (3.7) and later "The Greatest Show in the Galaxy" (25.4), people are at the mercy of bored, godlike beings who "inhabit" stories and confront their characters. We only need to mention *Peter Pan* for the rest to fall into place. In the book and the original play, Peter inhabits a world stitched together from bits of old adventure stories, but like a child or a god he refuses to be bound by the logic of any one story. When he visits Captain Hook, he doesn't surrender the ability to fly even though the rest of this portion of the story follows the tropes, rules and indeed narrative style of a pirate yarn. Children's fiction, especially in this period, is closer to a game than a film; see "The Mind Robber" , "The Five Doctors" (20.7) and "The War Games" (6.7) for more on this.

As in the work of children's author E. Nesbit - and before her, Ovid's *Metamorphoses* - the precise definition of the rules is crucial, and the more amazing the ability, the more cruel the fate of anyone who gets the rules wrong. Above all, as anyone who's observed children playing will know, the solemnity with which the rules are observed is the point of the game, not the actual winning.

After all, a game is a set of seemingly-unnecessary, agreed-upon limits. Even games of make-believe (*especially* these, according to influential child psychologist Jerome Bruner and many others from the philosopher John Locke onwards) are "scripted" with clearly-defined roles and functions, and breaking these causes tantrums. The classics of children's fiction, from *Alice* to *Earthsea*, are about young outsiders looking in on worlds with bizarre rules which override reality. To say something is so is to make it so, and the consequences are all your own fault.

Of course, you could interpret the whole of human society as a set of "seemingly-unnecessary" rules. In which case the Eternals are just echoes of our adult selves, playing games that even a child would find ridiculous. Again, this reminds us of *Alice's Adventures in Wonderland*, in which Alice's "sensible" logic is constantly overruled by the more convoluted logic of the grotesque and threatening adults... at least until she grows "big" herself, at which point her logic begins to overrule *theirs*. The Eternals are, let's not forget, clearly depicted as the grown-ups of this universe rather than the reckless, imaginative children. Watching them indulge in their game is as unsettling in exactly the same way as watching your parents play *Twister*.

So let's look at it from an adult's point of view. As in "Terminus", there's a move away from the idea of villains being petty human beings with laser-guns and towards the notion that the powers-that-be are distant, amoral and unconcerned with the affairs of ordinary mortals. It'd be going too far to call this "political", but it's still relevant. On the English ship, at least, there's also a blatant class conflict going on. '80s Britain saw a massive shift in the way class was supposed to work, and from around this point it's increasingly common to find British culture portraying aristocrats as effete parasites, feeding off the labour (and in this case, the imaginations) of the proles.

Hardly a new thought, of course, yet "Enlightenment" treats the idea with typical '80s abstraction. "The Sun Makers" (1977) sees the Doctor explicitly advising the underclass to turn into Marxists and organise strike action, but here there's no sense of a gritty ground-level struggle, just the assumption that there's something very wrong with the natural order of the universe if the Eternals are supposed to be the crème de la crème.

And on the subject of abstraction... though the Eternals may have god-like powers, these *aren't* your typical gods of mythology, so for once there's very little lore-plundering going on here. These are inexplicable forces from a realm beyond space and time, part of an order of things that allows elemental powers to take on human form but remains obscure to both the viewers and the other characters. Anybody who'd watched ITV's near-prime-time fantasy effort *Sapphire and Steel* between 1979 and 1982 would immediately have spotted a certain resemblance (see also **The Lore** of 23.3, "Terror of the Vervoids"). *Doctor Who* had already adopted the same weekday-evening slot as the ITV series. *Sapphire and Steel* was aimed at an older audience than "the kids", and lo and behold, the interactions of the TARDIS crew in this era suggest a less obviously child-like set-up than the old "father-figure Doctor and one young / stupid / young and stupid assistant" formula. Even the image of the space-going sailing-ships suggests the kind of thing you'd find in "adult" fantasy romances, as does the pseudo-romantic subplot about Tegan and Marriner. A "hard" SF conception of solar sailing vessels had been suggested by Arthur C. Clarke's story "Sunjammer" a generation earlier, though what we see here - space-bourne ships presented as a deliberately absurd anachronism, rather than a scientific possibility - has more in common with *Baron Munchhausen* than with post-rocketry science fiction.

Things That Don't Make Sense The Doctor's claim that Wrack's gemstone multiplies in power when it's broken into pieces contradicts his earlier claim that it needs to be a certain size to do its job. Then he scoops the broken bits of the gemstone up off the rug, and throws them overboard before they explode, but if each tiny fragment works as a focus in itself then shouldn't the microscopic fragments be just as dangerous? Come to think of it, why doesn't the Doctor just shake the rug over the side of the ship instead of scraping around on all fours? Nor is it explained why he ends up crawling across the deck before throwing the collected pieces off the ship. Has he sprained his ankle on the way?

The guests at Wrack's party seem to include the crew of Davy's destroyed ship, who've supposedly all 'transferred' back to eternity by that point. Bloody gatecrashers. Dr. Science has been dosed with rum, but if they need to catch the solar wind then isn't using force-fields to keep the air in rather counter-productive?

And "oh, Wrack and her first mate fell overboard" really is a shocking cop-out of an ending.

Critique (Grudging Defence) Earlier we said that this has a premise so obvious, it's amazing it hadn't been done before. We'll go further. It's precisely for stories like this that *Doctor Who* exists.

Even in its primal state as a quasi-educational adventure yarn, a great deal of this story would have been unexceptional. Sailors' lore is relayed to us via "eavesdropping" and slightly condescending explanations from an adult. The current Doctor is taking on Ian's function as well, and Turlough is this year's Unearthly Child. Although writer Barbara Clegg isn't slavishly copying or - worse - "referencing" old stories, there's a familiarity to this story that comes from its being rooted in the same "soil" as '60s episodes.

Look at what it doesn't do. It doesn't revolve around the Doctor trying to figure out, before we do, which of his many former adversaries has laid a trap for him; it doesn't rely on him knowing something from before the story started; it doesn't introduce an interesting situation and then relegate it to being a backdrop when the main villain pops up; this story is about its setting, and the "people" in it. The Doctor figures it out at around the same time we do, and even after that we have "privileged" information he lacks (mainly about Turlough). Yet he begins to put the pieces together faster than us, because he's clever and observant. We're right back in the Hartnell scheme of things. Sort of. Because this Doctor is also brave, energetic, moral and tactful. Everyone in this story does exactly what the story requires, and although some of them are famous and some not, the ensemble playing is what makes it work. Even Leee John is pretty much what that character has to be like, and his worst fault is underplaying.

It has flaws. The biggest, according to many people, is a rushed climax that emphasises the wrong things. We wanted to see Wrack get her come-uppance, not two old geezers with silly hats exchanging perfunctory dialogue like a school nativity play. Fans knew all this, and non-fans? Well, the chess-match at the start told us most of what the end scene needed to say. There's a White Guardian who's in a bad way, and a Black Guardian who does the laugh-that-begins-with-N and is therefore the baddie. And Turlough works for him, but the Doctor *isn't supposed to know, shhh!* If there's a Davison story you can show to non-

fans, then… actually it's "The Caves of Androzani" (21.6), but for obvious reasons that's hardly a good start. For children of all ages, this was a taste of what *Doctor Who* could be like when it tried. For everyone else it was a reminder of how badly things had gone astray.

Critique (Defence) In addition to everything that's just been said about the Hartnell years, one other thing has to be borne in mind: the early programme's grounding in history.

In Season One, virtually every other story has its roots in the "real" past. Those who grew up with *Doctor Who Weekly / Monthly / Magazine* were taught that "historicals" were a category of story somehow cut off from the rest of *Doctor Who*, though comparison with other tales of the '60s shows that this was never really true. But it *is* true that by employing historical "materials", the programme changes the audience's expectations in a quite specific way, rooting the series in something complex, concrete and *knowable*.

Ideally even a story set on Planet X should feel like an exploration of a complete world-view, but an occasional foray into known history instantly gives the viewer a reason to believe in this universe; a reason to think that it might be worth applying the same scrutiny to "SF" that you might apply to "period drama". Without some grounding in the past, the Doctor's flair for empiricism and investigation seems abstract and unimportant. It's certainly noticeable that after the production team dropped historicals in 1967, it took less than a year for the programme to degenerate into endless scenes of monsters stomping up and down corridors, and throughout its run the series has repeatedly come unstuck by trying to pull off so many flashy-looking "space" stories that it forgets how crucial its period pieces are.

"Enlightenment" hints at a programme that's finally got the point. This is the period piece to end them all, a story that carries on the tradition of putting symbols from the world we know into disconcerting environments - sailing-ships in a vacuum, a spaceship inside a police box, the principle's the same - but completes the grand illusion of making the history and the fantasy feel like part of the same continuum. As soon as the Doctor steps out of the TARDIS in episode one, it all *works*; the ship's tight, claustrophobic spaces convince you this is the genuine article, yet there's a feeling of lurching unease below the decks even before we find out the truth. When we see "the reveal", the cut-and-paste of an Edwardian racing-vessel in orbit of Venus doesn't jar in the slightest. And on television, it so easily could. In *this* version of outer space there's the same attention to detail you'd expect from one of the BBC's "serious" productions, in everything from the space-wetsuits of the crew to the fact that the scenes on deck are shot on film to suggest location work in an impossible location (see also the previous story). Davison's Doctor is perfect for all of this, a gentleman-traveller who's prepared to spend months sharing quarters with the sailors when he thinks it's necessary.

But it's the Eternals who hold all of this together. This whole story is their game, and the *real* environment here isn't the physical one (Eternals can create rooms out of thin air, which removes the potential clichés of getting-captured-and-escaping right from the start) but their own system of formalities. For once we have villains who can technically do anything, so the story isn't about working out how to defeat them but working out how they think. We know all the answers *now*, yet on first viewing the script takes its time to feed us clues about these people's intentions, and about the way their desires create what we see on-screen. Wrack's ship is an extension of her will, just as Striker's is a parody of English Edwardianism, where the sailors share incomprehensible jokes below decks while the blank-faced upper classes go through the motions of social etiquette. As in "Snakedance", boredom (ironically) becomes a much more interesting motivation than megalomania. We're led to hate Striker and Wrack for being such amoral, hollowed-out creatures, even as we feel sorry for Marriner for… well, for falling for Tegan.

In the end, only the finale disappoints. The revelation that Turlough's Enlightenment is the choice between good and evil comes perilously close to tweeness; you got a lot of this sort of cod-mythic moralising in '80s fantasy, not least because of *The Empire Strikes Back*. The programme might have gotten away with it in earlier, less self-conscious times, but not now. That one point aside, "Enlightenment" manages to present itself as a fairy-tale in all the *right* ways, doing what good fantasy always does and connecting its flights of escapism to tangible, recognisable icons instead of setting itself in a distant and unreachable no-time. A much-underrated story, and the last of its kind.

The Facts

Written by Barbara Clegg. Directed by Fiona Cumming. Viewing figures: 6.8 million, 7.2 million, 6.2 million, 7.3 million.

Supporting Cast Keith Barron (Striker), Valentine Dyall (Black Guardian), Cyril Luckham (White Guardian), Lynda Baron (Wrack), Leee John (Mansell), Christopher Brown (Marriner), Tony Caunter (Jackson).

Oh, Isn't That..?

• *Lynda Baron.* Originally a singer (see "The Gunfighters", 3.8), and eventually the unattainable love of Ronnie Barker's life in seemingly endless BBC sitcom *Open All Hours*. Anyone watching this story on first transmission had only to wait half an hour for the chance to compare her performance with her role as Nurse Gladys Emmanuel. Her daughter was the *Doctor Who* office secretary.

• *Keith Barron.* Household name and star of all sorts of intense dramas (early Dennis Potter plays featured him as the author's alter-ego Nigel Barton), as well as somewhat less intense ITV sitcom *Duty Free*. He once listed his ambition as 'never to be asked to play *Doctor Who*'.

• *Tony Caunter.* One of the half-recognisable faces of '70s television, but now that he's been in *EastEnders* (yes, *another* one) he's a lot more noticeable. He'd been in "Colony in Space" (8.4) as Morgan, and was one of King Richard's troops in "The Crusade" (2.6).

Working Titles "The Enlighteners".

Cliffhangers The scanner in Striker's wheelhouse reveals to the Doctor and company that the racing-ships are actually heading through space; a spacesuit-clad Turlough hurls himself off *The Shadow* in an attempt to escape the Black Guardian's influence; Wrack plants one of her deadly gemstones on the frozen Tegan's tiara.

The Lore

• Barbara Clegg was inspired to write this story when distant relatives stayed at her house and demanded constant entertaining. Like Chris Bidmead, she'd acted regularly in *Emergency Ward 10* and submitted scripts to other soaps as the '60s wore on. She knew Saward, vaguely, from their days in BBC radio drama. Her adaptation of John Wyndham's *The Chrysalids* caused something of a stir in 1981.

• Delays dogged the production, a result of the electricians' strike which had been rumbling on during "Terminus". Rehearsals could proceed, but videotaping was impossible. As a result, the original casting for Captain Striker fell through, as Peter Sallis (Penley in 5.3, "The Ice Warriors") had to bail out in order to make yet another series of wrinkly sitcom *Last of the Summer Wine*. The director had contacted Donald Houston, Nigel Hawthorne and Michael Jayston (see 23.1, "Mysterious Planet" et seq) before recalling Sallis' "distant" performance in a classic serial she'd directed (you guessed it, *The Pallisers*). It was decided early on that the Eternals shouldn't blink.

• Cumming hadn't originally been assigned to this story, but original choice Peter Moffatt had been given "Mawdryn Undead" to handle as the dust settled over the "Space Whale" debacle. Whilst she'd enjoyed the script, the growing problem of simply getting a studio was her main worry. The solution was that the allocation for the season finale, Eric Saward's "The Return" (later "Warhead" and finally 21.4, "Resurrection of the Daleks"), was reassigned to "Enlightenment". Both Saward and designated director Peter Grimwade were furious (see 20.6, "The King's Demons", for the next instalment of the Saward / Nathan-Turner Punch-and-Judy show). Saward, despite thinking that the story lost direction once the first cliffhanger was out of the way, liked the way Clegg handled both television and *Doctor Who* at her first attempt. They collaborated on a pilot for a new series called *Gateway*, although nothing came of it. Saward was already thinking of moving on.

• Saward's only other comment was that the episodes were too short. Episode one was extensively rewritten, with all the "period" dialogue included after Clegg had gone away and looked it up. Practically no cuts were made, although the various publicity photos that were shot on-set have led to false rumours about "missing" scenes, including one of Wrack and her second-in-command hijacking the TARDIS.

• Cumming alerted the producer to another problem. The regular cast-members were playing the characters as written, and this made her - as an "outsider", seeing it the way a viewer might - wonder why these people were travelling together at all. This was resolved with a few quiet chats.

Similarly, Clegg and Cumming had a lunch meeting and decided on small details such as the names of Striker's ship and two anonymous crewmen who were getting more and more lines in the rewrites. Jackson's role was extended, but actor Tony Caunter was needed elsewhere, so in episode three the character's lines were restricted to scenes on film (to be shot at Ealing Studios well in advance). Rehearsals were apparently a bit giggly, in particular the miming of fumbling around in the dark, but carried on through October and November in the belief that shooting would go ahead.

• The story was finally remounted after "The King's Demons" and the completion of "Terminus" in January; Malcolm Clarke only got hold of episode one to score a week before broadcast. The music includes a recycled piece from a documentary about Argentine poet Jorge Luis Borges (for Wrack's party), and additional bangs and stings added by Dick Mills.

• Leee John's band Imagination had been responsible for three big chart hits by this stage. He told his friends that a psychic had predicted he'd be in *Coronation Street* and *Doctor Who*. As yet he's not been on the former, although he's doing well as a self-parody has-been and is probably more in demand now than then. (For the record, he replaced the unavailable David Rhule.)

20.6: "The King's Demons"

(Serial 6J, Two Episodes, 15th March - 16th March 1983.)

Which One is This?   The working title was "A Knight's Tale", which should help you figure out roughly what happens here (no Queen songs on the soundtrack, though). The Doctor meets King John, only to discover that His Majesty's being worked by remote control…

Firsts and Lasts   First appearance of Kamelion, the new robot "passenger" on board the TARDIS, voiced by Gerald Flood and represented on-screen by a spindly electronic android prop that doesn't work anywhere near as well as the programme-makers might have hoped. Partly for this reason, Kamelion is a first for *Doctor Who*; a companion who gets picked up by the Doctor, then completely forgotten about for the next five stories, only to turn up again for his tragic departure.

The Master wears a disguise for the last time, hallelujah. It's also the last involvement Terence Dudley has with the series, but most importantly of all, it's the very last time that the TARDIS doesn't take the Doctor exactly where he wants to go (without outside interference, time corridors, distress signals…).

Two Things to Notice About "The King's Demons"…

1. Yes, let's dwell on the Master's disguise for a moment. This time, Anthony Ainley's required to wear lumpy facial makeup and ginger hair to adopt the persona of Sir Gilles Estram, supposedly a French knight in the employ of King John. (To preserve the "surprise" of the Master's re-appearance, the *Radio Times* listed the actor playing Sir Gilles as "James Stoker", which is at least a more believable anagram than the one for "Time-Flight".) Now, if a TV programme were to feature a *proper* French character, then it'd be normal to hire someone who could actually put on a French accent. Perhaps even someone French. But here Ainley is required to play the Master playing a Gallic knight, in the vain hope that no-one watching has seen *Monty Python and the Holy Grail*. The result can occasionally set your teeth on edge, and for many first-time viewers the reaction on discovering Estram's true identity wasn't so much "good grief!" as "oh, that explains it".

2. For the second time, the Doctor gets involved with a (supposed) King of England at the time of the crusades; is mistaken for a minion of the Devil with supernatural powers; and ends up hurriedly escaping from the bemused witch-hunting locals in the TARDIS (see 2.6, "The Crusade"). Sadly Julian Glover isn't in it this time, but his wife is (see **Oh, Isn't That..?**).

The Continuity

The Doctor   Good enough with human history to know where King John is supposed to be on the 4th of March, 1215. Here the Doctor gets knighted by the King of England, but the monarch turns out to be a shape-changing robot so it doesn't count. He can, as ever, fence well.

• *Ethics.* Prepared to ask for mercy on the Master's part, when the Master's threatened with death by iron maiden. [As in "The Time Monster" (9.5), but see the Master's next major appearance in "Planet of Fire" (21.5).]

• *Background.* He's been to the Eye of Orion, and obviously liked it as he suggests taking the TARDIS crew there. [The Doctor actually manages to get to his holiday destination in the next story.]

The Supporting Cast

• *Tegan.* She's got a new outfit, so at long last she must have followed Nyssa's lead and found the TARDIS wardrobe. She doesn't know enough history to figure out who the King of England is in 1215, but she knows about Magna Carta even if her facts aren't all straight. Tegan doesn't trust Kamelion when he asks to join the TARDIS crew, claiming that he's 'just' a machine [she didn't trust Turlough either, so maybe she just doesn't want the competition]. She emphatically doesn't want to go back home to Earth.

• *Turlough.* Still claims he wants to get back to his planet. Now he's come through his whole "trying to kill the Doctor" phase, Turlough is notably less cowardly and whiny than he was. He says he's been to the Eye of Orion, and describes it as beautiful [he's well-travelled, again suggesting he might see his home as somewhere other than his place of birth]. He's familiar with horses, somehow.

• *Kamelion.* A slender, silver-skinned but rather static android, with a mask-like face and green gemstone-like growths set into his torso, Kamelion was found on the 'benighted' planet Xeraphas by the Master [see 19.7, "Time-Flight"]. The Master states he was produced as a decoy weapon by an 'earlier invader' of Xeraphas, and was instrumental in the Master's escape from the planet, but doesn't go into detail. Kamelion describes himself as a complex mass of artificial neurons. As the name suggests, he has the impressive ability to change his appearance, and is capable - so the Master says - of infinite form or personality. Here he poses as King John, the Doctor, the Master and Tegan, and he can play the lute while he's pretending to be the monarch.

Kamelion can be controlled by simple concentration and psychokinetics, which means he can be overcome by a strong will, so the Master has been using him to cause trouble on Earth. The Doctor and the Master eventually have a mental arm-wrestling match for control of Kamelion, which - naturally - the Doctor wins. At this point it seems clear that Kamelion does have a mind of his own; he's not only intelligent, but civil [because the Doctor's will has "formatted" him that way?], and he obviously doesn't feel culpable for anything he did while in the Master's employ.

He politely asks to join the TARDIS crew, and the Doctor doesn't hesitate to allow it, despite Tegan's reservations that he may still be under the Master's control.

[Yet in the next few stories Kamelion is forgotten, and it eventually turns out that he's been sitting around in a backroom of the TARDIS. This suggests that the Doctor doesn't see him as being part of the crew, and perhaps doesn't wholly trust him, even though a shape-changer would *surely* be a major advantage when exploring hostile alien worlds. It's possible that the Doctor sees Kamelion as a liability, as any strong will encountered outside the TARDIS could take hold of the android and turn him against the rest of the crew. Indeed, this is made explicit in the Missing Adventure *The Crystal Bucephalus*, which also insists on explaining why the TARDIS console room changes after this adventure. If Kamelion's personality here is a reflection of the Doctor's mind, then it might suggest that Kamelion doesn't have "free will" and isn't considered wholly sentient. This might explain the Doctor's rather cavalier attitude towards the robot's survival in "Planet of Fire".]

The Supporting Cast (Evil)

• *The Master.* Now on Earth in 1215, where he's instructed Kamelion to impersonate King John. His plan is to de-rail the signing of the Magna Carta, but the Doctor refers to this as 'small-time villainy' by the Master's standards. After this he intends to undermine the key civilisations of the universe, so that chaos will reign and he can become emperor, etcetera etcetera. [The implication is that this is a "test-run" for Kamelion, so it makes sense that the Master would choose to play with his new toy in the Doctor's favourite country on the Doctor's favourite planet.]

He's disguised as Sir Gilles Estram, his make-up and ginger beard vanishing mysteriously when he wants to reveal himself to the Doctor. [As in "Castrovalva", he's moved on from rubber masks. But in "Castrovalva" it looks as if his disguise is generated by block transfer mathematics, whereas here it can't be. Is he somehow tapping into Kamelion's metamorphic power, or has he just got some sort of pocket-sized holographic device?] His tissue compression eliminator is now affectionately being called 'the compressor'.

[While we're on the subject of naming… the name "Kamelion" seems to be the Master's invention. In this incarnation he's given to pretentious names for gadgets, whereas his previous incarnation simply demonstrated his devices without explanation. Which is why fans refer to the monitoring contraption in "Colony in Space" (8.4) as "the Cherry Bakewell of Doom" rather than, say, "the Tele-Asphixiatory Opticory Manifold".]

The Master's not quite up to the Doctor's standard in a fencing match [as in 9.3, "The Sea Devils"], but has a reputation [exaggerated, surely?] as the best swordsman in France and is good enough in a joust to pose as the King's champion. Indeed, he positively seems to enjoy the chance to fight people to the death. [Despite the obvious risk, and despite the fact that his opponents must *surely* know the weapons better than him.] He doesn't mind handing the Doctor a deadly weapon in mid-fight, because he knows the Doctor won't use it. Once again, he escapes in a TARDIS which isn't fully-functional. [He'll return in the next story, though in an unusual role…]

The TARDIS(es) The Doctor's Ship arrives in the thirteenth century by mistake, and no reason is given for the navigational error. [Is the Ship deliberately tracking the Master?] Tegan has no problem making it dematerialise when the co-ordinates are already set, but an alarm starts to sound, and after some thumping and stabbing at the console she gets it to materialise in the same room as the Doctor. Which is handy.

The Master's TARDIS takes the form of an iron maiden here, and can be carried by only four men. [The iron maiden isn't a thirteenth-century device, which again suggests that a TARDIS' chameleon circuit doesn't scan its surroundings for a suitable form but has a pre-programmed bank of options. As in 18.7, "Logopolis".] He can give remote instructions to Kamelion from his darkened console room. The Doctor ultimately leaves the Master's tissue compression eliminator on board the vessel, switched on, and expects this to affect the dimension circuits. [This only makes sense if the compressor also uses dimensional engineering to shrink its victims, rather than just crushing things into tiny spaces. Presumably the dimensional field it creates messes around with the TARDIS' dimensional technology. This thought is picked up in "Planet of Fire".] This means the vessel won't go anywhere the Master wants it to go.

Once again, the Doctor doesn't recognise the Master's disguised TARDIS when he's staring right at it. [He did in "Terror of the Autons" (8.1), and Gallifreyans seem to have this ability in "The Deadly Assassin" (14.3). By this stage we have to conclude that the Master's vessel has found a way of shielding itself from Time Lord senses.]

History

• *Dating*. It's the 4th of March, 1215, three months away from the signing of the Magna Carta. The Doctor points out that the King will lose the crown jewels next year. [For non-British readers: "The Wash" mentioned in this story is an area of fenland between Norfolk and Lincolnshire which, like western Holland, was drained in the seventeenth century but will probably be underwater again when global warming kicks in. King John tried to escape his opponents by crossing it while it was relatively dry, supposedly on stilts.]

At this point King John is in London, swearing the oath to take the cross as a crusader. The Doctor arrives at the Fitzwilliam Castle, Lord Ranulf's estate around four hours' ride from the capital, where Kamelion is impersonating the King and singing songs of war against the Saracens. Loyal to the King, Ranulf emptied his coffers to support the royal campaign six months ago. [Historically, at this point in time French is the language of the English court. We hear everything in English, but the supposedly French Sir Gilles speaks with a French accent. Whatever process translates for the TARDIS crew, does it take individuals' regional accents into account?]

The Doctor states that the *real* King John is in favour of Magna Carta, but the Master's version plans to alienate the barons, causing John to be killed in battle or deposed. This will stop the foundations of parliamentary democracy being laid, and the Doctor believes that King Philip of France may end up on the throne. [These days it's fashionable to point out that the importance of Magna Carta has been exaggerated over the centuries, making the Master's scheme seem even pettier than it does already. However, Magna Carta was - and is - such a potent symbol of the reigning-in of royal power that removing it *would* make an immense difference to history. Though it wouldn't necessarily lead to a dark age of chaos and barbarism, which is what's implied here.]

The Analysis

Where Does This Come From? It comes from the history books. Not from *history*, but from the history *books*. Does this format seem familiar, at all?

Every British schoolchild knows about Magna Carta, or at least, they did before educational standards took a tumble. The Doctor arrives at a key point in English history, at a moment in time which younger viewers might just have finished reading about in school, but finds that somebody's meddling there and acts as if this means the end of the universe. The programme is making yet another attempt to reinvent one of its "standards" for the modern audience; it's "The Time Meddler" (2.9) with an '80s-style shape-changing robot thrown in.

Of course, the audience knows more about the basics of SF than it used to, so this time there's less exposition. The Meddling Monk had to explain his plan to change history by *literally* signposting it to the audience, writing it out on a big piece of paper in front of our eyes, but here - as in the '70s exploration of the idea, "The Time Warrior" (11.1), and as in the more recent "The Visitation" (19.4) - the whole interfering-with-history problem is more or less taken for granted. Does this make it seem suitably modern, though…?

No. Because the audience has changed in more ways than one. *Doctor Who* in the '60s was never xenophobic, and always had a mandate to educate its viewers about foreign cultures and "alien" ways of thinking. Consider "The Crusade", and the way Saladin's shown to be Richard's equal in honour, nobility and insight (and it's Richard who's doing the cliché of dodgy Arabs, "you like my seester?"). But the Hartnell stories were made at a time when the older members of the population still hadn't come to terms with the shock of World War Two; a time when Britain still, somehow, saw itself as the seat of civilisation. When the Monk threatens to change the outcome of the Battle of Hastings in 1066, it's implicitly acknowledged that derailing British history will have consequences not just for the world but for the natural order of creation itself, and even watching it again *now* it seems to make a sort of sense.

Those watching "The King's Demons", on the other hand, had largely come to terms with the fact that Britain's primary function on the global stage was to act as an American missile base. Despite all the Conservative government's talk of British "greatness", time had robbed us of the idea that we were at the centre of history. Just about everyone who's analysed "The King's Demons" has pointed out that the Master's scheme seems like petty malice, and that the Doctor's 'small-time villainy' comment sounds like a chronic understatement when you remember that two seasons earlier the Master was giving ultimatums to the entire *universe*, but it's not so much a problem with the plot as a problem with the time in which it was made. The Master's presented as evil because he's the enemy of all things British, and therefore the enemy of all things right and proper. Twenty years earlier, that would have been enough. In 1983, it just seemed silly.

However, in America this was exactly what Britain was *for*, televisually speaking. As in much of Season Twenty-One, you get the feeling that even if the production team isn't deliberately aiming at the American market, then it's still thinking "internationally" enough to make the story look like a stereotype of British drama. This was the golden era of US television shows doing "specials" in Merrie Olde England, cashing in on the Lady Di fad and the pop videos on newly-launched MTV - Tenpole Tudor and Adam Ant, hang your silly heads in shame - while the low point of Peter Davison's career in the years after *Doctor Who* was the *Magnum P.I.* episode set in Heritage Themepark Britain. (And *Magnum's* trip to Britain was only the tip of the iceberg. UK viewers of *Murder She Wrote* were astonished to discover that we still had music-hall stars in this country; *Remington Steele* went one better, and had us using steam trains; others of the oeuvre reconstructed modern London streets with gas-lamps, and hired Australian actors to play Cockneys.) We'd played into their hands by fighting a Union-Jack-waving naval war against Argentina for a mudpatch full of penguins, sheep and guano just after a royal wedding. Nay, *the* Royal Wedding. All "The King's Demons" lacked was Perry Como and reindeer.

Things That Don't Make Sense The Master, obviously chuffed with his new shape-changing robot, acts as if Kamelion will give him the power to conquer galaxies. In fact, all Kamelion can do is impersonate people. It's not unreasonable to think that the Master can do this anyway, what with all his seemingly-impenetrable disguises. Surely, the technology which allows Kamelion to change form can't be *that* difficult to find in this universe? Besides, if the Master wants to get in the way of Magna Carta then wouldn't it be simpler just to hypnotise the *real* King John? You get the feeling he's just using Kamelion because the robot's there, not because it makes sense to.

When the benevolent Sir Geoffrey's apprehended, the Master gets him into the great hall in less time than it takes the Doctor to get downstairs. Ranulf's uncertainty as to whether to trust the Doctor verges on the comical in episode one, thanking the Doctor for saving his son, then accusing the Doctor of bewitching the King, then opening up to the Doctor about his concerns, then announcing that the Doctor must be some kind of sorcerer (as if being a sorcerer is somehow worse than being a demon who can appear out of nowhere in a 'blue engine').

Why, precisely, does the Doctor challenge Sir Gilles to a duel at the end of the episode? Apart from the obvious "take things to the cliffhanger" reason? At this point he doesn't seem to suspect that the knight is really the Master, so isn't such a duel just forcing him into a life-or-death situation for no real gain?

Then there are the anachronisms. We can brush a lot of them under the carpet by claiming that there's something wrong with the way the Doctor's 'Time Lord gift' translates language, but much of this just seems sloppy. Aside from using terms like 'kidnap' (and speaking English at all is a bit weird... we're nearly two centuries before Chaucer here), whose idea was the iron maiden? There *was* a thing called an iron maiden then, a sort of glorified tin straightjacket, but the model we've got here is pure melodrama; we're in Hellfire Club territory once spikey coffin-shaped death-machines are wheeled out for "entertainment". And singing in praise of 'total war' so long before the Nazis coined the term would have been puzzling even in French.

And an odd glitch in dialogue delivery... when Turlough's trying to convince the natives that the Master's the bad guy and the Doctor isn't, Mark Strickson delivers the line that's clearly supposed to be '*he's* the evil one!' as 'he's the *evil one!*', as if he's been waiting for the antichrist all his life. As this section is called Things That Don't Make Sense, it's tempting to include every single sentence "Sir Gilles" says; one line comes out sounding like 'his end was to knife pleasant bitches, and newspapers will be forfeited'. He's actually asking what's for breakfast.

Critique So, we know we've seen it all before. There's English history, there are English character actors, and this time there's an unconvincing android waiting for us at the end of it. It doesn't

What Happened at Longleat?

BBC Enterprises, the merchandising, overseas sales and franchise overseers, had been using props and costumes from the series for years. "The *Doctor Who* Experience" was a proven money-spinner. Since 1974 there'd been two exhibitions, one on Blackpool's Golden Mile and another at Longleat House, home of the Marquis of Bath. It was only natural that as the merchandising of the series reached record levels, some anniversary event would be staged. Indeed, as Nathan-Turner had finally managed to get an extra £2,000 per episode from Enterprises, the crossover potential was inevitably going to appeal to him as well.

So over Easter Sunday and Monday, 1983, the BBC was granted use of six acres of the Longleat grounds and the Conservatory for a bit of a do. The organisers braced themselves for up to 50,000 visitors over the weekend. Almost that many arrived on the first day.

If the visitors got in, they found mud and tents. In the tents were props and costume displays, special effects demonstrations (if they timed it right), a chance to see the Radiophonic Workshop's staff at work (or at least chat), on-stage interviews, autograph sessions and the sets from "The Five Doctors". And lots of other people all there for the same reasons. John Leeson worked the PA, in character as K9, requesting people to move from dangerously congested areas. Nobody got hurt, though. It was good-natured, and even Tom Baker seemed at ease with the "rival" Doctors. (But more-so with the children, asking five-year-olds 'are you married?' One managed to leave him speechless by replying 'no, I'm waiting for you'.)

One small tent was converted into a cinema. In the pre-video age, the chance to see old stories was oddly more appealing than seeing what was coming next. The queues led to conversations. Seasoned viewers told children about Hartnell. Hardcore fans gave opinions at odds with *DWM*'s rather over-excitable view of the recent stories. American fans (there were fans in America!) told us they were bored with seeing Hinchcliffe stories over and over again. For many people, the sheer scale of what had seemed a personal affection was astonishing. Anyone who got past the army cadets - issued with UNIT badges and acting as stewards - saw the old footage. (For the record, the stories shown were 2.2, "The Dalek Invasion of Earth"; 6.1, "The Dominators"; 8.1, "Terror of the Autons"; and 13.1, "Terror of the Zygons". An odd selection, but less existed in the archives.)

And there were things to buy. The Radiophonic Workshop tent could supply you with two LPs, one released to celebrate its twenty-fifth birthday and one specifically for *Doctor Who*. And there was a special stick of seaside rock, which tasted horrible. You missed out on one of the Target novelisations? They were there, on sale. *All* of them. And there were membership forms for the Doctor Who Appreciation Society. The group's membership rocketed as a direct result, and the consequences of this would haunt the rest of the series.

But in the interviews several things emerged which, with hindsight, were worrying. John Nathan-Turner had increased his personal profile, and from this point on there was a public figure called "JN-T", who had catchphrases and trademarks like a character in the series. He gained huge rounds of applause for announcing forthcoming "returns" of popular items (Daleks, UNIT, the Master, etc). This became a problem later. A straw-poll at Longleat rated Davison as the least popular Doctor, and public opinion - based on what was said here - suggested his "blandness" was the problem (see 21.7, "The Twin Dilemma", for the "solution").

Worse yet, the sheer scale of public affection and apparent willingness to fork out for anything bearing the logo made "selling" the series as important as making it. This had always been the case to a small extent (see **Why Was There So Much Merchandising?** under 11.4, "The Monster of Peladon"), but whereas having "hard copy" of things like Vega Nexos or the Giant Robot was exciting for children, Joy Gammon's *Knit A TARDIS* and Gary Downie's *Doctor Who Cookbook* were seriously aimed at adults. *Doctor Who* was now something you bought, perhaps even if you'd stopped watching it when they'd moved it from Saturdays. If proof were needed, the BBC Enterprises market research team canvassed opinion on which stories to release on video. People seemed to like Cybermen, but "The Tomb of the Cybermen" wasn't in the archives, so they released a one-hour edit of "Revenge of the Cybermen" for £40. And a lot of people bought it.

The cliché is that "Longleat was our Woodstock". People's mums didn't tag along at Woodstock. And Woodstock was the end of something. Longleat was more like (if we're stuck with this analogy) our 1967 Monterey Festival, when a load of people who thought they were lonely one-offs realised they were a movement, and the people making big-money decisions recognised that the rules had changed.

matter how much time they've spent on the period sets, it doesn't matter how many dogs and horses they've drafted in to make this piece of Medieval pageantry seem "alive", at the end of the day we're being asked to watch a *Television for Schools* production with Time Lords.

Opinion still rages as to whether *any* fifty-minute *Doctor Who* story can function properly, though what you can say for sure is that in a two-part format like this… the Doctor never gets the chance to explore, to investigate, to *question* anything other than to point out the One Big Mystery at the heart of the plot. So the script gets into a terrible rush to plant him in King John's presence, then realises it doesn't have anything else to do with him, at which point things seize up until the Master arrives. Once the Master's in place, there's just time for the Doctor to make one escape from the angry locals before he wanders straight into the room where Kamelion's being kept and has the whole plot explained to him. Follow that with a shockingly weak ending, which basically comes down to "everybody makes a run for it", and all viewers over the age of nine are guaranteed to feel as if they've misread the phrase "second of a two-part story" in the *Radio Times* and it's somehow going to carry on next week.

What's sad here is that even its good conceits misfire. It looks for all the world as if Terence Dudley started out writing a sparkling, all-out romp - ah yes, that old defence of failed historicals, *romp* - but then realised it didn't work and lost his enthusiasm. The Doctor gets some nice performance-pieces when pretending to be a royally-approved demon, but even Peter Davison can't make this seem urgent. Kamelion the walking, talking TARDIS is this season's second attempt at a more interesting kind of companion, but so limp that nobody involved in any of his scenes looks as if they're taking him seriously. Since there's no overt SF content in the whole of the first episode, the sudden appearance of the Master is a twist, but the fact that it's so easy to disguise him just makes you realise how bland Anthony Ainley can be. Try to imagine them hiding the presence of Roger Delgado, and you immediately see the problem.

Ultimately, as with "Arc of Infinity", the *real* trouble isn't that anything here seems utterly, unforgivably ghastly (again, except for the horrible squeaky music) but that it's got nothing to do, nothing to say and nowhere to go. Criticise "The

Time Meddler" all you like, at least it's got Peter Butterworth to cheer things up.

The Facts

Written by Terence Dudley. Directed by Tony Virgo. Viewing figures: 5.8 million, 7.2 million.

Supporting Cast Anthony Ainley (The Master), Frank Windsor (Ranulf), Gerald Flood (King John / voice of Kamelion), Isla Blair (Isabella), Michael J. Jackson (Sir Geoffrey), Christopher Villiers (Hugh).

Oh, Isn't That..?

• *Isla Blair.* Had been in *The History Man* (and if you don't know about that, then what have you been doing all your life?), and had done the obligatory token *Blake's 7* episode ("Duel") in the early '80s. She was, and is, married to Julian Glover (17.2, "City of Death"; but more pertinently 2.6, "The Crusade").

• *Gerald Flood.* Had been in the proto-*Doctor Who* ABC series *Pathfinders* as the morally-ambiguous Harcourt Brown, planning his chicanery while the children explained photosynthesis to the viewers.

• *Frank Windsor.* Less than a year after Stratford Johns dressed up as Mr. Toad (in "Four to Doomsday"), his *Z-Cars* / *Softly Softly* partner also comes to the programme in an attempt to avoid typecasting. He'd already been in *Doctor Who's* antecedent-series *A for Andromeda*, and he'll be back later as the policeman in "Ghost Light" (26.2).

Working Titles "A Knight's Tale", "The Android", "The Demons", "The Demons Keeper" (and different punctuations of this last).

Cliffhangers Sir Gilles ends his swordfight with the Doctor by pulling out a tissue compression eliminator and changing his face into that of the Master. Ta-daah!

The Lore

• The trouble with Kamelion started when Mike Power, the software designer, was killed in a motorboat crash just before filming. The design had been modified from a robot built with a view to inclusion in the film *Xtro*, and semi-regular effects honcho Richard Gregory offered to help with the refit, having sold Nathan-Turner on the idea of a "real" robot. Even though it couldn't walk, there was clear potential in being one-up on all the other robots that were clearly men (or children) in suits. According to one report, it took a fortnight to program the lip-synch, and none of the technical staff could agree on whose job it was to run the thing. As it was the electricians' union EETPU that was delaying "Terminus" and "Enlightenment", including this prop was an almost suicidal move by Nathan-Turner…

• The jousting scene had been intended to go on longer, but the delay moved filming to the shortest days of the year. Bodiam Castle, the nearest "right" one to London (other than Windsor, obviously), was chosen. Tony Virgo had been a production associate, and had worked alongside Peter Grimwade on *Tinker, Tailor, Soldier, Spy*; he later wound up as producer of *EastEnders*. He left the joust until last, but it began to rain, after a perfectly fine day of shooting the "pick-up" shots. He'd consulted a colleague who'd done something similar for American TV, and had planned an elaborate storyboard, but they ended up getting as much done as they could and piecing something together in the edit.

• The rehearsals were punctuated by rehearsals for *Cinderella*, produced by Lovell Bickford, written and directed by John Nathan-Turner, starring Peter Davison, Sandra Dickinson and Anthony Ainley. This was at the Theatre Royal, Brighton, only a few miles from Bodiam Castle. Meanwhile Eric Saward got confirmation from Terry Nation that Saward's Dalek story "The Return" was acceptable, provided that Davros escaped and the pepperpots seemed less vulnerable. When the strike caused this to go belly-up, Grimwade took Saward and the crew he'd assembled to lunch. Nathan-Turner wasn't invited (being busy elsewhere), and when he found out became furious, haranguing the "guilty" parties about loyalty.

• Saward hadn't been enthusiastic about reusing Terence Dudley as a writer, but Nathan-Turner had been keen on his script for *K9 and Company*, strangely.

• When the second episode was broadcast, the BBC showed a promotional clip for the forthcoming event at Longleat House in Wiltshire. On *Nationwide* the next day, Davison appeared with Jon Pertwee and Patrick Troughton to discuss the series, the event and "The Five Doctors", which had been filmed on location that week and which

would begin studio shooting a fortnight later. Which brings us to…

20.7: "The Five Doctors"

(Serial 6K, One Ninety-Minute Episode, 25th November 1983.)

Which One is This? Have you seen the title? It's the TV-movie extravaganza starring three Doctors and two nearly-Doctors, trapped in a gloomy wilderness (Wales) and heading for the Dark Tower of Rassilon. (If you're British, then you may remember it being shown in the middle of the *Children in Need* telethon and Terry Wogan stepping out of the void after the end credits.)

Firsts and Lasts Not technically part of Season Twenty, but a one-off special shown in the gap between the 1983 and 1984 seasons, "The Five Doctors" is unique in several ways; it's the only "feature-length" episode of the original series, the only one shown out of season and the only one pre-Paul McGann to have been shown in America before the UK. (PBS stations broadcast it on the exact day of the series' twentieth anniversary, whereas BBC1 didn't find space for it until two days later.)

It's the first time the novelisation was released before the broadcast of the story, the first time fans could get really close-up to the sets (see **What Happened at Longleat?** in the previous story) and the first one to be shown after Davison's impending retirement - and the identity of his replacement - was announced. Less obviously, this was the last time that a *Doctor Who* episode was widely perceived as a big *event*, and in the programme's own lifetime the last occasion on which it got onto the cover of the *Radio Times*.

Since this is the twentieth anniversary get-together, various old faces from the series' history make their last appearances here. So it's goodbye to Susan Foreman, Sarah Jane Smith, K9, Zoe Heriot, Liz Shaw and Mike Yates (although the last three of these appear as phantoms, not as "real" people). It's also goodbye to Jon Pertwee as the Third Doctor, who gets to talk about reversing the polarity of the neutron flow for only the second time in his on-screen career, and to the Yeti. Perhaps thankfully, we bid adieu to the planet Gallifrey, as well as to President Borusa.

Off-screen, it's farewell to Terrance Dicks, penning his last ever script for the series, although in

ABOUT TIME 1980–1984

later years he'll fill up his spare time writing novels, appearing on nostalgia documentaries and devising the *Doctor Who: The Ultimate Adventure* stage-play. But at least Rassilon, definitive founder of Time Lord civilisation since "The Deadly Assassin" (14.3), gets his one and only on-screen appearance here. And it's hello to the new TARDIS console, replacing the incredibly cheap-looking one that's been in service since Season Fifteen. You can tell the Doctor's proud of it.

This was also the first *Doctor Who* story to be "remixed". The version re-released on BBC video in 1995 is a new cut of the story, cleaned up, re-mastered and with computer-generated special effects (two years before *Star Wars* tried it, but with similarly controversial results…).

Twenty (Yes, Twenty!) Things to Notice About "The Five Doctors"…

1. It's called "The Five Doctors", but only three of them are really there. William Hartnell died in 1975, of course, so stepping into his check trousers to play the First Doctor is Richard Hurndall. He does his best, but is somewhat thwarted by the clip of Hartnell we see at the very beginning of the story (taken from the last episode of 2.2, "The Dalek Invasion of Earth"). In the days before the series was cancelled, Hurndall's presence in this story made it harder than ever to answer that old pub-quiz question, "how many *Doctor Who*s have there been?".

2. Tom Baker isn't really here either, although he gave various excuses for his non-attendance (see **The Lore**) and at the time rumours ranged from "he's in a monastery" and "he's in prison" to the *Abbey-Road*-style "he's dead". Publicity shoots for this story featured Baker's waxwork from Madame Tussauds, and nobody on Earth was fooled. His appearances in "The Five Doctors" are, for those of you who slept through Volume IV, all cannibalised footage from "Shada" (17.6).

3. Season Twenty opened with a story in which a member of the High Council of the Time Lords turned out to be a traitor, and the first three-quarters of the story made sure we only got to see this mysterious figure's hand as he fiddled about with sinister technology and tried to use the Doctor as his pawn. Now we get to go through the same routine all over again, watching the Doctor's various incarnations being menaced by a black-gloved fist that does everything it can to "emote" at us (hovering over controls to suggest thought-fulness, slamming itself against control panels to suggest anger, etc). As in "Arc of Infinity", this whole "who's the traitor?" question is rather brought down by the lack of credible suspects, since the Council now consists of fewer Time Lords than ever before.

4. And inexplicably, Borusa the renegade President changes into an entirely new set of clothes whenever he has to do this "sinister hands" routine in his secret control room, wearing black instead of white in order to underline the fact that he's gone evil.

5. The timescoop, which snatches the various Doctors from their rightful places in space-time, manifests itself on-screen as an all-consuming rectangle of solid black. Technically speaking it's not the greatest of effects, but it is at least a striking image, a big square hole in the sky that tracks down its victims and swallows them whole. This wasn't good enough for the people responsible for the 1995 re-edit, however, who replaced it with a crap CGI cone that looked crass and out-of-date even then.

6. Not only that, but the remixers decided to electronically treat the voice of Rassilon, changing Richard Mathews' sneering, wizard-like tones into a horrible moaning noise that's apparently supposed to be "scarier". This is, of course, the *Doctor Who* version of "Greedo fires first".

7. But one cut made to the story by the re-edited version has caused less controversy; the moment when one of the Cybermen wanders over a hill in the Death Zone and spots the Doctor and company in the valley below. Its reaction to this discovery, an unusually satisfied-sounding 'ahh!', again makes you wonder if the Cybermen are actually quite chatty when nobody's around and like talking to themselves when they're on guard duty (see 19.6, "Earthshock").

8. Then there's the Cyberman who, wounded by the Raston warrior robot, does his best to shamble after the Third Doctor and Sarah but topples over and makes an 'uuuuh' noise that sounds like someone recovering from a hangover. One of his associates even throws up, while another is visibly wearing jeans when grabbing the Brigadier's arm. Not to mention the Cyber-Leader so short-sighted that he fails to spot Tegan and the Doctor running for cover when he enters the Dark Tower, even though they're right in front of him, and so stupid that he lets the Master casually pick up one of the dead Cybermen's weapons immedi-

ately after the Master turns out to have betrayed them all. Then he looks surprised when he gets blasted to death. As much as a Cyberman *can* look surprised.

9. The first scene in the chamber of the Time Lord High Council witnesses one of the series' oddest mis-delivered lines. The conversation goes something like this. Castellan: 'The constitution clearly states that when, in emergency session, the members of the inner Council are unanimous -' Flavia: '- which indeed we are -' Borusa: '- the President of the Council may be overruled.' But Paul Jerricho, as the Castellan, doesn't seem to realise that he's only delivering the *start* of a sentence and urgently announces 'the constitution clearly states that when in emergency session the members of the inner Council ARE UNANIMOUS!!!!', as if he's making an important statement. As Borusa says, 'what a ridiculous clause'. Add to this the sheer risibility of Anthony Ainley's delivery (enunciating the line 'I may be seated?' as if it's one word), and it's no wonder this scene is so often performed as a party-piece by drunk fans.

10. The Castellan also gets to deliver most of this story's everybody-join-in lines: 'We have a power-boosted, open-ended transmat beam'; 'I... am... IN-occent!'; and, after a comedy moment in which he tries to resist handcuffing with a Ronald Reagan gesture, 'no... not the mind-*probe*!'.

11. The Doctor's address to Chancellor Flavia in the last scene deserves attention, as well. He tells her to return to Gallifrey, even though that's the planet they're both standing on (he means the Capitol rather than the wastes of the Death Zone, but even so...), then orders her to summon the Council even though she's the Council's only surviving member. At least, as far as we've seen. He does this to keep her busy while he makes his escape from Gallifrey, but how long does he think it's going to take her to carry out his instructions...?

12. Arriving in the Death Zone, the Third Doctor meets up with Sarah when he has to dramatically save her from rolling down a small slope. You may want to marvel at the world's least perilous natural hazard, and at the fact that Lis Sladen can scream as if she means it anyway. (There's an edit of "The Five Doctors" that slices the story up into four episodes, and this is actually turned into a cliffhanger. There's an even worse one involving the Master and a musical staircase.)

13. And those who've been following the odd effects of transmat beams in *Doctor Who* - see especially 12.5, "Revenge of the Cybermen" - will be interested to note that when the Master uses one to enter the Death Zone, he arrives in the bleak, frozen wasteland wearing a cape that he didn't have when he started his journey. It's nice to see the technology making sure everyone's wrapped up snugly.

14. There's also a scene in which the Master discovers a similarly cloak-wrapped corpse in the Death Zone and declares it's one of his 'predecessors'. Presumably this just means that it's one of the two Time Lords sent into the Zone before him, but the sinister cape makes it look as if one of his former incarnations died here at some point. There's a BBC novel in that idea somewhere.

15. The Death Zone is - all together now - "a place of ancient evil"; the opening line of the novelisation, which had been committed to memory *before broadcast* in some cases. And the Eye of Orion is the most relaxing, beautiful place in the galaxy. Both of them look like a wet afternoon in Wales. We imagine a return to at least one of these exotic locales is on the cards for Eccleston's Doctor in 2005, given that the multi-kerjillion-pound BBC Wales production has so far only left Cardiff to go to London and Swansea.

16. The music goes out of its way to get the theme tune in by any means necessary. Even the sheet music for the Harp of Rassilon features a bit of it. (Or at least, it does in the original mix... the "dub" version has something sounding like the backing track for "The Boy is Mine" by Brandy.)

17. Colonel Crichton, the Brigadier's replacement at UNIT, is the one who gets to do the age-old 'who?' gag when someone tells him that the strange little man at UNIT HQ is the Doctor. Even though he was *talking* about the Doctor just a couple of minutes beforehand. No wonder Bambera got the job (26.1, "Battlefield").

18. Time is not a kind mistress. By 1983 many of the actors recalled to reprise their old companion roles hadn't been seen in the series for six, thirteen or even seventeen years, so if the story's going to make sense then you have to make allowances for wrinkles. It's not unreasonable for Susan to be all grown-up when she's reunited with the Doctor, but it's hard to explain why the Doctor sees ghostly illusions of his old friends that make them look like even *older* friends.

Similarly, it's doubtful that any theory of *Doctor Who* continuity can explain the state of the Third Doctor's hair.

19. As has already been noted, an explanation for the changes between "The Kings' Demons" and "The Five Doctors" - the disappearance of Kamelion, for example, and the new-look TARDIS console - is provided by the novel *The Crystal Bucephalus*. Though it's in no way wholly canonical, the book *is* exactly the same width as the gap in the middle of the video boxed set of "The King's Demons" and "The Five Doctors", so it plugs a hole in more ways than one.

20. The story goes out of its way to end where the series began: with the Doctor going on the run from his people in a rackety old TARDIS ('after all, that's how it all started'). The credits roll to the original *Doctor Who* theme from the '60s, which fades into the '80s version halfway through. So there's a real feeling of coming full-circle here, the sense that we've been promised a new start now the celebrations are over. We'll come back to this thought later…

The Continuity

The Doctor When the timescoop begins snatching the Doctor's other incarnations from his own past, the current version feels it as a terrible pain, and he comes close to the point of collapse. He loses consciousness after the Fourth Doctor becomes trapped in a time eddy, and starts to fade in and out, appearing and disappearing from the TARDIS console room due to 'temporal instability'. He claims he's being dragged into a time vortex, as part of him is there already, although he stabilises after a while. When the Doctors gather together in one place, the First, Second and Third incarnations can concentrate to link their minds as one and break Borusa's mental hold on the Fifth.

The current Doctor describes himself as being in his fourth regeneration, and appears a little wary of upsetting the cranky First Doctor, but they end up arguing over strategy anyway. The First seems less inclined to rush off into danger [and was the only Doctor to have died of old age]. The new boy claims that two versions of the same person only meet in 'the gravest emergencies' [he's remembering the events of 10.1, "The Three Doctors"], but he can safely touch his other selves without ill effects [q.v. **What is the Blinovitch Limitation Effect?** under 20.3, "Mawdryn Undead"]. He can read Old High Gallifreyan, although the Second Doctor notes that not many

people understand it these days. When he's offered the Presidency of the Time Lords, he's typically horrified, passing the buck to Chancellor Flavia and then escaping in the TARDIS.

As for the *other* Doctors…

(a) The First Doctor is in a large, formal-looking garden when the timescoop gets him. [It could well be the garden where he was observed by the Time Lords in "The Three Doctors".] Meeting Susan, he's not surprised to see that she's grown up and acts as if he hasn't seen her in a while. [So he's been taken from a point in his life after 2.2, "The Dalek Invasion of Earth".]

He's as impatient with his older / younger selves as with everyone else, and only Susan gets off lightly. Curiously, it's the First Doctor who works out the meaning of the "riddle" in the tomb of Rassilon, and even the Fifth Doctor doesn't seem to understand why the less experienced version of himself should be wiser. [Maybe Time Lords get cleverer as they're allowed to settle in to their bodies. The First Doctor's lifespan is much longer than that of any of the others.] The First Doctor doesn't recognise the Master at all, and has to be reminded that they were at the Academy together, but he knows the Second Doctor as 'the little fellow' before they meet [so he remembers the events of "The Three Doctors"]. He sees himself as being old [even though Time Lords can apparently live for thousands of years, so he must perceive each of his regenerations as a different "life"].

(b) The Second Doctor is taken from UNIT HQ during a UNIT reunion, apparently in the 1980s. He claims he read about the affair in the next day's *Times*, and came back to see the Brigadier. He remembers his trial by the Time Lords, and believes that Jamie and Zoe shouldn't recognise him as they had their memories of him erased [6.7, "The War Games"]. He also remembers meeting Omega and the Third Doctor; is familiar with the current UNIT HQ [all from "The Three Doctors"]; and says that he's bending the laws of time to be there, if not actually breaking them. He states that 'for once' he was able to steer the TARDIS to get to the HQ.

[This is hard to comprehend for so many reasons. In the first place, if he remembers his trial then he must have been scooped from a point after "The War Games" but before he appeared as the Third Doctor in "Spearhead from Space" (7.1). This would seem to lend credence to the theory that there are "unseen" Second Doctor adventures after "The War Games" - see **Is There a Season 6b?** under 22.4, "The Two Doctors" - but this raises new problems, as we'll see in that essay. The alternative is that he gains some of the Third Doctor's memories when the two link minds in "The Three Doctors", so he knows about his trial even before it happens. Which may be even stickier. And why is he bending the laws of time by meeting the Brigadier? Because the Brigadier knows so much about his future adventures? Because the Blinovitch Limitation Effect shouldn't let him go back a day to attend an event reported in the press? Or what?]

The Second Doctor's instincts aren't as sharp as those of the First or Third, as he doesn't sense it when something's obviously wrong with the Fifth Doctor.

(c) The Third Doctor and Bessie are snatched from an unidentified road, evidently in Britain. He recognises Sarah when he meets her [so it's after 11.1, "The Time Warrior", on his timeline], and isn't surprised when she turns out to be from a different time, or when she tells him that she saw him change his appearance. [His suggestion that his replacement was all 'teeth and curls' is a guess based on Sarah's hand-gestures, not a premonition of the Fourth Doctor, although he does accept all of this *very* quickly. As the Doctor knows Sarah and is busy going for Bessie-rides on Earth, he was most probably scooped in the gap between "The Monster of Peladon" (11.4) and "Planet of the Spiders" (11.5).] It takes him a while to realise who the new-look Master is, and unlike the others he's paranoid enough to believe that it might be the Time Lords *en masse* who are responsible for abducting him. As on their last meeting, the Second and Third Doctors get on each others' nerves.

(d) The Fourth Doctor and Romana are scooped from a punt in Cambridge, and eventually get put back in the same city. [Thus preventing the adventure they should have had in "Shada" (17.6), which explains why that story has such dubious canonicity. Sort of. See "Shada" for a bigger discussion of this.]

None of the Doctors seem particularly bothered by the fact that Borusa, their old mentor and occasional friend, is condemned to an eternal living death for his own folly [the Fifth Doctor, at least, must feel less well-disposed towards Borusa after the events of "Arc of Infinity" (20.1)].

It's not established whether the Doctors will retain any of their memories of this affair when they're returned to their proper places in space and time. [Or whether their histories will be changed if they do. Again, see **Is There a Season 6b?** under "The Two Doctors". A quick memory-wipe seems likely, and surely can't be beyond Rassilon's powers.]

• *Inventory.* The Second Doctor uses a firework called a Galactic Glitter to light up a Yeti. Meanwhile the First Doctor throws away several coins when testing the energy-beam trap in the Dark Tower.

• *Bessie.* The Doctor's car is equipped with some handy rope for lifting companions out of trouble. Bessie's damaged by an energy-bolt here, and left in the Death Zone [but presumably returned to Earth by Rassilon... does he valet her, as well?].

• *Background.* The Doctor knows the legends of Rassilon and the Death Zone, including the fact that Daleks and Cybermen were never brought there, and the Second Doctor sings an old nursery-rhyme about possible ways into Rassilon's Tower. The Second Doctor also reminisces about an adversary called the Terrible Zodin, but remembers that the Brigadier never met her; he states that she happened in the future, and continues the anecdote with the words 'covered in hair, and used to hop like kangaroos...'. [See 22.1, "Attack of the Cybermen", for more. If you care.] The Third Doctor recognises a Raston warrior robot on sight.

The Fifth Doctor claims to have known the current Castellan of the Time Lords for a long time. [We've only seen them meet once before, in "Arc of Infinity". But "Arc" itself hinted at there being at least one unseen visit to Gallifrey. See also **The Time Lords**.] Strangely, Chancellor Flavia tells the Doctor that 'yet again' she has the honour of informing him he's to be President. [She certainly didn't have that honour in 15.6, "The Invasion of Time", and this is the first time we've ever seen her. So what have we missed?]

The Supporting Cast

• *Tegan.* She's visibly heartbroken when she thinks the Doctor is going to give up adventuring and become President of Gallifrey, and visibly overjoyed when it turns out he's not. She's still very "into" this whole lifestyle, although she's not inclined to play the hostess role for the tetchy First Doctor.

Once again, Tegan has an instinctive knowledge of the names of flashy pieces of technology, identifying the 'entry-coder' at the door to the

Dark Tower as if it's the kind of phrase you'd use every day in Brisbane rather than in *Star Trek*. [See also her unexpected familiarity with transmats in 20.3, "Mawdryn Undead", and her insistence on using the full name of the tissue compression eliminator in the last story.]

• *Turlough.* Cocky enough to think he can tell whether all the TARDIS' instruments are in working order. After all the complaining and cringing of recent times, Turlough is entirely at peace when he visits the Eye of Orion, spending some time sketching in the tranquil atmosphere. Judging by the Doctor's reaction, he isn't very good. He's not quaking in the face of immediate danger any more, although a bomb placed outside the TARDIS still makes him edgy.

• *Susan.* Reunited with the First Doctor after all these years [2.2, "The Dalek Invasion of Earth"], and she's still calling him 'grandfather'. She's grown-up now, though, apparently middle-aged rather than in her teens. She's delighted when she meets the old Doctor, but she makes no attempt to tell him what she's been doing recently. [There's no indication of how long it's been for Susan since she left the TARDIS, or whether she ages like a human being. The fact that she's so happy to see the Doctor, and doesn't blame him for forcing her to stay behind on twenty-second-century Earth, suggests that she's had quite a good time there.] Her clothing hints that she's come directly from somewhere Earth-like. She doesn't recognise the Master, gets on well with the "modern" TARDIS crew, and accepts that the Fifth Doctor is the same man as her grandfather without anybody having to explain regeneration to her [in the "extended" mix she practically ogles him…]. She recognises the Tower of Rassilon on sight [not from personal experience, as it's part of Gallifreyan folklore]. Like the others, she's returned to her own time after events here.

• *The Brigadier.* The retired Brigadier is seen visiting the UNIT reunion, where he's giving a speech as the guest of honour. [This is clearly after the events of 20.3, "Mawdryn Undead", as he recognises the Doctor and Tegan. Curiously, he doesn't comment on Turlough's rather protracted truancy.] He's grown his moustache back [since being cured of his long-term mental problems]. Despite some griping at the Second Doctor, here his relationship with the Doctors ultimately seems stronger than ever, and he gets the chance to sock the Master one last time.

• *Sarah Jane Smith.* Currently living in a house in the suburbs [not necessarily Croydon, but not right out in the sticks]. On finding herself transported to a hostile environment on another planet, she gets back into the old routine almost immediately, not being overawed or whinging about being abducted. She treats the big get-together of Doctors and companions as just one of those things. She's never heard of the Master before.

• *K9.* Sarah's K9 senses the timescoop coming to get Sarah long before it happens, and even deduces that the Doctor's involved [just playing the odds].

The Supporting Cast (Evil)

• *The Master.* Called to Gallifrey [by what method?], he's happy to walk straight into the High Council's chamber as if he's got nothing to fear, and doesn't seem to doubt that they want to make a deal with him. [Unusually trusting for him, surely? He used to be raving paranoid.]

He initially believes that the Time Lords have nothing to give him, and isn't interested in their pardon, but agrees to work for the Council when they offer him a new regenerative cycle. As ever, his own survival is all he cares about, although naturally enough he tries to steal the prize of immortality when he finds himself in the tomb of Rassilon.

Interestingly, the Master states that a universe without the Doctor 'doesn't bear thinking about' [he doesn't sound sarcastic, as if he realises he needs the competition], and the idea of rescuing the Doctor obviously amuses him. Crossing the death-trap inside the Dark Tower, the Master unexpectedly proves to be better at puzzles than the First Doctor.

Ultimately Rassilon returns the Master to his proper place in the universe, along with everyone else. [Which is strange, as the Master wasn't timescooped here but was sent by the Time Lords. What does Rassilon consider his proper place? Moreover, the Master's TARDIS is on the verge of suffering dimensional damage in "The King's Demons" (20.6), but there's no mention of it here. Do the Time Lords bring him to Gallifrey through some means other than his TARDIS?] Rassilon believes that the Master's sins will eventually find him out [which probably wouldn't be of much comfort to all the people he's going to kill after being set free].

The TARDIS The Doctor has just finished fixing up the TARDIS, so the central console now looks much busier and shinier than it did. He believes it'll work properly once it's 'run in', and says the Ship's not merely a machine but more like a person, needing coaxing and persuading. It also needs a thump to make the new door control work. There are obviously sketching materials on board the Ship for Turlough to use.

Fixing up some sustenance for the First Doctor and Susan, Tegan and Turlough provide actual, proper food and drink, including fruit and cocktails. [From the TARDIS kitchens, mentioned in 17.6, "Shada"? This certainly isn't the product of the food machine from 1.2, "The Daleks".] After the Doctors set up the computer-scanner, a computerised diagram of the Tower of Rassilon is called up on the small screen on the console, and blinking dots appear to mark out the positions of the various Doctors. This scanner is said to be keyed to his brain-pattern. [The Doctor is the only person the TARDIS knows well enough to carry out this particular kind of scan. This means, logically, that his brain-pattern doesn't change when he regenerates.] At one point the Doctor speaks of sending a recall signal to call his other selves, but nothing comes of it.

Departing the Death Zone for their own times and places, the various Doctors and companions all bundle into the same TARDIS. The outlines of other TARDISes then split off from the Ship, each of them going in a different direction. The "current" Doctor expects this, and obviously believes it's perfectly normal for Rassilon to send them home in this way. [Is the TARDIS *really* splitting off pieces of itself, or is the Ship just being used as a focus for Rassilon's power, or… something?]

The Time Lords The Time Lord High Council now seems to consist of three people, but two other members have recently vanished in the Death Zone. This body is also referred to as the 'Inner Council' [meaning that the five-person Council we're used to seeing is just the core of a larger body, which explains why the Doctor later tells Flavia to summon the Council when she's the last of the surviving five]. Borusa is still President, the other two members being the Castellan and Chancellor Flavia. [The Castellan is the same as in "Arc of Infinity", and it's not too much of a stretch to suppose that Flavia was originally a replacement for Hedin. If the Doctor's time passes at the same rate as Gallifrey's, though, then it can't have

been more than a few weeks since the Omega crisis. What made Borusa regenerate? Stress?]

The Council has noticed that the Death Zone has been reactivated, as it's somehow been draining energy from the Eye of Harmony to an extent that threatens all of Gallifrey. They've found that the Doctor 'no longer exists' in any of his regenerations, and that the time-traces of his various selves all converge in the Zone. Two members of the High Council ventured into the Zone [Thalia and Zorac from "Arc of Infinity"?], but neither returned. When they call in the Master as an 'expendable' agent, it's done against the President's wishes, but the constitution states that in an emergency session the President can be overruled if the other members of the inner council ARE UNANIMOUS.

The Master is given the Seal of the High Council, a golden disc which proves him to be on official Time Lord business, and promised a whole new regeneration cycle - as well as a pardon - if he rescues the Doctor. ["The Deadly Assassin" indicates that *nothing* known to the Time Lords can stop them dying after their twelfth regeneration, but now it seems there's a way that requires the Council's consent. This effectively proves that Time Lords are only mortal because they *want* to be, an idea backed up by Rassilon's objection to the concept of immortality. Still, see **Things That Don't Make Sense**. This may at least shed some light on what the Minyans do with Time Lord technology in "Underworld" (15.5), and what Mawdryn does with it in "Mawdryn Undead" (20.3).]

Events here end with the Council in disarray, again. The Chancellory Guard shoots dead the Castellan when he's suspected of being a traitor and tries to escape. [The guards don't shoot to stun, and it all happens off-screen, so it's possible that Borusa gives the guardsmen secret orders to have the Castellan killed.] The Doctor states that he knew the Castellan of old, and that the man was fiercely loyal to his oath of office; mention of the dark days of ancient Gallifrey filled him with horror. [That settles it. He's definitely *not* a regenerated Kelner from "The Invasion of Time".] Once Borusa's imprisoned, the Chancellor forces the Presidency on the Doctor, the Council having used its 'emergency powers' to give him this position. The Doctor grants Flavia full deputy powers until he returns, and then runs away, but he's still technically President again [he loses this position by 23.1, "The Mysterious Planet"] and expects the

ABOUT TIME 1980-1984

Time Lords to be furious about his flight.

Found in the room of the Castellan, and apparently planted there by Borusa, are the Black Scrolls of Rassilon. These Scrolls are contained in a small casket, marked with the Seal of Rassilon. [The sideways-infinity-symbol was only referred to as the *Prydonian* seal in "The Deadly Assassin", so maybe Rassilon was the founder of the Prydonian Chapter. Then again, we never saw the Doctor's Prydonian seal in close-up, so it may have been a variation on Rassilon's symbol rather than exactly the same design. Certainly, non-Prydonians use the Seal of Rassilon. What's interesting here is that the guards find the box suspicious just *because* it's marked with the Seal, as if anything bearing Rassilon's mark is a significant artefact of some kind. This obviously won't be the case by the time of the TV Movie.]

The scrolls burst into flame when the box is opened. The Time Lords act as if these documents are well-known from legend, while Borusa states that they contain forbidden knowledge from the Dark Time. Their origin remains a mystery. [The implication is that Borusa learned everything he knows about the Death Zone, the timescoop and the Game of Rassilon from the Scrolls.] When it comes to legends, the Death Zone is referred to by the Master as 'the black secret at the heart of your Time Lord paradise' [meaning, everyone knows about it but they don't like to mention it].

Amazingly, Flavia still finds it inconceivable that there might be a traitor in the ranks of the High Council.

• *Borusa.* The current President has recently regenerated, again [see "The Deadly Assassin", "The Invasion of Time" and "Arc of Infinity"], but the Doctor indicates that he still has some regenerations left. In this new form he's a lot tougher than he was the last time the Doctor visited Gallifrey, and as stubborn as ever, but he's still not quite the canny politician of old. In fact he's become a rather grim, sombre figure, grumbling at his subordinates on the High Council instead of giving them the sharp edge of his tongue.

In fact, it turns out that he's gone power-mad. He suggests that he was ruling Gallifrey from behind the scenes even before he became President [this much is at least credible], and believing that he'll soon have to retire - his work half-done - he wants to be President Eternal. It was Borusa who reactivated the Death Zone on Gallifrey, and who's been kidnapping versions of

the Doctor to play the Game of Rassilon in the hope of gaining immortality; see **Ancient Time Lords** and **Planet Notes**. When exposed, he has no qualms about using the Coronet of Rassilon to emphasise his will and mentally control the Doctor's actions. This ability can freeze a whole bunch of humans with a single word. Eventually Borusa gains the immortality he seeks, when Rassilon turns him to stone inside the Tower in the Death Zone.

[All of this is massively out of character for the Borusa we know. Terrance Dicks has since suggested that Borusa was unstable after his regeneration, and to be fair, so many regenerations in such a short span of time can't have been good for the man. He *sounds* unstable, when he's describing his plans to the Doctor. By way of apology Dicks has released Borusa from his imprisonment in the Tower on two separate occasions, in the Virgin novel *Blood Harvest* and the BBC novel *The Eight Doctors*.]

Ancient Time Lords

• *Rassilon.* The Time Lords weren't always "noble". In the days before Rassilon they had 'tremendous powers' which they misused disgracefully, abducting beings from across space and time, and forcing these victims to fight each other in the Death Zone on Gallifrey. [Ergo, the timescoop predates Rassilon. Were the Time Lords actually *called* Time Lords in those days? It's a bit of a grey area.]

The Doctor points out that Daleks and Cybermen were never used in the Death Zone even during the Time Lords' most corrupt period, as they 'played the game too well'. [He says this as if it's part of the ancient stories, not a historical fact he's picked up on his travels, and he expects the High Council to know it already. This would indicate that the Doctor knew about Daleks and Cybermen before he left Gallifrey. He certainly knew about Mondas the first time he was seen to come into contact with the Cybermen (4.2, "The Tenth Planet"), but whether or not he knew about Daleks on his first meeting with them is open to debate (see 1.2, "The Daleks").]

Rassilon eventually put a stop to the games, sealing off the Death Zone and forbidding the use of the timescoop. But while the official history says he was a good man, there are rumours that his fellow Time Lords rebelled against his cruelty and locked him in the Dark Tower in perpetual sleep. [Engin in "The Deadly Assassin" never even considers the latter option, and takes it as read that Rassilon was the founder of Time Lord civilisation.] He's believed to be dead, though nobody really knows how extensive his powers were.

The truth is, Rassilon still exists within his Tower in the Death Zone. As Borusa knows [from the Black Scrolls, though it doesn't seem to be a well-known legend], anyone who braves the Zone and reaches the Tower can claim the great prize of immortality. This gauntlet is known as the Game of Rassilon, and the Second Doctor has heard of it. [It *doesn't* seem to be the same as the 'games' that were played in the Death Zone in the olden days, so Rassilon set up his own challenge here after the timescoop was officially shut down. This suggests that despite the claims of the stories, he *wanted* to take up residence in the Death Zone.]

When the Doctors successfully reach Rassilon's tomb within the Tower, an image of Rassilon himself appears above the ornately-robed, perfectly-preserved body that rests on the central bier. It's a huge, Cheshire-Cat-like head, a man with an evil grin, an elaborate moustache and a little conical hat. He knows who the Doctors and Borusa are without being told, and doesn't seem to object to being stuck here in the Tower [again, he obviously planned this fate].

At this point Borusa steps in and claims the prize on the Doctor's behalf, although he apparently needs the permission of at least one Doctor to do this. He takes the ring from the hand of Rassilon, at which point he becomes immortal by turning into one of the stone heads on the side of the casket. The eyes of the other heads are capable of looking around while Borusa's being transformed in this way, and the ring returns to Rassilon's finger afterwards. There are at least three "living" Time Lord heads on the bier already [all former Presidents?], while Rassilon himself is said to possess the same kind of immortality. [Does he normally only exist as a statue, but come to life when energy is fed into the Death Zone?]

Rassilon vanishes again soon afterwards. The Doctors speculate that Rassilon knew immortality was a curse, and set up the Game to trap those who sought everlasting power. [One thing that's not addressed here… before now the Time Lords have apparently never penetrated the Death Zone, possibly for cultural reasons as they have no problem transmatting people into the area. But after the Doctors switch off the force-field, the High Council has easy, convenient access to Rassilon's

tomb. Do the Councillors ever try to raise Rassilon? Do they ever consult with him, or try to analyse the quasi-mystical technology in his Tower? Or would too much power be needed to keep him "alive"? Then again, they might just get scared and reseal the Death Zone as the First Doctor suggests.]

The Non-Humans

• *Daleks.* There's one, at least, in the Death Zone. It recognises the First Doctor on sight, firing wildly even though it's surrounded by reflective surfaces that make its bolts bounce back at it and blow it up. The creature inside the Dalek is seen to be a large green mass with several stringy tentacles, which thrash wildly after the casing's destroyed.

• *Cybermen.* There are plenty of them in the Death Zone, led by at least two black-handled Cyber-Leaders, one of whom sounds exactly like the last Cyber-Leader the Doctor met [19.6, "Earthshock"]. This Leader knows of the Doctor and the Time Lords, wanting to capture the TARDIS for himself, although he's eventually destroyed. At one point the Leader states that promises made to non-Cybermen have no validity, but at least one of his subordinates doesn't know this instinctively [so the Cybermen have a code of practice among themselves]. Likewise, they understand the concept of trust but don't trust aliens.

As ever, these "new-look" Cybermen are obviously prone to emotion, especially anger. They're carrying some impressive hardware with them, most notably an enormous black bomb which they try to use to blow open the TARDIS. It takes two Cybermen to carry, and has to be hooked up to an energy source by a cable, while inside the TARDIS Susan and Turlough seriously believe that the bomb could threaten them. [See **How Indestructible is the TARDIS?** under 21.3, "Frontios". Note that neither Susan nor Turlough are experts on the TARDIS, though both have some knowledge of its workings, so they may be worrying for no reason.] The Cybermen can home in on the signal given out by the Master's equipment.

• *Yeti.* There's one of *these* in the Death Zone, as well. It angrily attacks the Second Doctor and the Brigadier, as if in an uncontrollable rage, and it doesn't seem to like fire. [It's apparently one of the robot Yeti, as in "The Abominable Snowmen" (5.2) or "The Web of Fear" (5.5), but surely it can't be controlled by the Great Intelligence while it's on Gallifrey? Whoever brought it to the Death Zone may have programmed it to attack anything that moves.] The Doctor believes it's probably left over from the games [assuming that time runs at its normal speed in the Death Zone, this might mean that Yeti can survive for several million years on their own].

• *Raston Warrior Robots*. The Raston warrior robot found in the Death Zone is described by the Doctor as the most perfect killing machine ever devised [he's exaggerating]. It's humanoid, but utterly featureless, looking like nothing so much as a rather graceful male dancer in a white all-over body-suit. It fires spear-like bolts from its wrists, so powerful that they can penetrate Cyberman armour, although judging by the bolt it fires at Sarah it's not a great shot. The robot is so fast that it seems to teleport from place to place, but the Doctor speaks of it moving 'like lightning'.

In the Death Zone it doesn't move from its position, as if it's been designed for guard-duty, killing anything that comes close. It keeps its extra arrows in its cave. It never speaks or shows much sign of intelligence, and when they're on the edge of its territory the Doctor warns Sarah to stay absolutely still as its sensors detect any movement. It's not clear whether the robot can withstand Cyberman firepower, as it doesn't stay still long enough for anyone to get a good shot at it.

Planet Notes

• *Gallifrey*. The High Council members are now discussing matters around a table in one of their usual spartan chambers, this one's fitted with a power-boosted, open-ended transmat beam that can transport people to and from the Death Zone. When believed to be a renegade, the Castellan is to be interrogated in a security section and exposed to a mind-probe, which is obviously hideous as the thought of it terrifies the man. There are potted plants and fountains in the Time Lords' city.

In the Council's chamber is a golden harp, the Harp of Rassilon, and on the wall nearby is a painting which depicts somebody playing it. Possibly Rassilon himself. When the musical score shown in the picture is played, one wall of the room slides back and reveals the darkened chamber where the timescoop equipment is held. It's common knowledge that use of the timescoop is prohibited, though it's suggested that the High Council knows the machinery still exists, but this is hazy. ["Harp of Rassilon" suggests that the secret room was equipped with the timescoop controls in the time of Rassilon, and therefore that only Borusa realises what happens when the Harp is played in the room. If so then the Harp and the painting must have been brought together by Borusa, and certainly we've never seen them in the Council's chamber before.] Here Borusa wears the Coronet of Rassilon, an ornate-looking headpiece which enables him to control the actions of anyone in his vicinity, another item he seems to have uncovered recently. [Not the same as the circlet which puts the President in touch with the Matrix, though the circlet *is* referred to as a 'coronet' in "The Invasion of Time".]

The timescoop room is a darkened area lined with computer banks and throbbing with energy. From here Borusa can seize anybody from space and time, and ditch them in the Death Zone. Victims of the scoop find themselves pursued by a spinning black trapezoid of pure black, which swallows them up before transporting them to the Zone. Whenever this happens an "action figure" of the victim materialises from a slot in the timescoop room, and Borusa places it in the middle of a glowing central display. [It makes sense that the technology should have been programmed to make little models of the "scooped", since the device was originally designed for an elaborate war-game. Then again the display has five sides, one for each Doctor, which may be Borusa's design.]

It's indicated that the timescoop isn't a normal piece of Gallifreyan technology, and modern Time Lords can't replicate it. [Time Lords don't normally seem to be able to interfere in their own pasts. In "The Three Doctors" (10.1) they cross the Doctor's time-stream, but that seems to be a subtly different thing. This may well be one of the few artefacts that can actually re-write Time Lord history. Even so, it would seem that the same individual can't coexist with him- or herself in the Death Zone, as Borusa wants as many Doctors as possible to play the Game but there's only one of each incarnation.]

A fault in the timescoop results in the Fourth Doctor and Romana getting stuck in a time eddy, so they never make it to the Death Zone [a similar thing happened to the First Doctor in "The Three Doctors", though back *then* it didn't cause the "current" Doctor to fade in and out of existence]. Borusa's the one who apparently brings the Fifth

Doctor's TARDIS to Gallifrey, and he even has models of the Fifth Doctor and companions to complete his set, but the TARDIS is only drawn to the Death Zone after the Doctor sets the Ship in flight.

The Death Zone is a blasted wilderness, with the Dark Tower as its only noticeable landmark, and it's implied that it isn't a "normal" part of Gallifrey as the TARDIS registers no place and no time when it lands there. Also, everyone there speaks of Gallifrey as if they weren't on it. The sky is the same colour as on Earth [compare with "The Invasion of Time" and 18.3, "Full Circle"], and it's walled around with an impenetrable force-field. Though the Fifth Doctor's TARDIS is allowed to land there [thanks to Borusa's intervention], it can't take off until the force-field is lifted, and the Time Lords send in the Master by a power-boosted open-ended transmat beam.

Dumped in the Zone by the timescoop, the First Doctor and Susan arrive in a labyrinth of reflective corridors, with the Tower visible nearby once a Dalek conveniently destroys the outer wall [we never see the exterior of this strange mirror-walled building]; the Second Doctor and the Brigadier arrive on a barren plain, with ruined brickwork structures nearby; the Third Doctor and Sarah arrive on a track that leads to the Tower through a miserable-looking wilderness; while the Fifth Doctor's TARDIS materialises in an area full of crags and valleys. Energy-beams from the sky, described by the Master as 'thunderbolts', occasionally try to fry those within the Zone.

There are three routes into the Tower of Rassilon. It can be entered from below by a series of torch-lit, Yeti-occupied caves, unfortunately prone to rockfalls. There's an entrance on one of the Tower's turrets, which can be reached from a nearby promontory with ropes and climbing-hooks, these tools being found in a cave that's guarded by a Raston warrior robot. Alternatively the Tower's great double-doors can be opened by using the entry-coder at the entrance, although the floor of the hall beyond is marked with a chessboard pattern which fries the unwary with energy-beams if crossed in the wrong way. The safe route across the grid changes with each journey, and the Master indicates that working out the formula has something to do with pi, but this is never explained.

The Tower's interior is riddled with passages and stairways, eventually leading into the tomb of Rassilon itself. The oppressive power of Rassilon's mind holds back those approaching the tomb, though the Doctor has no difficulty overcoming this fear. The Tower also tries to distract him with misleading visions of old friends, but these vanish when ignored. Within the tomb is Rassilon's body, and a small obelisk marked in Old High Gallifreyan, supplying the warning "to lose is to win, and he who wins shall lose". [Old High Gallifreyan looks remarkably like Greek. Compare with the **Additional Sources** of "The Three Doctors".] The Death Zone's defences are switched off from the tomb when the Doctor inspects the systems and reverses the polarity of the neutron flow, allowing TARDISes and transmatting Time Lords to enter.

• *The Eye of Orion.* The setting for the Doctor's holiday with the TARDIS crew, although it's not clear whether the Eye of Orion is a planet, just one area of a planet or something else entirely. It *looks* like a pleasant, natural landscape on Earth, where the Doctor and company relax and soak up the high bombardment of positively-charged ions. This atmosphere means that for some it's the most tranquil place in the universe. There are signs of civilisation here, moss-covered walls that looks like parts of an old castle, but there are no people anywhere to be seen. Naturally, the holiday doesn't last.

History

• *Dating.* The Gallifreyan present. Sarah is taken from Earth sometime around the present day [after 1981 according to 18.7-A, *K9 and Company*], as is the Brigadier [it's after "Mawdryn Undead" for him, so 1983 at the earliest].

The UNIT reunion is being held at UNIT HQ, which still has a big Ministry of Defence sign outside to announce its presence. The Brigadier's speech is covered in *The Times* the next day, as there's a reporter present [so UNIT's existence is once again well-known, and its senior personnel probably are as well]. The Brigadier's replacement is Colonel Charles Crichton, who's not too sharp and - inconceivably - seems to know nothing of the Doctor but his name. [Such poor briefing suggests that repelling aliens is no longer a UNIT priority. See 26.1, "Battlefield", for further lapses.]

The Analysis

Where Does This Come From? Well, it *primarily* comes from a need to do a feature-length birthday knees-up which draws in as many old faces and favourite monster costumes as possible, but let's try to go beyond that. Indeed, let's try to go beyond Terrance Dicks, because in "The Five Doctors" we can see two influences that are becoming increasingly obvious in the series at this point. Dicks (who was, in a very real sense, *Doctor Who*'s oldest writer at this point) doesn't appear to have consciously referenced either of them, but they're both coming through loud and clear here.

The first is comic-books. The impact of cinema on the early Nathan-Turner era, and the producer's own interest in TV lore, are so blatant that the comic-book overtones are easy to miss. But for over twenty years, the boy-spawn of the English-speaking world had been weaned on the complex, self-referential universe of Marvel Comics (and DC Comics, publishers of media favourites Batman and Superman, had started picking up some of the same tricks).

The series' dependence on returning villains and ongoing supporting characters in this era is often seen as pure fannishness, but it's a tendency that comes at least as much from comics as from an obsession with *Doctor Who* itself. The fanboys of the '60s and '70s had grown up thinking of cross-overs and surprise villain returns as perfectly normal parts of fiction. The arrival of British comics like 2000 AD, and the tendency of 2000 AD's writers and artists to work for *Doctor Who Weekly*, just made the connection more overt. The Master keeps popping up during the Davison years in exactly the same way that Magneto keeps popping up in *The Uncanny X-Men*. The Brigadier's sudden appearance in "Mawdryn Undead" is pitched to the audience in much the same way as an unexpected team-up between Spider-Man and the Fantastic Four. While the various Marvel titles like to lend each other their cast-members, *Doctor Who* has nothing to cross over with but itself, but by now it's got enough history to make that possible and the audience can at least be relied upon to remember *certain* things about the series' past. (This story even opens with a nineteen-year-old black-and-white clip of William Hartnell, and when you think about it it's remarkable that *any* programme could get away with such a thing.)

"The Five Doctors" - and indeed the very *idea* of "The Five Doctors" - is a point-for-point match for one of Marvel's anniversary team-up stories, even down to the fact that the Doctor's arch-enemy is the one who's given the task of trying to

rescue him, a staple of the Marvel oeuvre. It's enough to say that if the late '80s comics boom had happened just half a decade earlier, then the BBC would almost certainly have released a tie-in graphic novel.

The other big nerd-influence is game culture. It was almost inevitable that this would have an impact on *Doctor Who*, one way or another. There was still a feeling that the series' core audience was made up of bright fourteen-year-olds in glasses. By the early '80s those fourteen-year-olds were playing with home computers, and before long the technology was cheap enough to spread to "ordinary" people. The ZX-Spectrum Generation (see **LOAD "What Did the Computer People Think?"** under 21.6, "The Caves of Androzani") knew all about dealing with traps and monsters in Dark Towers. And if you wore *really* thick glasses, then there was *Dungeons and Dragons*, plus its many, many imitators.

These things were less of a ghetto interest than it might now seem. Games about slitting open goblins were getting mainstream TV exposure. There were Fighting Fantasy Gamebooks on the best-seller lists, and articles about software-designing whizzkids on the news. And from this point on, any teen magazine show worth its salt had to have a regular games round-up. In 1980 the BBC had launched *The Adventure Game* (see 18.2, "Meglos"), which drew heavily on both video-game and dungeon-exploring ideas.

It's hard to believe that anyone involved with "The Five Doctors" really cared about any of this, but at the same time the imagery was already taking root in the popular media, especially in children's television. However much you try to tell yourself that the journey to Rassilon's tomb is a take on *The Wizard of Oz* with overtones of *The Lord of the Rings*, the obstacles inside the Tower still make you wonder if the Doctor's going to overcome the Death Zone's defences by rolling 8 or above on a twelve-sided die. Previous logic-traps in *Doctor Who* - most obviously in "The Tomb of the Cybermen" (5.1), "Death to the Daleks" (11.3) and "Pyramids of Mars" (13.3) - had come across as the kind of puzzles you might find in a children's annual, but now there was an entire culture of this sort of thing. (As it happens, the following year Games Workshop planned an elaborate boardgame based on "The Five Doctors". The license fell through, so they changed the artwork and turned it into a game about a pyramid full of mummies instead.)

All this talk of tie-ins brings us to the other big influence on this story: cross-promotion and co-production revenue. This story was made by the BBC, but much of it was paid for by the Australians. $60,000 (Australian) was given to the BBC, apparently unbeknownst to the production team, on the understanding that no credit went to the Australian Broadcasting Commission... until the 1990 video release, at least. This story was part of a merchandising bonanza. Not a big one by today's standards, admittedly, but the next three years were the high-point of revenue for BBC Enterprises. As we've seen, the Drama department pooled all the income from such schemes, and it was only by special negotiation that *Doctor Who* got extra funding for this one-off. Amazingly, however, the secrecy surrounding the deal meant that from the production team's point of view this story wasn't specifically *aimed* at being merchandised (yes, in spite of Borusa's action figure collection). Yet the entire project was given the go-ahead, and conceived as a ninety-minute story rather than a serial with the cliffhangers removed, specifically to get the Australian cash. What the Australians thought they were getting for their money is a harder question to answer.

This being an early '80s story, there are the obligatory cinema allusions as well. As an attempt to turn *Doctor Who* into a feature-length, return-to-the-old-days spectacular, there's an obvious suggestion that this is *Doctor Who: The Motion Picture*, as if the programme's trying to do the same thing on television that both *Star Trek* and Superman had done on the big screen. In fact the appearance of the timescoop seems to be a direct lift from *Superman: The Movie*, a spinning rectangle that traps its victims as wailing, two-dimensional images. This time the destination's the Death Zone rather than the Phantom Zone, but it just underlines the fact that this is a great big comic-book story. And needless to say, there are less explicit references to the *Doctor Who* of yesterday than the Yeti outfit. "Timescoop" was the working title of "Invasion of the Dinosaurs" (11.2), commissioned during Terrance Dicks' stint as script editor.

There's also a final hint of Gallifrey being a Soviet system, something that came up quite a lot in the Time Lord stories of old ("The War Games", "The Invasion of Time", "Shada"...). The name "Rassilon" was always suggestive of "Rasputin", but here the connection's made more overt, with

Rassilon becoming a figure who's remembered by many as an insane sadist with diabolical powers; a figure who *might* have been overthrown by the other Time Lords, in much the same way that Rasputin was bumped off in the months leading up to the Communist revolution. Nonetheless, when we see the founder of Time Lord civilisation lying in state on his bier, his body looks more like the preserved corpse of Lenin than a mad monk.

One more obvious allusion is that he's spoken of as "bound". The idea that he might be a sort of Prometheus makes sense when you remember how the gods punished the Titan in Greek mythology, and what he'd done to warrant it.

Things That Don't Make Sense Faced with an unknown environment spoken of in legend as a place of certain death, the High Council of the Time Lords responds by... sending two of its own limp, non-combat-trained members there, apparently on their own rather than with huge retinues of guards. Are the others really *surprised* that neither returned? Especially if, as we're led to believe, the two in question were the wet ones from "Arc of Infinity". It's like sending the President and Secretary of State of the US into a foreign country, without any troops or intelligence, to scout out the terrain before declaring war (although some might claim that sounds like a good idea). Have certain members of the Council developed a lust for danger after the rollercoaster adrenaline rush of the Omega crisis?

As the Doctor points out, Daleks and Cybermen were never used in the Death Zone in the olden days because they played the game too well. This means that Borusa must have put the Cybermen (and the one token Dalek) in place recently, and he eventually confesses as much. So, er... why? Why make the Doctor's job of getting to the Tower of Rassilon even harder? And why does Borusa stop the Fifth Doctor returning to the Zone after escaping by transmat, when an extra player in the Game would improve the odds of gaining immortality? It *might* be necessary to stock the Zone with monsters before Rassilon will acknowledge the victory of anyone who comes to claim the prize, but if so then why does Borusa pick monsters which were too powerful for the old games, instead of easier-to-beat monsters which would surely be acceptable under the "rules"? Why not go for Krotons and Taran Wood-Beasts? [Judging by the way Borusa gloats over his figurine collection, the suggestion might be that he's just gone mad.] But then, the idea that Cybermen are too good at this sort of thing is hard to credit in itself. Ultimately they're just cyborgs with guns, whose minds have always been fairly limited and who've been on the verge of extinction ever since the '60s.

The Second Doctor believes that the illusions of Zoe and Jamie can't be real, as they had their minds wiped by the Time Lords and shouldn't remember him. It never strikes him that if *he's* been scooped out of his own time to be here, then his former companions could have been scooped from a time before the mind-wipe, which to be honest would be a more logical (if wrong) conclusion to reach under the circumstances. [Maybe he just notices how old the two look, but see "The Two Doctors" for a similarly haggard Jamie.] The Second Doctor also attends the reunion at UNIT HQ in his big shaggy walking-around-on-Tibetan-mountains coat, handy as he's about to be taken off to a freezing, blasted wasteland, but a bit over the top for the short trip to Southern England he was expecting.

Oh yes, and this business about the High Council being able to grant the Master a new regenerative cycle. Well, if they really *can* - and he'd almost certainly know if they were lying about it - then it raises all sorts of awkward questions. Why isn't it used more often? Rassilon may believe immortality to be a curse, but everything we've seen of Time Lord culture suggests that they're happy to live in a sterile, unchanging society, so wouldn't this ability have been exploited before now? Why does Borusa feel he needs the prize of 'imm-mortality!' from Rassilon's tomb, if he can authorise an unlimited regeneration-boost for himself whenever he feels like it? It can't be because he needs the rest of the Council's permission, as he's wearing a crown that lets him control people's minds, and the Council dupes surely wouldn't be able to resist if the Doctor can't.

Why has the Master never tried stealing the secrets of endless regeneration from Gallifrey before, and why did he go through all that malarkey with the Eye of Harmony in "The Deadly Assassin"? [There's one simple suggestion that explains most of this: the ability to renew the regenerative cycle has only just been developed. This makes sense, when you consider that the last few years on Gallifrey have seen unprecedented bloodshed and disaster. Following the unexpected loss of life in "The Deadly Assassin", Time Lord culture may have been spurred into action after years of stasis, and the Council may be going to new lengths to ensure the safety of its population. If this is the case, though, then the Master must have heard about it as he's not terribly surprised by the Council's offer. Mind you, it still doesn't explain why Borusa wants Rassilon's help.]

Why does Terrance Dicks, script editor throughout the Pertwee years, suddenly think that the Third Doctor talks like Rhett Butler? 'Jehosephat!'... 'great balls of fire!'... why not go the whole hog and have him say 'frankly, Sarah-Jane, I don't give a damn'?

Critique (Prosecution, ish) It's a party, so they all do their party-pieces. Susan twists her ankle, Zoe screams, the Brigadier huffs, Sarah's scared of heights, the Master goes 'heh-heh-heh' and, oh look, the Doctors are joining in. Except that they get it all slightly wrong. Like the *Star Trek* movies, what we have here is an on-screen convention. In those terms, nobody's really in a position to grumble. But it could have done something much more radically odd, like *Doctor Who* used to do before it started playing safe.

These days, if the BBC wants to celebrate something like this then it shows a glorified clips-tape on BBC2, with loads of B-list celebs doing talking-heads and the people involved trotting out the same old soundbites. That's what we got for the thirty-year anniversary, and again for forty. What "The Five Doctors" represents is a halfway-house between this approach and the way "The Three Doctors" wrapped up the past in a box before going off and doing something new. Yet the detractors have missed a vital point about "The Five Doctors". It doesn't do much we haven't seen before, but it does it all better, more confidently and as a statement of what the series still has to offer. The general public were having their memories refreshed about why they'd all at some time watched this series. Even the ones who may have hated this specific story were judging it by the standards of other *Doctor Who*, not any other series, film franchise or ideal programme as yet unmade.

On this score, again, it delivers. But it doesn't surprise. Every box is ticked, but the footage of "Shada" is a reminder of a period before tick-boxes, continuity references, convention anecdotes, a TARDIS full of kids and whicker garden furniture. All the "old" elements are shoehorned into the new format, and yet they don't damage it. They don't get a chance to.

You may be detecting a certain ambivalence. Had "The Five Doctors" marked the end of the cycle of "retro" stories then we'd look back on it with genuine affection, not the sort we reserve for kitsch merchandise or terrible dialogue. But this year's "something from the past in every story" approach will lead into a year which begins with a team-up of old monsters, then moves on to a remake of a Pertwee "classic", then a Hartnell's Greatest Hits package, then a Dalek story, then (dear God) a sequel to practically everything at once… "The Five Doctors" is tainted with the associations of what the next five years would bring.

Critique (Defence)   Let's have that last Critique again, but this time without the ambivalence and from a slightly younger party-member's point of view.

This is a big slice of cake, nothing more, nothing less and nothing else required. If there's a problem with "The Five Doctors", then it's not in the story itself but in the season preceding it. This is supposed to be the end-of-year get-together, a chance for everybody to romp around the place being chased by the top stars of the monster world, and if it had come at the end of a more substantial run of stories then its indulgences would seem a lot less indulgent. As it is, though, Season Twenty has already given us the retro get-togethers of "Arc of Infinity", "The King's Demons" and (more successfully) "Mawdryn Undead". Nevertheless, on its own it's still one of the series' finest "forget the details, pass the booze" moments.

Key to that, perhaps, is the fact that almost everyone is allowed to do exactly what they're comfortable doing. Nobody except Borusa is acting out of character, but they're bouncing off each other in ways we haven't quite seen before, which is surely the whole point of this kind of shindig. The First Doctor gets to insult the current incumbent. The Second and Third get to carry on their feud after ten years, so much so that you're expecting Pertwee's first line to Troughton to be 'and another thing…', but this time they're doing it in front of all their "relatives". The Brigadier gets to be more Brigadiery than at any point in his prior history, the Cybermen get to threaten the Master, the Dalek gets to shout 'exterminate' and the Yeti gets to chase some people down a tunnel

going "raaah".

Almost everyone is allowed to do what they're comfortable doing. The exception would seem to be Peter Davison. By this stage he'd already reached the conclusion that the programme wasn't going to get any more interesting (a conclusion which wasn't entirely accurate, as he discovered when "The Caves of Androzani" was made). On top of which, Terrance Dicks doesn't quite know how to write for this "new boy". So Number Five's starting to sound unsure, to sound less convinced of the sanity of doing this for a living.

Even *that* can't stop him, though. Dropped into a scene with two of his legendary predecessors and one impersonator, he succeeds in the appalling challenge of looking as if he really *is* the lead character around here, and all without trying to upstage the others. God only knows how it would have looked if Tom Baker had agreed to join in. As a result, Davison's final word on the Doctor's other selves - 'I'm definitely not the man I was… thank goodness' - comes across as an affirmation that even after eighty-odd minutes of meeting the old gang, this is still a programme that's happy with itself in the present.

So really, does this disappoint in *any* way? Barely. The non-appearance of the Fourth Doctor seemed like a let-down at the time, but now we know better. Borusa is (as in "Arc of Infinity") unbelievably tedious compared with his earlier selves, but this is the last time we'll be seeing him or his boring old planet. A line is drawn under the "Gallifrey" cycle at this point, or at least, that's what we're led to believe. Yes, that's got to be the last word here, and the previous Critique has already homed in on the problem. However much "The Five Doctors" may seem let down by the stories preceding it, it's *really* let down by the stories to follow. If the series had been rebooted here, as the ending hinted… if they hadn't tried to keep the celebratory party going into the next season, and then into Season Twenty-Two… then things might have turned out beautifully. But it'll all end in tears. And in "Attack of the Cybermen".

The Facts

Written by Terrance Dicks. Directed by Peter Moffatt. Viewing figures: 7.7 million (that's what you get for going up against *The A Team* in 1983). It was repeated in four episodes, the following summer, with an average of around 4.3 million viewers.

Supporting Cast Patrick Troughton, Jon Pertwee, Richard Hurndall, Tom Baker, William Hartnell (The Doctor), Elisabeth Sladen (Sarah Jane Smith), Nicholas Courtney (The Brigadier), Carole Ann Ford (Susan), Anthony Ainley (The Master), Phillip Latham (Lord President Borusa), Dinah Sheridan (Chancellor Flavia), Paul Jerricho (The Castellan), David Banks (Cyber Leader), Mark Hardy (Cyber Lieutenant), Richard Matthews (Rassilon), Lalla Ward (Romana), Frazer Hines (Jamie), Wendy Padbury (Zoe), Caroline John (Liz Shaw), Richard Franklin (Captain Yates), David Savile (Crichton), John Leeson (voice of K9), Roy Skelton (Dalek voice), John Scott Martin (Dalek Operator), Keith Hodiak (Raston Robot).

Cliffhangers For the repeated four-episode format… Sarah rolls gently downhill, yelping; Susan and Turlough watch the Cybermen laying some wires around the TARDIS; the Master prances down a staircase just as the First Doctor announces that 'there's nothing here to fear'.

Working Titles "The Six Doctors" (see **The Lore**), "Maladoom".

The Lore

• It had been planned for over two years that the twentieth anniversary would be marked somehow. When the move to weekdays in spring was announced, Nathan-Turner had asked that Season Twenty be shown from September, but Davison's other commitments made this impractical. When a "special" was suggested for November 1983, the possibility of co-production was raised (see **Where Does This Come From?**), and from this point of view it can be seen as separate from the rest of the series. Even now, any overseas station buying the Davison run from the BBC doesn't get "The Five Doctors" as part of the package.

• Originally the plan was for Waris Hussein to direct; he'd made the first story, 1.1, "An Unearthly Child". Robert Holmes was asked to write it, as Saward was keen to have him return after reading *Doctor Who: The Unfolding Text* (see 19.3, "Kinda"). When Hussein proved to be unavailable, Douglas Camfield was approached. Camfield had asked to direct for the series again in 1980, when Nathan-Turner had taken over and announced that he wanted "new blood" where

possible, so the production office received a dusty answer.

Meanwhile Holmes found Nathan-Turner's "shopping-list" approach to what should be in the story risible. He gave it a go, though, and came up with a storyline which could accommodate all of the expected guest cast, explain why the first Doctor looked odd and allowed Saward to use Cybermen (Saward's pet obsession and Holmes' pet hate… see 12.5, "Revenge of the Cybermen"). In Holmes' version, the Cybermen were attempting to gain control of time by isolating the genetic sequence of Time Lords, an idea that Holmes would eventually resurrect for "The Two Doctors" (22.4). They lure the various Doctors to the planet Maladoom, using a device based on the Master's TARDIS, and build less-than-perfect android replicas of the First Doctor and Susan. Some accounts hold that Sutekh would have turned up at some point (13.3, "Pyramids of Mars"). Saward soon twigged that being told what to do by a producer for whom he had nothing but contempt wasn't suiting Holmes, and so contacted Terrance Dicks.

• Unfortunately Dicks was at a convention in New Orleans, so for him it was 4.00 a.m. when the phone rang. His reaction was to try to get everything into the plot, and assume that no-one would be too worried by the details. He was amused by Saward's obsession that the Cybermen had to be active whenever possible, but with Tom Baker still blowing hot and cold on the project it was hard to deliver a script (and Baker insisted on seeing a script before making a decision).

Baker was touring in the original stage production of *Educating Rita* and was then at Brighton's Theatre Royal, where Nathan-Turner was working on that year's panto *Cinderella*, and thus had several meetings with the producer. He was interested in working with Elisabeth Sladen and liked Dicks' idea that the Fourth Doctor might be the surprise villain (or seem to be), but was daunted by returning so soon and sharing the screen with his precursors. Dicks had been asked to keep Doctor-on-Doctor action to a minimum in case of ego clashes, although this proved to be far from the case. Baker finally declined the offer, fearing typecasting and "swamping" the production. He did, however, agree to use of the "Shada" footage; some reports even have him suggesting the idea.

• The Third Doctor and Sarah were to have been reunited in a ruined street and menaced by

Autons, but this was judged to be pushing the budget too far. Hence Sarah and the Shallow Embankment of Evil. In one version the Pertwee Doctor was to have taken the spears of the Raston warrior robot and used them as struts, converting his cape into a hang-glider (hence his enthusiastic reaction to Sarah's crack about 'flying').

The robot, a last-minute "filler" element, was an "Earthshock" android costume resprayed. The silver paint needed retouching, and the cast were amused to see Keith Hodiak's crotch being administered to with hairdriers to get that part of the suit the same colour as the rest. A persistent rumour has it that Nathan-Turner directed the entire Cyber-massacre, and the producer did film a couple of the close-up shots to save time.

• Jamie was a last-minute addition, as Frazer Hines was thought to be too busy on Yorkshire soap *Emmerdale Farm*. At the same time Deborah Watling announced that she'd been cast in a new series with comedian Dave Allen, although this never reached the screens. Watling, as Victoria, was supposed to give away the fact that she was an illusion by calling Lethbridge-Stewart "Brigadier" (he was only a Colonel when the real Victoria met him in 5.5, "The Web of Fear").

• According to Paul Jerricho, Peter Moffatt told him that the line 'no, not the mind-probe!' had to be delivered as if the Time Lords had several different types of mental surveillance device, and this specific one was the most intrusive and painful.

• The name "Charles Crichton" may be familiar. When Dicks worked on *The Avengers*, former Ealing Comedies director Charles Crichton was also on the series. Five years after "The Five Doctors" he came out of semi-retirement and had a hit with *A Fish Called Wanda*. Originally the Colonel was to have opened a file with a photo of Troughton on the front, only to find it empty.

• As the novelisation was rushed out for the anniversary, Dicks adapted his script as he went along. Troughton's ad-lib about the Terrible Zodin was included at the last minute. However, the book actually reached the shops days before the UK broadcast.

• The "horn" or "shawm" sound for the Dark Tower is a sample of the Queen Mary's fog-horn, processed by a Fairlight synthesiser.

• Janet Fielding had been pressing for Tegan to be given a fur coat for location filming. This finally happened when they went to Bodiam castle (see "The King's Demons"), although the producer was less than thrilled with the look. Anthony Ainley's method of keeping warm on the shoot involved being cuddled by the make-up girls.

• Nathan-Turner kept the effigies of the Doctors and companions. (He took very few souvenirs; the only other one we're aware of was the Six Faces of Delusion mask from 20.2, "Snakedance").

• Set designer Malcolm Thornton was given a copy of 1972's *The Making of Doctor Who* as a reference for Old High Gallifreyan, which is why the Doctor's Greek-style "name" appears on the plinth in the tomb. Although the cost of the new console wasn't part of this story's budget, Thornton undertook the job on the understanding that it was to be retained for subsequent stories. He also took the "thunderbolt" idea and made it the motif for the Dark Tower and the torches; the script has the Brigadier's lighter as the illumination in the caves.

• The costumes raised an interesting problem. The BBC had signed up to international protocols on transmission standards for colour, and thus was advised not to use tight checks on clothes which might lead to strobing. Neither the original trousers for Hartnell or Troughton, nor the McCrimmon tartan (technically he counts as a Cambell), met this regulation.

• The DWAS reference department issued a book on the making of this story, which detailed all sorts of other aspects to the production, including the use of rat-traps to make the dying Dalek's tentacles undulate and where Sarah's costume was bought. A few of these have been included in what you've just read, and our debt to them is duly acknowledged…

21.1: "Warriors of the Deep"

(Serial 6L, Four Episodes, 5th January - 13th January 1984.)

Which One is This? For those familiar with *The Fast Show*, this story can best be thought of as the *Doctor Who* equivalent of Cheesy-Peas: 'You like Silurians? You like Sea Devils…?' For anyone else, it's the one with the dinosaur pantomime horse.

Firsts and Lasts Last appearance of the Silurians (7.2, "Doctor Who and the Silurians", unsurprisingly) and the Sea Devils (9.3, "The Sea Devils", ditto), here working together for the first and only time. It's also the first story since 1969 - and therefore the first story of the colour era - to be set in the twenty-first century. (This may sound incidental, but isn't. The "future" stories of the 1970s tend to be set on distant colony worlds in the far future, and if there's any link to the *real* world then it's usually a parable about the long-terms effects of pollution or a generic statement about imperialism. "Warriors of the Deep" is set in 2084, exactly one-hundred years after its transmission, in order to make a direct connection with modern-day politics. Which is a very '60s kind of conceit.)

Last appearance of the original Davison "uniform", the jacket of which was donated to the Children in Need appeal just after the debut of "The Five Doctors" (20.7).

Four Things to Notice About "Warriors of the Deep"…

1. Not for nothing has it earned the nickname "Warriors on the Cheap". There are all-new Silurian and Sea Devil costumes for the reptile-people's '80s comeback, and they're actually rather good, but that's obviously where the budget went as everything else has that *frisson* of "sticky-backed plastic" about it. The security doors on Sea Base Four are made of polystyrene, the computer graphics are done on a BBC Micro, and… no, there's no way you can talk about the design misfires here without mentioning the Myrka, a monster which makes even the Doctor say 'oh dear'. (See also **Bad Costume Decisions: What Are the Highlights?**.)

But what's entertaining is that however bad the

Season 21 Cast/Crew

- Peter Davison (the Doctor, 21.1 to 21.6)
- Colin Baker (the Doctor, 21.7)
- Janet Fielding (Tegan, 21.1 to 21.4)
- Mark Strickson (Turlough, 21.1 to 21.5)
- Nicola Bryant (Peri, 21.5 to 21.7)

- John Nathan-Turner (Producer)
- Eric Saward (Script Editor)

Myrka might be, the human beings around it can be even worse. For an easy laugh, watch the scene in episode three in which it zaps four Sea Base personnel at once, and behold the sight of four extras all going "argh" and trying to fall over in synch. Yet perhaps the funniest moment comes when an aged Ingrid Pitt (as the treacherous medic Solow) attempts to defeat this looming sea-monster by kicking it a bit.

2. It's a massacre. Amid a story of man's inhumanity to man and man's inability to talk to reptile, the Doctor once again tries to make peace between humans and Silurians and fails, resulting in all the reptile-people dying in agony while virtually all the humans present are cut down in their prime. (There's at least one human survivor among the supporting cast, although he only gets off because he's not present during the climactic round of bloodshed.) The Doctor's final, heartbroken statement - 'there should have been another way' - is often regarded as a testament to the series' humanity, but from another point of view it could be seen as enormously two-faced. The script's spent four episodes getting everybody into a position where they can safely be gunned down and gassed to death, and then it tells us that there could have been another way? Wouldn't it perhaps have been a more challenging story if we *saw* this other way, instead of ending things with an easy mass-slaughter? Even so, Peter Davison yet again sounds as if he can believe every word he says, so the story very nearly gets away with it.

3. The breakdown in human / reptile relations isn't the only old favourite being presented to us here. As in "The Sea Devils", the last episode sees the creatures taking over a naval base and then guarding the Doctor's companions so badly that

Bad Costume Decisions: What are the Highlights?

"Warriors of the Deep" is the start of a run of pseudo-military uniform designs which have lumps and flashes of colour in unorthodox places (we note Trau Morgus' oddly-padded collar in passing as the point where things start to get really ludicrous). It also features a spectacularly daft monster. Whilst acknowledging that styles change, and that earlier generations of fans mocked unfashionable looks which we now find acceptable - '80s criticism of "The Ark in Space" (12.2), for example, was largely founded on the premise that people in the future would never wear flares - we offer a few examples which have stood the test of time as "classics" of flawed judgement.

• **Brian Cant in a nightie (6.1, "The Dominators").** The diaphanous, knee-length, sleeveless robes worn by the Dulcians were meant to suggest a decadent, pampered society. When Arthur Cox (as the "rebellious" Cully) is clambering about in a quarry taking on killer robots, it *does* suggest that he's not cut out for this kind of thing, although he was woefully miscast to begin with.

But in the council chamber, Tensa is supposed to be the respected "hawkish" Elder. He's supposed to look as if he belongs there. His death is supposed to be serious. And worse, they've cast *Play School* presenter Brian Cant in the role. A man who makes a living impersonating jellies on plates or cows in fields shouldn't look embarrassed doing "straight" acting.

• **The Vervoids (23.3, "Terror of the").** Three things to note here:

1. As most people know, when the Vervoids die their leaves blow away, revealing the Adidas logos on their tracksuits.

2. These are killer plants, and thus have less reason to look like people in suits than any other monster. Ironically they look *more* like people in suits than any other monster.

3. The idea was that they should resemble Venus flytraps, but they actually ended up looking like... well, depending on who you ask, the Vervoid heads are either deranged tulips or ladies' naughty bits. In tracksuits. With a few leaves stuck on them.

• **Peri's leotards.** Wrong in so many ways. Not only is it completely out of character for this girl to suddenly take an interest in aerobics, or to start flaunting herself at every opportunity (according

to the notes, she's driven by low self-esteem), but the idea - if you recall - is that she's the representative of "normal" against which gaudy alien worlds and the "tasteless" Sixth Doctor are to be measured. Her choice of outfit in "Attack of the Cybermen" has an obvious appeal from a hetero-boy point of view, especially when she's required to make her chest heave dramatically, but *it's pink lycra for God's sake.*

• **Madeleine Issigri's metal hair (6.6, "The Space Pirates").** According to the black-and-white version of the future, everything will be reflective. Doors will be covered in sheet metal, fearlessly showing everybody the cameras, especially in the BBC's *Out of the Unknown*. Zoe will don a catsuit with glittery bits. When seeking to suggest the Issigri Mining Corporation's wealth, the designers opted for a sort of Egyptian look, and gave Madeleine a beehive hairdo made of space-alloy. (Still, Madeleine is in charge of an ore-mining operation. Perhaps all businesspersons in the twenty-second century wear wigs made of their own companies' output.)

This may have been intended as "futuristic", but with hindsight it makes her look like Marge Simpson. A decade later, bands like the Rezillos and the B52s liked to flirt with this look as an ironic comment on "the way the future used to be", but in 1969 it seems as if the director and designers actually meant it.

• **Fiske and Costa (17.4, "Nightmare of Eden").** In among the roaming Mandrels, the passengers in tinfoil babygro rompers and Tryst's Roger McGuinn glasses, we forget that the waterguards who come to arrest everyone are dressed like the biker from the Village People, in spangly leathers and dinky little caps. The more butch they try to sound, the more one wonders about the hankies in their back pockets, if you catch our drift. And on a related subject...

• **The Ice Lord Grand Marshal (6.5, "The Seeds of Death").** Nice idea, making the Grand Marshal look different from the Ice Lord and have a voice that suggests a different atmosphere aboard the flagship. Less nice is how it looks. Unless the vicious inhuman killers are competing in ballroom dancing to while away the nine months' journey from Mars, there's no reason for

continued on page 253...

they manage to slip away through a ventilation shaft. And as a nod to the Second Doctor, the Doctor gets to use a favourite '60s catchphrase when the Sea Base guards come for him and his associates: 'When I say run, run… run!' Sadly there's no good *reason* for him to say this, as he just wants everyone to get away from the guards as quickly as possible and he might as well have just said 'run!', but it was a nice thought.

4. Most "How To" books on the plotting of drama quote the old adage that if a gun is introduced in Act One, then it's got to be used in Act Three. Having established that the Silurians are this fortnight's monsters, the first episode of "Warriors of the Deep" then has the Doctor exploring the depths of Sea Base Four and discovering a large supply of hexachromite gas, which he describes as being lethal to marine and reptile life. Can you see where this is going…?

The Continuity

The Doctor With neither of his companions demanding free rides from him any more, the Doctor seems driven by pure curiosity again, happily taking Tegan on a tour of her future and exploring Sea Base Four even though he doesn't *technically* have a reason to. He doesn't seem to entirely trust Turlough, appearing wary of the boy's reasons for wanting to stay on the TARDIS. The Doctor's once again using physical violence to stun guards, although he insists on apologising to them afterwards, and he can hold his breath underwater for some time.

• *Ethics.* The Doctor considers the Silurians to be 'honourable' [a rather upbeat view], and believes he let them down when he met them before ["Doctor Who and the Silurians"]. Once again he does everything he can to try to engineer peace between the humans and Silurians, giving the Silurian leader Icthar every chance to think twice about wiping out humanity. [What's interesting to ponder is whether the Doctor would give these Silurians such leeway if he *hadn't* met their kind in the past, and didn't already know that some of them can be quite civilised. In many ways these Silurians act like the Zygons in 13.1, "Terror of the Zygons", and the Doctor was happy to let them be killed without a second thought.]

He doesn't put human life above Silurian life, only helping to kill the Sea Devil army when the whole world hangs in the balance, and he observes the death of a Sea Devil with the same sadness he'd usually reserve for humans. He sounds both hurt and angry when he sees the carnage around him and delivers his 'should have been another way' line.

• *Background.* The Doctor knows more about Silurian culture than expected, given his brief encounters with them before. He recognises the design of the Silurian battle-cruiser, identifies the Myrka on sight and knows the Silurian leader personally, though until now he thought Icthar was dead. He claims that in an earlier regeneration he attempted to mediate between Icthar's people and the humans, and Icthar was apparently in favour of a peaceful solution then. [The script seems to suggest that the reptiles' leader is the scientist from "The Silurians", but he doesn't look or sound anything like the scientist, nor does it explain the other things the Doctor recognises here. He even knows Icthar by name, and the scientist certainly *wasn't* in favour of a peaceful solution in the 1970s. Pretty much the entire Virgin novel *The Scales of Injustice* is an attempt to explain how the Doctor knows so much in this story, describing the Third Doctor's first encounter with the Silurian Triad and making sure he's shown a photo of a Myrka at the end of the book.]

He's also familiar with the Sea Bases of the twenty-first century, having been on one before.

The Supporting Cast

• *Turlough.* Happy to stay on board the TARDIS a while longer rather than going home, as he claims he wants to 'learn', although he doesn't sound too convincing. [As we later learn, he doesn't have anywhere that great to go to. The script seems to be setting things up for "Planet of Fire" (21.5), in which it turns out that Turlough's homeworld isn't a good place for him to be, but that doesn't explain why Turlough has been trying to get home *before* now.]

He now believes that the Doctor's competence with technology is beyond his own [also a bit of a change from last year]. However, when the Doctor's in an apparent certain-death situation and there's nothing he can immediately do to help, Turlough stoically announces 'he's drowned' while Tegan's more inclined to stand around getting upset. Nor does Turlough show much sorrow when he thinks the Doctor's a goner, and he's still inclined to save his own skin rather than make a 'futile gesture' to save other people.

Bad Costume Decisions: What are the Highlights?

...continued from page 251

the Marshal to have sequins and a star-filter on the lens of his video-phone. Whilst a strict-tempo paso doble routine may have enlivened "The Monster of Peladon", it raises all sorts of questions about Ssorg wearing stilettos and clingy dresses (see 9.2, "The Curse of Peladon", for more suspect activities from this species).

• **Jo's Spiridon ensemble (10.4, "Planet of the Daleks").** Jo Grant's groovy gear has been the butt of many a fan joke. The trouser-suit in "The Sea Devils" is a classic of early '70s excess, and her frequent knicker-flashes are well-documented, not least because they seem to change colour between shots. But at least some of the outfits that were most notorious in the 1980s now seem fairly sedate, and occasionally fashionable again.

There's no way, however, that the look adopted in Season Ten's jungle jaunt on Spiridon will *ever* come back in. Several fashion no-nos have coalesced into one hideous lump. There's the hair, a Rod Stewart-style feather-cut and borderline mullet (except on location). There's the jacket, with '80s-style big shoulderpads, '70s-style lapels and '50s-style green tartan. There's high-waisted flared trousers with a tight crotch and, finally, cork wedgies. She at least has the consideration to cover this with a flasher-mac, but when the very plants of this world projectile-vomit as she passes, she takes it off - along with the nasty gloves - to reveal the catastrophic total look. Each individual garment is bad, but nobody would have put them together at any other time, six weeks before or after this was made. (Actually... the combination of flares, shoulderpads and big collars is attempted again by the Seers in "Underworld", but they're robots and can't be blamed for lousy fashion sense.)

• **UNIT leisurewear (6.3, "The Invasion", and most of Season Seven).** What's the well-dressed member of a top-secret world-saving organisation wearing this season? A beige one-piece romper-suit, made even campier with the little beret at a jaunty angle. Incredibly, it takes the gentlemen of the press a while to work out that Lethbridge-Stewart is part of UNIT, despite this rather obvious clue (and the badge on the beret is a bit of a give-away, too). Just try to imagine what Colonel Faraday or Major Beresford (13.4, "The Android Invasion" and 13.6, "The Seeds of Doom") would have looked like if they'd kept this style. And Corporal Bell (8.2, "The Mind of Evil"), with her not-very-military hairdo.

• **Peter Pratt's Master (14.3, "The Deadly Assassin").** The idea of a semi-regenerated, "damaged" Master was fine, but the costume was a botch-up. The hands were supposed to be fitted with transparent tubes, containing different-coloured liquids at different stages, yet they wound up looking like gardening gloves. The robe was the same plastic weave used for the Kraals ("The Android Invasion"), which was already familiar from the Vogans (12.5, "Revenge of the Cybermen"). Above all, the "poached egg" eyes made it seem like he was about to launch into an Al Jolson medley at any moment. These were removed when the original costume was (rather pointlessly) used again in "The Keeper of Traken".

• **The Sixth Doctor.** God save us. (See 21.7, "The Twin Dilemma", for more. If you can stomach it.)

Turlough doesn't have any difficulty handling a blaster-rifle, and he's good enough with technology to sabotage electronic locks [as in 20.3, "Mawdryn Undead"]. He carries his own hankie.

The TARDIS The Doctor doesn't have any trouble navigating the Ship to Earth, but goes too far into the future and says he should have changed the TARDIS for a type-57 when he had the chance. Materialising in orbit, the TARDIS is scanned by the Sentinel-6 defence satellite, and the Doctor acts as if the attack could harm the supposedly "indestructible" Ship. The Sentinel's warning is picked up in the console room, and the Doctor can communicate with the satellite when it's on the scanner.

A burst from the Sentinel's weapons causes the TARDIS to go out of control and makes the console room turn orange, but some quick fiddling with the console results in a 'materialisation flip-flop'. This dematerialises the TARDIS, and it lands on Earth after the Doctor messes around underneath the console. [But conveniently, it lands in exactly the same location that the Silurians are about to attack. For the umpteenth time you have to wonder whether the Ship's doing this deliberately. Then again, it lands on the Sea Base that's receiving data from the Sentinel, so maybe it's following the Sentinel's signal to source. It's also odd that the Doctor has to go through the elaborate flip-flop procedure, which involves Tegan holding down one button while he fiddles with some others, rather than just dematerialising normally.]

Repairs after this are likely to take some time. [So logically, the TARDIS crew are stuck on the Sea Base for a while, with all the corpses, after the end of the story.]

The Non-Humans

• *Silurians*. They've changed somewhat since their last appearance. Apart from the fact that their features are subtly different [are they a different ethnic group?], their third eyes now flash in a Dalek-like fashion whenever they're speaking, and they show no sign of being able to use these eyes to cripple people or melt rock. Their voices sound more synthetic, too. [Even the "old" Silurians displayed features that suggested cybernetic implants, so possibly this bunch have had more of the surgery. This raises the question of whether Silurians would have turned into Cybermen, if they'd been left to prosper on prehistoric Earth.]

Here the Silurians are led by a council of three, comprising of Tarpok, Scibus and Icthar, the latter being the sole survivor of the Silurian Triad. The Doctor describes this Triad as the custodians of the Silurian race. [Maybe just *this* faction of Silurians, rather than the entire species. It's possible, but unlikely, that this refers to the trinity of Old Silurian, Young Silurian and Silurian Scientist in "The Silurians"; see under **The Doctor**. "The Silurians" showed us that these creatures see the world as being split into three pieces, thanks to their third eyes, so it makes sense that they might mirror this one-at-the-top, two-at-the-bottom structure in their political organisation.]

It's not clear how these Silurians were revived from hibernation, or whether they've only recently woken up. As we only see Icthar and his two Silurian colleagues, it's hard to tell whether they're the *only* survivors of their faction, but Icthar states that millions of others are still in hibernation [across the world, so Wenley Moor wasn't their only bunker]. Though Icthar is determined to wreak revenge on the humans, he *is* concerned with the protocols of Silurian law, and it's said this law forbids warfare unless it's defensive. Needless to say, Icthar feels the war against the humans *is* defensive, claiming that the Silurians have long since abandoned mediation. He states that his

people have offered humans the hand of friendship twice, and been betrayed as a result. [A blinkered, but not wholly untrue, description of the events of "The Silurians" and "The Sea Devils". Or is this a reference to an unseen encounter, since "The Sea Devils" only features the marine branch of the family?]

Icthar's plan is to attack Sea Base Four, launching its proton missiles and provoking a war between Earth's two major power-blocs. The Doctor believes this will leave a dead world, but Icthar thinks his kind can prosper in such an environment. [Maybe they're planning on living underwater, or hibernating until the planet heals itself. Or maybe Silurians can survive proton "radiation"... assuming, of course, that proton missiles *do* have a kind of fall-out.] Icthar bears no malice against the Doctor, and is prepared to let him and his companions live after the holocaust.

Here the Silurians refer to themselves *as* Silurians, even though it was just a human name and wasn't scientifically accurate anyway. [Is everything being translated into sloppy human-speak for our benefit, as per usual? Or maybe they've adopted the pejorative human name, and are brandishing it like the Mau-Mau, the Bolsheviks and Niggaz with Attitude. Given that they know so much about humans and human politics, it's at least possible.] As before, humans and Silurians have no difficulty talking to each other, although this ability to communicate doesn't stop the two sides wiping each other out.

The reptiles arrive in a battle-cruiser, a bullet-shaped submarine that carries a whole unit of the Sea Devils as well as their Myrka, with interior walls that look as though they're made of seaweed. The Sea Base sensors believe the vessel's organic. It has a particle suppressor which can turn the Sea Base's external weapons system back on itself, and the Silurians carry a 'manipulator', a small box that can override the security systems on the Sea Base.

Silurians move very, very slowly here, and wear what look like armoured vests. The spines on the Silurians' backs seem to grow into these vests, as if they're more like carapaces than clothes. [On the face of it, this would indicate that the military "elite" of the species are somehow connected with the Ice Warriors, not to mention the apparent similarities to the Cybermen. A prehistoric connection between Earth and Mars is, in *Doctor Who* terms, not only possible but virtually certain. See also **What Happened to Mondas?** under 4.2, "The Tenth Planet".]

• *Sea Devils*. Also "ethnically" different to the Sea Devils of the past, their skins a greenish-brown colour instead of bright green or orange. They also have narrower eyes. While the Silurians are busy running things, the Sea Devils seen here act as their military. Sea Devil Elite Group One has been hibernating for 'hundreds' of years, although the Silurians note that they didn't wake up as planned, and Icthar has to rouse them manually. [Hundreds of years, not millions. Although it's stretching the word "hundreds" slightly, this may once again suggest that the Silurians and Sea Devils seen here originally woke up in the twentieth century, then went back into hibernation after making their plans.] They're "stored" on board the Silurian battle-cruiser in a single cavern-like chamber, where they hibernate, frozen like statues. [In "The Silurians" the reptiles hibernate lying down in caskets. Are the Sea Devil Elite just trying to prove how hard they are by sleeping upright? Note that the Silurian ship lands in an undersea crater before the Sea Devils are revived, suggesting that the Silurians are picking the soldiers up from some kind of underground base. But the novelisation holds that the Sea Devils are kept in the bowels of the battle-cruiser, and that the ship stops at the crater purely because it's close to Sea Base Four. There's nothing on-screen to contradict this, as it's not clear whether the architecture of the Sea Devil chamber is supposed to represent part of an organic vessel or just a cave.]

Like the Silurians, the Sea Devils refer to themselves by their human nickname. Rather than the string vests worn by the last batch, these warriors wear blaster-proof armour and helmets that verge on the Samurai-like. They carry their usual disc-shaped hand-held weapons, but these don't seem to generate intense heat any more, as their unit is also armed with a large and rather slow laser-like cutting device for slicing through doors. The Sea Devils' hissing, non-electronic voices suggest less enhancement than the Silurians, but their commander Sauvix states that 'battle-orientation commences' as soon as they revive from hibernation [which sounds almost like an automatic conditioning system]. Hexachromite gas kills all the reptile-people and makes their insides turn to goo.

• *The Myrka*. The Silurian / Sea Devil "heavy artillery", the Myrka is a green-skinned dinosaur-like beast that looks sort of... like a pantomime horse. Well, it does. The Silurians can control it from their battle-cruiser using the devices they wear on their wrists, although it doesn't have much intelligence of its own. It's lethal to the touch, killing anyone who makes contact with it in a burst of energy, and blasters merely surprise and annoy it. It can apparently use its energy charge at long range, but it seems to take the creature a while to remember this.

The Doctor states that the Myrka is a creature of inkiest depths, or was until the Silurians 'tinkered' with its biology, so it has no tolerance to ultraviolet rays, and ultraviolet converters on the Sea Base can kill it. Its fins suggest it's amphibious.

History

• *Dating*. The Doctor believes it's around 2084.

At this point Earth is once again in a state of Cold War, and according to the Doctor there are 'still' two power-blocs pointing missiles at each other. The missiles in question are proton missiles, the kind that kill life but leave everything else intact. [The power-blocs are never named, although this is obviously based on the US / USSR model. See **What's the Timeline of the Twenty-First Century?** under 5.4, "The Enemy of the World".] Sea Base Four is a colony structure somewhere on the ocean bed, most of its crew having English accents but with at least one member who sounds Polish. And *she's* a traitor. The enemy bloc doesn't know where the base is, but the political situation's unstable, so the crew are half-expecting an attack.

The operation is run by Commander Vorshak, and staffed by uniformed personnel with blasters and not much imagination. The base is equipped with unmanned probe vessels and 'energy tracers' that can fire at nearby underwater targets. The proton missiles can't be armed or fired without a synch operator, a technician who can plug himself directly into the computer thanks to a surgically-implanted socket in his head. A psychologically unfit operator can be out of action for hours after doing this, but the station contains a psychosurgical unit.

The base has no military function without a synch operator, so when Sea Base Four's operator has a breakdown the psychosurgical staff - actually agents of the enemy bloc - persuade the Commander to release the conditioning disc, a small CD-like object that's inserted into a machine which feeds information straight into the control centres of the operator's brain. This makes the synch operator better, but it also means that the enemy agents can reprogram him to obey their signals. The disc's said to contain knowledge that's useful to the enemy, and usually it can't be released without authorisation from Sea Base Command. A synch operator is meant to be a safe-guard against unauthorised missile launch, though the Silurians have the technology to over-come this, and the Doctor can synchronise him-self with the computer by hooking himself up to the machine even without a head-socket. The Commander initially refuses to contact the out-side world for assistance, as he has to maintain radio silence to prevent enemy listening-posts locating the base, but the synch operator is once again necessary if contact has to be made.

The Cold War also involves orbital weapons, including the Sentinel-6, a robot satellite which sends an audio warning to the TARDIS and appar-ently does some damage to the Ship with its ener-gy-beams. The Sea Base can receive reports from this Sentinel. The idea of non-human intelligences surprises the people in this era, but they're pre-pared to accept it when confronted by both the TARDIS and the Silurians [as if they know there are aliens but haven't seen any].

Eye make-up's obviously in fashion again. The Sea Base staff are all slaughtered in the Sea Devil assault, but the base is equipped with large sup-plies of hexachromite gas, a sealing compound for undersea structures that's also lethal to marine and reptilian life. So nobody really wins this one.

The Analysis

Where Does This Come From? So, *Doctor Who* heads back into the Cold War. As previous vol-umes of this work have already pointed out, the series fretted over the possibility of World War Three in just about every era of its existence, from the "nuclear bombs cause mutants" strand of the '60s episodes to the "bureaucrats have to sort out their differences" phase of the early '70s and the "logical stalemate" ideas of "Destiny of the Daleks" (17.1). But now Ronald Reagan's in power, squar-ing off against the 'evil empire' of the USSR, and Britain's become an off-shore missile-base just like Sea Base Four.

Doctor Who didn't really live to see the end of the Cold War - it began with Kennedy's assassina-tion, and ended four weeks after the fall of the Berlin Wall - so this is its last chance to worry

about the consequences of nuclear / protonic armament. And since "Day of the Daleks" (9.1), its disrespect for the political classes has become even more pronounced, just as the public's had. The two power-blocs here aren't even given names; there's no indication that one side is made up of Commies, no hint at whether the people on the Sea Base are working for "us" or "them". All governments are equally stupid, and the Doctor's assessment that nothing at all has changed since the 1980s is perhaps the most pessimistic thing in the series' entire run.

Lest we should think that this view of politi-cians as universal time-wasters is in some way radical, it's worth remembering that the plot here (third party tries to provoke an apocalyptic war, then take over in the ruins) just puts the Silurians on the same level as the terrorist organisation SPECTRE in the '60s Bond movies, and on top of that some of the set-pieces here have obviously been pinched from sources like *Dr. No* and *The Spy Who Loved Me*. And the idea of the Cold War reaching into outer space is at least as old as Sputnik, but it's significant that the first overt death-satellite to appear in the series should turn up a year after the US formally announced the "*Star Wars*" programme.

But when it comes to the Cold War, the *really* big shift here is the use of computers. Machines are no longer cold, rational minds working out optimum battle-plans, but tools that might trigger a catastrophic war by mistake. Fear of an acciden-tal World War was perhaps the greatest anxiety that anyone had, by 1984. The popular con-sciousness, and the popular media, was just com-ing to terms with the fact that if computers were involved in launching missiles then the computers could be tampered with. The word "hacking" was re-entering the English language (see 21.7, "The Twin Dilemma", for a slightly different spin on this).

It gets lost amongst all the reptiles, but a large slice of the plot here is about the base's synch operator, a walking piece of hardware who makes *Doctor Who*'s long-standing obsession with the body / machine divide more explicit than ever. To be generous, you could see it as the series' first dabbling with cyberpunk, although comparing "Warriors of the Deep" with the more popular SF literature of the mid-'80s - a time when such liter-ature was increasingly desperate to look hip - shows you just how far behind the times the series was starting to fall. Computer games were on the rise at the same time, of course, so many were of the belief that America's nuclear armaments worked in exactly the same way as the kind of thing you saw in amusement arcades. Here the Sea Base's targeting system looks for all the world like *Missile Command*, and to make matters worse the graphics are done on a home computer.

When it comes to the series' own mythology, what's immediately obvious about "Warriors of the Deep" is that despite the Doctor's waffle about 'noble' Silurians (and, admittedly, their unusual willingness to let the Doctor go free once all the humans are dead), the reptile-people are really just generic evil aliens. In both word and deed, they're barely any different to the Cybermen, even bringing a 'manipulator' with them that overrides human control systems in much the same way as the mysterious time-travelling navigational device in "Earthshock" (19.6). All monsters are created equal; they are, in short, all Stormtroopers now (just look at 21.4, "Resurrection of the Daleks…").

Things That Don't Make Sense Maddox, Sea Base Four's psychologically unfit synch operator, describes himself as a 'student' with no hard-core military experience. Fair enough, military command might put this kind of raw recruit on a Sea Base during an unstable political situation *if* qualified staff were hard to come by. But we're repeatedly told that the Base's military capacity is reduced to zero if the operator's out of action, so much so that they can't even contact home without him. So the purpose of the entire facility hangs on this one clearly-unfit individual. And there's no contingency plan for him falling ill. And nobody's keeping a careful watch on his mental state, least of all the Commander, who just takes a "stiff upper lip" approach when Maddox is close to breaking point. And the death of his precursor wasn't properly investigated. Moreover, what kind of student-temp has a jack-plug surgically implanted and major deep-level psychological conditioning?

Meanwhile the traitors Nilson and Solow have risen to astonishing heights in this organisation, which - as it has synch-ops and control discs, and Turlough's threatened with some kind of (ahem) mind-probe - must have some pretty efficient lie-detection equipment. Yet the pair of them might as well be wearing T-shirts saying I'M NOT A SPY, BUT MY PARTNER IS.

The Doctor leaves the TARDIS and starts wandering around Sea Base Four because the Ship's going to be stuck there for some time, and he wants the Commander's permission to stay while carrying out repairs, which is a somewhat optimistic plan since he *knows* this is a time of Cold War and must surely realise that he can't prove himself to be harmless. Wouldn't it be safer just to lock the TARDIS doors (which he never does when he leaves the Ship, incidentally), given that the TARDIS is supposed to be unbreachable? Then, when station security goes to find the intruders, the Doctor suddenly thinks it's a good idea to hide from them instead of introducing himself and decides to head back to the TARDIS. In fact he's so keen to do this that he overloads one of their nuclear reactors, just to distract them. Is he feeling quite well?

In episode three, the security officer who reports to Vorshak knows what Sea Devils are called before anybody on the Sea Base uses the term. [Hinting, perhaps, that the Sea Base staff have some knowledge of what happened in the 1970s.] Having deduced that Nilson is an enemy agent, Vorshak doesn't even bother checking the man for weapons and promptly gets taken hostage as a result. Security is a touch lax even before this. The guards blithely march past a half-naked, unconscious colleague; the guard whom the Doctor elbows (and to whom he then apologises) later knocks on the door that's been sealed by the fugitive saboteurs, just as politely; and this has to be the last time that a high-security base in *Doctor Who* is shown to be lacking in any kind of CCTV.

Aptly, the "aliens" mirror the humans for ineptitude. The Sea Devils kill everyone they come across in the Sea Base, at least until they meet the Doctor, at which point they start taking prisoners for no explained reason. Repeatedly, the reptile-people prove very good at turning their backs on dangerous captives.

Special mention also goes to the moment in episode two when Turlough's caught by the guards and shouts 'go, Tegan, save yourself!', a line which (a) seems somewhat out of character, (b) is delivered very badly indeed and (c) sounds as if the writer's just noticed how drab all this chasing-around is and wants to make things seem more urgent. (It wasn't long after this that *The Lenny Henry Show* ran a *Doctor Who* parody that pointed out the "pointlessly running up and down lots of corridors" problem for the first time, at least in public. With hindsight "Warriors of the Deep" just looks like it's supplying ammunition.)

Critique First, let's look at what it *isn't*. One of the most oft-stated criticisms of "Warriors of the Deep" is that it's dragged down by the series' past, and that it's little more than an excuse to team up the Silurians and the Sea Devils. But this really doesn't hold water. The two races are used as separate castes, one political and one full of "grunts", a standard of sci-fi cinema at the time that makes perfect sense even if you've never heard of the '70s versions. In fact the dialogue here seems to go out of its way to *ignore* past continuity, wilfully disregarding the details of the other Silurian stories while sticking to the same general principle of "reptile-men, they're just like us".

What's odd, with hindsight, is that on paper the story's got so much going for it. Despite the occasional line of testosterone-muddled dialogue ('you'll get no help from me, Silurian!') and the monsters' depressing lack of personality, a lot of the time the script has a fair idea of what it's doing. From the general public's point of view, the Cold War posturing and base-under-siege storyline aren't just comprehensible but suitably *direct*. The Doctor's disgusted with the humans, but burns his brains out trying to stop them killing themselves anyway.

In fact, if the power-cut engineered by the invaders had happened as scripted (see **The Lore**) then this would have been remembered fondly by anyone who was a child at the time. Into the gloom they send a luminous, unstoppable beast… not a grafted-on effect, with blue lines or obvious wires, but a physical behemoth. Some have even argued that if this had been swapped with "The Caves of Androzani", then it'd have the same reputation that "Androzani" has now. This is meant to be a grand tragedy, a tale of human-and-reptile folly which sees the people of the future hatching convoluted plots against each other while greater forces move in to engulf them, and which ends with a body-count of operatic proportions. It *should* be great. It *should* feel like Hamlet with dinosaurs.

The trouble is that in execution, nothing comes off. The hallmark of the early John Nathan-Turner era (at least, at its best) is that the script, direction, design and performance are all supposed to work to a single aesthetic. Yet this is a story in which nobody's communicating with anybody else and everyone's run out of ideas anyway. The result is a production that's off-the-case in almost every way, from the steaming great cock-ups (Myrka) to the small details (they went to all the trouble of building nice new Silurian suits, then decided to give them flashing third eyes for that B-movie "I-am-a-robot" look). The performances are among the worst in the series' history, with nobody except Davison sounding as if they can understand why they're here at all. The design is sloppier than it's been for years, hinting at the shallow, half-finished futures of Season Fifteen.

But perhaps most surprisingly, it's just very badly directed. Pennant Roberts was never the series' most dynamic director, but in the '70s he *did* have a decent understanding of the form, a working knowledge of how to tell a story within the boundaries of the programme. Now, with the BBC directives on picture-quality preventing him from dimming the lights, the set-designer flatly refusing to make the base look as shoddy as the script dictates and the producer over-riding his decision to cut out the big green sea-cow, there isn't much he can do. Even the scenes which *might* have worked seem mis-paced, especially when the reptile-men have to threaten people in slow-motion, so you get the feeling that for Roberts it's just become an exercise in damage limitation.

He certainly made an effort *before* the shooting started. As he'd done before, he decided to make one of the male characters female without changing the lines (for a more notable example see Marn in 15.4, "The Sun Makers"). These days this is unremarkable, but if he hadn't done it then you'd immediately notice how odd this base is. As it turns out, the base is quite odd anyway; the erratic design and make-up at least suggest a deliberately, consciously 1980s kind of oddness, but then Ingrid Pitt decides to show off the karate moves she learned from Elvis and it quickly degenerates into the *wrong* kind.

The worst part is that, like "Arc of Infinity", this story launches the season. For casual viewers, who might just have been drawn to the first couple of episodes by trailers that emphasised the expensive-looking latex masks, it must have been like watching a confirmation of everything they ever suspected about *Doctor Who*; that it was a universe of bad actors, monotone monsters and extras dropping dead in corridors. As we've already seen, this was the period when people stopped treating *Doctor Who* as a family favourite and started sneering at its limitations. Two years earlier the season opener had proved the series could still be surprising by giving the audience a world built by M. C. Escher, and the ratings had stayed up all season. At this point, the programme isn't just failing to capitalise on that new lease of life, but undoing all the half-decent work it's already done. Everybody say "argh" and fall over.

The Facts

Written by Johnny Byrne. Directed by Pennant Roberts. Viewing figures: 7.6 million, 7.5 million, 7.3 million, 6.6 million.

Supporting Cast Tom Adams (Vorshak), Ian McCulloch (Nilson), Ingrid Pitt (Solow), Nigel Humphreys (Bulic), Tara Ward (Preston), Martin Neil (Maddox), Norman Comer (Ichtar), Stuart Blake (Scibus), Vincent Brimble (Tarpok), Christopher Farries (Sauvix), Nitza Saul (Karina).

Cliffhangers The Doctor's body floats limply in the drowning-pool of the Sea Base, and Turlough insists that he's dead; the Doctor and Tegan get trapped in an airlock with the Myrka; having already killed Nilson in a corridor-based shoot-out, a Sea Devil levels its weapon at the Doctor and says 'your turn' (then spontaneously decides not to kill him in the next episode).

Oh, Isn't That..?

• *Ian McCulloch.* Not the lead singer with Echo and the Bunnymen, though this can cause confusion. *This* Ian McCulloch had been the male lead in Terry Nation's dreary post-holocaustly "mainstream" drama *Survivors.* He wasn't too bad in that. It's been reported that Pennant Roberts, who'd worked on the series, had originally wanted McCulloch as Commander Vorshak.

• *Ingrid Pitt.* Hammer films icon (her standout role was *Countess Dracula,* but she's notable also for appearing opposite Jon Pertwee in *The House That Dripped Blood*) and author of one of the most peculiar showbiz biographies around (*Life's a Scream*). By this point she was attempting to leave her past behind her. For an idea of the usual sort of thing she did, see "The Time Monster" (9.5), where she plays Queen Galliea.

Some viewers may have identified Maddox as Martin Neil, who'd been one of the kids in Southern Television's seemingly interminable *Freewheelers* (with Wendy Padbury and Eric Flynn; see 5.7, "The Wheel in Space").

The Lore

• Here come the excuses. The main problem with "Warriors of the Deep" was that Margaret Thatcher called a surprise election in 1983, so the BBC was obliged to cover the result on the day the studio had been booked. The other available studio slot for the first recording block was about a week too soon. Mat Irvine, assigned to special effects, was delayed on another production in Scotland. Usually the effects team on a given story had a month or so to prepare; Irvine had nine days. His later memo to the BBC effects head Michealjohn Harris spelt out all the problems and commended his assistant, Stuart Murdoch.

Many of the effects in this story were technically unproven, and in particular the decision to use a "live" Myrka rather than a post-production effect caused endless problems. John Asquith and William Perrie had a regular gig as a pantomime horse on the seemingly-endless children's show *Rentaghost,* and were thus on BBC contracts anyway (so they'd accept a lower fee than outside contractees). The plan was that they'd have a week's practice inside the Myrka with Irvine on hand. In reality they didn't get into the costume until the last few hours of the shoot. In the studio, not only did they find the latex too heavy to comfortably stand up in but the fluorescent paint wouldn't dry. Some of it came off on Janet Fielding's dress, causing a delay while a replacement costume was found.

Alerted to the potential snags with the Myrka, Irvine and Roberts advised Nathan-Turner to remove its scenes entirely. But he opted to attempt them on the grounds that the beast was potentially the story's unique selling-point, and had tied up so much of the budget and resources that scrapping it would be a waste.

• Nathan-Turner also insisted that an underwater stunt scene should be included. The practicalities of this involved the loss of a day's studio shooting to do a location scene. As Roberts had discovered (see 15.4, "The Sun Makers" and **Which is Best, Film or Video?** under 12.3, "The Sontaran Experiment"), viewers could see the "join" between film and videotape, so it had to be a VT location shoot. This ruled out the usual option, the studios at Ealing, as the BBC had designated the site for film use only. Roberts took an outside broadcast crew to a naval training base in Southampton, where Davison overcame his reluctance to do his own swimming. Gareth Milne executed the stunt of the fall and "drowning".

• The production team had contacted Roberts as a result of reusing his "Shada" footage (20.7, "The Five Doctors"), and as he was now free after the end of *Tenko*, he was offered this story.

• Johnny Byrne's starting-point was, simply, seeing "Earthshock" (19.6) and wanting to try something similar. Eric Saward was keen, and arranged for Byrne to view "Doctor Who and the Silurians" and "The Sea Devils". Byrne admired Malcolm Hulke's pacing, and the way in which the Silurians were motivated. But from the lack of any characterisation among the Sea Devils he surmised that these were "drones". In conversations with Roberts and others, Byrne let slip that he was basically recycling an old *Space: 1999* script (but no-one can positively identify a single "source"). Saward rewrote vast tracts of it, to Byrne's dismay. Turlough's characterisation was all wrong, apparently, and the Doctor's desperation to avoid conflict was emphasised. Typically, Saward ensured that practically all non-regular characters were killed, though it seems he forgot about Bulic, the Sea Base's token survivor.

• Byrne had imagined a sort of giant, rusting, dimly-lit submarine - think of the space freighter *Nostromo* from *Alien* - with the Myrka barely visible in the shadows. Yes, *now* it makes sense. Ian Levine also had his say, commenting that the author had misunderstood the monsters and had let them know too much about the Time Lords. Though Byrne was less than pleased, he submitted one last story, "The Guardians of Prophecy" (see 18.6, "The Keeper of Traken").

• The frantic shoot caused problems with the cast morale. Fielding and Tara Ward (Preston) played what they thought was a rehearsal for laughs, only to find it was a take and there was no time for another go. Ingrid Pitt, hired to play Preston (or possibly, although this is unlikely, Karina), got her agent to "promote" her to Solow. She insisted on demonstrating her karate skills, and was also anxious to do a "serious" acting role, deliberately having herself appear aged and unglamourously-dressed.

• The script had originally involved Tegan and Turlough hiding in the base's sun-lounge (where the UV generator is kept) by stripping into swimwear. Strickson will be seen in his Y-fronts later this year - in 21.5, "Planet of Fire" - but the scene was removed long before Fielding got a chance to complain.

21.2: "The Awakening"

(Serial 6M, Two Episodes, 19th January - 20th January 1984.)

Which One is This? Roundheads and Cavaliers in present-day England, for reasons other than a time-slip, plus a big smoke-belching stone face in a church crypt and a little puppet hobgoblin sticking to the ceiling of the TARDIS. And it's only fifty minutes long, so there's time for you to catch the display of falconry in the next field.

Firsts and Lasts First appearance of the Fifth Doctor's costume, Mk. II. We presume that Mk. I is still drying out (see the last story). This has a red-and-green shirt detailing around the collar, and he's now wearing the jumper of the Gloucestershire Second Team. Unfortunately this is also the start of that irritating habit the Doctor fails to shake off throughout his next life, introducing himself with 'I am known as the Doctor'. As the young lad Will Chandler says, 'b'aint be a proper name'.

This is the last story to feature a design by Barry Newbery, who's been working on historical yarns since the stone age (well, "The Tribe of Gum"... see 1.1, "An Unearthly Child") as well as the occasional, less-successful space story (13.5, "The Brain of Morbius" and 15.2, "The Invisible Enemy"). His church set here is among his best, even though the main nemesis here - the Malus - itself was more impressive in the "flesh", according to visitors to the studio sessions.

Two Things to Notice About "The Awakening"...

1. For the third and final time, one of Tegan's relatives wanders into an alien-occupied danger-zone apparently by sheer chance. Following her aunt's unfortunate encounter with the Master and her cousin's fluke discovery of Omega's TARDIS, here it's her grandfather who coincidentally uncovers a centuries-old psychic warhead hidden in a sleepy English village.

What's oddest about this, though, is that Tegan's grandfather never really makes a difference to the plot. She wastes a couple of minutes being worried about him, but as things turn out the Doctor doesn't need an excuse to get involved in events here, and Turlough stumbles across the old man by accident instead of tracking him down for Tegan's sake. Which means that the whole story's constructed on a monumental coincidence even though it's hardly necessary (q.v. 19.5, "Black Orchid").

2. It's a rule of historical and pseudo-historical productions that everyone born in the seventeenth century speaks fluent yokel. The village of Little Hodcombe is, in the present day, wholly inhabited by people who use perfect BBC English. Then a local peasant is sucked through time from the 1600s, and ey, 'e be 'avin' the same Mummerset accent as one o' them villagers from "The Daemons" (8.5). Or a variation thereof.

The Continuity

The Doctor Likes tea, naturally. On this occasion the Doctor takes the unusual step of getting both his companions to wait in the TARDIS while he goes exploring, and funnily enough he does this on the one occasion when something manifests itself inside the Ship. At the end of events he plans to take a misplaced villager from 1643 back to the seventeenth century [something he's obviously done by the next story].

• *Inventory.* He's carrying at least one coin on his person, but it looks like a pretzel and it's apparently not from this world. [As with all the other currency this year. See 21.3, "Frontios" and 21.5, "Planet of Fire".] He also has a slim pen-torch [but not the same one he carried when he was Jon Pertwee, nor the one his first self used to demonstrate TARDIS malfunctions in 1.3, "Edge of Destruction"].

• *Background.* He knows of the Malus purely as a human superstition, but also knows all about Hakol probes and tinclavic mines (see **Planet Notes**).

The Supporting Cast

• *Tegan.* Still travelling with a handbag, though a different one from her Air Australia days. It turns out that Tegan's [maternal] grandfather, Andrew Verney, is English and the local historian in the village of Little Hodcombe. [Meaning, presumably, that Tegan's mother was English.] It also turns out that the village is falling under the influence of a psychic probe from the planet Hakol. [It's not clear whether Tegan met up with Verney while she was on Earth after the events of "Time-Flight" (19.7), but he never brings up the subject of Tegan's late aunt, or asks where she's been recently. See **Who Went to Aunt Vanessa's Funeral?**. The fact that Tegan's relatives keep stumbling into

extra-terrestrial danger is also striking. Coincidence, or something else? After all, Tegan's arrival on board the TARDIS looked like pure chance but seems to have been staged by the Watcher (18.7, "Logopolis"). Have the Watcher's arrangements somehow affected probability, at least with regard to her bloodline? Stranger things have happened.] No other relatives seem to be in the vicinity.

• *Turlough.* Tea is the one thing he misses about our planet.

The TARDIS As the TARDIS heads for Earth, Turlough is helping the Doctor solve problems with 'time distortion' by fiddling about under the console. During this process, designs that look like circuit-diagrams for the Ship are displayed on the console screen [not on the scanner, as they were in 19.2, "Four to Doomsday"]. But the TARDIS is well on course to visit Tegan's grandfather, as requested, even if there's some turbulence when it hits the Malus' energy field. The date of the landing can be checked on the 'time monitor'.

When the Malus manifests on board the Ship, the Doctor uses the console to lock the TARDIS' signal conversion unit onto the frequency of the psychic energy that feeds it, claiming there's a remote chance of being able to direct the Malus that way. This doesn't work, but it at least stops the entity fuelling itself from the psychic angst of the village.

The Non-Humans

• *The Malus.* The occupant of [or a part of?] a computer-controlled reconnaissance vehicle from Hakol, described by the Doctor as a living being re-engineered as a weapon. The Malus arrived in the village of Little Hodcombe some time before the 1640s, the spearhead of an invasion fleet that never came, for reasons the Doctor doesn't know. During the English Civil War it was activated by the psychic energy of the locals and worsened the fighting, then became dormant again.

There's a green-eyed gargoyle-like stone head bricked up behind a wall in the local church, and this is the Malus' face. Awakened by Sir George Hutchinson's unbalanced mind, it begins affecting the psyche of Sir George and his followers, making their "war games" increasingly violent and even spurring them on to attempt a May Queen sacrifice. It also causes pale, luminous ghosts of the Civil War to appear, which at first seem insubstantial but soon become malicious. On the other hand, at least two figures from the past are less aggressive [so the Malus isn't wholly in control of these projections]. One is a projection of a disfigured thief, who acts like a human being but seems to have the ability to teleport over short distances. The other, Will Chandler, is a real person brought to 1984 when the Malus briefly intermingled the two time-zones [do the people of Hakol really have time-warping technology, or was this a freak effect?]. Other bursts of psychic disturbance can cause the traditional ominous roaring winds, plus auditory hallucinations of the Civil War. The Doctor states there are varied forms of psychic energy, but this type requires a focus point or 'medium', in this case Sir George. His reconstructions of Civil War battles are creating energy for the Malus, and as per usual he believes the entity can give him great power.

The Doctor describes the Malus as 'pure evil', and believes it'll destroy everything if left unchecked. [As it did in 1643, although people must have re-settled the village afterwards. "Everything" would thus seem to mean "everything in the region" rather than "the whole world". It's likely that the Malus' graven image was made by those it possessed in the seventeenth century, as its full form only seems to exist as a psychic projection and it's hard to believe the people of Hakol bothered to sculpt it into the likeness of a local demon. Likewise, "Malus" is probably just the name given to it by the villagers, and it's first used by one of the locals.] The Malus' face slides forward when it's revealed, and the slab that leads to the subterranean part of the church lifts itself from the floor with electrical smoothness [machinery installed by humans on the Malus' behalf?].

Though only the Malus' stone face is seen in the church, an insubstantial 'parent image' of the entire being manifests itself at various energy-gathering points around the village, one of them on board the TARDIS. It appears as a stone gargoyle with stiff limbs and a malicious grin. [The power to breach the TARDIS again demonstrates huge amounts of psychic potential, as in 13.3, "Pyramids of Mars".] It never speaks or shows any real signs of intelligence. When the Doctor blocks its psychic feeding, it begins to suffer and uses the last of its psychic energy to try to kill anyone it can find. Ultimately Sir George dies when he's pushed into the smoking maw of the stone face, and with its medium gone the Malus is programmed to self-destruct and cause the maximum possible damage, taking the church with it.

[The BBC Books offering *The Hollow Men* attempts to resolve the question of the abortive Hakol invasion, the back-story of "The Daemons" and the events of "The Visitation" while at the same time linking it all to a council estate in Liverpool.]

Planet Notes

• *Hakol.* Source of the Malus, the planet Hakol is in the star-system of Rifta. The squishily malleable metal known as tinclavic is mined by the Terileptils on Raaga [19.4, "The Visitation"] almost exclusively for use by Hakol's inhabitants. This means tinclavic scraps are found in Little Hodcombe from the vessel that brought the Malus here. On Hakol, psychic energy has been harnessed much like electricity on Earth.

History

• *Dating.* It's 1984. [Meaning that Tegan's been missing from Earth for about a year, even if she hasn't spent that long on board the TARDIS. As Sir George is planning on burning a Queen of the May, it could well be the 1st of May when the Doctor arrives, or the first Monday after this.] The Doctor and company take a brief holiday in Little Hodcombe after the crisis.

The Malus arrived on Earth long before the Civil War started, but required a massive burst of psychic force to become active. On the 13th of July, 1643, the War came to Little Hodcombe when a Parliamentary force and a regiment of the King wiped each other out there. The Malus woke up and promoted hate among the troops, making the fighting worse, and they even burned a woman alive as Queen of the May. The village was destroyed as a result, though in the doomed church there are still unusual carvings of people being chased by the Devil.

The Analysis

Where Does This Come From? Pageantry was a big thing in the 1980s. This was a time when the *now* was officially all that counted, when nobody really cared where they'd come from. Politicians and fashion designers repeatedly called on "history", but it was a theme-park kind of history where the past was signified by statues of Churchill and re-enactments of battles helped the tourist trade.

Who Went to Aunt Vanessa's Funeral?

Tegan has more relatives than any companion, at least until Ace's connection to the whole of Yorkshire and the Soviet Union becomes apparent in "The Curse of Fenric" (26.3). Yet these people never act as if they're in any way related to one another. Her grandfather Andrew Verney doesn't ask after her "favourite cousin" Colin, who in turn - understandably, perhaps, given the time allowed between our introduction to him and his "possession" by the Ergon - fails to mention Aunt Vanessa from "Logopolis" (18.7).

Now, this may not be such a big omission, as we don't know how long Tegan was on Earth between "Time-Flight" (19.7) and "Arc of Infinity" (20.1). It's snowy in the first story and spring in the second, and she's had a haircut and a fashionecto-my, so it could be three or fifteen months. We also know that she can walk out of the warehouse - and the Doctor's life - in 1984, confident that she's got somewhere to go, despite leaving her passport in the TARDIS. Assuming she's thinking straight, that's quite a big admission (21.4, "Resurrection of the Daleks"). As an Australian in London, she can stay for two years unless she gets work or marries a local. We don't know when in 1984 the Dalek infiltration attempt takes place; it's raining, so it could be any time except three weeks in May. So either she has another job lined up that she didn't know about in "Arc of Infinity" (and in mid-'80s Britain, anyone who could just walk into a job must have been sleeping with the boss), or she was confident that the work permit from 1981 was still valid. This seems to push the "gap" in her time-travelling career towards one-and-a-quarter years.

We have, therefore, a gap long enough for a funeral. However, Andrew Verney appears not to have seen Tegan since she was much younger. Her "favourite cousin" Colin can be left in hospital without a visit once the Doctor wanders back into her life, so perhaps it's not such a close family. (Or perhaps the TARDIS crew stayed in Amsterdam for a fortnight after the "Arc of Infinity" crisis was over. This seems unlikely, given the Doctor's apparent reluctance to have her back full-time - watch that last shot - and the whole scene suggests that she's giving him a *fait accompli*.) It would seem that Tegan is the only connection between these three rather distant relations.

Then there's that name. John Nathan-Turner admitted that it was the result of a misunder-standing, but we're stuck with it. We can state with confidence that back in the 1960s, nobody would have called a child "Tegan Jovanka". This kind of excessive multiculturalism is quite popular now, and in the early '80s "Tegan" would have seemed reasonably trendy for a baby girl, but Tegan herself wasn't born into that kind of world. If you were a parent with a surname like "Jovanka" - and espe-cially if you'd left what was then Yugoslavia for Australia - then you'd pick a nondescript first name, often a saint (ex-pats from Eastern Europe, particularly Soviet satellites, cling to the church for social reasons but also for a sense of belonging).

Similarly "Tegan" is a Cornish name and as such tends to accompany Celtic surnames. "Tegan Frazer" makes sense; "Maria Jovanka" makes sense; "Tegan Jovanka" doesn't make sense. So maybe her parents divorced and remarried. Mum's maid-en name was Verney, dad was a Frazer. Mum remarried, became a Jovanka, got custody and moved to Brisbane. This explains a number of stray remarks, not least Tegan's six-year-old self under hypnosis talking about 'moi gaadin' where 'people always come back' (20.2, "Snakedance"... note how her accent gets thicker as she regresses). Then there's the apparent contradiction between her description of her dad's farm in 'the outback' and her comparison of Brisbane to the zero room (19.1, "Castrovalva"). It also makes her attempts to talk to Kurkudji slightly more plausible (see 19.2, "Four to Doomsday"), as a late-'70s liberal upbringing confronts the more... er... *pragmatic* Aussie farming community.

More interesting is what she doesn't say; for a "mouth on legs" she's remarkably tight-lipped about her mother, in an era when women in their early twenties were pretty much encouraged to slag off their mums whenever possible. If we assume that the writers had some feedback from the script-editors when adding family members, then it must have occurred to someone involved that she had a mother. *Doctor Who* girls tend to be orphans, in effect, but they also tend to lack any relatives or old friends at all. Turlough, Adric, Peri and Nyssa all have - or had - nuclear families in var-ious stages of diminution, so it wouldn't have been such a radical departure.

So which side of the family was Aunt Vanessa on? Well, she's not Colin's mum. Any middle-aged woman driving an old Triumph Spitfire hasn't had to raise children. (And she's got a house north-east of London; Nyssa states in 20.3, "Mawdryn Undead" that Tegan found the TARDIS on the

continued on page 265...

The current British generation's failure to understand that history is an ongoing, unfinished process - rather than just a series of films starring Mel Gibson - is largely rooted in the thinking of the Thatcher years. In that respect, "The Awakening" is actually quite clever. The opening scene, in which a woman in (reasonably) modern dress is chased by seventeenth-century horsemen, automatically makes the viewer assume that this is some kind of typical *Doctor Who* timeslip scenario when it's really just the sort of leisure activity you could find all over the country by then.

Civil War re-enactments had hitherto been the preserve of enthusiasts like those who formed the Sealed Knot. These societies weren't just fancy-dress troupes but dedicated, scholarly bodies, trying to comprehend the mind-set of a period from which Britain (as we understand it) sprang. They'd been instrumental in supporting the eight-year filming of Kevin Brownlow's documentary-style film of the Levellers' dispute with Cromwell, *Winstanley* (with one professional actor, Jerome Willis… he's Stevens in 10.5, "The Green Death"). But as the '80s ground on, the emphasis was less on the political and social aspects and more on the spectacle, and the "authenticity".

History - as it's taught to us now - is a series of battles and acquisitions, and everything has to be presented as "The _____ Experience". Even the BBC fell for this idea. The key thing to understand about the Civil War, unlike all the other photo-genic conflicts, is that it was ideological. A King declared war on his subjects to defend a view of the universe, and was opposed by people who were fighting for their souls as well as their own scheme of a Godly society. But theme-park history is uncomplicated and apolitical. It's also hygienic and painless. "The Visitation" (19.4) makes even the plague seem like a charming Olde Worlde custom, and that story's author has apparently script-edited away any hint of the suffering of 1640s Britain in *this* one. Arguably the "moral" of "The Awakening" is that the past isn't just a bunch of war games and we're all still living with the consequences, but if that was the starting-point then it's got a bit lost in the final edit.

Beyond that, most of the roots of "The Awakening" lie within the field of television itself. The buried, psychic horror once again suggests *Quatermass and the Pit*, and its later *Doctor Who* offspring "The Daemons" (8.5), although the ghost-like apparitions of the Malus come straight out of Nigel Kneale's teleplay *The Stone Tape*. And as in "The Daemons", there's more than a little of *The Wicker Man* here. Although if anything the influence is more explicit in "The Awakening" as this time the villagers are planning on burning their sacrifice alive. (The scene in which the ghosts of the Civil War decapitate one of the villagers by forming a pattern of swords around his neck is a direct lift from the movie.)

But the big influence here is another fantasy / SF hybrid of the early '80s. The idea that the past is somehow "buried" in the present, and can be brought to the surface by re-enactment, is a common theme in this era and suggests the same play of symbols and portents that's used in virtually every episode of *Sapphire and Steel*.

Things That Don't Make Sense The seventeenth-century thief who turns up in Little Hodcombe, with the mutilated face and the ability to teleport… what's *he* all about? Why is he a part of the story at all, and why does he make a brief, pointless reappearance *after* the Doctor figures out what's going on in the village, as if he's going to be terribly significant?

Tegan turns out to be one of those adventure-show heroines who can be surprised by someone standing right in front of her when she's walking along in broad daylight. Meanwhile, Little Hodcombe turns out to be one of those villages where everybody's prepared to accept the existence of aliens with the bare minimum of evidence, and nobody's particularly surprised by the TARDIS' insides. Likewise, everyone acts as if "Malus" were a familiar term, like "Jack Frost" or "hobgoblin". It isn't. In fact, it's just another word for a crab-apple.

It's May, and the weather's sunny, ish. Yet at least twice, the sky clouds over in the time it takes someone to walk five yards and look back. Perhaps this is why Sir George has a roaring fire in his study on a summer's afternoon. Hiding under the stairs in the tunnel, the Doctor and school-teacher Jane Hampden start planning their next few moves while the soldiers searching for them are still within earshot; we can still hear the men talking, just as loudly as the Doctor.

One might, even in a BBC family series, have expected a beheading to be accompanied by at least a *little* blood.

Who Went to Aunt Vanessa's Funeral?

...continued from page 263

Barnet Bypass. If Tegan and her aunt were on their way to Heathrow via Barnet, then they must have been coming from somewhere east of North London / Hertfordshire, and not the traditional Australian hang-out of Earl's Court. Besides, Tegan would've known what a police box was if she'd lived there, as there's one outside the tube station.)

In "Arc of Infinity", Colin's seeing the world and has hooked up with Robin to sample Amsterdam's delights. While he may be her favourite cousin, Tegan's mainly using his proximity as an excuse to go somewhere else after being fired. Maybe she *did* have to leave the country. Maybe she ran back to see the TARDIS dematerialise at the end of "Resurrection of the Daleks" because she abruptly remembered that she wasn't supposed to be in Britain any more, and needed her papers.

Anyway, to return to our original query... Vanessa appears to have been the only member of that branch of the family living in the UK. Perhaps she was a Jovanka by marriage. Tegan would have been around, probably taking on the upkeep of the house, but none of her other relatives were really that close to Vanessa. Tegan, on the other hand, has Vanessa's photo by the bedside in Brisbane (20.5, "Enlightenment"). Perhaps the policemen who tried to arrest the Doctor in "Logopolis" (18.7) contacted Tegan as next-of-kin, and she arranged a private cremation, with no pallbearers for obvious reasons.

Critique Despite all the New Romanticism of Season Eighteen, despite all the *Alien*-ness of "Earthshock", despite all the worst make-up decisions of "Warriors of the Deep"... this is, perhaps, as '80s as '80s *Doctor Who* ever gets. Which is to say, this is exactly what the BBC *did* then; quiet, small-scale dramas about quiet, small-scale places, with the occasional streak of period colour (not too much, mind, the age of the great historical epic is over) and enough references to tea and history to give it a surface layer of "English charm" and make it saleable overseas.

This time there's a psychic alien force making everyone want to kill each other, but even so it's a surprisingly *genteel* psychic alien force, and if anything what the story needs more than anything else is for the Civil War to look much less civil. Will Chandler's description of a human sacrifice, and the last-minute decapitation of a villager, just isn't good enough. But to an extent, this production's doing what *Doctor Who* has repeatedly done throughout its history, giving us a TV programme that looks like other TV programmes and then sabotaging it with something unfamiliar. The trouble is that the familiar has, to us, become all too familiar. Like last year's two-parter, "The Awakening" looks almost like a primer, an experiment to see if "classic" *Doctor Who* can be squeezed down into fifty minutes.

The result is that it can, but that doesn't mean it *should* be. As in "The King's Demons", the Doctor never gets to investigate properly here, and the first half comes across as a straightforward series of clues without the lurking menace needed to make things seem urgent. Unlike "The King's Demons", the least you can say about it is that here things aren't profoundly irritating. On first viewing, there's enough century-meets-century flavour to snag the attention, enough curiosity-value to make it worth watching; only the answers to the questions, and the talk of alien psychic probes, leads to disappointment. Twee final scene aside, it's a reminder of how audience-friendly the series could be, even though it seems like a five-finger exercise for a kind of *Doctor Who* that never quite came into being. And was the exploding church a deliberate reference to "The Daemons", or just a coincidence? It's difficult to tell.

That barely mattered to 1980s viewers, though. They were well-versed in piecing things together without verbal explanations. The connections between the odd items (notably the one-eyed man who takes Tegan's bag, and the smouldering cracks in the church wall) are implicit, not excuses for another lecture. When a lump of exposition finally becomes unavoidable, it's done as a comic interlude between the Doctor and his new companion, Jane. What's more interesting, from the point of view of film technique, is how the studied artificiality of most '80s *Doctor Who* is used against itself here. The domestic details, like pylons, 'phone boxes and cans of Jeyes Fluid, are "invading" the fiction-space of the programme.

Compare this to its almost-twins, "The Daemons" and more especially "The Android Invasion". In the two '70s stories the world is clearly the *Doctor Who* world, with space-centres and BBC3, so all the small details used to "root" it in the real, present-day Britain are brandished as evidence that this is something-like-our-world-but-not-quite. Here, except for one scene in which the 'phone boxes are deliberately introduced so that we can see the troopers conscientiously ignoring them, such details appear in the frame almost accidentally. It's not a separate world, it's part of ours, which the local magistrate is attempting to cut off from us... although he's not quite succeeding.

Considering that the previous two-parter was set in 1215 but couldn't have looked more early-'80s if it had featured Spandau Ballet as the King's minstrels, this might almost be a deliberate taunt.

The Facts

Written by Eric Pringle. Directed by Michael Owen Morris. Viewing figures: 7.9 million, 6.6 million.

Supporting Cast Polly James (Jane Hampden), Keith Jayne (Will Chandler), Denis Lill (Sir George), Glyn Houston (Colonel Wolsey), Jack Galloway (Joseph Willow), Frederick Hall (Andrew Verney).

Working Titles "Poltergeist", "War Game". (Reports that this was to be called "The Darkness" are garbled. This was possibly the title of Pringle's rejected Dalek script.)

Oh, Isn't That..?

• *Polly James.* One of the original *Liver Birds* (see also 19.3, "Kinda" and 4.8, "The Faceless Ones"). She'd done other things, but this was her first prominent non-Beryl role for a while.

• *Dennis Lill.* Has done a bit of everything, from *Survivors* to Mapp and Lucia. He was also Professor Fendleman in "Image of the Fendahl" (15.3).

Look very carefully, and the other-other trooper - not the one the sadistic Sergeant keeps ordering about, but his associate - is Chris Wenner, who was dropped as a presenter on *Blue Peter* under mysterious circumstances...

Cliffhangers The Doctor finds the face of the Malus behind a wall in the church, but smoke floods out and envelops him.

The Lore

• The bulk of Eric Pringle's work had been for radio, but his agent Peter Bryant (yes, the one who produced ten of Patrick Troughton's stories) had recommended that he try writing for *Doctor Who*. The author's first attempt, "The Angurth", was a casualty of the debacle surrounding Sarah's departure and the various drafts of "The Hand of Fear" (14.2, and see also 13.6, "The Seeds of Doom").

Like "The Awakening" this was a two-parter, but unlike the broadcast story it was written as such. The first draft of "The Awakening", entitled "War Game", was four episodes long. It was conceived with Adric and Nyssa in mind, and Saward found that with cast changes making rewrites necessary anyway, it could be condensed into two parts. At this point Saward was still busy attempting to fix "The Song of the Space Whale" and then rush "Mawdryn Undead" through, so the revised script was in the works for six or seven months.

• A cut scene featured Tegan encountering Kamelion in a TARDIS corridor. Speaking in the Doctor's voice, he explains that he's plugging himself into the computers to learn about the Ship's operations (see 21.5, "Planet of Fire").

• Significant character names come from real figures in the Civil War (Hampden, Hutchinson and Verney... Wolsey is from another century, but it's still a significant and "typically" English-sounding name). The name of the village where most of the story was filmed, Tarrant Monkton, suggests yet another Roundhead general.

• John Horton had been designated as effects designer, but was replaced at the last minute by Tony Harding. His previous form included less-than-satisfactory productions such as "The Power of Kroll" (16.5, though this was hardly his fault, as we've seen), "The Invisible Enemy" (15.2) and "State of Decay" (18.4). His work on "The King's Demons" (20.6) had been praised for the way he'd coped with exceptional hardship, i.e. Kamelion. Horton had fallen out with Michael Owen Morris, who made his debut here as a *Doctor Who* director (presumably the falling-out had happened on something like *Juliet Bravo*, as Morris' only prior role on *Doctor Who* was PA on 16.2, "The Pirate Planet").

• During filming, Denis Lill (Sir George) fractured a rib when a horse barged him into a wall. He'd got the part at almost the last minute, as the other possible candidates admitted they were unfamiliar with horses (one of these was Clifford Rose, seen in 18.5, "Warriors' Gate" as Captain Rorvik). The horse also caused the most widely-seen element of this story, the out-take in which it decides not to stop at the gateway to the church and promptly demolishes the whole prop.

• Will Chandler's dialogue was written in phonetic Mummerset, with "z"s for "s"s and zo on.

21.3: "Frontios"

(Serial 6N, Four Episodes, 26th January - 3rd February 1984.)

Which One is This? The TARDIS comes down with a bad case of worms, going to pieces on a planet at the edge of space-time and leaving nothing behind but the hat-stand.

Firsts and Lasts First appearance of *Blake's 7* costumes (the orderlies' helmets), after years of *Blake's 7* pilfering leftovers from *Doctor Who*. Last involvement of Christopher H. Bidmead in the series, although many unlikely rumours link him to "Timelash" (22.5) and "Silver Nemesis" (25.3). It's the last time Paddy Kingsland does the music, and the first time the Emulator's pan-pipes setting is used. The Radiophonic Workshop developed this by blowing across ketchup bottles, and it's now everywhere. Tegan says 'rabbits' for the last time.

Also, this is the first of four stories in Season Twenty-One to feature an actor called "Maurice". Which doesn't sound like a big thing, except that there are no Maurices anywhere else in the whole colour era of *Doctor Who*. How's *that* for trivia?

Four Things to Notice About "Frontios"...

1. The most obvious thing to mention is that the TARDIS gets destroyed. In retrospect, this doesn't look like a big thing, because it's obvious that the Doctor's going to find *some* way of putting it back together again before the end of episode four. At the time, though, things weren't so clear cut. John Nathan-Turner had publicly been talking about the possibility of changing the TARDIS' shape, and rumour insisted he was getting rid of it altogether.

And it was a time for burning things; it hadn't been that long since *Blake's 7* had ended its run by slaughtering all the regular cast. This wasn't a time for sacred cows. So when the TARDIS was blown to bits at the end of episode one, and the Doctor

got on with his usual planet-saving duties in the following episodes anyway... let's just say it was a matter for concern.

2. The other thing people noticed at the time was how horrid it all was. On Frontios, the earth eats people and corpses are used to drive brutal-looking tunnelling machines, making this one of those stories that small boys talked about in playgrounds the next day and said "bloody hell, did you see *that*?". At the very least, it proved that the series still had the power to get people writing letters of complaint to the *Radio Times* and *Points of View*. Of course, it was nothing like as yukky as had been planned (see **The Lore**, if you dare).

3. The villain here is the Gravis, leader of a race of giant slug-creatures that make their plans against the universe from the tunnels beneath Frontios. Some of the best moments here come when the Doctor pretends to be interested in the Gravis' work and chats with the creature as if they're comparing house-prices. The highlight arrives when the Doctor tries to convince the Gravis that Tegan is an android personal assistant: 'I got it cheap because the walk's not quite right. And then there's the accent, of course...' The other thing to notice about the Gravis is that although the rest of his species are "straightforward" slug- / insect- / worm-beings, the Gravis has a great big nose in the middle of his face. Smell is obviously a rare privilege in Tractator society.

4. It's official: *Doctor Who* has started getting affectionate towards the lurid movies it used to affect to disdain. Much of this story's look is retro, with the space-monsters resembling the Zanti Misfits from *The Outer Limits*, the ship interiors and Gravis' lair using big "atomic-age" glass shots, and the gravity beams making buzzing noises like the weapons and spaceships from *Flash Gordon*. (That's original 1930s *Flash Gordon*. See 23.2, "Mindwarp", for how director Ron Jones remade the 1980 version.) Even Turlough's "freak-out" on seeing the Tractators is taken from the little girl who gets menaced by giant ants in *Them!* (1954).

The Continuity

The Doctor In a bit of a funny mood, he's sorting things out on the TARDIS and starts by deciding where to put the hat-stand. He seems positively flustered when his Ship has to materialise on the limits of known history, displaying serious anxiety about the idea of landing on Frontios. Once he's there, he can't resist tending to the sick but asks the locals not to tell the Time Lords that he made any 'material difference'. He states that this is because of the 'laws of time', as the colony's too new, one generation at the most; too much hangs in the balance. [In other words, this is a nexus-point in history. Most of the Doctor's interference in the universe is unsanctioned by Gallifrey, so this is something *really* serious.] When the TARDIS is destroyed, he doesn't display grief or anger but looks as if he doesn't want to have to think about it [much like his reaction to Adric's death, in fact].

• *Ethics.* After being threatened by the leader of the colonists on Frontios, the Doctor has no compunction about ignoring the crisis there and leaving the humans to their fate [only because he's not technically supposed to interfere anyway]. Even so, he clearly can't bear watching individuals suffer and can't help ministering to the wounded.

• *Inventory.* He's carrying spectacles again, and uses them when examining fiddly equipment. And he's still got his cricket ball.

The Supporting Cast

• *Turlough.* Positively relishes the chance to tell Tegan what he's read about the 'doomed planet Earth' in the TARDIS databank. Though he's mostly over his "running away" phase, he displays an uncontrollable, atavistic terror when confronted with the Tractators. He knows the creatures from his own world [meaning Trion, or the possible adoptive home he seems to have been trying to get back to in Season Twenty?], where they infested the place 'long ago', although it takes him a while for this to come back to him as it's an ancestral memory rather than a personal recollection. [Earth-born humans are capable of this too, but in Turlough's race the memories are particularly clear.] After this he's in a disturbed psychological state for some time, and later begins to brood over his "failure", demonstrating that he's sick of being the token coward among the TARDIS crew.

In the pocket of his school uniform he's carrying two triangular coins, known as two-corpera pieces [again, probably from one of the worlds he's called home], each of which has a hole in the middle. It's good luck to blow through one of these coins. He knows quite a lot of odd details of cosmic history, including Hieradi's Twenty-Aeon War. [This anecdote is interesting, as it implies that he knows something from well after our time. See **Things That Don't Make Sense**.]

The TARDIS As the Ship heads into the far, far future, an alarm sounds on the console and the computer screen displays the warning "BOUNDARY ERROR... TIME PARAMETERS EXCEEDED". The Doctor states that they're on the 'outer limits', having drifted too far into the future, and puts the Ship in hover mode [so it comes out of the vortex and materialises in space]. The Doctor states that the future of the humans in the Veruna system is beyond the reach of 'our' [the Time Lords'] knowledge.

[In other words, this is about as far as the TARDIS can go. There are two obvious explanations for this, as we've seen in **When (and Where) is Gallifrey?** under "Pyramids of Mars" (13.3). The first is that Gallifrey exists in the distant future, and the TARDIS can't go beyond the Gallifreyan "present", which is what the Ship is approaching here. The second is that Gallifrey exists either in the distant past or outside normal time altogether, and this is simply as far as TARDISes can reach; this would explain the comment about the limits of 'our' knowledge, and gels with the Doctor's concern about the TARDIS nearly crashing through the time-spiral in 15.4, "The Sun Makers". Compare also the Doctor's statement about Frontios being outside the Time Lords' 'sphere of influence' with **What is the Blinovitch Limitation Effect?** under 20.3, "Mawdryn Undead". Is this as far as the Eye of Harmony can "see"? If so, then it's not impossible that other powerful forces - equal to, or opposed to, the Time Lords - monitor events beyond this boundary. That would certainly help to explain the Doctor's obvious anxiety.]

The TARDIS' stabilisers fail as Tractators draw the Ship towards Frontios. The Doctor gets his craft to materialise on the planet, but afterwards the internal doors won't open as they've been buckled by outside forces. And when the TARDIS is caught up in one of the meteor storms that ravage Frontios, the Ship is smashed into pieces, proving that it's less indestructible than the Doctor might have believed. There's no sign of the police box exterior, but shattered fragments of the architecture are scattered across the landscape, as are the hat-stand and various other items. [And Kamelion's around somewhere, one supposes. Sheer brute force has never even dented the Ship before, so does the effect of the meteorites on its structure have something to do with the extreme gravitational conditions created by the Tractators?

How Indestructible is the TARDIS?

Once upon a time, it was obvious. The TARDIS was a temporal manifestation of something outside time, so it couldn't be damaged.

This was more or less said out loud in 9.5, "The Time Monster", but had been sort of implicit throughout the series. *Sort of* because there were many occasions when the Ship ran into trouble, and the Doctor insisted on talking about imminent disaster. A selection would include "The Edge of Destruction" (1.3), obviously, but also "The Wheel in Space" (5.7) and the first few scenes of "The Mind Robber" (6.2… up to the point when the doors open onto nothingness, after which the whole story's of questionable veracity). Intriguingly, though, each of these features a different kind of threat. The first is to the Ship's power-source, and thus to the Ship as a whole; the second is to the vessel's dimensions; the third to the entire Ship as a result of a seemingly-paltry external threat.

So in the black-and-white days, the TARDIS interior is inside the police box. The box, whilst seemingly made of wood, is impermeable and unbreakable but *not* totally invulnerable. The problem with the volcano in "The Mind Robber" is the power-drain on the Ship, not lava per se. Had the lava piled up when the Ship was at peak efficiency, the Doctor could have stayed put. The internal dimensions are sustained by the time vector generator (and when this is removed, the Ship reverts to the internal configuration of a police box). However, even this is contradicted by other black-and-white stories. The lock of the Ship is removable in "The Sensorites" (1.7), but clearly part of the TARDIS systems in "The Daleks" (1.2). 'Space pressure' affects the external dimensions in "Planet of Giants" (2.1), and the crewmembers are reduced to fit this, but it's apparently not connected to the normal processes of internal dimensioning.

The colour stories begin to open up the question. Whilst "Pyramids of Mars" (13.3) has the outside world clearly visible through the doors, as in Season One, most stories after "The Time Monster" stick to a convention that there's an atrium area - in black - between the console room and the outside. (6.5, "The Seeds of Death", has curved mirrors there. Remarkably similar to the ones on the moonbase.) After "The Masque of Mandragora" (14.1), the concept of the Ship alters profoundly. In the new model, the TARDIS is a dimension, and the blue box is a gateway. The "interior" hovers around in some other kind of time and space, while the police box is relocated in different parts of the universe we know. The two are linked, but one isn't inside the other in the conventional sense, hence the Doctor's pseudo-explanation in "The Robots of Death" (14.5). The console room is located near the atrium zone, which leads into the box; whenever the Doctor changes from one console room to another, the atrium relocates accordingly.

"Logopolis" (18.7) cements this within a total theory, wherein the 'outer plasmic shell' is treated much like a computer-generated event in space-time. Though it's not explicitly said to be done with the same block transfer computation used by the Logopolitans, the implication is that it's still a product of "pure" mathematics, while the internal features are raw energy modelled in a not-dissimilar way. The further implication is that the TARDIS exterior can't be damaged, in the same way numbers can't be damaged, though it's reasonable to think that things which tear or distort space-time might have an effect in a way that (for example) just falling off a mountain wouldn't. As we've seen, the breaking-up of the Ship in "Frontios" only occurs under extreme gravitational conditions. The Cybermen's bomb in "The Five Doctors" (20.7), which at least *two* fairly knowledgeable companions see as a threat to the Ship, might well be capable of ripping a hole in the continuum instead of just causing a big explosion. Ergo the TARDIS can't be damaged the way "normal" matter can, but a black hole would still be a problem… as it is in "The Horns of Nimon" (17.5).

So that's the early-'80s, Neo-Platonic approach to TARDIS design. And we've seen several strong hints that this is indeed how the Ship functions. The notion of being outside time and space is implicit in the suggestion that its occupants are in 'a state of temporal grace' (especially in 14.2, "The Hand of Fear", where this 'grace' is treated as a side-effect of the vessel's mechanics rather than a deliberate security device). The Season Seventeen all-purpose doohickey, the conceptual geometer, hints at this in both its name and the ways it's deployed. In 17.6, "Shada", it allows Chronotis / Salyavin to be not-dead long enough to get Claire to fix it. Thereafter he can leave his Ship with no apparent ill effects.

But things keep invading this elsewhere dimension. Sutekh seems to have left a gaping hole in the TARDIS continuum in "Pyramids of Mars", allowing everything from exiled Karfelons (22.5, "Timelash") to robotic junk-mail (25.4, "The

continued on page 271...

The novelisation is more explicit about this, and see **How Indestructible is the TARDIS?**. If the TARDIS really has the 'power of a sun' under its console, then it's obviously not unleashed during this process.]

There's a brief flash when Turlough moves the hat-stand, described by the Doctor as residual energy from the Ship. The console is later found to be intact, and still has power, although most of the systems aren't functional. A second computer screen on the console displays the location of the scattered TARDIS components, once the switches that control the spatial distribution circuits are activated. The Gravis eventually uses his gravitational powers to draw the pieces of the Ship back together. The plasmic outer walls of the Ship seal, meaning that the console room is back in its own dimension rather than on Frontios, severing the Gravis' link with the Tractators. Within mere minutes it's whole again, and there aren't even any cracks in the walls. [It's as if the severed bits of the Ship *want* to come back together. Compare this with the casual way Nyssa builds the zero cabinet in 19.1, "Castrovalva".] After the TARDIS is restored, the engines aren't working properly and the Ship's drawn towards the 'middle of the universe' [i.e. towards Earth, as Frontios is at the edges], but this is the effect of an outside source [revealed in the next story].

The TARDIS databank is used again, and contains data on Frontios. Here the Doctor claims that TARDIS stands for Time and Relative *Dimension* in Space, singular. [As in Season One, though this version hadn't been used in years until "Mawdryn Undead"... Ian Levine's been issuing memos again.] Turlough is sent to fetch the portable mu-field activator and five argon discharge globes as a light-source, plus the Ship's medical supplies, though these are never seen as they're beyond the Ship's buckled inner door. The hatstand, meanwhile, is left on Frontios as a gift. The Doctor says there's another one somewhere on the Ship [see the "green wellies" scene in "Castrovalva"].

The Non-Humans

• *Tractators.* Great worm-like creatures that live in burrowed tunnels beneath the ground, with hard carapaces, faces that aren't *quite* humanoid and hands emerging from beneath their shells. The Doctor believes they're insects.

Though the Tractators display signs of intelligence and use machines, they're only sentient because of the Gravis, their leader. The Gravis does all their planning, and seems to be the only one capable of speech, as well as the only one with a nose. The Tractators are obviously a space-going species, as Turlough recognises the signs of their presence on Frontios from his own world, but this bunch have been marooned on Frontios for nearly five-hundred years. The Gravis drew the human colonists to the planet, letting them establish a colony before putting his plans into effect. Obviously well-travelled, he knows the Doctor by reputation, having heard of both Gallifrey and TARDISes. He reaches the conclusion that the Doctor has been sent to investigate by the Time Lords [so even if this era is on the limits of Time Lord knowledge, the Time Lords have at least made their presence felt there].

However, the Tractators' most notable feature is their seemingly-innate ability to affect gravity, something which seems to involve wiggling their antennae. A single Tractator can use its gravity-beam to pin someone to the wall, but they can pull as well as push, dragging human victims down to their lair through the soil of Frontios. The Tractators are the ones who've been causing the meteor storms on the planet's surface, snatching the rocks out of the sky to keep the colony under control. Humans are being pulled underground and used as central elements in the Tractators' excavating machines, powerful engines which use the captive mind and body of the victim as a motive force, though these drivers seem to get worn down quite quickly.

Other than the two excavating machines, the Tractators don't appear to have much in the way of technology, and their lair is little more than a smooth-walled burrow with just a few occasional signs of complex architecture. The walls have to be smooth, as the Tractators plan to use them as wave-guides, to concentrate their gravitational forces once their plans are complete. The planet will be given a gravity motor, so that Frontios can be steered through space, allowing the Tractators to breed on other worlds. How they normally travel, and how they got to Frontios, remains a mystery.

The Gravis' powers are such that he can single-handedly pull together the shattered TARDIS fragments. He becomes dormant when separated from the Tractators, as he draws his power from them, but it's indicated that he recovers some time later. The Doctor finally strands the Gravis on the

How Indestructible is the TARDIS?

...continued from page 269

Greatest Show in the Galaxy") to barge in unannounced. Things from "orthodox" space-time seem to intersect with the TARDIS continuum via wherever the outer plasmic shell happens to be located, even if it's not fully-materialised. (The issues arising from this are dealt with in **Does the TARDIS Fly?** under 5.6, "Fury from the Deep".) Exterior events are often seen to affect the interior, like the lopsided landing in "Castrovalva" (19.1), and the overheating in the same story when the Ship's heading towards Event One.

Later on, writers seem happy to continue with the idea of the TARDIS as a physical spaceship when it suits them, and have its exterior really made of wood. In "The Happiness Patrol" (25.2), it's defaced by graffiti and should - in theory - leave a puddle of pink paint behind, yet the Doctor and Ace still feel obliged to repaint it blue. In "Silver Nemesis" (25.3) an arrow sticks into the side of the police-box exterior (or into the new paintwork, perhaps?) and travels with the Ship to a place where the plot requires a gold arrowhead. In the black-and-white era the Doctor's always cautious about materialising in real-space, except on a planet or inside another vessel. The HADS in "The Krotons" (6.4) wouldn't be useful if things like acid sprays were no threat at all, but the only time we see this is shortly after a similar gadget is improvised to relocate the Ship a few miles from its previous arrival-point (5.5, "The Web of Fear"), as if the Doctor's trying out a new feature. Maybe acid is no real threat, but the device is like a car-alarm that goes off whenever there's a strong wind.

It may be significant that "The Krotons" was repeated while "Castrovalva" was being written. If we assume that the break-up seen in "Frontios" is some form of extreme HADS, displacing the Ship's interior across a planet as a result of hostile activity under extreme conditions, then the two different versions of the TARDIS functions can be resolved.

To sum up. The TARDIS is another dimension, contiguous but not continuous with our space-time. The way in or out is a mathematically-generated physical object which can be moved through the space-time vortex. At points in the vortex, strong influences from the related portions of space and time can influence the irrelevant continuum via the physical portal. The most powerful of these forces can affect the Ship's interior - that is, the dimension accessible through the portal - and damage, distort or drain that dimension. If this effect is severe then the operation of the portal is impaired, perhaps permanently.

A further supposition: the console is the source of the dimensioning forces. Although there appears to be a "centre" to the TARDIS (see "Castrovalva" especially), the TARDIS power is operated from the main controls. Originally the source was beneath the time rotor ("The Edge of Destruction"), but later the console can function even when it's removed from its natural setting ("The Mind Robber"; 7.3, "The Ambassadors of Death"; 7.4, "Inferno"; 9.1, "Day of the Daleks"). So the console is the part of the Ship that's able to move across space and time. The outer plasmic shell is generated from the console, but it's not in need of continuous projection like a television picture. Once materialised, the exterior isn't sustained by the chameleon circuit unless a revision's made, something we see happening to the Master's vessel from time to time.

The answer to the question seems to be that the TARDIS is occasionally indestructible, and occasionally at risk from heavy-duty forces. The exterior is remade but not continually, and the interior can be attacked from within orthodox space-time.

None of this explains what Striker does to the Ship in "Enlightenment" (20.5).

---

uninhabited planet of Kolkokron, believing that without his influence the other Tractators will be harmless too. [But there are presumably other Tractator colonies around the universe...]

Planet Notes

• *Frontios.* A stark, meteor-ravaged world in the Veruna system, home to both the Tractators and a colony of human beings who've escaped the doomed planet Earth but crashed here thanks to the Gravis' influence. There's a heavy asteroid belt in the system, which the Tractators use as a source of material for their meteor bombardment, but there are no other signs of life in the system. Even by TARDIS standards, the Doctor describes this place as being 'far out'. Apart from the Tractator abductions, the humans are under pressure here, as most of their technology was lost in the crash and they're reduced to lighting their settlements with phosphor lamps. On Frontios they don't even have wood or any other combustible materials. The food's rationed, which is why the crashed ship is always guarded, and the atmosphere's quite thin. The constant meteor showers, caused by the Tractators, have kept the colonists' numbers small and many human beings - both alive and dead - have been seen to vanish beneath the earth, hence the saying that 'Frontios buries its own dead'. There have been an increasing number of deserters, retrogrades, or "rets", who leave the colony to hunt out in the wastes. The military tend to shoot these people. [This militia consists of 'orderlies', suggesting the ship may have been a hospital vessel before being fitted for colonisation.]

The colonists' leader, the son of original leader Captain Revere, is named Plantagenet [hinting at the start of a dynasty of rulers]. Revere learned of the Tractators' existence before they abducted him, but chose not to tell the colonists, simply passing a law forbidding them to dig underground.

• *Kolkokron*. The uninhabited planet where the Doctor dumps the Gravis, apparently nothing but rocks and boulders.

• *Heiradi*. During the Twenty-Aeon War, the Arar-Jecks of Heiradi burrowed out a huge subterranean city beneath their planet, at least according to Turlough.

History

• *Dating*. The far, far, far future. The Frontios colonists are refugees from the 'doomed' planet Earth, due for a catastrophic collision with the sun according to the TARDIS databank. [This suggests c. 10,000,000 AD, as the Earth meets the same fate in "The Ark" (3.6), although the people on the Ark seemed a lot more sophisticated and better-prepared than the Frontios colonists. There's an argument to be made that the colonists could have been fleeing the apparent end of the world described in "The Mysterious Planet" (23.1), c. 2,000,000 AD, which is a bit of a stretch but would explain the humans' relatively primitive status.]

The Doctor notes that the colonists are one of the last surviving groups of humans, though they seem to believe themselves to be the last. They crashed on Frontios forty years ago in a supposedly failure-proof ship, the Tractators' influence overcoming the autonomous guidance. The ship carried technology capable of rebuilding civilisation, and there were thousands of people on board, though most were killed in the crash and many others were lost to an outbreak of disease.

The colonists had ten years to grow food, but the bombardments from space began thirty years ago. The population's now fallen below minimum levels for guaranteed growth.

Even this far into the future, Plantagenet doesn't believe that a craft as small as the TARDIS is capable of traversing the universe. Tegan can read the seemingly-English words on the colonists' documents.

The Analysis

Where Does This Come From? As he had been throughout Season Eighteen, here Christopher Bidmead is keen to show the process of scientific enquiry, the asking of questions as a subversive activity in the face of what "they" tell you. Now, however, the idea that overthrowing repressive regimes is automatically a good thing is itself questioned.

As a child of the Second World War, Bidmead would have grown up with an assumption that the government always had its reasons and that lives were always at stake; the Churchillian poster of Captain Revere and his son's "Let Us Go Forward Together" speeches both hint at this. The experience of the Blitz is a crucial element of many *Doctor Who* stories, from "The Dalek Invasion of Earth" (2.2) to "Resurrection of the Daleks" (21.4) and beyond. (Some accounts hold that the latter was originally set in 1944. Compare also with 26.3, "The Curse of Fenric".)

The interesting thing is that whilst Frontios is in many ways the standard-model Bidmead world, where knowledge has been lost and the work of reclaiming the science of the previous generations is officially frowned upon, this time it's the ones doing the frowning who are the most clearly-delineated. The science officer, Mr. Range, is never really allowed to explain why he's collating all this material about "Deaths Unaccountable", but Chief Orderly Brazen is given two or three speeches on what the alternatives are. For once, the threat of death for dissidents is a simple statement of fact, not a policy decision. So whilst this story would have fit into the E-Space trilogy almost too well, it's considerably more mature, as far as a story about steering a planet around the cosmos to spread a plague of giant slugs can be.

And this leads us to another element of Bidmead's past. As script editor, he'd sat down and watched an awful lot of Hartnell stories. The notion of giant insects being controlled by a central intelligence is at the heart of "The Web Planet" (2.5) and the Blitz element "The Dalek Invasion of Earth" has the Daleks wanting to burrow into the planet to enable them to steer it around the universe. However bizarre this idea is, it's a well-established part of the programme's lore (especially as the film version, *Daleks - Invasion Earth 2150 AD*, was re-shown almost annually). Similarly, the ideas introduced in "The Ark" (3.6) are re-examined here in the light of later known science. As with the TARDIS, it's there in the *Doctor Who* universe, so why not explore the possibilities rather than wish it away?

Ah yes, the TARDIS. Although the idea here is rather at odds with the account of the Ship's workings in his previous two scripts, Bidmead is trying something out. Apart from "The Awakening", each story of Season Twenty-One has the Doctor deprived of some element of his usual life, and here - possibly as a publicity stunt, inspired by Nathan-Turner - the first cliffhanger is played up as a possible drastic shift in the programme's dynamic. In some ways this is a missed opportunity. Developing a new world in as much detail as UNIT-era Earth was the sort of thing Bidmead might have proposed while working as script editor. The planet may have been turned into Earth's last refuge in order to make subsequent stories more urgent.

The starting-point, Bidmead's infestation of woodlice, wouldn't have led most writers to the idea of gravitic waveguides made by corpse-constructed mining machines. The science isn't quite as out-of-control as in "The Leisure Hive", but isn't wildly outside what's known (although the idea of making a surface "mathematically-smooth" would be questioned by anyone interested in Fractals... doubtless Bidmead himself would be one of the first to comment, if anyone wrote this today). The name of the aliens is allegedly a pun on "traction" and an anagram of sorts, but once the similarity to Ludwig Wittgenstein's *Tractatus* was pointed out, Bidmead incorporated it into the novelisation. Wittgenstein argued that maths is a human language-game and not a pre-existing condition of the universe, so you can see how the author of "Logopolis" might consider it the work of a monster. And Wittgenstein wrote a famous thought-experiment about a beetle in a box...

All this and corpses, too. Because despite its retro touches - see **Four Things to Notice** - "Frontios" is a specifically '80s kind of production,

and making "nasty" versions of old sci-fi favourites was one of cinema's minor obsessions at this point. This is a closer relative of Carpenter's *The Thing* than of *The Outer Limits*. Like so many stories of this period, the big stylistic influences here are the movies that followed in the wake of *Alien*, and once again there's a sense that the programme's trying to keep up with the excesses of modern culture by taking as much from contemporary horror as it thinks it can get away with. By now the world has moved on from the out-and-out butchery of *The Texas Chain Saw Massacre* and become obsessed with all things parasitic and biologically invasive, so whereas in times past a man-machine hybrid would be a nice, clean-looking monster like a Dalek or a Cyberman, here it's a clunking great drilling machine with a human head poking out of it. The implied cannibalism of Frontios - the planet consumes the dead, the Tractators use people for spare parts, and to be honest it's a shock when we find out that the aliens *aren't* literally eating the humans - would strike a chord with anyone who'd glanced at the top shelf of any video rental shop. For the first two episodes we're led to believe that the colonists are at war with an alien enemy that's bombarding them from above, and even when it's being a war story it's more visceral than most. The scenes of the Doctor tending to the sick in the colony's badly-prepared medical unit may be vaguely reminiscent of *M*A*S*H*, but it's hard to imagine the series presenting us with this many desperate, wounded people in the early '70s (at least until "Genesis of the Daleks", anyway).

Things That Don't Make Sense Despite the fact that the TARDIS crew have always been able to pick up outside communications (e.g. 21.1, "Warriors of the Deep") and even telepathic transmissions (e.g. 16.2, "The Pirate Planet") while they're in the console room, the Ship conveniently starts blocking off these sorts of signals when its extra-dimensional status is needed to break the link between the Gravis and the Tractators. [Is it something to do with the force-field? Or can transmissions normally only get in via the scanner?] In fact the logic of the ending involves a theory about TARDIS construction that's radically opposed to the one floated in previous stories by the same author. Everything depends on the TARDIS interior emphatically *not* being created and sustained by mathematical modelling, but now they're "beyond" the limit of Gallifrey's observation this doesn't appear to apply (see **How Indestructible is the TARDIS?**).

The guard who chases Tegan out of the medical shelter is so slow that she's got time to close the shelter's doors, look around, find an iron bar and slip it through the door-handles before he can get out of the building. It then takes some minutes for Brazen to command the man to try to break the door open, by which time the iron bar has mysteriously moved from being in the middle of the door-handles to resting on top of them.

Due to a scene being cut, Tegan appears to know the Doctor's plan in episode four without being told (when Turlough and Brazen rescue her and she tells them off for their pains... see **The Lore**). When Tegan and Turlough sneak aboard the ship, at least three onlookers - not including the guard they're trying to elude - can see them clearly.

So far into the future, it's pleasing to note that Brazen can mention a 'waxworks museum', fully confident that people born and raised on this remote and backward world will know what he's talking about (likewise, Range's daughter Norna calling Turlough a 'chicken'). We also note that pita bread is easier to come by in the future than it was in 1984, and that they have ballpoint pens which don't run out after forty years. If there's no electricity, then how does Mr. Range use a key-pad to open his filing cabinet? If this world has a thin atmosphere and no vegetation to speak of, then how can the colonists breathe? From the look of the soil, it's rather unlikely that they managed to grow enough even in the ten years of good harvests. It's also odd that the hospital complex lacks a concrete floor, what with all the rumours, to say nothing of basic hygiene.

The Arar-Jecks of Hieradi had something called the 'Twenty Aeon War'. Our universe is coming up to thirteen aeons old, and Turlough speaks of the war in the past tense [Arar-Jeck hyperbole]. He's also surprisingly adept at dating local rock specimens.

Critique (Defence, ish) A lot of people were uneasy when details of this story were announced. Christopher Hamilton Bidmead, author of two ponderous, self-consciously "important" scripts and editor in the year the series lost the ability to speak intelligible English, teams up with the director of "Time-Flight" and "Arc of Infinity". How can this be even remotely entertaining?

Fortunately, in both cases the track-records were misleading. Bidmead and Jones were both, to some extent, victims of a belief in "high-concept" stories where the one-line pitch ends with an exclamation mark. ('The Master's back and he's unravelled the Universe!', 'The Master's back and he's disguised himself as a conjurer, hidden in the Jurassic Era and stolen Concorde!'... see 2.1, "Planet of Giants", for an earlier bout of this.) But were it not for the cliffhanger leading into "Resurrection of the Daleks", this would have been the first "stand-alone" story for years, and only the decision to tease the viewers with yet another attempt to make the Doctor more "vulnerable" marks it out as mid-'80s.

Bidmead has finally got the hang of characterisation, plotting and what the programme can and can't do. Despite the obvious snag that the resolution of the big mystery of this planet is botched, everything leading up to the machine's appearance is paced and disclosed efficiently. A cynic might ask why such a seasoned veteran made so much of the plot revolve around two elements that couldn't possibly have worked (flexible monsters and unbroadcastably gruesome concepts), but considering that they'd got away with less in the past, it was worth a shot. It's interesting that for all the emphasis on rational inquiry and observation, it's revealed truth - in the form of Turlough's race memories - which provides the answers.

Where this story really scores is with the direction. Ron Jones had hitherto had the leftover scripts, poisoned chalices like "Arc of Infinity". His next few stories would see him taking vaguely pulpy scripts and getting them to work, emphasising the gaudiness but working from the actors up, not the "high-concept" down. And it's his casting which makes this special. Even a relatively small part played slightly OTT, like the Ret who proclaims Cockerell to be the messiah, is tolerable within the confines of what he has to do. As Brazen, Peter Gilmore is at the heart of the story, and his combination of dignity and pragmatism says more about how this world works (or doesn't) than any amount of info-dump dialogue. Mr. Range gets the bulk of this to deliver, and actor William Lucas manages to make it seem like it is who this character is, not what he's in the story for. The sidelight on this, from Norna, could have been irritating but Leslie Dunlop makes it entirely natural.

Against this background the regular cast perk

up; Mark Strickson in particular looks like he's having a better time than of late. "The Awakening" was visibly the point where Davison figured out how to play the Doctor, and now he's putting it into practice. With the cast believing what they're saying, a certain leeway is permissible in the sets and monsters. "Frontios" looks the way we'd like to think 1960s *Doctor Who* looked to viewers at the time, and for once the lighting is right. In fact, the "Main Street" set looked to some viewers like location OB footage, and only the subterranean sets (and obviously the TARDIS) looked studio-bound.

The most frustrating thing about "Frontios" isn't the mess they made of the machine and the Gravis' use for the dead (see **The Lore**), but the delay in making this kind of story up until now. If Bidmead, Jones and Saward had pulled off something like this instead of "Terminus" then we could have had five years of Davison.

Critique (Different Kind of Defence) It comes *perilously* close to being the point where the Nathan-Turner era descends into self-parody. After all, one of the series' hallmarks in the post-Alien era has been its reliance on "outer-space gothic", and "Frontios" has more dark spaces, suffocating tunnels, borderline-functional pieces of technology and cod-horror overtones than any other story of its ilk.

And yet… yes, in parts it looks more like a rebirth, as if this story was supposed to open Season Twenty-One and remind everyone of *Doctor Who*'s roots as something startling, claustrophobic and alien. This is no banal colony-under-threat-from-monsters story, but a tale that's trying to turn the genre inside-out, which starts from a premise of faulty assumptions (the people of Frontios believe they're being attacked from outer space, only to find that the real problem is the exact opposite) and then sets about demonstrating it in ways that seem tangible rather than cerebral.

Bidmead's style hasn't changed in the slightest. As in "Logopolis" and "Castrovalva", his talent as a scriptwriter is to know how to turn his ideas into visual events. The TARDIS is shattered, but rather than being blasted into another dimension it's worked into the cavern-walls of Frontios like a fossil, and its familiarity has never been so disconcerting. The Tractators are parasites, but rather than being banal eaters of life-energy (stand up, the Nimon) they're builders of diabolical engines.

The earth on Frontios is hungry, and we see it eat, even if the effects aren't *quite* up to it. Then Turlough gets to threaten the natives with a hatstand.

There's a palpable sense of doom here, with all the physical materials we see on-screen falling apart at the same rate as the colony's social system, so as in much of Season Eighteen there's no solid line between the props and the ideas. The similarities to "Full Circle" make you suspect that Bidmead had an even bigger hand in the writing of that story than we might have thought, but whereas "Full Circle" revelled in its monsters-and-spaceships setting in a way that seemed pleasingly childish, this is the horrible, visceral, grown-up version.

But you can tell the writer hasn't worked on the series for a while. His last script was "Castrovalva", and the Doctor's almost as erratic here as he was in his debut. This is a good thing. The TARDIS has become altogether too cosy of late, and the Doctor's manic spurts just give you the feeling that this series could go *anywhere* from here, a feeling reinforced when the Ship falls apart in the entirely unexpected first cliffhanger. It's lost some of its momentum by episode three, the part of the production that (so often the way) starts to pad things out with random tunnel-wandering, yet on this occasion the slowness of the story is a boon. Like us, the Doctor has to figure things out from scratch here, and we're asked to reason things through.

When events drag, it's mostly because the direction isn't up to the job. Contrary to the previous Critique, this Defence finds it hard to acquit Ron Jones; individually the actors are giving it their all, but Jones doesn't know how to put them together to make a complete picture, despite the script's best efforts. The scene in which Brazen leaves a deserter to be torn apart by starving retrogrades should be one of the most memorable of the decade, but ends up as a mess of bad staging and distracting cuts. The moment when Brazen himself stumbles into the clutches of the excavating machine is so clumsy that it's almost pantomime. The "revolution" of the retrogrades is made to look like an afterthought, as if it's vastly less important than what the Tractators are doing, and that's not the way it's written.

Still, so many of the rules of space opera are bent here that you can't expect *everything* to look as good as it does on paper. The Doctor uses pure bluff and trickery to beat the monster, no explosives or technology required. The colony leader is put out of action not by some alien plague-virus, but by simple heart problems (again, Bidmead's always been good at this kind of close detail). Plantagenet's rants to the Doctor make him sound like a stereotypical *Doctor Who* villain, yet he's just a frightened child in a man's body. And as in the author's other work, there's an obvious love of language and custom, right down to Turlough's wholly believable superstition about blowing through two-corpera pieces for luck.

All of this and top performances from just about everybody involved, too, so for once even the traditional daughter-of-local-scientist character seems to have a personality. Perhaps it was never going to cause a revolution in the art of *Doctor Who*, but as a template for what the series *should* have been in the 1980s, "Frontios" comes nearer to the mark than just about anything else.

The Facts

Written by Christopher H. Bidmead. Directed by Ron Jones. Viewing figures: 8.0 million, 5.8 million, 7.8 million, 5.6 million.

Supporting Cast Peter Gilmore (Brazen), William Lucas (Range), Jeff Rawle (Plantagenet), Lesley Dunlop (Norna), Maurice O'Connell (Cockerill), John Gillett (Gravis).

Working Titles "The Wanderers".

Oh, Isn't That..?
• *Peter Gilmore.* Aside from the occasional *Carry On* film, he's best known for two things. One: being the star of Victorian nautical soap *The Onedin Line*, in which he scared and impressed a whole generation of younger viewers with his monumental sideburns. Two: playing the lead in '70s adventure flick *Warlords of Atlantis*, the only film of its oeuvre which doesn't star Doug McClure.

• *Jeff Rawle.* Now he's almost as ubiquitous as Martin Clunes (20.2, "Snakedance"), but in 1984 he was best known for the early '70s series based on the book *Billy Liar*. Those familiar with '90s sitcom *Drop the Dead Donkey* may find the idea of the aggressive young leader of Frontios being played by timid, prematurely-aged newsroom boss George Dent to be somewhat hard to accept.

Cliffhangers After the meteor shower on Frontios, the Doctor finds his hat-stand in the middle of the colony and realises that the TARDIS has been destroyed; the Tractators pin the Doctor to the wall; the Doctor and Tegan face the Tractators' excavating machine, driven by the body of Captain Revere.

The Lore

• Bidmead's original plot makes a lot more sense. The Tractators are building a whole machine from snatched human corpses, and also using a severed head with a pendulum as the Gravis' translator device, a notion that's restored in the novelisation. Another cut was the opening scene, in which Tegan and Turlough use the TARDIS' controls as chess pieces (see 20.5, "Enlightenment"). When the Doctor persuades the Gravis that Tegan is an android, he quietly whispers his plan to her, saying that he's doing this to 'stop the Gravis adding you to his human Meccano set'. Tegan suddenly starts acting like a robot, and the Doctor "adjusts" her by putting a screwdriver in her ear. (The scene may have been trimmed to stop children copying this, although in itself the mention of Meccano breaks BBC regulations about product advertising. However, as scenes relating to this - with the Doctor telling the Gravis about the 'poly-directrix' lenses in his glasses - were also removed without the episode noticeably under-running, the cuts may have been made for reasons of time.)

• One of the stories considered for this season was "The House That Ur-Cjak Built" by Andrew Stephenson. Whether any mention of a Twenty-Aeon War was made in this is unknown (though compare the name "Arar-Jecks" to the villain in 21.6). Other stories submitted at around this time include "The Macromen" by Ingrid Pitt and her husband, which resembled the film *The Philadelphia Experiment* in many ways (she offered this to Nathan-Turner at the wrap party for 21.1, "Warriors of the Deep", and later mentioned story in a TV appearance as if it had already been made); "Hex" by Peter Ling and Hazel Adair (see 6.2, "The Mind Robber"); and what later became "Vengeance on Varos" (22.2) by Philip Martin.

• It was at around this time that the gentlemen of the press were introduced to the Sixth Doctor, Colin Baker. Most of them had already "discovered" that Brian Blessed was to be the replacement for Davison. Davison himself had figured out his stand-in's identity after a chance meeting with Baker, where the latter was just slightly too vague about his future plans.

• The original casting for Mr. Range was veteran film actor Peter Arne. Shortly before rehearsals, on the day he was due to have his costume fitting, he was found murdered at his home. One of the people who read the lurid tabloid treatment of this story was William Lucas, an occasional colleague of Arne's, who was contacted by the BBC that same day and only later realised the connection between his casting and Arne's death. Another death afflicted the production; designated designer Barrie Dobbins committed suicide a month before. His assistant, David Buckingham, was hastily promoted.

• The tunnelling machine was made by outside contractors, a company called Any Effects. Jones was unhappy with the result. Bidmead was unhappy with almost everything, especially the Tractators. He'd based the beings on the woodlice which had infested his first flat, and had envisaged more agile creatures. The director cast dancers in the hopes of allowing the Tractators to wrap themselves around their victims or crawl on their bellies through crevices, but the finished costumes were inflexible and encumbering (compare with 17.5, "The Horns of Nimon"). Only a couple of shots display the front axial projection inlays in the underbelly of the Gravis.

21.4: "Resurrection of the Daleks"

(Serial 6P, Two 45-Minute Episodes, 8th February - 15th February 1984.)

Which One is This? It's the Peter Davison Dalek story (they get one each from now on). As is traditional, there's a scene in which the Doctor has Davros at his mercy, but this time guns are involved.

Firsts and Lasts It's the first story to shown in 45-minute chunks instead of 25-minute instalments (see **The Lore** for the reasoning behind this), which means it's the first sign of Doctor Who taking on the America-friendly format that becomes the all-purpose length for drama series from the late '80s onwards, a format that's going to curse the whole of the next season and that's due to

make a big comeback in 2005. Terry Molloy makes his first appearance as Davros, a role he'll reprise whenever the Daleks turn up in the programme from now on, and Maurice Colbourne makes the first of two appearances as Commander Lytton. The TARDIS cloister bell rings for the last time, but most importantly of all, Tegan leaves the crew.

The shots of the attack on the space station are the first use of a motion-control camera in Doctor Who. No, it is interesting (see 23.1, "The Mysterious Planet").

Four Things to Notice About "Resurrection of the Daleks"...

1. All the violence. "Resurrection of the Daleks" has the highest on-screen death-toll of any Doctor Who story (see **Which Stories Have the Best Body-Counts?**), involving a seemingly-endless parade of casual shootings, off-the-cuff murders and nonchalant facial scarrings. Some of the victims get killed, duplicated by the Daleks and then double-killed, just to be on the safe side. Whereas the Doctor pointed a gun at his captors in "Warriors of the Deep" (21.1) and then handed it over in order to make them trust him, here he feels compelled to draw firearms on two occasions, and looks as if he actually means it.

But despite picking up criticism from "concerned parents" - perhaps for the last time in the series' history - what *really* sticks in the mind about the story isn't so much the horror as the wide variety of unbelievable death scenes, as no end of minor supporting characters are called on to look agonised and fall over. And it doesn't help that a lot of them are wearing space-uniform hats that make them look like the staff of International Rescue. If it gives you any idea what kind of story this is: it ends with Rodney Bewes, known for years as either "Mr. Rodney" from Basil Brush or the wet one from The Likely Lads, heroically hurling himself onto a self-destruct mechanism in slow motion to defeat the Daleks. He does this with the typically adolescent Eric Saward line: 'Hello boys! Just in time for the fun.'

2. A much more satisfying casualty is the first Dalek the Doctor encounters, which is destroyed when he and his new army friends push it out of a warehouse window and watch it smash open on the street below. This kind of wanton destruction was, of course, exactly the kind of thing that all twelve-year-old boys in the audience wanted to do. (But having accomplished this, the Doctor

then orders his colleagues to bring the Dalek's remains back up the stairs so that he can examine the pieces, which definitely has that feeling of "well, if you've finished playing with your toys then you can clear them up" about it.)

3. On much the same tack, the conclusion sees Davros turning the age-old playground chant on its head by maniacally shrieking: 'I-AM-NOT-A-DA-LEK!' He says this whilst dying of an anti-Dalek virus, with a gush of foam from beneath his "skirt" which is *unbelievably* rude-looking and makes you wonder why his other hand is always unseen.

4. It's time for this year's flashback sequence. There's been one of these every year since John Nathan-Turner took over, a way of bringing back old memories of the programme without it impeding the plot (unlike, for example, most of "Arc of Infinity"). In Season Eighteen, the pretext for this was the Doctor's life flashing before his eyes just before his regeneration; in Season Nineteen, it was a brief round-up of Cyber-history on the Cyber-Leader's scanner; in Season Twenty, it was the amnesiac Brigadier getting his memory back. Here the Doctor's wired up to a Dalek machine that scans his mind, although in the end all we get are static shots of all the companions so far, demonstrating that the Doctor remembers the 1960s in black-and-white. Except... where's Leela?

The Continuity

The Doctor Appears to have fillings [raising all kinds of questions about what happens to his teeth when he regenerates]. He guesses that Davros is around when he sees the Daleks [so he's come to think of Davros as the *real* enemy], and he sounds genuinely shaken and horrified when he learns of the Daleks' plan to assassinate the High Council of Time Lords. Which might explain what he does next...

• *Ethics.* However appalled he is by all the carnage around him - or perhaps because he's horrified by all the carnage around him - he finally decides that he has no choice but to kill Davros, taking a great big gun and going off to do the deed. But he's all too willing to listen to Davros' blather about making a new race of less offensive Daleks, and eventually fails to pull the trigger. [A curious parallel with 12.4, "Genesis of the Daleks", in which he initially chickens out of

blowing up the Kaled nursery when someone suggests there's a diplomatic option.] He obviously has no respect for Dalek life, shooting a Kaled mutant dead with a pistol, and regrets not destroying the Daleks when he had the chance ["Genesis of the Daleks" again, although he *did* eventually wipe out the Dalek nursery]. After this he seems to acknowledge that he's become too mired in violence, stating that he might have to mend his ways.

• *Background.* He states that he left Gallifrey because he grew tired of the lifestyle [18.7, "Logopolis", suggests there were also more pressing reasons]. He seems to know, without being told, all about the Movellan virus that defeated the Daleks.

The Supporting Cast

• *Tegan.* Things have finally got too much for her. Her Aunt Vanessa told her to give up being an air stewardess if she stopped enjoying it, and similarly, the TARDIS life has ceased to be 'fun'. Faced with the needless horror of the Dalek assault, she finally decides to leave the Doctor for good and stay on Earth. [To be fair, things have been getting on top of her ever since she rejoined the Doctor; see 20.2, "Snakedance". But things didn't stop being 'fun' when Auntie Vanessa *herself* was horribly murdered?]

Here she gets at least one innocent bystander killed, which might be the moment when she makes her decision. Alternatively, her faith in the Doctor is obviously shaken when he announces that he's going to murder Davros in cold blood, which is as plausible a last straw as any. She's obviously upset on leaving, and she even tries to return to the TARDIS as it's disappearing, as if she wants a better chance to say goodbye [or even to give the Doctor a chance to change her mind]. She's last seen in London, 1984. [It's lucky that her family never seems to ask awkward "where the hell have you been?" questions, as we learned earlier in this season.]

• *Turlough.* He's curiously un-cowardly here, and has no compunction about killing "bad guys", although he doesn't seem to know about Daleks. [Understandable, if his people aren't time-travellers... Daleks don't have an intergalactic empire by the twentieth century and are only making occasional journeys into their past.]

The Supporting Cast (Evil)

• *Davros*. For the last ninety years he's been trapped in suspended animation on board a prison ship belonging to the Earth authorities [where we left him in 17.1, "Destiny of the Daleks"], but he's been conscious while he's been frozen, and he certainly looks older than he did [his support system interferes with the freezing process]. When he awakens he's got a hand-held device concealed in his chair which can be used to jab human beings in the neck, instantly turning them into willing servants. It works on Dalek mutants, too. [He must have had this even in the old days, although it's strange that he's never been seen to use it before now. You would have expected him to try to jab the Doctor with it in "Destiny of the Daleks", at the very least.]

He somehow knows about Time Lords and TARDISes, even though he's never discussed such things with the Doctor before [it's fair to assume that the Daleks briefed him about the Doctor during "Destiny", as he *did* spend a while consulting their records before the humans captured and froze him]. Unsurprisingly, he sees the Time Lords as 'soft'.

Here Davros is his usual monomaniacal self, although his long imprisonment has made him more vengeful and prone to ranting than ever, and he's sharp enough to realise the Daleks aren't really loyal to him. [Since the humans have set up an entire penal station to keep him alive and imprisoned, it's likely they're planning to interrogate him at some point. They may also be hoping to exploit his knowledge, much like a captured Nazi scientist.] He now plans to genetically re-engineer the Daleks, and create a new and better race of the creatures [he's doing this by his next appearance in 22.6, "Revelation of the Daleks"]. The Movellans' Dalek-eating virus also causes Davros' chair to malfunction and makes foam spurt out of the systems, although he's prepared an escape route from the prison station and might just have a chance of using it...

• *Lytton*. Commander of the Daleks' human troopers [described by the Doctor in 22.1, "Attack of the Cybermen", as the Dalek Task Force], some of whom disguise themselves as policemen on twentieth-century Earth. Lytton is a hard-faced killer, has no compunction about working for the Daleks and guns down the opposition without mercy. There's a suggestion that the Daleks conditioned him, but that his own will is too strong for him to be fully under their control. He and his

men try using non-anachronistic machine pistols on Earth, but later break out the stun-lasers, and also use canisters of gas that make a bad smell and cause victims' skins to become horribly disfigured. The uniforms used by many of the troops under his command [those conditioned by the Daleks, rather than Lytton's hard-core elite] have shiny black helmets fitted with Dalek-like eye-stalks.

Despite playing a major role in the Daleks' plans, Commander Lytton's never introduced to the Doctor here and they only meet each other briefly [but see his next appearance in "Attack of the Cybermen"]. Once the Daleks are defeated, Lytton guns down one of the Daleks' troopers and makes his escape onto contemporary Earth, along with two of his "policeman" friends.

The TARDIS The Doctor can set a timer on the console to make the Ship dematerialise after he leaves it [Turlough uses the same feature in the next story]. Caught up in the Daleks' time corridor, the TARDIS experiences such severe turbulence that the cloister bell starts ringing. Weaving in time, the 'time-stress' on the Ship varies greatly, so the Doctor has to wait for the right moment to pull the TARDIS free or risk break-up. In this crisis, the TARDIS is described as going 'too fast' [compare with 1.3, "The Edge of Destruction"]. The Ship then finds itself travelling parallel to the corridor, eventually arriving at its end on Earth.

The scanner can pick up events in the future, apparently via the time corridor. Both the prison ship's destruction and the Supreme Dalek's taunting of the Doctor are somehow relayed to 1984.

The Non-Humans

• *Daleks*. More murderous, paranoid and sadistic than ever. Their long-but-bloodless Cold War against the Movellans was brought to an end when the Movellans created a virus that only attacks Daleks, and makes foam spurt out of their shells as they die. ["Destiny of the Daleks" suggested a logical impasse with the Movellans, so it's not clear how the Movellans managed to break this, or come up with a virus that the Daleks couldn't immediately cure. Outside intervention might have been involved, but see **War of the Daleks: Should Anyone Believe a Word of It?** under "Destiny".]

The Dalek fleet was destroyed, and those who survived scattered to far-flung parts of the universe to avoid the risk of infection and attempt to find a cure. Now they're making several plans at once. They aim to rescue Davros from his imprisonment, in the hope that *he* can deal with the virus; conquer Earth; trap the Doctor, so that they can copy his brainwaves; and then wipe out the High Council of Gallifrey. Daleks recognise the Doctor on sight, and instinctively try to exterminate him, but can confer with the Supreme Dalek through some form of built-in signalling device to receive more specific orders. They tell Davros that it's 'forbidden' for him to experiment on live Daleks.

The Daleks' plans are overseen by the Supreme Dalek, who's stationed on board a battle-cruiser in the far future (see **History**), a blocky grey warp-drive vessel that's connected to twentieth-century Earth by a time corridor. The Supreme Dalek is black in colour [rather than the more elaborate Supreme Council design seen in 10.4, "Planet of the Daleks"]. They're storing sample canisters of the Movellan virus on Earth itself, in a warehouse in London, as keeping the virus on their ship is too much of a liability. There are human prisoners on board the Dalek ship, taken from various eras in Earth's future [compare with Dalek tactics in "Destiny of the Daleks"… it may even be the same ship mentioned there]. Some of the prisoners escape to Earth, only to be hunted down by a group of Dalek troopers led by Commander Lytton. Here the Supreme Dalek wants Davros to believe that the Daleks serve their creator, but in fact they just want his knowledge [this may have been the case in "Destiny of the Daleks", though it was never clear], and Davros can't be that essential to Dalek plans as the Supreme is prepared to kill him when he proves untrustworthy.

The Daleks have the power to create duplicates, genetically-engineered copies of human beings [not robots as in 2.8, "The Chase", so *these* duplicates actually look like the people they're supposed to represent]. The Daleks need to examine their subjects' brainwaves to do this properly, so prisoners must be taken to the duplication room on their battle-cruiser, but subjects' bodies can be copied without close examination [they already have copies of Turlough and Tegan, suggesting that they've been tracking the TARDIS crew through space and time] and it apparently doesn't take more than a few minutes to create the doubles from scratch.

When the Doctor's hooked up to the slab that scans his brainwaves, images of his past appear on a display screen, and he believes his mind's being destroyed. The duplicate Stien, despite being Dalek-built, has been brainwashed into doing the Daleks' bidding; the conditioning can be broken, as Stien displays an obvious streak of guilt and eventually sacrifices himself to foil the Daleks' schemes. [It may take him a while to remember he's an agent, as at first he seems genuinely scared of the Daleks' troops. He has a stammer when he's undercover, but loses it when he's doing his masters' bidding.]

The Daleks of this era know something of Time Lord culture, and intend to use duplicates of the Doctor and companions to assassinate the High Council. They've also placed a number of duplicates in strategic positions on Earth, and these are still operational at the end of events here, though the Doctor - somewhat optimistically - believes they're unstable and sure to be found out before long. [This could mean twentieth-century Earth, future Earth, or both.] The Supreme Dalek has no trouble sending a message to the Doctor on board the TARDIS, appearing on the Ship's scanner without the Doctor's permission. Ultimately the Dalek battle-cruiser is destroyed, presumably with the Supreme on board.

The brown-green mutant blobs inside Daleks can survive even after the Dalek casings are pushed out of high windows. One of them throttles a soldier into unconsciousness, and the man is violent and delusional once he recovers. [His neck-wound may suggest an injection of some kind of venom, although he could just be in shock.]

History

• *Dating.* In the "present", it's 1984. In the "future", it's ninety years after Davros' capture. [In other words, ninety years after "Destiny of the Daleks". See "Destiny" for a discussion on the dating of this story. The rehearsal script for "Resurrection" ostensibly suggested a date of 4590, although there's just as good a case for setting it somewhere around the fortieth century.]

Although Earth in this era is described as if it were a significant power, there's no mention of it being an empire, a federation or anything else. The prison station has been in a poor state since regular inspections ceased, and Davros is its only prisoner, despite a large staff with medical personnel who are obliged to perform two-year tours of duty. The defence system's a mess, the emergency

Which Stories Have the Best Body-Counts?

Doctor Who has never held its extras in great regard. People may make jokes about the doomed Federation security officers in *Star Trek*, but at least only one or two of them die in the course of the average episode. *Doctor Who*, having the entire history of human suffering at its disposal, can comfortably bump off dozens of minor supporting characters in a single fight scene and still have time to get one of the speaking parts to heroically sacrifice himself.

What follows is a log of the stories which feature the most (and least) wanton carnage. Three rules have been put into effect here:

1. A "death" is the passing-away of a mortal, sentient life-form, organic or otherwise. "Sentient" is almost impossible to accurately define properly in this universe, but for our purposes it's enough to say that Daleks and Cybermen count. Voc robots probably don't, although D-84 might.

2. Only stories which exist in their entirety in the BBC archives are included here. This may seem unfair, but there's no other way of doing it. No matter how closely you listen to the audio soundtrack of "The Smugglers" (4.1), you're never going to be able to figure out exactly how many people drop dead during the swordfights. And it may *seem* that a story like "The Savages" (3.9) features no fatalities, but all we've got are the audio recordings, and for all we know Jano and Exorse are casually strangling babies while they're discussing their plans for the Doctor. (For the record, the other potential '60s applicant for the "no-claims bonus" is 5.6, "Fury From the Deep". All those scary moments when people disappear into the foam, and scream as they're dragged down tunnels? No need to worry. They all turn up at the end, safe and sound, and have a nice supper at Maggie Harris' house. Even the seaweed-monster is only in abeyance at the end, not dead but no longer at critical mass. A bit like Kroll.)

3. "The Edge of Destruction" (1.3) doesn't qualify for the list of lowest body-counts. Having no supporting characters is just cheating.

The Five Highest Body-Counts (Individual Deaths)

5. "The Curse of Fenric" (26.3). 38 deaths. And those are just the ones we see. The fact that the climax of the story sees the Doctor beating Fenric in a game of chess and getting on Ace's nerves distracts us from the fact that no end of human soldiers and advancing haemovores (yes, haemovores are people too) are being slaughtered outside. It's safe to say that there are plenty of off-screen casualties as well as the 38 who are seen to snuff it in the course of the story, and that's before you even begin to tackle the awkward question of whether all the haemovores who *aren't* transported to the twentieth century - and who cease to exist when the Doctor prevents their timeline - can safely be added to the list of the fallen. And remember: *The Godfather* only has a body-count of nineteen.

4. "Genesis of the Daleks" (12.4). 39 deaths. Just beating "Fenric", although there's room for some argument here as counting the deceased will require you to freeze-frame your video and try to work out exactly how many Kaled scientists are dropping to the floor when the Daleks start exterminating them. "Genesis" also makes it onto the list for mass deaths, which makes this story just as nasty as everyone said at the time. And remember: *Pulp Fiction* only has a body-count of seven.

3. "Attack of the Cybermen" (22.1). 41 deaths. This *isn't* counting the unseen hordes of Cybermen who are presumably blown up in the climactic explosion, but it *is* counting the many others who are shot, stabbed, decapitated or mauled into submission before our eyes. All the humans get it in the neck too, as do a lot of the indigenous Cryons, and yet the Doctor ends the story by lamenting the fact that he misjudged Lytton the murderous space-mercenary. And remember: *The Texas Chain Saw Massacre* only has a body-count of five.

2. "The Monster of Peladon" (11.4). 47 deaths. And it seems like such a nice, safe story, as well. But there's an awful lot of bloodshed when the miners meet the Ice Warriors (once again, you'll have to count the corpses in the tunnels), not to mention those who get disintegrated by the Ghost of Aggedor. Ironically the most moving death of the story is that of Aggedor himself, and he's not smart enough to be included in the tally. And remember: *Seven* only has a body-count of just over half a dozen.

continued on page 283...

switch that's supposed to destroy the prisoner in a crisis doesn't work, the Captain isn't bothered by the low level of morale and the supply ship is usually the only vessel the crew sees. The crewmembers appear to be drawn from the ranks of the military, dressing in uniforms and carrying blasters, though they're not expecting to be attacked and they're outgunned when the Daleks board them. Their side-arms don't damage Daleks, but their mines do, while the station's laser cannon is put out of action by the enemy attack and fighters are useless against the Dalek battle-cruiser. There's a distress signal that can alert the attention of near-by patrol ships, and naturally the station's fitted with a self-destruct mechanism. Just as naturally, it gets used at the end of events here.

Stien mentions a Constitution [of Earth], and he was taught at school that either the twenty-fifth or twenty-sixth amendment has something to do with freedom of choice. [We're assuming that Stien comes from the Dalek "present" here, although it's not explicitly stated as the Daleks have prisoners from several time-zones.] Davros claims that by now humans have no stomach for judicial murder. Daleks are a well-known menace, and the humans know they're capable of time-travel [but humans aren't, another reason the authorities might want to keep Davros alive for interrogation].

In 1984, humans have found the Movellan virus canisters on Earth and the regular army is investigating. [UNIT really has fallen out of favour.] Plenty of Dalek casings are left in London for the authorities to clear up.

The Analysis

Where Does This Come From? Back in the early '70s, Euston Films - a division of Thames Television - began making hour-long dramas entirely on film. With faster lenses and a management style which admitted that anything on time and on budget was fine, the company made *Special Branch* (see 1.4, "Marco Polo") and then *The Sweeney*. Grotty parts of London were the setting for fast, violent, earthy dramas with a cynical view of the authorities.

So while in 1971 the idea of policemen being killers was shocking and questions were asked in the House of Lords (see 8.1, "Terror of the Autons"), by 1984 the surprise was that these trigger-happy goons in uniform weren't real policemen. Within this new genre, the 1980 film *The Long Good Friday* has to be mentioned. Bob Hoskins' character has a dream of getting in on the redevelopment of Docklands, the part of London that forms the backdrop for the Earthbound scenes of this story. In 1984 it was believed

that an area associated with post-imperial decline and Victorian opium dens (see 14.6, "Talons of Weng Chiang") would become a shiny new haven of investment, enterprise and Yuppie flats.

By the time this story was broadcast, Wapping - the locale named in the script for "Resurrection" - was in the news as the site of a conflict between this particularly '80s mercantile view of the world and the traditions and livelihoods of the "real" East End. Rupert Murdoch moved the presses of his newspapers, *The Times* (once the flagship of the British press) and *The Sun* (then at its most xenophobic and reactionary) to Wapping from their traditional location on Fleet Street. News reports that year conveyed the impression that "The Battle of Wapping" was an all-out conflict between overzealous riot police and desperate workers spurred on by extremists. In fact, both sides went to the same pubs once the picketing had finished for the night.

As for the "space" parts of the story... no, there's no getting away from it. *Star Wars* has been mentioned in this volume over and over and over again, but we really do have to mention it just one more time, because this patently is the series' attempt to do *Star Wars* with Daleks. It's all here; the blaster fights, the shiny-helmeted space-mercenaries, the insane compulsion to try to get away with epic space opera on a BBC budget... and of course, the moment when the Daleks burst through the airlock door while the humans / rebels cower behind the nearest available cover and prepare for battle (although to be fair, "Revenge of the Cybermen" did something similar nearly a decade earlier).

The other film that keeps making its influence felt in this era, *Alien*, is also thoroughly plundered here. The tendency for things in outer space to be obsolete, dysfunctional and in need of a good thump - once the hallmark of amateur lash-ups like the TARDIS, not of professional military technology - is made more obvious than in any other story, with the staff of the prison station spending much of the first quarter complaining about poor morale and second-rate equipment. Even the station's complicated self-destruct mechanism suggests that Sigourney Weaver was here before Rula Lenska.

But reality's also impinging on the space opera here, odd as it may seem. "Earthshock" (19.6) had already hinted at the rising military culture in Britain, at a world where professional soldiers

Which Stories Have the Best Body-Counts?

...continued from page 281

1. "Resurrection of the Daleks" (21.4). 74 deaths. The winner in this category by some considerable margin, and Eric Saward's second entry in this list. Saward is often said to have been the most brutal of *Doctor Who*'s writers, but to be fair, most of the time he *was* writing war stories. If you've got a plot which involves soldiers from Earth running into the Dalek Empire then obviously it's a recipe for high mortality rates. But it should be noted that better-regarded writers than Saward had at least as great a flair for wiping out supporting characters when they got in the way, and if we had a list of the stories in which the highest *proportion* of characters die then Robert Holmes tales like "Pyramids of Mars" (13.3) and "The Caves of Androzani" (21.6) would be sure to warrant a mention. And remember: "Horror of Fang Rock" only has a body-count of eight. Oh, not including the shipwreck. Or the Rutan mothership.

The Five Highest Body-Counts (Mass Deaths)

5. "Silver Nemesis" (25.3). Certain sections of fandom are still horrified by the Doctor's actions in "Remembrance of the Daleks", claiming that it's morally unjustifiable for the Doctor to blow up an entire planet. These people don't seem half as bothered by "Silver Nemesis", in which he uses the same reprogram-an-ancient-Gallifreyan-death-machine ploy to eradicate an army of Cybermen which he describes as numbering in the thousands. Is it just that a planet seems so much more dramatic?

4. "Genesis of the Daleks" (12.4). The Kaled dome goes up in smoke and very nearly takes the whole Kaled race with it, and even assuming the millennium-long war has depleted the Kaled numbers, the population must still number in the thousands. Once again the Doctor's partly culpable, although at least this time it's not his finger on the trigger. Another city collapses in on itself in "Castrovalva" (19.1), though as block-transfer projections it's not clear whether its inhabitants count as "real" sentient beings or not. The conclusion of the story would suggest that they are, but if they

aren't then "Castrovalva" might well qualify for the list of lowest-ever body-counts.

3. "Remembrance of the Daleks" (25.1). Leaving aside the 32 individuals we see being butchered, blown up and talked to death, and the hundreds of Daleks on board their doomed mothership, there's the small matter of the Doctor tricking Davros into destroying Skaro. The story's status as "the one where the Doctor kills a planet" guarantees it a mention on this list, though in fact it might not belong here at all. Assuming that the Thals have left the place (oh, *surely* the Doctor must have checked before wiping the place out?), "Destiny of the Daleks" (17.1) indicates that the Daleks long ago left their 'ancestral seat'. If Davros has established a base there, then it's possible there are no more than a few hundred Daleks on the planet, if not less. Still, it's a nice big bang.

2. "Inferno" (7.4). The one story in which modern-day Earth bites the dust, and the fact that it's a parallel universe doesn't change anything. Nor does the fact that we tactfully cut away from the doomed alter-world just before it's flooded with lava. As Earth's population in the *Doctor Who* universe/s seems to be greater than that of the world we know (q.v. 11.2, "Invasion of the Dinosaurs"), we might conclude that at least 6,000,000,000 human lives are lost here. Which would make it a clear leader, if it weren't for the horror of...

1. "Logopolis" (18.7). We *have* to assume this has the highest body-count of any *Doctor Who* story ever made, even though we're given painfully little information as to what the death-toll might be. The universe is overcome by entropy, and we see it destroy the whole of the Traken Union, which - as an association of several inhabited planets - in itself would suggest a body-count of billions upon billions. Then we're shown an image on the TARDIS screen which would seem to indicate that the entropy's all over the place. Even if the picture's an exaggeration, and two-thirds of the continuum *isn't* instantly destroyed, there's still an inestimable amount of damage being done here. See the entry on "Logopolis" for all the many, many problems this causes.

continued on page 285...

were obsessed with cleaning their guns rather than making the tea and watching rugby. In 1975, "Genesis of the Daleks" redefined genocide and race-war for an age which had grown used to news reports about Pol Pot and the "troubles" in

Ireland, making the clash between Thals and Kaleds seem genuinely brutal instead of an outer-space children's story. Nine years later, full-colour global TV news had made instant footage from the world's war-zones so ordinary that it was barely even noticeable. Cinema-based space opera got away with neat, clean, consequence-free gunfights by making the whole thing seem fairy-tale, but *Doctor Who* was too rooted in contemporary Britain to pull off the same trick. The public had become almost-comfortable with the idea that somewhere in the world, someone in khaki was bound to be shooting someone else through the head.

At first sight much of the violence in "Resurrection" seems unnecessary - the soldiers are unremittingly brutal, innocent bystanders get shot with machine-pistols and bodies are shown to be fleshy and vulnerable - yet anything less than this wouldn't even have registered with the audience. Certainly, by this stage Lytton and company would have seemed ridiculous if they *hadn't* been depicted as no-nonsense professional killers. A couple of years later the sequel to *Alien* would set a kind of standard for this type of future-militarism, the difference being that in *Aliens* the gun-obsessed space-marines are treated as if they're actually heroic in some way. (In fact, if you want to see a "humans under siege" story that's *really* critical of '80s military culture then try Romero's *Dawn of the Dead*, which is a bit like Season Twenty-One with American accents and more zombie blood-splatter.)

Eric Saward, meanwhile, clearly wants to write a bigger story than one that's just about the Doctor meeting the Daleks. In fact that the Doctor does surprisingly little here, and much of the screen-time is spent setting the galactic stage, establishing that the war between Davros and the Daleks (never mind the Daleks and the humans) is quite capable of going on without the central character. None of the TARDIS crew even meets Davros until the final quarter. Again, *Star Wars* made this sort of large-scale cosmic politicking fashionable, although *Doctor Who Weekly / Monthly* may have played its part. Many of the *DWM* comic-strips explored the idea of what Famous Monsters like the Sontarans and Silurians did while the Doctor wasn't around, and on top of that the magazine had started reprinting the stories of the Dalek Empire that had first appeared in TV21 in the 1960s, so by the mid-'80s the *Doctor Who* universe seemed to have a tangible off-screen back-story.

Saward would try this sort of thing again in "Revelation of the Daleks" (22.6), in which the Doctor doesn't even get involved in the adventure until the halfway point, although it'll take Robert Holmes to do it properly (21.6, "The Caves of Androzani"). And Saward's attempt to make this "big" is hardly helped by all the Nationisms that haunt this story. Nobody who'd been watching the programme for any length of time would have been surprised to learn that the Movellans beat the Daleks with a *virus*. Indeed, Saward is careful - one might say "neurotic" - to ensure that a lot of the character names echo those in earlier Dalek scripts.

One last thing worth noting. The Supreme Dalek's final message to the Doctor claims that there are still Dalek duplicates in 'strategic' positions on Earth, the implication being that these are people in positions of power, i.e. politicians and military officers. Since the Doctor immediately points out that the duplicates are too unstable to be a threat, this looks more like a joke than an attempt to set up a sequel. Taking into account the public mood in 1984, and the kind of heads-of-government we had at the time, it's not surprising that gags about world leaders being robots and / or disguised aliens were a staple of stand-up comics, newspaper cartoons and *Spitting Image* on ITV. More than at any other time in living memory, those who ran the western world were perceived as being close to insane, so the description of the duplicates as less-than-stable seems carefully chosen.

Things That Don't Make Sense The Daleks' decision to keep the Movellan virus on Earth, thus supplying the humans with an easy way of killing Daleks, has got to be considered unwise even if it *is* part of a trap for the Doctor. The decision to keep Tegan prisoner on Earth, instead of on the rather more escape-proof Dalek ship, is similarly flawed. Nor are there any Daleks to greet her when she finally *is* sent to the ship, as if their opinion of human beings is so low that they're happy to let their enemies wander around the place.

The Daleks have the ability to make lifelike duplicates of humans, and yet they hire Lytton and his fake policemen to do their dirty-work on human-occupied planets rather than using humanoids of their own construction, which doesn't seem a terribly reliable strategy (especially in light of "Attack of the Cybermen", where we find out just how fickle Lytton is). You *could* argue that real humans have better instincts for hunting than Dalek constructs, but this is massively out-

Which Stories Have the Best Body-Counts?

...continued from page 283

**On a More Positive Note...
the Five Lowest Body-Counts**

5. "The Ultimate Foe" (24.4). One implied death. Many stories involve a single token blood-letting ("Planet of the Giants", "The Rescue", "Invasion of the Dinosaurs", "The King's Demons" and others), although in "The Ultimate Foe" things are ambiguous. Everyone makes it to the end of the story in one piece, but then the Keeper of the Matrix turns around to face the camera and... dan-dan-*daah*, the evil Valeyard has taken his place. It's probably safe to assume that the Valeyard, being the very embodiment of evil, has killed the Keeper to gain this position rather than just tying the man up and leaving him in a cellar. (Although one account suggests that the Keeper was the Valeyard all along. Has he *no* regard for the Blinovitch Limitation Effect?)

4. "The Three Doctors" (10.1). Either two deaths or none at all. The revelation in "Arc of Infinity" (20.1) that Omega mysteriously survives the end of "The Three Doctors" led to it being designated a happy-go-lucky mortality-free story, but look more closely. During the gel-creature attack on UNIT HQ, the wobbly invaders blow up a bazooka. Once the smoke clears, the two stalwart UNIT troops who were manning that bazooka can be seen lying quite still on the ground. Are they dead, or simply stunned? We'll never know for sure. Unless one of the writers of the BBC novels insists on mentioning it, in which case we'll accept their testimony as a tie-breaker.

3. "The Mind Robber" (6.2). Either one "death" or none at all. The problem is that we've defined a "death" as being the demise of a sentient being, and does the computer in "The Mind Robber" count or not? We don't know anything about the machine, except that it satisfactorily blows up at the end, so we can't tell whether it's just a fiction-processing device or has a will of its own. Nor can we tell whether the machinery we see is the whole of its being, or just a "terminal". It certainly deserves

to be mentioned in dispatches, even if nobody's going to shed any tears over it. A similar question-mark hangs over "The Celestial Toymaker", which either features five deaths or none at all, as the final state of the "players" isn't clear. Do they really die, did they effectively cease to be sentient beings when they first entered the Toymaker's realm, or are they returned to their former human lives when the realm's destroyed?

2. "Kinda" (19.3) and "Time-Flight" (19.7). One death each, but neither of them really counts, as in both stories the deceased party is later reincarnated. Panna's personality is transferred to a teenager's body post-mortem, while Professor Hayter turns up as an aspect of the Xeraphin mass-mind after his body's disintegration, and surely that's not what you'd call *proper* death? (By a similar token, you could argue that stories like "The Deadly Assassin" and "Arc of Infinity" have their body-counts greatly reduced if you assume that Time Lords are always "reincarnated" inside the Matrix. Do their personalities still exist as discrete entities, though? This is a whole philosophical can of worms, which we'll ignore for the time being.)

1. "Terminus" (20.4). The only *Doctor Who* story of the fully-archived era with an indisputable, unambiguous zero body-count. Well, just about. It's *possible* that some of the Lazars on board the leper ship die while waiting for treatment, but if so then they've got nothing to do with the story and we never see it happening. And you can't count the people who *might* be dying while the Doctor's visiting a given planet, or you'd have to boost the already-impressive death-score for "The Curse of Fenric" with all those who might be suffering on the Russian Front while the Doctor's busy fighting vampires. It's also possible that the radiation-scarred Bor might die during the course of "Terminus", as he's in a bad way the last time we see him and Nyssa doesn't seem to be hurrying to him with medical aid, but nobody's delivering the "goodbye, sweet prince" elegy either so we don't have to assume the worst.

of-keeping with the usual Dalek "we-are-the-superior-beings" philosophy.

Then again, it's unclear why the Daleks bother making duplicates at all, since they have to be conditioned to do the Daleks' bidding and the conditioning can be broken. Wouldn't it be easier just to condition the originals? In the Doctor's

case, fair enough, it's probably easier to brainwash a duplicate than the real thing. But Stien...? On top of all that, the Dalek high command hasn't bothered telling any of its "grunt" Daleks what the plan actually is, thus running the risk that they'll shoot the Doctor dead instead of sending him to the genetic photocopying suite.

ABOUT TIME 1980-1984

Dalek weapons keep failing to produce visible beams in episode four, giving the extras yet more opportunities to make "oooh!" noises and fall over for no apparent reason. Davros acts as if he's surprised to hear about the stalemate in the Dalek / Movellan war, even though he spent ages deliberating on it in "Destiny of the Daleks". (In fact this is mainly a fault with Terry Molloy's delivery. His statement about 'two totally logical war-machines unable to out-think each other... fascinating!' is delivered with surprise, whereas it's *supposed* to be delivered as if Davros is just ruminating over old events. Mind you, it's not what you'd call a great piece of exposition under any circumstance.)

In the warehouse, Professor Laird is given a pistol which the Doctor has just emptied into a Kaled mutant... and she takes it by the barrel. Shouldn't it still be piping hot? She also carries test-tubes in her pocket, in case anyone needs knocking out, and is rendered unconscious by the sound of the time corridor being activated even though the noise is barely noticeable whenever anybody else hears it.

Critique (Prosecution) It's a mess. The story looks like it's going to resolve itself, dovetail all the subplots together and make the ninety-odd minutes up to the big shoot-out look like it was going somewhere, but this is an Eric Saward script, so anyone not due to be in a later story is simply removed.

That isn't a climax, in a story where people have been dying violently throughout, and it isn't a conclusion. We have the beginning of a story-arc (if we can call it that) with Davros creating a new brand of Dalek, and this blights the next two Dalek stories, as the casual viewer is assumed to be up to speed on the differences. (Certainly this is true of Saward's next effort, "Revelation of the Daleks", but the big plot twist of "Remembrance of the Daleks" relies on everyone being slightly confused as to which side is which.) It's also the story where Tegan leaves, but this isn't really made lucid; and it's the one where Lytton is introduced, but that's not really important to anyone but the author.

But we persevere because the story keeps things going, and the direction makes it all seem like it's going to be important. Director Matthew Robinson keeps the camera moving, not in the pointless way of most contemporary dramas but because it's always got something else to show us.

Within *Doctor Who* this is almost retro, recalling the style of "The Sensorites" (1.7) and the unscreened pilot episode. Within mainstream BBC drama this was novel in 1984, and when Robinson shot the first few episodes of *EastEnders* in this manner it was hailed as a breakthrough. In a lot of ways the fusion of Euston-style grime and thuggery with space opera and overtly non-representational effects is new, and the cast are gamely trying to pitch their performances to suit whichever genre that particular scene appears to be in. By and large, the actors work well, and the fact that a whole raft of them never encounter the Doctor is less of a weakness than it could have been. We have to admit, though, there are two moments when the casting of Rodney Bewes as the conflicted Stein is a bit of a liability (no, see if *you* can spot them).

Critique (Defence) Let's get one thing out of the way first. Certain people would have you believe that Saward was a writer / script editor who had no idea about moral integrity, who saw nothing wrong with the Doctor packing a gun and who enjoyed slaughtering supporting characters in order to try to make his stories more exciting. This is drivel, at least in this period of the programme (though we'll reconsider the issue when we get to Season Twenty-Two).

Yes, of course it feels wrong when the Doctor shoots a Kaled blob with a pistol, but look at what happens *after* that. He decides he has no choice but to kill Davros, he picks up a blaster, he points it at the arch-fascist's head... and, despite Davros' taunting, backs down. Then Tegan sees ordinary, everyday people being murdered in cold blood, and realises this isn't a game any more. The final scene - so often overlooked, even though it's the very *point* of this exercise - has the Doctor realising that he's become too mired in violence, and that he's going to have to change his methods.

It's ironic, given what's going to happen next year, but it's in no way a betrayal. For once the brutality's *supposed* to make us feel queasy, and in this respect it's far less hypocritical than the usual claim-a-moral-triumph-then-blow-up-the-monsters fare. At a time when "army chic" was on the rise in Britain, this is a story which is more honest about the military than almost any other, a story in which enthusiastic young grunts get their faces melted off and the Daleks gun people down without pity rather than finding flimsy excuses to keep them alive. This time even Davros' mad ranting is enough to scare children.

That aside, what have we got here? Nothing too deep. But like "Earthshock" and "The Five Doctors" before it, the problem isn't that it's light-weight, it's that we've had far too *many* lightweight stories to make it seem spectacular. And it is, at least, a guts-out, no-holds-barred attempt to do fast-paced space opera within the *Doctor Who* format. It's hard not to like it for trying. It wants to show us Daleks bursting their way onto the station like Imperial Stormtroopers, but they keep bumping into each other. It wants to stage raging pitched battles, but the guns are rubbish. Repeatedly, it oh-so-nearly gets away with it. Yet as with "Earthshock", with hindsight the big surprise is how *coherent* so much of it is.

Let's not entertain this "it's just a mess" idea any longer; it's awkward in parts, but for most of the time this is a solid piece of visual storytelling, and even the logic's no worse than most other *Doctor Who* stories. One look at the **Things That Don't Make Sense** column tells you that it's only the details of the Daleks' plans that are faulty, not the grand sweep of the production. It's frequently been accused of having too many subplots and too much reference to past continuity, but this really only applies to one single scene, the one in which the Daleks unexpectedly announce their plans to invade Gallifrey. Many of the supposed "complications" here are so well-recognised from previous Dalek stories that they become background details rather than plot-points.

So what we've ultimately got is a story that just wants to be a rip-roaring space-adventure, not exactly within *Doctor Who*'s usual field of scientific inquiry and careful investigation, but not drastically opposed to the programme's basic principles either. It's fitting, it's dynamic and it's suitably of-its-time. It's also occasionally clunky and cheap-looking, but in 1984, it made us happy. No, more than that; in 1984, even the casual viewers regarded the Daleks' return with a sense of nostalgia, and the BBC's unexpected mid-season trailers for the story made this feel like a real *event*. It was, perhaps, the last time anybody could really say that about the series.

The Facts

Written by Eric Saward. Directed by Matthew Robinson. Viewing figures: 7.3 million, 8.0 million.

Supporting Cast Terry Molloy (Davros), Rodney Bewes (Stien), Maurice Colbourne (Lytton), Rula Lenska (Styles), Del Henney (Colonel Archer), Les Grantham (Kiston), Chloe Ashcroft (Professor Laird), Sneh Gupta (Osborn), Jim Findley (Mercer), William Sleigh (Galloway), Brian Miller, Royce Mills (Dalek Voices).

Working Titles "The Return", "Warhead".

Oh, Isn't That..?

• *Chloe Ashcroft.* Yet another *Play School* presenter, but unlike Brian Cant (Space Security Service agent in 3.4, "The Daleks' Master Plan" and Tensa in 6.1, "The Dominators") or Chris Tranchell (the Abbot's secretary Roger in 3.5, "The Massacre"; the public servant Jenkins in 4.8, "The Faceless Ones"; Andred in 15.6, "The Invasion of Time"), she never returned.

• *Rodney Bewes.* As we've already said, best-known as either the neurotic one from *The Likely Lads* and its more popular sequel *Whatever Happened to the Likely Lads?* or the straight man to Basil Brush, although at this point Bewes was still smarting from not getting the part he was born to play. Southern Television had big plans for its production of *Dan Dare* before a series of rights problems and mishaps prevented it from reaching the screen in 1980. Bewes would have played Digby to Simon Williams' Dan (see 2.3, "The Rescue", for more on the importance of the Pilot of the Future).

• *Maurice Colbourne.* At this stage he was best-known for playing Kline in the Birmingham-based surrealist crime drama Gangsters, although he'd also been in the BBC's 1981 version of *The Day of the Triffids* (now all but forgotten, and the big pink man-eating plants stole every episode). Later he starred in quintessentially '80s BBC series *Howard's Way.* Contrary to what's been said on many internet sites, he's visibly not the same Maurice Colbourne who appeared in various British movies of the 1950s; *this* Maurice Colbourne was born with the less-than-theatrical name of Roger Middleton, and on becoming a professional actor thought it'd be a good idea to take the name of an established performer who (a) shared his birthday and (b) had recently died. "Our" Maurice passed away in 1989, and as yet nobody has taken up the mantle.

• *Leslie Grantham,* here trading under the name of "Les" Grantham. Every man, woman and child in the UK would recognise him *now*, but this was his first broadcast TV work. While in prison (just don't ask what for), Grantham started taking acting lessons from Louise Jameson, her first job after "The Invasion of Time" (15.6). She recommended him to Matthew Robinson, with whom she'd worked on *Tenko*. So when Robinson directed the first episode of *EastEnders* a year later, Grantham was his suggestion for the key role of Den Watts, AKA "Dirty". You know the rest.

• *Sneh Gupta*. She was one of the dolly-bird hostesses on *Sale of the Century*, the archetypally naff 70s game-show (its host will be joining us for 26.3, "The Curse of Fenric"). That this was thought to be a big step forward in race relations tells you a lot about the 1970s.

• *Rula Lenska*. Had been one of the stars of ITV classic *Rock Follies*, though in America she became well-known for a series of TV ads which depicted her as an internationally-renowned actress despite the fact that nobody there had ever heard of her. She's easily the biggest star to be cast in a *Doctor Who* role which doesn't involve ever encountering the Doctor or the main villain.

Cliffhangers It was originally supposed to be four episodes instead of two, and was shown as a four-parter overseas, so... a Dalek materialises in the warehouse and threatens to exterminate all those present; on the Dalek ship, Stien holds the Doctor at gunpoint and reveals that he's a Dalek agent; with the Daleks holding all the cards, Davros screeches that nothing can stop them becoming the su-preme be-ings of the u-ni-verse.

The Lore

• The two-part edit was designed to get around the mess that the Sarajevo Winter Olympics made of the schedules. Originally this story had been planned as the finale to Season Twenty, to be directed by Peter Grimwade and designed by Malcolm Thornton; see 20.4, "Terminus" and 20.5, "Enlightenment" for more. Terry Nation, whom Nathan-Turner had met at a US convention, looked over the scripts and vetoed a few details (mainly Davros' apparent death and the inclusion of the Dalek Emperor). Michael Wisher had let it be known that he'd be interested in playing Davros again, but by the time the story was made he was committed to a tour in a play.

• Janet Fielding had put in her resignation before Peter Davison. With all three leads departing in rapid succession, it was decided to stagger their departures, so Tegan was written out first and in a hurry. Once she realised that this might happen, Fielding expressed an interest in being the first companion to assist in two regenerations. Filming her last scene, she worked herself up into a state by kicking prop boxes, which unsettled the other regulars. It'd be nice to say that this was the last scene filmed - which it was, almost - and that what we see was the only take, but in fact it's the second take. Nevertheless, the tears are all real, and Tegan returns for the regeneration scene (21.6, "The Caves of Androzani") and "A Fix with Sontarans" (see 22.3, "The Mark of the Rani", and the Appendix in Volume VI).

• The script called for the wharves in Wapping, which were then being redeveloped as luxury flats. However, traffic, logistics, the exorbitant fee asked by the owners and the more picturesque locations available across the Thames at Curlew Street - already familiar to viewers from many crime series - made Matthew Robinson relocate.

• Robinson had used Leslie Grantham on stage before, and offered him either Galloway or Kiston. Galloway got better lines, but Kiston is in more than one episode.

• Although credited as "Crewmember" for the three episodes in which she appears, Linsey Turner's character is called "Zina" on-screen (or maybe it's "Xena"... the mind boggles).

• When American television took the syndication for this story, they got hold of an edit that wasn't properly dubbed, with no music or sound effects in the second half. The cliffhangers were also edited differently to the version that's now commercially available.

• The helmets worn by the Dalek troopers were made by Unit 22 (or Imagineering, as the company was called by this stage), and were only seen by the producer after it was too late to veto their use.

• Sources close to the programme have suggested that the original draft of "Resurrection of the Daleks", written to follow on from "The King's Demons" (20.6), featured Kamelion as a key character. This has led some to conclude that the robot was originally supposed to fill Stien's role, which would explain a lot: why the Doctor's "sidekick" starts following enemy orders as soon as he comes within range of the Daleks (even though he's never shown any sign of being their agent before, almost as if they're overriding his will); why the Doctor has to struggle to break Stien's conditioning (as he does with Kamelion in the next story, "Planet of Fire"); and why no attempt was made to explain what happens to the robot between "The King's Demons" and "The Five Doctors" (because he was supposed to sacrifice himself, as Stien eventually does). But evidence for this is thin on the ground.

21.5: "Planet of Fire"

(Serial 6Q, Four Episodes, 23rd February - 2nd March 1984.)

Which One is This? Volcanoes, beaches, religious types dressed as nativity-play shepherds, pert young men in next to nothing and a pert young girl in even less. It's this season's *Doctor Who* holiday special, and what better way of celebrating than by ceremonially burning the Master…?

Firsts and Lasts Time for a big clear-out, just in time for the new Doctor's arrival. Turlough leaves the regular crew here, as does two-story companion Kamelion. That means it's time for some new blood - and, indeed, flesh - and it arrives in the form of Nicola Bryant as Peri, who taints the air of the TARDIS with her fake American accent but delights many fourteen-year-old boys with her bikini-related antics. (This is, in fact, the last time the TARDIS will have anything approaching an ensemble crew. From this point on, to the end of the original series and beyond, *Doctor Who* will return to the old '70s formula of Doctor-and-one-female-assistant.)

It's the last story directed by Fiona Cumming, the last written by Peter Grimwade and the first appearance of the Doctor's question-mark braces.

Four Things to Notice About "Planet of Fire"…

1. It's the Fifth Doctor's last squaring-off against the Master, so obviously there has to be some twist to their relationship. It comes in the Master's final moments, just before he's supposedly burned to a cinder on the planet Sarn: 'Won't you show mercy to your own -' Needless to say, this has been controversial, as it obviously sounds as if it's meant to end with something like '- brother' but could just as well end '- species', '- arch-nemesis' or even '- ex'. Some have claimed that the Master actually finishes the sentence, and that by 'your own' he just means 'another Time Lord', but that's certainly *not* how the line's delivered. Tactfully, the nov-

elisation drops the line altogether.

2. Here it turns out that Turlough has a brother, who arrived on Sarn as an infant when his family's spaceship crashed among the primitive locals, and has since been raised as a 'chosen one'. Which begs the question: do spaceships do anything *but* crash on primitive planets in the *Doctor Who* universe? (It's worth mentioning that this is the third script Peter Grimwade writes for the series, and that all three of them feature spaceships having accidents and alien travellers getting marooned.)

3. It's the second story in a row that seems to lead directly on from the story before it, suggesting that the Doctor deals with the Tractators, the Daleks and the Master all in the course of a single day and making you wonder if the TARDIS crew ever need sleep (although Turlough asks if the Doctor's missing Tegan, confusingly). The Doctor's slightly pointless way of reminding the audience what happened in last week's episode results in a line that's presumably meant to suggest a seething Time Lord rage: 'Daleks! I sometimes think those mutated misfits will terrorise the universe for the rest of time.' So very wrong in so very many ways, although it does at least stop the makers of spin-off novels and audios coming up with a series of Fifth Doctor / Turlough stories and slipping them into the gap. Doesn't it…?

4. The destination for this year's *Doctor Who* staff holiday: Lanzarote. Cunningly, this locale is used for both the beach scenes (actually set in Lanzarote) and for the rocky, volcanic slopes of the planet Sarn. The irony, of course, is that in the latter sequences the programme-makers seem to have gone all the way to the Canary Islands to shoot scenes that look a lot like traditional quarry-scenes filmed in Southern England.

The Continuity

The Doctor Can identify Greek relics at a glance, and explain their origin in pedantic detail.

It hasn't been long since the TARDIS left Tegan on Earth, as the Doctor's still grumbling about Daleks. Missing Tegan, he admits to being depressed, and once he's abandoned by Turlough he doesn't need *too* much convincing to give Peri a three-month try-out aboard the Ship.

• *Ethics.* The Doctor tends to treat Kamelion as a machine here, not a friend. He wastes no time in setting up the mechanical equivalent of a 'heart attack' for Kamelion, and once the robot's disabled he's prepared to kill Kamelion with the Master's tissue compression eliminator. He's obviously sorry about this, but doesn't need to be asked twice. [Even given that Kamelion wants to die, there's no way the Doctor would agree to this if it were a human being instead of a robot. Kamelion doesn't seem to count as a fully-formed "person" in the Doctor's philosophy.]

He's then prepared to stand and watch the Master die in the flames of Sarn, and looks rather shellshocked afterwards. [Compare this with - for example - 9.5, "The Time Monster". So much for the mending-of-ways mentioned in the last story.]

• *Inventory.* He's finally shown to be carrying some coins, although they're weird alien coins, all of the same style but with different polygonal shapes and in various colours. He's too absent-minded to realise that they're not going to be acceptable currency in Lanzarote, and leaves them as a tip.

The Supporting Cast
• *Turlough.* Panics when the TARDIS picks up a distress signal from his own people, so much so that he's prepared to shut down Kamelion - causing the android severe pain - to prevent the truth being revealed. Nonetheless, he insists on rescuing Peri when she nearly drowns herself. He's obviously a capable swimmer.

It's here that Turlough's past begins to reveal itself. His home planet is Trion, and his upper arm is marked with the Misos Triangle, a Trion symbol that's used to mark prisoners. There was a civil war on Trion, in which Turlough's mother was killed; his father was on the wrong side, and sent to the prison-planet of Sarn along with Turlough's younger brother Malkon. Turlough was sent to Earth, where he was watched by a Trion agent, so the Trions know he's absconded. See **Planet Notes** for more. On discovering that Malkon's his brother, he's instantly protective of the boy.

Turlough's full name and rank is Vislor Turlough, junior ensign commander, VTEC9/12/44. [If he had his own rank then he must have been of age before he was exiled to Earth. Malkon was a baby when he was exiled to Sarn, so assuming they were exiled at the same time, Turlough would seem to have been a full-grown adult about eighteen years ago. Some schoolboy. The Trion captain asks if Turlough's 'still running away', so it's possible that Turlough may have fled the regime for many years, but if so then how did he get an official rank?]

One of the relics from the crashed Trion ship, believed to be a 'gift of Logar' by the Sarns, is immediately identified by Turlough as the coded circuit-release key that lets him use the transmitter on the crashed Trion vessel. He finally decides to face the Custodians from his own world, but it turns out that things have changed on Trion and former political prisoners are no longer persecuted. His exile ended, he elects to leave the Doctor and go home, feeling he has a duty to return to his people even though he claims to have learned 'so much' in his time on the TARDIS. The Doctor is obviously expecting this decision.

• *Peri.* Perpugilliam Brown is an American college student who's just gagging to be called "brash", and every indication is that she comes from a wealthy family, although her 'allowance' isn't substantial enough to let her go swanning off all over the world. She encounters the TARDIS in Lanzarote, where her surprisingly young stepfather Howard Foster is part of a diving expedition that's exploring a wreck off the coast. Peri's getting bored here, and plans to gallivant off to Morocco with some nice English boys she's met, as she's not due back at college for three months. But she's got an ecology project to think about and exams coming up, and she's already got a ticket back to New York [where the college is?], although the address on her passport is given as "St. Michelle, Pasadena".

Obviously impulsive, she's not only willing to jet off to North Africa with people she's only just met, but is prepared to jeopardise her life by trying to swim ashore from Howard's boat in an attempt to catch the flight. And she's not that good a swimmer. Her mother's also in Lanzarote, but busy visiting sites of archaeological interest with other rich Americans and is never seen here.

[Peri never says goodbye to either her mother or Howard, who presumably never find out why their daughter vanishes off the face of the Earth. Here we should point out that much fan-lore, not to mention the Telos novella *Shell Shock*, has raised the possibility that Peri was sexually abused by her stepfather. The only thing on-screen to support this idea is Peri's solo scene in the TARDIS bedroom, which sees her having an ugly-looking nightmare and squealing Howard's name, but this hardly proves anything as she's just had a traumatic near-drowning experience after disobeying his orders.]

Peri gets involved in the Doctor's affairs by accident. She's remarkably quick to accept the idea that she's left Earth, and to work out how things work on board the TARDIS, even if she's occasionally prone to panic. Despite the Master repeatedly threatening her, Peri soon reaches the conclusion that she wants to travel with the Doctor for a while. She has little more than her clothes and her passport when she arrives on the Ship.

• *Kamelion.* Capable of connecting himself to the TARDIS databank with a cable, although he ends up screaming in pain when he does this. In fact he's just feeling the agony of the Master, with whom he's always shared a mental link. Soon he's being contacted by his old "owner", who urges him to mess around with the TARDIS' navigational systems. He does his best to resist the Master's influence, but the Master's using some kind of helmet-like will-boosting device, so Kamelion succumbs before long.

Kamelion turns into Peri's stepfather when she's dreaming about him, as her 'energy' overwhelms his personality circuits, and afterwards he knows her name. In fact he seems to feed on the energy all around him, while the Doctor uses sheer force of will to briefly cut the 'energy link' with the Master [as in 20.6, "The Kings' Demons"]. The Doctor describes the shape-changing process as 'psychomorphic printing', and can't immediately spot that it's Kamelion when the robot's posing as human. Kick Kamelion while he's disguised and he feels like metal, but he can still be knocked unconscious by a blow to the head. In disguise as the Master, he appears to have hair which can be blown by wind, but he's unable to hypnotise.

Tortured by the Master's influence, Kamelion sounds distinctly forlorn, and seems to believe that his own personality has been lost. The Doctor raises the local radiation in the control room on Sarn to induce a sympathetic reaction in Kamelion's psychocircuits, giving him the electronic equivalent of a heart attack, and once he's crippled Kamelion requests that the Doctor destroys him. And so the Doctor does.

The Supporting Cast (Evil)

• *The Master.* Curiously, he's now started wearing eyeliner. While experimenting with his tissue compression eliminator in an attempt to create an 'even deadlier' version, the Master somehow managed to reduce himself to around four inches in height, and is now making his plans from a well-equipped little box on board his TARDIS. [The box is actually supposed to be his workshop, miniaturised at the same time. Even by the usual standards of shrink-technology, it's bizarre that he managed to survive this accident, though his TARDIS may have played a part in things. Compare with "Planet of Giants" (2.1), and see also **How Hard Is It to Be the Wrong Size?** under "The Armageddon Factor" (16.6).] The old tissue compression eliminator is still serviceable, and works on inorganic objects as well as people. The Doctor warns him against using the device inside the confines of a TARDIS.

Naturally, the Master's more than willing to exploit barbarous alien religions in order to get his way, and he enjoys ordering people to be burned alive just to annoy the Doctor. He admits to having spent a lot of time working out sadistic deaths for his arch-rival. He's eventually restored to his full size by the numismaton flame on Sarn, but the Doctor's tampering makes the flame lethal, and the Master apparently disintegrates [he'll be back without explanation in 22.3, "The Mark of the Rani"]. His last words to the Doctor before he burns: 'Won't you show mercy to your own -'

The TARDIS(es) Kamelion opens a roundel in a corridor not far from the console room and connects himself to the systems, something which apparently links him to the Ship's databank. It also hooks him up to the computer and lets him reprogram the co-ordinates. When Kamelion starts screaming, the Doctor believes that programming an alpha-rhythm into the console should calm him down, although Turlough later uses the same controls to knock him out completely. The console also picks up a distress signal from Earth, which Turlough immediately identifies as being of Trion origin, and he rips some cables out of the bottom of the console to hush it up.

The Ship isn't fully operational without its comparator, an element from the console that looks like a circuit-board, and later on the Master disables the TARDIS by removing the Doctor's temporal stabiliser. [The Doctor calls this an 'old trick' of the Master's, perhaps meaning the general theft of TARDIS-parts rather than the theft of the stabiliser. See 19.7, "Time-Flight", by the same author.] The Doctor eventually takes the Master's temporal stabiliser, believing it'll be compatible with that of his own vessel and apparently stranding the Master's TARDIS on Sarn. The Doctor can program realistic images on either of the two console screens, which appear to be either computer-generated or drawn from some sort of memory bank, as he comes up with a "photofit" of a Trion protective suit.

The Doctor arms himself with a hand-held device for tracking the Trion distress signal when he leaves the Ship, while Turlough arms himself with a towel. The Doctor believes he can discover the place where the Trion distress beacon originated by hooking its cylinder into the console. The computer assures the Doctor that the volcanic mountain on Sarn isn't about to blow, and the 'seismic scanner' later issues an alarm, telling the Doctor that the Master's doing something inside the volcano. After rescuing her from drowning, Turlough dumps Peri in a chamber near the console room that's furnished with a single bed. [Apparently Tegan and Nyssa's old room, cleared out, so possibly the Doctor's just finished emptying it when he begins his rant against Daleks at the start of the story.]

The interior of the Master's TARDIS looks much like the Doctor's, but black instead of white. The Master describes it as 'superior', while the Doctor believes he can stop the vessel escaping by materialising his own TARDIS around it [as in "The Time Monster"]. According to the Doctor, Kamelion's interference remote-parallels the two TARDISes, so one goes wherever the other goes.

Planet Notes

• *Sarn*. A planet of sweeping, wind-blown deserts and at least one volcanic mountain, Sarn has a single city-community, home to the remnants of an indigenous population who live in the shadow of the volcano. The natives are terribly Old Testament, dressing in the robes of desert-dwellers and suffocated by their religion. Their architecture looks classical, but dilapidated, as volcanic activity is on the rise and the Doctor indicates that the entire planet is unstable.

In fact the people of Trion - Turlough's world - created a colonial civilisation here which ended 'ages ago', although in recent times Sarn has been used as a prison-planet for Trion's political exiles. Turlough's father, had he lived, would have been the natives' leader. [Giving a political prisoner an army of primitive zealots to play with might be considered an odd punishment, but odder is the fact that Turlough's relatives seem to have been the only prisoners sent here.] As it is, the locals know that Sarn is one of many planets and aren't surprised by visitors from beyond their community,

but know nothing of any other world or the influence of Trion on their society.

The Sarns worship Logar, Lord of Fire, as their only god. He's said to live in the middle of a volcano, but the religion demands the death of anyone who ventures onto the mountain. The planet used to be verdant, and the Trions did their best to keep it stable with their technology, their silver-clad vulcanologists having been mistaken for holy manifestations by the locals. However, the Chief Elder of the Sarns - Timanov, effectively their high priest - believes the planet's decline is due to a lack of faith. The Chief Elder is technically out-ranked by the Sarns' leader, the young Malkon, who's actually Turlough's brother. The infant Malkon was found on the slopes of the volcano, his arm marked with what the local religion believes to be the Sign of Logar, actually the same Misos Triangle that Turlough bears. Malkon has dreams of his past, but has been brought up in the local faith as a 'chosen one'.

Since the days of Timanov's father, unbelievers have been sent to the flames, but times are hard and the people are starting to question the religion's belief that an 'outsider' will come with food and gifts of technology. Burning the occasional freethinker is regarded by the Chief Elder as a way of encouraging faith, though only a chosen one can order it. [So it may not have happened in Malkon's lifetime, as we never hear of any other chosen ones before Turlough arrives. The practice could well have been introduced by previous Trion visitors.] The crash of the Trion spacecraft which brought Malkon to Sarn [and presumably killed Turlough's father] was taken as a sign from Logar, and the planet's littered with pieces of advanced technology, including energy weapons and a transceiver unit. Turlough takes one look at the relics from the ship and deduces that it was his father's craft.

Long ago the people from Trion tapped the planet's volcanic gasses for energy, and the machinery for controlling the volcano is still in place, hence the great flame in the Hall of Fire that's used for making sacrifices. Down in the heart of the volcano is the seismic control chamber, equipped with silver protective suits. These suits explain why Logar is believed to be a shining silver figure, and Timanov was once told to inhale the rejuvenating gases from the volcano by one of the silver-clad Trions. The seismic controls can make the volcano issue a blue flame that hasn't

Who Decides What Makes a Companion?

It's become increasingly obvious over the course of this volume that the Doctor has little or no choice as to who travels with him. Indeed, over the years he's only really chosen K9 Mk. II, and possibly Susan. Moreover, many people have journeyed on the TARDIS or been significant in the Doctor's life without ever being included in the roll-call of "official" companions.

For a start, the word "companion" is a problem. It's a fanboy word, popularised by *The Making of Doctor Who* in the 1970s, not the word the general public used[14]. For the average viewer, the Doctor had "assistants". This was a post invented by the UNIT job, and reinforced by the Key to Time mission, so it covers the whole of the '70s except for Leela. Prior to this we had a string of Susan-surrogates and strapping lads. While the Doctor seemed old enough to be the uncle or grandfather in this family-group, no-one questioned this or found it remotely suspicious.

Only in 1972, with "The Curse of Peladon" (9.2), did the Doctor actively invite one of his associates along for a ride and get her to come. Somewhat against her will, it seems. And only in 1974, with the ending of "Invasion of the Dinosaurs" (11.2), did we actually see such an invitation being made and - again, half-reluctantly - accepted. There had been orphans and lost waifs and strays, but Sarah had a home to go to.

But consider how she met the Doctor. She wandered into the TARDIS. Like Ian and Barbara, and Steven, and Dodo, and Ben and Polly and Zoe and Leela and Adric and Tegan. This is a vessel crafted by a culture that verges on the neurotic, a vessel with a twenty-one position trimonic lock on the door and the ability to telepathically mess with people's minds, yet it never does a thing to defend its integrity when any of these people come blundering into the console room. Nor does it try to warn its owner when he takes off with stowaways on board. It's starting to look as if the TARDIS is acting as a dating agency for the Doctor. Assuming that to be true for a moment... why would the Ship do this?

Two possibilities present themselves immediately. One is the option suggested in "Image of the Fendahl" (15.3), namely that the TARDIS likes some human telepathic traces and not others. This may account for the otherwise baffling events of "The Edge of Destruction" (1.3). In this, the Ship contacts the occupants with coded warnings, after apparently removing their recent memories. It emerges that the power-source of the Ship is somehow

conscious and, through the various computers aboard, aware in some sense. Consciousness, memory and time-travel seem to be intimately connected (see **What *is* the Blinovitch Limitation Effect?** under 20.3, "Mawdryn Undead"). So the TARDIS might take on board certain humans as a psychic vitamin supplement. The impact of these people on the Doctor's life may be a side-effect. It may also be the Ship's deliberate policy to give its master a playmate or two, possibly his mind has the biggest influence on TARDIS functions. This has a sinister ring to it; the TARDIS keeps its occupants, even the Doctor, as pets.

The other possibility is even more bizarre, but seemed increasingly likely as Season Eighteen unfolded. The TARDIS may be sensitive to disturbances in the timeline, and selects those people who'll have the most influence, perhaps even manoeuvring itself into the right position for them to "accidentally" come aboard. They become the Doctor's companions because history says they do. "Castrovalva" (19.1) pretty much admits this is how Adric, Nyssa and Tegan ended up as crewmembers, although in this case much of it is apparently down to the Watcher's intervention rather than the TARDIS. But the Watcher is part of the regenerative process, and regeneration is 'part of the TARDIS' (4.3, "Power of the Daleks"), so where do you draw the line?

This makes it seem as if the Ship is the best candidate for allotting "companion-ness". What if it's the Doctor, though? Even if he doesn't choose who comes aboard, he may select individuals with the Right Stuff from among those who *do*. Duggan didn't join the Doctor, Romana and K9 (17.2, "City of Death"). Tegan, whom the Doctor never really seemed to like much, stayed and indeed rejoined (19.7, "Time-Flight" and 20.1, "Arc of Infinity"). People the Fifth Doctor likes aren't in the regeneration pep-talks (21.6, "The Caves of Androzani"), just the official companions. Todd (from 19.3, "Kinda"), Will Chandler (21.2, "The Awakening") and the Brigadier (20.3, "Mawdryn Undead") might have shown their faces otherwise, and instead of the treacherous Kamelion, why not the sonic screwdriver back from the grave?

Even travelling on the TARDIS isn't quite the same as being a companion. Liz Shaw is in the flashback sequence in "Resurrection of the Daleks" (21.4), despite never travelling. Mike Yates might

continued on page 295...

been seen in generations, taken to be a sign of Logar's mercy to the sick and the injured.

In fact the system is drawing numismaton gas from the planet's core, described by the Master as one of the greatest energy sources in the universe, an immensely rare catalytic reagent. The numismaton flame heals Malkon after he's wounded by an energy weapon, while the Master aims to enter the flame and absorb its 'infinite transforming power' in order to regain his normal size. [The similarity of the sacred flame on Sarn to the sacred flame on Karn (13.5, "The Brain of Morbius") is obvious, but it's hard to believe they might be the same planet, especially since Sarn's due to explode soon. Unless the Time Lords shift it across space, a la Ravalox (23.1, "The Mysterious Planet"), in order to protect the 'elixir of life'? The novelisation of "Planet of Fire" mentions Karn, and has the Doctor speculate that the same process might be involved on both worlds.]

The climax of events here sees a Trion rescue ship relocating the Sarns, their destination unknown, and the less-than-religious Amyand looks likely to be their new leader. Timanov insists on staying behind on Sarn, even if it's apparently doomed.

• *Trion.* In the crashed Trion ship on Sarn is a transmitter, giving Turlough direct access to the Trion Communications Executive, and the Custodians send a rescue ship for the Sarns [indicating that the Trions feel they have a responsibility towards their former colonial charges]. The ship arrives in next to no time, and the uniformed captain expects Turlough to recognise him as a superior officer. Trions have agents on 'every civilised planet', including an agrarian commissioner on Verdon and a tax inspector on Darveg, while Turlough's watcher on Earth was an eccentric solicitor on Chancery Lane. [The solicitor's mentioned in 20.3, "Mawdryn Undead". "Verdon" suggests a planet covered in plants, although the novelisation changes it to "Vardon", a world that's also name-checked in Peter Grimwade's script for "Time-Flight". Are they the same place? The Vardon in "Time-Flight" had a space-faring civilisation 140,000,000 years ago.]

Meanwhile, on Earth… there's a sunken sailing-ship off the coast of Lanzarote, and among the relics brought up from it is a silver signalling device from Trion. [Maddeningly, this isn't explained anywhere in the story. See **Things That Don't Make Sense**.]

History

• *Dating.* On Earth, and presumably on Sarn, it's somewhere around the present day. [1984? If so then the change to the political system on Trion has happened sometime in the last year, since Turlough was in contact with his "solicitor" in 1983 and wasn't informed.] It's summer, as Peri says that 'fall' is three months away.

The Analysis

Where Does This Come From? Like "Snakedance" a year earlier, it's a story so casual about drawing on religious imagery (holy mountains, shining visions from God, purifying flames, etc) that the biblical "props" are barely distinguishable from the sci-fi ones. Like "Snakedance", it has a chosen boy-leader who isn't terribly keen on his duties and a vigorous heresy which the authorities attempt to suppress. Unlike "Snakedance", it doesn't have any doubt at all that religion is basically *wrong*. Back in the '70s, Chris Boucher got away with writing two separate stories in which the creator-god turned out to be wholly malevolent and worshipped only by stupes (first Xoanon, then the Fendahl), and later stories of the Graham Williams epoch were just as contemptuous of the idea that humanity might have divine origins. In Season Seventeen, a story in which life on Earth is revealed to have started with a chance combination of glop and alien radiation is quickly followed by a story in which Eden is inhabited by disgusting, primordial swamp-monsters. Here, though, the stakes are raised… or at least they would have been, if the script editor hadn't intervened.

It had been a long time since the church had been a potent force in Britain, and by the mid-'80s religion meant nothing more to most people than Harry Secombe singing hymns on Sunday night ITV, but AIDS and a second generation of immigrants were starting to make dogma an issue again. Peter Grimwade wrote a story about the risks of authoritarian religion, his ostensible target being Fundamentalist Islam. The thought-processes of such patriarchs - interpreting everything as "signs" to back up previous conclusions - were becoming familiar, with the Ulster Protestants, a deranged Chief Constable in Manchester and evangelical cults in inner cities all proclaiming that 'undesirables' (of whichever group the individual church happened to denounce) were bound for Hell. Grimwade

Who Decides What Makes a Companion?

...continued from page 293

be thought to have a similar claim, and Rassilon seems to think so in "The Five Doctors" (20.7).

Just to muddy the waters further, Leela's missing from the "Resurrection" flashback despite appearing in the one for "Logopolis" (18.7), as if the Fifth Doctor's come to see her as a bit of an embarrassment. Maybe he's guilty about missing the wedding. Some have suggested that the Doctor's telepathic ability, arguably used to translate everything into English, may have the side-effect of boosting endorphins; in short, a companion is someone addicted to the Doctor's presence, whether they like him or not. Of course, the converse might also be true, and a rather more sentimental possibility is raised by "The Curse of Fenric" (26.3). The haemovores can be shut out with a psychic barrier generated through faith. The Seventh Doctor's faith is in... Ian, Barbara, Susan, Vicki, Steven. Perhaps significantly, the Fourth Doctor seems to have less interest in companions than any of the others (q.v. 16.1, "The Ribos Operation"), and he's the one who puts the most faith in inanimate "props" like the sonic screwdriver and jelly-babies.

But ultimately this is a decision made by the producer and script editor, and as such it's inconsistent. Donald Tosh decided against making Anne Chaplet a companion (3.5, "The Massacre") because girls from Earth's past weren't "right". Yet he'd introduced Katarina two stories earlier, as if she were going to be a permanent addition. In the first year we had a number of one-story figures who did the work of a companion, such as Ping-Cho (1.4, "Marco Polo") and Sabetha (1.5, "The Keys of Marinus"). The final cliffhanger of "The Sensorites" (1.7) sees the abduction of space-girl Carol, and the fact that she's in peril is apparently as important as the endangerment of a regular like Susan. The big difference seems to be whether these people have homes to go to. Anyone caught pondering how much they want to get away from their humdrum lives less than ten minutes before the TARDIS arrives is fair game, but people with families, relationships and good jobs are stuck where they are. Unless they're journalists, or played by Billie Piper...

belonged to at least two such hell-bound categories. As a result there's no middle-road here, no suggestion that religion might have something to offer us even if it's scientifically invalid. The Chief Elder burns people for no good reason, and his ultimate decision to stay on a doomed planet looks like sheer pig-headedness, not a noble act of faith.

On a less spiritual note... those who've been following the series' shift towards soap opera might want to take note of the scenes between Howard and Peri in the first episode. The sight of attractive, wealthy Americans / pretend-Americans arguing about their personal lives in sunnier climes than Southern England is more likely to remind viewers of *Dynasty* than *Emmerdale Farm*, although it's closer to the late '70s *Nancy Drew* than either. As if to confirm the "soap" thesis, the story we have here is... well, it's not really a story. This is three or four subplots unfolding next to each other. More than ever before, even in Season Three, the programme's format - as a series about the Doctor and his chums, rather than a series set in the *Doctor Who* continuum where the Doctor's just one figure - is under attack. We can trot out all the reasons we've already hinted at, not just the soap opera connec-

tion but the existence of *DWM*, the influence of comic-books and the belief (common from the 1970s onwards) that every story needs a whacking great back-story to make things seem "bigger" than the individual characters, a trend that would later see authors writing 900-page prequels to "classic" SF novels and lead to the '90s obsession with story-arcs.

Since we've also been charting *Doctor Who*'s relationship with contemporary technology, this is as good a time as any to note a trend that's been common in this era, especially when Peter Grimwade's doing the writing duties: the reliance on TARDISbabble. Ten years earlier, hi-tech equipment was portrayed as so exotic that the Third Doctor apparently felt he'd be able to turn a video recorder into an anti-matter engine with nothing more than a sonic screwdriver and one line of technical gibberish. But now that there's no end of affordable electronic merchandise in every home, and vaguely ordinary people are finding out how to program computers as something other than a work-skill, it's not going to wash. Since the TARDIS is firmly embedded in the public imagination as a "magic box" that can do just about anything, from about 1979 onwards it's the Ship that provides most of the unlikely techie-talk. By this stage the Doctor's name-checking new console functions practically every week, and that's even before Kamelion plugs himself into the systems as if it's perfectly normal for robots to have SCART leads.

Things That Don't Make Sense The sequence of events here is... puzzling. The Master has his shrinking accident at the same moment that the TARDIS picks up the distress signal from the Trion beacon on Earth, a beacon which in itself is never explained. According to the Master's account, Kamelion then goes straight to his aid, but what the robot *actually* does is steer the TARDIS towards the beacon for no particular reason. After that Kamelion remote-parallels the Master's TARDIS to the Doctor's, to make sure both vessels end up on Sarn, and by the time the Master gets there he already knows about the all-important numismaton gas. For this to make sense, Kamelion must analyse the beacon, cross-reference it with information in the TARDIS databanks and conclude that the gas is a handy way of restoring his shrunken controller, but this is never made explicit and leaves us with the remarkable coincidence that the Ship picks up a signal leading to Sarn at exactly the same moment that the Master needs a cure.

Besides, why does the beacon lead the TARDIS to Sarn and not Trion? If there's data on the numismaton flame in the TARDIS records, then why has the Master never thought about using this astonishingly potent healing-force before, not even when he was horribly crippled in "The Deadly Assassin"? And assuming that the shrunken Master's box *is* a miniaturised workshop, why is it in such a neat little package? Why are there no doors? How did he get the lid on? Isn't it convenient that the device he uses for controlling Kamelion, a device he's apparently never tried to use before [though we might guess that his pain during the compression experiment opened up some kind of empathic link with his former mind-slave], just happened to be in that room? It's not as if it's a *big* workshop, even before the accident.

On rescuing a drowning girl in Lanzarote, Turlough decides to drag her inside the TARDIS where she can ask a lot of awkward questions instead of lying her down on the beach and getting a doctor. And one other, really obvious, question: when the Master's begging the Doctor for help in the final episode, and slowly burning to death inside the numismaton flame... why doesn't he just step out of it, like Kamelion does? His TARDIS is a whole three feet away, just behind him.

Critique (Prosecution) Watched as a four-part story, this is nothing much. A couple of good performances, notably Peter Wyngarde's portrayal of Timanov; a couple of shockingly bad ones (various boys in shorts); and one that, as a portent of things to come, makes the heart sink (Nicola Bryant... fortunately first impressions were misleading).

Watched as part of Season Twenty-One, week after week, it's the crossover point between two different versions of what the series is like. In that regard, it's like "Terminus" (20.4). One week we're in rainy Southwark, watching Daleks and replicas corrupting even the Doctor. Then we're in wholly new territory for the series, the Canary Islands and an alien planetscape shot on location. And if we think it looks like the bog-standard quarry, we get one of these for comparison a fortnight later, along with a totally different approach to four-part *Doctor Who*. As we hinted earlier, it's misleading to think of this as "a story" at all, but the culmination of various story-arcs running over the last few years.

Seen in that light, it's interesting as a restatement of various old themes and ideas from the programme's back-catalogue. How does Turlough reveal his cryptic past? By contacting his own people and asking for their help in evacuating innocent victims of their "black sheep". How did we find out about the Time Lords? The Doctor contacted his own et cetera et cetera. Flame of healing restoring sick Time Lords? Check. Von Daniken cargo-cult mis-interpreting wrecked spacecraft as celestial benefactors? Been there, done that.

For the hardcore fan this is thin stuff. Some might think that the hardcore fans were the audience, but there's a public out there too, and in dreary February 1984 a glimpse of sunshine, vast uninhabited plains and crystal blue waters was exactly what they wanted to see. We're cynical about it now, but Lanzarote was to Season Twenty-One what Adric's death was to Season Nineteen, a jolt to anyone who thought they knew what *Doctor Who* couldn't do. Interesting comparisons with "Frontios" can be made as well. This story has a society on a knife-edge, relying on a boy-king and his *eminance grise* to prevent catastrophe.

The Doctor sides with the rational, sceptical "heretics" who are threatening to mortally destabilise the world. And in both cases Turlough's memories provide answers where examination would have taken too long.

What happens in front of the location is almost irrelevant. There is actually a clever script attempting to come through. When the Master and the Doctor are each exploiting the local religion for their own ends, the Master's cunning is at last allowed to threaten the Doctor in real-time, rather than in the form of elaborate traps laid ages ago. He's far more formidable here than he has been since "Colony in Space" (8.4). Yet even with all the odds stacked in favour of this being a satisfying four episodes, things go wrong. Sarn, when we first see it, is a planet with its own Holiday Inn. Fiona Cumming's direction, never anything more than workmanlike, is almost entirely ordinary here. The shots of Peri sneezing are especially crass, and resemble a 1930s musical comedy. Just as it's seeming like the series has outgrown its "kiddy show" reputation, it has directing and acting of a piece with *Rentaghost*.

But for once, the music isn't the usual squeaky irritant, the effects all come off and we don't have to make allowances for outside forces. What we get is what they intended to make. It's not very good. It's not too bad. It's almost completely unmemorable, unless you were a teenage girl in love with Turlough or a teenage boy lusting after Peri. In that regard it is extraordinary that a woman directed something so close to being outright exploitation.

Critique (Defence) Once again, Peter Grimwade gets the nightmare brief: explain Turlough, find a reason for him to leave the TARDIS, introduce the new companion, deal with the wobbly robot, give the Doctor a "final" confrontation with the Master before his regeneration (because at the time, we really *did* think this was going to be the last showdown… "The Mark of the Rani" was a disappointment in so many ways) and make sure everyone's got the chance to go on holiday somewhere sunny.

The traditional response to "Planet of Fire" is to say that it's a reasonable way of tying up loose ends, but not a particularly good story in itself, yet that's doing a disservice to the approach Grimwade takes here. We've been through this argument before, with "Mawdryn Undead" (20.3). Here, as there, the programme's pitched as an ongoing serial rather than an adventure story. It's not leading up to a big bang, not even *trying* to lead up to a big bang, and tellingly there's no colossal explosion on Sarn to end proceedings. Is that a problem…?

Well, if so then the problem's this: it's in the nature of "soap opera" that it only works the first time round. There's an irony here, of course. Those who criticise what happened to the programme in the '80s are always keen to point out that the series was pitching itself at the fans rather than the general public, but here it's the fans - that poor minority which insists on watching the episodes over and over again on video - who are going to feel short-changed. Now we *know* Turlough's from a family of political prisoners, we can't get involved in the question of why he's maniacally sabotaging the TARDIS. Now we *know* Kamelion's not going to stay around, we can't find it in ourselves to care about his death scene. Now we *know* the Master burns up while screaming in agony… and so on.

Shown over two weeks in 1984, when it was part of the ongoing *Doctor Who* saga rather than that-story-just-before-"Androzani", this was intriguing and slightly askew from the norm; a story which seemed to be going in odd directions, but at the same time really had a sense of pushing Davison's time on the series towards its conclusion. In a word, it worked. This Critique would agree with the Prosecution's argument that its weak spot is Fiona Cumming, who on this occasion doesn't seem particularly interested (although the Defence certainly *wouldn't* agree that her work is always this ordinary… "Castrovalva", "Snakedance" and "Enlightenment" all display an instinctive understanding of how to make elsewhere-spaces work, and all in very different ways), yet the fact that so much of it feels suitably folkloric tells you that at the very, very least the majority of those involved are doing their jobs properly.

Still, a serial-story only works if it exists in the context of something much bigger. As is so often the case in this season, the *real* hitch is that however much it tries to twist and turn, this phase of the series just doesn't have much left to say. "Resurrection of the Daleks" was a good crowd-pleaser, but in the days before we had the hindsight to realise how of-its-time it was, it didn't really seem to be *about* anything. "Planet of Fire" doesn't really seem to be about anything either (and remember, even "Mawdryn Undead" felt like a rumination on the programme's own past), though perhaps it would have done if Grimwade had been allowed to dwell on the "evil religion" side of things as much as he'd intended. So even at the time, it felt as though this sort of thing was only acceptable as long as the *next* story was something big, beefy and important.

And as luck would have it…

The Facts

Written by Peter Grimwade. Directed by Fiona Cumming. Viewing figures: 7.4 million, 6.1 million, 7.4 million, 7.0 million.

Supporting Cast   Anthony Ainley (The Master), Peter Wyngarde (Timanov), Barbara Shelley (Sorasta), Gerald Flood (Voice of Kamelion), Edward Highmore (Malkon), James Bate (Amyand), Dallas Adams (Professor Howard Foster), Jonathon Caplan (Roskal).

Cliffhangers   Peri is left alone on the TARDIS with Kamelion-posing-as-Howard, only for Howard to transform himself into the Master; the 'unbelievers' cry out for the Doctor's help as the Master orders them to be burned in the sacrificial flame; Peri opens the Master's "control box" and finds the shrunken Master within, still threatening her despite being teeny.

Oh, Isn't That..?

• *Peter Wyngarde.* In 1971, "Jason" became the most popular boy's name in the UK; in 1972, Peter Wyngarde - the actor who played Jason King - was voted the man that most Australian women wished they'd lost their virginity to. In the ITC series *Department S* and clearly-labelled spin-off *Jason King*, Wyngarde was quite absurdly suave, even though many people thought he was wasting his obvious talents. Then, after a scandal which was mild by today's standards, nothing. His only other screen credit of the 1980s was as Klytus in *Flash Gordon*, and *that* was inside a mask.

The Lore

• Perpugiliam Brown was originally to have been blonde and - ostensibly - named "Chloe". The notes for the character had her losing her father at the age of thirteen, when he was the same apparent age as the Doctor (Howard was written

as being significantly older than Dallas Adams). The name Perpugiliam was found by the producer in a novel, and thought to be "typical" of the names that mothers in New England gave their daughters in the '60s.

• Nicola Bryant hails from Guildford. She had yet to gain an Equity card when she won the role (and several Americans flew in especially to audition). She told the press that she had dual nationality and that the accent was authentic; these were both true, sort of. She'd married a Broadway singer, Scott Kennedy - whose existence was kept secret, and note the ring on the "wrong" finger - and her flatmate was a New Yorker who'd coached her. On being short-listed she frantically took on any available work, mainly as a singer in nightclubs, to gain Equity membership. Her outfit at the first press-call, which saw her literally wrapped in the Stars and Stripes in some photos (it was the 5th of July, so there was a flag handy), was the basis for the shorts-and-leotard look in Season Twenty-Two. Various hairdos were tried before the "bob" was decided on, for practicality in filming as much as anything else, although Bryant kept her hair long and had plaits for the passport photo in episode one. Six weeks later she was at the photo-call for Colin Baker as the new Doctor. Finally, on the 14th of October, she got to do some filming.

• The idea was to follow Tegan with someone *else* from present-day Earth who wasn't English. Saward now alleges that Peri was intended to cash in on the huge US market, which had been maturing for five years. The convention circuit was a lucrative and relatively stress-free way of keeping in touch with the audience, and Nathan-Turner found time to attend at least two a year. However, Saward's theory - which was darkly muttered in UK fanzines, as well - is questionable, as the *Doctor Who* most popular in the States was the kind they made in the '70s. Attempts to make the new product US-friendly weren't going down well with the American market, any more than the British had really warmed to it, and the programme's un-Americannness was one of its key selling-points.

• Stop us if you've heard this one before… the filming of Peri's drowning and rescue was delayed when a tourist (legendarily a German nudist) rescued Bryant, unaware that it was just television. Another well-worn tale involves the last night of location shooting. The hotel had some turtles in the swimming-pool. Peter Wyngarde and Dallas Adams drunkenly decided they should be returned to the sea, and a full-scale search was called when the expensive reptiles were found to be "stolen". It's funny when Wyngarde tells it.

• 9/12/44, Turlough's code-number, is John Nathan-Turner's date of birth. (See also 22.1, "Attack of the Cybermen".)

• Wyngarde took the script to imply that Timanov was about two-hundred years old, and played it as such. With some location scenes having to be shot very fast, Cumming kept trying to gee up her guest star. Eventually they compromised on 120 years old.

• Much of the script needed vetting. The story was originally set on the fictional Greek island of "Aeschyllos", but the decision to film on Lanzarote rendered all of Peter Grimwade's careful research into Greek history utterly meaningless, and a reference to the island being a drab backwater was removed. Saward also toned down the anti-religious tenor of the script.

• Grimwade is said by Saward to have been on the script editor's "side", and it's been suggested that the writer was only given this commission as a consolation prize for missing out on the Dalek story in Season Twenty, even though the producer was still seething at him. However, he submitted at least one more story idea ("The League of the Tancreds", a historical adventure), which Nathan-Turner considered favourably before rejecting it on cost grounds. Later Grimwade wrote a number of children's books, the most successful entitled *Robot*, and a spectacularly waspish episode of the ITV children's one-off drama strand *Dramarama*. "The Come-Uppance of Captain Katt" was about the making of a family SF series, and featured Alfred Marks as an egocentric star not entirely unlike Tom Baker. The producer was depicted as a self-obsessed prima donna, so maybe Saward had a point. Grimwade died, after his second bout of cancer, in 1990.

21.6: "The Caves of Androzani"

(Serial 6R, Four Episodes, 8th March - 16th March 1984.)

Which One is This? The Phantom of the Space Opera. Guns, caves, androids, explosions, a sinister mastermind in a kabuki mask and the last gasp

for a leading man who still hasn't shaken off the title of "new boy".

Firsts and Lasts It's the end of the road for Peter Davison as the Fifth Doctor, which means that the flashbacks he suffers as he dies a death on the TARDIS floor (charmingly, involving newly-shot footage of all the actors who've played his companions rather than clips from old episodes) involve the last on-screen appearances of Tegan, Turlough, Kamelion, Nyssa and Adric. And of course, as this is a regeneration story the "replacement" has to put in a token appearance at the end of episode four, although the debut of the Sixth Doctor is unique in that Colin Baker gets to deliver a few lines rather than lying there unconscious until the next story. The closing credits superimpose the latest Doctor's face over the "starfield" background, just to make sure we understand what's happened.

Graeme Harper sits in the director's chair for the first time, in itself not such an overwhelming "first" as he only ever directs two stories (the other being 22.6, "Revelation of the Daleks"), but this small canon of work has become so well-regarded that it's worth mentioning anyway.

Four Things to Notice About "The Caves of Androzani"...

1. Take away the space-travel, and you could almost believe you were watching a historical. "The Caves of Androzani" isn't an all-out adventure in which the Doctor wilfully gets involved in the universe's affairs or has to save world X from threat Y, but a story in which his mere presence sets off a global-scale chain of events, with politicians being assassinated and local wars being brought to their conclusion while he's just trying to save his sick companion (q.v. **Working Titles**). In fact much of the Big Story plays out like a revenge tragedy, which barely involves the Doctor at all. This "operatic" feel may explain why the script can so easily get away with lines of dialogue that'd choke actors elsewhere, culminating in Sharaz Jek's shriek of hate to the man who left him hideously burned and disfigured: 'You stinking offal, Morgus, *look at me!*' (Mind you, even Christopher Gable's top-drawer performance as Jek can't quite get away with 'even I can't bear to see or touch myself' without at least 40% of the audience smirking.)

2. This being Peter Davison's last outing, there's got to be an explanation for his "celery bling", but

at this point it's also worth stopping to contemplate how little else the Doctor's been carrying in this regeneration. The Fourth Doctor used to lug around his own bodyweight in pocket-matter, and even the Third wasn't averse to pulling out the occasional gadget, yet since the destruction of the sonic screwdriver the Fifth's entire escape-kit has consisted of a cricket ball, some string, occasionally a pair of glasses and a few dodgy alien coins. No wonder he dies so quickly.

3. If there's a design "theme" in this season then it's the abuse of computer graphics, apparently the abuse of a BBC Micro. In "Warriors of the Deep", missile command looked like *Missile Command*; in "The Awakening", the electronic effects around the Malus made it look as if might have been programmed in BASIC; in "Frontios", the font on the TARDIS console screen seemed chillingly familiar; and here the neo-gothic gloomery of Sharaz Jek's control centre is somewhat broken up by the computerised, multi-coloured map of the cave system, complete with blobby little symbols to mark the locations of enemy troops.

What's notable here isn't just that it looks like a computer game c. 1983, it's that it looks like a beefed-up version of one specific computer game c. 1983, namely the official *Doctor Who* one. Exclusively compatible with the BBC Micro, naturally. See also **LOAD "What Did the Computer People Think?"**. (And that's not the only piece of distractingly cheap-looking technology here. Episode one makes the mistake of giving us a close-up of Trau Morgus' computer-control unit, a bad move as it's blatantly a TV remote control. You can even see the volume, brightness and colour buttons.)

4. A word should be said about the Doctor's regeneration, of course. The first regeneration to be treated simply *as* a regeneration, without any other mitigating factors (as in the previous four) and without any kind of "story arc" to proclaim it (as in the previous two), it works by presenting itself as an inevitable part of the plot rather than an inevitable part of the series. This is a story which ends in a bloodbath *and* a mudbath, with only two of the supporting cast surviving - Morgus' aide Krau Timmin, and the mysterious agent whom Morgus sends to blow up a copper mine - so the Fifth Doctor's passing looks like part of the same terrible, inexorable process. This can easily be overlooked on first viewing, however, as the moment when the Doctor prepares for death coincides with the moment that Peri leans over his body and gives the audience its best-ever look down her cleavage. For the fourteen-year-old boys mentioned under "Planet of Fire" (21.5), this must have been emotionally rather confusing.

The Continuity

The Doctor Allergic to certain gases in the praxsis range; see *Inventory*. He knows something of android engineering [much as in 16.4, "The Androids of Tara"], and has no trouble programming a course for a spaceship, although he says he's out of practice when it comes to manual landings. Again, he's capable of storing oxygen for several minutes.

The Doctor starts exploring Androzani purely because he's interested in the terrain, and he states that 'curiosity's always been my downfall'. And so it proves to be. When he puts Peri's life in danger by inadvertently exposing her to spectrox toxaemia, he's more desperate than ever to make sure she lives, acknowledging quite early on that finding a cure could kill him and ultimately giving her the antidote rather than using it to save himself. Toxaemia causes him to regenerate, though he states that it feels different this time, and he's not sure whether he's going to survive. As he regenerates he hallucinates the faces of all the companions he's had during this regeneration, plus the Master. [As in 18.7, "Logopolis", the fact that his memories are restricted to friends of *this* incarnation suggests that Time Lords see each regeneration as one "lifetime".] The companion roll-call ends in Adric - apt for a death scene - and indeed, 'Adric' is the Fifth Doctor's last word.

Once it's all over, the blond, curly-haired, well-built individual who finds himself occupying the Doctor's clothes wastes no time in sitting up and examining himself. [He's up and about almost instantly, whereas every other regeneration has seen the Doctor collapse as soon as he tries to get up, and judging by the next story this lack of rest isn't a good idea.] The first thing he does is be sarcastic to Peri. The second thing he does is insult her. His statement 'change… and it seems not a moment too soon' suggests that unlike many of the others, the Sixth Doctor is immediately inclined to think of himself as an improvement.

• *Inventory*. At last, an explanation for the celery on the lapel. According to the Doctor it detects certain gases in the praxsis range, and turns pur-

LOAD: "What Did the Computer People Think?"

Home computers have been mentioned a lot in this volume. This is perhaps not surprising, given that we started it with the first *Doctor Who* story to be script-edited by Chris Bidmead. But there's a reason to dwell on the subject, and it's not pure techno-fetishism. The truth is that nothing shapes the psyche of a population like new technology, and for those who grew up with the first generation of "cheap" personal computers in the early '80s (we really can't call them "PCs", in the modern sense of the term), these machines didn't just develop a culture of their own but seemed to introduce new ways of thinking. Let's not forget that prior to the arrival of the video game *Pong* in the late '70s, nobody could control what happened on their TV screens except by changing channels. Before VCRs were commercially available or Ceefax was widespread, the idea that you could flip a few controls and actually *steer* the little shapes on the set was honestly astounding. Television, and indeed the media itself, suddenly seemed… manipulable. Home computers, which allowed you to enter simple commands in BASIC and fill the screen with all sorts of pictures, colours and swearwords, took this process a step further. Home video took off at about the same time, which meant that the media was suddenly becoming non-linear. By 1984, the TV wasn't the one giving the orders.

But these machines weren't like games consoles. Here it's worth underlining that especially in Britain, the computers of the early '80s were specifically designed to encourage children to figure out how they worked (see the **Where Does This Come From?** of 18.7, "Logopolis"), and as a result quite a few teenaged boys became unexpectedly wealthy after writing their own games software. These included the creators of the BBC's first *Doctor Who* game, the one that looks like the model for Sharaz Jek's monitoring system in "The Caves of Androzani". These days it takes a Hollywood-sized programming team to create a saleable computer game, but back then it was a cottage industry for whizzkids, in the same solo-inventor-messing-around-with-gadgetry tradition as the BBC Radiophonic Workshop or… well, *Doctor Who* itself. As we've already seen, machines like the ZX-Spectrum and the BBC Micro weren't just part of a trend - though nothing says "early '80s" like the kind of graphics you see on the TARDIS console in this period - but theoretically a way of making you smarter, and at times *Doctor Who* and the home computer boom seemed to be joined at the hip. Bidmead's run as script editor… the radiophonic music in Season Eighteen, virtually indistinguishable from the kind that the BBC used on every "educational" programme about computer technology… the fact that the only good reason to own a BBC Micro was *Elite*, the first computer game to be advertised on TV, with a voice-over from Tom Baker[15]… all of these things felt like part of the same process. (*Elite* obviously had a long-term effect on the minds of the twelve-year-old boys. Much of the space opera in the 1990s *Doctor Who* novels, for example, comes not from *Star Trek* or *Star Wars* but from the *Elite* version of how outer-space battles should be fought.)

Now, the ZX-Spectrum Generation was a short-lived one. By 1990, programming was "out" and games consoles were "in"; big business took over from the amateur inventor, appropriately at the same time that *Doctor Who* itself died; and the Youth of the Nation was suddenly being taught to swear allegiance to Nintendo rather than to figure out how to use computers creatively. It's worth taking a moment, though, to consider how those early computer-literate boys and girls (mostly boys, let's be frank) ended up seeing the world.

By the 1980s, the British education system couldn't in all honesty have been described as inspirational. The Thatcher government wanted an emphasis on business and technical skills, and had little interest in art, culture, history, or anything else that didn't have an immediate cash value. It was at this point that the gulf between "arts" and "sciences" began to widen, and the idea took root that you either did one or the other, preferably the latter if you wanted a decent living. From the government's point of view, the computer explosion was a good thing because it taught schoolkids important "work-skills".

Needless to say, this isn't the way the computer people saw things. And here we're not just talking about the twelve-year-olds, but those members of the older generation who were becoming obsessed with RAM-packs and floppy discs (which, in those days, really were floppy). Two names immediately spring to mind: Christopher H. Bidmead and Douglas Adams. The kind of people who liked messing around with machine-language weren't Thatcher's profit-driven technocrats at all, but the same kind of people who listened to Bach and saw Leonardo da Vinci as the poster-child for all human genius. (In which con-

continued on page 303…

ple as a warning. [Why *this* Doctor is particularly worried about gases in the praxsis range is another matter. Is only this body allergic, but if so, then how did he find out?] The Doctor also states that celery is a powerful restorative 'where I come from', and tries to revive Peri by sticking it under her nose, but unfortunately the human olfactory system is relatively feeble. So Time Lords must have good noses. The celery is eventually left behind on Androzani Minor.

• *Background*. The Doctor has been to this part of the universe before, and states that Androzani Minor hasn't changed. He can't remember exactly when he was here, but he's fairly sure it wasn't the relative future. Having been told that a certain Professor Jackij has found the cure for spectrox toxaemia, the Doctor later speaks as if he's familiar with some of the Professor's work. [Androzani Major doesn't seem to have flourishing relations with the rest of the galaxy, so Jackij might be from this neck of the woods.] He's never heard of spectrox before now.

The Doctor states that he tried keeping a diary once, 'not chronological, of course' [which could mean either the Second Doctor's five-hundred-year diary or the old time-logs consulted by the Fourth]. But he could never find the time for it.

The Supporting Cast

• *Peri*. She's clearly developing a bond with the Doctor, as they're already engaging in an effective "double act", and he's protective of her even before he knows she's contracted something lethal. Having said that, his enthusiasm often irritates her, though it's notable that she's the only companion of the Fifth Doctor who's had the wit to ask him why he wears a stick of celery on his jacket. She's initially excited about exploring an alien world, even when the world in question is just a rocky dump. [This indicates that Peri's still new to the TARDIS, despite the attempts of later audio and novel writers to insert eight-hundred other stories into the gap after "Planet of Fire". Her line 'makes a change from lava' seems to confirm this.]

Planet Notes

• *Androzani Minor*. A desolate, cave-riddled world with an Earth-like atmosphere but no signs of plant life, described as being one of the 'Five Planets'. The Doctor says it's been a billion years since there's been any sea here. The core of Androzani Minor is superheated primeval mud,

so when its orbit takes it close to Androzani Major the gravitational pull causes mudbursts, when the hot mud erupts from the ground and briefly makes the surface uninhabitable. Hence the cave-like blow-holes, the cavern passages being polished as smooth as glass and lit by natural phosphorescence. The Doctor believes the mudbursts are the reason Minor was never colonised.

However, the planet's real significance is that it's the only known source of the drug spectrox. The caves are inhabited by large winged creatures known as 'bats', and these leave spectrox nests, fuzzy balls of a cobweb-like substance that are harvested and refined to create the spectrox drug. The bats have a three-year life-cycle, and spend their chrysalis stage in their nests. The people of Androzani Major believe refined spectrox to be the most valuable substance in the universe, as it prevents ageing and offers its user at least twice the normal life-span if taken regularly. It's a white powder when refined, though it's imbibed in a drink. In its raw form it contains a toxic chemical similar to mustard nitrogen, and anyone who touches one of the nests develops spectrox toxaemia, which causes rashes, cramps, spasms, slow paralysis of the thoracic spinal nerve and finally thermal death.

The only known cure for this is the milk of the queen bat, probably containing an anti-vesicant, although all the queen bats have gone down to the oxygen-free depths of the cave system to lie dormant. The milk cures a victim of toxaemia in moments, and its use as a cure has been noted by no less a luminary than Professor Jackij. The only other native life seen roaming the caves is a bulky, bipedal, dragon-like creature which lives down in the magma but comes up to feed on any flesh it can find.

But the most notable inhabitant of Androzani Minor is Sharaz Jek. He was once a partner of Trau Morgus, a leading figure on the twin planet of Androzani Major, and built an android workforce to collect the spectrox in the belief that they'd share the profits. But Morgus betrayed Jek, giving him faulty detection equipment and leaving him to die in a mudburst on Minor's surface. Jek was appallingly scarred and burned, which is why he now wears a stylish facemask, and he's been seeking revenge ever since. He describes himself as having been a doctor before he made the study of androids his life.

From his well-equipped headquarters deep in

LOAD: "What Did the Computer People Think?"

...continued from page 301

text, the Doctor's aged appearance in the first computer-era story - 18.1, "The Leisure Hive" - takes on a certain significance. It's important to realise that in the '80s, schoolchildren generally *weren't* being taught who Leonardo was. You learned important things like that from either computer-culture or "City of Death". People of Adams' and Bidmead's "tribe" saw art and technology as parts of the same pattern. Look at the computer magazines of 1980-84 - magazines aimed primarily at an adolescent audience, usually with the emphasis on games rather than hard-core nerdery - and you don't see endless pages of Lara Croft pin-ups and big explosions. There were spaceships and monsters, no doubt about it, but there were also bizarre references to history, classical art, literature (usually SF, admittedly) and obscure music. Why? Because the *individuals* who wrote the software, individuals rather than companies, were "into" that kind of thing.

So the computer kids were learning things that a lot of other schoolchildren weren't being told about, but in a bewildering, non-linear order. In a time when the government had no interest in teaching people where they'd come from (q.v. 21.2, "The Awakening"), members of the Spectrum Generation were picking up bits and pieces of the past, and sometimes ended up making little digital collages out of them. This, in itself, should suggest that these people grew up to see the world in a subtly different way to those of an earlier age who (a) had a better "formal" education and (b) weren't brought up to think of either TV or the arts as something you *used*. (Research suggests that the children of this era remember less, but can process more, although this is open to all sorts of interpretations.) At the time, you could truthfully say that those who knew about computers had a better understanding of culture and language than the average teenager, *but* they only understood these things in their own terms. Everywhere you look in Season Eighteen, you see the same peculiar art / technology relationship. "The Keeper of Traken" (18.6) gives us a world in which every artefact is meant to be beautiful, but most of them turn out to be stuffed with hidden circuitry, up to

and including the Melkur. "Logopolis" turns the whole universe into a computer program, yet instead of being cold, sterile and mechanical it's full of curious, near-surrealist imagery. The next season opens with "Castrovalva" (19.1), inspired by M. C. Escher, the artist of choice for the new wave of bedroom-boffins.

It's reasonable to say that both Adams and Bidmead ended up thinking about things in much the same way as the younger computer-trained generation, though Adams only entered this phase after he left *Doctor Who*. In the '80s and '90s he often talked about the possibilities of a non-linear media, and spent a lot of time working out how to create a genuinely interactive novel, though annoyingly he died just as the technology was arriving to make it feasible. And as for Bidmead… the scripts he wrote / re-wrote for the series reflect the thinking of the computer people in one other noticeable respect. Remember, those who learned about Charles Darwin or T. S. Eliot or the Renaissance from computer-culture saw themselves as having access to vital information about the "old" world that wasn't being taught to them properly by anyone else. And in almost every Bidmead-influenced script, there's an elite of techno-literate thinkers who believe themselves to be the guardians of ancient and endangered knowledge, from the Deciders in "Full Circle" (18.3) to the Consuls of Traken, from the Logopolitans to the rulers of Frontios (21.3).

Lalla Ward's acerbic comments about the '80s series pitching itself at teenage computer-nerds aren't entirely unjustified, and the criticism that *Doctor Who* became vaguely elitist in this period holds some weight. It has to be remembered, though, that these were troubled times for British culture. The techno-happy "elite" didn't want to rule the world any more (compare with the SRS in 12.1, "Robot"), they were just terrified of a rising wave of ignorance. Bidmead, especially, saw the passing-on of knowledge as a moral mission rather than just an incidental aspect of the programme. His interest in the fiddly technical details of his own beloved home computer may make him sound rather drab, but it's also telling. Computer people were, after all, obsessed with explaining how things worked.

the caves he controls the mute, faceless androids which patrol the tunnels, simple models that use their projectile side-arms to kill any human intruders who aren't wearing one of Jek's special belt-plates. Fortunately the Doctor doesn't count, as the androids have infra-red vision and can see that his biology doesn't match human normal. But Jek also has the power to create android duplicates of human beings. The caves are wired with his surveillance systems, and he can create a robot which mimics the face and voice of any subject he sees, a process that takes mere minutes for basic, none-too-intelligent duplicates. Guard androids have to be shot several times before they're destroyed, though they can be deactivated by cutting the solenoids at the neck.

As Jek controls the caves, he also controls the supply of spectrox, a problem for all the people on Androzani Major who are crying out for the drug. There's a growing public feeling that the authorities ought to bargain with him, but Morgus isn't hearing any of it and is sponsoring the federal forces, which have already moved in to the caves to try to find Jek's lair. The caves are vast, however, so the campaign against the androids has lasted for six months and cost hundreds of lives. It doesn't help that the general's aide de camp is actually one of Jek's androids, his finest creation, with a cortex containing five-million responses. Also present on Androzani Minor are gun-runners from Major, mercenaries who've come to supply Jek with weapons in return for spectrox, though the mercenaries' boss is none other than Morgus himself.

• *Androzani Major.* A heavily-populated world, apparently in the Sirius system, though all that's seen of it here is Trau Morgus' office. Morgus is purportedly 'the richest man in the Five Planets', and the chairman of the Sirius Conglomerate. ["Frontier in Space" (10.3) has already made mention of Sirius V.] A despicable power-mad businessman and descendant of the first colonists [a sign of status, as in 14.5, "The Robots of Death"], Morgus already has the ruling presidium in his pocket. But the President himself is close to bargaining with Sharaz Jek, at least until Morgus pushes the man down a lift-shaft. It's a measure of the effect spectrox has had on this world that the President is 84 but looks as if he's in his fifties. His apothecary recommends a dose of 0.3 of a centilitre every day, although he's been without any for three weeks and has begun to feel his age.

The Sirius Conglomerate owns Androzani Minor, which means that Morgus already has stocks of spectrox and that the price has conveniently risen. Morgus has recently increased unemployment by closing plants in the west, and he suggests shipping those without valid employment cards to eastern labour-camps, which he just happens to have been building himself. Copper output has increased despite a limiting order, which is bad news for Morgus economically, so he sends an agent to the Conglomerate's own Northcawl mine to arrange an explosion. The death of one executive in the mine is seen as more important than the deaths of any of the workers. Morgus can order minor personnel to be shot without anybody arguing, and has private fortunes on the outer planets of the Sirius system.

Ultimately, just about everyone involved in this clash of egos is butchered; Sharaz Jek takes his revenge on Morgus, then gets shot dead, while the soldiers and the mercenaries kill each other off, or are slain by the androids, or buried by the mudburst. Morgus' personal assistant, Krau Timmin, becomes Chairman and Chief Director of the Sirius Conglomerate after the presidium issues warrants for Morgus' arrest and seizes his private assets.

History

• *Dating.* The future, date unspecified. [It seems virtually certain that these people are Earth-spawned humans. The Sirius system doesn't have any stated links to the outside galaxy, and there's no talk of trading spectrox beyond the Five Planets, so communications with other systems can't be good and it's unlikely to be the age of the Earth Empire. The fairly primitive weaponry on show here might indicate that it's not far into the future, and that Androzani is one of Earth's earliest colonies, although the existence of spectrox - a substance never mentioned in any other future-tale - might indicate a time in the far, far future when human civilisations have been cut off from each other and technology has started to degenerate. Since this is a Robert Holmes script, the latter seems likely, and this could well be a time of dispersed humanity much like that seen in its sister-story "The Power of Kroll" (16.5). But if Androzani is in orbit of Sirius then an earlier date is at least possible, as Sirius is less than nine light-years from Earth and likely to be one of the first systems investigated by Earth-people. The novel *Lucifer Rising* hints that the story's set somewhere around the twenty-second century, which is quite feasible, although Jean-Marc Lofficier's claim in *The Terrestrial Index* that the mention of 'federal forces' indicates the Federation from "The Curse of Peladon" (9.2) is clearly silly.]

Sharaz Jek initially assumes that Peri comes from Earth. Among the humans on Androzani

Major, "Trau" would seem to be the form of address for men and "Krau" the form of address for women. The guns used are mainly projectile weapons, machine-pistols and the like, though among the weapons being shipped to Jek are gas weapons and volatisers [q.v. 8.1, "Terror of the Autons"]. The gun-runners' spacecraft is nothing to write home about, and the Doctor can tell that such ships are only meant for interplanetary travel as they're too small for long-range journeys, while Morgus' private vessel uses 'beta drive' to get from world to world quickly [c.f. 6.6, "The Space Pirates"].

Transmissions are sent from Major to Minor by 'interplanetary vid' which appears to be holographic, and personal vehicles on Major are known as 'floaters'. The federal forces have military artificers and a radio-satellite, while androids are referred to as 'droids'. It's a military tradition that those to be executed are given Death Under the Red Cloth, which basically means being shot by a firing squad while wearing red robes. This seems to be an honourable way to die as the President says that in *his* day gun-runners would be shot in the back while the Red Cloth was reserved for soldiers. Those who die in this manner are then cremated, their remains wrapped in the aforementioned robes.

Picking chacaws is, according to Stotz, a worse profession than gun-running. [If you're interested, the novelisation describes chacaws as 'a fiercely-spiked fruit grown on the penal plantations of Androzani Major'.]

The Analysis

Where Does This Come From? Robert Holmes has always had a thing about making businessmen, bureaucrats and petty officials look like sadists and sociopaths, but now the rest of the world has caught up with him. It's the 1980s, and *everybody* hates big business; corporations are the new Hitler.

"Terminus" (20.4) handled this kind of subject-matter by making the evil slave-driving company an invisible, near-godlike force, but Holmes takes the other tack. Morgus is a calculating, dehumanising empire-builder, not simply grey-faced and short-sighted like most of the threatening businesspeople of past stories, but an amoral killer who sees his victims as mere statistics. Hundreds die, and thousands more are reclassified as unemployed scum, all according to the whims of the

aggressively self-interested. (And when Morgus falls, his Conglomerate remains standing. We're not expecting things to be any nicer under Krau Timmin. As in "Terminus", beating the company is harder than dealing with a single individual or a single crisis.)

Is it *really* necessary to explain how this connects with the mood of Britain circa 1984? The mention of plant-closures here, and the idea that those without valid employment cards are to be used as slave labour, is telling in the context of a time when unemployment was through the roof and there was widespread mistrust of the various "schemes" created by the government to bring the figures down. And once again there's a ruthless, professional military in action (as in 21.4, "Resurrection of the Daleks"), acting on behalf of the self-involved but being spun to the public as patriotic.

This is post-Falklands *Doctor Who*. There's little or no deliberate satire here, but compare it with Holmes' last script, the thematically-similar "Power of Kroll" (16.5). "Kroll" seems like an abstract exercise, or at best a piece of historical conjecture, comparing the plight of the Swampies with that of the Native Americans without a great deal of enthusiasm. This, on the other hand, feels like a product of the *now*. It helps that the motives of most of the characters are so wholly material, not rooted in ideology but in the dog-eat-dog mentality of its era, with the Doctor and Peri surviving (well, ish) purely because they refuse to be part of the process at all. This is a morality play, in which virtually everyone's obsessed with ambition and revenge.

We've already mentioned how much this story resembles a historical drama, but specifically we're in Jacobean territory, the cycle of seventeenth-century revenge tragedies by people like Middleton and Fletcher where greed and wrath always lead to a massacre. No-one is immune. The "nicest" person here is General Chellak, who genuinely seems to believe he's Doing It for Androzani Major and who at least comes to believe in the Doctor's innocence, but even *he's* prepared to send one of his men on a suicide mission just because the soldier knows things that could compromise his career. As with Eric Saward's later scripts, the Doctor's a catalyst here rather than a protagonist, but that makes sense. This isn't his world, and it really isn't his decade.

Even apart from "Kroll", Holmes' own back-catalogue supplies many of the "recycled materials" here. Nobody who knows the series well has ever been able to see Sharaz Jek's unmasking without thinking of Greel in "The Talons of Weng-Chiang" (14.6). There as here, there's a strong undercurrent of *The Phantom of the Opera*, especially given Jek's obsession with Peri. Still, it'd be another three years before "Weng-Chiang" would be released on video, so it didn't seem so obvious at the time. The mercenaries are dealing in gas-based weapons (because it wouldn't be a Holmes story without gas) and small-but-lethal devices called volatisers (as used by the Master in "Terror of the Autons"). There are also notable similarities to the style of latter *Blake's* 7 episodes - a recurring problem, in this period - although the Doctor does his usual trick of landing in someone else's programme and messing everything up instead of playing along. Moreover, the debt Holmes owes to Frederik Pohl and Cyril Kornbluth has never been more obvious (see 15.4, "The Sun Makers", for another example), but a more blatant source is the seemingly-inescapable *Dune*. As you may know, *Dune* involves a drug that extends life and allegorically represents oil, amongst other things. You might also see hints of Ursula LeGuin's *The Dispossessed* here, not least in the character names and the twin planets that represent different political systems.

There's also the little matter of the soldiers referring to Jek's robots as 'droids', but we'll gloss over that.

Things That Don't Make Sense Lots of trained mercenaries with machine-weapons fail to hit the Doctor on open terrain. Jek's androids never had any trouble making it down into the lair of the queen bats and recovering their milk, so why doesn't Jek have some of the substance in storage, just in case of spectrox-related accidents? Which must be quite likely, in his line of work.

Jek also seems to believe that spectrox is the secret of eternal youth, and that it can keep Peri young 'n' pretty forever, which isn't what anybody else believes [as ever, Jek isn't thinking straight]. And where / how is Jek getting spare parts for this seemingly-endless army of androids? It's not as though Stotz is going to motivate his rebellious crew by smuggling wigs and WD40.

The Doctor begins showing Peri the wonders of the universe by taking her to a planet which, as far as he knows, has no interesting features whatsoever. Finding traces of a recent spacecraft-landing,

he then asks why anybody would want to come here, apparently not spotting the irony. In itself, it's hard to understand why he doesn't know about something as historically monumental as spectrox, despite having prior knowledge of this corner of the cosmos. Even if the supply ends with the fire at Jek's lair, the long-term effects (all those people who lived longer than expected…) would last a century or more, and be as big a part of history as cars.

Once the Doctor's picked up Peri and the bat's milk, he carries both to the TARDIS and safety, but spills half of the goop. As this stuff is so effective so quickly, why not give it to her, take some himself, *then* leg it to the Ship? He'd get off the planet quicker if he didn't keep falling over from spectrox toxaemia.

Critique (Grumpy Defence) All right, it's not quite perfect. Just very, very close.

If a monster like the magma beast is considered a liability (when it's easily the best monster of Davison's tenure, and almost of the whole 1980s), the rest must be pretty nifty. So what's it doing that's so different from everything else this year, or this phase in the programme's development?

The most obvious change is that, with a couple of lines at the start and the final scene excluded, it doesn't refer to any other story. This is a self-contained adventure in a world which follows its own rules. It even has its own narrative rules, with Morgus addressing asides to the viewers and (more subtly) Jek controlling what we see, either though his monitors or - in one extraordinary scene - with an illustration of Jek's point inserted. We fade across from Jek laughing to Major, see Morgus being a git, then fade back to Jek still laughing as he had been when we left him. The "death-knell" running for eight minutes in episode four highlights the fact that this is very obviously melodrama, but done with absolute conviction. The humour is from the situation, not the performances per se.

Holmes was working on a different theory from everyone around him. In his experience, viewers could handle SF concepts if the "hook" was something familiar. By making Sharaz Jek obviously an echo of the Phantom of the Opera, he could extrapolate two whole worlds secure in the knowledge that everyone could follow at home. In this he's diametrically opposed to the tack Bidmead took when condemning "State of Decay"

(18.4) for looking and sounding too familiarly Hammer-ish. From this point of view Bidmead and Douglas Adams are working from very similar starting-points; once they've made up a world, what can they do with it? Holmes is coming at it from the other direction. We have a story, what kind of world suits it best? In this regard he's taking the series back to its roots, which is itself paradoxically the one thing that the last two continuity-choked seasons had failed to manage.

The irony is, of course, that Nathan-Turner didn't want this one made. Whilst he was happy to associate with people like Pip and Jane Baker or Terence Dudley, he never grasped the importance of writers, and particularly not Robert Holmes. Saward came to believe that for Nathan-Turner, scripts were a pretext for costumes, sets and guest-stars who were mainly there to be photographed with the producer. Holmes knew that within the confines of what was do-able, the programme was about storytelling and characters, with spectacle as an overlay. What Holmes originally wrote would have worked in Season Seventeen, or Season Ten, or Season Three. For good or ill, Saward encouraged Holmes to go just a little further than usual, to be more like his own reputation. Harper took the script and ran with it, and Nathan-Turner was kept out of the way as far as possible.

For the majority of viewers, though, it was run-of-the-mill. There's not much on the surface to distinguish between this and most of Season Twenty-One. It's got a quarry, a rubbish monster, garish uniforms, lots of pink in the set design and BBC Micro graphics. If they shut up and listen they might note a lack of overstatement, faux-macho lines and people saying 'this is madness'. They might find they can follow the story a bit more easily than usual. They may even laugh occasionally, and not at the spaceships. Sadly, though, for most people this was the one in between the one with the volcanoes and the one with the bird-men.

Critique (Less Grumpy Defence)   What's not in question is that this is the most fitting way possible for the Davison run to end; the pity is that we didn't get here before now. A rapid-fire, multi-textured tale of human angst and high politics, with a script that suggests cultures beyond the confines of the sets and a director whose instinct for the modern medium is so good that the story's rhythm is very nearly visible on-screen... this is what the programme's been aiming at ever since Season Eighteen.

The early Nathan-Turner stories have frequently tried to do "space-gothic" properly, and you can see it even in much less... well... convincing stories like "Earthshock". But before now they never had Robert Holmes behind the typewriter, and more importantly - *more* importantly, because this is the film-maker's triumph far more than it is the author's - Graeme Harper behind the camera. And in a final, tragic twist, the finished product only turns up once the audience has stopped caring and started taking *Doctor Who* for granted.

The reason "Androzani" works is simple: it believes every word it says. Just look at the way Peri gets poisoned by spectrox. Giving diseases to companions is nothing new, but more often than not it's a way of padding out the story, of getting the Doctor from point A to point B ("Revenge of the Cybermen", "Mawdryn Undead"...). Here it looks like it bloody well *hurts*. On first viewing, we could believe that the New Girl might really die - just look at Adric, we told ourselves, just look at Kamelion - and we see her body start to tear itself apart even as Androzani Minor goes to hell around her. Or consider the scenes in which the Doctor and Peri await their execution, which would be pure filler in most stories but honestly feel like the build-up to a funeral here. Every threat the Doctor faces looks like a *real* threat, not something he might be able to gab his way out of at a moment's notice.

This means that his levity finally *means* something. When he refuses to take the ranting, gun-toting, militaristic opposition seriously, it's not just a bit of a laugh; this time he's playing with fire, he really *could* get shot in the head, and every one of his asides is used like a weapon. Such a thing would have been unthinkable when Tom Baker was in the lead role. (Yet Holmes wrote much of the script with Baker in mind, which again suggests that what we see on-screen is far darker and far more dramatic than anything the author was imagining.) Davison's performance here is probably the best of his entire career, a savage poke in the eye to all those who seriously believed he was a "bland" Doctor just because he didn't goon around the place trying to steal every scene. And then there's Nicola Bryant, whose position as companion during the Great Fall from Grace - see Volume VI - has blinded many to the fact that she's extraordinarily good at her job. Here she works wonders with the script's fairly standard companion-banter, and makes Peri seem likeably sarcastic from the very first scene.

But yes, this is Harper's show more than anyone's. A lot of commentators, including Davison himself, have praised the director's "interesting camera angles". This is perfectly true, and his use of the lens is fittingly exotic, but it's only a fraction of his achievement here. He gives this story a pulse. Holmes' script stages the action so that all the strands of the plot accelerate at once, and reach crisis point together; Peri's near-death, the military's doomed last assault, Sharaz Jek's vengeance-play and the planet bursting-open all feel as if they're part of the same organism, and Harper understands this perfectly. His eye for striking visual "arrangements" has led many to compare him to Douglas Camfield, but with all due respect, Camfield never understood light, space and motion this acutely. As in all good film, action and characterisation are indistinguishable. Even the "terminal" cliffhanger, which sees the Doctor hurtling towards the planet and not caring about the consequences, leaves us in no doubt that he's heading towards his own personal Armageddon and that we're right there on board with him.

So, it's the end of another era. Davison didn't stay on the series long enough to become part of the folklore, not in the same way that Baker did. The '80s being what they were, it's doubtful that he could have managed it even if he'd been around for another half-decade. But "Androzani" forces you to put that out of your mind, and assume that this is a grand tragedy even if you've never seen the series before. As Androzani Minor shakes itself to pieces, the Doctor's death looks both apocalyptic and inevitable without any pretence that it's a moment of revelation. In this kind of ever-accelerating, high-gravity environment, villains who might otherwise have been screeching dullards take on the kind of operatic intensity that the series was so desperately trying to reach in Season Twenty, so in the end - as we, and so many others, seem to keep saying over and over again - only the magma beast disappoints. The word is "masterful".

The Facts

Written by Robert Holmes. Directed by Graeme Harper. Viewing figures: 6.9 million, 6.6 million, 7.8 million, 7.8 million.

Supporting Cast Christopher Gable (Sharaz Jek), John Normington (Morgus), Martin Cochrane (Chellak), Robert Glenister (Salateen), Maurice Roëves (Stotz), Roy Holder (Krelper), Barbara Kinghorn (Timmin), David Neal (President), Colin Baker (The Doctor), Anthony Ainley (The Master), Matthew Waterhouse (Adric), Sarah Sutton (Nyssa), Janet Fielding (Tegan), Mark Strickson (Turlough), Gerald Flood (Voice of Kamelion).

Working Titles "Chain Reaction".

Oh, Isn't That..?

• *Robert Glenister.* Played Peter Davison's brother in the sitcom *Sink or Swim*, so seeing them teamed up again here was quite distracting at the time.

• *Christopher Gable.* Formerly of the Royal Ballet, he'd been Twiggy's co-star in Ken Russell's film *The Boyfriend*. He was originally cast as Salateen, but asked if he could play Jek. Graeme Harper had already considered this, but had thought that Gable would refuse a role in which his face was never seen.

• *Roy Holder.* As a kid he co-starred with Hayley Mills in *Whistle Down the Wind*, and as an adult he was Chas in ITV's *Doctor Who* rival *Ace of Wands*. Come the 1990s, he'll turn up again in *Middlemarch*.

• *John Normington.* He'd played a lot of officials, bank managers and such, and was on occasion a "professional Yorkshireman" (in at least two Alan Bennett projects, most recently the 1983 film *A Private Function*).

• *Maurice Roëves.* Had been the local policeman in *The Nightmare Man* (see 13.6, "The Seeds of Doom"), and was in SAS cash-in flick *Who Dares Wins*. Later he'd make a splash in *Tutti Frutti* (penned by a scriptwriter called Johnny Byrne, but not that one). He also pops up in *Cheers*, and in an episode of *Star Trek: The Next Generation* called "The Chase", which is - amazingly - even more embarrassing than the Hartnell story of the same name.

Cliffhangers The Doctor and Peri are covered in red hoods and shot by the firing-squad; the magma beast rears up over the rock that the Doctor happens to be hiding behind; the Doctor steers the gun-runner's ship into a crash-dive towards Androzani Minor, insisting that he's not going to let anyone stop him now.

The Lore

• Saward commissioned the script for this story sight-unseen, partly as a thankyou for Holmes' patience during the "Six Doctors" debacle (see 20.7, "The Five Doctors"). Nathan-Turner was keen to write out the Fifth Doctor before the season break, to give the audience time to get used to the new style. Saward decided that "Chain Reaction" would be ideal, and his brief to Holmes was simply 'kill the Doctor'. Holmes later admitted that he didn't really know much about Davison's Doctor, and was imagining Tom Baker when writing a lot of the script.

• Davison was worried about the fact that he was being removed four episodes before his contract ended, and was eventually paid for the full season. He was by now expressing regret that he'd opted to leave just before getting comfortable in the role, and had established himself well enough to suggest changes. He'd never been happy with the "uniform", and now he was cautious about the apparent pandering to the overseas market (see 21.5, "Planet of Fire").

• Graeme Harper claimed that his original casting for Morgus and Timmin was Alan Lake and Diana Dors (see 15.5, "Underworld", for why this didn't happen). Ian Holm (Bilbo in *The Lord of the Rings*) was approached to play Morgus, as was Ronald Lacey, then typecast after his role as Toht, the bespectacled Nazi in *Raiders of the Lost Ark*. Some reports claim that the part of Salateen was offered to Roger Daltry, the founder of *The Who*.

• Harper's instruction for John Normington (Morgus) to turn more towards the camera when making a sotto voce "aside" was relayed incorrectly, but the full-on address to the screen was kept. (Saward in particular loved this, and Seasons Twenty-Two and Twenty-Three will see him experiment further with this style of narrative.) The concept for the regeneration was based on the end of the Beatles' "A Day In The Life". One detail missing in the screened version is that as the Doctor dies, the lights on the console go berserk.

• There was - guess what - a scene-shifter's dispute, causing a delay in the completion of this story and thus in "The Twin Dilemma". As Maurice Roëves (Stotz) had been flown in from America, the budget was stretched still further to retain his services for the remainder of the shoot.

• Saward had a Praxsis 35 electric typewriter (q.v. the Doctor's reference to the 'Praxsis range'), which he later cited as proof - when fans claimed that Holmes was a genius and Saward a hack - that he'd written a large amount of the script. A lot of the "continuity" dialogue - celery, the comments by past companions in the regeneration and all the Sixth Doctor material - was penned by Saward. The "flashback" scene was written for the cast-members available; Ainley and Sutton were the ones in doubt, as Sutton had chickenpox and Ainley had a rapacious agent. But they were all invited to the wrap party anyway, so lines were written for them and their sequences were added later.

• All the episodes overran, and this was *after* the scripts had been pared down considerably (including a final editing session in the BBC bar, when Nathan-Turner sent Saward and Holmes to sort it out). As written, the Doctor fights the magma beast to get to the nest; the North Caul copper mine's boss has five widows; Salateen tells Peri that the soldiers are lectured on the risks of raw spectrox (and that many people join the army rather than work for Morgus); and the Doctor knows Salateen's an android from the start, as the caves are warm but Salateen never sweats.

• Colin Baker is reported to have been hopping up and down in the wings, anxious to film his debut. He had to wear Davison's spare costume with the flies undone in order to get into the trousers. In a moment of glee he "mooned" Sandra Dickinson, which - allegedly - endeared him to all the production staff she'd alienated over the previous three years.

• Peter Davison went on to appear in several classic serials, beginning with *Anna of the Five Towns*, and starred in *Campion*. After a brief spell in the wilderness, the last few years have seen him once again starring in two hit series at once, *The Last Detective* and *At Home with the Braithwaites*. Janet Fielding's TV career petered out eventually, despite some high-profile appearances in *Minder* and a major role in children's series *Murphy's Mob* (opposite Keith Jayne, who played Will Chandler in 21.2, "The Awakening"). With the spectacular fall-out from her marriage, she was in the public eye until the early 1990s and later went into artiste management. She eventually became Paul McGann's agent.

Mark Strickson went to Australia and studied marine biology, and he's now a documentary producer. Matthew Waterhouse made a few straight-to-video horror films, although he's best-remembered as the worst Hamlet in living memory; that's not just our opinion, but the unanimous opinion of London's theatre critics. The story of how this production came to happen is bizarre and involves the Greek Orthodox church, Richard Franklin and a sweet-shop in Yeovil. Gerald Flood died of a heart attack a few months after the voice-over for Kamelion's last message, part of the "Curse of Kamelion" which has seen almost everyone involved in the robot's creation die prematurely (his software programmer, both his scriptwriters and all three actors who played him for any length of time). Sarah Sutton started a family, and only recently returned to acting, although she had a cameo in "Dimensions in Time" (see the appendix in Volume VI).

21.7: "The Twin Dilemma"

(Serial 6S, Four Episodes, 22nd March - 30th March 1984.)

Which One is This? 'Doctor Who turned into a cowardly madman with funny clothes, and there were two teenage boys who could move planets, and bird-people with plasticine noses, and a giant slug on a throne, and… and… oh, Auntie Em, it was such a *strange* dream!'

Firsts and Lasts It's the first adventure for the Sixth Doctor and his amazing technicolour dreamcoat, and the change in style is as immediate as it is obvious. The revamped titles have a chromatic filter on the stars, in an attempt to re-introduce the old "tunnel" look without it seeming like a climb-down. The Doctor appears in his jacket (previous renditions of the "starfield" titles just had a face) and is beaming inanely. Welcome to the Age of Kitsch…

Four Things to Notice About "The Twin Dilemma"…

1. With "The Twin Dilemma" regarded in its day as one of the worst *Doctor Who* stories ever made, the *real* killer here is that after the moody, brutal politicking of "The Caves of Androzani" this almost looks like a pantomime, with awful clothes, gaudy sets and atrocious make-up. In fact there's almost - *almost*, mind you - a sense that the series is wilfully sending itself up, or at least being so confident of its status as part of the British psyche that it thinks it can get away with a pulp sci-

fi story full of bad science and funny aliens. That something's gone a bit strange becomes clear when a professor from the twenty-somethingth century inspects the area where his children were kidnapped by extra-terrestrials and urgently announces: 'I've found zanium on the floor, it looks serious!'

2. These missing children, the twins of the title, are another of the story's key problems. On paper the idea of two adolescent geniuses whose equations have the power to punch holes in space, who seem utterly removed from the rest of the human race around them and who can even finish each others' thoughts, is potentially quite disturbing in a *Through the Looking-Glass* sort of way. On-screen, of course, it looks like two inexperienced child actors with pudding-bowl haircuts and space-tunics being nauseatingly smug at everyone. Since their role in the plot is actually quite minimal, for most of the time they're at least bearable, but then they try delivering their lines in unison and you're guaranteed to want to punch someone.

3. *More* slugs…? Yes, that's right; only a month and a half after "Frontios" (21.3), the series gives us another species of half-humanoid slug-creatures with astonishing mental powers, who want to spread their seed across the universe and who prove to be useless without their psychically-gifted leader. The most obvious difference between the two is that whereas the Gravis' authority was somewhat dented by his comedy nose, Mestor is wearing deely-boppers (weirdly popular in the early '80s, so the monster's at least trendy this time). And as if to rub in the fact that this series is cannibalising its own back-catalogue, here the Doctor allies himself with yet *another* kindly old Time Lord who turns out to have been a friend of his during some never-before-mentioned episode in the past.

4. There doesn't actually seem to be a dilemma in it.

The Continuity

The Doctor The new Doctor isn't entirely… stable. At first simply erratic, confused and forgetful, like most newly-regenerated Doctors, he later attacks Peri in a fit of angry paranoia, breaks down in hysterics and decides to cleanse himself by living on a desolate asteroid as a hermit with Peri as his disciple. Whether she likes it or not.

The John Nathan-Turner Era: What Went Horribly Wrong?

*Being the Case for the Prosecution. For the opposing view, see **The John Nathan-Turner Era: What Was the Difference?** under 18.1, "The Leisure Hive".*

The question presupposes that the Nathan-Turner era was ever "right". In fact it was woefully misconceived from the outset. Right from the start he selected staff whose notions of how television worked, how science fiction worked and above all what Doctor Who was "for" were in keeping with his own, not the public's. Quite simply this was a man who did not understand television in the 1980s.

Ask the public.

If you were sixteen in Britain in 1980, you had better things to do on a Saturday night than watch Matthew Waterhouse. The viewing figures show that about a fifth of the viewers in 1979 were 8-11 year-olds, slightly less than that for 30-49s and fewer still among 12-15s. People aged 16 to 19 made up 7.9% of the viewers. In case the rest of this volume hasn't made it abundantly clear, Britain in 1980 was an exhilarating place to be sixteen, with a combination of wildly varied youth culture and a sense of moral outrage at what was happening economically, socially, politically and educationally. Nevertheless, the new regime at Doctor Who decided that making the series for sixteen-year-olds was a sensible policy, and that making it didactic again would automatically enthuse the Youth of Britain to abandon their silly ideas of forming bands and get jobs at ICI instead. Those teens actually doing A-Level science found the results patronising, inaccurate, silly and slow. And whilst the programme may have been all these things in the past too, this time it took itself so-o-o seriously.

No, not "seriously", "solemnly". The issues in earlier stories had been quite intense, but handled with a certain elan. Some commentators have found hilarity in the preposterous notion that men in stuck-on beards bleating about Source Manipulators is someone's idea of primetime entertainment, but the actual fact of "The Keeper of Traken" isn't at all funny. A year ago we were laughing *with* (or at least, as Bart Simpson would say, "towards") the series. Now anyone not laughing *at* it is weeping, or just doing something else. It thinks it's being profound; it thinks it's visually impressive. It's barely competent.

It would be nice to provide external reasons for the fall in ratings: the series was shown too early in the evening, people remembered "The Horns of Nimon", it was on opposite Buck Rogers, that year's run of *Basil Brush* wasn't much good… when all of these factors were removed, the ratings for Doctor Who rose, but as the story being shown then was "Warriors' Gate" they fell again, pronto. The much-publicised departure of an iconic figure in British folklore got ludicrously small numbers. People whom it might be argued had been discouraged by the series' "cheapness" and "silliness" came back to see the new-look, "serious", "glossy" stories, and were driven away for good. People *liked* "cheap" and "silly". Pretentious, earnest and dull were the turn-offs. (Note that the one concerted attempt to do something less po-faced was made back-to-back with "Warriors' Gate". "Meglos" has all the faults alleged of Williams' stories, but without the panache which kept people watching. It was not, as is often thought, a Williams legacy but especially commissioned and made *after* "Full Circle". If they can't do frivolity properly, what hope was there for serious drama?)

Fortunately, "cheap" and "silly" made unannounced cameos over the next ten years. What Nathan-Turner lacked in ability to gauge the mood of the public, he more than made up for in his zeal as an impresario. Every producer had made at least one story where what had worked before was pushed way beyond the limits of what was worth doing. Barry Letts, in particular, let success (as defined as "not monumentally screwing up") go to his head when attempting stories like "The Time Monster" (9.5) or "Invasion of the Dinosaurs" (11.2). Where most producers learned from this mistake, or were thwarted by external factors - usually budgetary or union difficulties - all of Nathan-Turner's worst moments were self-inflicted. He remained unrepentant for most of these. After all, they got his name in the papers. We might giggle at a slightly silly effect like Erato the Tithonian (17.3, "The Creature from the Pit"), but the story wasn't commissioned to introduce Erato as a companion (see 20.6, "The King's Demons"). Gimmicks, "High-Concept" stories and daft publicity stunts seem to have been the motivation for commissioning scripts, not viewer enjoyment.

As the production unit manager, Nathan-Turner had been in charge of getting stories made on budget. Whilst he managed miracles in this regard as producer, overall his strategic skills seem to have abandoned him. Quite simply, if you've got 26 episodes a year and you know that you're

continued on page 313…

But least sane of all, there's the new costume he picks for himself from the TARDIS wardrobe, a horrible multicoloured mish-mash and a small cat-shaped brooch for the jacket lapel. In the end he only drops the "hermit" idea when it turns out there's something to investigate on the asteroid, but even then he's dangerously unpredictable, narcissistic, selfish, violent and occasionally cowardly, arrogantly taking the lead in the battle against the Giant Gastropods even though he barely seems to have any idea what he's doing. He has no time for the "niceness" of the Fifth Doctor, seeing the old persona as 'effete'.

[An interesting feature of his breakdown is the hysteria he undergoes in the TARDIS costume room. He free-associates on the idea of "no change", and becomes agitated at the idea of the eternity of boredom ahead of him, 'the grinding engines of eternity'. It's similar in substance, if not tone, to Sherlock Holmes' explanations of why he solves crime (and uses cocaine when nothing's available to prevent his great mind from becoming stagnant). It also suggests that the Doctor feels imprisoned by his position as a Time Lord. This is similar to the rejected two-part story Douglas Adams once proposed about the Doctor retiring; see 17.6, "Shada".]

For once, though, the Doctor actually approves of his change. He describes the regeneration with the words 'I call it a renewal' [a line which offhandedly confirms that the Doctor's first change in "Power of the Daleks" (4.3) was also a regeneration, as 'renewal' is the way it's described there]. He claims that in *his* case regeneration is a violent biological eruption, in which cells are displaced, changed, renewed and rearranged [suggesting that it's not so violent for *other* Time Lords]. He claims his instincts warn him that there's some great evil afoot when he reaches the asteroid Titan 3, but this may be sheer paranoia... even though he turns out to be right, on this occasion. He also considers the TARDIS' exterior form to be 'hideous', not a feeling that any other Doctor has been known to share [which explains why he's trying to fix the chameleon circuit in the next story].

The Doctor suggests a 'mind-link' with the Time Lord Azmael in order to overcome the telepathic powers of Mestor. [The only time that two *different* Time Lords are said to be able to do this, at least on television; see "The Three Doctors" and 20.7, "The Five Doctors".] He plans to give the twins Romulus and Remus a lift home in the TARDIS after events here. [This has obviously been done by the next story, unless anyone seriously wants to suggest a whole series of "missing adventures" involving Peri and a couple of adolescent number-nerds.]

• *Ethics.* Claims he has an in-built resistance to any form of violence, except in self-defence, so when he discovers that he tried to kill Peri he considers himself a living peril to the universe. While still in his unstable state, he refuses to save the life of someone who's threatened him, at least until that person's revealed to be a 'policeman'. Thereafter he's smugly proud of saving a life.

He has no hesitation at all about slaying Mestor with a bottle of slug-killing fluid. His manic assault on Peri stems from the belief that she's an alien spy, sent to kill him. [After Turlough and Kamelion, this isn't entirely unwarranted...]

• *Inventory.* There's a hand-held mirror in the Fifth Doctor's jacket, and Peri immediately knows it's there [suggesting some unseen time between the two after 21.5, "Planet of Fire"].

• *Background.* He knows of Vesta-95 as a good place for a holiday, knows of Titan 3 as a good place for meditation and has been to Jaconda before, remembering enough about the local mythology to recognise the traces of Giant Gastropods. The Doctor knows Azmael as the Master of Jaconda, regarding the old Time Lord as a friend and the best teacher he ever had. Two regenerations ago there was a night on Jaconda when Azmael drank too much and the Doctor had to push him into a fountain to sober him up [yet another missing chapter of the Fourth Doctor's life]. The Doctor can still find his way around the planet's palace.

The Supporting Cast

• *Peri.* Finds the Doctor's metamorphosis 'terrible'. Despite being threatened and at one point almost strangled by the Doctor, she's obviously still concerned about him, possibly just for the sake of the *old* version. Whom she describes as 'sweet'.

Before long she's settled into a routine of being exasperated by the new incarnation rather than scared of him. She doesn't insist on leaving his company, even though he's still fairly manic by the end of events here [the next story hints that she stays with him because she thinks he needs help]. Peri never thanks the Doctor for throwing away

The John Nathan-Turner Era: What Went Horribly Wrong?

...continued from page 311

going to make a big space-adventure with new-look Cybermen, you do not under any circumstances follow this with a script like "Time-Flight" (18.7). Even if you've blagged Concorde for free, this is the type of tale which - to do it justice - requires the sort of filming they used in "The Five Doctors" to avoid it looking like people milling about on a small tussock. If you're going to do both in a year, spread them out (at least in production order). This sounds like backseat driving, but as someone who'd been in the thick of Season Sixteen's budgeting crisis and had been de facto producer of "The Power of Kroll" (16.5), it should have been obvious to him. It's admirable that we got to see practically all the expense on-screen, but this leads to miscalculations like Season Twenty-One's last three stories. If you want to showcase your new star then don't make his debut the runt of the litter, financially and aesthetically. If it is that important to have him appear at the end of a year's run rather than at the start, make *his* story the one you film in Lanzarote. (That said, JN-T remained proud of "The Twin Dilemma" to his dying day.)

Visual storytelling had developed during the 1970s, and even BBC in-house directors knew this. A story like "The Face of Evil" (14.4) relays its visual information ahead of the verbal confirmation, showing how the world works before telling us (and not always telling all it shows). The dialogue can therefore go off into tangents, and we get characters rather than just data-dispensers. Williams-era stories developed this. You want a for-instance? "The Pirate Planet" is resolved by the Doctor telling Romana (and us) that he's done something very clever. We don't need to know any more than that he's turned the Captain's plan on itself. A perfunctory explanation is offered, but in such a way as to make a character point about the rote-learned Romana and the experienced, innovating Doctor. For our purposes, however, the Doctor did it by thinking of a bent fork and getting the local spook-men to smash things up with a spanner that they levitated with the last ounce of psi-power. The constant explanations as to what's happening in "Warriors' Gate" constitute the bulk of Romana's dialogue in parts three and four, yet this wasn't enough for many viewers... even hardcore fans with video recorders. It doesn't make her decision to stay any more comprehensible but it does remove any inducement on the part of the

viewers to settle back, watch the pretty pictures and accept that it's "symbolic". Viewers were perfectly happy to accept non-mimetic drama in 1981, even for family adventure shows, but our attempts at following it on an aesthetic level were thwarted by this info-dump dialogue constantly reminding us that it's all "real". We just aren't paying attention. (See **Is Realism Enough?** under 19.3, "Kinda", for a more detailed consideration of what audiences can take. Or could then.) We could mention the obsessive continuity, but that's a whole nother essay; see **Is Continuity a Pointless Waste of Time?** under 22.1, "Attack of the Cybermen". Just the dialogue pertinent to that specific story was impenetrable enough.

Or, for a more controversial example, consider "Nightmare of Eden" (17.4). In this, as anyone watching would realise even if they didn't speak English, the problem is that two ships are inside each other; you can tell because there's an electronic effect. One ship had a machine to "sample" bits of other worlds, and as a side-effect of the crash things from an alien planet are able to wander around a space package holiday flight. The Mandrels look out of place anywhere but the swampy planet. Compare this to a near-identical set-up in 18.3, "Full Circle". The Marshmen don't look much "wronger" in the Starliner than the Outlers or the Deciders, but that's not the point. The visuals are telling a different story from the dialogue. In the dialogue we're being told how regimented everything is, and how repressive the Alzarian life has become. On the screen we have a rag-tag assortment of young folk ambling about, only one of whom has a parent of any description, and a few old men whom no-one salutes or even stands aside for in the tight corridors. Even the Mistfall is not shown as a crisis; there's no urgency, even though the director is of the generation who experienced the Blitz. Even the Trogs in "Underworld" (15.5) had more thought put into them than this.

Bidmead has said in interviews that Nathan-Turner had no conception of how modern scripts worked (although later script editor Andrew Cartmel states that the producer had learned this by 1987). "The Leisure Hive" shows this clearly. Nathan-Turner removed portions of the script he thought held things up, then found himself with under-running episodes - which were filled with visual "vamping" - and unmotivated characters.

continued on page 315...

one of his lives to save her, but then, he's too busy being rude to her to give her a chance. She's happily raiding the TARDIS wardrobe by now.

The TARDIS The TARDIS wardrobe - or at least, *a* TARDIS wardrobe - is just one corridor away from the console room. It contains numerous clothing-racks, and outfits hanging around the walls willy-nilly [and doesn't seem as well-ordered as the wardrobe used in 16.4, "The Androids of Tara"]. Among the items on offer here are the Second Doctor's big shaggy coat and one of the Third Doctor's velvet numbers, while Lieutenant Lang appropriates a truly ludicrous glittering multi-coloured top that's even worse than the Doctor's jacket.

The TARDIS has a medical kit which includes a deep-healing beam, a hand-held device that occludes post-operative shock and closes wounds when run over the wounded Lieutenant's skull. The Doctor claims it's a great improvement over the old laser-scalpel.

The Time Lords

• *Azmael.* An elderly-looking and apparently benevolent Time Lord, as well as a friend of the Doctor's, Azmael is now posing as "Professor Edgeworth" and working as an agent for Mestor the Giant Gastropod. [No reason is given for him to be working under an alias. He's probably embarrassed.]

In fact Azmael believes in the sanctity of life, and is only following the despot's orders because he believes it's the only way to save the Jocondans. He was once the Master of Jaconda, and still sees the natives as being his people. [Does "Master" indicate that Azmael actually used to *rule* Jaconda? If so then it's curiously out-of-keeping with supposed Time Lord "non-interventionism", but presumably Jaconda is of so little note that Gallifrey isn't particularly bothered by the idea of one of its own running the place.] Azmael puts green marks on the arms of the twins Romulus and Remus, giving them selective amnesia and briefly making them pliable, but he can remove these marks with a touch [possibly Mestor's technology rather than his own].

Azmael doesn't recognise the Doctor, whom he hasn't seen in two regenerations. [Because he's getting on a bit, and his senses aren't that sharp. In 14.3, "The Deadly Assassin", Runcible recognises the Doctor after *three* regenerations.] He describes

himself as old, and he's used up his power to regenerate. There's no sign of him owning a TARDIS [17.6, "Shada", suggests that old Time Lords are allowed to "retire" to the outside universe but can't take TARDISes with them]. He dies, lamented by the Doctor, during the struggle with Mestor.

The Non-Humans

• *Giant Gastropods.* Creatures half-humanoid and half-slug, with arms but no legs, dark eyes and wobbly antennae. Their leader, Mestor, is now ruler of Jaconda.

Here he holds court in a palace of tunnels, surrounded by Jocondan lackeys including a chamberlain, condemning any who break his law to death. Azmael states that Mestor's thoughts affect all of Jaconda, so it's possible that the natives are being held in slavery at least in part by mindpower. Through sheer force of will Mestor can surround his victims with a lethal green light and cause 'death by embolism', a painful and much-feared fate, or throw up defensive energy-barriers. Obviously paranoid, Mestor can monitor the thoughts even of the Time Lord Azmael, though the Doctor can resist this telepathy. [Azmael's mind may also have been muddied by Mestor in order to stop him noticing the obvious holes in the plan to "save" the planet.]

Mestor can telepathically use a Jacondon as a 'monitor', seeing what the subject sees at long range, though this is fatal for the subject as it burns out the mind. He can mentally communicate with people, or manifest himself as an apparition, even across vast tracts of space; and he can use an energy beam to destroy human fighters in the vicinity of Titan 3 [he may be using technology to boost his mind-powers]. Most impressively of all, his power unlocks the TARDIS doors at long range.

Royal hatcheries on Jaconda contain incubators for Gastropod eggs, but these eggs are dry and 'designed' [engineered] to withstand the heat of an exploding sun. Mestor's plan is to tap the mathematical powers of the Sylvest twins from Earth - see **History** - and use their calculations to move two lesser planets in Jaconda's system across space with an immensely powerful tractor beam. The planets are supposedly to be placed in three different time-zones, as Mestor knows something of time-travel thanks to Azmael, and the Doctor believes that one tiny miscalculation in this plan

The John Nathan-Turner Era: What Went Horribly Wrong?

...continued from page 313

Bidmead himself compounded this through his terror of technobabble. This may sound odd, given that he is responsible for some of the least comprehensible, most unsayable lines in the programme's history, but it seems he seriously believed that a made-up solution was worse than anything else. The snag was that he used the accurate but tedious explanation where an earlier story would have had something visual followed by a viewer-friendly piece of whimsy where a lecture would simply not do.

The "new blood" Nathan-Turner employed took the narrative style right back to 1965. In the case of Lovett Bickford, 1935 was nearer the mark. The digital effects provided a smokescreen of "now"-ness. A cursory examination of the average shot-length and use of inserts reveals how staid the grammar of the shots was even in something "fresh" and "pacy" like "Earthshock" (19.6). It looked fresh, because it had never been done in colour before. Terence Dudley learned his craft in the '50s, and - the "look at me" Scene-Synch sequences aside - "Meglos" looks like a Hartnell, and not a good one.

Meanwhile, the entire style of the production was looking anachronistic. As we hinted in the last volume (**Which is Best, Film or Video?** under 12.3, "The Sontaran Experiment"), viewers were getting used to a new TV production grammar which said that VT was somehow the poor relation, even in the pop videos the programme was often attempting to resemble. And after ten years of science fiction films using synthesizers, because they sounded "futuristic", most space movies were going for the orchestral sound; synths sounded like a bloke in his bedroom, or local radio jingles (most of which, in those days, actually *were* by Paddy Kingsland and Roger Limb). Barry Letts had earlier forced Dudley Simpson to score the whole of Season Eight for primitive synthesizers, and the results stank. Hiring the BBC Radiophonic Workshop was an obvious cost-cutting move, and made the series sound amateurish. Characters and situations got "themes", and the programme's title music was pressed into service rather crassly. A story like "Arc of Infinity" might almost pass muster with the sound down (if we ignore the Ergon, the bump 'n' grind "bonding", the costumes, the sets...) and even with the dialogue it might almost have been tolerable, if rather long-drawn-out. The music just puts the tin hat on it.

Where *Doctor Who* had once been the slickest, most adventurous drama production the BBC made, it was now creaky, embarrassing and uninviting. If you switched on halfway through an episode there was no incentive to sit back and see what would happen. In the '70s it was written and directed so that anyone could pick it up at almost any point. Many commentators singled this out as the defining quality of the programme's appeal (see, for instance, the *Radio Times* feature to mark the start of Season Eleven). By 1981 this wasn't immediately apparent, and the music and sets, the pace of the directing and the wall-of-sound that served for dialogue was positively repellent. This was not a programme for casual viewers.

But that didn't matter, because there was a fandom, guaranteed to watch anything with a police box in it. We have to take it on trust that the Season Twenty "something from the past in every story" policy was really an accident, but why make such a big deal about it in the publicity? At conventions in the 1980s it became almost a ritual that teasing announcements of returning monsters, characters or writers were greeted with enthusiastic applause. It seemed by 1985 that the programme was made largely to garner this approval, like government policy being determined by the party conference. It has to be said here, and we've been avoiding it for most of this volume, but this is the point at which "the *Doctor Who* Fan" of popular mythology - in anorak and cheap trainers - comes into view. Obsessively buying any old crap (Gary Downie's *Doctor Who Cookbook* needs to be mentioned again, a cheap laugh but a good 'un, and Joy Gammon's *Knit a TARDIS*) and having no life, this wasn't just the Trekkie myth transposed. *Star Trek* was - God help us all - glamorous and halfway respectable. It looked professional even in 1980s BBC kiddie slots. That anyone might not have outgrown *Doctor Who* when the rest of the country did, in 1980 when they got rid of the "proper" titles and theme music, that was just tragic. With Ian Levine on board vetting the series for any inadvertent creativity or imagination, Bidmead trying to make Open University modules and then Saward attempting to make the type of stories that usually starred Stallone or Schwarzenegger (ignoring the fact that the cast was now Mr. Sitcom and his child brides), and the resulting mess sounding like '70s Public Information films about road safety but

continued on page 317...

could blow a small hole in the universe. But in truth Mestor just wants the two smaller planets to be drawn into Jaconda's sun, creating an enormous explosion. This will scatter the eggs throughout space, allowing the Gastropods to invade the universe. [Inevitably, see **Things That Don't Make Sense**.]

Gastropods are accompanied by the stench from their gastric tracts, the overpowering smell of rotting vegetables. Their slime-trails fasten like concrete, only faster, so anyone who steps in fresh slime tends to get stuck. Inconceivably, Mestor apparently finds Peri attractive, and indeed seems to be embarrassed by the limitations of his own shape as he intends to take over the Doctor's. His consciousness moves from his own form to Azmael's when his body is destroyed by chemicals from Azmael's lab, and when Azmael dies a black "spirit" is seen to dissipate into the air [so Mestor's mind may still survive somewhere].

Planet Notes

• *Jaconda.* [Note: the spelling varies wildly in the script, but in general it's "Jaconda" the planet and "dans" the people]. Once a beautiful planet, but now covered in desolate landscapes of barren soil, stripped trees and Giant Gastropod slime-trails. The Jocondans are a starving, oppressed people, though some of them are working for Mestor. They're humanoid, but evidently related to birds, with silver faces, black feather-like manes, extended beak-like noses and two "horns" emerging from their heads. There are two smaller planets in the same solar system as Jaconda [and possibly others that we're not shown on the diagrams].

Found in the depths of the Jocondan palace are wall-paintings which tell an ancient story: the queen of Jaconda offended the sun-god, who inflicted a terrible revenge by sending a creature half-humanoid and half-slug, the offspring of whom ravaged the planet and starved the people. The sun-god relented by sending a drought that destroyed the slugs, but it must be more than a story and some dormant eggs must have survived, as now the Gastropods are back. Once Mestor is dead, the locals begin to rise up against the other Gastropods, while Lieutenant Lang stays on the planet to help with the situation. [The Doctor speaks of Jaconda being 'galaxies' from human-occupied space, but he may be speaking figuratively, as Mestor sees humans as a potential threat

and they almost certainly don't have intergalactic travel in this era.]

• *Titan 3.* A craggy, desolate asteroid a long way from civilisation. The atmosphere - 'what there is of it' - is breathable, but there's a high level of radiation. Mestor has a 'safehouse' there, a dome-like base equipped with a 'revitalising modulator' for Azmael. This cubicle-like device breaks down the molecular structure of the body and reassembles it, usually a refreshing process, though it takes the Doctor mere minutes to re-jig it so that it sends himself and Peri ten seconds back in time and returns them to the TARDIS. [If the technology's so close to time-travel, then it's virtually certain that Azmael helped to design it.] A self-destruct mechanism eventually blows up the base, leaving Titan 3 uninhabited.

• *Vesta-95.* A marvellous place for a holiday, according to the Doctor. It's also yet another holiday destination which the TARDIS never actually reaches.

History

• *Dating.* The computer used by the human authorities states that freighter XV-773 was reported missing-believed-destroyed in "12-99", and that was eight months ago. [If "99" suggests a year, then the story probably takes place in a year ending in "00". 2300 is the date given in the script, and it'd fit the rest of the history of this universe, though oddly the novelisation plumps for 2310. The names "Romulus" and "Remus" have an obvious hint of empire about them, as if Earth's just about to enter its "bombastic" phase. But though every indication would seem to be that the planet from which Romulus and Remus are abducted is Earth, it's never actually stated in the story.]

In this era there's something like an interplanetary police force, which takes orders from a minister. The symbol of this service is a silver eight-pointed star. The HQ seen here is a humble office, with people milling around in unflattering pale blue tunics, though it may not be on Earth as the map on the wall is unfamiliar. They're obviously worried about trouble from aliens, and faced with a crisis the Commander launches all the pursuit crews, ordering all unidentifiable space vehicles to be investigated.

Lieutenant Lang pilots a one-man fighter with "wings", and is the leader - and last survivor - of a squad of five. His ID describes him as belonging

The John Nathan-Turner Era: What Went Horribly Wrong?

...continued from page 315

looking less exciting[16]... who in their right mind would watch this?

What did the British public want to see in 1980? Something retro; most of the successful adventures were either pastiches of earlier styles, or set in a period we thought we knew but with an ironic, modern hero passing judgement on the time. Hollywood had worked this out by updating Superman's opponents (and girlfriend) but not the premise nor the character, and that was only one example. Indiana Jones was an '80s man in a '30s world, saying all the things we knew old-fashioned heroes were thinking but couldn't have said in Republic serials. Nevertheless, he was a hero, because he acknowledged weaknesses and got on with saving the world anyway. In Britain, we were still a few years away from Blackadder but a great deal of "youth" TV re-dubbed or decontextualised old footage with cheerful irreverence. In France they were calling this "postmodernism", and about five years later America caught on, but in Britain it was "punk" or "satire" and anyone who'd grown up with Python could join in. Less talk, more visuals, but the talk has to be multi-layered and not just functional. Is this sounding familiar? If not, go back and read volume IV again.

At precisely the point when "vulnerable" heroes were being cast aside by audiences looking for unambiguous good guys, the BBC neuters its very own realistic superman. First they put him in a superhero costume, with question-marks on his clothes to replace any mystery the character had. Then they stop him from surprising anyone, and turn the Doctor into an extra in his own series. They then recast the main role as a juvenile. (N.B: This is not a dig at Peter Davison, who coped admirably. "Juvenile", in theatrical terms, is the male lead who isn't answering questions. Hamlet is a juvenile, regardless of the age of the actor. So is James Bond. The Doctor isn't, or wasn't.) The Doctor is now the kind of person who asks apparently older people for advice or guidance, and who has knowledge but not insight. We've had characters like this before; most recently K9.

Doctor Who had always been based on an idea of literacy as power against the powerful, developing the individual's self-knowledge and ability to understand others, and above all conveying the basic message that things-as-they-are isn't all there is. Now it all goes philistine and illiterate. The boy-Doctor and his teen-titans only ever read instruction manuals. The real Doctor read real books, for their own sake. He was a hero because he had the Big Picture. Doctor Who presupposed that art existed to ask questions, to convey a world view. The TARDIS auxiliary power station (15.6, "The Invasion of Time") had works of genuine feeling and integrity. They weren't just "pretty" or "well-executed", they had something to say to anyone with the ability or inclination to appreciate them. Chagall's "Snail" takes what might seem like random junk and makes of it something joyous and creative; the programme's ethos up until now (see 2.1, "Planet of Giants"). The Doctor and Romana go to the Louvre to see a painting, and the Bad Guys go to take it. In the Bidmead scheme of things, only one artist - M. C. Escher - is ever mentioned, and that is because there's been a maths textbook about him. His pictures are simple puzzles; they are prints, made to be mass-produced. They are product, not expressions of anyone's soul.

Thus far we've looked at the stories covered in this volume as though this was the whole story. The phase just about to begin is the height of Eric Saward's influence on the programme's direction, but more significantly this is where the personality cult of JN-T (even the name, to anyone familiar with twattish breakfast DJ Dave Lee Travis or "DLT", is a huge alarm bell) grows out of control. The concept of the Sixth Doctor is largely a self-portrait by the producer. After this high-water mark the "trademarks" - the Hawaiian shirts and catchphrases such as 'stay tuned', 'the memory cheats' and 'wit rather than slapstick' - all go. Indeed it is significant that Seasons Twenty-Five and Twenty-Six show him with regained enthusiasm and hands-on involvement (at least, if the Saward account of the later portion of their partnership is to be believed, and this is not the time to go into all that).

This is the part of Nathan-Turner's reign which deserves all the praise heaped onto Season Eighteen, and by this stage he is trapped on a series he's given his all to for almost a decade. We will examine this in detail in Volume VI, but the programme was only made because he was prepared to surrender any promotion or other ventures; the BBC would not hire a replacement and so his departure would have ended Doctor Who. Typically, he sought to mask this with more catchphrases: 'I've been persuaded to stay... I'm sur-

continued on page 319...

to Interplanetary Pursuit "A" Squadron [though this just seems to be the name of his unit, not the police force as a whole], and he carries a small energy weapon. The ship used as a base for Mestor's Jocondans is a spacehopper mark three freighter, an impressively large, rectangular vessel. It's been fitted with a warp drive, even though freighters of that type aren't built for it. Ships have registration numbers in this period.

The irritating twin sons of Professor Sylvest, Romulus and Remus, are teenage geniuses with a flair for maths. They like to 'play equations' on their computer, a game which terrifies their father as their powers in higher mathematics are so great that they could 'change events on a massive scale'. Because of this they're kept in seclusion when their parents aren't around, and Sylvest has his own security clearance, immediately calling the Special Incident Room when they're abducted. Lang's superior Commander Fabian is already aware of the danger posed by the twins falling into extra-terrestrial hands. [Mestor believes the twins are vital to his scheme, and never considers using a computer to do the calculations. This suggests that only the subtleties of a human mind can accomplish his goal, which is reminiscent of the block transfer mathematics used in 18.7, "Logopolis". Do the twins' equations have the ability to warp space-time? That seems to be the implication here, but if so then the human species never exploits or develops the idea. Maybe the twins would have been recruited by the Logopolitans, if any had survived.]

When Azmael appears out of nowhere before the twins, they believe it's just the kind of illusion they've seen at the theatre, suggesting that everybody in this era has forgotten about matter-transmission. However, Professor Sylvest immediately recognises the deposits of zanium on the floor as signs that the twins have been spirited away by teleporting aliens. Still, at least there are theatres in the future.

And people in this era are still saying "leftenant" instead of "lootenant" [as in 11.3, "Death to the Daleks"].

The Analysis

Where Does This Come From? It looks so much like a work of lightweight, disposable sci-fi, so much like *Doctor Who* entering the realms of self-parody, that it seems odd to even try to put it in the context of the real world. However, one thing is immediately noticeable: the idea that the planet could be threatened by mathematically-gifted teenagers, a notion that in the mid-'80s was starting to seem much less "escapist" than anyone might have thought.

As "Warriors of the Deep" has already demonstrated, the big fear at this point was that nuclear war might start by accident, and this coincided with the rise of the home computer. Friend-of-a-friend stories were claiming, as early as the days of the ZX-81, that some bright adolescent or other had already succeeded in hacking into America's missile systems. Before now the idea that child prodigies could build a doomsday weapon had been a staple of comic-books, but when Professor Sylvest warns his children against using their computer to play 'equations' there's suddenly a streak of paranoia behind it. The previous year had seen the release of *War Games*, a Disneyfied version of a near-apocalypse scenario in which a teenage nerd (played by Matthew Broderick) accidentally starts the countdown to World War Three while playing video games in his bedroom. Given the public's obsessions in 1983, this is a strong contender for the title of "Most Inevitable Film Ever Made".

"The Twin Dilemma" is on the same tack, although it keeps nuclear missiles out of things and instead resorts to the very Season-Eighteen-like idea that raw mathematics equals power. Indeed, as written in the script, Romulus and Remus almost come across as characters from Lewis Carroll; the Tweedledum and Tweedledee of higher mathematics, harking back to the playful logic of Douglas Hofstadter (see "Logopolis").

The other possible film influences are somewhat obscured. If the twins had been girls, as Moffatt wanted, then the similarity to *The Shining* would have been hard to ignore. Fear of bright children is one thing, but fear of identical bright children speaking in unison is altogether different. Basically, we're in the same territory as John Wyndham's *The Midwich Cuckoos* (filmed as *Village of the Damned*, although you probably knew that). There'd be little point in writing a story about twins if it could be avoided, so we have to ask ourselves what in Anthony Steven's script required *two* juveniles, and what Saward removed to render this pointless.

The best guess, based on interviews, is the idea of a genuine "twin dilemma" (think of the Riddle

The John Nathan-Turner Era: What Went Horribly Wrong?

...continued from page 317

prised and delighted to still be producer...' Compare the photos: the vigorous young man in 1980 taking the helm of one of the most sought-after jobs in the business; the camp, overblown self-parody of 1985, as famous as some regular cast-members and apparently making the series as something to do between conventions; the sharp, pensive figure of 1989, who's tried most of what the writers suggest at least once before and

knows if it'll work this time.

The question isn't so much "where did it go so horribly wrong?" as "why did it take so long for him to get it right?". The series he inherited had its faults but came with a vast residual affection, a guaranteed place in the BBC's line-up and an unspoken agreement with the viewers that if the story was worth their while then a few flaws in execution were tolerable. By 1988, in the main, the stories were again worth the viewers' while. But they'd all left.

of the Osirans in 13.3, "Pyramids of Mars"); one of the twins is evil, but which one? Could this have been the original storyline? It'd make more sense of the working titles than what we're left with here. Nathan-Turner was adamant that boys should play the twins, and the script calls for them to be darkly saturnine and arrogant.

But back to the old-school sci-fi. Back in the 1970s, the BBC's screenings of the old *Flash Gordon* serials had been the surest sign that Christmas was coming. Elements from these had cropped up in '60s *Doctor Who*, but when things went a bit solemn in the early '70s - and then knowing and sardonic later on - this strand was disowned. Jaconda is the sort of planet that either William Hartnell or Buck Rogers might visit, and it's not hard to see how the '80s trend for affectionate, semi-ironic space-operatics (see 21.3, "Frontios") would be an excuse to bring that sort of thing back for a new audience. The court of Mestor, an alien throne-room where prisoners are forced to their knees before a bloated, lascivious tyrant, is a favourite of old-fashioned pulp SF (although Peri never actually gets stripped half-naked and held in chains for his pleasure), which was back in fashion at this point after the appearance of Jabba the Hutt in... oh, you know.

And for old-timers, the name "Inspector Fabian" - the name of Lieutenant Lang's boss - may be a tad familiar. *Fabian of the Yard* was a mainstay of TV drama when Steven started writing in the mid-1950s.

Things That Don't Make Sense Mestor's plan is as bizarre as anything heard in the series since the days of the Kraals. Firstly, it's taken as read that getting planet-moving calculations wrong can blow a hole in the universe, which is a stretch in itself. [Possibly it's the method being used to shift

the planets around that can have unfortunate continuum-ripping effects, feasible if the twins are engaging in something akin to block transfer computation.] But the only reason Mestor wants to cause an explosion in Jaconda's sun is that the blast will scatter his people's eggs across the universe. Well, it might do, *if* a couple of doomed planets were enough to cause such an explosion. But so would... for example... taking the eggs into orbit and pushing them a bit. The blast might propel the eggs across space at high velocity, but certainly nowhere even close to light-speed, and when it comes to interplanetary travel even light-speed is (sorry about this) sluggish. It'll take the eggs unfeasible lengths of time to reach even the closest solar system; the overwhelming emptiness of space makes it hugely unlikely that any particular egg will actually *get* to a planet; the planet probably won't have an ecosystem capable of supporting slugs, even if an egg gets lucky; and since each egg will be heading in a different direction, any baby Gastropod who makes it to a suitable home will have to raise itself and infest that world single-handed.

Besides, if Mestor just wants to spread his eggs around the universe then he'd be better off sucking the secrets of space-time travel out of the Time Lord "teacher" Azmael than bothering with a couple of human whelps who know how to number-crunch. Come to that, he'd have a better chance of propagating the next generation with a common-or-garden spaceship, like the one his own servants are using.

Episode one sees Lieutenant Hugo Lang, ace fighter pilot and squadron leader, answering the 'phones at the police station as well as attending to his duties as guardian of the spaceways. The guards on Jaconda reach new heights of incompetence, knocking out Hugo in a tunnel and then reporting to their leader that they've left him 'half-dead' before being told to go back and get him, as if it's standard procedure to leave intruders lying around the palace and giving them a chance to get away. It's reasonable that Azmael may never have considered using his handy flasks of slug-killer before now - since he is, after all, both terrified of Mestor and convinced that only the tyrant has the power to save the planet now it's been devastated - but it's harder to believe that the telepathic, all-knowing Mestor would let him keep the stuff lying around in his lab.

And precisely *how* does the device that sends Peri ten seconds back in time make her re-appear on board the TARDIS? [Unless the TARDIS is pro-grammed to lock onto anyone in the vicinity who's transported out of their normal time-stream by primitive equipment, as a sort of safety meas-ure. Something similar happens to the Doctor in 9.5, "The Time Monster".] The Doctor's insistence on adjusting the time-factor, so that he arrives at the TARDIS at exactly the same time as Peri, does-n't seem particularly necessary either. Then he arrives ten seconds in Peri's future, supposedly, except that he then has to mess around with the TARDIS console in another time-zone entirely in order to get back to the time where Peri is. Suddenly, the UNIT HQ scene at the start of "The Ambassadors of Death" (7.3) looks very nearly logical.

Critique Even now, it's hard to understand exact-ly what happened. Some would argue that the worst excesses of *Doctor Who* in the mid-'80s were inevitable, the result of ongoing problems ever since the change of producer in Season Eighteen (see **The John Nathan-Turner Era: What Went Horribly Wrong?**), but in itself the whacking great gulf between "The Caves of Androzani" and "The Twin Dilemma" seems startling. It felt wrong at the time, and it still feels wrong now. Those who'd given the thumbs-up to the series in the early '80s felt cheated. Those who hadn't been happy since the days of K9 had a chance to say "told you so".

So what *did* happen? How could anyone have thought that this story, of juvenile space-monsters, meaningless plans and never-ending cop-outs, was ever workable? How could anyone have thought that a script so full of pulp-fodder (Fabian's line of 'may my bones rot for obeying it!'), which reaches its conclusion when the Doctor strolls into the villain's throne-room and throws a big flask of acid at him, was in any way finished? How could anyone have thought that the costume designs were remotely acceptable, or that it was reasonable to suggest "headquarters of the space-police" by taking a mismatched office set that wouldn't be tolerable in a daytime soap opera and putting some toy spaceships on the desks? Perhaps more importantly: how could the producer still believe, a decade later, that this was an exemplary and much-underrated story?

Perhaps the answer is that by this stage, John Nathan-Turner was under a gigantic misconcep-tion as to how the series worked. For those who'd been "there" with the early Nathan-Turner stories, his great success had been to understand that *Doctor Who* was a television programme, and should thus use every advantage of television. But by now he's so wrapped up in the job that he's started to believe in the myth of the series; he's started to think of it as a national tradition rather than a workable piece of TV, and that means he's making *Doctor Who* that's like *Doctor Who*. And of course, that's the last thing we want. Given a new leading man, the programme wisely pulls away from the "space gothic" feel of much of the Davison run, but… it's got nowhere else to go, nothing to draw on but its own legend. To Nathan-Turner, "The Twin Dilemma" is a story that fulfils his mandate to make a programme that's just like its old self, but in a fresh, upbeat new style. To everyone else, it's unwatchable.

No… not quite unwatchable. In one sense, "The Twin Dilemma" deserves some slack. There are times in the programme's history when the cast and crew are left to run on automatic, when the regulars end up doing the same old shtick over and over again and nobody involved feels the need to even try. It happened with Pertwee in the latter UNIT stories, it happened again when Tom Baker got too cosy in his role. That's not the case here. Colin Baker's performance isn't great, and it'll certainly get better, but you can tell he's getting a kick out of this and he's not taking anything for granted. His manic laughter in the costume room is genuinely unsettling. Nicola Bryant is stagger-ingly good, looking more scared in the Doctor's presence than most companions do in the pres-ence of the monsters, and accidentally becoming the focus of the story as a result. But ultimately even the Doctor / Peri scenes start to drag, as end-less arguments are inserted to hammer home the point that this is a dangerous, unpredictable new Doctor. And what's the point of him being unpredictable, if he's trapped in an "adventure" that just requires him to go through the motions until an opportunity to kill the villain turns up?

The miserable truth is, there's no way of taking "The Twin Dilemma" seriously. Every now and then you'll realise how hard some of those involved are trying, and you'll desperately want to reappraise it. But even if you treat it as a kind of gaudy, over-enthusiastic B-movie then it's still only semi-bearable. Much of Season Twenty-One has required us to be patient, but now our patience has worn thin. It's the beginning of the end.

The Facts

Written by Anthony Steven. Directed by Peter Moffat. Viewing figures: 7.6 million, 7.4 million, 7.0 million, 6.3 million.

Supporting Cast   Maurice Denham (Edgeworth), Kevin McNally (Hugo Lang), Gavin Conrad (Romulus), Andrew Conrad (Remus), Edwin Richfield (Mestor), Dennis Chinnery (Sylvest), Barry Stanton (Noma), Oliver Smith (Drak), Helen Blatch (Fabian), Dione Inman (Elena), Seymour Green (Chamberlain).

Working Titles   "A Stitch in Time", "A Switch in Time".

Oh, Isn't That..?

• *Maurice Denham.* On radio he'd mainly been a comic actor, in shows like wartime hit *ITMA* and *Much Binding in the Marsh*. In films he'd played serious roles in epics like *Sink the Bismark* and *Nicholas and Alexandra*. He was in his seventies when this role came up, and soldiered on in programmes like *Minder* for another few years afterwards. His appearances in *Porridge*, one of the '70s sitcoms on the BBC's "repeat until doomsday" list, have guaranteed that he's still a familiar face on British television to this day.

Cliffhangers   On board the TARDIS, Lieutenant Lang unexpectedly recovers from unconsciousness and prepares to shoot the Doctor; Peri sees the Titan 3 base explode on the TARDIS scanner, apparently with the Doctor still inside; the Jocondan guard stops the Doctor running off to save Peri from Mestor, and Azmael announces that if necessary, she'll have to die (N.B. this may well be the least-memorable cliffhanger of all time).

The Lore

• For the remodelled titles, Nathan-Turner had a brainwave that the Doctor should wink at the audience. The photos used to make the "smile" work were the second attempt, as the winking made it seem that the Doctor was blowing a kiss once the pictures were animated. (As we'll see under 24.1, "Time and the Rani", the "wink" idea was tried again and eventually used.)

• As has already been mentioned, the media buzz was that Brian Blessed would be the new Doctor. Some have taken the story's final line, 'I am the Doctor, whether you like it or not,' as a rebuke to the fans who expressed disappointment at Baker's casting. Baker was somewhat put out that the rumour appeared to have BBC sanction, as he'd already been told he had the part before the reports began. During the delay, Baker's son Jack died suddenly; the actor devoted his period on the series (and much time since) to raising funds for the Foundation for the Study of Infant Deaths. The cat-badge worn in this story was originally a one-off, but the makers made a bulk order to sell to fans as a fundraiser.

• Ian Levine came up with the idea of the Doctor having an ex-Time-Lord mentor. Earlier drafts variously called him "Aslan" (guess why that was dropped) and "Azazael" (another fallen angel; see 8.5, "The Daemons").

• Nicola Bryant had been due to wear a trouser-suit, as in "Timelash" (22.5), but Nathan-Turner overruled this as not being revealing enough. The location shoot in February was bitterly cold. Bryant had been rather subdued when Baker first met her, and he formed the idea that she was a touch stand-offish. The location work, and the quick trip to America for yet another convention, broke the ice.

• The Conrad twins were a last-minute casting choice after every possible alternative had been explored. Their father, Les Conrad, had been one of the gun-runners in "The Caves of Androzani". Maurice Denham was struck by how daunted they were, and took it upon himself to keep an eye on them.

• Another consequence of this year's industrial action was that the location work was filmed between the studio sessions, not before them as was customary.

• Anthony Steven had been writing for television for thirty years when Nathan-Turner approached him. They'd worked together on *All Creatures Great and Small*, and Steven had also written for Maigret and the Scots period medical series *Dr. Finlay's Casebook* (including the episode "Comin' Thro the Rye", where elderly, plump Dr. Cameron accidentally invents LSD in 1934...). His ill-health and odd delays left little time for rewrites or revisions, and Saward eventually rewrote a large amount of the final version. Despite this, Steven wrote to congratulate Saward and offer his services again.

• Saward's biggest revision was the ending, which originally would have been a showdown in deep space, and Mestor was hardly in it. A couple of cut passages indicate that there was more to the Doctor's instability than post-regenerative confusion. He announces himself to Mestor as 'a rather special Time Lord' (see 25.1, "Remembrance of the Daleks") and in one free-associative ramble suggests that he shouldn't have left Gallifrey, then claims that if he'd been a better student then he might have become President, then recalls that in fact he *is* President and immediately heads off to rejoin his "team".

Moreover, he claims that his previous self was repressed and heading for a breakdown through trying to be more human. This is in keeping with the ideas Baker and Nathan-Turner had thrashed out, that this Doctor was nursing a secret which made him seem abrupt and callous (the model Baker offered was Mr. Darcy from *Pride and Prejudice*). The plan was to mellow this Doctor as time went on, and eventually reveal his secret, at which point everything would make sense.

Nathan-Turner also believed that each regeneration led to a rift with the companions. Saward thought that so soon after "Castrovalva" it was important to have a Doctor who wasn't just a bit feeble but emphatically "wrong" for the first few episodes. In this, he was speaking from the heart. Saward felt that Baker was woefully miscast, and that the entire series was taking the wrong direction, with the "guest-star" policy and the "knicker-elastic fund" (see 18.1, "The Leisure Hive") shifting the series from drama to light entertainment. Nathan-Turner's frequent public references to the series as 'like Morecambe and Wise' did little to reassure him. Saward later wrote "Revelation of the Daleks" at least in part to prove a point to Baker about how to play a character like Bayban the Butcher (Baker's role in *Blake's 7*, but see 22.6 for more).

1 It's tempting to say that Jeremy Bentham is "no relation" to the other Jeremy Bentham, the father of utilitarianism who came up with the word "Panopticon" in the eighteenth century (see **Does This Universe Have an Ethical Standard?** under 12.1, "Robot"). It's tempting, but it's not true. He is.

2 On this note… at the risk of becoming self-indulgent, one of the authors of this present volume would like to point out that although the ongoing series of *Faction Paradox* novels is set in a universe very much like that of *Doctor Who*, *Faction Paradox* firmly takes the "fantasy" approach rather than the "SF" one. Hence all that messing-about with totems instead of machines. *Sapphire and Steel* works in much the same way.

3 It has been argued that Grimwade gets "auteur" status for this, as nobody else would have directed episode three of "Earthshock" as so flagrant a bun-fest. One scene is wall-to-wall cyberbuttocks, shot from a camera at waist height. And it's repeated in part four! We, of course, would simply point out that he's the only director other than Terence Dudley to get scripts accepted. But in none of these cases did the writer direct his own work. Imagine what he would've done with the public school setting in "Mawdryn Undead", the airline stewards in "Time-Flight" or the Turlough-in-trunks beach scenes in "Planet of Fire"…

4 Made in 1976, and featuring a child actor named Gary Russell as one of its lead cast. Extensive research has been unable to discover what happened to Mr. Russell after this.

5 Actually not the most disgusting thing that's ever happened in the TARDIS prop, but further details are unpublishable.

6 The last vestige of the Victorian-style "realistic" acting was William Hartnell as the Doctor. The lapel-clutching, eye-rolling, stance-striking perform-ance we all grew up ridiculing was the way the gen-eration of actors before him thought you were sup-posed to depict stern, patrician leaders. Neville Chamberlain's newsreel interviews as leader of the opposition show him looking like he's facing a fir-ing-squad, but once he was Prime Minister someone had the bright idea of coaching him. They hired an elderly, distinguished actor, but one unused to working with cameras. The result is pure First Doctor.

7 *Denis Healey:* Former Chancellor of the Exchequer, and one of the most-impersonated pub-lic figures of the 1970s, since to most people he sounded exactly the way a hippo might sound if it could discuss the value of sterling. See **Why Couldn't They Just Have Spent More Money?** under 12.2, "The Ark in Space", for more.

8 Oh yes they have. As anyone who's seen Denys Fisher's 1976 Cyberman action figure will know.

9 *Ali Bongo.* One of the leading figures in the UK's Magic Circle, and an expert at adapting illusions for television, but he has a habit of appearing in a false moustache and comedy *Arabian Nights* costume in public. He presented a lot of early '70s children's programmes, although more recently he's been interviewed in all of the six-thousand documentaries about stage magic that have been made in Britain since David Blaine became fashionable, and even when speaking earnestly about the history of his profession he *still* insists on wearing the turban.

10 You'd think that, anyway. But funnily enough, "Mawdryn Undead" was the first *Doctor Who* story watched by the publisher of this present work, and *he's* still here.

11 To clarify for non-UK readers… a "public school" is a school set up before the reforms of the nineteenth century, but after there were enough wealthy people around who weren't related to royal-ty. The name is therefore confusing; for "public", read "posh". Most of these schools are registered as charities for tax purposes, though the inherent elit-ism means that they're still very much more expen-sive than schools which admit the *general* public.

12 *The Boys from the Black Stuff*: hit drama, despite the apparent bleakness and gallows humour, written by Alan Bleasdale. His later series *GBH* features a corrupt Liverpool city administrator having a nerv-ous breakdown at a *Doctor Who* convention. The lecherous Dalek yelling 'fornicate, fornicate' is

drawn from life; Liverpool conventions got like that sometimes.

13 "Tannoy" is the name of Britain's best-known man-ufacturer of public address systems, which means that a great many people refer to all public address systems as "Tannoys" in the same way that they say "Bacardi and Coke" instead of "rum and cola". However, you can see how the Tannoy people wouldn't want to be associated with lepers.

14 The 1976 edition of *The Making of Doctor Who* was the first book to present a list of past companions, although there were notable omissions, Ian and Barbara amongst them. The original 1972 edition used the c-word, but didn't go into detail, while the 1973 *Radio Times Doctor Who Special* called them "assistants" and only singled out a few of them for "where are they now?" interviews. The "canon" of companions that fandom generally accepts - which includes both Katarina and Sara Kingdom, even though the former only appears in five episodes (less than, say, Lady Jennifer Buckingham in "The War Games") and the latter only appears in a single story (by which token, *anybody* who ever takes a trip on the TARDIS might qualify) - seems to have been an invention of early issues of *DWM*.

After the "controversial" ending of "Earthshock" (19.6), one reader wrote to the *Radio Times* letters page to point out that Adric wasn't the first companion to die, but the third… indicating that by 1982, this officially-sanctioned companion list was already firmly established in the minds of pedants. In "Resurrection of the Daleks" it's given the on-screen stamp of approval, as the faces of Sara and Katarina are amongst those dragged out of the Doctor's mind by the Dalek brain-scan. Yates and Benton aren't, as far as we see.

15 Tom Baker did a lot of advertising voice-overs he left *Doctor Who*, the most memorable being for *Man and the Masters of the Universe* action figures. T was, of course, something massively undignified a the man who used to be Our Doctor trying to sell half-human half-skunk creature called "Stinkor".

16 *Public Information Films.* The Central Offic Information, a wartime body concerned with kee everyone alive and well-fed, became a peacetime t ing-camp for a curious mix of film-makers, civil ser and safety experts. Their thirty-second films off advice and information had, by the 1970s, develor style of punchy worst-case-scenario domestic hor There was nothing in the home that couldn't beco death-trap. Patrick Troughton narrated one in w polishing a wooden floor and placing a rug on top was built up like Hitchcock on fast-forward: '… at think, he'd only just come *from* the hospital' he pur a newborn baby is narrowly spared its father's grisly

To save on cost, the music was either from sto often familiar to viewers from adventure series - or sisted of Moog synthesizers making menacing gr and whoops. The catch-phrases from these films, the sight of once-familiar actors or celebs (forget *Wars*, Dave Prowse is the Green Cross Code Man and foremost), ensure that commercially-available pilations of the films are an instant nostalgia-trip for one who grew up here. Non-UK readers should k that these compilations, "Charley Says" and "Ch Live", are the one-stop guide for anything in these b you still don't understand about British Pop Cul And they even show someone using a police box fo original purpose of calling the police…

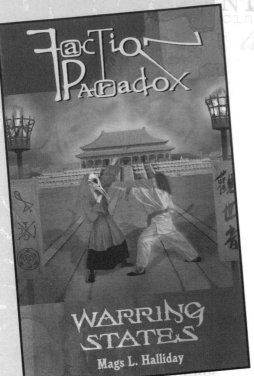

introducing the all-new novel...

Faction Paradox

WARRING STATES

The air in the Stacks races through the tunnels, pushed by the ghost trains rattling over the dead tracks. Posters for films that never were, and adverts for beauty products that give new meaning to "age-defying", flutter blindly. Occasionally, the icy air slams into abandoned platforms, where insubstantial suicides stand, clothes swirling around them as they stare into the abyss of the permanent way.

Deep in the Stacks, Cousin Octavia welcomes the intermittent blasts of air. She likes it down here, safe not only from surface-level War offensives but also from the tedious internal politicking of the Eleven-Day Empire itself. Down here in the Faction's huge repository of knowledge, beneath a bloodlit London, she could lose herself in research. And if people got lost in the Lobokestvian geography of abandoned underground tunnels whilst looking for her, even better.

Unfortunately, Prester John is good at remembering the way.

'You could visit me in Westminster,' he remarks as he arrives, swirling flyers for *The Defective Detective* in his wake. Octavia shrugs.

'I've found it,' she tells him.

In the city square the crowd gathered, jostling not only to get a good view, but for their eagerness to be seen by the officials. Four men and a woman knelt, hands tied and heads bowed. A mandarin of the sapphire button stepped forward, peacock silks as stiffly formal as the condemnation he was making.

'- are hereby executed, for the most heinous crime of attempting to disrupt the Most Exalted One's Heavenly Kingdom, for the circulation of pernicious and corrupt ideas promulgated by the heathen foreign devils, for -'

As he continued, guards hacked off the queues of the men, holding the plaited hair high. The woman's hair had already be shorn, and not gently. All five waited silently as the official finished his denouncement.

In the crowd, Liu Hui Ying felt the hand of her father tighten about her upper arm. He was scared, she had realised this morning. Terrified that his laxity, his trade with the foreigners, his schooling of her, would lead to his own beheading. These five had been brought down from the north for this, but Chin Liang-Yu had been a school friend of Liu's. So now her father made her watch her friends kneel in the dirt for their ideas.

Five swords fell, the edges shearing through the second and third vertebrae, through the thick muscles and flimsy vessels of the throat. Chin's head rolled, tainting the dust with blood, until its force was spent and it came to rest staring upwards at Liu with something like hatred.

Walking back to the dockside factory, where her family's fortune had been made selling antiquities, Liu felt her jaw tingle with the promise of vomiting, her mouth filling again and again with the taste of it. She swallowed it down, urgently wishing she'd managed to close her eyes. Her father's new-found distrust of her education didn't yet outweigh her cheapness as a translator, and there was a new shipment of vases going to Britain. She set to work.

'Please, convey to your father my gratitude for continuing his business with us at this time,' Atkinson said. He took a sip of pai mu tan. Liu's father nodded with satisfaction as she translated.

'We are always honoured by your visits,' he said, then excused himself to supervise packing the crates. Atkinson took another sip of tea. Liu liked these moments, her chance to practise her language without being watched.

'How was the voyage from India?'

'Easy enough. We had an interesting party on board. Your father might want to contact them.'

'Really, how so?'

'It was an archaeological expedition, from Oxford, who hope to find the Great White Pyramid of China. I told them that it was just a myth, but Professor Grieves seems quite sure.'

'What is it this time? The stars aligned to bring down heavenly fire? Prehistoric germ warfare? Godfather Morlock's birthday?' Prester John is sidling through the room, letting his long coat brush against the precarious mounds of research material. Just reminding her that he can bring it all crashing down, make her go back to the fighting. 'Actually, that last one would be of some use. He'd be really pissed off if I threw him a party -'

'The Holy Grail.'

'Again? We've got a storeroom full of the things.'

'The metaphorical Holy Grail: live forever.'

'Given that we've already given history the slip, why would we want that?'

'Think about it. We give history the slip but it always catches up. Always. Remember the Noose?'

Prester John winces. 'Yes, that was embarrassing. So, what's the plan?'

'I'll need to mount an expedition into linear time to retrieve it. And I can only trace it to China. During the Boxer Rebellion.'

Prester John nods agreement. The distant rumble of a train swirls Cousin Octavia's clothes about her, and her shadow dances.

Release Date: June 2005. **Retail Price:** $17.95.

info@madnorwegian.com

www.madnorwegian.com

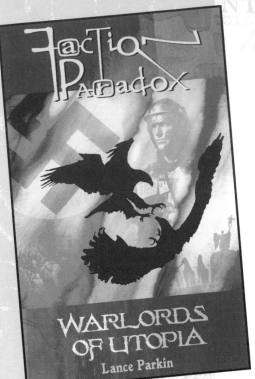

Faction Paradox

WARLORDS OF UTOPIA

Lance Parkin

Faction Paradox

WARLORDS OF UTOPIA

Adolf Hitler, the Gaol.

In the exact centre of the island was a tower. It was an ugly concrete stump four storeys high, a brutalist version of a medieval keep. There were tiny slits for windows. There wasn't a door. Around the tower, thorns and weeds had grown into a jungle. The tower held one prisoner.

Surrounding it was an electric fence. And the guards. Millions of strong men and women with the bodies they should have had, unmarked by armband or tattoo, allowed to grow up and grow old. Proud people, many with names like Goldberg, Cohen and Weinstein. Men and women who would never forgive. Men and women who lived in the vast, beautiful community that surrounded the tower, keeping him awake with their laughter, their music, the smell of their food, the sight of their clothes, the sound of their language and their prayers and the cries of their babies. They felt they had a duty to be here. They had always been free to leave, but few had.

On Resurrection Day itself, some had realised that as everyone who had ever lived was in the City, then *he* was here. It had taken longer to hunt him down. Few knew where he'd been found, how he'd been leading his life. Had he tried to disguise himself? Had he proclaimed his name and tried to rally supporters? It didn't matter. He had been brought here, his identity had been confirmed and he had been thrown in the tower that had been prepared for him.

Some of those living in sight of the tower had wondered if they were pro-tecting him from the people of the City, not protecting the City from him. And it was true: the City - the glorious, colourful, polymorphous, diverse City, with uncounted races of people living side by side - was the ultimate negation of the prisoner's creed. The vast, vast majority people of the City didn't care who he was and couldn't comprehend his beliefs, let alone be swayed by his rheto-ric. Individuals who'd killed, or wanted to kill, many more people than he had remained at liberty and found themselves powerless. Had imprisoning him marked out as special? Such things were argued about, but the prisoner remained in his tower.

Every day bought requests from individuals, organisations and national groupings who had come up with some way to harm him within the protocols of the City. There were also representations from his supporters, or from civil liberties groups, concerned that his imprisonment was vigilante justice or that no attempt was being made to rehabilitate him. There were historians and psychologists and journalists who wanted to interview him. There were those that just wanted to gawp at or prod the man they'd heard so much about. All of them were turned away.

One man had come here in person. An old Roman, in light armour.

The clerk, a pretty girl with dark hair and eyes, greeted him.

'Your name?'

'Marcus Americanius Scriptor.'

While she dialled up his records and waited for them to appear on her screen, she asked: 'He's after your time. You're a historian?'

'I was,' the old man said. 'May I see him?'

'The prisoner isn't allowed visitors, or to communicate with the outside world. He is allowed to read, but not to write. Oh, that's odd. Your record isn't coming up.'

'It wouldn't.' The Roman didn't elaborate.

He looked out over the city to the tower. The young woman was struck by how solemn his face was. Most people who came all the way out here were sightseers, sensation seekers. Even some of the gaolers treated the prisoner with levity. Mocking him, belittling him.

'Don't you ever want to let him loose?' he asked, finally. 'Let him wander the streets, let his words be drowned out. On another world he was an indifferent, anonymous painter.'

'It sounds like you know that for certain,' she said, before checking herself. 'To answer the question: no. He stays here.'

'I met him,' the Roman told her. 'On a number of occasions.'

She frowned.

'A long story,' he told her. 'I suppose I'm concerned that you torture yourselves by having that monster in your midst.'

The woman had heard many people say such a thing.

'Not a monster. A human being.'

'But the only human being you've locked away for all eternity.'

'The wardens have ruled that he will be freed,' she told him.

Americanius Scriptor seemed surprised. 'When?'

'First he must serve his sentence, then he will be released.'

'When?' he asked again.

'In six million lifetimes,' she told him.

Marcus Americanius Scriptor smiled.

'I'll be waiting for him,' he told her. He turned and headed back to the docks.

Release Date: OUT NOW

info@madnorwegian.com

www.madnorwegian.com

TIME
UNINCORPORATED
THE DOCTOR WHO FANZINE ARCHIVES

Vol. 3: Writings on the New Series

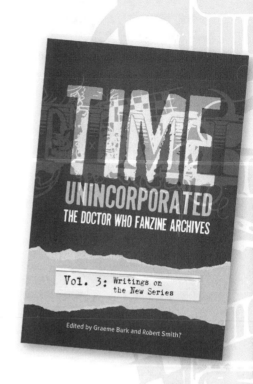

Coming soon...

Time, Unincorporated 3 compliments its predecessor by presenting an astounding array of fanzine material on the new *Doctor Who* – including essays on Matt Smith's first season, *Torchwood*, *The Sarah Jane Adventures* and more.

Works included in this volume stem from such publications as *Enlightenment*, *Tides of Time*, *Shockeye's Kitchen* and more. Also included are a number of essays on new *Doctor Who* that were written exclusively for this volume, from such writers as Andrew Cartmel, Jon Blum, Kate Orman, Lloyd Rose, Steve Lyons and more.

ISBN: 978-1935234036
Retail Price TBD

www.madnorwegian.com
1150 46th St, Des Moines, IA 50311 . madnorwegian@gmail.com

MORE DIGRESSIONS
PETER DAVID

A new collection of 'But I Digress' columns

FOREWORD BY HARLAN ELLISON

Out Now... The first compilation of its kind in 15 years, *More Digressions* collects about 100 essays from Peter David's long-running *But I Digress* column (as published in the pages of *Comics Buyer's Guide*). For this entirely new collection, David has personally selected *But I Digress* pieces written from 2001 to the present day, and also included many personal reflections and historical notes.

Topics covered in this collection include Peter's thoughts on comic book movies, his pleasing and sometimes less-than pleasing interactions with fandom, his take on the business aspects of the comic-book industry, his anecdotes about getting married and having children, his advocacy of free speech and much more.

More Digressions features a new foreword by the legendary Harlan Ellison, and sports a cover by J.K. Woodward (*Fallen Angel*) that highlights some of David's comic-book creations.

ISBN: 978-1935234005
Retail Price: $24.95

www.madnorwegian.com

mad
norwegian
press

1150 46th St
Des Moines, IA 50311
madnorwegian@gmail.com

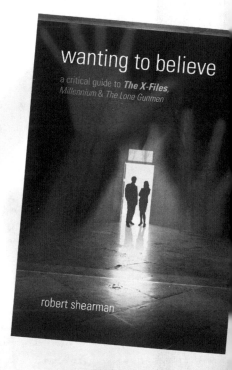

who made all this ?

Lawrence Miles is the author of... hold on... yeah, *eight* novels now, the most recent of them being the first volume in the ongoing *Faction Paradox* series, *This Town Will Never Let Us Go*. After co-writing *Dusted* - a guide to *Buffy the Vampire Slayer*, also published by Mad Norwegian - he suddenly found that he'd been cured, and didn't want to see another episode of *Buffy* ever again. So once *About Time* is finished, he's planning on constructing a great ceremonial pyre and burning the complete collection of *Doctor Who* videos and CDs that's taken him nearly twenty years to assemble. Favourite story in this book: "Logopolis". Least favourite: "Arc of Infinity".

Recovering academic **Tat Wood** is the person most compilers of previous guidebooks went to for advice and cultural context. Despite having written for *Film Review, TV Zone, Starburst, SFX, Dreamwatch, Doctor Who Magazine, X-pose* and just about every major fanzine going, he has a rich, full and complex life. Currently lecturing and tutoring, he is busy mentoring mature students from across the Commonwealth and the new Europe whilst attempting to break into mainstream "literary" fiction. Tragically, this is interrupted by people wanting to get the lyrics to half-forgotten 1960s TV themes ringing him rather than bothering with the Internet (because he's quicker). Although culturally adept and well-rounded, he has lived in Ilford for the last ten years. Favourite story in this book: "Warriors' Gate" ('for all its faults'). Least favourite: "Terminus".

Mad Norwegian Press

Publisher/Series Editor
Lars Pearson

Copy Editor
Fritze CM Roberts

Interior/Cover Design
Christa Dickson

Cover Art
Steve Johnson

Associate Editors
Marc Eby
Dave Gartner
Val Sowell
Joshua Wilson

Technical Support
Michael O'Nele
Robert Moriarity

1150 46th Street
Des Moines, Iowa 50311
madnorwegian@gmail.com
www.madnorwegian.com